SENATE
MAGIC

SENATE MAGIC

A NOVEL BY

JEANNE MOZIER

HIGH STREET PRESS

BERKELEY SPRINGS, WEST VIRGINIA

SENATE MAGIC

© 2013 Jeanne Mozier

Published in the United States of America by

High Street Press
49 Rugby Lane
Berkeley Springs, WV 25411
http://highstreetpresswv.com

Book production by Black Walnut Corner Book Production
Cover design by Jennifer Mallory

ISBN 978-0-9898018-0-5

The Characters

Kiley Albright Tomasso, aka Kat, Congresswoman from Rhode Island/U.S. Senate candidate.

Roxy Holland, Kat's longtime friend; comes to work on campaign as speechwriter.

Liz Barnes, friend of Roxy's from Morgan Springs; comes to work on final months of campaign.

Max the Magician, stage magician and oracular advisor; longtime friend of Kat's.

Race Scarlatti, Rhode Island crime boss.

Thomas Jefferson Stuart, U.S. Senate/Virginia.

Celeste Albright Tomasso, Kat's mother.

Frank "Duke" Tomasso (deceased), Kat's father.

Mario De Palma, Kat's campaign manager.

Hayes Redcliffe, Kat's chief of staff.

Jake Hansen, artist, Roxy's Rhode Island boyfriend.

Reynolds Winston, U.S. Senate/Rhode Island.

Jasmine Elliott, Kat's press secretary.

Carrie Lange, Kat's office manager in Rhode Island.

Bruno "the Hose" Capaldi, Kat's Providence political operative.

SENATE MAGIC

Jamie Winston Caldwell, Kat's ex-husband

Emmett Douglas, Rhode Island governor/U.S. Senate candidate

Pete Hassem, food critic: *Providence Journal*

Harry Crast, political editor: *Providence Journal*

Consultants:
Lila Gravely, pollster
Hal Gould, media
Paul Reilly, Senatorial committee

Fast Forward
November 1990

Bolting upright in bed, Kat woke from the nightmare, heart pounding, limbs trembling in shock. Election day was over. She missed it. No one reminded her! She struggled to bring herself fully awake, to escape lingering dream images of sobbing crowds trampling on her Kiley for Senate signs littering the ballroom floor. The phone was ringing. She reached to answer it. Only one person would call at four in the morning.

"I was wrong about the diligence of your press secretary. You rate a full page in the *Washington Daily*, photos too." His voice greeted her.

Electrical current shot along her nerves. This was not good news. She pushed a tangled mass of black hair away from her face and pressed the phone closer.

"Do they name you?" Her voice filled with fear—residue from the dream.

"Oh yes, I make the list."

"List?"

"More than a dozen photos of you, each with a different man."

Kat was stunned. "What? What men?"

"It's distinguished company, and you look gorgeous in every picture, as usual. You and President Jamison are standing tanned and smiling on the deck of some boat. In the picture with Prince Charles they catch your nose at a bad angle but compared to him you're a sculptor's dream."

She moaned in dismay as he continued.

"And I thought we had something special. Here you are making eyes at Charlie Drummond from ABC, and in this one you're with some Hollywood hunk —dueling eyebrows."

"I don't want to hear any more," she said, attempting to halt his amused recital.

"Wait. The three best are coming up. You and the Dalai Lama, then you and three New Guinea mudmen. I think those three are mudmen, although they could be the Democratic Senate leadership. Finally, there's a picture that must be at least a decade old. Your face is fuller and your hair is long and wild, covered with white lace. You're standing with a demure look next to the Pope."

"The Pope! You can't be serious." Kat rubbed her eyes and looked out the window at the dark sky. Was she actually awake?

"It's fortunate I'm a secure man. One with balls as you well know. I'm not shown until the bottom of the page. We do look good together though, better than you and the Holy Father. I'll admit to a bit of pride that my lady is able to tempt the Supreme Pontiff of the Roman Catholic Church. That should win you a few undecided votes in Rhode Island."

Muttering obscenities under her breath, Kat slid a long leg out from under her crazy quilt and onto the wood floor. She shuddered as she looked in the carved walnut dressing mirror that stood near her bed. Patting the hollows beneath her prominent cheekbones, she acknowledged he was right. Her face was more angular, gaunt in fact. The campaign had taken its toll.

Dark eyebrows, high-bridged nose, unruly mane of black hair—she resembled a pre-Mosaic Egyptian queen or goddess. Or an albino raccoon, she thought, rubbing the dark smudges beneath her large gray eyes. Her wide mouth, bare of its usual red lipstick cover, added to the impression.

"I'm bringing copies of the paper with me for your memory book. I'll be there in a couple hours. Have someone meet me at the Charlestown airstrip, and assemble your staff for a meeting, probably by seven a.m."

Kat barely heard his words. There were only two days until the election. What could she do to counter this in such a short time? As if reading her mind, his voice became serious.

"The headline says it all: *Who's the Lucky Man?* Either their source doesn't know about me, or he's waiting to up the suspense—and the price—by exposing us piecemeal."

"He? Do you know who?" Kat's voice was strained.

"Preventive measures have been taken," he said quickly. "I'll tell you when I get there."

An angry flush crawled up her face and emerged in her tone.

"What do you mean 'preventive measures'? What have you done? Why do you refuse to talk with me before going ahead and..."

"There's no other way, Kiley." His deep, rich voice was patient but firm as he interrupted. "This is my scandal, too. It's come down to war and I'm committed to getting you out alive. I'm sorry I didn't consult you before drawing my sword. That's the problem with us heroes, we take all this chivalry to heart. I'll be there soon. You can berate me in person."

As he hung up, Kat lowered her head into her hands. "Men," she muttered.

1

Milady's Secret
November 1989

Morgan Springs
Washington

Roxy was only halfway up the steep hill that led from the hot springs when she regretted her decision to climb the stone steps cut into Warm Springs Ridge. The scripts she was delivering were heavier than they seemed when she set out. She should have driven to the castle.

Max was introducing a new murder mystery for the winter season. He called about her final edits insisting she deliver them to the Circle Room at the top of the castle tower at dusk. Magic. She smelled magic. Max kept his magic in the tower room.

Soon she would be leaving for Rhode Island and Kat's U.S. Senate campaign. Roxy wondered if his insistence had anything to do with offering her advice—oracular advice, she presumed.

Maybe he would tell her this was the year she could streamline her naturally rounded shape and he would give her a potion to do that without having to give up the pleasure of food. She snorted her way up the last few steps. No chance Max would reveal to her the path to self-indulgence without consequence.

She caught her breath admiring the remarkable stone structure with its towers and battlements. It did not seem at all strange for Max, oracle and magician, to live in a castle. It was somewhat miraculous that they all found their way to the small town built in the mountains of Virginia, and found a century-old castle there.

When Max first saw it in the late '70s, it was in serious disrepair. He spent a year using his predictive skills to make money in commodities, enough money to buy the place outright. He maintained a small apartment in the south tower but used the castle mostly as a showcase for his magic theater. Kat was part owner and financed many of the renovations and furnishings.

Turning the last twist of ornate metal stairs that led to the tower-top room, she saw Max looking out one of the round windows facing the town. He bounced his large, powerful body lightly on the balls of his feet as he rolled a silver dollar across his knuckles, palming it to reappear and roll again. Just a prestidigitator practicing my art, Max would explain when anyone asked.

Roxy knew the coin rolling was both a familiar trick Max used in his magic performances as well as a nervous habit. The number and speed of the marching coins served as indicators of his psychic tension. Light from sconces mounted in the stone walls cast shadows on his square face and made his almost white hair gleam as he passed in front of one. His full mustache, several shades darker than his hair, swept from under his narrow nose into two magnificent arcs. Three small emeralds studded his left ear.

Max seemed distracted as she chattered about the scripts, flashing her dimples and flipping her bright blond hair in her own version of tension release. "Aren't you going to Washington tomorrow for the first round of campaign meetings?" he asked.

He walked over to the rosewood library table that was a prized possession. It had a globe and stars inlaid at each end in brass and mother-of-pearl. The top was embossed with a celestial field. He picked up a file with her name on it and another marked Campaign. Roxy's heart sank. This was not a casual question. Max was going to talk about trends, patterns, aspects and who knows what else, predicting what would happen. She did not want to hear it. She was anxious enough about this undertaking. His prognostications would only make it worse.

"Are you concerned?" He was looking directly at her, his voice filled with a knowing tone that made it impossible for her to dissemble.

"A little." Her answer was more hesitant than she meant it to be and she hurried to explain. "Campaign politics is new to me. I know I've written material for Kat in the past but it was never this important. She's surrounded by high-powered professionals who'll think I don't belong in the game, and frankly, they may be right. I'm not sure I know what I'm supposed to be doing."

Max leaned against the table and motioned for her to sit facing him in a carved walnut chair with arms that ended in lion heads. Roxy squirmed her hand into a lion's mouth and waited for him to begin.

"Stop worrying about whether people will like you or not. They will. They always do," he said. His smile was surprisingly kind.

"You're fun, accommodating and don't compete. They're going to love you on the campaign. It won't take them long to recognize that you write Kat better than anyone. Besides, you're a published author with six novels to your credit. They'll be impressed. Most political writers are hacks."

Her green eyes brightened.

"You're there because Kat needs you. I'm not sure she could do this without you." Roxy waved dismissively

"She can buy political talent. You'll remind her of the personal and intimate when she gets too abstract. You're a loyal friend and she can trust you with her life."

Roxy's skin began to prickle at the ominous tone in his voice.

"Do you see terrible things happening?"

Max flipped the silver dollar he was rolling in the air and caught it, slapping it on the back of his hand.

"Heads" he said, describing the coin's lay. "Is that terrible?"

The only thing she hated worse than Max the mind reader was Max the Zen master. She threw up her hands.

"OK. I give up. What do I need to know?"

He gestured to the folder.

"Kat and I will discuss the specific timing and context of the campaign predictions. There are general directions you need to understand as well as your part in it. Kat's senate race is more than a political campaign. It's mythic. Myths have rules and laws peculiar to that form and these are mythic laws you'll learn by living them. Think of this as practical experience for your secret fantasy to write new myths for children."

Max looked up at her. "The personal tests prohibit you from standing aside as an observer. You're an important part of the pattern." She had an uneasy premonition that mythic laws were like gravity, hard to resist once set in motion.

"Are you saying this will be a literal myth with heroes and goddesses and terrible monsters? Are you going to do magic so Kat wins?"

"I serve destiny, I don't threaten it," Max said. "As for the myth," he chuckled and muttered almost to himself, "I'm not sure the Republican party is ready for Kat's vision of herself as Athena prepared to infuse the political process with the twin lightning bolts of truth and feminine wisdom."

Roxy did not like the sound of that at all.

"I want to hear more about my personal tests," she said.

"It's one of those difficult phases when you have to make choices. Not easy, I know, for someone so devoted to the path of least resistance." He cocked an eyebrow at her shudder.

"Sorry, Roxy. The tests will be emotional in nature—and unavoidable."

Max spread out papers covered with arcane symbols and glyphs written in his almost italic hand.

"The book on the campaign is short and sweet at this early stage. It will be a mythic quest for Kat, for you, for several other figures that appear in my scrying. Some parts will be glorious, some will be painful; much of it is still shielded from sight."

"Just so long as it doesn't involve men, I can tolerate anything. I've given up men forever."

Roxy pouted, drawing her already bow-shaped mouth into a tiny pucker and collapsing her dimples into minor creases.

"There are definitely men involved. But that's to be expected. Politics, sex, magic—they're all a quest for power. The dark side will be present with jealousy, deceit, and betrayal in abundance.

"Why don't you want men around? I thought they were your favorite oppo-site sex."

She refused to be teased out of sulking.

"I've sworn off men since that bum, Clancy, set off to work on oil rigs in the Gulf of Mexico. All his talk about my being his little pillow and he still disap-peared. I had to stop seeing Greg when Clancy left. It didn't seem right to use a nice man like him to soothe my broken heart."

When he didn't respond, Roxy continued.

"You know how irrational I am when it comes to falling in love. Snap! One word from a man with the right voice and chemistry at a weak moment and I'm in his bed and obsessed for months. What if it's the wrong man, someone who can hurt Kat or the campaign?"

"This is your year for profound adventures of the heart. Learning to say no could be one of your big lessons."

Roxy grimaced. No was a seldom used word in her vocabulary. Only her teen-age heroines in the adventure novels she wrote were virginal and able to resist sensual lures. If there was sexual energy on the campaign trail, it would find her. Kat would be happy with the magic and power.

"It's like I have an on / off button activated by voice control, only I don't get to choose whose voice. Can't you do some spell that will turn my love sensor off for the next year?"

When Max reached into a basket on the table and pulled out a pink velvet bag, Roxy was elated. Could he really do that kind of magic?

"I created a special batch of Max's Fortune Strips for you. There are thirteen, one for each month. Pick one for November now."

She sighed, wanting more substantial assistance than Max's often obscure messages.

"I have several volumes of medieval magic. I could probably find a chastity belt in one that might work," he offered, once again responding to her thoughts. Her pout deepened as she reached into the bag and drew out a folded piece of paper.

Opening it, she read: *Your choice makes possibility real.*

★ ★ ★ ★ ★

It was weird to see Kat's opponent speeding alongside her on the Whitehurst Freeway the morning she drove in from Virginia. Senator Winston occupied her thoughts the rest of the way to the Capitol. As Roxy walked the hall of the Longworth building, she reviewed what she knew about him. Winston was the longtime senator, very popular and had one of those convoluted personal con-nections with Kat that came in modern society—he was the uncle of her ex-husband. According to Kat, he was not a bad senator, he just did nothing and, in her mind, there was much that needed doing.

For the hundredth time, Roxy wondered why Kat was running. Her congressional seat in the House of Representatives was safe after eight years; she could be re-elected forever with virtually no effort. It seemed easier for her to wait until the other senate seat came up in four years.

A young intern directed her into the private office where Kat presided over a staff meeting, looking serene and controlled as usual. Roxy slipped into the empty chair next to Mario De Palma, Kat's young political chief in Rhode Island. He was her favorite of all the staff, an almost universal female sentiment. She could never decide what made him so appealing—liquid black eyes in a cherub face with soft black hair, his perfect manners, or the absorbed attention with which he greeted all women as if they were treasures to be discovered.

Roxy noticed new faces among the familiar ones, additions geared to the upcoming senate campaign. Kat nodded a greeting and turned to the man on her right, asking him to summarize her current political situation. He began, the cold precision of his words softened by the honeyed cadence of his drawl.

"It's early November. While the incumbent senator, a Democrat, has not officially announced his intent to run again for what he terms 'the best job in the world,' there is little question that he will. Reynolds Winston is very popular. He is also the powerful chairman of the Senate Finance committee with a virtually unlimited capacity to raise money. With his party only two seats away from losing control of the Senate, the Democratic leadership will do everything they can to keep that seat.

"On the other hand, there are vague rumors of fraudulent tests of a controversial tranquilizer his family's pharmaceutical firm produces. At this time, Senator Winston has not been implicated in the savings and loan scandal except through inaction, his greatest skill as we've come to know. He has more than 2 million dollars in his re-election account that he could pocket should he choose to retire.

"Our candidate," he nodded to Kat, "is personally committed though undeclared. She is as popular as Winston, and as well known in Rhode Island. Her record of activism on health, environmental, and women's issues is matchless. Her work serving constituents is superlative."

Roxy could barely distinguish the words as his voice sent waves of pleasure through her body. She groaned. Who was this guy? Everyone was listening with rapt attention, so he must be a key player. Not that it mattered. She was sure Kat would consider anyone on her staff to be an inappropriate choice for one of Roxy's love obsessions. She tried to concentrate on anything except his voice, but nothing could distract her from that seductive sound.

"At a minimum we need to raise three million dollars, probably more. The National Republican Senatorial Committee will help. They see the current two-vote margin as a not-to-be missed opportunity for regaining control of the Senate. They're thrilled Kiley Tomasso has chosen to run.

"Our task during the next year is to convince one more than fifty percent of the voters that Rhode Island can no longer afford Winston's affable do-nothing style. Kiley Tomasso must be their next senator."

Responding to Kat's almost imperceptible tightening, he added smoothly, "Of course, our real margin of victory will be much greater."

"Then let's think that way from the very beginning," Kat said abruptly.

Roxy tried to sort out the detailed exchanges about what issues to stress, how to win various endorsements, and methods for invading the other district, the half of the state Kat did not now represent. When disagreements began, the points were easier to understand.

"Hayes, my position on this is clear," Kat's tone was firm.

Hayes Redcliffe. Roxy remembered from her study of Kat's staff list that he was the new chief of staff. A man named Hayes with southern comfort in his voice was running Kat's office. Obviously, it was one of the personal tests Max predicted. She better find a way to avoid falling off this cliff. Kat would strangle her if she became entangled with one of her staff.

"No negative campaign. No dirty tricks. No spreading rumors of scandals to humiliate Winston. If there are investigations and they demonstrate illegal or dishonorable actions on the senator's part, I'm sure it will be revealed. No one is more affronted by public and media acceptance of Winston's charm and good nature as sufficient evidence of his worthiness to remain in the office than I am, but how we conduct this campaign is as important to me as its outcome."

Kat launched into a recital of complaints about the senseless, mean-spirited rhetoric of the previous year's presidential campaign.

"I'm determined that the 1990 Senate campaign in Rhode Island will show the country, and the world, that electoral politics can be about issues. No demeaning or degrading the opponent. In fact, I don't have an opponent. I am running against no one. I am running for the United States Senate and the people of Rhode Island need me there. Let's convince them of that."

Roxy caught a glimpse of cold blue eyes and a tight frown as Hayes leaned forward to scowl at his boss. Maybe ignoring him would not be so difficult after all.

"Political reality favors inertia," he replied, the drawl sharpened almost completely out of his voice. "You may think Winston has accomplished little, but he's accumulated significant clout and done enough for the state that voters will need a compelling reason to unseat him. You may not be thinking of him as an opponent but voters are simple. They have to choose you or Winston. Conventional wisdom says you lose without a negative campaign."

Kat's eyes narrowed.

"Conventional wisdom bet against me in '82 when I became the first woman

MILADY'S SECRET

in the state's history elected to federal office. Conventional wisdom predicted defeat for most of the legislation I've gotten passed. The only thing conventional wisdom has right is that in order for me to accomplish what needs to be done, I need to be in the Senate."

She suddenly smiled and her voice lost its edge.

"Besides, I thought electing a Republican Senate was the driving force of your life, the reason you're here."

He nodded in agreement.

"Then let's talk about how we win this seat."

Graciousness returned to Hayes' voice.

"We all agree that press will be essential to our victory, not just state coverage which Mario handles brilliantly, but national media as well. Kiley Tomasso must become such a superstar that people will beg for her to be their senator. To develop our national media image," he waved to his right, "our new press secretary, Jasmine Elliott."

Kat was disappointed when her long-time communications director left to write screenplays in Hollywood. He had handled all press duties as well as writing most of Kat's speeches and statements. His departure was the official reason for Roxy's presence.

Roxy examined Jasmine closely. Even if the press secretary was officially congressional staff, she would also be involved in the campaign. The overlap was unavoidable. Score another point for incumbency, thought Roxy. No wonder more than ninety-five percent of the members got reelected.

Jasmine looked to be in her early thirties, tall and thin with short auburn hair. Henna or natural? Roxy decided the color must be a cruel act of nature. Who would ever choose it? Her blouse and skirt were severe but in bold colors. She peered at people sitting around the office over a pair of half glasses. Her tight, narrow face looked like she spent more hours in any one morning making it up than Roxy had accumulated in her thirty-eight years. Thin lines in the corners of her eyes and lips hinted that smiling was not a favorite exercise.

The meeting concluded with briefings from Mario about politics in Rhode Island and some heated discussions about policy from several of Kat's more radical staff. Kat had gathered a group of idealists who reluctantly worked for a Republican because they trusted her continued opposition to the party's various backward positions. She repeatedly assured them that Republican money to finance the senate race would not buy automatic party-line votes once she won the seat.

Roxy stayed in her seat, waiting until the staff left so she could check in with Kat.

Mario leaned over and whispered to her, "I'm not flying back until tomorrow night. Several of us are planning to meet at the Irish Times about six. Why don't you come along? Kat has a formal dinner on her schedule, so she won't need you."

Smiling agreement, she wondered if Hayes would be there, too.

★ ★ ★ ★ ★

Mario was holding court surrounded by a bevy of the bright young women that populated the congressional world, known universally as the Hill. The place reminded Roxy of her college hangouts: wood paneled, noisy, filled with excitement, and packed with scores of ambitious young people in booths and around heavy wooden tables marked with cigarette burns and the stains of countless glass rings. She noticed Hayes sitting at one end of the table engrossed in conversation. Slipping onto the empty chair at his other side, she joined in a conversation led by Kat's vivacious secretary Maggie, who was the mainstay of daily office routine.

They were swapping horror stories about outrageous behavior by members of Congress. One young woman confessed a drunken encounter with a congressman when she was a sixteen-year-old page. After a staff softball game, he lured her up to his apartment where he attempted sexual advances.

"He passed out before he could do any serious damage," she explained matter-of-factly. Another discussed her reign as the "office wife" of a long-time southern representative who fired her abruptly when his legal wife decided to move from Mississippi to join her dear husband in Washington. Both were thrilled to be working for Kat who was called the Ice Queen by fellow members whom she socially discouraged.

Roxy shuddered. She had been hassled less working in bars. The din was beginning to fray her nerves when Mario came over and stood behind her chair, poking Hayes to get his attention.

"I need a place to stay tonight. I've gotten several offers of spare couches," Roxy looked up at Mario, amused as he nodded to the table of girls, "but I'd hate to cause dissention in the ranks by making a choice. Can I stay with you, Hayes?"

"Of course," Hayes got up. "In fact, why don't we three go now. We need to talk about tomorrow's meetings. I have beer at home, and we're only a few blocks away."

Roxy was surprised that his invitation included her. She was certain he scarcely noticed her. He looked directly at her.

"I need to get to know you. I'm told you're Kat's resident confidante."

When he took her hand and raised her from the chair with an inviting smile, she groaned inwardly. He looked like all the men she ever loved, compactly built with light hair and stunning clear blue eyes that magnetized her interest. But it was that voice that pushed her over the edge. It was irrational but unmistakable. An intimate connection now lodged in every fiber of her being with Hayes' voiceprint on it.

As they drove, Hayes delivered a non-stop lecture on the passage of restoration and rehabilitation eastward through Capitol Hill neighborhoods.

"You can tell when a house has been renovated by the door; cut glass or elaborate antique wood ones have been transplanted from now-demolished mansions. This is the edge of acceptable territory," he explained as they parked in front of his row house just off 14th Street in Southeast.

"The streets seem peaceful and tree-shaded as you move further east, but it's deceptive. Crack houses, drug deals and gun-toting punks lurk everywhere. I love this street. All the houses here have front porches and backyards. Mine is the only one with a swing, in case you need to find your way back sometime." He leaned toward Roxy suggestively as she turned off the car.

Once inside, Hayes pointed them to the dining room table.

"This is a special occasion. It's initiation time for you two." He disappeared and returned carrying an elaborate wooden tray with three intricately carved narrow silver goblets, a silver bowl of salt, another of sliced limes, and a bottle of Mezcal con Gusano complete with agave worm.

"Have you ever done Mezcal shots, Roxy?" he asked as he poured the gold distillate and set a goblet in front of each person.

She shook her head, trying to appear unconcerned, gripping the can of beer she picked out of the refrigerator on her way in. It was obviously an honor to be included in this ritual, and she was determined to appreciate it.

"It's a different kind of liquor. Distilled from Maguay, the same plant that provides mescaline, Mezcal gives a high that is almost hallucinogenic. This is the real thing. I bought it in Oaxaca where it's made. There are shops everywhere that exclusively sell Mezcal. You go in with your bottle and get it filled for less than fifty cents.

"As for shooting it, this is how it's done." He pried the beer from Roxy's hand. "Moisten this area between your thumb and index finger."

A quiver shot up her belly as he ran his tongue slowly across the crotch of her hand and deliberately caught her eye.

"Sprinkle some salt there." Her hands shook as she followed his direction. Hayes sat down next to her, prepared his own hand and instructed: "Lick it off. Now all together, we shoot the Mezcal."

Roxy licked her hand, tasted the salt then bolted down the liquid as the two men did. She was jolted by the sensual flavor and powerful body rush; it felt warm from her throat to her stomach.

"Finish it off by sucking on the lime."

She completed the ritual and sat very still, waiting. He quickly poured another round and he and Mario began sprinkling salt on their hands again. She lasted one more round before her spinning head hinted at the need to stop if she wanted to talk, or at least be able to mouth the words should she think of anything to say.

If this stuff could make her see visions, she needed to be careful. She didn't want that icky worm in her glass. No biting any pickled worm in half, bonding or no bonding. The men finished their third round then settled in to solve world problems. In this case, the world was limited to Kat's senate campaign.

It took a few minutes for Roxy to decipher the white noise she heard coming from them. Mezcal was potent stuff. A salty taste stung her lips and a burning sphere hung just under her heart. Mario was grinning.

"Now we're getting down to the real stuff of politics—good, serious gossip. What about this Jasmine Elliott, our new press secretary. What do you think of her, Hayes?"

"No causing cause more gossip than you hear," Hayes warned the younger man. Mario shrugged his shoulders, unconcerned.

"People know I always have good stories to tell. It makes them more ready to tell theirs. And since all my stories are told on myself, there's no one to retaliate."

"And it's your version that gets spread." There was admiration in Hayes' voice and an affectionate look on his face.

"But back to Jasmine," scolded Mario. "Did you check her out yourself? And did Kat really want her?"

The chief of staff seemed defensive as he answered.

"She has impeccable Republican credentials," he began. "She worked on all the presidential campaigns since Ford in '76. Her father is Michael Elliott, the ultimate cliff dweller, Washington insider, and important Republican moneyman.

"Jasmine's been her father's hostess since her mother died. She knows everyone worth knowing, and everything about them," Hayes concluded.

"Are we buying insurance by hiring her?" Mario asked. "If she's working for Kat does that mean she won't talk about her?"

Something made Roxy uncomfortable about Hayes' look.

"Or do you expect Daddy Elliott to make a big contribution to Kat's campaign for hiring his darling daughter?"

"I wasn't thinking about money when I recruited Jasmine and you know Kat would never have hired her if she didn't think she could get the job done."

"Well, I don't like her." Roxy was startled by what she said although as soon as she heard herself say it she knew it was true. She didn't like Jasmine Elliott.

"She gives me the creeps. She kept examining everyone at the meeting today like they were dinner."

Mario smiled as he reached over to pat her hand.

"I don't like her either. But I think she spent most of her time watching you, Roxy. I've heard she likes smooth legs."

She looked puzzled; he patted her hand again.

"Girls, Roxy. She likes girls."

"What's the matter, Mario, couldn't get a yes out of her so you think she's gay?" Hayes mocked the young man who smiled disarmingly.

"It has nothing to do with whether a woman responds to me or not. I can tell. There's something. She looked at every man in the room like she was erasing everything between their belt buckle and their knees."

The Mezcal began to take effect and Hayes shimmered in a golden light that made him increasingly resemble her lifetime image of Prince Charming. Roxy decided she needed to find out more about him before her sexual compulsions drove reason totally away.

"How did you come to be in politics?" she asked as the gleam in his eyes made her head spin.

He said his Piedmont family and classic education at Wake Forest directed him to a career in the church.

"But I loved strategy and Confederate military history. I wanted to affect the future. So I chose politics instead."

Hayes took another sip of Mezcal and continued his story.

The local Democrats were chaotic and divided. His Republican senator needed campaign volunteers, so Hayes signed on. The old man liked the way he thought and his responsible attitude. Soon he was the senator's 'round the clock driver and protégé, learning the workings of electoral politics from a master.

As the senator got older, he didn't share Hayes' view that women and environmental concerns were the future of politics.

"I left with his blessings. I had my pick of campaigns, politicians or appointments. I heard that Kiley Tomasso was planning to run for the Senate. If she won, the Republicans would control the Senate. If I helped make that happen, my political career would be guaranteed."

"I read those articles about what an odd choice you were to be Kat's chief of staff and political advisor," Mario said. Hayes nodded agreement.

"Conventional wisdom gets it wrong again. It may be an unexpected choice but it made everyone happy. The Republican Senate committee saw me as one of their own, Kat needed my campaign expertise, and I'm appreciative of the chance to make a major contribution. Besides, I like her politics and her integrity, no matter what some of the staff think."

"I was one of the doubters," Mario confessed, "but no longer. You've convinced me of your superior managerial and political skills a dozen times over."

Hayes poured himself and Mario another shot of Mezcal. As he downed it, he smiled at Roxy and sighed, "Mutual admiration, nectar of the gods."

They all laughed. This was her idea of a great meeting: people sitting around drinking, laughing, and doing business.

"When I asked Kat about you," Mario continued, "She claimed you were a master strategist. I think it was the two different dog-eared translations of Sun

Tzu's *Art of War* on your desk that convinced her you were the one she needed. And that you quoted, in perfect context, the passage she chose for the campaign: 'It is as though all the forces of nature are working towards one's own objective.'"

Hayes smiled. "I must admit, I was equally impressed by her acquaintance with the sage of strategy. It's a little disconcerting that she uses him as a guide for personal growth."

"Mutual admiration, nectar of the gods," Mario mimicked as he downed his Mezcal then stood and announced he was ready for bed.

"We have meetings all day tomorrow," he reminded his host.

Hayes whistled as he saw it was almost midnight, pointed Mario upstairs to the spare room then walked Roxy to the door.

He lifted her long blonde hair outside the jacket he helped her put on, running his hand lightly along the back of her neck. Roxy's knees weakened as she felt the bottom of her stomach drop. She was horrified. Maybe it was the Mezcal. Maybe she was hallucinating. There was no way Kat would allow a consuming infatuation with her chief of staff.

"Are you OK to drive?" he asked, looking into her eyes, his hand moving slowly up her arm, his voice low and intimate.

"I'll take you back to Kat's and you can pick up your car here in the morning. We don't want anything to happen to you." When he kissed her lightly, but with a hint of more than a collegial good-night, Roxy fled out the door.

It was not his fault, she rationalized, driving through the deserted streets. Her love chemistry was as addictive as any drug and his seductive voice triggered it. She couldn't even blame the liquor. She knew the burning would not go away when she was sober.

★ ★ ★ ★ ★

The morning ritual when Roxy stayed at Kat's Washington house was always the same. She slept in what Kat called the playroom. Two walls were lined with books and electronic equipment and a third was paneled in mirrors. There was a thickly padded carpet, trapeze, and ballet barre for exercise. Kat treated her possessions as art and loved looking at them. Her fabulous jewelry and scarf collections hung on the fourth wall and into the large dressing room that opened from it.

This morning, as on most others, both women were up at dawn.

Roxy rolled over and switched on the television as she prepared to spend her usual ten minutes getting ready for the day, a daily pattern that made her the object of undying irritation for several of the roommates she had during her life. She sat cross-legged in front of the wall of mirrors and creamed her face. Her mother told her years ago that a woman's skin was more precious than jewels. She often wondered if her freckle-dusted peaches and cream complexion was as valuable as Kat's porcelain perfection.

She breathed a prayer of thanks to whatever guardian angel granted her thick blonde hair that needed little but the flick of a brush to hang smoothly, and curly dark lashes that framed her startling green eyes. She never wore lipstick; it made her tiny, bow-shaped mouth look ridiculous. But she did smile a lot, partly because she was a naturally happy person. Smiling also expanded her mouth and created her dimples. Her chin was rounded and her cheeks were rosy. Her nose was too pert for a dignified profile. She often accentuated her smooth brow by pulling her hair back from it. All the pieces were acceptable, it was the overall effect she continually lamented. Cute. She was cute. Roxy hated the word. Just once she wanted to be described as exotic, interesting, bold—anything but cute. She was almost forty and men still told her they wanted their daughters to grow up to be a nice girl like her. When she took them to bed, they stopped saying it.

It did not help when Kat regularly reminded her that cute little blondes with big tits were her worst nightmare as rivals since high school days.

She was watching Headline News, occasionally switching through the channels to see whether she was missing anything on another station when Kat came in and began stretching and twisting on her ballet barre.

Whenever the rhythms of their distinct lives brought them together on a daily basis, Roxy knew what her role was: she fed Kat gossip both celebrity and personal. The prodigious information bank in Kat's head was crammed with important knowledge about scientific principles, historical patterns, and arcane facts. She was an avid reader with a remarkable library at her Rhode Island house filled with literature, art books, science texts, philosophy, history, and esoteric volumes. She wasted no time on the passing stream of trivia that captured the scattered attention of mainstream culture. Still, Kat could summon every fact she needed from minor amendments attached to whatever bill was on the House floor to the name of the Soviet Foreign Minister's new granddaughter.

"Osmosis" was Kat's explanation whenever Roxy questioned her, usually mildly annoyed at having her know another news tidbit that she thought was hot off the press.

"I'm fortunate to have a life full of wonderful people like you, and my staff, who absorb all this information so I can pick it up by osmosis. I skim the headlines as I walk by news boxes, half listen to radio, television, and conversations in elevators or movie lines then imagine the worst and stupidest possible actions humans could take. I'm usually right on target with the news."

Kat came over and stood by the futon her friend used as a bed.

"Let's talk about the campaign and what I need from you."

Roxy fixed back on Headline News, muted the sound, and prepared to listen.

"You know that Max described the campaign as a mythic quest. One of the requirements is to think in new ways. When the Berlin Wall came down last week, I saw the door to the future open wide. The Wall was the epitome of all that was old, dead, and corrupt in the world. If it could crumble, anything could. Now is a time when those willing to ignore the old rules, see with new eyes, ask the same old questions in new ways, can transform the world.

"Some of the old-ways folks will be nominally on my side in the senate race," she warned. "With only a two-seat margin, every senate race this year is to the death." Kat's voice tightened.

"The Republican Senatorial Committee is lining up their issues people to push me as far to the right as they can, and their hit men to target Winston's weaknesses and draw blood. Every time there's a vote on the floor, someone calls to remind me what the acceptable party line is. It seems there's little room in the GOP they know and love for social libertarians and ecologists like me. They must take a secret oath to uphold the divine right of rich white men to rule in the U.S. Senate."

Roxy smiled, imagining the picture she had seen of a prune-faced old senator who was identified as the man controlling the millions that got doled out by the Senatorial committee to promising campaigns. His penciled eyebrows would reach for the ceiling if he could see Kat parade around in her underwear pronouncing such political heresy.

Lingerie was one of Kat's obsessions. Rumor had it she heavily financed the initial expansion of Milady's Secret, whose catalogs and mall stores made sensual an accepted quality in women's underwear and sports clothes. If she didn't, she should have, thought Roxy. She had a body that was made for displaying lingerie and owned an extensive wardrobe of it but in only two colors at a time. The colors changed, always simultaneously, and never more than two. The current phase was silver gray and forest green. Kat was wearing the green. Roxy never knew what happened to the underwear once new colors were selected; it was not an item you handed down to friends.

"One of the main reasons I begged you to come work with me was to provide a different point of view, as a woman, an artist, and a good friend. You understand how I feel about intuition, magic, and working for higher purpose. You're not caught up in the glamour of power and money."

Kat sounded anxious. Hanging lightly from her hands on the trapeze with her knees grazing the soft blue carpet, she continued earnestly.

"I need you to write for me, to help me have fun, and to be there for me when I haven't time to ask."

Much of Kat's concern came from the stress and conflict of being a beautiful woman in a bastion of male power. For all her abstract arguments and lack of enthusiasm for amorous adventures, she agreed with Roxy that men and women were different and both were needed for a balanced world. From the time her first boyfriend kissed her, Roxy knew without question that balls and a swinging dick gave males a certain approach to life that was unlike the attitude wombs gave females. She often thought about the distinctions between men and women, treating the subject as an almost scholarly pursuit, one she used occasionally to defend her active and varied social life.

Standing tall and shapely in a lacy demi-bra and flutter bikinis, Kat left no question of her qualifications to represent the value of unique feminine traits in the political world. There was also no question why Roxy was needed. What male on Kat's staff would be able to handle this scene with professional detachment?

"Women in power go against the grain." Kat was still talking, brush in hand, sporadically stirring up her unruly hair with it. "All this power that everyone in Washington craves is simply another form of sexual energy. I guess it's threatening for some people to see women exercising it freely."

Kat walked over to the window.

"Sometimes I catch one of the more entrenched members of Congress looking at me with horror in his eyes. I know he's thinking that soon there will be more of me, more women wanting power, surrounding him and his kind, cutting them off forever from the dominance they think should belong exclusively to them."

Roxy secretly thought it was far more disturbing for some of those good ol' boys to catch a whiff of Kat's perfume in the members elevator or watch the curve of her ass as she walked up the steps in front of them.

"He's right to be afraid. He knows what I know. A Congress that's half female will no longer be his Congress. It may not be Congress at all." Kat looked at Roxy with an ironic smile on her face. "More heresy, I know," she sighed.

Walking over to the mirrors, Kat began brushing her hair in earnest, trying to coerce it into modest behavior.

"I wanted more women around on the campaign."

"Is that why you hired Jasmine?"

"In part. She's also an outstanding press secretary and committed to the idea of helping women advance in the political world."

"Mario says she's gay."

Kat turned away from the mirrors and gave her a piercing glance.

"And how did Mario come to that conclusion?"

Roxy shrugged.

"He said he could just tell. Do you know if she is?"

"Considering Mario's effect on women, he's probably right," Kat responded. "When he moves over to campaign, I hope to find a woman to replace him in my Rhode Island congressional office."

"Couldn't you find a woman for the chief of staff job?"

"Hayes is the best. He has an uncanny political sense, understands the Hill perfectly, and knows all the Republican players. This is one time my independence isn't paying off. I need the party for this race. I need to raise millions. I need the prestige and favors the administration can provide. They want another Republican in the Senate. Hayes is my broker. In the eyes of the Senatorial committee, his pragmatic attitude guarantees my idealistic fervor won't get out of control."

Kat continued to tick off what she saw as the important qualities of her chief of staff. "He's charming, intelligent and able to constructively disagree. He has an incredible amount of knowledge and is adept at passing it on to me in useful and concise ways. He also has a biting edge to his mind. I don't trust men who are too nice."

Roxy breathed a sigh of relief as Kat walked into her room-sized closet to pick out the clothes she would wear. She did not want Kat to spot the blush that was spreading over her cheeks as she thought about Hayes and how she would like to find out if he was indeed the best. Her graphic speculation halted when Kat walked back into the room pulling a forest green silk skirt over a gold medallion printed jacquard blouse.

The narrow skirt was slit up the back several inches above Kat's knees. The tailored suit jacket had a snug waist and tiny peplum that grazed the top of her hips. She broke all the limiting rules about dressing for success. No gray or dark suits with white blouses and silk scarves; no modest pearl earrings and black leather flats. Glamorous and memorable, she blazed even brighter in a city and business where glamour meant power not beauty.

Kat touched up the red polish on her nails and painted a matching color on her generous lips then turned and faced Roxy.

"There will be a lot of people wanting pieces of me during this campaign, trying to push me in one direction or another. We've been friends for almost twenty years. I trust you with parts of my life few other people even know exist. I need you watching for me when I can't do it for myself. That's why your specific role in the campaign will be vague. Officially you'll be there to write my words —speeches, brochures, statements—but in fact you'll be one of my guardian angels. I have a feeling I'm going to need a few. No detailed job description for you my friend, and no real title. I hope your ego can take it."

It was an easy sell. Roxy had accepted Kat as a teacher/guide years ago when they met in college. There had been periods where one or the other of their lives took them to different parts of the country or even the world, but the bond was never broken. It took but a shared breath for it to seem as if they had tea together just yesterday.

"You know I don't care about job descriptions and resumes or about politics," Roxy answered. "I'm doing this for you."

"Maybe you can get material for your next book," Kat replied with a knowing smile.

"Maybe. But I would have to switch genres. There's not much call for senate campaigns in teen-age adventure novels."

"But there is if you're writing myths."

Roxy began to get herself dressed.

"If only I could be back at St. Patrick's wearing a uniform every day," she sighed. "I wouldn't need to worry about how I looked, what I wore, did it send the right message."

Knit leggings and an oversized sweatshirt were her idea of the perfect outfit. It served well in her study where she spun out Shane Marlow adventure stories. Working with Kat forced major changes in her wardrobe. She was thrilled to find a line of soft knit skirts with matching pullover tops that were passable in professional Washington and acceptable to her.

Kat took an exquisite brooch from the wall and attached it to the soft petal collar of her blouse. It was a female face cast in gold, snake-like spirals of hair streaming from her head, garnets set as her blazing eyes.

"Medusa," Kat murmured as if in invocation. "Her head was fixed on Athena's breastplate for strength."

It always jolted Roxy when Kat calmly switched to the role that had earned her the nickname "high priestess" long before she ever dreamed of politics and the Senate. Even after years of sharing some incredible experiences, Roxy found this side of Kat a little weird and implausible.

Kat was an authentic mystic or occultist—Roxy could never understand the subtle difference that allegedly existed between the two—and considered it a destiny not a choice.

"It was all part of the package. When I stood in line waiting to be born," she would say, "they gave me great legs, electric shock hair, Duke as a father, and an assignment sheet that said channel your magic through politics and you can change the world. I guess I must have asked for a life of challenge."

Kat adopted the Greek goddess of wisdom as her model years ago when she began exploring the ancient myths as a way of understanding female energy. She often suggested to Roxy that her patron should be Aphrodite, goddess of love. Thinking about Aphrodite started Roxy thinking about Hayes again, wondering if there was a way around Kat's iron-clad ban on collegial consorting.

★ ★ ★ ★ ★

She hung out in Kat's office observing Hayes at work as he briefed the con-gresswoman on strategy for a committee mark-up later that morning and a meeting with the Rhode Island Peace Mission. Roxy contributed a few remarks as they reviewed the next day's speech on health care to a national nurses' group.

When Hal Gould arrived, Kat included Mario and Jasmine in the meeting. She had selected Gould as her media advisor for the campaign over the objections of Hayes and the Senatorial committee. Although he was acknowledged as one of the grand old gurus of political consulting, he tended to choose his clients by their views rather than their party. In a year where all senate races were critical, being bipartisan was a cardinal sin.

"We'll save planning strategy until the meeting this afternoon with Senatorial. I wanted you to meet the rest of my personal team first and see if there were any last minute questions we needed to resolve." Kat directed her remarks at the short, bald, wise looking man who sat facing her on the couch. Roxy thought of the bronze Buddha she had in her garden. Later Mario told her Gould reminded him of Yoda in the Star Wars movie.

"You know my chief of staff, Hayes Redcliffe." The two men nodded cordially.

"He will coordinate all aspects of the campaign from Washington while Mario De Palma will soon be named campaign manager and run the operation in Rhode Island. Jasmine Elliott is my new press secretary and will work closely with you on coordinating the press coming from this office. Roxy Holland is a dear friend and author who has generously consented to put her work on hold for the next year and move to Rhode Island. She'll be my speechwriter and emotional support. Think of her as 'first friend.'"

Pleased at Kat's introduction, Roxy bestowed a warm, dimpled smile on Gould, making sure Hayes caught a glimpse of it as well.

"Mario and Roxy have known me forever; they will be your sources on personal background. Mario also knows my political history better than anyone."

For several minutes they discussed the roles of other players outside the immediate campaign team both in the state and on the national level.

"I have what may seem a rather strange question," Gould grinned apologetically. "Exactly what name do we use when referring to you?"

Kat's eyes sparkled as she laughed.

"My full name is Kiley Albright Tomasso. My mother always called me Kiley Albright hoping I would forget the Tomasso part, or change it at the earliest possible moment to a more appropriately aristocratic surname."

"Didn't I read that you were divorced?"

"My ex-husband's name is Caldwell, and it was aristocratic enough for my mother. Unfortunately the man did not measure up. We were married for so short a time, I never changed my name. Here in Congress, I am Kiley Tomasso. In Rhode Island…"

"I know," Gould interrupted, his droll tone matching his expression, "When you've said Kiley, you've said it all." They all laughed. Her name recognition and voter approval ratings were legendary.

"So who's Kat?"

"Without delving too far into sordid family history, my father agreed to allow my mother to name me but hated the name. He wanted something personal, ethnic, and Catholic. The thought of me wandering through life without a namesake saint was too much for him. As soon as he saw a silver baby cup engraved with my initials, he had his name—K.A.T."

"I'm Jewish so I'll plead ignorance. Is there a Saint Kat?" Gould asked perplexed.

"Duke's mother...."

"Your father is named Duke?" Gould's eyebrows jumped towards the broad expanse of skin that lay above them.

"Was. He died several years ago. His legal name was Francis but as the only son among five children in an Italian family, he was Duke from birth. His mother was named Catherine, after Catherine of Sienna, a noted Church scholar. As far as my father was concerned, I was named Kat after his mother and Saint Catherine would look after me as well."

"Who calls you Kat?"

"All my family and friends, my staff except when we're trying to maintain a semblance of professionalism in official meetings, and everyone in Rhode Island when they talk about me."

"So, who calls you Kiley?"

"Other than the press, officials, strangers, bumper stickers, and my mother —no one."

★ ★ ★ ★ ★

While Jasmine huddled with Gould reviewing media contacts and press lists, and Kat dashed off for a luncheon speech to a group of state energy officials, Roxy joined Hayes and Mario. They walked across the still-green Capitol lawns, splashed with colorful chrysanthemums, to Tortilla Coast, a Mexican restaurant only a block from where they were having the afternoon strategy meeting.

Roxy ignored the fast-paced political discussion that bounced back and forth across the table between the two men. She was engrossed in the tasty chicken fajita and the rushes she felt wherever Hayes casually touched her. They sat side by side in a darkened back room, facing Mario. Throughout lunch his leg brushed hers and his fingers dangled against her shoulder as he sporadically stretched his arm across the back of her chair. By the time they were leaving and he brushed her hair away from her jacket collar as he had the night before, she was leaning against him in an attitude impossible to misunderstand. Blood chemistry was at work and Roxy had no will to resist.

They crossed Massachusetts Avenue, discussing the renovation of Union Station that updated the historic train station with two floors of chic shops and restaurants.

He pointed to the skeleton of a concrete giant being erected in the parking lot between the Republican Center and the train station. Soon the building would be filled with the ever-expanding number of secretaries, aides, and assistants needed to serve five hundred thirty-five congressional emperors and empresses.

As they climbed the steps to the Ronald Reagan Republican Center where the Senatorial committee held court, Kat drove up. Roxy fled inside while Hayes and Mario waited to greet the congresswoman.

Roxy smiled and nodded to everyone as they arranged themselves around the table. She assumed the jumble of unknown faces, all male, would sort themselves out eventually. As she expected, Kat sat at the table's head with Hayes on one side and Hal Gould, her media advisor, on the other.

A skinny, bespectacled dark-haired man from Senatorial interrupted Hayes' summary of their opponent's weaknesses.

"We've prepared a detailed fact book on Winston. It fits in the category of opposition research. I have several comments to add to Redcliffe's assessment. The investigation into the senator's pharmaceutical business is quite extensive although still top secret. Needless to say, the Democrats are desperate to keep it that way until after the election. Fraudulent test results are suspected in several areas, gays are claiming AIDS research is being ignored, and Winston's Finance committee ties with various banks are rumored to have led to special loans for several questionable products. Senior citizen groups are up in arms because he led opposition to generic drugs. Finally, the sins of the father are visited on the son, and we found well-concealed traces of young Winston's drug use. You can make mincemeat of him for using his public position to benefit his private coffers, and worse, for allowing private benefits to influence his vote against the best interests of his constituents."

Kat's face darkened at Paul Reilly's assumption that she would attack her opponent as a matter of strategic policy.

"There are the barest whispers that Winston actually considered retiring although his numbers show he could be re-elected easily. Winston wanted to walk but the boys made him run. The persuading by our esteemed Majority Leader and his henchmen apparently got quite brutal. If David Canton is going to be president in '92, he needs to remain majority leader in '90. He has his heart set on breaking the Republican stranglehold on the White House," Reilly said.

Kat barely suppressed her disgust as she responded.

"Mr. Reilly, I am truly appreciative of all the assistance the Senatorial committee has given and hopefully will continue to give me in this race, important as it is to both me and the party. However, you must understand, this is my campaign and I have certain guidelines. My campaign does not exist to investigate Reynolds Winston. If we come across factual evidence that Winston has been abusing his position, it is our responsibility to let this be known to the proper authorities. If these alleged abuses are under investigation then we can await the results. There will be no attacks on family members, no personal attack of any kind. Frankly, I don't want to be the target of all-out retaliatory war by the Democrats. I intended to focus this campaign on informing people of my positions, my accomplishments, and my qualifications to be their choice in November."

There was little doubt that Kat meant every word she said and that she would demand obedience to her wishes. But smug looks around the table expressed better than any words how absurd and impractical most of the men found her position.

"We've assembled a fact book on you as well, as if we were working for the opposition," said Reilly.

"And what did you find?" she asked coldly.

"Nothing corrupt, nothing immoral. Just too much flash and trash."

"What?" Kat was audibly irate although her face remained deliberately blank.

"You look like a movie star and talk about nothing but pollution controls."

Hayes tapped his pencil on the table for several minutes before the amused chatter wound down enough to yield the floor to him.

"It's obvious we have to develop a strong background of accomplishment for Kiley. It's there in her years of congressional work; we need to be certain people know about it. At the same time we cannot overlook the obvious parallel technique of educating the voters about the questionable legislative positions and competence of their beloved senator. We need a hit man."

Kat's attempt at serenity—eyes partly closed, chin resting on her steepled hands—disappeared with Hayes's suggestion.

"Haven't we discussed this before? Didn't you hear what I just said? No hit man. No negative campaign." Her voice was harsher than Roxy had ever heard it.

Hayes looked surprised.

"Someone needs to guide the press in certain directions, suggest fruitful questions. You're right, you can't do it, nor can any of us on your team but someone needs to keep the opposition honest."

"Any information Senatorial develops on Winston's vulnerabilities goes to Mario. He's the only one I trust to handle that loaded gun. I don't want any negative attitudes to come back and bite me in the ass. "

"President Jamison will be visiting Rhode Island on my behalf later this month. We need to capitalize on this for money, publicity, and credibility, especially within the Republican party. We can also use the event to start up our campaign mechanism in the state. Roxy, I want you to go to Rhode Island next week and help Mario pull off this presidential visit."

"We'll be sending Paul Reilly," interjected a man from Senatorial. "We have some suggestions to maximize the fundraising potential of the event."

Rhode Island was a small state that would see several major, and expensive, campaigns in 1990. There was only so much money to be raised in-state. Kat's own modest fortune was not liquid. Everyone realized she would be reliant on this committee to raise the millions she needed.

★ ★ ★ ★ ★

Kat gestured for Roxy to follow her into her private office.

"Are you planning to drive back to Morgan Springs tonight?"

"Unless you have something you need me to do here. I was waiting for rush hour to end before I leave."

Kat fought to balance the harsh tone of a command with the affection she felt for her long-time friend. Unfortunately, Roxy's personal life continued to lack discrimination.

"Max tells me your friends can still pick from any group the man who will draw you instantly, panting and willing. From what I remember, Hayes fits the profile perfectly. It can't happen this time, Roxy. A campaign stirs up enough tension and emotion on its own. Sexual games make it even more difficult. I need both of you clear headed and totally focused on the task at hand, which is winning this election. I've seen what happens when you fall in love, or become infatuated, or whatever you call it. You become useless and the man seems to think of nothing but finding a time and place to drag you off to bed. The bottom line is not now, not Hayes."

★ ★ ★ ★ ★

Much of the next day Kat spent on the phone touching base with her own private network of contacts in Rhode Island. She never completely trusted the politicos who mostly talked to each other. People spoke repeatedly about Winston's inaction and seeming disinterest in the dramatic changes taking place in the world even though he sat on key committees. A few whispered about how easily his pharmaceutical firm had their drugs approved. They were reverent about his committee chairmanship, his power, and what a nice man he was—so kind and polite. They remembered all he did for Rhode Island.

"We don't want to have to choose between you," voice after voice said, begging her not to run. "Rhode Island needs you both."

By mid-day, Kat was only half listening to the conversations. If she heard one more person cite Winston's clout and tell her they did not want to choose she would scream. Her mind wandering she recalled her warning to Roxy about Hayes.

"As usual, you have your finger on the pulse of the people," she said mechanically to the woman with whom she was speaking. "Thanks for your ideas. Let's see each other soon."

Kat quickly hung up and dialed another number.

"Hi," she said when the phone was finally answered on the fifth ring. "Got a minute?" When he said yes Kat made her pitch.

"I need a favor. Actually this is more like a favor to you. I have a friend coming up to work on the campaign, a dear friend. She'll be staying at my house in Narragansett and I'd like you to keep an eye on her."

Kat laughed at the response then continued.

"Trust me. This will not be a chore. I can't risk her getting too deprived of male companionship and rampaging through my staff, or among the general male population for that matter. And it's only for a year."

Kat listened to his response and said seriously, "Well, maybe it's about time you did have a relationship. She's worth it. There's lots you can teach her and maybe a few things you can learn."

They closed their arrangements and Kat leaned back feeling she accomplished at least one valuable strategic move that day.

2

A Presidential Visit
November

Rhode Island

They were huddled in a corner of the cavernous hall at Rocky Point running through the countless details that had to be right. The president of the United States would be arriving in the morning.

Roxy found herself shredding the edges of her notepad strewn with doodles and reminders about flowers for Kat and extra bunting for the bandstand. Side conversations checked off security plans, high school band approval, sound system and decorations. There were costs she never imagined. Every light socket at Palladium Hall was checked and hundreds of phone lines put in, requiring miles of multicolored wire, junction boxes and cables. Every minute of the visit was planned in great detail. Routes over which the president would travel had been gone over and over repeatedly by Secret Service and local police. Emergency routes to hospitals or the airport were worked out.

She stared at 135, the number of people involved just in Rhode Island to make this visit happen. Then she picked up a red pen and circled forty thousand dollars. That was Kat's share of the visit. President Jamison would spend about eighty minutes with Kat's campaign. Roxy hoped he was worth four hundred dollars a minute.

Paul Reilly had dollar signs all over his notepad. Every few minutes he would shake his head, push his glasses back up the bridge of his nose, cross out what he had been writing and start over. He believed the entire point of campaign finance rules was to find ways around them.

"I've assigned Roxy to the VIP room. She'll be handling the two thousand dollar donors, lining them up backstage for their photos with the president," Mario was telling them.

Secret Service looked at her and wrote down her name.

"We'll have a special badge for you tomorrow so you can go in the holding area where the president will be," he said. "You'll need to get us lists of everyone in the receiving line, on stage and in the motorcade."

Roxy nodded. The lists were ready now except for last minute donors. Kat would probably be calling people trying to raise more money while she waited for the president to land.

"We have twenty-five photos," said Reilly. "Do we have them all sold?"

For the millionth time, Roxy listened to Mario and Reilly complain about Dan Burkhart—current attorney Attorney General and prospective Republican candidate for governor—creaming the presidential visit. One week on the job and she knew the essence of electoral politics was money. There was no such thing as a free election in America. Everyone could vote freely, that was true. But no one could run for office freely. So here they were, in a gargantuan relic of another age when crowds would flock to the amusement park to dance away the night, trying to raise thousands of dollars selling people the chance to have their picture taken with the man who supposedly served them.

The meeting ended and Roxy brushed the pile of tiny bits of paper into her purse. The sheet with her notes was reduced by half. They adjourned to Jeanie's, a local bar near Rocky Point with worn out waitresses, a couple pool tables, and cheap beer.

★ ★ ★ ★ ★

On her first morning at Kat's house in Narragansett, Roxy was up before dawn so she could begin her program of daily walks on the beach.

The cluster of expensive new houses on the street that led from Kat's turn-of-the-century mansion toward the ocean looked like scenery for a model train set. In fifty years they might look real, if they were still standing. She walked towards the stone towers on either side of Ocean Drive and the sandy beach beyond. Inspired by medieval French architecture, they were all that remained from a grand casino that was the social center of Narragansett during its Victorian heyday as a seaside resort. A fire in 1900 had destroyed the casino, leaving only the towers, now memorialized in Christmas tree ornaments and note cards as Narragansett's premier landmark.

As she passed under the stone archway across the road that connected the pair of towers, the wind disappeared. Rubbing her hand along the rough stone walls, she emerged almost immediately on the other side, greeted once again by moisture-laden breezes that smelled distinctly of fish. A weak sun emerged, barely smearing the gray skies with shades of pale pink. By the time she walked along the seawall and down stairs onto the beach, she was lost in thought about the day's event and her responsibilities. Her mind churned like the turbulent slate gray sea tinged with green and she automatically danced away from surf that blew too far up on the sand.

A PRESIDENTIAL VISIT

She was going to meet the president. Up until now, Roxy had not given it much thought. It was all selling tickets, rounding up volunteers, and working on Kat's remarks. But Mario had given her the best job, standing back stage while the photos were taken. She would be hanging out with the president for at least half the time of his visit.

Thank goodness she brought her best dress and the pearls her mother insisted she wear.

Roxy arrived at the halfway point in her walk, the end of the beach where Narrow River entered from the left and flowed into the ocean in a natural estuary sprinkled with giant boulders. She stood for a moment on the soft sand and gazed across the river to a weathered old building surrounded by green scrub. Someday before this campaign was over she wanted to explore the far side. On this day she turned and walked back, writing and rewriting Kat's remarks in her mind.

★ ★ ★ ★ ★

The frayed look of the ballroom was hidden along with the gold lame. The room was festively draped in the red, white and blue of Kat's colors with a fair smattering of her trademark blue stars. A huge KILEY 1990 banner strewn with stars hung so no camera shot of the president would be without KILEY as background.

The Woonsocket High School band—all seventy-two pieces—were sitting proud and excited, waiting for their moment of glory. People were streaming through the doors. Dead time, that moment when the president arrives, was still two hours away.

★ ★ ★ ★ ★

"We had a call," Mario told Kat as he greeted her at Green Airport. "The president's going to be about a half hour late."

A slight smile formed on her face.

"Too bad, that will up Burkhart's bar bill considerably."

There was no love lost between the self-righteous attorney general and Kat. He was a drug-war minion of the president's much-loathed White House chief who Kat repeatedly branded as a neo-fascist Neanderthal.

"Do we know what the president will be saying about you?" Mario asked.

"He grants me reproductive choice," Kat said with a feeling of success, handing him a copy of the remarks sent from the White House, "and respects me for disagreeing. There's not much else he can do. Most of his best chances for winning the Senate come in the form of pro-choice female candidates."

Secret Service and Warwick police hurried them into the hangar. Paul Reilly fell in with them.

"I wanted to check on your ticket sales so we can give the Secret Service an exact list of who's allowed backstage."

She handed Reilly a scrap of paper with several names on it.

"A group of homeless advocates are picketing the president's parade route near Burkhart's house," Mario reported. "They claim it's obscene that only people with hundreds of dollars to spend can see him."

Kat asked a few quick questions about the organizers and numbers of protesters then ordered him to bring them to Rocky Point. Reilly stopped walking, shocked.

"Are you crazy?" he shouted. "You can't bring a bunch of street people to see the president."

"They have a right to see Jamison. He's their president, too, at least the way I learned civics," Kat said. "Mario, get those people to the Palladium."

"You can't do this! Secret Service will never allow it." Reilly's eyes were bulging behind his thick glasses and his balding forehead showed blotches.

Kat looked at him steadily while telling Mario to get more metal detectors and as many additional security forces as Secret Service might think this threat required.

★ ★ ★ ★ ★

Twenty or so people watched from the hangar as the blue and white 707 known as Air Force One set down with the president of the United States on board. Lights for television crews illuminated the American flag on the plane's tail. There was a stiff wind as Kat stepped out on the tarmac with the other greeters. Standing tall with her blowing black hair and braid-trimmed plum cape behind the stooped Burkhart and his scrawny wife, it was her magnetic image that captured the cameras and filled television screens as people all over the state waited to see the president.

Sam Jamison descended from the plane waving to the cameras and walked over to the official delegation. Greeting the saturnine Attorney General and his wife, he kissed Kat and bundled her ahead of him into the waiting limousine.

★ ★ ★ ★ ★

A PRESIDENTIAL VISIT

Roxy smoothed her hands over the soft velvet of her dress and scanned the VIP room.

The people who had paid two thousand dollars each to Kat's campaign fund so they could be photographed with the president were an interesting lot. Kat's contact in the Indian community, Dr. Rastogi, was there. So was his Hispanic counterpart: a young realtor and his flamboyant wife who was draped in hot pink, sparkling with jewels and adorned with a pink bow in her hair. Several women professionals, a car dealer or two, and a half-dozen of Duke's cronies were lined up smoothing their hair and straightening their ties.

They all had different reasons for spending the money. Some would have given it to Kat for the asking. Others would hang the photo on the wall of their emerging-from-the-ghetto office to show they were on their way up too, slipping into the mainstream through a crack opened by Kiley Tomasso, their next U.S. Senator. More established supporters wanted to show their connections were still good and have a chance to lie about what they whispered in the president's ear while they were at his side. In reality, there was no time for any of them to have more than a moment of introduction to the president. Smile, shoot, shoot, then move on.

There was a swirl of activity by the door and suddenly they were there. Kat was radiant in a suede-trimmed raspberry Lagerfeld suit with a skirt that flared just enough to flatter her spectacular legs. Her hair was scooped atop her head, and gold chains hung around her neck and at her ears. She looked imperial yet at ease leading the tall, graying president over to her guests. A quick hello and the photographer had Jamison and Kat posed in front of the backdrop which showed her outfit off to perfection. Roxy wondered if someone had told her what color the backdrop was.

The final donor moved away and Kat waved Roxy to take her place in a photo. Roxy blushed as she stood between the two people who towered over her. She barely heard Kat introduce her.

"Roxy's the heart of our campaign," Kat told the resident who murmured something, and then it was over and Mario was pulling her out of the way.

The band struck up "Ruffles and Flourishes" and for the first time in more than a decade, those historic words were heard in Rhode Island: "Ladies and gentlemen, the president of the United States."

Television cameras rolled, people cheered and the band played as Kat stepped up to the podium, quieting the crowd.

"Less than three weeks ago, people were held captive behind the Berlin Wall. Today pieces of this horror are being chipped away and sold as souvenirs of an enslavement we hope never to see again. New ideas, new freedoms, new opportunities are on the march. Walls are tumbling so fast there's no time to pick up the pieces—we can only walk through, keeping our hearts pure and purpose clear. This new wave can sweep the world, as in Germany, without a shot being fired."

The audience cheered and screamed then held their breath as Kat said softly, "Communism collapsed in a whimper. Did guns bring it down? Was it simply time for the Iron Curtain to melt away? Or was it prayer, determination, and the unquenchable desire for freedom in the human heart?"

Kat moved to her social agenda. She spoke of using the spirit that brought down the wall in Germany to revive democracy and freedom in America. The president visibly winced.

She challenged the audience with her platform.

"Our friends will no longer be hungry and homeless." A ragged group waved their signs and cheered. "Our aunts and grandmothers will no longer live in fear about medical bills and cuts in Social Security. Our children will be born healthy and protected from having their minds and bodies polluted. Our sisters will have control over their own bodies."

The president was clearly pained as the hall rocked with cheers for Kat's words but he rallied to the occasion. Shaking his shaggy head, he told the crowd he occasionally disagreed with Kiley, but admired her persistence in demanding pollution controls, especially against ocean dumping. He noted her push for adequate health care then concluded by praising her work for Rhode Island in the House of Representatives.

"She's been a great congresswoman, and she'll be a great senator." As the crowd cheered, he took a step towards Kat, lifted her hand and said, "I want you in the United States Senate. I need you there. Rhode Island needs you there. America needs you there."

It was several minutes before the cheers died down and the president plunged into the crowd that had lined up along the ropes to shake hands and kiss babies. Kat followed close behind him, people reaching out for her touch. Her media team was pleased: the president's strong praise of Kat, great crowd shots, her own bold remarks, a final moment as Kat got onto Air Force One with the president. Several ten-second bites could be used in commercials capturing credibility and stature with a frosting of independence—a combination ideal for Rhode Island.

★ ★ ★ ★ ★

Roxy sat with a cluster of young volunteers in the cleared and deserted hall. One had emerged as a star during the event. She sold nearly $20,000 worth of tickets, and managed all the escorts and other volunteers. Her name was Carrie Lange and she was a Kat worshipper. She was stocky with dull red hair and a horsey face. As unattractive as Carrie was by most male standards, she was more appealing to Roxy than the sisters who sat across from them with their permed and moussed Rhode Island big hair and too tight, too short outfits. Their eyes were glued to Mario. All types of people worked for Kat's election.

A PRESIDENTIAL VISIT

After discussing and rejecting nearly a dozen places, the group agreed with Carrie's suggestion: Sh-Booms, a club in downtown Providence where DJs sat in a cut-off '57 Chevy body and played old time rock and roll. Roxy voted with the rest; they had earned a good party. She had no more responsibilities before leaving on Wednesday for home. She smiled at Hayes and Reilly as they nodded agreement. Hayes had come from Washington with Kat and there had not been a moment to talk with him.

★ ★ ★ ★ ★

They all looked so young, Roxy thought as she waited at the bar for pitchers of beer. They were young. At twenty-six, Mario was the oldest member of Kat's Rhode Island staff. For these kids, the music of the '60s and '70s were old standards. Bright and clean, they sat around the table, yelling and bouncing in their seats with the excitement of having seen the president.

A burly, dark-haired man at the bar turned in her direction. As he looked her up and down, Roxy moved away, uncomfortable. The beer arrived; she grabbed the pitchers and quickly joined Carrie and the staff kids at their table. Noise and music flowed around her, drowning out any thought. She smiled when someone directed a remark at her, but watched Hayes huddled in a corner with Reilly and a couple White House staff.

There was a flurry of movement as Mario led several of the girls to the dance floor, leaving Roxy with Carrie and the big hair sisters. She was wondering how to slip out when a greasy-looking man in tight pants approached the two girls. He brought along the thug from the bar, who slid into a chair next to Roxy. Before she could engineer an escape, he was leaning over with a hand on her arm introducing himself as Vito someone or another, a big jewelry manufacturer with money to burn.

"They say you work for the congresswoman, helping her raise money and stuff."

Roxy looked around desperately for a way out but Carrie had vanished, Mario was still dancing, and the big hair sisters were draped around the greaseball.

Vito leaned closer and leered. She reeled back from the smell of cheap Scotch on his breath.

"Your candidate can always use another check-writing friend, don't you think honey?"

Roxy did not like the growl of his voice, or his hand stroking her arm. She definitely did not like the look in his eye as he brushed his hand along the curve of her breast and lifted her pearls.

"Nice. These are real. I like real."

Outraged, she pushed his hand away and tried to jump up.

He held on, breaking the strand. Roxy cried out, grabbed the pearls cascading around her feet and fell to her knees trying to save them before they rolled away and were lost. Vito was practically on top of her, one hand grabbing at her breast, the other pulling up her skirt. She screamed and pushed away. He lost his balance and knocked both of them over along with several chairs.

Hands pulled her to her feet, and she was crying about the pearls and kicking at Vito, still crawling around under the table. As he stuck his dark head up between two chairs, Roxy grabbed one of the pitchers of beer and dumped it on him. Suddenly Hayes was there and spun her out of the way as Vito roared and lurched, knocking over tables and sending glass flying everywhere.

"Now I'll never find the pearls," Roxy sobbed as Hayes rushed her across the dance floor to a dark corner behind the DJ's car. "They're my mother's, a present from my father. She wanted me to wear them to see the president. Now they're gone. She'll kill me. And all because of that drunken pig." Roxy was ready to go back and continue her assault on Vito, but Hayes' arms held her tightly. When Mario found them, he reassured Roxy they would collect the pearls.

The DJ never stopped during the ruckus. A soft, sweet song that Roxy remembered from college began playing and she found herself swaying to its tune in Hayes' arms. Two more songs played before he drew back to look at her.

"OK, now?" His voice was gentle and full of concern. Roxy nodded her head. She felt terrible. What a scene. And her pearls! Tears came to her eyes again. Hayes brushed them away, kissed her lightly, and led her back to the table.

There was no trace of Vito; the greaseball had taken the two girls and left. Carrie was apologetic about disappearing and presented a plastic beer cup filled with all the pearls she could find.

"I've talked to the owner," she said, sympathetic. "He'll check tonight after they close and send over any more they find. I'll take care of the pearls for you, don't worry."

Roxy nodded her thanks and barely whispered to Hayes who still had his arm around her. "I'm sorry to have caused such a problem. I don't know what happened. That guy Vito—" Roxy felt her anger building again, her eyes filling with tears.

"I think you'd better go home. I'll take you."

She started to argue but he insisted.

"It's pouring rain and you're in no condition for that long drive back to Narragansett. Kat would skin me alive if anything happened to you. Besides, your hulking friend could be out there waiting."

They were lost for almost twenty minutes in Providence, circling around ripped up streets and the river relocation project. Hayes laughed as he explained how only in Rhode Island would they spend millions of dollars and tolerate years of chaos to move a river running through the state's capital city. So much effort to shift it a few feet this way and that so it would meet another river and create land for downtown office space.

Roxy sat in embarrassed silence. She wanted to hide from him, but was painfully aware of how he rescued her and was now taking her home.

"I walk on the beach every morning," she said when they reached Kat's house. "It's very calming and inspires my ideas. I think I need a walk right now. Will you come with me?"

He smiled and pointed to his shoes and suit.

"I'm not quite dressed for the beach, but maybe we can walk along the seawall and watch the ocean from there."

A nearly full moon lit up dark clouds that hung along the northern curve of the shoreline and carved shadows on the waves. No one was out. The fresh smell left by the rain lightened the usual salty breath of the sea. They sat on the wall along the beach, waves crashing against the giant rocks at their feet, spray covering Roxy's hair and sparkling on Hayes' mustache. He spoke fondly of his home in North Carolina.

Since his first view of the ocean on a school trip, he was entranced. Every year since, he managed a couple weeks on the Outer Banks. He claimed the ocean in Rhode Island was different, more accessible. For thousands of people who lived along its many curves and inlets, it was part of their property, scenery like the woods in the western part of the state.

"One of the most important cultural facts about Rhode Island," he told Roxy, "is that you can be at the ocean in less than half an hour from anywhere in the state, except for Woonsocket. They have no idea the ocean is out there," he said with a chuckle. She slipped her arm through his as they walked back to the house, feeling comfortable and secure. Fat raindrops sparkled on bushes, splashing against them as they brushed by. She was pleased that the vagaries of her heart were once again born out.

With her in Rhode Island and him in Washington, any liaison would be both infrequent and discreet. It should not be difficult to hide from Kat. She obviously needed to end her self-imposed abstinence. Vito probably smelled her pent-up desire; animals are uncanny like that. And who better than Hayes, she thought, as she watched him open the front door. He had been her hero tonight and that earned him some reward. Her fire was already lit for him.

Once inside, his attention was drawn to Kat's house. He wandered around the huge entry hall, admiring the design and craftsmanship of the stone fireplace and exclaiming over the wide stairs of dark mahogany curving up to an arch that framed the entrance to the second floor, cozy seats built into its railing halfway up the stairs.

"We can tour the house then pick out a room for you," she offered, seeing his interest.

The opportunity to live in Kat's splendid, turn-of-the-century mansion near the beach was a prime inducement for her coming to work on the campaign. It would not have been nearly so desirable had Kat been running in Ohio or Nebraska.

Kat had been meticulous in restoring traces of complex and elaborate Victorian decorations. Most of the walls were painted in soft colors. Hayes admired the Japanese matting in the oddly shaped room used for television-watching, and commented on Kat's wisdom in allowing the stone fireplaces to stand unadorned. Polished wood floors were covered with room-sized rugs from Turkey, India and Persia. Stained glass windows gleamed luminously in the moonlight.

Roxy led him through the kitchen towards the back stairs. The illicit feeling that always arose when she used them made her suddenly shy. She barely pointed to the closed door of the master bedroom she occupied, not wanting him to see the interior of the room she had chosen as her own. It was not a chaste Victorian bower like the several other bedrooms on the second floor, all furnished with brass beds and quilt racks for clothes and towels.

"Kat has her bedroom and library on the third floor," she explained gesturing towards a second set of stairs. "She plans to use the rest of the house as office space and for staff to stay whenever necessary."

He had not touched her or used the intimate tone that melted her will since they arrived at the house. Roxy decided Kat must have warned him as well, and he was being particularly circumspect in her house, even though she was safely back in Washington. When he selected the back bedroom, at the far end of the hall from hers, Roxy interpreted it as an omen and surrendered her hopes for a wanton adventure. She began babbling to cover her disappointment.

"You use this bathroom," she indicated a door next to his room. "I'm going to turn off the lights and lock up. I'll leave keys to the campaign car on the hall table; the entry card for the parking lot is in the car. The cupboard is bare, so you'll have to get coffee on the way. There are sheets and blankets on your bed, towels in the bathroom." She turned and hurried downstairs before he could say a word.

She puttered around on the first floor for a few minutes. When she went back up to her room, the bathroom door at the end of the hall was closed and light showed beneath it. Resigned to sleeping alone that night, she closed the door to her room thinking how sad it was to waste both the opportunity and the setting.

The bedroom Roxy occupied looked like an elaborate sexual fantasy from the early '70s. She could never imagine what Kat had in mind when she papered the walls. Black paper was printed with languid white and pink flowers and streaks of silver foil. Piles of pillows were strewn around the carpeted floor and on the bay window seat. An art deco lamp of two nude women softly lit the room. The black lacquer bed had black satin sheets and a heavy throw of white rabbit fur.

A collection of mirrors covered the wall by the bed from floor to ceiling. There were gilt-framed beveled ones, silvery art deco ovals, stained glass trimmed ones, and a dozen or more oddly shaped mirror pieces without frames.

Reflected in them was another wall filled with paintings, drawings, and even some sculptures—all female nudes.

Roxy tossed her dress and underwear on the overstuffed chair beside the bed and stepped into the bathroom where the fantasy continued. A clawfoot tub was set on a shiny tile floor, silvery paper reflected in another mirrored wall. Huge, fluffy pink towels were stacked on shelves, and a few rested on the floor where Roxy dropped them.

Back in the bedroom, she looked despairingly at the king-sized bed. At least four times in the past week, as her dreams became more intense and sexual, she had decided she could not spend another night in the room. Yet it held her, slyly intimating that she might yet need its decadent splendor. All indications were that her intuition was failing.

Roxy slipped into a short pink satin robe, enjoying the cool feel of the fabric against her naked body. She watched her multiple images in the mirrors, then closed her eyes, smoothing her hands down her sides, rubbing the satin against her skin. She never saw Hayes until he put his hands on her shoulders.

"I tried every door until I found you," he said, amorous breath filling her ear. He was standing behind her, looking in the mirrors. He moved his hand across her chest and up along her throat; his other arm pulled her tightly. Roxy did not resist. She cupped herself against him, grateful for the support; her knees were so weak from his touch she was afraid she would collapse in a heap. Moving her hair aside, he kissed her neck with quick, light touches, his mustache brushing her nerve endings into a frenzy. Her breathing became rapid and shallow. Her nipples leapt up to meet his hand as he slid it under her robe and lightly massaged first one and then the other. Watching through her lowered lashes, Roxy savored every move. She breathed in his tangy odor; he must have just stepped out of the shower.

His hands slid lower, pulling free the tie around her waist. The robe hung open, exposing her to his view. He pressed his palm to her smooth, slightly rounded stomach as his chest swelled against her back.

"So soft, so soft," he kept murmuring. His fingers traced a slow downward path then buried themselves in the blonde curls that swirled to a point between her legs.

Roxy gasped; the pleasure was so intense. His lips continued to dance lightly across her shoulders and she melted against him, parting her thighs, inviting his fingers to continue their exploration. She was always thrilled to have a man worshipping the goddess at her most intimate shrine.

As the robe fell from her shoulders, she turned in his arms and began kissing him—long, luxurious kisses. He was wearing only a shirt which she had off in a second. No need to waste time.

Shock waves rippled through her as she sprawled on the fur throw, his body on top of hers. Pushing the throw aside, both of them sighed as they slid between the satin sheets wrapped in the subtle perfume that invaded her dreams.

Three hours later, Roxy lay in a stupor. The promise of his ravishing voice had been fulfilled and no threat of Kat's displeasure could dampen her enthusiasm. There isn't a square inch of his body I haven't touched or licked or rubbed or had inside me tonight, she thought, as she began to wonder if the sheets were washable. She rolled over to look at him. He was asleep. Reaching across to turn out the light, her breast pushed against his cheek; he smiled and burrowed deeper into the pillow. Roxy was sure this would not be their only fling.

Contented, she fell asleep.

★ ★ ★ ★ ★

Feeling sun on her face, she sat up. It was eight o'clock. The bed beside her was empty; Hayes was practically in Washington by now. Roxy put on her robe, looked around the room then ran downstairs. The car keys were gone but there was nothing else—no note, nothing.

Standing there foolish and forlorn, she began to make up excuses: he had to get back, he was being considerate not to wake her at six when he had to leave. It did not matter; no excuse was going to be enough. What happened last night should not have happened. Granted, it was not all her doing. Hayes did come into her room, he did start the lovemaking.

Roxy perched on the wicker couch in the odd shaped room just off the central hall. She clicked on the local news in time to catch the tail end of coverage about the president's visit the previous day: "President Jamison came calling and left some Rhode Islanders a lifetime of memories, and others a pocket full of cash."

As weather charts filled the screen she looked around the room thinking once again how much she liked it. The bamboo wall covering, large windows, and plants made it almost tropical. A collection of perfectly preserved Victorian green wicker filled the room—a couch, two chairs with fluffy cushions, a lounge and several tables. In the corner was another of the distinctive stone fireplaces, this one featuring an over-the-mantle arch of the small round beach stones that could be found all along the shore. When a fire destroyed the Green Inn along the beach, Kat's fireplaces became the best remaining samples of a noted stonemason's work dating from the early 1900s. Roxy could not remember his name but he carved the date 1909 in the hall fireplace. The cornerstone for the house was dated 1902.

It was early and Liz did not like being awakened before noon but Roxy needed to talk. She called her friend in Morgan Springs. After initial grumbling to indicate she did not like the world so soon after dawn, and that being out of state was not sufficient excuse, Liz was ready with her advice.

"What are you whining about? You've been desperate to get laid for weeks, and this Hayes character was one of your top ten choices wasn't he?"

"But Kat told me not to get involved with him."

"All of a sudden you're listening to what people tell you to do?" Liz was practically shouting. "It must be from hanging out with all those Republicans. And besides, what's involved got to do with it? All you did was screw the poor boy once."

"It was more than once," Roxy interrupted.

"Well then," Liz continued, "go carve a notch on your bedpost for every time he brought you off and trace the number in the sand. You're a woman of the '90s. You probably straddled him and screamed out your own name when you came."

There was nothing like a quick dose of Liz to prove introspection useless. Roxy knew she was right, or at least comforting, and it was far too gorgeous a day for her to sit around moping.

She would drive to the congressional office later and volunteer to help answer phones. Hayes called at least five or six times a day. She would answer the phone, they would have a perfectly innocent conversation, and from his tone of voice she would know what the previous night meant to him. Roxy put her head in her hands and groaned. Was it all starting again? Another man, another few months of passion and anguish and then, over. She would get bored, his looks would no longer please her, his voice would grate on her ears. But this was not any man. This was Kat's key political person and Roxy was committed to a year working with him. She could not burn him up then toss him away like all the others.

★ ★ ★ ★ ★

Surf was high from the previous night's rain when she walked out to the beach about an hour later. She was exhausted from examining her encounter with Hayes from every possible point of view. Walking along the shore would clear her head.

Spray from waves crashing into the rock beach along the south end of the seawall wet her face. She drew her light jacket tighter around her, remembering it was November in spite of the bright sunshine. She passed the Coast Guard House, a restaurant and bar in a stone structure adjacent to the Towers with a huge anchor mounted under the eaves.

There was a man near the rocks hauling a large silvery fish out of the water. He quickly slipped the fish off the hook, threw it back, and cast again. The line was scarcely in the water when he had another strike and was pulling another fish onto the rocks. Roxy stood fascinated as the fisherman repeated his actions, each time pulling another fish out of the boiling surf then tossing it back. For a while she wondered if he was catching the same few fish, then noticed all the silvery bodies thrashing around churning the water. She was stunned; there must be hundreds of fish swimming around the rocks.

When several other men with poles moved out along the rocks to join in the sport, the first man packed up and moved towards the seawall. He saw her and waved. Roxy waved back; he had been great entertainment. He was loading his gear into the back of a pick-up as she passed by. When he smiled and greeted her, she decided to find out if the fish convention happened often and if he always threw back what he caught.

They leaned against the truck bed and looked out across the seawall chatting for several minutes about waves and sunshine, hearing the traffic pick up behind them. He was friendly and Roxy told him about being in Rhode Island to work on Kat's campaign, living in her house and walking on the beach each morning. He told her the fish were striped bass and that Kat had a lot to do with there being so many of them back in Rhode Island waters again. That such a mass of them would be roiling around in the shallow water and rocks below the Coast Guard House was unusual. It was the first time he had ever quit while the fish were still biting.

"I was tired of pulling them in, and I saw you up here watching. You seemed more interesting than hooking another dozen or so striped bass."

Even though Hayes had sated her for a while, she was never one to pass up an opportunity to flirt. His name was Jake Hansen.

"Vintage Swamp Yankee, born and bred here in South County," he told her.

"I'm heading over to my favorite place for breakfast to celebrate an already wonderful day and it isn't yet noon. Want to come? It's a real Rhode Island institution."

Roxy was not sure if he meant breakfast in general or the place he was planning to go but she did not care. She was not going to the office until two or so, had plenty of time to kill, and thought Jake Hansen seemed the ideal companion for that chore.

"Sure. I'm ready for whatever will help me understand Rhode Island better."

"Guaranteed, you can't even aspire to being a real Rhode Islander until you've eaten at the Bait Shop." Roxy assumed he was kidding but discovered that was indeed the name of the tiny restaurant at Middlebridge.

There were people sitting around over coffee even at 9:30. Jake was obviously a regular, rating quick service and a broad smile from the hefty woman who waited on them. He reviewed the menu for Roxy and applauded her choice of American pancakes filled with blueberries, strawberries and bananas. He ordered hash browns and sausage for both of them, and a spicy omelet topped with salsa and guacamole for himself.

Jake was delightful, the food was great, and Roxy was disappointed when he looked at his watch. It was nearly noon.

"I'd better get you back. There must be lots to do after a big presidential visit, and I have some work myself."

In all his stories, Jake mentioned nothing about what he did for work. When she finally asked as he was paying the bill, he told her he was a carpenter.

"Actually, I work in stained glass," he said as they got into his truck, "but that's my art and I've never been able to support myself with it. You can starve for your art only so long then compromises need to be made. My compromise was to build spectacular frames, or renovate whole rooms for which I would charge a living wage. The stained glass window, or panel, or lamp I throw in practically free."

Roxy examined him. It seemed a peculiar way to make a living. Jake Hansen did not look peculiar, though. He had an engaging smile that crinkled his eyes and flashed a stunning set of white teeth. Slim and straight with dark hair and eyes and a crisp, defined edge to his looks that made people think immediately of clean, he was *Gentlemen's Quarterly* all the way even dressed in worn jeans, a pocket teeshirt and a windbreaker. Roxy realized he did not smell of fish, but had a slight pine aroma. He was interesting but not her type. He spoke with the most obvious Rhode Island accent she had heard so far. It was classic New England with broad, long vowels and dropped r's plus an added bonus of Brooklynese gangster tones that seemed endemic to the Ocean State. As she listened, comparing his cadence to Hayes' southern drawl, she realized the difference was as much pace as pronunciation.

Jake could be a fun playmate while she was here and maybe distract her enough that she would not turn one night with Hayes into an obsession that could wreck the campaign.

"I'm impressed," he said turning into Kat's driveway, "you ate everything on your plate, a true accomplishment with the amount of food Sandy piles on. Have you been starved for the past few days?"

"It's true. I love to eat," she laughed, dimples flashing. She was notorious for her appetites, and food ranked right up there with sex.

"Thanks, Jake. That was a real treat. You've made my visit. Can I look you up when I get back in January? I need some inside sources in the state who aren't politicians. You seem to know everything and everybody. You could be my pulse of Rhode Island."

He looked pleased.

"There's someone else you should meet if you're interested in surveying the dining wealth of our state. Maybe I'm pushing it, but if you can stand another meal with me in the same day, I know my friend Pete would love to have you join us. We're going to Jack's for our weekly feast. It's truly one of Rhode Island's tastiest man-made attractions. Kat's congressional office is on the way. We could meet you there."

Roxy accepted eagerly. She had no plans for her last night in Rhode Island. If she sat around alone she would either brood about whether she was foolish last night in sleeping with Hayes, or worse, she would be on the phone worrying about it. Dinner with Jake and his friend offered a perfect alternative. She was already hooked on the local food and eager to taste more.

★ ★ ★ ★ ★

The phone rang incessantly the entire afternoon but Hayes never called. Mario was at campaign headquarters and Hayes must have been calling him there. When she finally contacted Washington, Maggie reported he was in meetings at the Senatorial committee and not expected back in the office that day. Roxy welcomed the distraction when Jake and his friend Pete arrived and they set off for East Bay and Jack's.

Peter Hassem was a witty man with a wicked gleam in his dark eyes. His bristling beard, hawk nose, and longish hair looked foreign and exotic next to Jake's chiseled face. Their banter was the relentlessly abusive teasing that men often used to display affection for each other.

As the notoriously picky but widely admired food critic for the *Providence Journal*, Pete often produced anxiety among restaurant staff, but not at Jack's. This was his home base. Victor, son of Jack and warden of the dining room, whisked them to a corner table, though in the huge open room crammed with wooden tables and chairs, there was no real privacy. No menus appeared and Roxy considered what she should eat. When she mentioned to Jake and Pete that she thought she would have the lobster, all conversation stopped. They looked at each other and Pete said "you tell her. You brought her."

Solemnly, Jake looked over at Roxy and explained.

"When we come to Jack's we eat a certain way. No lobster," he waved his hand in dismissal. "You can get them anywhere. Put your dinner in our hands and we'll introduce you to Jack's as only we know it."

Roxy was more than happy to oblige.

Soon waitresses were streaming out of the kitchen with platters of food and pitchers of beer. Neighboring diners would fall into a hush when yet another dish was carried past.

"We have quohogs in garlic and oil, fried squid, steamers, snail salad, and here—Jack's greatest accomplishment, available nowhere else—smelts. They have the best sauce ever. I've tried to duplicate it a dozen times. It's not even the same when you take them home and reheat them." Pete's discourse on the meal was barely interrupted as he ate from various platters. She had to admit, the tiny fish she always considered bait were delicious in the tangy red sauce. She lost count at the fourth platter of them and cringed when their waitress placed a huge bowl of spaghetti with white sauce on the table.

"Dinner," said Pete, "we never eat only appetizers."

"Do you rave about Jack's in your column?" asked Roxy, pausing to let the seafood settle before attacking the spaghetti.

"Never! Some places are sacred. The masses are simply unworthy. Jack's belongs to those who know. Victor understands my reticence. This place has hour-long waits every weekend night anyway: people packed in that small lobby and stretching out the front door and down the steps. He doesn't need my help."

They sat at the table eating for hours as other patrons came and went, Jake and Pete regaling her with stories of their youth.

"We met in high school," Jake told her. "We didn't have class together, Pete's much older."

"Only a year. Let's keep this story straight."

"But we did share the same corridors, that's where everything important happened. Pete came heavily advertised by friends we had in common. The only chemistry we felt in our initial meeting was suspicion. I remember we circled each other like street curs sniffing behinds. But true love won out and we've been like brothers ever since."

Pete smiled over empty platters strewn with bits of onion floating in remnants of spicy sauce. Occasionally, he would remove the pipe from his mouth and add a footnote to Jake's commentary, but mostly he sat sucking and gurgling with a contented smile.

"Pete's the master rod man," Jake smiled mischievously, "both with fish and women. He looks at every woman, and every fish, as if it's the only one he's ever seen. And they respond by jumping onto his hook. He never goes anywhere without his rod, rule number one for a serious fisherman. I could tell hours of stories about being on the way to someplace with Pete when he would see suspicious activity in the water, stop the car, leap out, get his rod from the trunk and proceed to catch a few. One thing about Pete, he always knows the best places to go for fish—and for women."

Taking the pipe from his mouth, Pete leaned towards her conspiratorially.

"Let me tell you a fish story that will explain my attitude about women, as well as about fishing. I don't want you to think I'm a slut." They sat expectantly as Pete began his tale.

"One time in college, my fraternity had a party near a nameless lake in the Big River area where the Girl Scouts had a summer camp. Everyone was drunk, hanging out on the beach and in the water. There was an easy slope with a sand bottom that stretched from the beach about a hundred feet into the lake, then it dropped precipitously. I was determined to fish even though people kept getting in the way. Finally I got a big hit, nearly pulling the pole from my hands. I must've worked that sucker for an hour, in and out, in and out. But it would never come far enough in to the shallow water that I could get a look at it. That's all I really wanted was to see it, not to land it, and certainly not to eat it. Finally the line broke and the fish disappeared without my ever having gotten so much as a glimpse. It was one of the few regrets in my life that I never saw it or found out what it was. That's how I feel about women. I don't want to catch them or keep them, I only want to play them on my line for the sport and catch a glimpse before they get away."

Roxy nodded her agreement; she could empathize with Pete's quest. Jake then continued with his commentary.

"Don't let Pete's story make you think he's shallow and superficial. He has political views. He's very concerned about water quality. It's where the fish he loves live and he wants them to have only the best."

"That's why I've been a big fan of Kat's since her Baywatch days. No telling how empty of fish Narragansett Bay would be if it hadn't been for her crusade during the early '70s," Pete added.

"Of course, Pete feels the same way about Warwick Mall where all the young girls he loves live." As the two men grinned at each other across the table, Jake kept talking.

"The only thing that competes with women and fishing for Pete's interest is his work—food. We spent several days on a trout stream in Maine once trying to decide which was most important: fishing, sex or food. We concluded that we needed more time to research the question properly."

The waitresses had cleared all the other tables, placed the chairs up on them, and were sitting in front of the kitchen eating. The one who had been commanding service to their table came over and asked if they would consider going home.

"We need to commend the chef first," Pete responded as the two men took Roxy into the kitchen to meet the remarkable Jack. Small and wizened, wrapped in a dirty apron, he did smell of fish. He and Victor were gracious and claimed Kat was their favorite politician. They urged Roxy to bring her along next time.

"We'll take down Senator Winston's photo from the bar and replace it with Kiley Tomasso if you'll bring us one." She agreed immediately.

Riding back in the car, Jake pointed out it was a doubly successful evening for her; not only was she introduced to Jack's smelts, but she made a political conquest.

"That's how you win elections in this state," he explained, "one vote at a time. It's the last of the retail states."

Roxy looked over at him in surprise. She heard the distinction between retail and wholesale vote getting for the first time only last week at the strategy meeting.

"Let me illustrate how life in Rhode Island works with a quick story." She nodded eagerly and they sped back across the bay.

"I had a friend in college whose father was head of research for Electric Boat, where they make submarines. They lived in Middletown and he was a recreational lobsterman. The family had this rambunctious golden retriever who could not be kept on a leash no matter what the law said. Regularly the dog catcher would pick up the dog wandering through town or along the beach and bring it home. Just as regularly, he would be rewarded for his trouble with a couple of lobsters. No one keeps track, but everyone knows—favors beget favors."

3

Max's Magic Circle
December

Washington
Morgan Springs

Hayes had been friendly but detached as they walked with Kat over to the Republican Congressional Committee building where they were having the initial meeting of the working campaign team. This was the first Roxy had seen or spoken to him since the president's visit.

People settled into the wood paneled room that smelled of cigar smoke and leather chairs, laying out papers, notebooks, clippings and other paraphernalia. Scanning the conference table, she was glad to see the two new faces in the room were female, and that only one of Senatorial's battalion of white shirts remained—Reilly. Kat had complained bitterly on the walk over about Senatorial's assigning of Reilly to her campaign and his pit bull approach.

An attractive woman with waved gray hair was introduced as Jill Everhart, the finance director. Roxy recognized her as the wife of Kat's longtime legislative chief. Kat had stolen Jill from a national women's organization to raise money for the campaign. The other woman was Lila Gravely, a pollster who had worked with Kat since her first race. Her name suited her serious face and business-like exterior. After listening to her presentation of a recent poll, Roxy understood why Kat trusted her advice.

"The numbers in this race are unlike those in any other race I've seen. But that's to be expected. Rhode Island is not a conventional state, and Kiley Tomasso is not a conventional candidate." Lila acknowledged smiles at her understatement and continued describing the two candidates as equally well known and beloved.

"The good news is people love what Kiley's doing, trust her absolutely and are proud she's their representative. The bad news is that's where they want her to stay. Our other bad news is that they're not mad at Winston and have no reason to kick him out so they won't." Lila looked pained as she explained.

"What they really want is both of them. They asked endlessly 'why can't she wait?'"

No one missed the silent screaming of Kat's frustration as she responded.

"There is no time to wait. Everything is happening too fast. There may not be a next time. We can't afford to waste our chance on a nice man who does nothing."

Lila nodded and continued describing an unusually high number of undecideds that she interpreted as unwilling to choose. The best news she delivered was that fewer people wanted to re-elect Winston. She ranked groups pointing out that support for Kat among women was weaker than it should be and white males were weakest of all.

"You need to hold your own Italians and regain the men you lose there, pull in French Canadians, and keep Republican East Bay Yankees in line. The campaign needs to sell each of these groups on the idea that you're one of them."

Proceeding to issues, the pollster reported no surprises.

"Your issues are hot for the '90s and voters strongly identify you with action and challenging the status quo. He trounces you in business, economics and clout. Other than exposing him as a crook and a fraud, which I understand you refuse to do, I'm not certain you can win."

Kat allowed the buzzing to continue a few moments after Lila's conclusion.

"I understand Senator Winston is very popular and that people will not desert him short of a major scandal, and this being Rhode Island, maybe not even then. If I cannot take votes from him, that leaves the undecideds, dissatisfieds and new voters.

Kat waved away several attempts to dismiss her idea. "We have little choice."

"So we go after burnt-out hippies and boat people, those who have dropped out and those not yet invited in?" derided Reilly.

"We go after all those people who care about their future," Kat responded coldly.

They took a short break. Roxy stayed in her chair and watched people connect and ricochet around the table like bumper cars at the carnival. Hayes was on the phone the whole time, and Kat huddled with Jill and several Senatorial committee finance staff who had appeared on cue. As people began to retake their seats, Hayes tossed her an intimate look that assured he remembered their night wrapped in black satin sheets. She curled her toes and felt waves of pleasure sweep up her legs.

"Poll numbers explain current reality, they neither create it nor predict its future form," said Kat, reopening the meeting. "Lila gave us a clear picture of the Rhode Island electorate today. If we don't give them a compelling reason for choosing me over Winston, they are not going to change their longtime voting pattern. "

Roxy felt the air change as Kat spelled out the mission.

"We need to find that reason today and spend the next eleven months selling it."

Kat's media guru, the Yoda look-a-like Gould, folded his arms on the table, leaned towards Kat and proceeded to outline his game plan. As he described a year of slow building tremors exploding in an earthquake, he flung his arms into the air.

Gould restored his usual calm and outlined a series of phases that began with building stature, highlighting the need for action and neutralizing the voters.

"At the end of summer, we hammer voters with the need for choice. We force them to accept that they must choose."

Everyone watched Gould as he unfolded the final phase although he sat almost motionless.

"We go for the heart and close the sale. We make them feel a compelling need for Kiley Tomasso in the Senate. We move them to her side, exploiting whatever issues Lila tells us will make them sit up and pay attention. We peak election night." There was no arm flinging at this earthquake.

Roxy scanned the faces around the table as they focused on the round little man's words. Kat and her team watched him intently. Senatorial staff looked bored, except for Reilly who scowled and shook his head at every sentence. Gould looked only at Kat.

"This will be the hardest choice voters have made in the state for a long time: both candidates are beloved, both are respected, both are viewed as accomplished. Of course, your achievements are real, his a façade." Kat nodded graciously.

"We have to hold a mirror up to him so everyone can see the emperor has no clothes. As much as it may irritate you," he reached over and grabbed Kat's hand, "people don't want to make a hard choice and they will avoid deciding until the last minute. Our final television spot will be the one that wins it."

"I suppose you have a spot in mind," Reilly said snidely.

"Not exactly," Gould smiled slightly. "But I'll know it when I see it."

Reilly continued his sniping, underlining Senatorial's distrust of this man who played both sides of the political street.

"And the whole winning strategy will be contained in your broadcast ads, right?"

"Wrong," said Gould. "Whatever we do in a thirty or sixty second spot must be reinforced over and over again with activities here and particularly in Rhode Island. There's plenty for everyone to do. Your committee's job is to raise us the money we need."

Gould smiled beatifically at Reilly, who sneered at the notion that Senatorial served solely as a money source.

"We'll keep our ears open on Winston, too. Everyone's devotion to sweetness and light may begin to fade when poll numbers show him twenty points in the lead."

As Reilly once more pitched the need for negative campaigning, Roxy noticed Jasmine taking a quick survey of the expressions in the room and making some notes. When their eyes met, Roxy turned away. In a flash she knew she did not want Jasmine Elliott taking her measure, or to notice at all that Roxy was a player in this drama. Jasmine seemed the type of woman who kept score, and she did not want to be a name on any of her lists.

Mario spoke up. "Can we select an announcement date?" he asked. "Then we'll know how much time we have to get phase one off the ground."

Everyone nodded agreement. "It can't be much earlier than the end of January. There are the holidays, Congress out of session, the Super Bowl, the president's budget and the State of the Union address," Hayes ticked off.

"February 14," Kat said.

"Is that a suggestion?" asked Hayes.

"That's when I'm announcing," Kat replied.

She and Max must have worked out the date, thought Roxy. I wonder if they picked a time.

As if reading her mind, Jasmine spoke for the first time.

"I don't suppose you know the time?" she asked, an edge in her voice.

"Late morning so we can catch the noon news. Sometime between 9:45 and 10:30."

"It's a little late for the noon news, but I'm sure the television stations will stretch it for this major an event." Jasmine was not giving up. "That time is obviously appropriate for your purpose."

Roxy gave Jasmine the same stare the press secretary was receiving from Kat, wondering what Jasmine knew, or thought she knew about how the day and time for the announcement were chosen. It was not so unusual to use arcane devices to predict the future. Roxy recalled being surprised when Kat told her how many politicians in Washington did so.

Gould clapped his hands.

"Valentine's Day. Perfect!" he crowed. "Hasn't Kiley been characterized as having a love affair with the people of Rhode Island?" he asked Mario.

"It's getting them to marry her that'll be the hard part," Reilly answered.

Roxy glared at him in disgust. If he were what was available to her in the male line, she would retire from the fray and build a shrine to her vibrator.

With the date decided, planning began in earnest.

"Mario is moving over to the campaign after January 1," Kat announced, "although Hayes remains deeply involved. For now, I'd like all official information channeled through Hayes. I've hired a well-connected young woman from Woonsocket—a target area, we know—" she nodded to Lila, "to handle day-to-day management in the Rhode Island office. Mario remains the Rhode Island contact for this level of the campaign but you should at least know who she is.

Her name is Carrie Lange. She was our star volunteer for the president's visit, is a computer whiz, and started today."

Kat paused and looked around the table engaging each person.

"This is a difficult race. There is no easy or assured victory. You're here because you are the best and that's what it takes. I'll listen to your wisdom and advice. In return, you must trust my vision. The future between now and November is ours to create. We can't afford to reject information because it doesn't fit our preconceived notion of how a campaign should unfold." She stared directly at Reilly.

"There is no guarantee we can run the perfect and seamless campaign we need to win, no matter how hard we try. What we can guarantee is that we learn from our mistakes. The way to triumph is clear." Kat sat up straighter. "We align ourselves with larger trends and exploit the power of their momentum. Reynolds Winston is not the wave of the future—I am."

As Hayes smiled knowingly, Roxy guessed Kat was quoting from their old friend Sun Tzu.

★ ★ ★ ★ ★

Roxy stood in front of the mirrors in black bikini pants and a red and black stretch velvet jacket, holding pants in one hand, skirt against her waist with the other.

"Should I be elegant and fancy in the skirt or sporty in pants?" she yelled to Kat who was blow drying her hair.

"With that jacket, what makes you think anyone will ever look below your waist?"

Kat turned off the hair dryer and walked over to the wall hanging with necklaces. Selecting one she put it around Roxy's neck.

"If you got it, flaunt it," she said as she stood back and smiled. The tiny onyx beads were strung so the carved figure hanging from them fit perfectly at the top of the soft valley formed by Roxy's breasts. She picked up the figure, admiring the shiny blackness. It was a primitive female form, mostly breasts and rounded hips; her arms were outstretched.

"The goddess we both serve," Kat said.

★ ★ ★ ★ ★

Roxy stopped on the open staircase to survey the staff Christmas party trying to find Hayes. It looked like he hadn't arrived yet. Kat was elegant as usual in a plum silk blouse and softly pleated pants dramatically highlighted by an embroidered velvet vest and necklace of raw amethyst set in silver.

Once downstairs, Roxy hovered by the food, sniffing at homemade pizza and clams casino, wondering what could be nibbled on before official feeding time. When she heard Hayes' voice, she looked up in time to see him slip a luxurious fox jacket from the shoulders of a perfectly-groomed woman with black hair cut very short. Kat walked over and gave the woman a warm hug. Roxy knew she was in trouble. Was there a serious girlfriend? Who was this woman? And why did Hayes bring her? No one ever brought a casual date to staff parties; the work talk drove them crazy.

"Oh, there's Cindy Michaels!" exclaimed Kat's secretary, Maggie, who was standing next to Roxy.

"Who is she?"

"Our financial angel in New York and one of the hottest investment bankers in the city She's committed to raising us half a million dollars from the financial community. We've had two breakfasts in Manhattan for Kat so far and each raised fifty thousand. Cindy has a golden touch."

Roxy pressed for more.

"Kat met her at some networking seminar for fast lane women and it was love at first sight. Cindy's been great at everything from turning out professional women for Kat to managing exposure in serious business magazines. Hayes could be an irresistible bonus. For half a million of other people's money, Cindy gets a senator for a close friend and her right hand man in bed. No wonder she's a success on Wall Street, she understands leveraging her position."

Roxy felt like throwing up.

Maggie dragged her from the corner behind the food table.

"C'mon. Stan's ready to do his Christmas spirit review then play Santa Claus and hand out presents. You don't want to miss this. He calls it seasonal training for lapsed religions mixing the magic oil in the Temple at Hanukkah and Druid rituals of solstice with all the old familiar Christmas stuff."

The gifts were small, most connected to jokes. Stan built up the humor as he handed each recipeint their package. Jasmine caused a stir when she opened hers to find a sleek blue lace trimmed nightgown. There were howls and whistles with several men pointing the finger at Mario who shrugged his shoulders. Roxy noticed Jasmine look at Kat who smiled back.

When her name was called, Roxy was surprised. Moving from her safe perch she slid around several people and reached for her package. She missed Stan's remarks but everyone was laughing then urging her to open the present. Tearing off the paper she lifted the cover of the box and gasped. There were her pearls, restrung and looking good as new. She turned to Mario with tears in her eyes but he nodded over to Hayes who sat smiling at her.

"We can ask only so many sacrifices from our loyal friends," Hayes said. Roxy burst into tears and fled upstairs.

By the time she flung herself on a coat-covered bed, she could hear laughing start up again downstairs.

The door opened quietly and Kat walked in. "Roxy, what's the matter?"

Sitting on the bed, she pulled coats from around Roxy's face.

"I don't understand why you're upset. When Hayes told me about that horrible incident at Sh-Booms, and how he wanted to get your pearls restrung and give them to you tonight, I was touched—after I finished being enraged. We've never had a chance to talk about it. I told Mario to track down that Vito character and teach him some manners." Roxy sniffed away her remaining tears. It was a wonderful gesture for Hayes to make and there was no way to explain to Kat how devastated she was that he could do it and still bring another woman to the party without confessing what happened that night back at her house.

"I'm sorry. I guess I was overcome by how nice everyone on your staff treats me. I don't deserve it."

"Of course you do. You're our heart, our beam of sunshine. We all need that love you throw around so freely. It gets tense and serious on the Hill. You represent normality and fun for all of us. I, for one, couldn't do this campaign without you."

Kat motioned Roxy off the bed and towards the door. "Let's go back downstairs. You've been hiding in corners all night depriving these flesh-starved boys of the sight of a real woman."

Mario was in the midst of winning twenty dollars from two young staffers who bet he couldn't throw a deviled egg in the air and catch it in his mouth. Roxy held the bet as Mario moved over towards the fifteen foot high stairwell, tossed the egg almost to the ceiling and gracefully caught it as it headed back down. Within a moment he swallowed it and turned to collect the money. There was applause, a flurry of activity, then Kat was standing next to her holding their coats. Hayes and Cindy were gone.

★ ★ ★ ★ ★

They worked very late preparing for Max's upcoming Magic Circle which he presented at the castle to a select group each season, so Roxy was not up at dawn as was her habit. When she reached over to answer the ringing phone, she noticed how bright it was outside and checked the clock. No growling. She would have to be polite; 9 a.m. was not too early for a call.

"I just spoke with Kat. She's driving out here in a little while. She wants to meet us at Magnolia's for lunch." Roxy was surprised to hear Max's voice. She knew nothing about Kat coming to Morgan Springs for the Magic Circle although it made sense. Max staged the theatrical events to make pronouncements about each season. He claimed the winter one began the magic year, so he used it as a platform for his annual predictions. Kat would certainly be interested in what he had to say about 1990.

Roxy assured him she would be there, then called Liz. This was a prefect opportunity to get them together. She desperately wanted Liz to come to Rhode Island for the final months of the campaign. Liz was an absolute genius at making things run smoothly while having fun. Max had agreed with her assessment that Liz would be indispensable, although his reasons were chilling.

"Kat's blazing light tends to draw dark forces in some sort of baffling cosmic balance. Not only would Liz guarantee Kat ate enough to live but she has a sixth sense about creeps and is absolutely fearless when it comes to running them off." She shuddered when Max had told her this, and shuddered again now. She did not like to think of the campaign coming down to confronting bad guys in ways that demanded Liz's brand of courage.

She sold the idea to Kat. Now all Kat had to do was convince Liz to accept.

Hearing the blood chilling snarl as the ringing stopped, Roxy suddenly remembered it was hours too early to be calling Liz.

"I've had three hours of sleep and two phone calls already. This better be good or your life is over."

"Don't yell at me, I didn't wake you up."

"You would have if two more sadistic and vicious people hadn't beat you to it. Besides, I expect better of you."

"I'm sorry. I wasn't thinking. Max just woke me up."

"At 9 a.m? Isn't that the middle of the day for you? Are you sick?"

Roxy ignored Liz and gave her the information without commentary.

"Kat's coming. She'll be at your restaurant by noon. If you met up with us, we could talk about your working on the campaign."

"Now let me get this straight." Roxy knew from the tone in Liz's voice there was no escape. She was a bird captive to Liz's claws, and she was about to be mauled.

"You steal hours of precious sleep from me, the first I've had in days. You want me to come down to that fucking restaurant where I'm imprisoned day and night, on my one day off. As my reward, I get to spend a couple of hours with you and that Amazon witch friend of Max's who pretends to be an elected official. You two will proceed to manipulate me through flattery, money, appeals to my patriotism, voodoo, and anything else that might work to give up my action-packed life here and exile myself away from the mountains in some ministate where they have quohog festivals and unkempt, second-rate Mafia figures.

"I assume I'm on the right track here." There was a brief pause but Roxy was too wise to take the bait. Liz was inexorable once in motion

"Once in this paradise, my job will be to keep all of you sane, entertained, well fed, organized and functioning like a well-greased machine instead of a block and tackle with frayed rope. And knowing the moral code of our favorite 'goddess,' I'll be prohibited from sampling the ambitious and accommodating young Apollos she collects around her. Sounds like fun to me. I'm so glad you dragged me out of bed for this." The sarcastic tone oozed out of the phone.

"Have I thanked you lately, Roxy? You know, for letting me be your friend?"

"I know Kat wants to talk to you, Liz. We'll be at Magnolia's for a while then probably come back to my house. We'll be at the castle tonight." Roxy hung up. Liz would continue in the same vein as long as anyone would listen.

★ ★ ★ ★ ★

The waiter removed the last of the bean soup, for which Magnolia's was deservedly famous, and refilled their basket with Liz's equally praised homemade sourdough rolls. He brought them each a Magnolia Virgin, a secret mixture of fruit juices and ginger ale. A Magnolia Slut added vodka, without taste but effective.

They exchanged pleasantries about the food and Magnolia's décor then Kat confirmed Roxy's assumption: she was here to consult Max about the senate race.

"I also need some advice about a performance I've been asked to do at the upcoming Press Club dinner. It's a major event, filled with media heavyweights. Politicians always provide the entertainment and this year's bright idea was to feature the five female House members who are rumored to be running for Senate.

"Comedy is expected but Hayes told me point blank that I was too earnest to be funny and no amount of great writing would change that. I thanked him for his insights and told him not to worry, I would handle this project myself. I may not be a comedienne but I am a credible performer. Hopefully, Max can help me develop a bit I can do."

Roxy was willing to dispute any position Hayes took.

"Mario and I disagreed with Hayes' assessment that you couldn't handle comedy. Reilly said, 'a broad like that should do nothing on stage but take off her clothes.' The man is so vile! Why did Senatorial assign him to your race?"

Before Kat could respond, Liz arrived. One look at the steel edge to her face and Roxy cringed. Liz was "primped" full-tilt. Her mane of frosted hair was curled and tied with ribbons, her face painted on, long silver earrings brushed her shoulders, her lush body was packed into skin tight jeans and a denim jacket that was silver-studded and fringed. Her trademark false eyelashes made her big blue eyes look permanently startled. She carried a Gibson guitar on her shoulder and looked equally ready to sing or swing with it.

Smiling, Kat seemed not to notice the "I want to kill" cloud attached to Liz's shoulder. Kat was so obviously delighted that Liz began to relax.

She wasted no time in idle chit chat.

"Max told me that when you were road warriors in the '70s, you'd occasionally sing together in bars to earn gas and food money. I'm singing at his Circle tonight and invite you to join me. I came over here to pick a few numbers we all knew and see if you wanted to practice."

Liz walked over to the bar to pick up a mug of light beer the bartender drew when he saw her come in.

"Light beer. It's all I drink now. Cheapest way I know to keep up this magnificent bulk." She patted her mounded stomach. "There's lots of money in here."

Searching for common songs, Liz grilled Kat about the repertoire she and Max had. Since Liz knew more than five hundred tunes, from country ballads to low down blues, they quickly picked five with two more for encores. It seemed only a few minutes before Liz was tuned up and she and Kat were belting out the honky tonk sound of "Queen of the Silver Dollar" as if the two of them worked up the act months ago. Kat's pure perfect-pitch soprano wove around Liz's remarkable torchy twang; it was grace balancing power. They did a couple Linda Ronstadt numbers: "Different Drum" and what Liz called her determined "Willin'". When they practiced the haunting minor keyed "House of the Rising Sun," Roxy shuddered—that was playing the night at Sh-Booms with Hayes.

"OK, Kat." Liz broke off the playing. "We finish up with a trio of girl songs, what I see as the three faces of women. First 'Silver Threads and Golden Needles' for the motherly side, then the raunchy, slut side in 'Love Me Like A Man,' and finishing up with 'Amazing Grace' as the angel."

"You're exactly what I need on the campaign, Liz; what we all need," Kat said. "Whatever it takes to get you to Rhode Island by August, I'll do it. Name your price."

"Let's finish these songs and then we can talk about it." Liz picked up her guitar and strummed the opening chords to "Silver Threads."

After Liz insisted on running through each song at least three times, they finally came back to the table, pitcher of beer in hand.

"So, tell me how this campaign really works and who's who," she began. "Let Roxy tell it. She sees everything as a book plot with characters defined by their roles: the Candidate, the Lover, the Bad Guy. It's like a *Reader's Digest* version of life."

Liz sat, chin in hand, an innocent tell-me-everything smile fixed on her round face. Roxy was not intimidated; scripting the campaign was a favorite pastime.

"I guess Hayes and Mario are the two main players, besides Kat of course.

Hayes is the strategist and premier among the hired guns. That's how I see all the consultants and most of the staff which doesn't mean I don't think they're devoted to you, Kat, but they're professionals and they'll go on whether you do or not."

Roxy blushed slightly as she talked about Hayes then panicked when she remembered confessing their passionate liaison to Liz. Desperately she studied her friend and realized she would say nothing now; she would wait and make Roxy sweat meanwhile collecting more and more incriminating evidence.

"How's Mario different?" Liz asked, breaking Roxy away from her self-torture.

"First of all, he's in Rhode Island. He knows the state, the people, the real reasons Kat's in Washington. But the most important difference is that he's there primarily for her and not the politics."

Kat nodded in agreement.

"I don't know about other candidates and other campaigns, but it seems to me that Kat is truly in charge of her senate race. I never get the idea that anyone pushed her into running as the press keeps saying, and no one seems to be a handler. She relies on Hayes and Mario to do their jobs and for their good advice but I see Kat making the final decisions. She has the clearest and fullest vision of the campaign and its purpose."

"Good observations, Roxy, but incomplete. I rely heavily on Max to give me perspective. In many ways, he holds the broadest vision because he keeps the cosmic patterns in mind. He's in charge of determining the critical factor of timing. He never gives political advice, although I know his thoughts on the issues. His code holds that any magician who seeks political power will be destroyed.

"I find you invaluable Roxy, for keeping me tuned in to how people are feeling, not one of my strengths, unfortunately. And it's only in the words you write for me that I can clearly hear my voice."

Kat turned to face Liz directly and continued, "I need you for your reality. We need to be fed, motivated, and hopefully have a good time. You'd be perfect as social director and campaign mom, common sense and whip in hand. Please, Liz."

Kat reached out and grabbed Liz's hand then clasped Roxy's, "we'll be three hearts beating as one."

Liz smiled. "You mean you'd be the angel face, I'd be the mother, and Roxy would be the slut. You always get the best parts, Rox." As Liz laughed, Roxy made a face and wondered whether having her on the campaign was such a hot idea after all.

Liz said she would consider the offer and see what arrangements could be made to turn Magnolia's over to someone else for four months.

They stood at the main square with its beautiful clock tower above the colonial brick courthouse, their backs to the ancient hot springs that made the small Virginia mountain town a noted resort.

"Tell me about Liz. Is she a native here?" Kat asked as they walked uphill to Roxy's.

"Her story is colorful. She's one of those naturally larger-than-life people that easily become legend, especially in small towns like this." Roxy had condensed Liz's life to its important highlights years ago. It was easy to recite it as if it were part of one of her novels.

Liz grew up in Tucker County, West Virginia, a couple mountain ranges away. There was nothing there for anyone the least bit different or special so she left as soon as possible. She went to Cumberland and started working in a restaurant. Soon she was their featured entertainment as well as the best waitress in the place.

An engineer on the highway crew cutting their way through the mountains heard Liz sing, fell in love and brought her back to Morgan Springs. His name was Joseph Barnes the 5th or 6th or something absurd like that. Everyone called him Barney. He was the first son of the town's oldest and most important family. His namesake was some 18th century builder in Morgan Springs who was named emissary to France by his good friend, Thomas Jefferson.

Liz sat around being social as befit the wife of an important local prince but got bored. She persuaded Barney to let her work in several of his family businesses. None of them really interested her although each prospered under her care. They were never able to have children so her restlessness grew. Finally she decided to start singing again professionally instead of at parties and in the choir.

About six years ago, Barney built Magnolia's as a showcase for Liz. It was a huge success, the most important meeting place in town from the day it opened. In November of 1985, about six months later, Barney was killed rescuing people in Tucker County from the worst flood in a hundred years. For almost two years, Liz was a permanent fixture at Magnolia's. Staff would whisper about coming in at 9 a.m. on weekday mornings to find her sitting on her stool at the far end of the bar, drinking, unmoved from when she closed the night before. No matter how much she drank, Liz was able to function perfectly in her restaurant. The food was the best for miles around, the bar friendly, and she still sang on occasion.

One day, when she had ballooned up from the alcohol so that she was barely recognizable, grace struck. No one knew why, but Max claimed he was there when it happened. Liz was sitting in her usual place at the bar. She finished a bottle of bourbon, peered into the empty bottle, then swore, throwing it against the back of the bar where it shattered.

"There's no goddamn prize in the bottom of that one either." Addressing no one in particular she yelled, "There's no prize in any of them."

She never took another drink of hard liquor from that day on.

As they reached the house, Roxy held out her hand and stopped Kat.

"Liz is one of the most savvy women I know. She's an organizer, a motivator, and incredible cook; she sings like a superstar, is totally loyal to her friends, and does great hair. She could probably get even yours under control." Kat smiled indulgently, knowing that her unruly hair was a perpetual topic of concern in Rhode Island, a state where most beauticians drove Mercedes.

★ ★ ★ ★ ★

There were no unfamiliar faces among the fifteen or so people seated with them on period couches and at small tables in the castle's upstairs parlor. The room was rich and splendid with its narrow strip stained oak paneling trimmed along the wood ceiling by an ornately-carved frieze.

The seasonal Magic Circles were by invitation only and Max selected carefully to arrive at a discrete and appreciative audience. Since there was no required dress for the ritual, people were arrayed in the usual range of personal costumes. Roxy was casual in jeans and a hand knit sweater. Kat's chocolate brown knit body suit was topped off by a short, leopard print skirt, thigh-high suede boots, and a sheepskin tunic casually draped off one shoulder. All she needed was a bandolier and rifle and she would be central casting's notion of guerilla chic, and the Senatorial committee's worst nightmare.

The candle-shaped lights set on circular chandeliers darkened, a Tchaikovsky overture played softly in the background. There was a blinding flash of light, a blaring of horns and drums and Max stood before them, framed by twisting smoke in the wide doorway of a small circular room opening off the parlor. Resplendent in white tie and tails, he drew all attention with his force and magnetic presence. For several minutes he spoke seriously of the year about to begin, parading predictions as if he was reading them from cosmic cue cards along the back wall. All the while, he displayed his remarkable skill as a prestidigitator.

The coins disappeared and Max pulled a rope from the air.

"In honor of our special guest this evening—" he flung a ball of green light from his finger which came to rest, glowing over Kat's head "—one of my favorite rope tricks, called Little Rhody. The man who taught it to me named it for his home state and the state of my dear friend, Kat."

Max's voice increased dimension as he executed the rope trick's complicated process, seemingly not hampered by the missing joints of his pinky.

"This will be a difficult year for Rhode Island, born a Gemini and condemned to a path filled with deceit and misuse of power. A pure heart, dedication to high ideals, and powerful women have been—and will continue to be—its salvation. In 1990, there will be calamitous shocks and the crumbling of treasured and trusted institutions. Many will suffer loss."

Kat frowned at his words as Max completed the trick to great applause. Picking his harmonica from behind the ear of a woman at a front table, Max shifted gears from magic to music and gestured for Liz and Kat to join him. The spotlight grew to embrace the trio: Liz with her guitar, Kat sitting on a high stool, Max behind them. A carved breakfront that skimmed the ceiling formed an elegant backdrop

They were decidedly a hit. Max's wailing harmonica was the perfect contrast to the pure blend of women's voices. After playing the seven songs they rehearsed, Liz and Kat yielded to the crowd's demand and sang "Amazing Grace" again, this time a capella.

Their clear angel energy hung like sparkling drops of light as Max moved immediately to the magic part of the ritual.

"When I asked for guidance in selecting the core of the Circle, I was told," Max pulled a small sheet of printed paper from the air and began to read. "The colorized version of *Miracle on 34th Street* will be shown. No, no, no!" he exclaimed in dismay, peering at the dark ceiling as if rebuking some unseen spirit. "This is the television listing. We want serious. We want profound."

Roxy laughed along with the rest. Max crumbled the paper, tossing it into the air where it was consumed in a puff of smoke and a loud pop. He waved his hand, sending off sparks, and a life-size tarot card was brought into the spotlight.

"Does that mean it's time to serve drinks?" Liz quipped loudly as she examined the card. It was the four of cups: a youth being offered a golden goblet by a hand suspended in space.

"First we tell miracle stories and drink wonders from the magic cup, then we adjourn to Magnolia's where you can serve us the real thing," Max responded good naturedly.

Various people told of unexplained events and dreams, then Kat moved to the spotlight from the divan she shared with Liz and began to speak.

"My strange experience occurred almost a year ago, just down the road in Harper's Ferry, a ghost-filled town if there ever was one. It was sunset and I was standing in front of historic Saint Peter's Church. I had been restless all day, a state I attributed to the meetings and briefings I attended. One of the senators who was there came over and gestured to a path circling behind the church. He said something which I didn't hear because as he touched my arm I saw a Confederate soldier standing in his place with a drawn sword, blood dripping from its tip. I was terrified, wrenched my arm away, and ran up the footpath. Reaching the end of the bluff, I sat on a rock bench trying to catch my breath and make sense of what happened.

"When I looked back at the path, I saw him standing there watching me, once again a 20th century man dressed in navy pinstripes and a gleaming white shirt. I recognized him as your senator, T.J. Stuart. He appeared to be waiting for me to say something, probably afraid if he moved closer I would jump. I muttered an apology for my rude behavior and he walked over to the base of the bench."

"'This is Jefferson's Rock,' he said touching the bench. 'In 1783 he came here and wrote about the incredible view from this spot. The idea of natural wonders always fascinated him. He purchased Natural Bridge from King George in 1774 and was delighted to find this bench in Harper's Ferry.' He began reciting Jefferson's words.

"'On your right comes up the Shenandoah having ranged along the foot of the mountains a hundred miles to seek a vent. On your left approaches the Potomac in quest of a mountain passage also. In the moment of their junction, they rush together against the mountain, rend it asunder and pass off to the sea. This scene is worth a voyage across the Atlantic.'

"By this time, sunset was flaming along the cliffs across the river and he reached to help me down from the bench. I shrank away, afraid of what might happen if he touched me again. He seemed surprised but stepped back, letting me slide down unassisted. Reluctantly, I told him about my vision. He nodded and said 'places that have known much death and disruption often have strange psychic fields around them.'"

Roxy could see her own shock reflected on the faces around her. There was probably not a person in the admittedly fringy crowd who voted for the notably conservative Stuart as Virginia's senator. Even Kat acknowledged surprise at his comment and the commonplace tone in which he made it.

"He apologized for frightening me, promised to remain in the present, then led me back down the path, talking all the while of Jefferson, 'for whom I was named,' he explained."

Comment on miracle stories was not allowed; Max believed they lost the power of their message if analyzed rationally. He signaled that Kat's was the last they would hear by conjuring his white top hat from thin air.

"And now for dessert, a bon bon of the future."

He circled through the group, chanting softly as each person reached into the hat and removed a folded piece of paper, opening it to find their message.

The bounty of love is limited only by interrupting its flow. Roxy blushed as she read her message and wondered if Kat would accept divine guidance as an excuse for her lusting after Hayes. Kat beamed with relief showing Roxy her message: *Before the year is out, you shall know your heart's desire.*

Kat elected to stay at the castle with Max to review his predictions about the campaign. Everyone else left for Magnolia's and serious partying.

It was a clear night with the stars shining within reach as they walked down the terraced hillside to the springs and town. Threads of wood smoke hovered like lost shades in the narrow valley, the aroma skimming their nostrils. Antique streetlights glowed softly around the park and a scattering of white and red lights streamed through on the grid of streets. The new Renaissance Spa hovered to the left, interior light making its pentagonal, window-lined shape gleam like a polished chunk of rosy quartz. Where the path curved, Roxy looked back and saw Max and Kat turn from the battlements on the castle roof and go inside.

★ ★ ★ ★ ★

"I've spent hours casting charts, laying out cards, and consulting the runes about your campaign. I even pulled out a crystal ball I hadn't used in years. Doors kept slamming in my face," Max said. Kat felt goose bumps on her arms.

"I can see no clear path leading from now to election night; something happens this spring that changes everything, altering the destiny of the campaign. I tried to penetrate beyond that force but I can't tune it in clearly."

"Does the announcement date matter?"

"Not really. The date we picked, February 14, gives you the best array of forces available unless we wait until much later—April or May—to begin. It's an extremely powerful day for you personally.

"I'm not sure what this means but you should know the forces behind the change are somehow sexual."

She blushed and walked stiffly to the round window that overlooked the small town. After a brief moment she turned back to face him.

"Max—" she spoke reluctantly.

He stood and held out his arms. "We don't need to talk about this, Kat. You know I'm here for you, whatever you need, whenever you need it. We've shared love before and we certainly can do it again. It would be my pleasure. I'm not sure the sex refers to you, though."

Kat allowed his arms to enfold her. When she relaxed a little, they sat at the library table.

He picked up a polished gray stone, manipulating it in his hand, making it appear and disappear. Finally he spoke.

"The unexpected, the unknown, the unplanned—this is the recurring pattern. It's why I can't see the outcome. It showed up in every method I tried. The runes were particularly dramatic."

Ceremoniously, he laid the gray stone on the star Regulus, marked by a glowing point on the celestial field of the table top. It was blank. He turned it over—also blank.

"Three times I drew a rune, three times it was this one, the unknowable. This is destiny, baby, and the fates are not ready to let us see it no matter how much it hurts my pride not to have an answer."

Kat picked up the stone rubbing its smoothness. A faint shadow of resentment lurked in her eyes.

"What does one do with the unknowable?"

"Leap into the void with absolute faith." Responding to her withering look, Max protested. "I don't write destiny, I only read it and then only when the fates turn on the light."

"Maybe I should listen to what everyone is saying and wait six years."

"You can't wait. All the forces we can muster must be in place by '93—the critical point. It's the time of mutation when the force of evolution can take a radical leap, hopefully forward. The patterns will be set by '95 that determine how we approach the next millennium. Wrong choices could be disaster, now and for centuries. You can't delay, '96 will be too late." Max spoke as if he were reading from pages written on her soul.

"Whatever happens with the campaign, this year is clearly one of personal victory for you. When you walked up to me tonight, I could see you on a giant white stallion leaping through the sky to levels you never before imagined."

Max laid out several cards.

"I did dozens of readings on various questions about the campaign and you. These seven cards continually appeared."

They examined the evocative images printed on the tarot cards. Kat picked each up in turn as Max recited what he saw as its meaning for her.

"The High Priestess and Empress are you."

He pointed to the first two cards, one of which looked like Kat with dark hair and a detached expression on her face. The other was warm and bountiful with long blonde curls. "The Emperor and the knight racing with drawn sword are your hero."

She tossed down the two cards.

"I don't need a hero."

"One or the other showed up in almost every reading. I'm open to other interpretations but these two guys sure look like heroes to me. And with these cards"—he picked up the remaining three and handed them to her "heroes may be a necessity."

Slowly she laid down the first card.

"The Devil is your opponent, not a surprise," Max said blandly then paused as she set the next. They both stared solemnly at the unmistakable Death card and Kat chided herself for the spark of fear that the black armor clad skeleton sent careening through her brain.

"It turned up so often and in such a way that I'm forced to conclude it should be taken literally: someone is going to die. And this," he tapped the final card, "is once again you."

She gasped involuntarily. A black haired woman was tied and blindfolded, eight swords struck in the ground around her.

"You may finally confront the limits of your will; destiny promises to be un-swayed."

While she sat silent, Max pulled out a small envelope.

"In here are word charms I created affirming Kiley elected to U.S. Senate. Give them out to whomever you trust to summon their magic."

"I have one last question," she croaked. "Will the outcome be worth the pain?"

"Yes!" Certainty filled his voice. "Yes."

★ ★ ★ ★ ★

"I knew you would be the perfect person to help," the voice on the other end of the phone gushed.

It was Carrie Lange. When she first introduced herself, Roxy made no connection. As the conversation continued and Carrie reported how pleased she had been to help Hayes in his quest to have Roxy's pearls restrung, it dawned on her who this stranger speaking so familiarly was.

"I'm so excited to have the job. Kat's been my ideal for years ever since she spoke to my high school class right after she won her first race. She was so inspiring. I credit her with motivating me to escape the French ghetto in Woonsocket where I grew up.

"You're so lucky to have her as a friend."

Roxy recognized the ardor in her voice. Kat often had this effect on young women, particularly the plain ones like Carrie. She conjured up the slightly equine features of Kat's new office manager and reaffirmed her initial judgement—worshipper. Fortunately it did not take long for most staff to realize Kat was not a personification of the goddess, especially since Kat actively discouraged the attitude. They soon became devoted co-workers and treated their former idol with the amiable disrespect endemic among political staff.

"I've been given the responsibility of selecting a Christmas gift for Kat from the office. You know her better than anyone. Do you have any suggestions?"

After several moments of blankness followed by a quick flash of gratitude that she had a handcrafted silver and ebony star pendant for her, Roxy did have a suggestion. Before leaving Morgan Springs the previous day, Kat mentioned how she recently discovered her dressing mirror in Narragansett mysteriously cracked. Carrie was elated when Roxy suggested replacing the mirror and promised she would get a quality antique piece at a reasonable price from one of her many contacts.Wanting to insure it would be appropriate to the décor, Roxy described Kat's bedroom.

"The walls are pale rose trimmed in stained oak. She has a mahogany bedstead carved with ocean waves and jumping fish. Two panels on the headboard are painted with mermaids. I think the mirror was also mahogany and stood next to the bed. There's a cabinet, almost nine feet tall, made from walnut with decorated door panels."

Once the gift issue was resolved, Carrie readily reported on announcement activities, recent coverage of Winston's campaign in the local press and staff gossip. Her manner was bitingly funny. Although she worked with many of Kat's people during the president's visit, Roxy was still surprised at how much information she knew. Promising they would have dinner as soon as she came to Rhode Island, she hung up. Within an hour, Roxy once more forgot Carrie Lange.

4

Yankee Doodle Dandy
January 1990

Roxy grabbed the ringing phone as she came back to load the last of her clothes into the car before leaving for Washington.

"I'm glad I caught you," Kat said, "I need your help with my routine for the Press Club dinner tonight." Roxy had not discussed the event with her since she left Morgan Springs. She had no idea what Kat planned for her performance.

"I'm not going to have to go out on stage and do anything, am I?"

Public appearances were not Roxy's idea of fun. She was happy to leave the spotlight to Liz, Max, Kat and whoever else had the desire and talent for it.

"Don't worry. I know what a bashful puppy you are," Kat chuckled. "I need you to pick up three guys who are my back-up group. Bring them to the Press Club. They'll be ready by 9 p.m. at a sports bar in Georgetown called Winners."

"I know where that is," Roxy replied. "How will I know them?"

"They'll be in New York Yankees baseball uniforms."

Roxy had a queasy feeling that Kat was freelancing.

"Have you talked to Hayes about your performance?"

"No. But he's my escort, so he can drag me off stage if I get out of hand. He's bringing Harry Crast from the *Providence Journal* along." Kat paused briefly then continued, "This is our secret for now, Roxy. Trust me."

Her heart sank. Whenever people felt compelled to tell her to trust them, it was because they were about to do something foolish.

★ ★ ★ ★ ★

Peeking from a draped-off area behind the podium, Roxy scanned the room. Kat was sitting calmly at one of the large front tables with a collection of senators and important media figures. Somehow she always managed to look serene even when chaos was about to descend. Roxy had pumped the baseball trio, who turned out to be musician-singers, about the content of Kat's act. She thought it sounded great but had a feeling that Hayes would disagree. He was sitting at one of the side tables with an older man who looked like an overgrown pixie—pointy ears, shaggy hair and all. It was Harry Crast. Political editor of the state's most important newspaper, he was the man shaping the public view of politics in Rhode Island. Who knew what he would think of Kat's performance?

Roxy's eyes lingered a moment longer to watch Hayes lean over and listen carefully to Harry then laugh appreciatively. He does his job well, she thought.

The petite congresswoman from Maryland, Rachel Palczeski, won a round of applause teasing the media-filled audience with tales from her previous life as an English teacher. The political columnist who was acting as host rose to introduce Kat.

She walked up to the podium, ruby red heels tapping on the wooden floor, tossing a baseball up and down, catching it deftly then throwing it in the air again. Her curls were bunched up and spilling out from under a baseball cap she had stuffed on her head. Her frilly red chiffon dress danced around her knees and shoulders. Since she looked unlike any other senator, there was no reason to expect that she should behave like one. Resting the ball on the podium, she greeted the crowd.

"When my staff heard I was invited to entertain you tonight, they tried to dissuade me, insisting I was not funny."

Kat screwed up her face and posed like a rag doll tossing the baseball. The audience roared its approval—this was not funny?

"Like all good members of Congress, I rely on staff advice. I cast about for an alternative to comedy. Again, like a good member, I turned to the press to check my image; what could I do to entertain a roomful of editors, columnists, television and radio commentators?"

Kat began tossing the baseball again.

"In Rhode Island, the preeminent political voice belongs to my dear friend Harry Crast of the *Providence Journal*."

The cameras obediently followed the arc of Kat's hand as she waved at Harry. "A few months ago he said there were two things I could do to improve my standing as a candidate for the Senate. One was to throw out the first ball."

Kat waved.

"On your feet Harry. The first ball is being thrown out to you."

She threw the baseball easily into his hand.

"It's signed by our number one baseball fan, President Sam Jamison."

As the audience applauded, Kat continued.

"The second piece of advice was to wrap myself in the flag."

The three men in Yankee uniforms moved into the spotlight. One began softly playing "Yankee Doodle Dandy" on the harmonica.

"Here's a flag waving tribute to a remarkable American songwriter born in my hometown of Providence, Rhode Island on the Fourth of July—Mr. George M. Cohan."

Her shoes tapping rhythmically, Kat joined the three men, all of them now singing. They sounded great giving a bouncy tempo to the song. The tempo increased and a part of the act the singers never described, unfolded.

Kat began tap dancing to the song, and with an opening spin, ripped off her dress. Hands on her waist, she tapped out a dazzling array of cramp rolls, toe heel brushes, and flap ball changes, clad in a red, white and blue star studded and spangled dance leotard cut high on her legs. Traveling with a shuffle she took a baseball bat from one of her back-up group and danced around it. Her red shoes flashed and pounded as she twirled the bat like a baton, step kicking through the final verse and concluding by tossing the bat high in the air and catching it as it spun back down.

She cakewalked through a repeat of the final refrain, and as the dance ended with Kat in a classic pin-up pose—ankles crossed, leaning against her bat, the baseball cap held high in her right hand, her locks spilling around her smiling face—there was a split second of shocked silence in the room.

Then a piercing whistle from the back gave a signal and the blinding light of dozens of prohibited flashbulbs caught Kat's pose. By the time the whistler began to applaud and stomp his feet, his ear splitting Appalachian hog call was nearly drowned in wild cheering from the packed audience. Virtually everyone was on their feet clapping their approval.

In the tumult, Kat snatched up her dress and ran off-stage. Roxy slipped along the wall to slide into an empty chair next to Hayes. He and Crast were looking at a tall, well-built man, leaning against the back wall, arms folded, a pleased smile on his long face. The whistler.

"T.J. Stuart, Republican senator from Virginia," Hayes told Crast, admiration in his voice.

"Is he a political supporter of our girl, or just an appreciator of fine female flesh?" Crast asked with a cynical tone.

"Probably both."

The two men laughed and looked at Stuart who nodded slightly to Hayes then walked out of the room. They turned back to the table and Hayes barely acknowledged Roxy before proceeding to describe Stuart to the journalist as if he were more important than Kat's performance.

"Stuart defies categories in his political orientation almost as much as the congresswoman does. There's no doubt he's a fiscal conservative and supports a strong hand both in international affairs and in dealing with domestic violence and crime. He continually rails against too much government control except for the environment. His particular crusade is pure water.

"No one wants him in their little group because he's too smart and refuses to take orders. Senator Thomas Jefferson Stuart has this notion of restoring Virginia's ante-bellum pre-eminence in national affairs and is fierce in representing his state. His personal honor is above reproach."

The cynical tone remained in Crast's voice as he asked, "And he's an ardent feminist of course, can't wait to have more women in the Senate. Right?"

"Stuart says repeatedly he's tired of looking at those same old ugly ties and paunchy bellies every day on the Senate floor. He loves ladies, he wants more of them around.

"The women's groups hate it. He votes fairly, and often with them. He's out working to elect more women, but they claim his basic attitude is sexist. He insists on referring to them as 'ladies,' which drives several noted female leaders to distraction. And he delights in pointing out inconsistencies in their rhetoric— another maddening trait, according to some."

From her quick look at him, Roxy thought the problem might be that he radiated maleness like few men in Washington did. That look seemed almost as threatening as Kat's curves and curls and probably to the same people.

"Frankly, Harry and strictly off the record, of course. "

Hayes paused as Crast nodded agreement, "Of course."

"I think the Senatorial committee doesn't know what to do with either one of them and figured they deserved each other."

Both of the men laughed. Belatedly recalling his manners, Hayes turned to Roxy introducing her to Crast as Kiley's friend.

"Roxy and I have met before. In fact, we've enjoyed Kiley's dancing before." Hayes looked quizzical and Roxy searched her memory for the event as Crast settled in to tell the story.

"Each year the *Journal* sponsors a Follies—skits, poking fun at various public figures, the usual. One year while still at Baywatch, Kiley was the emcee. She worked several dance numbers into her role including one that lives in local legend—Kiley Tomasso, the dancing Clorox bottle, named as state mascot. It was part of her campaign to clean up the Rhode Island beaches; a highly successful campaign, I should add.

"The following year at the Folllies, when Kiley was a congressional candidate, she was target for one of the skits where she was elected overwhelmingly as the Legs of Rhode Island. My own memories of her dance career go further back. She and my daughter took dance class together and Kiley was featured in virtually every recital. It's good to know if she loses in November, she could still have a promising career in Las Vegas."

Hayes was not happy to hear Rhode Island's political dean casually discussing his candidate losing the senate race. But he recovered quickly and was smiling as Kat approached the table, stopping for greetings and applause along the way.

Roxy hung around, watching a parade of Washington power brokers come and pay homage to Kat's performance. Crast was dancing in attendance and beaming as many of the media celebrities greeted him as well and joked about the baseball. Charlie Drummond, ABC's new hotshot host of their morning show, approached with a huge bouquet of flowers. He presented them to Kat with a flourish and a look that made Roxy's knees weak second-hand. Then he leaned forward, whispered in her ear and with a brief kiss turned and left.

Roxy could not wait to force Kat to tell her what he said, or rather what words he used to say "fuck me baby," which was obviously what he was thinking.

★ ★ ★ ★ ★

After driving Kat to an breakfast meeting, Roxy went on to the congressional office. She was the only one there when the first dozen roses arrived. By the time Kat came and staff appeared for their 11 a.m. meeting, there were three dozen more. Roxy collected and numbered the cards as the roses came in and put them in water. Then she took the cards into Kat's office, peeking at each message. The first card was signed "Guardian Angel." The second read "Who says women are equal—they're better! I have neither the talent or nerve to do what you did. An Admiring Colleague." The third said "Beau" and the fourth was blank. The same person must have sent them. Roxy wondered if it was Charlie Drummond.

She handed them to Kat, who seemed amused rather than mystified as she opened each and read them. But she said nothing, forcing Roxy to keep her prying a secret.

Staff was buzzing about Kat's dance when they came in for the meeting. There were dozens of phone calls and most were positive with only a few predicting hellfire and damnation for Kat. Hayes reported the Rhode Island office was swamped with calls from baseball teams, veterans groups, and Yankee fans begging for copies of the finale photo appearing in the half dozen newspapers he spread across the table. Admiring comments were circulating when Jasmine interrupted, her disgust plain in her voice.

"It's difficult for me to get excited over press coverage with headlines that read 'SENATE PIN-UP! CAST YOUR VOTE HERE.' Gould is worried about the Democrats trivializing her. It seems they won't have to look very far for a way to do it." Jasmine glared at Kat, her face twisted with betrayal.

"Have you spoken with Gould about this?" Kat asked her press secretary. "Have other media expressed disapproval?"

"Gould is a man. He sees it like all of them do," Jasmine swung her hand around at the assembled staff, "something to drool over and make degrading remarks about. Didn't you hear Charlie Drummond this morning? He practically propositioned you on the air."

"Jasmine may have legitimate concerns and Gould was not particularly pleased," said Hayes.

"Did he say anything specific?" Kat asked.

"His exact words were: 'Didn't any of you political geniuses ever tell that broad not to take off all her clothes in the first act?'"

Kat looked amused.

"I've heard him say that before, but I never thought he meant it literally. Did Harry Crast seem appalled or horrified?"

Hayes shook his head.

"No, but like most Rhode Islanders, he smiles at your—ah, eccentricities. The out-of-state press may not be so tolerant."

"OK, we won't plaster the pictures around and I'll accept no offers of work in a chorus line. I guess we'll have a better reading on general reaction by the time of our strategy meeting tomorrow. If we have to do damage control, let's be ready to act fast," Kat told Hayes.

He decided humor was the only sane way to deal with this issue.

"We do have some complaints from Red Sox fans however." Kat looked uncertain. "But I tried to explain "'Red Sox Doodle Dandy" simply did not scan."

"I got a call this morning asking me to come over and meet with Susan Webb in Senator Groven's office. She asked for me by name," Roxy said. "Somehow I get the feeling it's connected with the show last night."

Kat and Hayes looked at each other and he muttered, "She's Groven's chief aide. I wonder what she wants with Roxy, or how she even found out about her."

"It's OK if you go Roxy, but talk to Hayes first—and afterwards."

Color danced across Kat's cheeks as Maggie brought in the latest dozen roses.

★ ★ ★ ★ ★

Hayes suggested they talk in his "window office," the low sills along the hall windows in the Longworth building that congressional staff used to escape the cramped quarters of their shared space. It would be more intimate than his desk with the entire front office staff able to hear and see them. Sitting in the corner of the window, Hayes leaning against her, yes, it could be the chance she wanted. They had not spoken alone since the night of the president's visit.

It started out the way I planned, thought Roxy as she carefully picked her way through an arcane route along the miles of underground corridors and tunnels linking the six congressional office buildings with each other and the Capitol. The polished concrete floors of the subterranean passages were deadly for women in heels. She had twisted her ankle or nearly fallen on the slippery surface more often than she could remember. She never traveled this way alone before and hoped she could recall the twists and turns, the elevators to take to which level, to get her from Longworth to Russell where Senator Groven had his office.

She was still smarting from the softly spoken but unmistakable tongue lashing Hayes had given her and almost forgot her standard worry as she moved along under the Capitol. What a nightmare to be trapped in these corridors with hundreds of staff, members and tourists if there was a nuclear war, having to survive together until it was all clear.

The possibility of the type of attack that would require months of living sealed underground was greatly lessened by Gorbachev's recent actions. He did the unthinkable. He refused to play nuclear nightmare with the Americans any longer. Roxy was a child of the '50s though, and habitual childhood fears die hard.

She had been close to tears when Hayes accused her of conspiring with Kat in staging her dance the previous night and seemed not to want to believe her denials. He talked about teamwork, and putting the brakes on any of Kat's ideas that might be detrimental to the campaign. Roxy was indignant that he assumed Kat would not know what was best. It was her senate race after all; her own safe seat she was giving up to take this chance. They would all find jobs if she lost. Kat was the one with everything on the line.

Roxy was really irritated when he said her political inexperience could make it dangerous for her to be Kat's sole confidante.

By the time he moved on to instructions and warnings about her imminent meeting with Senator Groven's aide, Roxy heard nothing. If she could shut out his voice, she could concentrate on how his blue eyes now seemed cruel and hard, and how she wanted to forget his soft, manicured hands roaming over her body.

Absorbed in reliving the painful interview, she was brought up short at the bottom of the escalator facing the entrance of the Senate subways. Which building? There were three tracks, each marked by the name of a different Senate building. Watching the small cars that looked like an amusement park ride, Roxy searched through her bag to find Groven's office number. She got on the train farthest left and resolved to concentrate on the meeting ahead.

Reaching Senator Groven's office, the sight of Susan Webb drove any other thoughts from her mind. The severe look on her thin face was intensified by a tight bun of gray-streaked hair. Black eyebrows plucked into wings, a blood-red mouth and matching claw-like fingernails completed the terrifying picture.

After the briefest of polite exchange, Ms. Webb—Roxy could not imagine calling her Susan—moved directly to her point.

"As you know, Kiley Tomasso's race is very important to all Republican senators." The woman stopped, uncertain how politically astute Roxy was, then added, "Her victory could mean the difference between a committee chairmanship or continuing in the minority." Roxy indicated she understood the impact.

"We were told you were Kiley Tomasso's best friend and she listens to you on personal matters." Her voice was brisk, cool and detached—almost soft in comparison to her face and stark black suit. Roxy managed a nod that she hoped conveyed agreement.

"The senators are concerned about the congresswoman's appearance."

"You mean Senator Groven?" Roxy asked.

"Senator Groven and others. They feel her clothes and shoes are not senatorial, and they want her to do something with her hair. It's very disturbing. Her look may be acceptable in the House but it's not in the Senate. Could you suggest she visit a personal shopper perhaps, or maybe your media people could find someone to work on her hair, make-up and wardrobe?"

Roxy kept waiting for her to crack a smile, to break a little and acknowledge how absurd this conversation was. She couldn't imagine Kat with anyone buying her clothes, and her hair was hopeless unless she pulled it back like Ms. Webb and posed as the Wicked Witch of the West after shock treatment.

"Does Senator Groven really stand around talking to other senators about Kat's hair and clothes?"

Noticing the perplexed look on the woman's face Roxy explained, "I mean Kiley—ah, the congresswoman. Kat is the name her friends and family call her." Ms. Webb looked even more disapproving.

Roxy ignored everything Hayes told her about saying nothing to Groven's aide and agreeing with whatever she said then coming back and telling him. She was outraged at the woman's presumption.

"Or did this concern suddenly come up after her dancing last night?" she said spitefully.

Ms. Webb narrowed her eyes and her mouth became so tight it virtually disappeared. "There was nothing senatorial about her display last night. I think most of the senators agree on that."

"Oh, I don't know," snapped Roxy, "Senator Stuart sure seemed to like it."

"Senators whose opinions matter do not agree with him." Her tone left no doubt in Roxy's mind that Stuart did not carry much weight in these circles.

Seeing no positive direction for the discussion, Roxy began to get up when a door opened to her left. The way Ms. Webb shot out of her chair led Roxy to conclude the man who emerged must be Groven. He was of medium height, desiccated and parchment skinned, with thinning hair combed over his skull. His eyes were small and seemed continually focused on something just over her shoulder. A slightly younger version of the senator with the obsequious manner that identified him as what Hayes called genuflect staff, followed close behind.

"This is Kiley Tomasso's friend. She seems unconcerned with the congresswoman's appearance." Ms. Webb was quick to inform the senator of the problem.

Roxy was fascinated by how repulsive Groven was as he stared back, pulling on his tie. He cleared his throat several times. He spoke in the rolling, elocuted tones of a radio announcer. Or, more likely, a preacher.

"Your friend, Congresswoman Tomasso," he said, continuing to stroke his tie, "is entirely too female." Roxy could almost see the "female" bold-faced and underlined in some script he was reading behind his eyelids.

"It would not be seemly for a senator to look like her. If she wishes to join us in the U.S. Senate, she must tone herself down."

He straightened his tie, mussed by his pulling on it.

"She could take advice from Ms. Webb," his hands were nowhere near his tie as he nodded towards his aide who seemed almost to be smiling. "She always looks quite professional." Without ever looking at Roxy again, Senator Groven left the office followed by his staff clone.

★ ★ ★ ★ ★

"Is she alone?" Roxy asked Maggie, nodding at the closed door. When Maggie said yes, Roxy escaped into Kat's office before Hayes could complete his phone call. She would tell her story directly to Kat.

The perfume of six dozen roses almost knocked her over. Kat was standing near the windows, holding a handful of florist cards as if she were about to draw one and bet on it.

"Do you know who's sending the roses?" Roxy asked.

She ignored the question, responding with one of her own as she walked over to the couch next to her desk.

"What happened with Groven?"

Roxy was agreeable to tackling the subject of Groven first. She could hear about the rose-sender later. She told Kat that Groven and his buddies, whoever they were, considered her too female. As she related the details of her conversation with Ms. Webb, Kat sat quietly, displaying no emotion on her face. With her hair pulled up, she could have been the model for the ivory carved cameo she wore on her dress.

When Roxy demonstrated Groven's obsession with his tie, both women flashed on what the image revealed.

"That's sick! What a twisted, repressed, slime bucket he is!" Roxy said, horrified.

Kat began laughing. Roxy stared at her for a second then shouted, "Too female for him! Just the thought of you had him jacking off his tie. I hope he was somewhere alone watching you dance last night."

She too started laughing and collapsed into the chair facing Kat. The two women laughed uncontrollably then Roxy felt tears coming. She thought about Hayes, and the legions of other men who had disappointed her over the years, and could not stop crying. She looked over to see Kat watching her then begin crying herself. Holding the cards in her hand, Kat waved them and sobbed as if her heart were breaking. The pain in her tone stopped Roxy's tears and she went to sit by her friend, wondering what could have caused the unusual display of emotion. Inexplicably, she thought of the advice in Max's fortune strip that she selected for January: *Always question what you think you know.*

They were sitting on the couch consoling each other when Hayes knocked and walked in. He leaned on the desk, folded his arms and asked, "As bad as that?"

Kat nodded encouragement to Roxy, who retold her story. As she relayed Groven's comment about Kat being too female, he unconsciously reached up and straightened his tie then smoothed back his hair. Roxy stopped in the middle of her sentence, looked at Kat and they both exploded laughing again.

The bewildered look on his face as Hayes stood away from the desk, threw up his hands, and walked out of the office made them laugh even harder.

★ ★ ★ ★ ★

Roxy attached herself to Kat's legislative director, Stan Everhart, during the fundraiser the Senatorial committee was hosting for Kat in their reception room that evening. Stan was the rock upon which Kat's legislative reputation was built. His shock of silver gray hair matched his wife Jill's equally splendid mane. He looked sober and staid on the surface but, as the Christmas party revealed, had an unrelenting sense of humor with people he knew.

Like most of Kat's staff, excepting Hayes, Stan was an unreformed liberal with a tinge of alternative politics. Although he and Hayes worked smoothly together, there was an underlying tension resulting from their diverse political views. Stan was leader of the staff clique who felt the need for eternal vigilance against too much Republican thought. They justified their concern by pointing out that Rhode Island was an overwhelmingly Democratic state and only Kat's flagrant independence allowed her the level of popularity she enjoyed.

She would be safe with him. Hayes would stay away and she could keep out of trouble and maybe do some good. She stood and smiled at the various PAC representatives. They were called lobbyists before the campaign finance reform of the '70s. They paid a thousand dollars to eat passable cocktail food, drink, and let their support be known not so much to Kat as to the senatorial committee. A roomful of Senators to shake attendees hands and listen to their pleas was the added bonus of committee-sponsored fundraisers.

As the senators gathered around and began making the requisite noises of support for Kat's candidacy, Roxy examined them. Senator Groven was not present but there were several others of the same type. Empty shells. Roxy guessed that two millenia ago, the Roman model for the U.S. Senate was also a parade of mediocrities and nonentities. No wonder the vision of Kat flashing through the Senate halls flicking off sparks from her high heels sent them into orbit almost as easily as thought of her voting record. The way each senator voted, however, was often less important than who got to the magic number of fifty-one first. She was a Republican, another R in the all-important column that added up to control of the Senate. It was a goal for which they were willing to sacrifice much.

Senator Stuart walked in as the elegant and popular Senator Grace Langley from New Jersey insisted on the need for more women in the Senate.

"The Republican party has the opportunity to enlist the invaluable alliance of a majority of the voting public—women—by capturing their imaginations with exciting and promising candidates like Kiley Tomasso."

"And with a shift in their policy on choice," Stan Everhart muttered, underlining one of Kat's prime arguments with her party.

T.J. Stuart stepped forward to address the group, and Roxy noted again how he radiated energy. He had the strong and graceful body of a man who preferred solid earth beneath his feet rather than concrete and carpet. Compared to the unimpressive collection of his fellow Senators standing before her, Roxy thought Stuart positively glowed. He was alive in a ring of corpses. He was not handsome as much as compelling. His nose looked as if it had been broken a few times and left to heal in place, his hair was light colored and cut short, emphasizing what could be kindly termed his high forehead. But it was his intense and expressive brown eyes that held Roxy's attention. They seemed to miss nothing.

"I'd like to second all my colleagues' wonderful and encouraging remarks with something more substantial—a little cash."

He walked up to Kat and held out a check to her. As she took it, he turned back to the crowd and explained, "My good friend Earl Beckham at Norfolk Steel and Shipyard woke me this morning to tell me he was wiring a five thousand dollar check to the congresswoman and asked that I deliver it in person tonight with this message."

Stuart unfolded a piece of paper and once again faced Kat as he read in a voice that filled the room.

"I saw you dance last night and you convinced me. We need more babes in the Senate. There's more where this came from."

A slight tilt to Stuart's lips indicated he might be smiling as he delivered the message. Everyone watched Kat's reaction. She beamed her appreciation, waved Hayes over and said in a voice Roxy swore was deliberately seductive, "Let's set up a breakfast with Mr. Beckham so we can thank him properly for his confidence and support."

She never took her eyes off Stuart who bowed graciously and began the applause that introduced her speech.

After a brief but enthusiastic review of her basic themes, Kat challenged her finance team and the other senators, to follow Stuart's lead in raising money for what would certainly be a too-expensive campaign. Even the most jaded of the political insiders responded to some magic Kat was able to weave through her voice when she spoke to groups of people. Noticing how intently Stuart was watching her, Roxy wondered if this was the first time he had heard Kat do what she called her inspirational injections. She insisted she could bombard people with thoughts to raise their energy, and they responded. The energy in the reception room certainly felt better to Roxy when Kat was talking than when Senator Bourn was wheezing along.

People applauded, then began making their way out, pausing at the door for a final word with Kat. Roxy asked Stan about Stuart.

"What do you know about him personally? Is he married?"

"Oh yes," Stan answered. "His wife Clarice is the daughter of Virginia's most important kingmaker. I expect she's part of the reason Stuart's in the Senate."

"Too bad," said Roxy. She went to stand near Kat so they could leave together. She was talking to Senator Stuart as Roxy moved close enough to be part of the conversation.

"I do appreciate your friend's check," Kat said sincerely.

"And his sentiment?" asked Stuart.

"It's a beginning. Maybe over breakfast I can convince him of my other talents. My senatorial talents."

"I'll suggest he invites several other businessmen. Norfolk's close, you could fly down and back and still make votes. But you shouldn't do it for less than fifty thousand."

"Fifty thousand," Roxy repeated, amazed.

He looked at her and smiled. "He gave her five grand after watching her dance on television. Breakfast should be worth at least fifty."

"I wonder what he'd pay her to….."

The look on Kat's face silenced Roxy immediately and she flinched as she remembered to whom they were talking. The strain of fast lane life in Washington was corroding her judgement. It was a good thing she was moving to Rhode Island.

Stuart leaned over to Roxy and whispered loudly, "I'd give her ten thousand myself." Roxy gasped and blushed. Stuart raised his eyebrows, cocked his slight smile and bowed to them.

"Ladies," he said, raising his hand in salute, then turned and left.

★ ★ ★ ★ ★

"I suppose we'll have to rehash my Press Club performance before we can move on to more pressing matters like the announcement." There was little tolerance in Kat's voice as she began the strategy meeting, once again at Senatorial committee headquarters. Gould backed off his initial horror when he heard from Mario and Hayes that calls and notes were running heavily in support of her.

"If we construct a good enough campaign emphasizing her accomplishments, this little aberration will be viewed as an assurance that she's not too serious, too staid and devoted to political work. We want to keep some charm and humanity in the picture," Gould explained.

"Our overnight tracking calls show an incredible shift of interest to Kiley among the middle-aged and older men who were our weakest sector." Lila Gravely sounded secretly pleased then hastened to caution that not too much stock be put in this as firm and lasting support.

Jasmine's disgust had not receded.

"We should have no trouble convincing Rhode Island voters to choose a showgirl with great legs instead of a businessman with a bank account."

Gould had a major plan to pitch to the group and he wanted the energy more upbeat. To counter Jasmine's negative assessment he produced a media coup.

"My good friend Charlie Drummond called me last night and begged me to schedule Kiley for his morning show on ABC. National exposure. It's just what we want." He was stunned when Jasmine hissed at him.

"She can't go on his show. The man is a total pig. He would sit and leer and drool, and what if he asked her out or something on the air. Then what would we do?"

"Don't be ridiculous," Kat said, her irritation obvious. "ABC is not going to allow Charlie Drummond to behave like a complete idiot and even if he does put the moves on me, I can assure you Jasmine, I am well able to deal with it. This would not be the first time I needed to deflect unwanted attention."

"Thank heavens you'd turn him down."

Kat's head snapped around as Senator Stuart's voice came from the open door behind her. Everyone else was equally surprised. They had all been so engrossed in the exchange between Jasmine and Kat, no one had seen him standing there.

"I've seen Drummond's little black book. He has names in the hundreds and carefully rated as to their performance. I'd hate to see you on his list."

Stuart was leaning against the doorjamb as he spoke. Dressed in faded and worn jeans, a navy flannel shirt hanging open over a Valvolene teeshirt, heavy work boots and a navy down vest slung over his shoulder, all he needed was an old Winchester rifle cradled in his arm to complete the picture of mountain hunter.

"Sorry to interrupt." Amusement was plain in his voice. "I'm off to Roanoke and home for the weekend and wanted to tell you arrangements have been made for your breakfast with the boys in Norfolk."

He spoke to Kat who was still facing him then handed a note to Hayes.

"Call Beckham. He's expecting to hear from you to finalize a date."

Breathing hard and tightening her fists, Jasmine lashed out at Stuart with pure venom in her voice. "I spoke with several important female leaders this morning who were horrified by your friend's insulting message last night, if indeed it came from anyone besides you."

The fierce look in Stuart's eyes did not deter the press secretary.

"They don't feel the money makes the sexist remarks acceptable. We may lose their endorsements and any further contributions from their groups."

Kat leaned toward her and said in a threatening tone, "This better not be true."

"I assure you the note was vintage Earl Beckham, as you will have the pleasure to find out for yourself, and it was meant as a compliment. Since my purpose is to help not hinder your efforts to reach the Senate, allow me to make up any loss you may suffer from the wounded egos of lady lobbyists. You'll have checks on your desk Monday for twenty thousand dollars and an endorsement from the national Chamber of Commerce in time for your announcement. If there is anything further I can do, including apologizing directly to any lady I may have insulted, please let me know."

He shot a parting look at Jasmine that clearly wished her a tortuous death at the hands of some biker gang and left, closing the door behind him.

There were several moments of silence before Kat turned slowly away from the door and faced Jasmine again.

"That was unforgiveable." Kat's voice could have cut steel. "You and I will discuss the situation with the women's groups later, along with staff whose job it is to deal with them. Please remember you are the press secretary and limit yourself to your appropriate duties. If you have free time on your hands, perhaps Hayes can develop some new assignments for you.

"Senator Stuart is very valuable to this campaign," Kat added after a tense pause. "He is helping us raise hundreds of thousands of dollars. And he offers a powerful appeal to conservative Republicans in the state, a group with whom we are notoriously weak. If you have problems with his attitude, or that of any other supporter of mine, speak to me about it. You will draft a formal apology to the senator to show to me. I'd make you grovel in person, on your knees, but obviously I can't trust your behavior."

Without allowing Jasmine, or anyone else time for response, Kat began discussing plans for the announcement.

Kat was especially delighted when Mario listed the various groups involved in the event and related activities. There would be more than a dozen, from Italian-American war veterans to nurses and teachers for Kiley, each with a banner, list of supporters, and endorsement.

When Kat showered Mario with praise, he graciously acknowledged that Carrie had been invaluable in helping put the details together.

"Carrie sold me on adding events in the north," he said.

"Do you think Woonsocket is more important to us than South County or Newport?" asked Kat, concerned that neither were included in the day's events.

"Not more important," Mario answered, "just more difficult. There are a lot of swing votes in the north. A lot of voters that are new to Rhode Island and haven't been voting for Winston most of their adult lives. They're ready for you, they just don't know you. The votes are there to be had, we'll just have to work harder. I want to get started day one."

When Lila Gravely nodded agreement with his assessment, Kat gave her approval.

"Our most pressing concern today is media. With less than five weeks before the announcement, we need agreement on our initial strategy and the themes we want to emphasize, then schedule production." Kat barely paused, continuing before Gould could launch into a sales pitch for his commercials. "I want to do the easy assignments first.

"Roxy is my word wizard. She'll write my announcement speech which will be one of our key documents for the next few months. She can work with you, Hal, to develop a brochure. Initial drafts of everything should go to Hayes by next week," Kat directed.

Since she would be working in Rhode Island starting Monday, Roxy had hoped to report to Mario rather than Hayes. Probably serves me right, she fretted, squirming in her seat.

"Everyone in Rhode Island knows Kiley Tomasso." Gould was scarcely exaggerating. Kat's name recognition, like her opponent's, hovered around ninety-nine percent.

"They know her as a Rhode Island girl made good, as her father's daughter, from her Baywatch days, and for the past eight years, as their Representative in Congress. Now we need to introduce them to Kiley Tomasso, U.S. Senator."

His plan addressed a number of problems, from Winston's perceived clout to people's vague notions about the difference between a seat in the House and a seat in the Senate.

It would be an easy leap from imagining Kiley Tomasso as their Senator to actually voting for her.

The immediate vehicle of Gould's plan was a biographical spot.

"We review who you are, reinforce your bond with voters then spin your work in Congress as senatorial." He checked off some key words on his stubby fingers: independent, solve problems, fight against the odds.

"We conclude with you taking the obvious next step to the U.S. Senate. Very straightforward," he continued, "but there's more. Something subtle."

When Gould said he was aiming to redefine their concept of U.S. Senator, interest rose.

"Convince them that Kiley looks senatorial, then her vision, activism, and new ideas seem exactly what they should expect of a Senator as we face the new millennium."

He described film lengths and usage.

"We excerpt a tight, two-minute spot that we broadcast twice a day for a week around the announcement." Kat nodded agreement. Gould hesistated, then added a piece of news.

"Winston has hired Roberts & Sondheim to do his media. They're brutal. Their routine philosophy is 'when your opponent is down, kick her, kick her, and kick her again. Aim to kill, not weaken.'"

Gould said almost in an aside, "I'm surprised Winston selected them. They'll never agree with his notions of a polite campaign. He'll be lucky to hold out until June before they convince him it's imperative to go negative."

"The Democratic leadership again," Hayes said.

"The plan may be to test out some attacks. If they backfire, Winston apologizes and the media guys are the heavies," Gould responded.

"I don't believe Winston would allow this campaign to disintegrate into mud-slinging and negative attacks," Kat protested. "He's told me so. Besides, it would be a greater risk for him. He has dirty linen to be exposed."

Everyone looked uncomfortable. Paul Reilly jumped in gleefully.

"Truth is irrelevant in negative campaigning. If an attack makes people question a previously positive opinion they had, it's working whether it's true or not. If you have linen—and we all do—a well-planned attack can make it appear filthy. Winston was telling you what you wanted to hear, a favorite ploy of his. I think Gould is right. By June they'll have him convinced the future of the Democratic Party, and his right to be laid out in state in the Rotunda of the Capitol, are more important than his outdated notions of gallantry and polite behavior."

Gould returned to the film.

"I know your father is deceased," he said, "but how about your mother? Is she available for us to film as part of your bio?"

The truth of Kat's relationship with her mother was obvious in both her sharp tone and her reply.

"Mario can provide you with footage we could use of me with my father. My mother is in Europe. She is not, nor should she be, available for inclusion in any campaign films."

From the looks on their faces, Roxy could easily tell who at the table knew Celeste, and who only assumed that Kat had a mother she would want to involve in the campaign. In twenty years, Roxy met Kat's mother fewer than a half dozen times. None of the encounters were pleasant. Kat's voice changed to a more neutral tone.

"As I told you before, Mario and Roxy are authorities on my personal and political history. Please check with them on the material you need and on what is appropriate to be included. When can I see a script?"

"We need to start shooting next weekend. I'll have an outline for you by midweek. The details will change as we see what the pictures look like but we should be able to agree on major directions." Gould interpreted Kat's remarks as approval of his idea.

As the meeting wound down with further discussion of key themes and particular issues to feature, Roxy drifted, occasionally jotting down an idea or phrase that appealed to her. There was a concept drifting around the edges of her mind. Six years. What could happen in six years if Kat was not in the Senate caring for Rhode Island? She liked the notion, would talk to staff about the specifics, and see how it evolved as an overall theme for the speech.

★ ★ ★ ★ ★

Kat was sitting on the floor in the playroom, papers strewn around her when Roxy returned from taking Mario to the airport. She recognized the pages with circles drawn on them filled with symbols and numbers—astrological charts. It must be material from Max.

"Are the charts for various staff?" Roxy knew little more than the general public even though she spent years listening to Kat and Max discuss their various esoteric ideas.

"This is my chart, the chart of the campaign as drawn for announcement time, Rhode Island's chart, various progressed charts for election day…" Kat's voice drifted off and she looked up.

"How about laying out the cards for me, Roxy? Sometimes they cut through all the intellectualization and provide a clearer picture."

Kat extracted herself from the pile of papers and reached into a drawer along the wall, pulling out the inlaid wooden box where she kept her tarot cards.

Sometime early in their relationship, Max and Kat discovered that Roxy was an ideal medium for the message of the cards. Both of them often influenced the turn of the cards by their own thoughts. They devised a technique where one or the other of them would think of the question while Roxy shuffled, cut, then laid out the cards in a modified Celtic pattern. Over the years, Roxy had learned what each of the positions in the pattern was supposed to represent, and she had an instinctive appreciation for the messages encoded in the colorful images and symbols inscribed on the seventy-eight cards. There were four suits of what were called minor arcana; they resembled modern playing cards. The twenty-two major arcana cards were treated with particular reverence; they represented sacred messages from the gods.

She sighed what could be taken as agreement, and plopped herself down next to Kat, picking up the cards to shuffle. She was a little clumsy; it had been months since she had handled the oversized cards. Kat spoke her question, and she laid out the familiar ten card spread.

"What about my U.S. Senate campaign?"

The center card, which described the situation or person was the High Priestess. Roxy was not surprised. She turned up in virtually every reading related to Kat. She even looked like Kat with her horned headdress, dark hair, and serious but commanding expression. The next card was laid across the first and symbolized the main obstacle. Roxy gasped as she turned it over. No matter how many times Max or Kat told her the Death card symbolized endings of all sorts, not necessarily physical death, the card terrified her. And in this case, she was not alone. Kat was staring at the card as if she saw herself in the faces of those kneeling before the black armored knight on a white horse. The next two cards represented the past and its contribution to the situation being described. Both were minor arcana, pentacles, and both represented Kat's hard work and real accomplishments.

Turning over the card at the top of the reading which indicated the energy that overshadowed the whole situation, Roxy was almost as surprised as she had been by the Death card. It was the Lovers. Kat mutely ignored the question in her eyes.

"Maybe this is the rose-sender," she suggested. "Do you know who it was?"

"Keep turning, Roxy." Kat had been avoiding that question for days.

The remaining five cards, which spoke to the future and ultimate outcome of the situation, were all reversed. They were not yet engraved upon the fated pattern; it echoed Max's discovery that the outcome was not clear. There was something yet to happen that could change everything.

"I guess Liz will be here this summer," Roxy said, smiling at the card that represented the future. It was the three of cups, three women dancing together.

Kat seemed to agree with her interpretation and examined the next card laid along the right hand side in a line of four read from bottom to top; it represented the hidden fears of the asker. Frowning as she saw the Strength card reversed, Kat quickly glanced at the remaining three. Temperance, the six of wands representing victory, and the two of pentacles completed the spread. She growled darkly and scooped them all up, placed them back in the deck and put them away.

After Kat went to bed, Roxy pulled out the cards and laid the spread again. She found an interpretive book on the shelf and checked each of the cards' meanings. There was little doubt as to the message being sent; even she could read it. There were hard times ahead, and victory was not assured. She wondered who would die.

5

Preparing the Way
January/February

Rhode Island

Maneuvering through stacked stone pillars entwined with ivy into Kat's curved driveway, Roxy sighed with relief and parked in front of the vast, gray structure shingled in weathered cedar. At the end of the block, the ocean was roaring and crashing whipped by wind and rain. Hopefully the storm would blow itself out and she could unload in the morning. Nine hours of driving through torrential downpours plunged her into despair. What if the weather were an omen, a dismal foreshadowing of her year in Rhode Island?

Her mood darkened as she searched for the key to Kat's house, pawing through the collection of rubber bands, paper clips, notebooks, mints, address books, brush, wallet, and wadded up receipts in her oversized bag—no keys. She ran through the rain onto the porch that encircled three sides of the house. Both corners curved out into room-size spaces and extended up into turrets on the second and third floors. Carefully she emptied her bag, checking in every corner, turning each pocket inside out. No keys.

Cold, damp and depressed, she reconstructed her departure from Morgan Springs and was able to clearly envision the keys sitting on her kitchen table waiting to be packed into her bag at the last minute so she would not forget them. She knew they were still there.

Her options were bleak. The house was impregnable. Kat was in California, raising money. Though fisherman Jake probably could have found a dry spot in his bed for her, she had no idea where he lived or how to find him except on the beach in the morning.

She could call Frankie, Kat's brother. They had been lovers briefly, after college, and stayed good friends until he married an insecure bitch a couple of years earlier. The wife, Connie, found some compromising pictures of Roxy that he kept as souvenirs and banned her from their house forever. She would not be happy for a phone call at midnight asking Frankie to come to the beach.

It was Saturday night so Mario could be anywhere but not home—at least not yet.

Carrie! She made Roxy her new best friend during the days of chaos after Kat's Press Club dance, calling every hour, reporting what was being said by everyone and anyone in Rhode Island. They had planned to meet for brunch at Amsterdam's in the morning.

Accepting Carrie's quick offer to come stay with her, Roxy headed north.

Surely Carrie did not live on the palatial estate that loomed before her. Rechecking the number on the lion shaped pillars, she saw the stocky young woman standing in the lighted doorway of a three-story gatehouse along the fence.

The house was warm, Carrie was friendly, and Roxy gratefully inhaled the pungent aroma of brewing tea. Yet, she felt uncomfortable. Something was lurking in the shadowy corners, something that set her teeth on edge.

"This is an unusual place. How did you come to live here?"

Carrie's stare as she told her story soon had Roxy examining the details of the kitchen where they sat; she felt uncomfortable returning the woman's gaze.

"I'm good at taking care of people, especially kids. I was still in high school when I moved in to work for the family in the big house," she waved vaguely in the direction of the pillars.

"I really want her to be our senator. She'd make everyone in Washington sit up and take notice of Rhode Island."

Drifting a little in the warm room, Roxy sat up with a start to find Carrie standing next to her, scissors in hand.

"You have a few straggly ends. I thought I'd trim it for you." Carrie had hold of her hair. "It's really beautiful and so thick."

Roxy jumped up, squealing. She babbled incoherently about never cutting her hair and pulled it free. She made some excuse and rushed off to bed, locking the door behind her. She stood shaking.

Roxy was up at dawn, exhausted from a night of vaguely frightening dreams. When she made her way back to the kitchen, Carrie was already there. The rain had stopped and everything seemed normal. When Carrie offered a quick tour of the grounds, Roxy agreed. It was a beautiful setting, the large stone mansion matching Carrie's tower. Both dated from the early nineteenth century. The house and elaborately landscaped gardens and lawns extended to a large pond surrounded by trees, a dock and raised deck with benches and tables off to the right.

Carrie explained in a conspiratorial whisper that Arnold Coleman, the owner, was a successful lawyer with strong ties to the Mafia. He and his wife spent most of the winter in Florida or the Caribbean, flying up occasionally for business.

"I've been working on Mr. Coleman to let us use the place for a fundraiser," she volunteered. Roxy flinched, sure that Kat would not allow a fundraiser at some Mafia's boss' house.

Unable to dissuade Carrie from accompanying her back to Kat's, Roxy spent the trip trying to rationalize away her discomfort. She almost succeeded until, having unloaded the car, Carrie went directly to the master bedroom.

"What a wonderful room. A view of the ocean and your own bathroom."

Roxy's New Year's pledge had been to avoid being horny and over stimulated. She had decided to move from the pleasure pen master bedroom to somewhere more sedate. If she was forbidden to consort with Hayes, she did not need constant reminders of what that consorting meant. Carrie was moving around the room, posing in front of the wall of mirrors and ruffling the fur spread.

"From what I've heard of your female charms, this looks ideal," Carrie was smiling slyly as she explored the exotic, black-papered room. "I heard you made our desirable chief of staff with his oh-so-luscious southern drawl number one on your hit parade."

"Who told you that?" Roxy blurted.

Carrie's homely face glowed smugly.

"When a person responds immediately with 'who told you that,' you know a rumor is true."

A half dozen mirrors reflected different views of Roxy's scarlet face. She was mortified. Who knew? Who would have told Carrie?

Laughing, Carrie bounced on the bed.

"Don't worry, your secret's safe with me. Did you do it here, in this pleasure pen?"

As she emphasized the words "pleasure pen," Roxy's mouth opened even wider. Was this woman some kind of mind reader? She told no one of her name for the room although it was written somewhere in her ever-present journals; they were buried away downstairs.

"No one is gossiping about you." There was a note of concern in Carrie's light voice.

"I guessed from the way you talk to him on the phone and from how anxious he was to have your pearls fixed. As far as I know, no one else has even a glimmer. Except maybe Kat." She paused as Roxy sank onto the bed.

"Did she say something to you about it?" It was certainly possible that Kat suspected. After all, she had warned Roxy to stay away from Hayes, and she knew about the pearls, and she definitely knew her patterns with men. But to talk with Carrie about it—a virtual stranger!

"I'll tell you a big secret about me if it would make you feel more secure," Carrie said reassuringly.

What difference did it make who knew? It was only once and would probably never happen again. She could always get Kat to forgive her one transgression, and there was no reason to think Carrie would tell anyone else. Besides, she loved people's secret confessions. Some of them made great scenes for her books. She propped herself up on one elbow.

"OK. You win. We'll trade secrets. Tell me."

Carrie fluffed up the pillows and settled against them.

"I was sickly as a child and spent most of my early years in bed at home or in a hospital. There were eight other kids in the family. I was in the middle. My parents worked in mills in Central Falls leaving me in the care of an older sister or elderly aunt. Two of my brothers turned into thugs. They work for crime bosses in Woonsocket. When my health improved by the time I was a teenager, I became involved in local theatre. I really want to be an actress."

Emphasizing her ambition with a dramatic look from under her almost non-existent lashes, Carrie continued.

"One night, when I was about fifteen, I came home late after play rehearsal and found my two older brothers and several other hoodlums partying at our house. My parents had gone on their first trip away from Woonsocket ever, traveling to Quebec for my grandmother's funeral.

"I thought I slipped in unnoticed, and went to my bedroom where I tried to sleep. Much later, I woke up to someone lying on top of me. He clamped his hand over my mouth as soon as he saw I was awake, pulled up my nightgown and raped me in my own bed. It was horrible." Tears streamed down her face.

"But that's not the worst part," she choked. "I got pregnant. I couldn't tell my parents. I had no idea which of my brothers' creepy friends it was, not that it mattered. There was no way I was going to have the baby. I was too young to go to a legal clinic by myself, and I had no money, so I ended up turning to my brothers after all. They were brutal and blamed me for being so stupid. They insisted that as ugly as I was, I should be happy any man wanted to fuck me. But they did bring me to Mr. Coleman who found a doctor and took care of all the costs. That was when I started working for him, as a way of paying back my debt."

Carrie was sobbing heavily.

"I would have had the baby if it happened any other way. But I just couldn't. Every time I see a child about the age mine would have been, it breaks my heart."

When she asked for a hug, Roxy was quick to comply. She was a chump for sob stories. "I've never told anyone this story before," Carrie muttered, her face buried in Roxy's shoulder.

After a couple of minutes, Carrie snuggled deeper against her and began fingering her hair. It must be this room, she thought. Everything feels like sex in here. She struggled to slide out from Carrie's hold.

"Let's go get some breakfast, then I need to start unpacking."

"I'll be happy to stay and help," Carrie said brushing away her tears.

"Thanks, but you've already done more than enough. Mario said he was coming down later to help me move any furniture." Roxy blessed her inspired lie when Carrie's look faded at the mention of Mario. She wanted to be alone to unpack at her own pace, with her own thoughts for company. She also had a few items Max sent that needed to be placed in Kat's library on the third floor. Without knowing why, Roxy was certain Kat would not want Carrie in the locked room.

★ ★ ★ ★ ★

Roxy's week was devoted to settling in at the house and office, and collecting background ideas for Kat's announcement speech.

Mario directed her to the second floor of campaign headquarters.

"Kat set this up," he said, indicating the well-supplied office. "She stored duplicates of everything plus a copy machine at the Narragansett house. She wants the dining room set up as a twin office to this. You know how Kat hates wasting time traveling. With a cellular phone in the car, and a laptop version of this machine, she can be working here, at home, or in transit."

Kat was a technology queen horrified by the still-Byzantine methods by which the U.S. Congress chose to participate in a computer driven world. Most of the members were computer illiterates, although the fax machine was universally revered. She, on the other hand, yearned for the day when a brain implant would allow direct access into main frame data banks.

"Imagine the intuitive leaps I could make then," she proclaimed.

It was obvious that Kat had considered her friend's preferences in setting up the office they would share. Not only was it packed with work toys, but it had a softly cushioned small sofa in warm pink, a matching overstuffed pink print chair, plus a window. Roxy's creative process often required hours of reclining while staring into space. She could construct lengthy dialogs, work out plot problems, flesh out a character, and now formulate deathless prose for Kat entirely in her head while lying on a couch. Putting it on the computer was almost automatic writing.

A large living room that looked like it had been transported whole from a rogue fraternity house was designated the conference room. A bathroom, bedroom, and kitchen completed the second floor. There was a garden out back, their own parking lot across the street, non-stop action downstairs in the campaign office proper, bedrooms and several full baths on the third floor so they could camp out for days if necessary. And to top off the perfection, Kat's campaign headquarters was located on Atwells Avenue in the heart of Federal Hill, arguably the most exciting and interesting neighborhood in the state.

The first couple days Roxy devoted to exploring the area, a task she had been anticipating since her last visit in November. Kat had spent her childhood on the streets off Atwells Avenue, in the same neighborhood where Duke grew up. They lived in a house that opened off the square behind the office. Kat and her brother now owned most of the buildings—including the one in which campaign headquarters was located—on that square and the block of Atwells it opened onto. A small alley connecting the two could be closed to the public by locking a large iron gate.

It was an exotic commercial neighborhood that, except for some recent sprucing up, looked unchanged since the early '20s when it became the center for immigrants from Italy who drove out the original Irish residents, the previous generation of newcomers. To advertise their loyalties, the Italians of Federal Hill painted the center stripe of Atwells Avenue their native colors of red, white and green.

While the pulse of Rhode Island might be in its ocean, its stomach was arguably in the streets around their office. Food was everywhere: real sausage, hanging cheeses, imported waters, mouth-watering pastries, more than a dozen restaurants that Roxy could not wait to try, including Chinese and Thai. Boards announced as lunch specials stuffed squid with spaghetti, tripe offrito, eggplant, and other Italo delicacies. Food markets—at least one per block—lured her in with their smells of cheeses, salamis, breads, oil and half-dozen different types of olives.

Old fashioned street lamps set off blocks of storefronts with apartments above that provided every need and most desires. There were clothing shops with tailors, barber shops and beauty parlors, an upholsterer, travel agent, laundromat, appliances, a bank, sewing center, newsstands with large window signs advertising the Numbers and smaller signs noting Italian videos. Even the empty storefronts appeared prosperous, simply taking a break from commercial use, or—as Roxy later learned—fronting for some private business venture that kept their parking areas full.

She knew the mountains of western Virginia were far away when she passed Angostino's Religious Supplies, a gift shop filled with statues of Mary, Jesus and a multitude of saints. It was almost directly across the street from headquarters. Mrs. Angostino, wrinkled and wrapped in a worn gray wool cardigan sweater, held onto Roxy's arm when she discovered she worked for Kat.

"She's a good girl, that one, a real Madonna." She fluttered a speckled hand at the life-size statue of the Virgin Mary standing in the shop window. "And that Duke, her father, he was a saint, God rest his soul." She crossed herself muttering a prayer for Duke, then hobbled back into her saint-filled shop.

Walking along peering into store windows, buying bits and pieces of food in several markets, Roxy tried to imagine what parts of Kat arose from this environment and what parts led her out.

For many of these people, especially on Federal Hill, Kat was family. Roxy wanted to guarantee they heard that in the speech. It should emphasize Kat's ethnic ties, how they made her like the majority of Rhode Island's population who still identify themselves with their own or their parents' homeland. The speech also needed to reveal what made Kat different—a star—because people expected their U.S. Senator to be someone special.

On Tuesday, she walked several blocks west to Holy Ghost Church—Rhode Island's first Italo church and spiritual heart of Federal Hill since its construction in 1890. Its orientation to the street underscored its paramount role; perched on a corner, it faced the diagonal looking down the hill. All parades on Federal Hill ended there. All Kat's political campaigns began there. Her cousin, John Tomasso, a Scalabrinian priest, was now pastor at Holy Ghost. On February 14, he would once again say a special Mass for Kat, this time to kick off her senate campaign.

The church was locked. As Roxy sat on the fountain looking up scores of steps, she could almost see Kat there, as a tearful daughter following her father's coffin, as a teenager crowning the Virgin Mary with flowers during a May procession, as a little girl dressed in white for her First Communion.

They had been looking through Kat's family albums recently, searching for photos Gould wanted for the bio film, when Roxy spotted Kat's First Communion pictures. She saw a solemn little girl with looping black curls that peeked through her white veil, long white stockings, hands clasped around her new white prayer book, new crystal rosary beads hanging from them. Roxy had the same exact pose in her own photo album except her hair was a platinum blonde page boy.

She and Kat laughed about their common experience, about the sacredness of the ritual that no seven-year-old could understand.

"Coming up with sins to tell the priest at my first Confession was really a struggle for me," giggled Roxy. "I had no siblings to fight with, my parents were wonderful, I've never been capable of lying, and I didn't have a clue about sex. For days I poured over the Ten Commandments and the Catechism pages explaining which sins arose from each Commandment. I couldn't come up with anything. Then in some story about one of the saints—I can't even remember which now—I learned about pride."

"That was it! I was proud of being such a good girl, I was proud of my parents, and my blonde hair, I was too busy being proud to worry about the starving children in China or South America or wherever the mission of the month was. That was my sin, and I was proud of it."

Roxy stopped to laugh again.

"Who knows what the priest thought when he heard this tiny voice saying 'Bless me Father for I have sinned. This is my first Confession. I've committed pride.'"

Kat laughed too, then became serious.

"To this day I don't feel I ever made a good Confession, even my first. I've always kept my gravest sin hidden. How can I be forgiven for anything when I hate my mother?"

As if to explain, Kat described how she walked out of church that day, after receiving Holy Communion for the first time. She saw her mother standing off to the side scowling at her.

"I had been trying to avoid her but she finally caught up to me and hissed, 'There's blood on your stocking, It's that awful skinned knee. You must have broken the scab kneeling. Now you look terrible. No more bike riding and tree climbing for you. It's time you started learning to be a lady.' I was so mortified," Kat said, "that I let her run my life for the next couple of years—ballroom dancing, etiquette sessions, piano and art classes."

They decided to include a First Communion picture in the packet sent to Gould.

Roxy picked up local color from her strolls along the streets of Federal Hill. She collected factual information from office files and conversations with staff, especially Hayes. Their several conversations a day were strictly campaign-related, yet she could not escape the intimacy in his voice. She soon forgot how angry she was and began to anticipate his arrival for the campaign announcement.

Morning walks on Narragansett Beach provided fruitful time for working on Kat's speech, and on her growing image of the campaign themes.

Roxy was filled with anticipation as she walked towards the beach that first morning, like going to meet a lover she had not seen for a while. She could glimpse a slice of the ocean from the house and for most of the way to Ocean Drive. She stopped at the seawall and caught her breath at the panorama revealed. Stone beaches and piles of boulders extended out to a fishing pier and an odd stone cupola standing guard in the intersection. The stone Coast Guard House, shaped like a ship, and the arched towers through which she would pass on her way to the real beach—the sand beach—lay to the north. Straight ahead was sparkling blue water to the horizon broken only by meandering boats and the low-lying land masses of Jamestown and Newport connected by their bridges.

Her standard walk from Kat's house to the north end of the sand beach where Narrow River entered the ocean took an hour, an ideal amount of time to thoroughly work through a concept, or a speech, or come up with a slogan.

Living along the ocean, as so many Rhode Islanders did, Kat became its ardent defender, claiming she never felt she was truly in Rhode Island until she was within sight of the water. Providence and its surrounding satellite cities were commonplace urban settlements with a smattering of historic and ethnic flavors to distinguish them from a thousand and one others scattered across the country. It was Rhode Island's endless coastline that made it unique.

Turning back at the estuary, Roxy admired the classic harbor curve duplicated in many other ocean towns from the Caribbean to southern France. If she focused only on the towers and the small green park at their base, she could have been back in the late 19th century when Narragansett was a posh resort.

There was a shift in time and space when she climbed the stairs from the beach, as if she were leaving a movie theater. The days were warm for winter, with sunshine and no wind. A one-legged gull strutted along the seawall. She sat on a bench facing the ocean and wrote the thoughts that came during the walk.

By the third day, she had most of the key concepts for the speech set in her mind. That morning, visibility was limited by a low mist that rose from the sand. She noticed two fisherman, dressed in orange slickers, rubber boots, gray sweat-shirts and baseball caps. She wondered if they planned their outfits to match or if that was what all Rhode Island men wore for a morning of surf fishing. They walked along, searching for just the right spot. Both held their poles parallel to the beach; both carried buckets and had fishing bags slung across their chests.

Roxy thought about the ocean as these two saw it, providing so many things: pleasure, sport, food and income. She knew fisherman, both sport and profes-sionals, were strong supporters of Kat's efforts to clean up the ocean. It was their world she was saving, and hopefully their livelihoods. She made a mental note to add economic factors as motivation for Kat's fight against pollution.

★ ★ ★ ★ ★

Roxy picked up the goodies-packed new campaign van and went to meet Kat at the airport. The van was painted in Kat's signature colors of red and white and sprinkled with blue stars. Once she declared, they would letter it Kiley for Senate and some magic slogan not yet developed. Her brother Frankie was the source of the van. He had gotten it for a camping trip out west, but Princess Connie vetoed the idea of living in a tent, thousands of miles from her mother, favorite hair dresser, and malls. Rather than return the vehicle, he loaned it to the campaign, asking only that it come back to to him the same steel gray it was when he bought it.

The cellular phone was already installed and there were power sources for computers and other equipment they might need, side facing back seats that could fold into a bed, even a small refrigerator. A sun roof would permit Kat to stand and wave to crowds as they drove through the state.

Using an entry card, she opened the gate to the VIP lot, left the van, and went into the airport to wait. The attendant at the metal detector struck up a conversation, noticing the new Kiley for Senate sticker on her jacket. It began as the usual profession of undying love and admiration, then the woman asked if Roxy knew Kat's birthday.

"I'd love to do her astrological chart," said the attendant. "It might be very helpful for her. I guess she's decided to run," she said, pointing to the sticker. She was older, a little faded but still had a lively light in her eyes. Her interest seemed sincere.

"Kat's had her chart done," Roxy answered.

"Wonderful! Do you know what she is? What sign I mean, and any other details?"

Roxy dredged through her memory. She had enough trouble keeping straight what Max told her about her own stars let alone being able to recite Kat's psychic genetics.

"I know she's an Aquarian and a Libra rising," Roxy began.

"Oh, that's why she's so lovely yet very unique looking," the attendant interpreted.

Roxy nodded. "And I think she has a Leo moon."

"With Libra rising that would put her moon right at the top of the chart," the woman asserted sagely, "ideal for an elected official in the spotlight."

The woman switched to her own stars and the problems she was having as a Capricorn with all those planets transiting. Disinterested as usual in esoteric details, Roxy slipped away as the woman launched into the story of her recent divorce and her daughter running away.

Kat's tired look vanished as she walked into the terminal and greeted Roxy. They were stopped several times by admiring constituents as they wound their way outside.

There was no arguing when Kat decided she wanted to drive the new van home.

"For the past five days, I've been driven everywhere, told where to go and when, told who to talk to and what to say so they'll give me money. I want to be in control for a change," she explained.

Kat attributed the success of the fundraising trip to the superb efforts of her finance director, Jill Everhart.

"She was exactly the right person for the California crowd," Kat said. "It galled me to beg for support from a room full of professional and wealthy Hollywood women as if I were a born-again eyelash batter. I've been an outspoken fighter for every issue they considered important including the environment. I'm pro-choice. I'm ardent equal pay. I'm a strong female candidate and he's…" Kat sputtered, "he's a Democrat."

Kat's irritation translated into more pressure on the gas pedal.

"Jill beat them into submission pointing out that the entire time she was running Women for Political Action she never had to come lobby me on any critical issue. I was out there leading the fight while Winston sat in his office stirring occasionally to cast a vote if sufficiently cajoled.

"I told them that if they truly wanted their views to shape the direction of national policy they needed strong Republican voices supporting those positions. They already had the Democrats and it wasn't enough. I hammered home that electing more women to the Senate—women who voted correctly—was the important task, not worrying about Democrats or Republicans."

"Did it work?" Roxy asked.

"Some. They've been scared into believing that the Republicans will gain control of the Senate, put a bunch of Neanderthals in as committee chairmen, and repeal fifty years of social legislation. But, they loved me, and we raised almost seventy-five thousand dollars and scheduled two more visits before June. Once their own senate and gubernatorial races heat up, money for candidates outside the state will become scarce."

Kat turned to look at Roxy.

"With control of the Senate at stake, my being a Republican is suddenly a problem. I can't ignore that. It needs to be set to rest in my announcement speech."

Kat talked as they sped south, Roxy jotting notes.

"With all the challenges we face, ordinary people want plain common sense. As far as I can tell, neither political party has a monopoly on that. In fact, most people wonder if politicians know what common sense and the public good are.

"I want to blur their lines. No more us and them, winners and losers, white hats and black hats. If we're going to compete in the world, we can't afford distinctions that shut out talent, we can't afford to view anyone as negligible no matter what their perceived handicap. Since a large part of the population still considers being female a handicap, make sure and put in a line that says women can—and must—be engineers, bricklayers, corporate executives, and even U.S. Senators."

Kat was on a roll. She obviously had been considering this issue and spoke in the precisely elocuted pattern she learned at Miss Williams' as if she were addressing a crowd of thousands.

"A world without walls is a world without obstacles. We must all be winners or we all lose. For this nation to be strong, we must demand first-class citizenship for everyone. To guarantee that Rhode Island, America, and all people of the world approach the 21st century as winners, we must rise above the old separations and work together. And that means selecting the best person to serve in the U.S. Senate whether Republican or Democrat," she concluded with a flourish.

They arranged to walk on the beach together in the morning and talk more.

★ ★ ★ ★ ★

"Don't make the speech all positive," Kat said as they turned at the river for the trip back. "I want them to feel a little fear, and know that I understand that fear. Then we can hand them hope. There's a Thomas Jefferson quote I want to use to close the speech: 'I like the dreams of the future better than the history of the past.'"

"What fears should I highlight?" Roxy asked.

"I liked your idea about all the terrible things that could happen in the next six years if I'm not there in the Senate—or in the House either—to save them. We can stir up their fear with all the usual threats: crime and drug statistics, the collapse of the biosphere if we keep polluting, drowning in trash, hospital care bankrupting families, no affordable housing, children who have no skills worth anything in a world economy, a degraded society holding nothing sacred, nothing worth fighting for."

"And what is the hope?"

"I'm the hope." Kat seemed surprised that she needed to ask.

"With all due immodesty," she continued "the polls, focus groups and whatever other methods my political consultants use to take the pulse of the people, continually indicate that for Rhode Islanders—and apparently an increasing number of people outside the state—I personify their hope for a better future. I want to jolt them out of their apathy and boredom. I want them to commit to constructive change, to see the future as I do: a challenge, an opportunity to make better choices, a time for converting frustration to positive action."

As Roxy trotted to keep up with Kat's long-legged stride along the beach, she flashed back to the Fortune Strip she selected at Max's castle and how aptly it reflected Kat's attitude: *Believe in your own magic, it is real.*

"I want all those who feel shut out of the process to see me as their champion, their chance to be part of a better future. I want them to know that I'm out there in front ready to lead, not waiting to see which way the wind blows, or which idea plays best in the press."

Kat continued to preach to the surf and sea gulls, stopping as they reached the Dunes Club.

"I'm not afraid, or uncertain. I know the future is bright! I want them to see me as their hero."

"What about the goddess?" Roxy asked, confused. Kat always insisted there were two paths in life—the path of the hero and the path of the goddess—and that she and Roxy were decidedly on the goddess trail.

"They're not ready yet for the goddess," she answered with finality and began walking again.

They reached the stairs before either spoke.

"Make sure you mention Rhode Island's 200th birthday in the speech. That two-bit crook we have as governor plans to ignore it. He's refused all funding and no one has any plans to celebrate. I want to ride in on my white horse and remind them this is too important to forget." Roxy made a note and added one to herself to ask Mario about Kat's relationship with the Democratic governor, Emmett Douglas; maybe negative attacks could be made on him as a surrogate for Winston. Still writing as she emerged from the beach, Roxy almost ran into Jake who was standing next to the open door of his truck. She had not seen him since she arrived in Rhode Island. Flustered by his unexpected appearance, and his delighted smile, she quickly introduced him to Kat.

"Jake and I are old friends," Roxy was surprised to hear Kat say in reply.

"We were in love in the eighth grade," he added, winking.

"Now that was a long time ago," Kat exclaimed. She looked horrified as Jake added, "Thirty years to be exact."

"This man is a gold mine of information about the state, its history, social customs, people's attitudes, and who's doing what to whom," Kat explained to Roxy. "Talk to him. He'd be excellent in one of our commercials—one about fishing, or maybe Beavertail."

"No, Beavertail was for Max. Have him do it." As they laughed, Roxy looked mystified. Jake knew Max, too? Rhode Island was a small place!

Jake smiled and walked over to Roxy, putting his arm around her shoulder.

"I would love to be your own personal chief volunteer. No task too difficult. Your wish is my command. May I begin this evening about seven? I'll take you along with Pete and me as we visit his favorite chef, Pierre. He's opened a new restaurant, the Mediterranean. We'll bring along an autographed photo of Kat, maybe even the lady herself?" he asked, engagingly raising an eyebrow.

Both women agreed, and he asked where they would be.

Kat answered as she dragged Roxy towards the house, "Campaign headquarters, 400 Atwells."

★ ★ ★ ★ ★

A hurricane of meetings and planning about brochures, issue mailings, and media filled the next week.

Gould's Buddhic calm vanished. He would scream at Kat that she thought too much, she was too analytical. His other major complaint was that she was too female and irrational. Kat smiled serenely at his conflicting attitudes and tore his scripts to pieces. By Sunday night they had achieved an acceptable collaboration and would begin filming commercials on Monday.

Roxy worked with Carrie to arrange thousands of details required to film at the fifteen locations they selected. Gould and crew interviewed possible participants for the person-on-the-street format they wanted and the media advisor sent Kat out to get her hair done.

"Buy some clothes that don't make you look like an intergalactic priestess on tour. No 'fuck-me' shoes, and no small patterns in the fabric," he ordered.

The only bright spots for Roxy were daily walks on the beach, and the dinner with Jake and Pete.

They presented a choreographed recital of their plans to win a thousand new votes for Kat by placing her posters in bars, restaurants, bait shops, auto parts, and hardware stores.

"Pete's taking care of first time voters under twenty-five," Jake explained dryly. "I'm organizing commercial fisherman for Kiley—my Dad's still active in their associations—while Pete's spearheading sports fishing."

Kat was smiling broadly.

"With twenty people like you, we could win easily."

Fueled by her approval, they competed to tell increasingly outrageous fish stories. The food was marvelous—each ordered a different country—and Pete shamelessly flirted with Kat all evening. Recognizing a professional snow job when it blew her way, she responded with an appropriate mix of appreciation and disinterest. They all went home early and slept alone; regrettably, in Roxy's estimation.

★ ★ ★ ★ ★

The team assembled to screen the film footage. Gould had almost final versions of the bio, long and short. He showed the two-minute commercial first.

While a warm bass voice reviewed the highlights of Kat's biography, the screen flashed with pictures of her at all ages, many with Duke. There was Kat posed in her first Easter bonnet and patent leather shoes, at First Communion, in her Miss Williams lacrosse uniform, and several dance shots, including the recent Press Club pose which drew a sharp breath from several in the room. Gould justified his choice as the spot continued.

"If we use it first, it provides less of a weapon for them to use against us."

Footage of her public image began with her days at Baywatch, continued through the congressional years, and concluded with the president's visit and his endorsement. The voices through this segment came from ordinary people talking about what she did for them; content was geared towards the issues she would be stressing—education, economics, and the environment.

It closed with the snapshot Gould wanted viewers to take with them—Kat sitting at a desk in the U.S. Senate chamber. Reminding people their choice in November would determine their future through the next millennium, she urged, "Choose wisely." Her commitment and dedication were clearly visible in her face.

"Choose for the children, choose for Rhode Island." Kiley Tomasso—U.S. Senate—the Right Choice! read the closing banner.

Roxy was stunned at how senatorial Kat looked. Her hair was positively docile, pulled back with a few shy tendrils softly framing her face. She had a deep rose tailored suit with a high collared lace blouse in a softer pink, one of her remarkable cameos pinned at her throat, and rosy quartz hearts in her ears. Her make-up was subtle, her usually red lips toned down to a dusky rose that reflected the overall tint of the image.

Applause filled the room and Kat was beaming with pleasure as Gould motioned to insert the long version, currently twenty minutes.

"This footage, and one of the constituents we interviewed, inspired a memorable ad series. We can talk more about it afterwards." Gould waved off Kat's incipient frown.

"I know you like one thing finished before starting another, but great ideas can't be scheduled. It's all here in writing, we only need to decide on the films today. But I want you to be thinking about this idea so I can start looking for the additional characters I need."

Having thoroughly confused everyone, Gould started the tape.

"The opening is the commercial we just saw. The end will be drawn from footage we take during the announcement, so this will not be ready for release until late February."

Kat nodded her agreement and settled in to watch the issues segment of the film. Roxy's surprise at Kat's senatorial appearance in the commercial was nothing compared to her amazement when Jake appeared on the screen talking about fishing and Kat's work to save Narragansett Bay and protect the ocean. He was remarkable on tape, obviously a Yankee of several generations standing. Equally obvious was his attachment to the sea. He stood like a man who learned balance standing on a boat. The hallmark of his endorsement was its heartfelt sincerity, clinched by a final direct look at the camera that made the viewer want to promise anything to the lovely, concerned man with expressive eyebrows.

Before the assembled group could do more than signal their approval with applause, Gould began talking.

"I know this is a lot to take in. We'll watch them both a couple more times so we can critique them. But first I want to say a few more words about the potential ad series."

He ignored the groans of several and plunged ahead.

"The man talking about fishing is a natural. If someone as sincere and obviously native is that devoted to Kiley, she must be OK, is what his endorsement says. I want to feature him in a series of spots, discussing key issues in natural settings—work, back yard, along the beach, in a store—with two other characters that I need you to find for me," Gould said, nodding over to Mario.

"I want an older man, an ethnic, maybe Irish since our Italian flavor is already so strong. We need a way to hook into the crucial white male contingent. Plus an old lady—the crone who lives next door. She'll deliver this message: : 'My children are gone, but Kiley's here. She understands, she'll take care of me, she's family.' The younger man is Kiley's champion. Through a series of dialogues on ordinary issues, he sells Kiley to these two—and groups they represent. We can start with a few basic issues and add more if something comes up or changes."

Gould noticed the smiles passing between Kat and Roxy.

"So, what do you think?" he asked Kat directly. "You like this guy? You like the idea?"

"I love the idea, Hal, and the guy—his name is Jake Hansen, by the way—is an old friend. He'll be happy to do whatever you want, and I agree, he's a natural."

"Are there any problems I should know about him? And that goes for whomever else we end up with in these spots. The press will be sniffing around wanting to know who these folks are. He's not on your payroll or anything is he?" Gould asked.

"No problems that I know of. No financial connection with me, although he did recently sign up as a campaign volunteer."

Roxy could hardly wait to tell Jake about this. He was going to be a star!

★ ★ ★ ★ ★

As countdown to the announcement continued, the office grew more cluttered with boxes and boxes of brochures, bumper stickers, sweatshirts, envelopes and folders stacked in an ever-changing maze of cartons. Volunteers streamed in and out at all hours, addressing invitations and solicitations, calling to recruit other volunteers. Star volunteers became part of the field organization, helping to assemble crowds for various stops planned throughout the state.

Roxy saw Jake a couple of times on the beach when they were both able to make it up at dawn, and at headquarters when he came by to pick up materials or meet with Gould. He completely captivated the veteran media advisor who was convinced that Jake's face—and particularly his eyebrows—would clinch the race for Kat. Buddha, as Roxy continually thought of him, told everyone how remarkable he found Jake's eyebrows.

"They're sincere and strong yet subtle and sensitive. Who could resist anyone with such eyebrows?" In truth, Roxy had not really noticed them until she saw the film.

One day, she took Jake to lunch with her at Tony's, just around the corner in de Pasquale Square. Tony had been one of Duke's many paisans and considered it his responsibility to feed Kat's campaign staff and volunteers.

PREPARING THE WAY

The entrance was a signless green door at the back of a mundane building. A sensitive nose may have guessed its location from the aroma of tomato sauce. Inside was an ordinary neighborhood bar room decorated with red-checked tablecloths, a row of booths along the wall, and a worn wood bar. Pool tables were visible in the next room. Upstairs, regulars played cards. The walls were covered with pictures of local celebrities and political figures. Leaving no doubt as to his loyalties, for every photo of a political figure, there were two of Kat with some notable or another. Tony's wife Gloria did all the cooking, which included a different pasta every day, and varying meats. After one bite from her laden platter, Roxy knew Tony's would be her campaign home.

Early February was most memorable for Kat's appearance on *People* magazine's front cover in her Yankee Doodle Dandy costume. It stimulated screams of rage from Jasmine which she swore arose from the heart of several women's groups, and another rash of phone calls—this time from all over the country— asking for copies of Kat's pin-up.

Jill Everhart swore she could trace at least twenty-five thousand dollars in campaign contributions directly to the *People* cover. Maggie told Roxy there were several dozen more red roses on the day the magazine hit the newsstand. In Rhode Island, all three television stations reported Kat's cover girl appearance and repeated the article's hokey branding of Kat as Rhode Island's "Senate Sweetheart" based on her planned Valentine's Day announcement.

Roxy spent the final week working around the clock with Carrie to nail down the details of more than thirty official events scattered in all corners of the state. Fortunately, the young woman's weirdness was overshadowed by her competence. Kat's supporters of every stripe were included in preparations, either as participants in announcement events or as guests at special briefings aimed at their demographic. At least a dozen times a day, Roxy wondered how people could pull off this type of campaign in bigger states, where every trip required a plane, hotels, and hundreds of travel miles. Nothing longer than a day trip was possible in Rhode Island.

On the last Sunday before the campaign officially began, staff and volunteers gathered at the Atwells headquarters to send out the last of the ten thousand postcards printed as invitations to the Wednesday announcement in Roger Williams Park Casino. They featured Kat's U.S. Senate portrait. Gould insisted it be the only official photo they use. The card proclaimed, "Choose a future with Kiley where fish still live in the bay, and all Rhode Islanders have a job."

Kat had a rock star mentality about public rallies. They had to be big to be good. She swore the mass of human energy determined how successfully she could transform their thinking.

"There's no way to whip a small group into a screaming frenzy and convert them on the spot to fanatical supporters. I can be informative and even inspiring in intimate gatherings but it takes a giant crowd to pull me—and them—over the top," she said. They promised to assemble more than a thousand people for the announcement.

Finished with mailings, the staff gathered to watch the final version of the commercial spot that would be shown during the morning, evening and late night news on all three stations for a week leading up to the announcement. Roxy caught brief snatches of discussion spelling out how many tens of thousands of dollars this media burst was costing, but the spot was great. Everyone left for a night of partying at Tony's enthused and ready to join the battle.

Roxy sat with Mario and Kat's legendary Providence operative, Bruno Capaldi. He was known as "The Hose" by everyone who spent more than ten minutes in the Atwells office. Raised in an ethnic tradition where women ran the household and raised the children, "The Hose" was a paragon of macho chivalry, practically ripping bundles from her hands to carry them for her. He was in his late twenties with a deceptively sweet face and mild manner, the son of another of Duke's many lieutenants. Casually stylish, with sandy hair and light eyes, it was only his unmistakable street tough accent that labeled him one of Kat's Italian connections.

After a brief stay at Providence College where he was politely asked to leave by the good Fathers who ran the Catholic school, Bruno, Sr. bought him a liquor store on Federal Hill so he could support himself with a minimum of effort while devoting his life to his true love, politics. The Hose excelled at making deals and specialized in the Byzantine and occasionally bloody manipulations that defined local politics in Providence. Kat was the only statewide race that interested him. For her he would win the city.

Using the telephone as an extension of his natural senses, he knew everything that occurred on the streets and in the back rooms of Providence. Like Kat, he was a third generation type who absorbed the technology, adapting it to traditional patterns.

His view of politics was a capsule of Rhode Island's attitude.

"This is the only state where people are more impressed if you know a city councilman than a U.S. Senator," he explained.

He relentlessly trashed the eager young attorneys from the neighborhood who begged to learn politics at his feet.

"These Guidos think they're somebody because they passed the bar exam on the fourth try." Then he would send them out to learn the nitty gritty of politics.

"You want to get elected in Providence you gotta take care of stuff like street lights and potholes. These boys all think it's nothing but glamorous parties and calls from the president."

His philosophy was unabashedly egalitarian. He disdained the Providence hill crowned by the classic buildings of Brown University and the elegant homes that surrounded it.

"They think they're in a different world behind those iron fences," he complained, "a world above. I don't like anybody thinking they're better than some-body else."

When Roxy objected, pointing out that indeed some people were superior in talent or energy, he amended his point.

"At least they should start off equal."

★ ★ ★ ★ ★

"I don't remember leaving any lights on in the living room," Roxy muttered as they pulled into the driveway. Kat was out of the van and into the house before she could give the matter further thought. The sharpness in Kat's voice brought her up short as she closed the oversized front door and looked into the formal parlor.

With few exceptions—Roxy's pleasure pen upstairs and the conservatory with its Jacuzzi—Kat's house was maintained in Victorian splendor. The deli-cate and shadowy pinks, grays, and blues of the parlor's fine old Aubusson rug matched the tinted light from rose velvet drapes. Lounging uncomfortably on a stiffly formal fainting couch, upholstered in tapestry, was Kat's mother, an almost empty bottle of B&B on the three-tiered muffin stand at her elbow. An ancient grandfather clock that stood in a corner leading into the dining room struck an ominous series of notes.

"What are you doing here, Celeste?" Kat asked brusquely. Nothing in her tone indicated that this chic, designer-clad older woman now sitting up with her legs carefully crossed, was related to her in any way. Other than her shapely legs and her skin, pale and luminous like fine china, there was little that Kat seemed to have inherited from her mother.

"I see your ambitious desire to advance in the crass and degraded world of politics has done nothing to improve the gutter manners you learned from your immigrant father and his countless relatives." Celeste slurred her words slight-ly as she waved her hand vaguely through the air, motioning Kat to approach. "That's no way to greet your mother. What would all those dear voters think of such disrespect?"

"Answer my question, Mother," Kat insisted, nearly spitting out the word.

"Why, my darling daughter, you're about to inaugurate a campaign for the U.S. Senate. In such a family oriented state, I assume a parent by your side would enhance your image. And when it's a parent who claims the bluest of Rhode Island blood as her birthright, I cannot imagine you could be anything but grate-ful. After all, it's my Newport friends and family that you continually turn to for money." Celeste sounded triumphant as she managed to complete her sentence.

"I don't want you here, not for my announcement, not for any part of this campaign. There are no contacts you can offer me that I can't claim for myself. You haven't set foot in the state since Duke's funeral, and that's the way I want to keep it. Plan to return to the Riviera tomorrow." Kat's voice filled with disdain as she began to turn away. "Besides, you're drunk."

Just then, the front door opened and Max walked in.

In all the years she had known them, Roxy was never quite certain how he and Kat stayed in touch. They did not appear to communicate in any conventional way—no phone calls, letters, faxes or whatever. Somehow they were connected and Max simply appeared at critical times.

Celeste's attention shifted.

"I see you have your faithful slaves surrounding you, as usual," she said snidely, pointing to Max and Roxy.

Kat scowled as Max pleasantly greeted Celeste, then leaned against the tiled mantelpiece of the fireplace, marching his ever-present silver dollars across the knuckles of his left hand. He must be moderately upset, Roxy observed, watching three coins rotating rapidly across his hand. There were several seconds of silence broken by Celeste's return to berating her daughter.

"Even this refugee from the '60s greets me more politely than the child to whom I gave birth. At great risk to myself," she added, looking around for support.

Roxy flinched at Celeste's insulting tone but Max retained his bland expression as he watched Kat's mother and continued to rhythmically roll his coins. Celeste poured herself the remnants from a bottle Roxy knew was nearly full the night before and quickly drank it all. Kat's face was twisted in rage and she moved towards her mother with the obvious intent of throwing her bodily from the house. The coins vanished as Max caught her arm and gave her a warning look. The effort of will she exerted to become calm and regain control showed on her face; her eyes remained flinty.

"Let me repeat my advice, Celeste. I want you on a plane back to Europe in the morning—one way, no return before the election." Cold dislike filled Kat's voice.

"Why does my daughter hate me so?" Celeste's whining was directed at Roxy and Max.

"I could have died giving birth to her. It was a bitterly cold night, with snow and sleet. I nearly fell trying to maneuver down a back street in Providence where her father insisted we go to visit some beggar or another he felt obliged to help. It took us hours to cross town and get to the hospital. But what thanks do I get?" She waved her empty glass at Kat, her voice beyond hysterical.

"She hates me! Her friends hate me! And no wonder. I'm sure she's poisoned your minds against me, hasn't she?" Celeste approached Roxy, screaming in her face. "Hasn't she? Don't be afraid. Kiley likes the truth. She's always talking about it as if it's some sort of holy grail."

Roxy shrank away from Celeste's wild eyes and malignant tongue. The shrieking woman turned back to her daughter.

"You think I killed your father don't you? That's what you've told these peasants, isn't it?"

A primitive look settled on Kat's face.

"Get out! Get out of this house, this state, this country!"

She screamed as madly as her mother. Fury poured from her and a pulsing vein stood out in her slender neck. She wrenched her arm away from Max's restraining hand and moved to grab Celeste.

Drunk as she was, Celeste retained her survival instinct and successfully dodged Kat's grasp. Standing behind a high backed chair alongside the couch, gripping its ornately carved trim, Celeste continued raving.

"I didn't kill him. I don't care what you think. You never loved me. It was always your father, always Duke!"

She nearly choked as she screamed his name, flinging her arm at the splendid portrait in oil of Kat's father that hung over the mantle. He was shown as a mature man with his two children standing on either side. Graying temples fringed his full head of black wavy hair; shrewd intelligence balanced with compassion shone from his dark doe-like eyes; his Roman nose and square chin defined strength. The long, slender hands resting on his chair were surprisingly elegant and graceful.

"I was nothing. Only an incubator to create half-breed children that he could use to climb his way to respectability. But it never worked. You couldn't do it. He was a guinea wop laborer and all the awards Miss Williams gave you couldn't change what he was. You were accepted only because of me. All your father had was his filthy money, and everyone knows how he got that!"

Roxy huddled on the window seat shrinking away from the sight of Celeste's now-deranged face. Max held Kat tightly, keeping her as far from her mother as possible. But Celeste kept up her raving.

"I didn't kill him, I tell you. When I heard the noise in his study, how was I to know he had a stroke. He kept the door locked. He swore he'd kill me if I ever tried to enter that room. I know that's where he took all his women. That's where he took you so you could plot against me trying to turn my baby boy against me, too. How could I know there was anything wrong? I turned and went about my business. How could I know?"

Kat stopped struggling and slumped against Max. It was clear from her blood-drained face that Celeste's words were a revelation—a confession that if his wife did not actively kill Duke, she certainly could be blamed for turning away and leaving him to die.

Celeste leaned her head down on the chair back and began sobbing.

"I didn't kill him, I didn't. How could I know? How?"

Kat's ashen face grew composed and she moved from Max's arms to stand facing her mother.

"I was given complete control of Duke's fortune. The money I choose to send you each month is just that, my choice. If you ever want to receive another dime from me, if you want to keep me from staging a raid on the few stocks you own, if you want to finish your life as anything but a bag lady in downtown Providence, I suggest you walk out of this house and get on a plane for Europe. If I see or hear from you ever again, I will cut off any further funds."

Kat's voice grew more frigid with every word.

"And if you try to manipulate Frankie into helping you, I will tell him exactly what you admitted here tonight. I'll tell my uncles, and Duke's friends, and you'll find no safe haven anywhere. They would track you down and kill you. Now get out!"

Kat nodded wearily and leaned her head against the mantle. Duke's hands in the portrait looked ready to reach out and stroke her wild hair.

"Just get her out of my sight," were her last words as Max led her mother away.

★ ★ ★ ★ ★

Rolling over, Roxy decided she could go back to sleep and walk on the beach that night after the final event. She was driving; there would be no sneaking home early. Once an event was confirmed on Kat's schedule, she went.

Before her resolve became reality, Kat and Max were knocking lightly on the bedroom door. They came in carrying a tray of muffins and juice. By the time they settled themselves—Kat on the bed, Max pulling a chair alongside—she was sitting up, mildly resentful but fully awake.

Kat's face bore the ravages of a long, sleepless night; her eyes were puffy and red from tears, her voice hoarse.

"Do you mind putting off your walk until tonight? Max is leaving for Key West as soon as possible and we need some answers first."

Roxy looked at Max, her distress obvious.

"I thought you were here for the announcement. It's the beginning. Isn't there a magic blessing or something you need to do?"

"Relax Roxy. Kat and I started the flow with inaugural rituals before dawn. I'll be with you in my heart. You don't need me in the flesh."

Unsatisfied, she persisted. "What could be so important that you can't be here?"

Max moved to a stream of sunlight flooding the window. Two silver dollars appeared and began their rhythmic knuckle march officially called "ducks on the water."

"I spent most of my life living and performing in Newport each summer. I'm notorious. People know Kat and I are," he waved his free hand vaguely, "companions. I don't think Rhode Island is ready for a Rasputin or even a Merlin. Max the Magician would not be a credible advisor for Kiley Tomasso, candidate for the U.S. Senate."

Roxy examined him. In the routine fashion of daily life, she forgot how bizarre he must appear to a world with boundaries of acceptable appearance and behavior far more rigid than hers. She flashed on memorable Max costumes. He was a most convincing pirate with eye patch and cutlass which he wielded fiercely. He was an equally convincing German baron with Napoleon hat and tight white breeches. He was an impeccable Merlin, with luminous robes and dazzling mind reading tricks. Roxy secretly thought that Max was occasionally tempted to recreate the worldly role of the legendary magician-advisor to King Arthur.

Years of acrobatics and stage magic developed in him a constant posture of total attention that intimidated most. His almost white hair was cut short with spikes in front and a thin braided tail hanging down his neck. Add the earrings and mustache and there was no doubt he and Kat made a striking pair that would not go unnoticed anywhere, let alone in a state the size of most large counties.

Max softened the blow of his absence by guaranteeing he would be around in private when needed. Roxy shuddered. Even in his simplest comments there seemed to be layers of meaning. He picked a deck of tarot cards from the air and tossed them on the fur spread, and she shuddered again.

They wanted her to lay out the cards. This would be no single question quickie, she felt certain. After last night there were several questions even she wanted answered. At least they brought food. She reached over and broke open a blueberry muffin, its warm smell improving her attitude.

As she shuffled the cards, Kat gave directions.

"We want this to be dialogue—quick follow up questions to each previous answer. As soon as I finish the question, lay out five cards, starting on your left and moving in an upward slant to the right. Max will remove them after we read them; you continue to draw from the top of a single pile. Are you ready?"

Kat closed her eyes briefly then fixed her gaze intently on the cards, asking the first question.

"How can I forgive my mother?"

Looking at the cards, the answer was obvious even to Roxy: she couldn't, at least not yet. She was bound until she could turn away and leave it behind, tempered by the pain.

Barely skimming the cards, Max dragged them off.

"Will this problem affect the campaign?" Kat asked.

Roxy noted the surprise on both faces as Max pointed to the Tower card and barely breathed, "Yes".

It was one of the twenty-two named cards that were most important, and it always made her uneasy. The picture showed a smooth stone tower being struck by a lightning bolt, a man and woman hurled from its windows in flames. It never meant anything but destruction and ruin. At least it did not look like her Towers, the ones she walked through almost daily. She did not want to feel threatened by them.

Immediately Kat asked "How?" The soft purr of a calm ocean was audible through the silence as they stared, absorbed, at the next five cards. Max pointed to the final card, a knight charging with a drawn sword—"Your hero," he interpreted.

"I told you before, I don't need a hero," Kat said sharply.

The Lovers card was first in the spread but not upright. Kat may think she doesn't need a hero, thought Roxy, but at some point there would be a man involved. She wondered who.

Kat took all the cards from Max and abruptly handed them back to Roxy. "Start another round."

Mixing all seventy-eight cards, Roxy waited for the next series of questions.

"How will the announcement go?" Kat sounded distracted. To Roxy's profound relief, the array of cards was positive. The announcement would be perfect.

Max earned moans when he followed-up with his question.

"Does it matter?"

Once again the cards returned to the theme of uncertain outcome.

"The campaign, will it be....?" Her voice trailed off before asking the obvious but Max signaled Roxy to lay out the cards.

Her hand shook as the Death card turned up in the second place. It was soon. The next two cards made her stomach tighten. Kat paled and even Max leaned forward in his chair to stare at the cards: the sinister Devil holding a naked couple in chains, then the Tower again. The final card echoed the last reading Roxy did with Kat, only this time the uncertain outcome was more harshly described by a blindfolded woman sitting with two crossed swords.

"Four major arcana," said Max pointing to the first four cards with their evocative pictures. "Destiny speaks loudly."

He looked at Kat intently. "This campaign is a mythic experience; it will unfold true to those rules and no others."

6

The Announcement
February

Rhode Island
Washington

Announcement day was distinguished by a geometric increase in the press. Roxy skipped Mass at Holy Ghost Church and went directly to the park casino. The day was clear, sunny and bright. Jake was equally dazzling as he handed out bumper stickers in a white sweatshirt with a large blue star and Kiley for Senate lettered in red. She hadn't seen him all week since the only beach walk she managed to squeeze in was after dark. He was enthusiastic in his responsibility to mobilize support for Kat on this first day.

The casino looked festive and inviting, strewn with Kiley for Senate posters, red, white and blue twists of crepe paper, and glowing blue stars everywhere. Hearts were banned from the Valentine's Day announcement except in posters people made for themselves. Overflowing trays of pastries and fruit provided by neighborhood bakers and grocers on Federal Hill were spread on long tables, staff and volunteers occasionally snatching a bite as they hustled past. Carrie directed the whole operation with the fervor of a regimental commander, her clipboard filled with lists and notes, her troops all volunteers. Some were students or grandmothers swept up in the thrill of their first major political campaign. Others were stalwarts from previous congressional campaigns, carryovers from Baywatch, or members of Kat's extended family.

Hayes and Jasmine presided over a press room packed with national media waiting for the candidate to arrive. Gould and crew were setting up equipment to film the announcement event for commercial use. Kat vetoed her media advisor's plan to send cameras to the church. The new Irish bishop repeatedly attacked her in private for rejecting his insistence that she renounce her pro-choice stance; there were rumors he was threatening excommunication. She was not about to give him additional ammunition by politicizing her attendance at Mass.

The ballroom began to fill up with hundreds of exuberant supporters, all boasting Kiley stickers. Many carried handmade heart adorned signs. Hundreds more stood in the sunlight outside waiting with media crews to catch the first glimpse of arriving dignitaries.

Roxy began to get nervous about the time. Max decreed Kat must announce her intention to run sometime between 9:45 and 10:31 a.m. It was her assignment to note the exact minute when it occurred. That moment would identify the key image of the campaign.

Horns and shouts signaled Kat's arrival. She was standing in the van, waving through the sunroof, leading a parade of festooned cars carrying volunteers and supporters.

Cheering crowds and flashing cameras added to a tangible swirl of energy that marked her passage up the stairs and into the ballroom. Her dress was a lush blue-green of soft wool clasped at the waist in an elaborately knotted gold belt; the full sleeves were appliquéd with exquisite gold dragons. Matching dragons with emerald eyes studded her ears. In the open throat of her dress hung a carved gold cross that Roxy knew she wore for Duke.

Kat's progression was triumphal, filled with outstretched hands and exchanged kisses. Even the dignitaries awaiting her on stage were caught in the frenzy. Her long-time political ally, Mayor Mike Zagarella, was emcee for the event. A born cheerleader, he almost fell from the stage in an enthusiastic welcome fueled by the cyclone of activity and excitement. Finally, the cheering abated, and a stream of dignitaries recited her many accomplishments, praising every virtue imaginable.

It was time. Kat moved in a flowing stream of green to the podium and appeared to swell into a shimmering column of light as the applause mounted. When it appeared their voices could shout no longer, she slowly raised her arms then brought them down, hands clasped to her chest, gathering all their love and aspiration into her heart. The room vibrated in expectant silence, and there was a smell of anticipation in the air, clean and sharp like ozone.

Her speech held no surprises. Everyone knew why they were there, why Kat was there. But they wanted to hear her say it; they wanted her to give voice to their dreams.

Roxy abandoned herself to the rhythm of the words. They were her words when she wrote them but irrevocably Kat's as she spoke them. Sparks of recognition flashed as Kat lovingly described her childhood growing up in a tiny flat on Federal Hill, how her father built their business by building Rhode Island—its streets, schools, sewers, and homes. Looks of identification grew more profound as Kat evoked her attachment to the ocean and the life it supported, empathy collecting into a poignant drop that hung in the air. Roxy felt the breath of the goddess brush her.

The tempo quickened as Kat recited her triumphs in Congress, reminding them of obstacles and difficulties overcome in their service. The audience was very patient. They knew her achievements. They were proud of the woman they sent to Washington. They waited to hear what was next. They wanted the vision.

After hours of wrangling, the decision had been made for frontal assault.

"When you present your weaknesses, it's in your power to make them strengths," Hayes said, arguing to mention the two concerns incessantly repeated—why did they have to choose between two wonderful people, and why could she not wait for six years.

The upbeat tenor of Kat's voice changed as she described the chaos of the present, the accelerating pace of change, and the need to be prepared with visionary and courageous leaders.

"As we face the countdown to the millennium, there are critical debates ahead and a compelling need to challenge the old patterns that are crumbling around us. We cannot wait six years for bold, effective ideas—it will be too late."

Their fear was palpable as she recited a litany of daily loss and destruction of the environment, statistics outlining the epidemic of crack babies and emotionally-ravaged children, relentlessly escalating costs of banking and insurance industry fraud and incompetence. She decried America's tragic failure in educating its citizens, old and young, for participation in the global society of the 21st century.

They were afraid. They recognized the darkness and it was close. Kat allowed them to absorb the fear a moment longer.

"Can we wait? Can we afford business as usual when destiny offers progress? Are you ready to make the choice, the right choice for tomorrow, for the glorious future we have before us?"

Roxy checked her watch, it was 10:03. She wrote it down.

"I announce my candidacy for the United States Senate. I challenge Rhode Island to choose between yesterday's failed policies and tomorrow's hopeful future."

Their shining faces and light-filled eyes agreed—she was their hope for a better future. Force and power poured from her as she outlined the future she chose.

"A future with drug-free bodies, waste-free oceans, and pollution-free air, where our place in the global economy is earned by our genius, not financed by selling off our birthright. Together we can choose a future where the emphasis is on creating and sustaining health rather than concern over who will pay for economically lucrative repairs."

"False barriers will continue to dissolve as we choose this future. We will learn the proper harmony of environmental protection and economic security; of freedom and responsibility; of men and women. But it will not come easily."

Kat paused and scanned the sea of upturned faces.

"The future is ours to choose today, to begin creating today. There is no time to wait! The '90s stretch before us, a final decade concluding the most astonishing millennium in the history of humanity. Come, let us face this momentous time together." Her voice was warm and reassuring, her face inviting as she held her arms out to them.

"We have the vision, the commitment, the energy, and the hope that guarantees our success. We need only make the right choice." Her arms remained outstretched as cheers and applause rocked the ballroom.

Tears of joy were flooding hundreds of eyes as they continued to scream their support of Kat. Roxy was startled when Hayes offered his handkerchief. She realized tears were streaming down her face as well.

Kat stood at the microphone radiant and unmoving, receiving their energy and sending it back electrified and uplifted by her vision. A messenger walked on stage and handed her an enormous bouquet of red roses wrapped in tissue that matched her dress. The joy in her face as she clasped the roses stirred Roxy's heart—these were more than stage props.

Hayes propelled her out of the crowd massing to greet Kat as she descended from the stage, and led her to a quiet corner where he could still watch the action.

"Mario and Jasmine will be accompanying Kat for the rest of the schedule. Would you stay and help me deal with press and other calls back at headquarters?"

Roxy was thrilled and quickly agreed.

"That was a brilliant speech, by the way. You accomplished every goal with incomparable clarity and style."

She let his praise fill her with pride for a moment then honestly reminded him that Kat's spirit made the words potent. She made it possible to even consider saying such things as part of a national political campaign. There was a respectful look in his eyes, as if he never considered that she understood the underlying truth of this race.

She should be irritated he took her so lightly, Roxy thought, but was too pleased at what his look meant for the future to worry about the past.

★ ★ ★ ★ ★

Hayes stretched his arm possessively across the back of her chair as the remaining celebrators finished the night at the Coast Guard House. The group was mostly Washington staff staying at Kat's, delighted to be partying within walking distance of their beds. Carrie had invited herself to overnight with them in Narragansett and was preparing to leave for the house, casting a knowing glance at Roxy resting comfortably in the crook of Hayes' arm. She straightened up. He was forbidden territory and she had to be discreet.

As Carrie said her goodbyes, Roxy's mind searched for a place she and Hayes could go. The walls at the house would be all eyes and ears with everyone staying there, Carrie particularly, since she knew—or thought she knew—there was something more than collegial cordiality between them. But it was too late, she was too tired, and her brain too blurred by an ecstatic day and several pitchers of beer to focus on any problem for more than a fleeting moment. Once Carrie was out the door, she forgot her concern and leaned back, ignoring the words and hearing only the honeysuckle scented tones that filled Hayes' conversation.

"I better get this girl home while she can still walk," Hayes said, nudging her awake. She barely noticed leaving the bar and walking across the street to the western tower. The cool air began to clear her mind in time to wonder why he was guiding her through the cave-like area under the archway to a door in the tower. It was locked. As she turned back to the street he took her arm and moved her to a corner, out of sight of the sidewalk.

It all happened so fast, Roxy scarcely had time to grab his shoulders and hold on as he none-too-gently lifted her onto a parapet, her back to the street. His hands slid under her skirt, and along the outside of her thighs, pulling her hips towards him as he positioned himself between her spread legs. Her head snapped back, grazing the rough stone tower walls. She turned it slightly to see the ocean heaving and rising, swelling then breaking into surf spraying the rocks next to the Coast Guard House.

She was praying he would not drop her the ten feet or so to the concrete sidewalk when he captured her full attention by ripping the crotch from her pantyhose and ramming himself into her. Now she knew why mothers always wanted their daughters to wear panties, but in this instance it would have slowed the action for only the briefest moment. She could not imagine what would have stopped him. Who wanted to, she thought, abandoning herself to the battering rhythm, surrounded by the damp musty fume of the stone spiced with ocean and sex.

Securely lodged inside her, Hayes moved his hands up her arching back as she leaned against his arms for support. Resting the top of her head against the stone wall, she wrapped her legs snugly around his waist, tightening her hold on him and quickening her motions to match the urgency she felt. As he plunged deeper and deeper, it was pounding ocean and pounding sex and she concentrated on holding on so she would not fall. His driving motions reached a frantic peak, and he pulled her to him in a final, rough thrust. She thought about knights and their ladies in secluded corners of some medieval castle. Then she stopped holding on and let a soft, shuddering convulsion sweep her body as his desire pushed her through the gates of paradise.

They walked back to the house in silence. Her arms and legs felt voluptuously present but not too functional. It took great effort to move them even slowly. The insides of her thighs were sticky as she walked, her shredded stockings stuffed in Hayes' pocket. He guided her past both entries to the driveway then pulled her gently into the shadows behind the far stone pillar. Stroking her cheek with a knowing touch he whispered his desire in a voice that felt like a thousand little flames licking her body.

"You're so soft and inviting, I can't resist. There's something about touching you, even being close enough to touch you that casts a spell on me. It drives me mad, and I have to take you, to touch you as deeply as I can." He kissed her, drawing her mouth into his. "I love women who are the color of honey with a blush of innocence spread across certain intimate places." Slipping his hand under her sweater, he brushed his fingers lightly across her breasts, laughing delightedly as her nipples hardened under his touch.

He led her into the lamp-lit night, dropping his hand from around her shoulder as they approached the house.

"You rate an A+ for today," he said with a satisfied grin as they walked up the stairs, "from beginning to end."

★ ★ ★ ★ ★

For the first time in two weeks, Roxy was thinking about something other than Hayes as she flew to Washington for meetings with the campaign team. Mario spent the flight reviewing decisions to be made, plans to be approved, crises to be faced.

He frowned each time Roxy cited Carrie as the source of various bits of information and voiced his growing distrust of her.

"She's weird and she makes me nervous," he said as if there were more to come. After brief consideration, he leaned over, his voice low. "I accidentally opened one of her computer files the other day and found a collection of bizarre notes. I printed it out." Mario handed her a page of cryptic sentences.

"Can you get these to Max? I know this sounds paranoid, but I think Carrie's into something ... evil. Look at this."

She followed his finger and read what seemed like a childish chant.

Jasmine, Jasmine, proud and free
You shall turn your will to me.
What I want, what I crave
You shall give me to the grave.

A list of herbs and flowers followed. Roxy felt her skin crawl. The thought of Carrie and Jasmine was decidedly perverse, but not hard to imagine. She remembered the crude approaches Carrie made to her the first day she moved to Rhode Island. She glanced at several more of the notes.

THE ANNOUNCEMENT

Green candles for wealth, black to destroy, red for sex.
Always work in dark of moon.
Need bit of hair, fingernails, a photo, clothing, some possession to penetrate another's mind.

Cold fingers gripped her heart. She never paid much attention to the more arcane rituals Max did but she knew without question that what she was reading had to do with magic, bad magic.

As she read the final entry, she began quaking with fear.

To make lie believed write it on paper, burn white candle on paper then burn paper and candle droppings. Sprinkle pinch of ashes when telling story. It will be believed.

Mario's name followed with cocaine and money after it, and her name with the word sex written three times.

What was Carrie's game? Mario was right. Max was the man they needed to ask.

"She's spreading those rumors, too," Mario said as Roxy looked up, pale and shaking. Her heart sank; had Carrie been talking about her and Hayes? She avoided Carrie for two days after the announcement hoping by then she could casually laugh off any suggestions about what they had done on the way home that night.

"She told more than one of the congressional staff that I have a serious cocaine problem and will have to declare bankruptcy soon to pay my drug debts."

Roxy's eyes widened at his anguished voice. Mario had a fierce professional pride in his reputation and was conscious of how everything he did reflected on Kat. He claimed his only excess was a desire to please women. Since he was successful—and always waited to be asked before proceeding—he did not feel that activity presented any threat to Kat's stature.

"Have you confronted Carrie with her lies?"

"I've tried, several times. Usually she sits and stares at me blankly then flatly denies she said anything. Even when I dragged in the person she told, Carrie continued to protest her innocence. This last time she looked me in the eyes and accused me of harassing her because she wouldn't sleep with me like every other woman on the staff. Now that I've seen this, I don't think anything I say will have an effect. Carrie's not into innocent gossip. She's set on destroying us. I don't want to worry Kat until you've talked to Max and find out what's going on. The last thing we need is having rumors around that anyone on our staff is practicing witchcraft."

They landed at National Airport as Roxy considered what a time bomb Carrie could be, not just for Mario or even for her and Hayes. What if she got some notion in her head about Kat? Who knew what her ultimate plan was, or whom she was really out to entrap?

★ ★ ★ ★ ★

Since the House went into session at ten that morning, and Kat could be called away for votes, the campaign meeting began early. It was at Senatorial committee headquarters again and Roxy was surprised to see Senator Stuart sitting at the conference table with Jill Everhart, campaign finance director. They were deeply engrossed in lists of names, Kat making notes in the green leather folder carved with mystical symbols that was her constant companion. In it she kept names, multiple phone numbers, and notes about several hundred people from whom she hoped to get two thousand dollars each. She worked the lists constantly, keeping in touch with people, updating information, adding new prospects.

"Why is it all about money?" Kat was complaining. "Are we like ancient Romans requiring proof of wealth before allowing entry to the Senate?"

Stuart laughed.

"No. We've modernized it. Now a senator need be capable only of raising great amounts of money that he or she can pass on to television stations and consultants. We'd be better off with the old Roman way. You and I would be eligible for the Senate and we wouldn't have to grovel for money."

"What grovel? I thought you liked the fundraising part."

"I tolerate it as a game of skill."

Stuart outlined his plan to help her raise two hundred thousand dollars from Cubans in Florida and California. The Virginia Senator's links to the exile community were well known. Their continuing fight against Castro, and the strongly individualistic attitude of their leaders appealed to his romantic philosophy of liberty and freedom. He developed strong personal relationships with several top Cuban leaders, flying regularly to Florida for both politics and pleasure.

The exile community saw a Republican Senate as beneficial to their cause. He suggested Kat appeal to them through a hard hitting op-ed piece linked to the current debate in the United Nations Human Rights Commission about violations in Cuba. It would be released in her name to all Rhode Island media outlets as well as several national and Florida newspapers.

"It doesn't matter whether anyone in Rhode Island cares about Cuba or not," Stuart explained, "it only matters that Cubans with money prefer you to Winston.

"We can demonstrate how recent revelations about noble Fidel serving as a drop point with Noriega and the drug trade have done nothing to strengthen

Winston's support of democratization efforts. Drugs are a hot button issue everywhere and he has potential trouble with both legal and recreational ones. I've heard his son has a serious drug habit."

Kat glared at him.

"I refuse to engage in personal attacks on him or his family. The people of Rhode Island should elect me because I will be a better senator, because they want change."

Looking quizzical for a moment, Stuart shrugged.

"This isn't Eastern Europe. Don't exaggerate the enthusiasm for change. Life still works in America for most people."

He returned to the topic of Cuba. There was a burning light in his eyes as he talked about divided families, torture, and political prisoners rotting in Castro's jails for daring to question his totalitarian rule. Roxy squirmed. She was decidedly a 'make love not war' person, and admitted to a soft spot in her heart for Castro's fatigues, his flamboyant and defiant oratory, and rumors of his extraordinary appetite for sex.

Stuart described the plans of Raul Diaz, the unofficial ruler of south Florida's Cubans and his dream of "next year in Havana." Roxy speculated on whether Diaz planned to restore Cuba as the free-market, free-wheeling pleasure capital of the Western Hemisphere and how the south Florida economy would react when millions of Cuban dollars returned home for reconstruction and development. Those good ol' boys in Tallahassee who ran the state probably pictured the liberating of Cuba as a way of sending all those folks back and making the Miami area English speaking again—a real cracker fantasy.

A fundraising trip to Miami was set for mid-March.

"What will they want from me for their money?" Kat asked.

"What does everyone want? We all accept campaign money with the vague understanding that we might, someday, provide a sympatic ear, a helping hand to the donor. In the case of the Cubans, the electoral defeat of the Sandinistas and Gorbachev's cold shoulder treatment of Castro have inspired them with hope.

"You can introduce in the House my Senate resolution condemning Cuba for repeated human rights violations and calling on Castro to release all human rights activists and political prisoners from his jails."

On a roll, with both Hayes and Kat obviously captivated, Stuart directed them to several other topics.

"Everyone knows how you stand on women and the environment. You need to tell them something they don't know. Emphasize your business background. People will respect your radical economic notions when you remind them you know how to provide jobs and make money.

"Start sounding tougher on drugs and crime."

Kat raised her eyebrows slightly.

"Tough is not one of the attributes I'm planning to emphasize."

"Maybe it should be. Not that your opponent is a macho figure but he is rich, prestigious, and most importantly, male." He ignored the flash of annoyance in Kat's face.

"Our polls show that eighty percent of the voters would be proud to have a female senator," Lila Gravely shot back at Stuart.

"That's what they tell you. Then they look at this lovely lady and in their hearts wonder if she's got what it takes to stand toe to toe with Gorbachev or some Middle East bandit. They don't expect that of her in the House, so the question hasn't been raised. The Senate is a different story. People expect their senators to play on a world stage," Stuart replied in a neutral voice.

"And you don't think I project the stature of one capable of succeeding on a world stage?" Kat asked irritated.

As if oblivious to the dangerous ground he was treading, Senator Stuart answered honestly.

"When health care and the environment are primary on people's minds, you fill their idea of a capable leader; but if there's a war, or an economic crisis, all their atavistic urges will be stimulated and they'll turn to dad. Winston exploits his image as a good and wise father."

There was authentic shock on Kat's face at his assessment.

Her hostility began to fade when he pushed for her support of a ban on chemical and biological weapons.

"This will become hot, soon. There may be military action against Libya or Iraq as the main terrorists," he predicted. "Push for a ban now, and you'll look remarkably prescient in November."

Kat was attentive. She often cited the Senate's responsibility in relation to treaties as one of the reasons she was seeking promotion to the higher body.

"The proliferation that is tomorrow's worst nightmare includes nuclear technology, chemical and biological weapons, and soon genetic engineering in the hands of every two-bit thug and power-mad dictator."

Roxy noticed the look of worship in Hayes' eyes as Stuart continued his discourse.

"The real foreign policy issue of the next several years is the economic unity of Europe. It's like a giant magnet pulling Germany together and the Communist bloc including the Soviet Union, apart. Few in America are prepared for the ramifications of European unity, whatever its form, on our economic future."

"Which are?" Kat asked.

"If the U.S. doesn't redirect its education system and begin investing in means of production, we'll lose whatever creative edge we still retain and end up a backwater of the global economy living off the fat of the land—but not for long." Considering his response satisfactory, the senator ploughed ahead.

"Last but not least, you can win points against Winston by supporting term limits. Push for twelve years in both houses and you squeeze him out. We need new faces. People get into a rut of believing a politician is good because he's familiar. They need to see with new eyes. Thomas Jefferson, my namesake," Stuart bowed his head slightly, "said 'God forbid we should every twenty years be without rebellion.' It's time."

Stuart handed her destiny with a flourish and Kat clapped her hands in delighted agreement. It was time and no delay could be tolerated.

"I'll get you facts and figures on all these issues as well as several others," Stuart said as he rose to leave. "We can portray your relative inexperience as the fresh, new vision that's needed in the topsy-turvy world scene we now face."

Once the senator left, Gould reported an anonymous tip he received about all campaign scheduling decisions being made by an astrologer. Kat brushed off the insinuations as trivial.

"Max and I have already agreed he will stay out of sight during the campaign. Our personal relationship is no secret in Rhode Island and if he's not visible, I don't think it will be an issue."

"You mean there really is someone named Max the Magician?" he asked in horror.

"Don't worry, Hal. I'll simply tell anyone who asks that you and Mario make all the relevant decisions and neither of you consult stars or tea leaves."

Roxy wondered how lightly Kat would take rumors of arcane practices if they discovered Carrie was actually dabbling in black magic. Gould accepted Kat's assurances. Engrossed in his own media plans, he was already impatient from sitting through Senator Stuart's monologue.

"Who cares about some magician when we have Jake? I had your commercials tested for Q-factor and he rated off the scale. People loved his eyebrows."

Kat looked irritated as she leaned over and asked, "How did I rate, Hal?"

"Oh, I didn't test you. This was for future commercial purposes."

"Do you think you could wait to launch Jake's career until you've finished with my senate race since it seems impossible for you to concentrate on both?" Her voice was sharp and became more so as she continued.

"While I'm not concerned about Max, I would be interested in your advice on how we can inoculate against this becoming a problem. That's what I pay you for, in case you've forgotten." Gould rapidly regressed to a ten-year-old being scolded by his mother.

"Keep quiet about pagan activities and stick to attending Mass and saying the rosary. In instances like this, telling the truth is almost never the best course of action," he whined.

Kat's beeper indicated a vote and she rose to leave, adjourning the meeting until two when they were to return and finalize commercial scripts.

Hayes was finishing his notes as Roxy moved around the table. Her plan was to convince him to have dinner with her, alone. From there, it should be easy to…Roxy stopped as Mario addressed them both.

"Well kids, are we ready for a night of wild and wonderful partying in our nation's capital?"

Quickly—too quickly for Roxy—Hayes declined, explaining he had a friend in from out of town. Mario shrugged and smiled, clapped him on the shoulder then went to join Gould standing outside the conference room. Roxy tried to slip by and leave, irritated that Hayes had not kept the evening free. He blocked her way. They were alone in the room and her breath quickened as he took a step closer and smiled down at her.

"How about lunch? We could grab some sandwiches and go over to my house."

He obviously had a date that night but there was no mistaking the look in his eyes. Lunch and dinner, what a man! Hiding her displeasure, she smiled seductively, lowered her lashes and purred, "I never eat lunch."

Then she reached between his legs and slid her hand along the front of his pants, feeling him swell beneath it. Let him eat standing up, she thought spitefully as she escaped out the door.

Dashing blindly across the broad plaza below the east front of the Capitol, Roxy nearly collided with Kat who was running to make a vote.

"Come with me, we can talk on the way," she said, scarcely breaking stride. Trotting to keep up, Roxy wondered once again how Kat managed to run up and down stairs and across marble floors in the high heels she perpetually wore. Standing outside the House chamber, leaning against the marble wall waiting for Kat to cast her vote and emerge again, Roxy seethed at Hayes' effrontery. Before she could contemplate more than two painful methods of torture for him, Kat was back and headed out the door, dragging her along.

"I have a treat for you," Kat said sounding pleased with herself. "There's a reception tonight at the Czechoslovakian Embassy honoring newly-elected President Vaclav Havel. Come with me."

Roxy was excited in spite of herself. The thought of a playwright replacing the repressive Communist ruler in Czechoslovakia was remarkable. She had read several of his plays and a book of his prison essays and felt deeply drawn to him as a writer. Nothing like a glamorous adventure to soothe bruised feelings, she thought, silently blessing Kat.

★ ★ ★ ★ ★

The afternoon meeting progressed smoothly. A different issue would be targeted each of the five months remaining until Congress recessed for summer break in August. Media, activities, and direct mail would be coordinated to reinforce the monthly message.

THE ANNOUNCEMENT

Since March was Women's History Month, it was decided to begin with Kat's incomparable work on women's issues. Unlike most of her female colleagues, Kat was never reluctant to speak out on behalf of her sex. Everyone agreed women were a group that should be brought solidly into her column early in the campaign.

"At Jasmine's suggestion," Kat nodded smiling at her press secretary, "we kick off the month with a week of power. I want to leverage every powerful woman I know, appear with them, and talk about nothing but women."

Roxy made her pitch for adding historical women of power. She had done research on Anne Hutchinson, one of Rhode Island's founders. A courageous leader, she was described as magnetic and aggressive. Tall, angular with a regal bearing, she was in many ways a sister spirit to Kat.

Anne had been banished from the rigid Massachusetts Bay colony in 1638 for her radical spiritual beliefs. Seething over her notions that personal connection with God was more to be sought than conforming to the rules imposed by men in their churches—which at that time and place were also the rules of the state—the elders drove her and her family out. Heading south, they settled on Aquidneck Island where, under Anne's direction, the first government in America with guaranteed freedom of religion was established. While Roger Williams practiced religious tolerance on the mainland, Anne Hutchinson drew up the first declaration of absolute religious freedom in America and wrote it into law across the bay on Aquidneck. Her declaration spread to Maryland and Pennsylvania and eventually became the basis for the French Revolution.

Kat shared with Anne Hutchinson the courage to develop a belief system from her own experiences and a willingness to put those beliefs into action. Freedom of conscience was a clarion cry for both, and Anne would have understood the religious freedom Kat demonstrated in her own spiritual system. Both believed no church should have power through the state to force obedience to its doctrines.

Roxy told the story with enthusiasm and Kat quickly agreed to make Anne Hutchinson and her independent ideas the centerpiece of her women's speeches and press in March. "She's been called the 'mother of twentieth century woman' for her exercise of freedom of thought and action in a time when that was enough to get you run out of town, if not burned at the stake," Roxy concluded.

"This may flush out Bishop O'Reagan on his intentions about ex-communicating you for being pro-choice," observed Mario. "The sooner we deal with this issue the better, and since Winston's also choice," he shrugged his shoulders.

"But Winston's not a Catholic with his nominal spiritual leader breathing down his neck," Kat replied, distressed.

As one who left behind all her years of Catholic schooling without a backward glance when she lost her virginity at seventeen and discovered how wrong they were about sex being bad, Roxy could not understand worrying about the bishop, as if he had any power to dictate Kat's relationship to God. That was the point of Anne Hutchinson's story.

Kat agreed that sooner was better to face down the bishop and she would be wise to choose the battleground. Anne Hutchinson seemed just right.

Gould jumped in with a script for his women's spot that featured Jake and an older man he recruited at a Warwick American Legion bar.

"The two men are taking a lunch break and talk about women in real life economic terms. Jake tells how his wife does the same job as the guy at the next desk but he gets five thousand dollars more a year because his title is something mostly men get in that company. 'We need two salaries to raise our family. I want my wife to have what she deserves, what she's earned. Why should our whole family get by with less money for the same work. Where's the fairness in that?' Jake asks. Big Mac—that's the older guy's name—and the rest of us wonder also and are delighted to learn that Kiley is doing something about it. Everyone deserves fair pay."

Kat reviewed the script boards while Gould raved about his characters.

"I was going to make Jake a construction worker but decided a fisherman was better; they're the cowboys in this state."

She suggested a few minor changes, then turned to Roxy who had been working with Gould on the script.

"What do you think?"

Roxy was pleased with the script she and Gould had developed together. She had seen Jake and Big Mac rehearse—no film had been shot yet—and they had great chemistry. She seconded Gould's assessment that the spots could make political history.

"I only want them to get me elected," Kat reminded them.

Gould had rough outlines for additional commercials to set the theme in each of the issue segments to follow women. "I want to test reaction to the first spot before I finalize any others—to see if there are any dramatic alterations needed. We can shoot all the background material now."

Kat expressed her pleasure at the positive notes Gould was striking.

"I asked Senatorial to assign someone other than Paul Reilly to our campaign," she said caustically, "after he outlined several commercial ideas to me, each more insulting and demeaning to Winston than the one before. He suggested a split-screen spot. On one side Winston is peddling his firm's tranquilizers and anti-depressants, while on the other a young man is peddling crack. His weak voting record on drugs and crime is then flashed on the screen."

Kat sighed and blocked any discussion of how effective a commercial like that could be.

"Don't any of you get ideas that this is a good direction for our commercials. I meant what I said about negative campaigning. If there are legal problems in either Winston's business or personal life there are authorities who should investigate. I want discussion to focus on his effectiveness, his ideas for the future."

Kat signed off on using spots on environment, health care, education, and taxes. Each would stress the need to restructure economic promises and include real costs for environmental degradation and social decay.

"Will all of these feature Jake and Big Mac?" she asked.

"We found a great old lady to be the third member of the cast," Gould answered. "She's white-haired, vital, no-nonsense—and we're making her a doubter. I'm convinced there are hard-core women decision makers out there who don't like the idea of any woman in the Senate. If we can sell you to them in a commercial, we can sell anyone."

Gould dropped his voice and unconsciously looked around the room, "I think these spots will create three believable characters whom we own. By September, having Jake, Big Mac, and Aunt Helen doing shameless plugs for Kat will be as good as celebrity endorsements!"

Everyone but Roxy expressed minor reservations about this prediction, but all were content to wait and see the finished product.

★ ★ ★ ★ ★

They were sprawled on the floor of the playroom, examining the few morsels of food they smuggled out of the Czech reception. It had been an incredible mob scene with half hour waits to get in the door, even with VIP tickets. Everyone there was a VIP. They managed to position themselves in the front of the line as Havel pushed his way up the stairs and into the embassy ballroom. Roxy was amazed to find herself looking directly into his eyes as he passed almost unseen between the two lines of bodies; he was decidedly short, and looked bemused but profound as he returned her smile.

The crush of bodies was too much for security and they immediately whisked him off to a back room. Kat and Roxy did not stay to see if he emerged to address the crowds later; they would see him in the morning when he addressed Congress.

"What did the chart of the announcement turn out to be?" asked Roxy licking the remains of cake frosting from her fingers. Kat had spoken to Max soon after they arrived back at the house.

"We selected the date because it keyed to my Aquarian energy. There are positive indications about money, and the structural philosophy of government and institutions. The strangest part is an abundance of indicators about relationships—dramatic and transformative relationships. The key image that came with the exact time is that of a new continent rising out of the ocean."

Roxy felt the tight prickling that came when she heard Kat speak with a prophetic voice; as usual it made the hair on her arms stand on end.

"Are there any problems?"

"There are challenges along every path," Kat said solemnly. "This one is filled with deception."

Roxy cleaned up the crumbs and empty glasses as Kat went over to brush her hair in front of the mirrors. When Roxy came back upstairs, she was shocked to find Kat sitting huddled against the cabinet, staring at a blank television screen.

"Tell me more about Anne Hutchinson," she said, turning a glassy stare on her friend. Roxy quickly pulled out some notes and began reading.

"The ministers taught terror, she taught love. They preached to impress one another, she talked to plain people.

"The church elders in 17th century Boston held their congregations in bondage with the power of both church and state. They pronounced the 'curse of Eve,' preventing women from taking their rightful place. Hutchinson wanted liberation. They were outraged when a woman challenged the natural order of their universe by daring to debate with them—and on spiritual matters no less. She left Rhode Island with only part of her family less than six years after arriving. She thought leaving would protect the settlement and its religious freedom. She was murdered by Indians paid by church elders in Massachusetts. As the first woman to make her mark on American history, her flame became a beacon for the world."

Roxy looked up and wondered why Kat looked so pale and still.

"What about her personally?" she asked in a hoarse whisper.

Shivering slightly, Roxy pulled on her robe.

"She was a visionary, literally as well as in her ideas. She was also a healer and midwife. These were not valued talents in 17th century Puritan Massachusetts. Nathaniel Hawthorne wrote a well-informed sketch of Anne early in his career. He alludes to her by name several times in *The Scarlett Letter* indicating that she served as a partial model for Hester Prynne."

"Anne was married and bore fifteen children, so she must have known something about sex. She endured an abnormal pregnancy while imprisoned in Massachusetts. Over forty at the time, she had a miscarriage that expelled what were clusters of malformed cells, never a fetus. They call it," Roxy checked her notes, "a hydatidiform mole. She almost died. The church elders accused her of 'thirty monstrous births at once, none of human shape', and claimed it was a sign from God decrying her monstrous heresy against His teachings. That's when she came to Rhode Island." The look on Kat's face made Roxy's blood run cold.

"Are there any pictures of her?"

"I don't know. I've never seen one, but I'll keep looking."

Kat walked stiffly to her room, dangling her hairbrush.

THE ANNOUNCEMENT

★ ★ ★ ★ ★

It was like starting the day by kissing a speeding bus. Roxy walked into the breakfast meeting of Kat's finance team at the Capitol Hill Club. Hayes was there, pouring cream into the coffee of an impeccably dressed and smiling Cindy Michaels. Of course, Roxy snarled inwardly, a friend from out-of-town. I hope the bitch raises enough money to keep me from throwing her out the third floor window.

She ignored the proceedings and indulged in personal torture wondering whether Hayes had done the same things in bed with Cindy that he had done with her. At least the one time they used a bed. The time in the tower—Roxy was certain Cindy had no comparable memory to cherish. She could not imagine the dressed-for-success financial witch sprawled against a stone wall listening to the ocean while…. Her cheeks flamed as she recalled the night, the sensation of doing something so possessed.

Hayes was watching her. The flush on her cheeks deepened. What was it about this man, about the look in his eyes as blue and translucent as marbles, that made her want to crawl under the table and bury her face in his lap? She wondered if he were free for lunch today? It was never too late to make up for past regrets. She probably had been too hasty yesterday. Roxy glanced at Kat's schedule and noticed that Hayes was listed as accompanying her to an Inner Circle lunch meeting. Campaign money, Hayes would go.

Roxy squirmed slightly trying to relieve the pulsing between her legs. As soon as the breakfast ended, she escaped, mouthing to Kat that she would see her at the final afternoon meeting.

★ ★ ★ ★ ★

Hayes came into Kat's office for the staff meeting and squeezed himself onto the couch next to Roxy, trapping her against its arm. Her heart doubled its beat as his intensity pulsed along every inch of her body where they touched. When he surreptitiously rubbed her hip, she felt a trickle of moisture along the inside of her thigh.

Fortunately she knew everything of substance discussed in the meeting as Hayes directed the staff in their part of the plan. She stared blindly at a printed outline of the scheduled issue segments and allowed herself to float languorously on the melodic sound, distinguishing no words, merely reveling in the tingling she felt as his voice brushed against her.

Reluctantly abandoning her state of acute stimulation when Hayes was called out of the meeting for a phone call, she listened to Kat's concluding pep talk.

"The campaign is about to hit its stride. From now on, everything we do here will be guided by strategic considerations demanded by the senate race. You are my secret weapon. It's your brilliant and dedicated efforts over the past eight years that have brought me to a position where I can legitimately consider advancing to the Senate. Now I'm going to need you to do even more, and to do it playing a secondary role. There's no alternative but that the campaign will claim all my time and effort as well as yours. Please respond as quickly and fully as possible to any requests from campaign staff, think politically in everything you do here, and direct your time and resources to those areas that can best serve themes we unfold in the campaign."

Kat looked around the room, appreciation misting her eyes.

"It may seem like I've abandoned you and the crusades we've undertaken as our part of the work. I haven't. We've chosen this new game—me overtly, you by staying here. We must play by the rules, at least until we understand them enough to break them with some hope for success."

The frowns on several faces, including Stan Everhart's, turned to smiles as they heard her message of reassurance.

She motioned to Hayes, leaning against the open door.

"Our general will keep us all on the correct path. He knows the strategy, the timing, whatever anyone here needs to know—so do I, so does Mario. If you have any questions, concerns, confusion about a direction or assignment, ask one of us. No one will be shut out of the campaign."

As the meeting ended, Roxy noticed it was almost five. She had about half an hour before she and Mario had to leave for the airport. Hayes followed her out into the hall and maneuvered her over towards the elevator.

"I have some papers in my car I need you to bring back to Rhode Island. Will you come get them with me?"

She was excited by the craving that showed clearly and found no will to resist as he demanded she follow him into the elevator and down to the garage. He unlocked the passenger side of his car and motioned her to get in.

"Where are we going?"

"Does it matter?"

Desire dripped from his liquid voice and he slid his fingers under her collar to stroke the soft skin where neck sloped into shoulder. Roxy moaned slightly and reminded him she had to leave for the airport in half an hour.

"There's time." He pushed her in, closed the door and walked around to the driver's side.

They circled down counter clockwise to an almost empty section on the lowest level of the concrete maze that was the parking garage of the Rayburn building, away from the continually watching cameras. Roxy thought every inch of space in this garage was fought over with great vigor, so she never imagined deserted areas like this. Hayes backed the car into a dark corner and turned off the engine. Reaching over to open her door, he drew his hand back across her breasts and kissed her deeply.

"Get in the back," he drawled, getting out of the car.

She balked momentarily, chagrined by the thought of fumbling around in the back seat of some car at her age, then obeyed. Briefly, they looked at each other. He reached over and pulled her to him.

"I surrender," he said, eyes glittering, his hands caressing the delicate, warm skin of her waist and reaching around to unhook her bra. He pushed up her sweater and the bra in the same movement as he lowered his mouth to her breasts.

"You are so delectable. I'm captive to your taste and feel," he muttered barely removing his lips from her breasts before returning with a hunger that made her doubt he had spent the night doing the same to Cindy.

His urgency ignited her own and Roxy slipped off her panties and loosened his pants as he devoted himself to her breasts. Moist and inviting, her sex drew him in, closing around him like a sea anemone. Bliss was not long in coming. She lasted only a few quick strokes before her tension exploded like plasma, streaked with color and moving thickly through all her cells. She could feel his mustache brush against her breast in a smile as he felt her climax and timed himself to push her along. Then his control was gone and the car rocked as they fought to blend their separate bodies into a single pulsing unit.

Sadly, Roxy felt her moment of time with him slip away as he wilted and withdrew tenderly, the fevered plunging over.

"I love it that you are so open to me, that I can go into you and feel satisfied," he said in tribute as he moved off her to sit up and check his watch. "We have five minutes to spare."

Hayes nudged her to the back of the empty elevator. Blocking the view from the door with his body, he pushed away a fallen lock of her bright blond hair.

"You have a most fetching just-laid look."

Her hands flew to her face in horror.

"What if someone notices?" Roxy groaned as she tried to smooth back her hair and erase whatever traces of passion remained.

Hayes led her off the elevator, laughing.

7

A Star is Born
March

Rhode Island

Each day the ocean sounded different and looked different. Even the debris washed up was ever changing. Usually she passed the sprawling white stucco house with its bright red roof and turrets before finalizing her reading of the ocean, pulse of Rhode Island and—in Roxy's mind—forecaster of her day. Haphazardly for the past couple of weeks, she had been collecting data on how the feel of the ocean each morning when she walked matched the feel of her whole day. If the link was real, this day should be terrific. The waves were active, surf spraying. A hot pink plastic buoy bounced gleefully. Cut loose from the concrete block mooring, it drifted towards shore. The sky was gleaming azure. The gulls looked spiffier than usual. A light breeze tore high white clouds into streamers. Roxy breathed in the salt air and sighed. She was ready for the great day her ocean oracle predicted.

The fluid pattern of the crashing waves reminded her of how she really wanted to do it on the beach; feel her mini-waves of passion amplified by the ocean waves, driven by the moon, connected in with the whole cosmic plan. It sounded like one of Kat's pet parallel laws. She doubted if Kat applied her scientific speculations to getting laid, however.

Finishing titillating reruns of back seat passion she felt someone walking along beside her. It was Jake, white teeth gleaming in the bright sunlight as he smiled.

"Mario sent me to find you. Gould is delayed, and we don't need to check in at headquarters until noon. If I provide breakfast, will you come and help me pick out clothes for the filming? Gould said to wear my own, I'd be more relaxed."

Jake's place was an old white farmhouse that boasted a country kitchen with handhewn beams and painted wood floors. They sat at his rough oak table eating warm and fragrant muffins bare—no jam or butter needed.

"It's less than five miles from the beach and that's a premier fishing stream," he pointed out the wide windows that made up the modernized east wall of the kitchen.

"It flows into Pettaquamscutt Lake which in turn becomes Narrow River—the end of your beach march."

Birds and squirrels frolicked along the stream bank as Jake went to assemble the wardrobe choices he wanted her to approve. At his call she left the kitchen and went upstairs. Walking through the wood framed doorway on the second floor, she marveled at the space she entered, an obvious addition to the nineteenth century farmhouse.

A loft extended over a two-story high atrium filled with plants. The south end was a wall of windows. A ceiling-high panel of stained glass bordered one end of an ornate metalwork railing; a second panel was mounted on the other end. Roxy walked towards the vividly green one which featured the ethereal features of a woman garbed and veiled in leaves.

"The forest deva," Jake said as he noticed her interest. "This is her mate, the opposite pole, the sky god."

Roxy crossed to the other end of the railing and examined the heroic posture and visage of the male figure; blue was the predominant color.

"Is this your work?" she asked, admiringly.

"My first major project." Jake continued to root around in his closet and through several open drawers. "It was my personal test of mastery. Once I completed this pair, I felt prepared to announce myself to the world as an artist."

"I guess so," Roxy agreed. "They're the most remarkable glass panels I've seen. The expressions on their faces are so stirring. And there's more shades of light and color than I ever imagined possible in glass."

She turned her attention back to Jake who was standing bare-chested in his jeans, a pile of shirts, jackets, and sweaters on the bed in front of him.

"Thanks," he said with a grin then waved his hand over the clothes. "Well, what should I wear?"

As they reviewed the script outlines to determine how the character should be dressed in each, Roxy was only half attentive. The rest of her interest was devoted to assessing Jake. He had the rounded biceps and muscled forearms of a man who swung a hammer, especially noticeable since the rest of his body was sleek and lean. He put on and discarded several tee-shirts that were indistinguishable to her before settling on a deep red that he claimed was his favorite. Posing self-consciously, he flashed his wide smile and focused his twinkling dark eyes directly on her. The smile changed his face, she thought. He became totally appealing—a born salesman.

She particularly watched his eyebrows, to see if Gould's assertion had any merit. He did waggle them for emphasis, they seemed almost to turn up on the ends when he was smiling, but it was sincerity they projected best. When he furrowed his brow earnestly, his eyebrows made you want to be concerned, too.

They assembled a full selection of shirts and sweaters, several types of footwear and even a couple hats. Jake's requirement, which Gould accepted, was that he wore only jeans. And well he should, thought Roxy, admiring his flat stomach and lean hips where the jeans rode snugly, accentuating his firm ass and thighs.

"Come with me." He piled the selected items on the bed, tossing rejects in a corner by the closet, and took Roxy's hand, pulling her from the chair. "I have something for you."

His workshop was built close to the stream behind the house. From the outside, it looked like a rough wood box with a high shed roof; inside she noted it was solidly built, well-insulated with a wood stove. One side of the building was devoted to woodworking equipment—a radial arm saw, a band saw for intricate work, a small planer, a sturdy workbench and a wall hung from floor to ceiling with hand tools and clamps of all sizes. Jars of screws, nails, bolts and other small items lined a floor to ceiling set of shelves. On the other side was the glass studio—several tables of varying sizes, open bins filled with sheets and pieces of glass boasting a profusion of colors and textures, drawings and sketches tacked up around the windows which dominated the space. Everywhere were pieces of his art.

Music greeted their entry—a rousing march that Roxy had heard countless times but could not name. She asked about it as Jake walked to a control box in the corner and turned it off.

"My own motivational program," he explained. "I used to come into the shop and spend an hour or more puttering around aimlessly—looking at glass, hanging up tools, sweeping sawdust—and still struggle to get started. So I installed an automatic switch on my tuner and CD and programmed the march to begin as soon as anyone walks in. It jump-starts me. Every so often I change marches but this is one of my favorites. It's John Philip Sousa's "Riders for the Flag." Circuses use it a lot. I saw *Stars and Stripes,* a '50s movie about Sousa, probably five times as a kid. Something in his marches closes a circuit in me and I'm in action."

He lifted a rectangular blue framed glass scene from a nail over his drafting table and held it in front of the sunlight pouring in. It was beautiful. She had never seen anything like it. A remarkable butterfly with curved multicolored wings rose three dimensionally from the plane of the rectangle. Swirling, colorful clouds, and a pieced and layered flower in blues and pinks completed the scene.

"This is for you," Jake said looking enormously pleased with himself. "Thanks for all you've done to get me ready for my debut."

A light blush crept across his cheeks and his voice was almost shy.

Roxy was effusive in her thanks and praise of the exquisite beauty and delicacy of the piece.

"I don't know that anything I've done deserves this."

Taking the rectangle in her hands, she examined the delicate swirl of colors in the butterfly wings and traced its unique curve.

"Recycling," Jake explained. "I have a friend who blows big glass balls. These are his failures."

They moved around the shop. Jake pulled out sheets of glass, explaining how he worked. Roxy examined tools used for cutting and grinding. She gingerly touched strips of foiling

"I love glass," said Jake. "I love the color and translucence. I marvel every time I see light make the images three dimensional. Everything in my life seems color saturated when I'm here working."

"How did you begin doing stained glass?" Roxy asked.

"My athletic career came to an abrupt halt senior year in high school when a motorcycle accident crushed my ankle. All sports other than swimming were off-limits to me."

"You couldn't even fish?"

"Fishing is not a sport. It's closer to a spiritual practice—or carnal appetite if you're Pete," he laughed.

"I always had an urge to create beauty so I sold all my sports equipment and went to RISD—Rhode Island School of Design," he said, deliberately spelling out the letters.

"Learn what RISD is if you want entré into the arts community in the state." Jake's expression got sheepish.

"I stayed for a while then set off to find some utopean artists' community."

"Did you find one?"

Jake nodded. "In California. It failed after a couple months. Destiny struck while I was on a bar stool in the Santa Cruz mountains. I noticed a piece of stained glass hanging over the bar. It was cluttered with magical forms surrounding a center panel that said FUCK NIXON in a rainbow of colors." He chuckled at the memory.

"I had an epiphany right there on the bar stool and said to myself, I'm a stained glass artist."

Jake described his work routine. "I do carpentry to pay the bills. Gould's paying us scale for the commercials so this week of filming buys me the time to finish my special project."

He gestured to several female figures in glass.

"This lush beauty is the rose deva and this is the delicate trillium. I've been looking for a peach blossom model. You'd be perfect. Would you pose for me?"

Surprised, Roxy examined Jake. They had been seeing each other regularly for a couple months—on the beach, Friday night dinner, on the campaign—but there had never been any sexual interest shown on either side. She was highly sensitive to the blood chemistry that aroused her desire and felt none rise for Jake. And since she felt nothing from him directed at her, she could not even muster up interest in response. He was an attractive man, there seemed to be no other female in his life, and she was certain he was not gay. He was much too charming and handsome to be permanently unattached so she chalked up his lack of interest to recent romantic trauma freezing his heart.

A STAR IS BORN

She agreed to pose.

★ ★ ★ ★ ★

The camera loved Jake. Diffident in person, on film he projected presence and substance while his natural charm radiated. He was so 'sincere' that Roxy could hear mothers all over Rhode Island directing their daughters to find a man like him, and fathers agreeing. People would believe Kat should be their next senator if Jake told them so. Gould was right, he had discovered a star.

For the next three days their happy caravan drove around the state. There were cameras, bags of batteries and film, lights and sound devices, props, scripts, and pages of directions, schedules and names of contacts. Gould was director and rode with Roxy and Jake. His partner, Rudy, who did all the filming, rode in a van filled with equipment and driven by his assistant. A second van with sound and light techies and their equipment followed; the still photographer rode with them. Big Mac brought up the rear driving Aunt Helen and the hairdresser.

They filmed in playschools and hospitals, at the beach, on Beavertail and Block Island. There were scenes shot against the backdrop of closed factories and crumbling buildings; other featured fishing boats and processing co-ops. Jake, Big Mac and Aunt Helen were troopers, never complaining, patiently waiting while their hair was fixed or their make-up applied. Roxy and Gould watched and listened, making minor changes in scripts while Rudy moved the trio through the scenes.

Everyone they encountered was friendly and voiced their support of Kat. Roxy calculated fewer than ten percent expressed any reservation or concerns, which made her wonder if anyone planned to vote for Winston. The press caught up with them at several locations seemingly intrigued by the notion of serial commercials.

"We'll get at least a week of earned press out of this, and an audience anxious to see what they've been reading about. Then when the commercials hit—pow! We'll be off like a rocket and Winston'll never know what hit him!" Gould was ecstatic.

Kat had a hectic schedule of church fairs, fundraising events, and constituent meetings. The only conversation Roxy had with her focused primarily on events in the state following the weekend fundraising trip to Miami that Senator Stuart arranged. Until she heard from Max, or until Mario uncovered something in his investigations, Roxy decided not to mention concerns about Carrie. Kat had more than enough on her mind.

SENATE MAGIC

★ ★ ★ ★ ★

Roxy took a night walk: the full moon demanded it. She started out with rock in hand, just in case. Who knew what monsters lurked on the dark, deserted beach? The light was soft but bright and she could see clearly enough to toss the rock away before going very far along the sand. Sounds were muted at night. The clacking of water as it withdrew over billions of rocks lining the beach almost dominated the mildly roaring waves.

She noted a different feel to the ocean, to her body as she walked in the moonlight. She felt pulled, magnetized, passions on the rise. Quickly she looked around. She did not want to be the object of misguided passion for some moon-crazed weirdo. Certainly there was no chosen magnet on her horizon.

Full moon madness waited for daylight to strike. Mario got a call from Harry Crast at the *Providence Journal*. He had received a packet of news clippings and releases highlighting examples of what the cover letter described as Kat's 'poor judgement.' The letter was signed by the purported head of an unknown citizens group. A little checking determined that the packets had been sent to more than fifty media outlets both in and out of state. An ardent supporter of the positive campaign both Kat and Winston had pledged to run, Harry was disturbed by the scurrilous attack.

The source of the negative material was ultimately traced to the Democrats. Hayes had Kat's approval to express hurt and betrayal over allegations made in the packet which included Max, astrology, dancing at the Press Club, and what big job the administration had promised her for running. She remained unreachable in Florida. Winston made it all easy by immediately and strongly denouncing the tactic and insisting it never be repeated. His call to apologize was the only one Mario put through to Kat.

An hour before Roxy was to leave and meet Kat at Green Airport, life got very weird. Liz called frantically from Morgan Springs.

"Max says it's beginners black magic and she's a Celtic witch who cannot be allowed around Kat. But if you think I'm keeping this weirdo here, you're crazy! She shows up after midnight on Friday, lurks around in a corner of the bar for a while then comes over and tells me you sent her. That Kat's in Florida hijacking Cubans for money and you thought she'd understand the campaign better if she came here and met Max and me."

Roxy sorted through the chaos, distracted by wondering why Liz was the first call she had from home. Why hadn't she heard from Max yet about Carrie's writings.

"Who is this Carrie creature, anyway?"

Liz's question made her wonder about mind reading before she focused on what the rant meant.

"Carrie's there? In Morgan Springs?" Roxy cried.

"She sure is. She's been underfoot every second of the time she's been in town. We got real busy late Friday night and she made herself indispensable, busing tables, washing dishes, handling drunks. After lunch yesterday, she was talking about leaving her job in Rhode Island and coming to run Magnolia's for me while I work on the campaign."

Roxy punctuated Liz's recital with exclamations and moans.

"Saturday morning I called Max figuring he might know what was going on. He'd just gotten back in town and didn't come down until later that afternoon. Of course, I knew nothing about your suspicions of the girl. Obviously our phone sex doesn't include sharing any real inside gossip. All I get to hear is what dark corner you've been felt-up in recently."

Roxy ignored Liz's assaults.

"When Max finally showed up, it was spooky."

The tremble in Liz's normally fearless voice took Roxy by surprise. She thought her friend was steel from surface to core.

"He saw Carrie from the far end of the bar and pulled out a single coin. He set it spinning across his hand and walked slowly towards her, staring intently. She shivered a little when he first looked at her, but she's a cool customer, I'll tell you. By the time Max was circling, looking her up and down, she was chatting away like a cute little girl trying to act flirtatious with her dad. The coin was spinning across his knuckles so fast it set up a breeze."

Liz paused, and yelled something off the phone.

"Sorry Roxy, they can't do anything without me. How I think I'm going to leave for four months is beyond me. Now, where was I?"

"Did Max say anything to her?"

"He looked at her, cold as ice, palmed his coin and began reciting some strange rhyme. 'You are Discord, twisted with fear. Chaos and lies brought you here. Bloody Kali, you must go. Your dark heart will stop the flow.' It was so quiet in the bar the words seemed to hang dripping in the air. There was no doubt in my mind. Carrie was bad news and Max was running her out of town, or in this case, off the campaign. Whatever you guys decide to do is only window dressing.

"Before he left the bar, he turned and warned me to be careful. 'An evil past makes it easy for her to do evil once again. Stay clear. She can see more than anyone would imagine.' Then he was gone.'"

"What did Carrie do?"

"She stared me right in the eye, barely blinked once, and said 'no wonder our consultants worry about the press finding out about him. They might believe all that hocus pocus is real.'"

"And after that, she's still around?" Roxy raised her voice.

"No. She went back to Rhode Island last night. She's your problem now."

She pumped Liz for whatever stories Carrie told during her visit. There were drug and sex lies about Mario and fantastic stories about Roxy's affair with Hayes that far outran the admittedly unusual path the relationship had taken so far. She even told Liz the story about being raped, only the circumstances and ending were changed. She claimed she lived with the Colemans in Florida until she had the baby then they helped her find a good family to adopt the little girl.

"She said she named her Elizabeth," Liz said.

Roxy ranted at Carrie's lies and her avowal that she had never told anyone the story before.

"She did have a romantic tale about Kat's lover who sends her the roses. You seemed to have forgotten that tidbit, as well." Liz huffed, indignant.

"That's ridiculous! Kat doesn't have a lover. If she did, I would know it. Who does Carrie claim this mystery man is?"

"Our very own Virginia senator, T.J. Stuart!" Liz sounded triumphant, thinking she had information—even if it was a deliberate lie of Carrie's—that Roxy had not heard.

"Stuart! That can't be true! He's married. Kat would never get involved with a married man."

"Oh please, Roxy. This is the '90s, girl. Majority rules, marriage is only temporary."

"Not for Kat. Not in an election year! Not during her senate race!" Roxy raved. "Why should we believe Carrie? We know she's a pathological liar."

"I think she exaggerates mostly," Liz observed. "There's usually a kernel of truth in what she says, as we know in your sordid case."

Roxy considered Liz's analysis, ignoring her barb about Hayes.

"Maybe you're right. I can imagine that Stuart would send Kat roses, more as teasing than serious seduction. He's being extremely helpful with the campaign, but I can't imagine he's dumb enough to risk his own career, and Kat's by—by—by fooling around with her."

"Fooling around?" Liz howled in disbelief. "Is that a technical term you use when your pure-as-driven-snow teenage heroines get poked by their horny football player boyfriends after escaping some idiotic danger. The act in question here is fucking, Roxy. We're not really concerned about relationships. The people want to know if that Cuban cowboy is fucking our favorite goddess on the campaign trail."

"He's not Cuban," Roxy muttered.

"Oh, sorry. Let me rephrase that: an Appalachian cowboy with Cuban friends. Is that more to your satisfaction?"

"Carrie's lying, we know she is," Roxy repeated.

"Remember what Max said: 'She can see more than anyone would imagine,'" Liz retorted.

A STAR IS BORN

★ ★ ★ ★ ★

Kat bounced off the plane, tanned and elated, greeting constituents and fellow travelers. She talked about Miami and the Cubans all the way back to the house, at one point pulling a handful of checks and substantial amount of cash from her bag.

"With Jill doing follow-up, we may top two hundred thousand dollars on this trip alone. They loved me! And I felt deeply connected with them, too. One old man took my hand, telling me in a paper-thin voice, how I look exactly as his wife did when they were first married. I wore my bright yellow suit and left my hair loose. I was overwhelmed with how Latin it all was. The airport is crowded with Hispanics dressed to kill: high heels, gaudy clothes, exotic tropical perfumes. There's a '50s look to everything there—even a giant mural of a Miami Beach scene at that time. I was swaying to a subliminal rumba when a lovely young woman introduced herself as Rosa, Senator Stuart's aide, and my designated companion for the events."

"Was Stuart in Miami, too?" Roxy was desperately curious.

"Only in the hearts of all the people I met. They talked about him as if he were their personal liberator."

No Stuart, no affair, was Roxy's conclusion. The situation was too ideal for lovers to ignore. She listened as Kat recited the weekend's activities.

She described the ranch houses sprawled sprawled across a monotone landscape where the occasional palm tree was decidedly outnumbered by swimming pools gleaming turquoise in the sun. Feverish Latin style was everywhere inside—gold flecked mirrored tiles on the walls, huge couches filling sunken living rooms, statues of naked women disguised as antique sculpture.

"My hosts were unfailingly gracious. The guests were friendly, charming, and exceedingly curious about what a woman like me was doing in the sordid world of politics. I told my story several times, and each time they reciprocated by telling me theirs."

Some escaped before Castro came to power in 1959, others in the early '60s when harassment and restrictions began. Most had been middle or upper class in Cuba. Most left a father, uncle or brother dead or lost forever in Castro's prisons. Many had been young teenagers or children when they arrived.

"America's been good to them," she said. "They've made fortunes, built comfortable homes and assured their children of bright futures—and they appreciate it."

They controlled Miami and were almost universally Republican.

"They blame Kennedy, Carter and the Democrats for allowing Castro to take and keep Cuba. They shower money on Republican candidates selected by Diaz, the leader Stuart told us about. It's how they show their thanks. I felt like a bride at an Italian wedding. People would come up to me and stuff cash or checks into my hand or my bag."

Kat went upstairs to shower and rest. Mario had arranged to screen the commercials at Terminisi's, Kat's favorite neighborhood restaurant. The commercials were good enough to celebrate and he wanted to be prepared. He also knew Kat would be grateful not to have to walk further than around the corner. Roxy managed to drag Mario off long enough to tell him Max confirmed their worst suspicions about Carrie.

"Well, I have a silver stake to drive through her heart, too," he whispered in return. "We can talk about it tomorrow and decide what to tell Kat. It seems unanimous—Carrie has to go."

The screening was a huge success. Everyone loved the three completed commercials, hailed Jake as the hottest new face of the decade, and howled with delight at Harry Crast's column praising Gould's genius and restraint while virtually accusing Winston's media guru of initiating the negative attacks on Kat.

"The spot with Jake and Big Mac discussing pay equity and family leave debuts two days after our women's press conference," Gould reported. "We don't want to step on our own stories."

Roxy smiled. She knew Gould had argued endlessly to debut the commercials on Sunday as a kick-off to women's power week, but Kat refused. The time would not be right. Kat won, but Gould was a master at turning every cloud's silver lining to his advantage.

"In April we do Jake and taxes—we'll have that complete next week. May is Jake and Big Mac discussing Kiley's accomplishments as a businesswoman. We'll tout her position on easing inheritance tax for within-family business transferences. June, we unleash Aunt Helen in that beauty you saw here tonight—worrying about the future of education and the environment for all her grand nieces and nephews. Our senior spots are not going to be whining recitals of selfish claims but what older folks also care about—the kind of world their descendants will face. By summer, we'll have a hit on our hands!"

"Is there an overall theme?" Kat asked.

"Several." Jake shows them how much you've accomplished and in a back corner of their mind they're asking what has Winston done for me lately? Hopefully the media will also ask that question and begin to slowly bleed him dry on his inaction. We use the same key phrases in each spot—Kiley looking ahead, her star on the rise, in touch with today, 'one of us'—whoever us is. Jake closes each spot with the line 'Imagine what she can do for us in the Senate.'"

Kat applauded.

Before leaving, Jake came over and invited Roxy to come watch the commercial's debut with him later that week.

"I know it starts with the news at 7 a.m. but I'll feed you breakfast and walk on the beach with you after. I'd feel much more secure if you were there. Maybe you could even pose for a while if you have nothing urgent that morning?"

Mentally reviewing her schedule, Roxy realized there were no specific assignments once the women's press conference was over. She quickly accepted.

★ ★ ★ ★ ★

The women's community health center in North Providence was packed with female volunteers, women connected with the clinic, and representatives of the five women's groups endorsing Kat's candidacy. Television cameras dominated the area, print reporters docilely keeping to their self-assigned place behind the cameras. Kat was electrifying, dressed in a wine colored knit dress and full length sleeveless vest ensemble that shouted 'power clothes.' Her hair was up and she wore garnets set in gold at her ears and throat.

As the cameras filmed, more than half a dozen women leaders—including two prominent Democrats—praised Kat and cited the reasons their group endorsed her candidacy. Whatever words they used, it boiled down to one reason, the one Kat pushed incessantly: there would be no equity, no guarantees for the women in any arena until they were fairly represented in decision-making bodies. Over and over they repeated that Kiley Tomasso was more than a politically correct vote, she was a leader and a voice undeterred by partisan pressure. She was a fighter for women who did not wait to be asked to join the battle.

They used horrifying statistics to describe a future only redeemable by the zeal of Kiley Tomasso in the Senate. One woman pointed out that seventy percent of new workers in the next decade would be women, but that training program enrollments did not reflect that change. Another from a more radical group took Winston on directly, flagellating him for keeping childcare legislation bottled up in his committee while publicly supporting it.

"Go for it," Mario muttered, delighted. Kat pretend not to hear the attack.

When a woman lawyer from one of the largest groups explained that women of the world do two-thirds of the work, earn ten percent of the income, and own one percent of the property. Roxy shuddered. Remove America from those statistics and the picture for global womanhood was dismal indeed. No wonder Kat thought there was no time to waste in reviving the goddess.

The bombshell was reserved for Ronnie Kilpatrick, in town from Washington to present her national group's endorsement. She said several major labor unions threatened to cut off all future money to the group if they endorsed any Republicans, regardless of their position on women's issues. That included female candidates.

She had flown to Boca Raton to meet with the labor council and beg them

to allow her organization to endorse Kiley Tomasso. One building trades representative, a long time ally of Duke's, rallied support. The unions made an exception—the sole exception granted—for Kiley.

Only Kat and Mario looked unsurprised by Ronnie's announcement. Journalists were madly scribbling while cameras darted from one female face to another, all registering the unions' attempted political roadblock.

Kat used their anger to launch a hard-hitting statement that called on women
throughout the country to focus on electing more women to Congress.

"At least there we get equal pay for equal work," she quipped. Kat then introduced a future that swept into the next century.

"In many ways, we live in the same old world. Women have made it if they
play by the rules and move up the ladder as men demand. Women smoke more,
die of stress-related diseases and deprive themselves of satisfying emotional support. We must move forward and sweep through the '90s on a wave of change
that will bring the world into balance. We must take the next step!"

Describing this next step, Kat cited the growing importance of so-called
women's issues like childcare, family leave, peace and ecology.

"Characteristics common to women—cooperation, sharing, recognition of
the importance of relationships and reconciliation—have to be embraced and
valued. We must join with men and lend our unique capabilities in bringing
balance to the world. Then we can proceed to the future together, with everyone
a winner.

"I endorse the words of Jeanette Rankin, first woman to serve in the U.S.
Congress: 'Men and women are like right and left hands; it doesn't make sense
not to use both.'"

Kat's face became intent as she began the final paragraphs of her speech. She
was reaching into people's minds, trying to turn their ideas in a new direction,
trying to implant the vision of another way.

"And what will be the shape of this future world where both men and women
are valued for their strengths and unique contributions? No longer will most of
the world's illiterates be women, nor the world's poor be women and their children," she predicted.

"Common defense for nations will depend on a strong economy, a healthy
and well-educated population, a caring and responsible world view rather than
fancy hardware and war toys. Health care will emphasize growing healthy babies
from the start so later costs of care can be dramatically reduced. Business and
government will recognize that day care and family leave are normal costs of
employee productivity.

"Recognition will be made of women as independent individuals, not some
man's daughter, wife or widow. No longer will women live in terror of being
alone, unable to care for themselves, described as 'one man away from poverty
and destitution'. And this reality will be reflected in our economy, in pensions,
and with credit."

She then pumped a final surge of energy, urging women to empower each other, to field, support and vote for women candidates at every level.

"It starts in one woman's heart, but it becomes inevitable when we support each other, promote each other for leadership positions, and stand together crying out in unison for the changes that must be made, changes to benefit everyone."

When the applause finally ceased, journalists shouldered ahead to Kat with their questions about Winston's clout and the threat of Republican takeover of the Senate. Asked about the differences between her and Winston on women's issues, she recalled the words spoken by women leaders earlier.

"Our goals are often the same, the real difference is in our approach, the difference between passive support and active leadership."

She reiterated her standard cry when faced with questions about abortion.

"The real need is not to make abortions impossible but for programs in sex education and contraceptive research to make abortions less necessary."

An anchorman for one of the television stations brought up the negative clippings sent by Democrats.

"Do you plan to hit back?"

Kat smiled sweetly and almost fluttered her lashes as she purred, "Ladies never hit back. I accepted Senator Winston's immediate apology for the hyperactive behavior of his party and trust that the issue of negative campaigning will be put to rest completely."

Kat selected the final questioner. The chief political reporter for several regional weeklies rose.

"Can the U.S. Senate replace a man in your life?"

"That question deserves no answer," she snapped as anger flashed in her eyes. She stalked away from the microphones ignoring the barrage of flashing bulbs attempting to catch her outraged expression.

★ ★ ★ ★ ★

The battle raged all afternoon and the following day, mostly on the call-in radio talk shows that were lifeblood of Rhode Island airwaves. From campaign headquarters and the homes of staunch volunteers, they tried to flood the lines with pro-Kat questioners who would focus on real issues and accomplishments.

Most of the effort was in vain. The public was suddenly obsessed with her personal life. Dozens of women callers to the radio shows urged her to find herself a man before it was too late. "A fancy title won't keep you warm on a cold night," one woman warned.

Fortunately, Kat was in Washington and could not hear the mindless dialogue on the radio. Roxy had several conversations with Hayes about it. He kept pressing to find out if Kat did have any personal life. Was there any romantic interest they could use to reassure the radio callers?

"We've been keeping track. Nearly fifty men have called offering to make Kat's life meaningful with their undying devotion. Does that help?" Roxy snapped, tired of the incessantly ringing phones.

Finally she managed to drag Mario off so they could compare notes on Carrie.

"Where is she? We can't have her lying about Kat and Senator Stuart when everyone in the state is obsessed about her love life."

He was as anxious to escape the ringing phones as she was.

"Carrie called in sick and reportedly is in the hospital with some chronic condition. Adding what I found to Max's reaction, I think we'll have no problem convincing Kat she's dangerous and must be fired immediately."

"What did you find?"

"The Mr. Coleman whose estate she lives on—she wasn't lying about his Mafia connections. He's a major mouthpiece for the biggest wise guys in the state. And it looks as though Carrie's part of the organization, not just an innocent nut case."

"You mean someone deliberately sicced her on Kat?" Roxy asked in dismay. "Who would do that? The Democrats?"

"I think this is personal," Mario responded, "and I think I see Race Scarlatti's fingerprints all over the scene of the crime."

"Who's Race Scarlatti?"

"He's the head OC, as the Hose would say. The undisputed chief of our state's criminal organization. He poses as a legitimate dealer in precious metals. Scarlatti is a longtime admirer of Kat's, a feeling that is not mutual."

"He has a strange way of showing his admiration, or do you think he sent us Carrie as a favor?"

Mario was already plotting his assault and muttered that he would tell Roxy the whole story when there was time. For now, she could leave the situation entirely up to him. He would tell Kat tomorrow and they should be rid of Carrie while she was still out sick.

"Do you think we should tell her what Carrie's saying about her and Stuart?"

"Not if we can avoid it, especially not with all Rhode Island playing the Dating Game for her. Witchcraft and Scarlatti should be more than enough."

★ ★ ★ ★ ★

Roxy picked up muffins on her way to Jake's the next morning, arriving in time to catch the first airing of the women's commercial at 7:05 a.m. She was intrigued to see how it looked in with regular programming. The opening seconds were Kat, announcing Rhode Island must make a choice in November. Gould titled this "Kiley Tomasso in a cameo appearance as the Senator." Framed in an oval, she looked like a cameo, an official portrait hanging in the Capitol. When Jake and Big Mac followed, it appeared as if they were news and only Kat's brief statement was a political ad.

Intently focused on his screen image, Jake seemed pleased. When his New England voice asked, "Where's the fairness in that?"—the r's disappearing along his palate—it was as if generations of Yankees past and future were speaking through him. He finished with his signature phrase: "Imagine what she could do in the Senate."

Roxy believed he'd convinced Big Mac and thought she could hear dozens of switches in dozens of brains all over the state being pulled for Kiley Tomasso, U.S. Senate. Gould had taken Jake's raw appeal and created a masterpiece.

They were congratulating each other on the obvious impact of the spot when the phone rang. Answering, Jake smiled and held the receiver away from his ear. Roxy could hear an angry female voice rapidly shouting in some foreign language. After a minute or two, Jake hung up the phone and smiled sheepishly.

"A Portuguese waitress I used to date. She wanted to know why I never told her I had a wife."

Laughing, they agreed Jake was decidedly believable in his role. There were three more calls within ten minutes—his mother, Big Mac, and Pete, who begged Jake to keep track of all the women who called and pass on whatever crumbs fell from his plate. When the phone rang again, Jake shook his head, grabbed Roxy's hand and fled to the beach.

Driving rather than walking to the beach felt strange. Once again she thanked the fates for the luxury of a house two blocks from a perfect stretch of sand and ocean.

It was a Kodachrome day. The ocean was calm, surf soundlessly lapping at the beach, barely a fleck of white showing along the vibrant blue edge. They laughed about the dogs that walked themselves each morning, slipping through holes in the fence.

"No dogs on the beach after May 15," Jake told her. "Even these independent mutts disappear. Someone must send them a notice. It's a good thing, because dog patrol trucks cruise by regularly looking for offenders."

Her normal hour-long walk took more than three as they pawed through shells along the surf line with their feet, examining a few outstanding and perfect specimens. They stalked the inevitable gulls, swooping and scavenging tidbits of sea creatures and seaweed from the sand, and cheered on three guys in chartreuse wet suits doing formations on jet skis about ten feet from the surf.

Burrowed into a hollow in the dunes at the north end of the beach, facing rock sentinels at the river mouth, they traded stories of their lives' defining experiences. It was only later that Roxy recognized the ritual of revelation as that moment which usually preceded a deeper intimacy. At the time, she was just engrossed in the simple pleasure of being appreciated.

Stopping back at the house before returning to Jake's to pose as the peach blossom deva, Roxy checked her answering machine and returned a call from Mario. He reported phones ringing off the hook, press excitement, and general positive reaction to the commercial, which was scheduled to air four times a day for the next two days then twice daily for the next two weeks. Assuring Roxy she could take the day off and support Jake through the initial impact of his incipient stardom, he told her Carrie was back.

"I scheduled a meeting tomorrow morning at headquarters while Kat's campaigning in Newport. I want you there."

★ ★ ★ ★ ★

Jake posed Roxy on a low stool in front of the jungle of plants and trees he grew in his atrium. He moved a fig tree—its bare branches just begin to sprout leaves—next to her so she could cradle a branch in her hand.

"It's only the line of your arm and upstretched face that I need. I can draw in a peach branch later."

She posed in the sweatshirt she had worn on the beach that morning. As the light softened, Jake decided he wanted to catch the pink tones slanting from the left playing on her bare shoulders.

He pointed to the bathroom. "Would you go and take off your shirt? Wrap it around so I can see the skin and curve of your shoulders."

Baroque music played melodically in the background and the phone was unplugged to stop its incessant ringing. Jake seldom spoke as he sketched. Roxy spent the hours wondering why he was attentive and charming but essentially treated her like a little sister. Deciding faint hearts never won any prizes, she deliberately stripped off her shirt and slowly wrapped it around her, the tied sleeves barely hiding her full breasts.

Pleasure, appreciation, recognition of her attempt to reach him all registered in his expression but no lust, no fire. He walked over, his face and body neutral, and asked her to turn slightly to the right.

"Don't worry about the branch, I'm only interested in capturing the light as it falls against your skin."

When he touched her shoulder to move it to the angle he sought, Roxy could practically see sparks arc from his finger. His lips parted slightly and she thought a brief flash of desire danced across his face. Then he turned, satisfied with her pose, and began to sketch again.

A STAR IS BORN

They ate white pizza from At My Uncles, one of their favorite South County eateries, as they watched the news and a repeat of Jake's commercial. The music, wine, and soft nest of pillow she nestled into on the large platform he used as a couch conspired to lull her into a barely conscious state. She must have dozed off and woke to find him sketching her.

"You looked so innocent and peaceful. It was an angel face I had to capture," he said smiling.

Enough of this teasing, thought Roxy. She had been having an erotic dream and felt aroused. She was ready to confront Jake with his…what? His restraint, his gentlemanly behavior? What could she say that would not sound stupid, and leave her open for total rejection?

Reclining against the pile of pillows, Roxy tried to look as voluptuous and alluring as her just-scrubbed looks allowed. She wrapped a few long strands of blonde hair around her fingers. "Don't you find me attractive?" she asked in a kittenish voice.

He smiled engagingly and took her hand.

"You are Aphrodite come to life and I am most pleased you have chosen to take abode in my lair."

"So why haven't you done anything about it?" She pouted, vaguely waving her hand over her body.

"In time. In time."

Roxy sat up and faced him. "Whose time?"

"I guess mine," he said as his face and voice grew serious. He sat and reached for both her hands.

"You have a very special gift, Roxy. Most women want a man but not the sex; so many of them seem to want to bring themselves off. But you appreciate that energy in a man, you recognize the phallus as the most direct route to link souls. Sexual energy is very strong in you, and very pure."

"So tell me something I don't know, like why it doesn't move you?"

Jake ignored the second part of her question answering only the first.

"Sexual energy can be trained, controlled, but most importantly, enhanced. You have the talent to play like a master. Are you interested in learning?"

"Would we learn together?"

"I've learned, now I'm practicing."

This was sounding too much like one of the obscure conversations Max and Kat had that she never understood. She wanted a straight answer.

"Does this mean we'd have sex together?"

"It certainly does."

Well, this was more like it, she thought, as she leaned closer.

"Can we start now?"

"There are some things we can start now, but no intercourse for another three weeks."

"Three weeks. Why? I know what to do. There can't be that much for me to learn."

Jake laughed. "I'm sure you're right. There's probably as much for me to learn from you. It has to do with rhythm. There's a rhythm to this work and the time won't be ripe for consummation until the full moon."

Roxy groaned. Not another person who plotted their life by the stars or some other calculator of time that did not map out on a seven day a week, twelve month a year calendar.

"It'll be worth the wait," he said with assurance.

Shrugging her shoulders, Roxy sank back into her nest of pillows.

"So what do we do until then?"

"We'll do things to you. I practice a type of sexual discipline known as White Tiger/Green Dragon yoga, and I'm in a period of willed abstinence, not just from ejaculation but from any arousal of sexual energy. I considered yielding to your very desirable charms," he reached over and ran his hand lightly along the inside of her thigh, "but decided I wanted to teach you the practice and it would be more propitious to wait. There are sexual practices we can explore in the meantime that will teach you some basic principles."

"Then it's OK for my sexual energy to be aroused?"

"Absolutely! Aroused and released. I want to save my initial orgasm for our first intercourse but there's no need for you to wait. We can spend the next couple of weeks building your sexual prana, although it seems to be close to peak naturally."

She had heard of tantric yoga but considered it a weird practice invented by a couple of Indian gurus to attract and hold followers. Once or twice in the early '70s guys had used it as a line to get her into bed. Since Jake needed no line to get her clothes off, and since he was delaying not hastening his gratification, she assumed he was serious. The thought of a man devoting himself to her sexual gratification exclusive of his own was an original experience. She melted into the pillow, legs falling open, arms loose by her side, eyes clouded. She was ready to begin.

Jake explained that tantric yoga considered sex a sacrament as he slipped off her sweatpants and shirt and began massaging her foot.

"With practice, sexual ecstasy can be extended for an hour or more."

Roxy peered at him under her lashes. Now that was worth practicing for, she thought.

"All the ancient mystery religions ritualized sexual union. In Greece it was Aphrodite who reigned over the magic of sex, the bliss that comes from joining male and female. There is great power in this union of opposites, power that is blatantly degraded and misused in our society where sex is treated like one more commodity to be exploited. All the unhealthy taboos come from misunderstanding and fearing the sexual power because the possessor is too weak to control and channel it. There is little doubt that sexual union with the right partner at the right time with the right state of mind can open the way to new dimensions."

Roxy recognized truth for her in what he said. Comforting warmth spread in ripples from his hand as he kneaded and rubbed her foot.

Pulling on each of the toes in succession, Jake continued his lecture.

"D.H. Lawrence embodied many of the principles of tantra in his writing. He urged a proper reverence for sex, a proper awe of the body's unique and marvelous experience. It wasn't sex that was a problem, it was the attitude that treated it as lightly as downing a cocktail. Lawrence believed that higher emotions could not be reached until extravagant sensuality burned away the body's dross. His words are poetry: 'shame and fear chased away by sensual fire.'"

Jake stopped for a minute and removed his hands. The pulsing stopped. Roxy leaned up to look at him as he spoke earnestly.

"A woman finds the fire outside herself, from a man. For a man, the fire is within, lit by a woman."

She felt the poles of her cells swim towards his magnetic pull. As he massaged her other foot, Jake's tone became almost scholarly.

"For the next few weeks, we'll practice treasuring every aspect of sexual activity from the touch and smells to the sounds and tastes. Each contributes to the ultimate flavor of the union. Once you learn this with sex, you can apply the enhanced sensory awareness to all aspects of your life."

Moving along her legs, he spoke about the breath and how learning control over the breath gave a person control over all her energies.

When he finally reached her sex, Jake began to speak of dangers.

"There is great power stored in the secret knowledge of sex—the power to attract or repel. Nothing can be denied a person who masters it."

He slid his hand under her hips, brushing his thumb along the outside of her panties, their crotch already soaked through, sending shock waves through her body. He leaned her over on her side, arranging the pillows to steady her in place. Telling her about the primal energy, the prana or kundalini that was aroused through sexual excitation and stored in the spine, he began stroking the curve of her tailbone.

"It's from this base that it all begins, the first chakra."

Roxy was absorbed in the glowing orange petals that spread under his hand and the buzzing she felt vibrate at the base of her spine.

"The serpent of sexual energy lies coiled here when at rest; aroused, it moves up through the other chakras until it bursts through the top of the head seeking completion in the cosmic. This happens unless there are blockages in the passage, an epidemic condition in modern life."

She only vaguely heard his descriptions of the other chakras as he moved his hands, front and back, up the centerline of her body. The colors and shapes that formed beneath his hands changed and the pulse of the column of light as it ascended towards her head increased.

"I want you to hold onto this energy as long as you can," she heard him say through the pounding in her ears. "When you can't hold on any longer, let me know."

His hand moved between her breasts, and Roxy heard the pure tones of a flute harmonizing with a drumming that surrounded her inside and out. Everything felt green and then a red flame began to lick at her neck.

As he stroked the soft hollow at the base of her throat, Roxy heard moans and whimpers that she realized were hers. And then she felt a consuming rush of molten fire and knew she could hang on no longer.

"Now. Please," she whispered.

He slipped his fingers under the wet silk of her panties and she sobbed as a jet of flame leapt from them and tore up her body, exploding from the crown of her head. He held his fingers in place as her body arced and tensed with the force driving through her. He placed his other hand on the top of her head and closed the circuit.

"Let it whirl around and through you, spinning around and around from the base to the crown. Don't hold back."

She could see his words streaming neon trails as they whirled around and around before her eyes. And then there was nothing but sound roaring through her soul. When the sounds became lightly tinkling bells, Roxy opened her eyes. She felt refreshed and invigorated as if she had slept for hours. But the sky was still a deep blue behind Jake's head so she knew the time had been short. He was sitting in a chair pulled up alongside the platform, his feet up on the pillows, watching her.

"I'm a fortunate teacher to have such a student," he said with admiration.

★ ★ ★ ★ ★

Roxy was in a daze the next morning. The beach was so fogged in she was confused about whether she had actually walked there or just dreamt it. The dull roaring of the waves merely echoed the internal roaring left from the previous day.

She was not much more coherent upon reaching campaign headquarters. It took her several minutes of phone conversation, instinctively reacting to the sexual tones in the male caller's voice, before she realized it was Hayes. Her immediate surprise to discover her heightened sensual response was not tuned exclusively to Jake dissolved when she considered that Hayes did have a sort of prior claim. Finding the earpiece back on its receiver, Roxy could not recall a single word of their conversation. She had better clear her head before the meeting with Carrie.

She escaped to the funny little park under the archway entrance to Federal Hill. She liked the symmetry: the arch in Narragansett, the arch on Federal Hill. There were often clusters of young people all in white sitting on the benches or standing around the paths. Today it was empty and there was nothing but dull gray outlines as Roxy looked across the highway towards downtown. She stood staring blankly at the bust of Garabaldi, heralded as a soldier of humanity and creator of modern Italy. Pull yourself together, she scolded. There's work to be done, time enough for play later. As she walked back along the restaurants and storefronts of Atwells, she rehearsed the questions she planned to throw at Carrie.

They met in Mario's office at the back of the first floor; neither wanted Carrie anywhere near Kat's private space upstairs. As she sat looking at the blank stare pasted on Carrie's blotchy face, Roxy remembered Max's warning that she was some sort of witch. She wondered if Carrie could read minds and blushed as she flashed back to her encounter with Hayes in a deserted corner of the Rayburn garage. Her stomach tightened as a twisted smile moved across Carrie's lips and she turned to Roxy with raised eyebrows.

The interview was useless. Carrie listened while Mario cited her lies and Max's warnings then concluded that her close liaison with Scarlatti brought corrupt energy too close to Kat. Roxy had convinced Mario it was to their advantage to say nothing about discovering her weird rhymes and spells in the computer. Carrie refused to respond and seemed resigned to being dismissed although she insisted neither Roxy nor Mario had the authority to do it.

"I'm a congressional employee. I want Kat to fire me."

"That will never happen," said Mario. "As your official supervisor, Hayes is more than willing to fly up and do the honors."

Roxy flinched. She did not want Hayes in Rhode Island. Not now.

Carrie shrugged unconcerned. "Have it your own way. He can send me a letter or tell me on the phone. I've got the message."

Impatient to resolve the issue of Carrie's lies about Kat, Roxy hurled her questions. "How could you tell people that Kat was having an affair with Senator Stuart? You know that isn't true. "

Carrie stared at her for what seemed like forever, before she agreed in a toneless voice, "I know it's not true."

"Then why did you say it?" Roxy was leaning out of her chair, her voice raised.

Once again, Carrie simply shrugged then stood up. "If you two are finished, I'm going back to the office and pack up my stuff. I'll stay and help you find and train a replacement if you want."

Mario quickly declined her offer, promised to send her severance pay the following week, and practically pushed her into the hall.

Before the door closed behind her, he was on the phone to a locksmith ordering the locks changed at both the congressional and campaign offices. Then he spoke with the Hose and asked him to watch Carrie.

"I don't think we've seen the last of her," he warned. Finishing his report to Hayes about their meeting, Mario waved Roxy over to the fax machine that was spitting out several pages of a news article.

"Hayes says there's a brutally frank article in the *Washington Post* about Winston's inaction on several key issues. It includes broad hints about careless drug testing in his manufacturing plants and cover-ups. He claims Jasmine was taken by surprise and wants to make certain no one here knew anything about it, or talked to the reporter. Supposedly the source is someone on the staff of the next senior senator on the Finance committee who would stand to be promoted to chairman if Winston was defeated."

They were reading the article with pleased smiles when Kat walked in. Roxy automatically handed her the pages she had finished while Mario explained what they knew of its source. Kat's face darkened and her brows closed in on the bridge of her nose as she read the slashing attack.

"They all but call him lazy, self-serving and hypocritical, rating him as one of the Senate's least productive members." She sounded outraged. "Are you sure we had nothing to do with this? No one at Senatorial decided to score a few points on their own?"

"I only know what Hayes told me but it makes sense. Senator Cushing has almost as much to gain from Winston's defeat as you do."

"Unless the Republicans win the Senate," she said, returning to reading the article. Suddenly she exploded. "I can't believe it! His mark is all over this."

Roxy quickly looked over to see what set Kat off. It was an allegation that Winston's company knew from their market research that eighty-three percent of the users of their new tranquilizer were women, yet they tested the drug solely on men.

"Whose mark?" Roxy asked startled.

"Stuart's! What could he be thinking? I'm committed to a positive campaign and he's out leaking moronic stories like this."

Agitated, Kat began pacing across the small room.

"All the committee staff adore him. He probably pumped up one of Cushing's people to leak this trash figuring no one would trace it to him."

"How do you know it was him?"

"He told me he uncovered this statistic about the testing last week."

Mario was unconcerned. "Even if Stuart did set this up, I'm sure he was careful about anyone tracing it to him."

"Not careful enough. I know."

"You don't count. He did it for you and probably figured you'd be grateful. This is invaluable. We've been wanting to say this stuff but can't risk it. Now it's here in black and white, and in the *Washington Post* no less." Mario could not hide his glee.

"You're as bad as he is," Kat exclaimed. "It must be the testosterone.

"Don't kid yourself that this is some sort of gift-wrapped treat for me. T.J. Stuart lusts after a Republican Senate. I'm simply one of the tricks he has to win." She picked up the phone and quickly dialed.

"Is he in? This is Congresswoman Tomasso." Kat's scowl deepened. "Will you ask him to call me as soon as possible? I'll be in Rhode Island all weekend."

Roxy heard a noise outside the door and walked to the window in time to see Carrie slipping through the alley. She must have been lurking outside and heard the whole conversation about Stuart. Before she could collect herself enough to tell the others, Kat was gathering up her papers and telling Mario that she was heading to Boston immediately.

"My speech is at eight tomorrow morning and I'm not ready to get up at dawn and drive to Boston." She waved away Roxy's offer before she could make it. "And I don't want anyone else getting up to drive me there. Call my friend Linda, tell her I'll be there in an hour and want to take her someplace for dinner. Give Stuart her number if he calls. Tongue lashing him will improve my disposition tremendously. Don't wait up, Roxy. I'll see you Sunday morning."

They stood, mouths open, as Kat blew out of the room.

★ ★ ★ ★ ★

The time to tell Kat about Carrie's eavesdropping never came. When Roxy returned from the beach early Sunday, planning to wash her hair before Jake arrived to take her to the Charlestown flea market, Kat was sitting in the bamboo room waiting for her.

"Do you have any lightweight clothes here?" she asked as Roxy walked in.

"I brought everything I thought I'd need between now and November" she replied, wondering what was behind the question.

"Good. Get packed. Tomorrow morning you'll take the early plane to Washington and from there fly to Key West. Max will meet up with you. You can stay with your friends Tweedle and Dee. They just had a baby, didn't they?" Roxy nodded agreement dumbly. "You'll like the chance to see them I'm sure."

"Why am I going to Key West?"

"My dear ex-husband Jamie called. He claims he has information about Winston he can tell only me. I haven't seen the creep since I divorced him twenty years ago and I don't want to see him now. Duke exiled him from the country but Jamie decided it was safe to sneak back when he died. He's been living in Key West for the past four years. I don't mind, it's easier to keep tabs on him there."

"Any idea what he knows?"

"None." Kat walked over and looked at her. "You're the only one I trust completely. Jamie loathes Max and would never talk to him. I need you to do this for me, Roxy."

"Turn down a chance for a free vacation in Key West in late March—do I look crazy to you?" She made light of the request. "I assume this is a free trip."

Kat smiled tightly. "Oh yes. Senator Stuart will fly you down and back. And Roxy, other than Max and Stuart, no one is to know where you're going—or why."

8

Wheel of Fortune
March

Key West
Washington

Senator Stuart's aide Rosa met Roxy at National Airport. She was, as Kat had described, petite with long dark hair and luminous black eyes, efficient and friendly. As they drove across the Potomac River and west along the Expressway heading towards Upper Marlboro, she explained that she was accompanying them to Key West. Her husband had been held for nearly a decade in a Havana prison and there was reason to believe Stuart's incessant pressure for his release would soon be successful.

Passing the exit to Andrews Air Force Base, Roxy asked where they were going.

"Senator Stuart keeps his plane on a grass strip owned by a longtime friend. He built a rough hangar, maintains the strip, and keeps fuel in tanks there. It's outside controlled air space for Washington so the senator can come and go as he pleases without notifying anyone." Rosa smiled as she relayed this last to Roxy. Apparently Stuart's rough and ready style evoked amusement and tolerance in his staff rather than despair over their inability to direct him.

They turned at an expanse of white wooden fencing around Travaille, a former tobacco farm in southeastern Prince George's County. A burnished brass plaque announced the brick colonial mansion was built in 1780. Rosa followed a dirt road behind the tobacco barn and parked near a beat-up blue Ford truck with Virginia tags, an empty gun rack in the back window, and a 101st Congress sticker on its front bumper. Senator Stuart looked up from the raised cowling of a tied-down plane.

The plane was small, a twin engine Piper Aztec with red nose and tail markings. Kat had explained that Stuart began flying when he was sixteen and brought to it the same precise attention and devotion to excellence that he did to everything. Her reassuring words faded when Roxy was confronted with the reality of a machine that looked far too fragile to fly the three of them more than a thousand miles down the East Coast, and the absence of a crew of mechanics and flight attendants to check every detail. She had never flown in anything but large commercial jets.

Roxy picked up her bags and followed Rosa over to join Stuart at the plane. He closed the cowling and greeted the two women—Rosa with a kiss on the cheek, Roxy with a wave.

"It'll be another minute or two while I top off the gas tanks and clean the windshield."

He untied the ropes that held the plane in place, loaded the luggage, and helped Roxy up the two steps onto the wing.

"Don't step off the black area," he warned, gesturing her to sit in the second row of seats.

Stuart scrambled in next, sliding into the pilot's chair while Rosa came last and climbed into the front passenger seat. The door remained open, a light breeze blowing through, as he made a final check of the instrument panel, radios, charts, and notes on little yellow stick-ums along the plane's dash. As the propellers roared into motion, spinning invisibly on each wing, Rosa closed and locked the door in place.

Bumping along the narrow grass strip, Roxy wished she had forced Kat to check the cards for her before going on this trip. She did not want that Death card to be hers. She was surprised by the powerful surge of lift-off as the small plane climbed over a stand of trees immovable along the south end of the runway. There was a decidedly sexual flavor to the driving thrust of the engines and the resulting push on her body. After her instinctive reaction away from the force, she thought about Jake's admonition that she devote the next three weeks to fully experiencing all aspects of sensation. She threw herself into the climb, letting the erotic energy charge up from her toes through her loins and into her head, sweeping her breath before it.

After several minutes heading west, they flew south along the edge of the Blue Ridge; too far south to see Morgan Springs, Stuart explained when Roxy asked. At sixty-five hundred feet in the early morning light, the mountains looked otherworldly—they could be on the planetoid Ceres or Asta—sharp and blue with lakes of silvery mist filling the valleys. There was scarcely a hint of the towns, cities and growing rural areas they sheltered. The interstate, with its traffic like toy cars on a programmed track, was once the Great Road cut through the Shenandoah Valley in the mid-18th century, running along the eastern slope of the variously named but geologically related foothills of the ancient Appalachians.

Stuart flew, keeping a watch on charts and instruments, calculating ground speed, adjusting direction. He spoke in Spanish to Rosa who sat making notes and asking questions. Occasionally he would describe their location, or a technical aspect of the flight in English, addressing his remarks to both women. The

sky was incredibly clear with miles of visibility. Roxy wondered how topograph-
ical maps were able to mimic the rolling reality of the planet's surface before
mapmakers had airplanes?

About an hour out, they flew over rugged mountains so sharp it looked as if
no more than a single row of evergreens defined the peak. Directly below was a
huge lake spread like a big puddle west from the mountains where a large dam
blocked the river. A fringed shoreline created miles of waterfront property. Stuart identified it as Smith Mountain Lake with Roanoke the city to the west.

"Will we fly over your place?" Roxy asked.

"The springs and bottling plant are too far into the mountains for us to see,
and my house in Roanoke is indistinguishable from the rest of the neighborhood. But we did fly over my father's family place, now below twenty feet of
Smith Mountain Lake water."

Roxy was curious about the bitterness in his voice but she was too intimidated by the senator to question him further.

She remembered reading about Stuart's background in the Congressional
Directory. He built a family spring water business into a world class competitor
for the bottled water market which expanded dramatically during the late '70s
and '80s. From this background he moved into politics, becoming an indispensable aide to Virginia's legendary senator, Curtis Lee. An old man, Lee's health
began failing. When he died less than a year before his term expired, Stuart was
named to caretake the seat. Although the Directory did not say this, Roxy assumed Stuart's unusual ascent was engineered by his powerful father-in-law.

Stuart decided to run for the senate seat. He stunned the opposition with
his well-organized campaign and charismatic style, sweeping into office on the
conservative flood unleashed by Ronald Reagan. He began making his mark as a
genuine conservative with little tolerance for those politically motivated charla-
tans who used conservatism as a cover for imposing their own rigid and narrow
social standards and petty hatreds. His re-election six years later was easy. Roxy
wondered, as she had when reading the biography, what possessed Stuart to help
Kat's campaign.

There was no more commentary on the flight until Stuart pointed out the
swamps that stretched south from Savannah along the Georgia coast. Light illuminated the maze of rivers and streams that traced calligraphied patterns of
silver across a hazy, dark gray-blue background of land.

Roxy dozed as they flew over the seemingly unbroken green carpet covering
northern Florida. When she awoke and looked out the window, they were along
the western coast of the state; blurred green and brown patterns of underwater
reefs showed through iridescent blue water. There were hundreds of small islands, beaches linked together in a white chain by bridges. Roadways seemed
to float in the ocean, fingers of water intruded into the coastline. Further south,
they flew over a vast area of undeveloped subdivisions with beige roads ending

in circles carved out of the green brush. There were no houses, only dreams of future growth that Kat often argued would surely push Florida's already fragile ecology over the edge to disaster.

The bottom of the peninsula was empty. The timeless green maze of the Everglades was cut into graceful shapes by winding rivers. It looked like a puzzle waiting for the gods to reach down and assemble it, locking each piece into place. Even this irreplaceable treasure was being eroded by the drive of development.

They flew over open water then saw the barest tracing of dark green strung east and west across the horizon, out in the middle of the gulf, out of sight of the mainland—the Keys. Beneath them, the panorama was surreal. There were brownish-green patches dotted with houses, encircled in white beaches, cut by strips of roads. The ever-present water was also green with brown swirls like the land where the bottom was close to the surface. There were channels where the green was clearer, and dotted with the dark spots of underwater islands—millions of them. It was disorienting how, in looking along the horizon, the color of the water blended with the color of the sky. A single glance couldn't discern which was which.

Roxy thought it was incredible that people found their way out there to live, and somehow managed to build the remarkable roadway she saw below which bonded the outstretched islands into a single drive.

As they approached Key West, Stuart concentrated on the radio. Traffic was heavy with military aircraft and sightseers. A red bi-plane flew beneath them as they made their approach, trailing a streamer announcing an upcoming concert. Posh hotels stretched along private strips of beach were dotted with umbrellas. A new shopping center was under construction along the northern shore. Unimpressive by commercial standards, Key West International Airport wore a typically tropical look with a single wide runway, about forty small planes, hangars, and a white stucco main terminal marked in both English and Spanish.

Stuart sent her with Rosa to wait in the terminal's Conch Flyer Bar while he dragged the plane with a long orange handle as if it were a giant toy, and tied it down to bolts in the macadam.

As they sat in big wicker chairs at a polished wood table, Roxy wondered if there was enough time to try some of the conch specials advertised behind the bar. She spotted Max at the same time Rosa waved to two swarthy men in open-neck shirts who stood in the doorway. They were completing a confused round of name exchanges when Stuart appeared, the two Latins greeting him effusively. Max rolled a single silver dollar across his knuckles as he examined the senator. Roxy introduced them and they nodded at each other with almost equal intensity and control.

Stuart said a few words in Spanish and the men left with Rosa. He waved Max and Roxy to sit down.

"My arrangement with Kiley was to meet you back here tomorrow afternoon at five. I need to be in Washington the following day. I'll be unreachable until then should plans change but here's a number where you can call Rosa. Should you not be here, I'll contact her."

Max nodded agreement and handed Stuart a card he plucked from the air.

"We can be reached here." Stuart smiled as he took the card.

"I understand why you're here," he said to Roxy. "Should you need my help, we can delay our schedule for a few hours."

Roxy shivered slightly; this was the first he had mentioned what she was doing flying around Florida. Kat told her to trust him. Roxy wondered what Stuart did know.

★ ★ ★ ★ ★

It was almost three, the time Jamie had set for the meeting. Max and Roxy headed to the Half Shell Saloon, a local hangout on the water in Land's End Village near the turtle kraals. The rough and ready look, with its picnic tables, hundreds of license plates from all over nailed among the beams, conch specialties and raw bar made it a magnet for tourists at night. At mid-afternoon it was deserted, only a meaty bartender shucking bivalves behind the bar. Max motioned for him to bring two beers as they sat at a table to wait.

"Why do you think Jamie picked this place to meet?" Roxy asked.

"It's a favorite among importers of his type." Max paused and looked at her knowingly. "With all these deep sea fishing boats coming in and out, it's an easy matter to slip in illicit cargo. A popular tourist bar makes a good cover for meetings with out-of-town distributors and it'll be jumping with college kids now that it's spring break. Lots of potential for recruiting there. Jamie may even own a piece of this place. I know he's involved in several bars in town."

Soon after they sat down, there was a shift change and the evening bartender arrived. Max looked surprised then smiled and waved. The large man came over and joined them while the daytime bartender closed out. Max introduced him as Wally, Tweedle and Dee's next door neighbor.

"Hope the smoke wasn't too bad last night," Wally said in a voice far too puny for his well-muscled body.

Max brushed off any concern and the two explained to Roxy about Wally's procedure for smoking fish. It had such exceptional flavor that the bar bought all he could make. He would bring tributes of the smoked fish regularly to his neighbors to compensate for the smoke.

He soaked whatever the daily catch was overnight in brine salt, garlic, vinegar and lemon juice. Then he placed the slabs of fish on racks in a gutted refrigerator on the back porch. His secret mixture of tropical woods smoldered in a giant cast-iron skillet atop a propane burner under the appliance, smoke filling the closed refrigerator through a hole cut in the bottom and escaping through a vent in the top.

"It's so good, just the smoke makes my mouth water," Max testified.

"Dolph's are running. You'll have some for dinner tomorrow," Wally promised as he made his way back to the bar to take up his station.

"The boys have a real find in Wally," Max explained. "Not only is he an honest bartender, and produces magnificent smoked fish, but he knows how to officially forget anything he hears or sees in the bar. It's a skill that keeps him alive."

Jamie was already fifteen minutes late. They ordered a large bowl of steamed shrimp; "Key West Pinks," Max called them. The shrimp were a nocturnal catch with a long season from November to July.

"Shrimp make up almost half the value of the fishing industry and probably a lot more from some fishermen's related nighttime activities," Max explained.

Wally brought a message along with their shrimp.

"I was told," he began, turning towards Roxy, "to tell blondie to come alone. Tomorrow, same time, same place. And tell her to wear something tight."

The big man blushed as he finished the message and went quickly back to the bar.

"Ah, Jamie. Always one to turn an elegant phrase." Max spoke sarcastically as Roxy shuddered and looked around the open room trying to peer onto the outside deck.

"He must be watching us," she said with a tremor. "Why doesn't he want you here?"

"Don't you know how Kat and I met?" Max asked, leaning his arms on the table.

"She's made references over the years to you rescuing her, and being her first teacher, but no details about how it came to be. By the time I met you both, you were together. I always assumed you knew each other from Rhode Island."

Max chuckled.

"My summers in Newport were not spent in the social circles which Kat's mother found appropriate for her daughter. I mostly worked fishing boats or in bars. I knew Jamie long before I met Kat, mostly by reputation."

Max talked about his years studying theater and Jamie's experimental film-making.

"I went to audition once in a small frame house near the Brown campus. It didn't take long for me to discover his films were more pornography than experimental art. I stayed to meet him. I saw a demon in his eyes and left. I was shocked a couple of years later when I read that he had married Kat. I heard he was still doing filming. It was easy to assume that she knew, and participated."

Roxy looked shocked. "How could you ever think that about Kat?"

"I'd never met her. It wasn't hard to believe that her public image was not the whole story. The black master bedroom dates from that period. It was Jamie's idea of the perfect bridal bower."

No wonder it felt like sex in there, Roxy thought.

"Kat went back to Cornell in the fall for graduate work and Jamie decided to go along. He told everyone that the spectacular natural beauty of the gorges and lake, the Gothic splendor of the turn-of-the-century mansions that dotted the campus, and the campus architecture itself, would inspire his films."

Max talked about his rock band playing at a Cornell fraternity and hanging out for a couple days. They went to a screening of some footage that had been shot the previous weekend at a supposedly spontaneous drunken orgy. Jamie was the filmmaker and relocation from the shores of Narragansett Bay to the shores of Cayuga Lake had not altered the genre.

"We were walking down curved stone stairs into what looked like a dungeon in a fraternity house overlooking the lake that had once been Ezra Cornell's 18th century mansion when Kat came blindly racing up them, knocking us against the wall. Her face was twisted in agony. I followed her into a dead end corridor. She stood absolutely still and looked at me, her eyes flipping from bleeding betrayal to raging madness."

An expression of wonder and tenderness replaced Max's usual look of radiant will and self control.

"I've never felt so strongly that I belonged in a point of time and space as at that moment when I faced this magnificent woman obviously distraught beyond tolerance. I stretched out my hands and said 'I'm here to help you.' Her eyes were almost serene except for a single point of madness. Her body was as tense as a twisted rope. Taking my hands she cried desperately, 'get me out of here.' I did, and it was nearly ten years before I felt it was safe to leave."

Max waved Wally over.

"Let's have something more to eat while we're here, then we can go down to sunset. I haven't been there in weeks and may even decide to perform. Tweedle and Dee won't be back from Miami until after dark."

They quickly ordered more shrimp and beer, and some conch chowder.

"What happened to upset Kat that night?" Roxy asked.

"Apparently Jamie's mother had been seriously injured in a car accident and Kat had come to tell him. When she opened the door to the room where they were watching the films, she was able to see several scenes before anyone noticed her. She recognized Jamie's apartment in Newport and two of the women who were engaged in rather perverse sexual activity on the screen. Then she saw Jamie, watching the film, enthroned in an antique bishop's chair with a nubile co-ed diligently sucking him off.

"I wasn't surprised to discover that she never had any idea of the types of films he made. People had hinted at his bizarre tastes but she never believed them. Jamie always showed her films that were weird and avant-garde but never sexual. To this day, I wonder why no one ever told Duke. He would have never let her marry Jamie."

Roxy urged him to continue the story.

"Seeing the films that night, she knew the accusations were true. Within hours, she had lawyers drawing up divorce papers and sworn not to tell her father until she could return to Rhode Island. We went to an all-night hardware store, bought two locks and mounted them on the door of their apartment. Then she pointed me to a couch in her study and spent the night in a chair facing the door, a loaded pistol in her hand."

Pausing for a moment, Max grinned at the memory.

"It was an old Ruger Blackhawk .44 magnum. Who knows where she got it or whether she knew it would blow a hole in Jamie big enough to drive a car through? Fortunately, he never showed up. We moved his few possessions out of the apartment the next day and locked them in a small trailer Kat rented and parked out front. She placed a note on the door telling him where the key to the trailer was, locked the new locks, and we set off for Rhode Island. I don't think she ever saw Jamie again. They had lived together as man and wife for all of four months.

"By spring the civil divorce was final, Duke had exiled Jamie from the U.S., and was greasing blessed palms to get an annulment from the Catholic Church. That's when we met you." Their food arrived as Max finished the story.

★ ★ ★ ★ ★

Key West was a banana republic strung out on the southernmost tip of the United States. They walked with mostly young tourists along the shop and bar-lined streets towards Mallory Square where hundreds of people gathered on the narrow pier outlining the harbor shore. Sunset watching had been a spectator sport in Key West as long as anyone could remember. It became ritualized in the late '60s. Sunset time was now posted prominently each day on chalk boards and wax penciled signs all over town.

Surveying the sleazy characters set up to work the sunset celebration, Max decided he would not perform. Instead, they wandered among the crowds. Vendors lined the side of the pier away from the water hawking exotically painted teeshirts, jewelry, art, and fruit smoothies. Palmists, fortune tellers, and card readers were set up in every nook and cranny selling their vision of the future. Performers worked in designated, staked out turf, with their backs to the harbor and the tour ships anchored there. Max chatted with a few of the old timers, casually asking a man playing bag pipes and one swallowing swords about Jamie. No one had anything new to report.

WHEEL OF FORTUNE

Improbable colors streaked the western sky as the glowing red-orange disk of the sun quickly plunged into the gulf. The colors matched the garish tie-dyed clothing designed and sold by several artists on the pier, an amusing replay of the '60s that suited Key West-end of the line paradise for many of that generation. Roxy caught herself waiting for the inevitable hiss as the fireball sank. All she heard was the incessant snapping of camera shutters, then cheers and applause from the audience as the sun vanished from sight. Fully-rigged sailboats moved, silhouetted against the color-drenched horizon, a distinct and recurring part of the daily sunset celebration.

Sitting along the pier, waiting for the crowds to thin out, Max told Roxy about a recent confrontation with Jamie in Key West.

"Now he has a personal reason to hate me."

Max's story began with his unsuccessful run for Mayor of Key West about a decade ago. "I lost the election, of course, but gained a network of conch-hippies—long time escapees to Key West with a smattering of natives. I know everything that happens."

When Duke died, Jamie decided his exile was over and moved to Key West. Kat chose to ignore his return, trusting that Max could keep tabs on him. Jamie became a coke dealer who made the common mistake of indulging in his product. He degenerated quickly

"About six months ago, one of my friends from high school called to ask my help in rescuing his teenage daughter from Jamie's clutches," Max said. "Without bogging down in sordid details, the upshot is we succeeded—an outcome that did nothing to endear me to Kat's ex-husband."

Walking to Tweedle and Dee's house along a side street near Duval, main artery of Key West nightlife, Roxy lost herself in the intoxicating perfume of a tropical spring night. The overpowering scent of pink and white flowers on skeleton-like frangipani trees mingled with mildly narcotic night-blooming jasmine while gaudy trumpet flowers and closed-bud hibiscus glowed in the lamplight.

A huge sopadilla tree filled the side yard between Tweedle and Dee's house and the one next door where Wally lived. They passed beneath its spreading branches—ideal for tree houses—onto the downstairs porch of the 19th century Bahamas-style frame house. It was painted pink and, like most others in this old downtown neighborhood, had shuttered windows and unique drops and perks of gingerbread trim.

Once the initial excitement of seeing her old friends and meeting their new baby lulled, they all sat in the lush side yard. It was a botanical wonder filled with giant palms, papayas dangling their breast-shaped fruit, a Banyan tree with a deck built around it about ten feet from the ground, and a Woman's Tongue Tree with huge pods that rattled in the breeze blowing in from the west.

The evening passed quickly, bringing each other up to date, telling stories about the campaign and admiring Tweedle and Dee's son Samuel. They were performers too, describing themselves as vaudevillians to Max's magician.

By midnight several other performers dropped by and the gathering moved into the house. Roxy always loved hanging out with her friends who were musicians or performers where even the most casual of visits could burst into a full scale show. Tweedle had built a large island in the center of their expansive kitchen so jugglers, magicians, and prestidigitators could stand around and impress each other with their skills.

As Max pulled out his coins to demonstrate one of his most dramatic tricks, usually reserved for on-stage performances, Dee asked if he still used the Kat silver dollars.

"Of course," he answered, proceeding to fan five silver dollars in his hands sticking between his fingers. He smacked the hand against his chest, passed it behind his back then brought it around with the coins back in place between his fingers.

An aspiring juggler induced Max to teach him a new coin technique and Roxy asked Dee why she linked Kat with the silver dollars.

"There are two reasons really," she explained. "Max claims that the Liberty goddess portrayed on the coins is really Athena, Kat's personal icon, and that the portrayal even looks like Kat with all those curls."

"Max—toss over one of your coins so I can show Roxy her candidate's profile," Dee yelled. She jumped up to catch the three coins Max sent spinning over. Not liking the boys to feel they were the only ones with nimble fingers, Dee executed a masterful Buddha's Delight, palmed each coin in turn then picked them one by one from behind Roxy's right ear. She bowed to well-deserved applause.

All three coins were the same. Dated 1883, they possessed the genuine weightiness of silver undiluted by the baser metals used in contemporary silver dollars. "See, she does look like Kat, the same high-bridged profile and full lips. There are even stars around her head." Roxy turned the heavy coin over. There was an eagle, wings outspread, and In God We Trust inscribed over its head. The letters along the bottom curve spelling out one dollar were nearly rubbed away.

Dee continued her discourse on the coins.

"Using real silver is best in coin tricks because it doesn't clank as loud as the new mixtures do. That's important since most of the secret of coin manipulation is in silently and invisibly palming more than one. What Max can do with nine of these large and heavy coins is impressive, a testimony to the size and power of his hands."

"What's the second reason?" Roxy asked.

"Apparently Kat found the coins for Max, one by one over a period of about eight months while they were on the road. The first one she discovered in a small rock shop near Wall Drug in South Dakota. She planned to keep it for herself so she could practice the tricks Max was teaching her. The 1883 added up to a two numerologically and she believed it was symbolic of their partnership. When she found the second one—literally found it outside their van after they survived a hellacious lightening storm near some lake in Montana—she was sure it was the first coin's mate and she gave it to Max. The rest of their trip, she haunted every little shop and moldy back room she could find, searching to complete the set. She wanted ten for him, and planned to keep the first one for herself, as the connection."

"I've never seen Max use more than nine."

"Kat found only ten total. She was planning to give Max the one she wanted to keep when they ran across this Basque shepherd in the Nevada mountains. I can't remember exactly why they stopped to talk with him, or how they were able to communicate with someone who spoke a language unrelated to any others on earth, but they did. Something about being Atlanteans together in a past life. He noticed the missing pieces of Max's finger. He said he must be a great shaman to bear the sign of his mutilation so proudly. He kept saying 'nine, nine,' and pointing to the finger then to Max. Kat never gave him the tenth coin."

When Wally arrived, bearing the smoked dolphin as promised, Roxy realized how late it was. She was preparing to go to bed when Max called her over.

"I asked Wally if he would go into work a little early tomorrow so he can be there when Jamie comes. I'll feel more comfortable knowing Wally is watching."

Roxy agreed and Max arranged to come back for her early the next afternoon. He owned the house next door rented now to Wally, but it was a houseboat anchored in mangrove swamps along the eastern shore that he called home.

★ ★ ★ ★ ★

She was glad for Wally's solid and secure presence behind the bar as she waited for Jamie to appear. Max decided to meet Stuart at the airport and bring him back to the bar to get her, in case reinforcements were needed. Roxy wasn't sure it was a good idea to involve the senator so directly but Max was adamant so she stopped arguing.

Roxy spent the hour reading tourist information. She read about the giant sea turtles she could see sleepily stirring in the wood pens called kraals, hunted no more since they were legislated an endangered species. The Victorian heyday of Key West—when its cigars, sponges and fishing made it the wealthiest and largest city in Florida—was described in another little book which told her the pina colada had been invented there. It also described the continued presence of voodoo among descendants of original Cuban and Bahamian settlers.

Suddenly, she remembered Jamie's message that she should wear something tight. Looking at her outfit, she was irritated that he would think she had worn the skimpy linen shift over a knit tank top for him. He wouldn't know that she had been in such pain from yesterday's sunburn that she had worn as little clothing as was acceptable.

Wally nodded his head toward the door. A stooped, almost emaciated man, slunk in. He had dark hair to his shoulders, a lank mustache, and a sneer on his lips. Removing his dark glasses, he stood blinking, trying to adjust to the bar's dim interior. Roxy could not imagine how Kat had ever seen this man as anything but a twisted and corrupt soul.

Before she could recover from her initial shock at his appearance, he had reached the bar and was sliding his hand along the inside of her thigh as she straddled the stool.

"Delighted to feel you, my dear," he cackled, his other hand reaching for her breast.

Roxy felt like a cattle prod had been rammed up her spine. She pushed him away and jumped off the stool. As he leered at her, a glazed look on his dilated pupils, she remembered she could not escape without discovering what he had to tell Kat. She stood frozen, glaring at him.

Effortlessly, his stance and attitude shifted, and in a patrician Newport accent he ordered a bottle of champagne from Wally and invited her to sit down.

"We have important matters to discuss."

She sat at the table as far away from him as possible. She was shaken but determined not to leave until he gave her the information. He motioned Wally to open the champagne then waved him away and picked up the bottle himself. He poured her a glass while discoursing on the virtues of the grapes.

"It's not the same as drinking other alcohol or even other wines. The effervescence raises it to another level where it may intoxicate the soul." He raised his glass and ran his eyes across her body, frankly appraising.

"Kat sent me here to get the information you claimed to have, then I have to leave." Roxy tried to sound cold and detached while she quaked inside. At least Wally was watching from behind the bar and Max would arrive soon.

"As you wish," he smirked.

"You may know that my lovely ex-wife's honored opponent in this upcoming senate campaign in my home state, which I miss so grievously, is also my most beloved and devoted uncle."

Not devoted enough to insist you could stay in Rhode Island when Duke ran you out, she thought as he waxed eloquent on how close he was to Senator Winston.

"My mother was a Winston, hence my distinguished name—Jamie Winston Caldwell. Much of my idyllic childhood was spent in his home since his only child, Sonny, was but a few years younger than I. My cousin Sonny and I remained close through my filmmaking career when we often used his father's home as a movie set. Of course the esteemed senator was in Washington approving dangerous new drugs that his companies made. When your good friend—and I assume Kat would send only a very loyal friend for this task—ended my career and I was forced to retire to the Bahamas, I stayed in touch with my cousin. Together we started a new venture, importing rare substances into Newport."

Jamie smirked again and pulled a narrow silver tube from his pocket, sprinkling some white granules from it on the side of his hand. As he rubbed his hand under his nose snorting the substance, Roxy realized with a shock that it was cocaine. She looked quickly around the room but it was empty except for Wally, who saw nothing. When he proffered the tube to her, she had no idea what to do other than decline and urge him to continue.

"We've both profited enormously from our family business. Making money from dealing drugs runs in the family, you know." Jamie cackled, a chilling sound.

"I provided drugs for my cousin and women for my uncle. After the senator's wife, the saintly Maureen, died so tragically a few years ago, my uncle realized he would have to be discreet about satisfying his baser needs. He turned to me. I arranged private weekends in Atlantic City with accommodating young ladies. Both he and Sonny were recently infatuated with a former starlet of mine, a personal favorite named Roberta Duschamps.

"The dear girl is pliant, lovely, and a coke junkie. She likes it through needles." He suddenly moved to the chair next to Roxy and began to hoarsely whisper. "She liked having Sonny shoot her up on the inside of her thigh. Said it got to her pussy quicker. The senator, as far as I know, got only sex."

As Roxy sprang back from him in gross dismay, he began cackling again and his eyes turned glassy. She was terrified but willed herself to be strong. She moved to another seat once again facing Jamie.

"What does this have to do with Kat?"

A cunning look slid over his gaunt features.

"My sainted mother, who is all I have left in the world, is not well. I desperately want to return to see her before she," he dropped his voice and lowered his eyes, "passes on. And now with my uncle sick also—perhaps Kat could see her way clear to let me visit?"

A deal, he was offering her a deal, Roxy thought. All she could do was agree that she would pass on his request to Kat.

"That is, if the information you have is worth anything to her."

"Oh, I think she'll be impressed by its dramatic and transformative nature." He appeared satisfied with the superficial promise Roxy made.

"A top secret investigation of fraudulent tests on one of Winston's wonder drugs is about to report out exceedingly damaging findings. You may know this already. What no one knows is that I received an urgent distress call from my dear friend Roberta just a few days ago. She was hysterical. It seems she's being punished by a righteously indignant God for her venal and promiscuous lifestyle. She's tested HIV positive, as has the senator. Somehow Sonny's escaped, but he's certain it's inevitable."

Through her growing shock, Roxy heard the unbelievable tone of glee in his voice.

"Does this mean Senator Winston has……"

Jamie finished the sentence as Roxy hesitated, unable to say it. "AIDS. Yes my dear, delicate flower. The silver fox has AIDS. It's doubly ironic because his insurance company has been playing politics with AIDS research for years."

Roxy sat stupefied by the information.

"What's going to happen now?" she finally asked.

"Who knows? Who cares? My uncle is obsessive about never dishonoring the family name." He stretched his mouth into a shape Roxy vaguely recognized as a gruesome grin. "I thought Kat should know."

She looked at her watch. Max was due any minute.

"Who else knows about this?" she asked.

"No one, as far as I know. The doctor has been pledged to secrecy until the senator decides what to do."

The news conveyed, a lecherous look filled his eye and he once again slid over to a chair next to Roxy. Thinking about what else she needed to know, Roxy barely noticed him move until he slipped his hand under her shirt and tweaked her nipple.

"You have great tits babe. Why don't we go take some pictures? I could give you something worthwhile to wrap that luscious mouth around."

She jumped up. She had what she needed and did not have to tolerate this monster another second. She screamed exactly what she was thinking: "You're such a pig! How could Kat have ever married you?"

His face darkened with a strange mixture of hate, betrayal and sadness.

"Bloodlines. It was all bloodlines. Her mother wanted to purify the immigrant pollution in her daughter's veins; her father wanted a dynasty. Who knows what the lady herself wanted?"

His face twisted and his voice became cruel.

"My exquisite wife—or ex-wife, I should say—is not the pure and enlightened being you all worship. She's a cunt with a mouth just like all other women." He almost spit the word—women. "Trust me, she knows how to use them both, thanks to my excellent tutelage. I'd be happy to do the same for you."

Disgusted, Roxy stumbled away from the table and towards the door just as Wally came from around the bar to keep Jamie from following her. Everything suddenly quieted. Max appeared in the doorway, Stuart right behind him.

Jamie began screaming as Wally dragged him into a back room.

"Ask your magician friend about Kat's talents. He's the one who benefited from all the tricks I taught her. He's the one whose cock she revered, the ungrateful slut!"

Roxy shuddered as she saw Max's face turn into the mask of someone ready to murder in cold blood. Then she noticed Stuart, dressed as if he had just returned from a week in some tropical jungle, start to pull a huge machete from his belt, his eyes fixed on Jamie. She had to do something to get them both out.

Roxy began sobbing hysterically, grabbed Max's arm and dragged him out the door, snagging Stuart with her free hand as they moved by him. From the corner of her eye, she saw Wally push Jamie into a back room and close the door.

★ ★ ★ ★ ★

They quickly drove the few blocks to Tweedle and Dee's where Roxy leapt out to collect her packed bags. When she returned, the men were leaning against the car. Max was spinning three coins across his knuckles, Stuart carefully running a sharpening stone in long strokes down the edge of his machete.

As they pulled away from the curb, Stuart leaned forward from the back seat.

"What did you find out from Caldwell?"

She was in a quandary. How much should she tell Stuart, or Max for that matter? Roxy could feel both men intently waiting for her answer. Kat sent her to Key West with them, so it must be OK, she reasoned. Besides, she did not want to bear the burden alone.

Skipping Jamie's dramatic shading and elaborate descriptions, she told them the drug company scandal was about to break and that Senator Winston had AIDS. Max whistled softly, while Stuart's expression was unreadable. His lips parted briefly in a suppressed gasp.

"That changes things," he said, the barest trace of disturbance audible in his tone. Roxy could almost see him replotting strategy for the campaign in his head.

"The Death card," she said to Max, agitated by her sudden insight. He shot her a piercing glance then concurred. Looking at Stuart in the rearview mirror, Max briefly explained.

"In several recent tarot readings referring to the campaign, the Death card turned up. We've been wondering who would die. There have also been indications that something would occur to change the face of the campaign. This certainly fits."

"Maybe you'll be able to see the outcome now," Roxy added hopefully.

Max shrugged. "Maybe."

Turnng to face Roxy as they sat at a stoplight, his voice serious, he directed her to tell Kat to buy television time on election eve.

"There will be a need for her to talk to voters one last time."

Roxy wondered why Max was speaking so freely of magic and their use of it on the campaign in front of a notably conservative U.S. Senator. Stuart sat unruffled in the back seat, continuing to sharpen his blade, attentive to all that was being said.

After a brief silence, the senator asked, "Why did she marry him?"

Roxy was startled by the change in conversational topic but quickly replied, "I asked Jamie that."

"What did he say?" Max asked, curious.

"He didn't know. He said that Duke and Celeste had some notion of blood-lines and dynasties, 'but what the lady herself wanted, who knows?' were his exact words." Neither man spoke so Roxy continued. "Then he got gross."

"Gross? How?" Max prodded.

She squirmed uncomfortably, not really wanting to discuss this in front of Stuart but she was caught in her own trap. She'd brought it up.

"He said she wasn't the pure goddess we all thought she was. That she was a cunt and a mouth like every other woman and that he had taught her how to use both. Then he offered to teach me."

"Why are you grinning at me like that?" Roxy demanded, indignantly glaring at Max.

"The man is such a slimy lizard, the thought of him with Kat—or anywhere near me—is beyond disgusting. I can't think of repugnant enough words to describe him."

She caught a glimpse of Stuart, who had stopped honing his machete. His smile matched Max's.

"And what are you smiling about?" she huffed. "Both of you are as bad as Jamie. I suppose you're going to tell me it's true about Kat, and suggest that maybe I could benefit from Jamie's instruction?" Roxy was working herself up to a frenzy as she directed her question at Max.

"Jamie has this perverse notion that coital sex is low on the evolutionary scale. Only animals do it," Max said, smiling. "He believes that humanity's evolutionary leap was defined by developing the organ of speech—the mouth—a divine leap according to Jamie. And that the second great gift accompanying this marvelous development of the mouth was oral sex. I suppose it was all justification for his peculiar bouts of impotence. According to Kat, technically they never consummated their marriage."

A shocked look pervaded Roxy's features. "Never?"

Max shook his head.

"Never. Duke wanted to use it as grounds for the Church annulment but Kat refused. She didn't want any official record of sexual perversity. They settled on using Jamie's very vocal and public disavowals of any interest in fatherhood as their justification for annulling the marriage."

"What are you smiling about?" she asked Stuart, who's face was a study in "thank God I'm a man." He put up his hands mockingly as if to stop an assault by her.

"Nothing personal. It's a conditioned reaction at the thought of a great blow job. I think it comes with the Y chromosome."

As they drove past the beach, Stuart repeated his initial question.

"Why do you think she married him?"

Roxy didn't answer, sullenly cursing men and their almighty dicks under her breath. Max answered instead.

"I didn't meet Kat until the final night of their marriage, so my view is somewhat slanted. Sparing you the technical astrological details, the short form answer is temporary insanity. Pluto transits to Kat's chart drew her to Jamie's very powerful, very mad Pluto energy. It all happened in less than a year when she was about twenty-two. Kat's an Aquarian. Madness is part of their genius. Pluto compels; no resistance is possible. A soul can only scramble to make it through the cyclone with as much humanity intact as possible. For Kat, the energy was transitory; for Jamie, it's permanent."

Stuart slipped his knife into its holder as they turned at the airport driveway. When they got out of the car and started walking to the plane, Roxy realized with a sinking feeling that she and the senator would be flying back to Washington alone. It will be dark soon, she thought. I can pretend to be asleep.

★ ★ ★ ★ ★

They reached the southern edge of the Georgia coast before Stuart spoke to her. Without prelude, as if he had been thinking over all he heard in Key West, and all he knew about Kat from their political work, he asked Roxy how the women came to be friends.

She was glad to answer. The silence, broken only by Stuart's cryptic dialogue with unseen flight controllers over the radio, was beginning to strain her already frazzled nerves.

"I was a junior at Cornell. It was spring semester and I was filling a science requirement by taking genetics. It seemed to demand the least scientific aptitude of anything else available, and least was what I had. It also fit with my personal quest, exploring the difference between men and women." It was dark enough that Roxy could pretend she did not see Stuart's amused grin.

"I wanted to understand about the Y chromosome and why it makes men, men. Everything scientific I learned was not as informative as what my friend Liz says. She claims it's not really a Y but an incomplete X and that men are missing all the stuff on that other leg of the X: the genes for setting the table or picking up their clothes or remembering birthdays. And their sexual equipment is compensation—shooting out, expanding like a missing leg, the missing leg of the X."

Roxy was involved in her favorite topic, forgetting that Stuart had asked her about how she met Kat.

"Geneticists claim that men and women differ in their DNA only by three percent. I don't believe it. More than that is visible and who knows how much plumbing entails not to mention our heads."

"Are you a man-hater, Roxy?"

She was shocked at his question and wondered what she could have said that would lead him to such a wrong conclusion.

"Not me! I love men. I can't imagine a world without them. Who would fix the machines and take out the garbage? I'm only kidding, except about being unable to imagine a world without men. I can hardly get through the week without...." Roxy was horrified at what she was about to admit to a U.S. Senator whom she scarcely knew. Fortunately, Stuart seemed more interested in understanding Kat than exposing Roxy's weaknesses.

"And Kiley?"

"She's less a lover of men than I am, that's for sure. I think she's waiting until the perfect hero arrives—a man who can live up to her father. I hope she finds him someday. It's sad to think of a beautiful woman like Kat wasting herself." Roxy paused briefly as she thought about Kat alone.

"Back to Cornell. The graduate instructor in my genetics class dropped out for some reason and Kat replaced him."

"Science is her academic background?" he asked, surprised.

"History of science, more precisely," she answered.

"The university was desperate to find someone to replace the instructor. Although Kat was enrolled in the History Department, she was well-schooled in hard science, a respected scholar and prize graduate student, and she volunteered. It was a few months after she and Jamie split up and I think she needed to keep busy.

"Early on, I was in the genetics lab counting fruit flies—the major scientific skill required of beginners—when Kat came in. We chatted for a while about my project which had to do with recessive red eyes or something, then she invited me to come along with her to Jim's Place, a Collegetown bar next to a laundromat while she did some wash. Max was working there, bartending. I'd seen him around campus—once you've seen him you don't forget—but this was the first I knew they were a couple. It wasn't really surprising. Kat was as exotic and unforgettable as he was.

"I'll never forget my conversation with her that day. She converted me to disciple on the spot."

Stuart lightly touched her arm and signaled her to wait while he talked on the radio to controllers around Savannah. A few minutes later, he asked her to continue.

"What did she say to enthrall you?"

"It was the scope of her ideas that was so compelling."

Roxy described Kat's scholarly quest as the search for parallel laws. She started in high school with hard science. Feeling that it was incomplete, she changed her focus to history of science at Cornell. Hard science denies nature by subjecting it to mathematical laws and measurement rather than accepting it as it is. Meaning, not measurement, is most important. Kat felt the answer was within reach when she discovered the antagonistic separation of magic and science that led to the Industrial Revolution. She met Max, learned about 'as above so below' and the circle was closed. She began her work on parallel laws. Max introduced her to the sons and daughters of Isis, the founders of science and philosophy trained in the eternal truths of life so they can cope intelligently with whatever emergency arises.

"It's remarkable," said Roxy. "Many of the ideas Kat was exploring twenty years ago are now an accepted part of new science: holistic, concentrating on connection rather than dominance and hierarchy. She always said intuition was an evolutionary step from intellect and that she was seeking a world view that allows both nature and mind, both same and other to exist.

"It's all about evolution for Kat. Evolution is the ultimate parallel law, the basic cosmic pattern. It's her version of a unified field theory. That day she told me that she had pledged her life to co-operate with evolution. Max says human evolution is driven by the force of ambition and kept on track by myth."

Roxy turned towards Stuart to make her point.

"Kat's not really a politician. She's more attuned to the inner life—a scholar, scientist, philosopher, occasionally an artist. She has the most amazing mind I've ever experienced. She forgets nothing. She can call up information as easily as any computer. She probably could have been a noted philosopher except that she's incapable of sitting back and thinking great thoughts without being compelled to act out her vision. That's how she ended up in Congress. Formulating public policy seemed to the next evolutionary step for her."

Memories of the year with Kat and Max in Ithaca streamed through Roxy's mind.

"They were just beginning their work together when I met them. Kat believed she could become a prototype for the new age scientist who would possess a wholeness and balance that came from inner and outer knowing. Max was her guide to the inner world.

"Somehow we all connected and they discovered I could channel clear information for them through tarot cards. They used the cards themselves but felt my manipulation resulted in more profound and unpolluted information. I saw them as remarkable characters from which great novels would spring. It was 1971 and the world was in turmoil, the revolution was happening, everything but normality was permissible.

"The three of us lived together the following school year. Kat had rented a house on the lake and she and Max encouraged me to share it with them. Rent was free in return for light maintenance work. I had no better option so I agreed. We've been friends ever since.

"After college, she and Max wandered around the country for awhile, then returned to Rhode Island. Some volunteer group needed a trained scientist to test samples. Kat offered her services and ended up founding Baywatch."

Roxy stared out the window at the blanket of lights beneath them, large black areas sprawled between the clusters. Again, the sky reflected the view beneath the horizon. She glanced over at the multitude of flowing dials, pulsing colored lights and switches and hoped Stuart knew how to fly when he could not see the ground.

They flew for a while in silence.

"What's the relationship now between Kiley and Max?" Stuart's voice startled her from daydreams and she looked over at him. He was comfortable in the seat, one hand lightly on the half steering wheel, looking at her intently. Roxy was curious about that herself—and wondered why he wanted to know.

"Kat says they're companion souls traveling the way. She also claims she owes her sanity to Max. They enjoyed an intimate relationship for years, separating before she went into politics. Kat says their spirits remained linked. I don't really know whether they continue to be lovers, but they are still connected."

Roxy examined Stuart's profile against the dark sky. How serious was he when he flirted with Kat, Roxy puzzled, as she looked for a reaction to her story in his face?

"Max always knows when there's a crisis in Kat's life. He simply appears when she needs him. After the tempest over rumors that he was making decisions for the campaign, they'll probably see each other seldom, and only in private, until the election."

"I was impressed with Max. I would certainly value his information and can understand why Kiley does." Stuart's endorsement of Max's arcane talents was matter-of-fact.

Roxy peeked at her watch trying to determine how much longer it would be before they reached Washington.

"I need to land at Blacksburg and meet one of my foremen. There's a problem at the main spring that requires my attention. It should delay us less than two hours. We'll be in Washington before midnight." Roxy was in no hurry to face Kat with the news about Winston. Being in the plane, talking about old times—it was so peaceful, so detached from the chaos she knew was about to erupt.

"I thought your home and business were in Roanoke?"

"Woodrum Airport, Roanoke's regional field has gotten too busy. I keep my plane based at Virginia Tech's airstrip in Blacksburg. The springs, water plant and the family homestead are actually located near Catawba, along the eastern base of Brush Mountain. "

"Were you born and raised in Roanoke?" Roxy felt he owed her some personal stories. He'd heard enough of hers over the past few hours.

"Me, my parents, my grandparents—I'm a mountain man for several generations."

"Don't you consider yourself a southerner, being Virginian and all?"

"Actually, I feel more like a westerner. There's this long history of conflict between the Tidewater planters who are the epitome of southern culture, and us ruffian types along the mountains. My great-grandfather on my father's side was the first of three generations of railroad men. He came south from Pennsylvania in the 1880's soon after the Norfolk and Western arrived. By that time, Virginia was back in the union and northerners were once again migrating into the area. It was my grandfather, another railroad man, who bought the land in Franklin County that was flooded by the Appalachian Power to make Smith Mountain Lake in the early 60's."

Roxy noted that same edge to his voice when he talked about the lake. This time, she felt ready to pry.

"Did they confiscate the land?" she asked. "You sound bitter when you talk about it."

Stuart looked over at her, obviously affected by the observation.

"When my father got the money—a reasonable price for the land, I admit—he left. We never saw him again. I was about fourteen."

Roxy was touched by the pain in Stuart's voice. She never imagined him as having personal problems. He continued with the story, returning to his ancestry, his voice warming as he began describing his mother's family.

"My mother's parents were both born along the Blue Ridge. He was a history professor at Hollins College, my grandmother was a librarian. Their big frame house on Wells Avenue was filled with books, stimulating conversation, and dreams of scholarly careers for my mother and her brother. But my grandfather died young, so my grandmother was forced to take in boarders to support her children. When my parents married, they lived in the same house in Roanoke with my grandmother and later my uncle's wife and son, and me and my sisters."

"They struggled to hold onto the mountain land with the springs and we often spent weekends there. My father and uncle educated me outdoors—hunting, fishing, working the land—all those manly things." Stuart tossed the last phrase at her. "I also learned about being a man from the toughs in town. We would hang out in the tunnel under the rail bed built over the salt lick. It was all very stimulating to my Y chromosome.

"The family plan during my childhood was to accumulate enough capital to set up a bottling operation at the springs. It belonged to my uncle and mother. Gordon—he's my uncle—was convinced the water had great value. My father's money from selling the land was supposed to be used to finance the plan. He agreed until the money was in his hand, then the temptation—the desire to be free—was too great for him.

"My uncle went ahead with the plan anyway, borrowing money wherever he could. He made my mother and me partners, same as if we'd had the money. From that time on, I devoted myself to the business. Gordon had to threaten me to get me off to college.

"If I could do what needs to be done from my cabin near the springs, I would. I go as often as possible just to breathe air that no one else is breathing at the same moment. When it's just a man and his land, there are few laws, and those are natural limits that are easy to follow willingly. Even the most essential laws impose outside will. They steal freedom in the name of humanity."

Roxy found herself agreeing with Stuart and understanding better how he arrived at his political positions.

"When my father left, it prevented me from continuing the family tradition of working on the railroad. But a love for motion, speed, the power of mechanical movement is in my blood. Adrenalin is my drug of choice."

"Is that why you fly?"

"I fly because U.S. Senators don't ride motorcycles."

Roxy looked at him surprised.

"Just a joke. I fly because I love it, the freedom from the weight and pull of the Earth, the closeness to the speed. Flying a small plane like this one is a lot like riding a motorcycle. It was a fortunate choice since pictures of me as a young pilot standing alongside my first Cherokee are more palatable to the voting public than a Hell's Angel with long hair and tattoos astride a Harley."

It was dark as they approached the southern tip of Virginia. The mountains were deeper shadows breaking the darkness of the sky. There were few lights. The area near Blacksburg seemed unpopulated until they were almost at the airport when lights began toward the north. As they circled to land, Roxy lost her sense of direction.

The small, private terminal was open until midnight during the week. Stuart explained it was due to the presence of Doug, who was a fixture at the field.

"We'll probably revert to dawn to dusk service like other small airstrips when he retires."

Stuart made a quick check of the weather on the computer inside the pilots lounge as Roxy dashed upstairs to the ladies room. Returning, she found him talking with an earnest young man.

"This is Chad, my chief troubleshooter at the plant. We're going to drive out to the springs for a look around. You're welcome to come along, or you can wait here. It shouldn't take more than an hour."

Roxy opted for the adventure.

She saw the rifle on the rack as she climbed into the truck. It was the .243 Winchester with a worn wooden stock that she imagined the day at Senatorial when Stuart and Jasmine duked it out.

Chad and Stuart talked over her as they wound their way north and west into the mountains along a narrow, hardtop road. It seemed that the Perrier scare the previous year had made spring owners paranoid. Insiders believed a toxic substance was deliberately introduced into the Perrier spring as a form of industrial blackmail. Chad was concerned it could happen to Crystal Spring, source of Stuart's notable Crystal Spring Water.

Arriving at the sturdy mesh fence surrounding the spring as it gushed from rock crevices at the base of the ridge, the men jumped out of the truck, Stuart grabbing the Winchester from its rack. He told Roxy to stay put. They were never out of sight of the headlights as they carefully walked around the area, pausing regularly to examine brush or marks along the ground.

They climbed in the truck, both satisfied that their trespassers were of the four-legged variety.

"Probably a bear," Stuart guessed, assessing the trampled grass and fragments of tracks they found.

On the drive back to the airport, Roxy hummed along with the tape Stuart played as the men discussed spring operations.

"Jefferson National Forest," Stuart reported, gesturing at the unbroken darkness to his left as they flew north toward Roanoke. "It's a huge expanse of forested mountains that straddles the Appalachians stretching well into West Virginia. There are important springs on both slopes of the range."

Stuart talked with the radio voices briefly then banked the plane to the right, causing Roxy to grab her seat with alarm. She saw the Roanoke airport behind the tipped wing as they headed southwest. "When I fly in from Washington, and see the star shining on Mill Mountain, I know I'm home."

She was astonished to see a huge red, white, and blue neon star glowing directly in front of them. Stuart pulled the plane up and over the star at the last minute, driving Roxy's stomach up to the back of her throat. As they turned to the left to begin heading north again, she thought about Kat, with her galaxies of star items. She would love this, a city-sized star.

Stuart recited the star's history.

"It was erected by the local Chamber of Commerce in 1949 as a temporary business promotion. Of course, once erected it was destiny. Roanoke began calling itself the Star City of the South. The star is a hundred feet tall, composed of thousands of feet of neon tubing, and stands more than a thousand feet above the city. I could see it from the roof of our house in Roanoke, and spent many nights wondering where it would take me."

"Do you know about Kat and stars—that they're her magic signature? She has a collection that will warrant its own museum someday," Roxy told him.

"I've noticed," he replied dryly. "Do you think she'd like this one?"

"She'd love it! More than that, she'd want it." They both smiled.

SENATE MAGIC

★ ★ ★ ★ ★

It was exactly midnight when Stuart dropped her off in front of Kat's Washington townhouse, waiting while she unlocked the door and went inside. Kat was up waiting; she could hear her moving around overhead. Roxy dawdled on the first floor, trying to pull her thoughts together about what Kat needed to know immediately and what could be discussed and savored under less frenzied circumstances. Included in the latter was Stuart's life history, although she never did have nerve enough to ask about his wife. She was surprised he never mentioned her or her father in all his talk of family.

Roxy realized she could stall no longer when Kat appeared at the top of the stairs. She went up and followed Kat into the large living room, settling into one of the white cushioned couches.

"Did you see him?"

"Yes."

"Did he have information worth listening to?"

"Let me get a beer and I'll spill my guts."

Fortified, Roxy repeated her conversation with Jamie at the Half Shell Saloon. When she got to the part where he sprinkled coke on his hand, Kat jumped up and began pacing the Kirim rugs strewn on pearly toned carpeted floors. She stopped and faced Roxy, staring intently when the deal for Jamie to return to Rhode Island to visit his dying mother was described.

"His mother died about ten years ago." Kat's tone was quiet though rage throbbed beneath the surface. "Duke flew him to Newport and back for the funeral."

Roxy was shocked.

"That scum! Why'd he even propose it to me? He must know you'd know it wasn't true."

Kat shrugged impatiently and waved Roxy on.

"What's the point?"

Taking a deep breath, Roxy spilled it out.

"Fraudulent drug tests are going to be revealed and Senator Wilnston has AIDS. He got it from a hooker Jamie's been providing him and his son. She's a junkie. No one knows but us."

Kat sank in shock onto the couch behind her.

"How does Jamie know this?" she croaked.

"He supplies the drugs."

She moaned and bowed her head to her knees. When she raised it again Roxy shuddered at the sight of her eyes. They looked lacerated with horror.

"It's the Death card."

Roxy nodded agreement.

"What did Max say?"

She repeated his words. Kat agreed she would tell Gould in the morning to purchase the television time.

"What did Senator Stuart say?"

Hesitating, Roxy calculated what to tell Kat now.

"His only comment was 'that changes things,' but I could see his brain considering strategic implications." She would save the personal commentary until later.

Kat paced around a few more times.

"I need to think about all this. I don't want the slightest breath to leak out. Don't tell anyone else, and we should speak about it only in person, and in safe places. You're going to Rhode Island on the early morning flight?"

Roxy nodded.

"Tell Mario everything and warn him, no talking about this on the phone, even hints. I want him to keep his ear to the ground and find out who knows what, and when. I'll try to be up there before Friday. I'll tell Hayes. No one else needs to know until Winston does something."

When Kat began thinking about political ramifications, the pain vanished from her face, replaced with a look of clear, precise focus. The feminine, sentimental side ran for cover. Common sense and ruthlessly analytical conclusions prevailed. Her miraculous powers of recovery from emotional shock always amazed Roxy.

"I'll be up early to see you off and give you further instructions, if I can come up with any." Kat smiled over her shoulder as she went up to bed.

★ ★ ★ ★ ★

It was after two and Kat was unable to sleep. Reaching over beside her bed, she picked up the phone and dialed a number. He answered on the first ring, his voice assuring her he had not been asleep.

"I need to talk with you."

"I'll come get you. We can drive around."

His strong voice always worked on her like chamomile, soothing her jagged nerves, making her feel secure and protected. The force of longing almost rocked her from the bed.

"No. I want to come there."

She could scarcely believe what she said. There was silence. He sounded pleased as he agreed.

"I'll leave the back door open. Let yourself in. You'll find me in bed, reading."

9

The Death Card
March/April

Washington
Rhode Island

Peeling off black spandex running pants, and shaking out her mop of hair freed from a neon pink sweatband, Kat outlined the instructions Roxy was to give Mario back in Rhode Island.

"If Winston chooses to ignore the scandals and his health crisis, he is a weakened candidate. Should he decide to retire, which is probable, it will take the Democrats some time to regroup and find a replacement. With everyone even remotely qualified already committed to some race or another, it could be a difficult process. Whoever the candidate, they won't be as formidable as Winston. We have an open field, at least for a while."

The morning run had restored Kat. Her voice was energized and her face glowed. She looked like a different person from the woman Roxy had briefed the previous night.

"We need to move fast and not miss a single opportunity. I want to be on the radio every day, in the press, speaking all over the state, and in general being senatorial. The House will be on Easter recess soon for ten days. Get Mario scheduling me to the max. I want a strategy meeting Saturday in Rhode Island. Tell him to include Bruno."

"Do you plan to tell everyone about Winston having AIDS?"

"No. You, me, Hayes, and Mario—no one else should know. We can use the impending exposure of Winston Pharmaceutical's drug tests as justification for juicing the campaign this early." Kat wrapped herself in a terry robe, ready for a shower.

"I never believed Winston would be my opponent. I didn't want it to happen like this, though."

"Who do you think your opponent will be?" asked Roxy, having no idea. She was shocked to see anger in Kat's face.

"Emmett Douglas, our esteemed governor."

"I can't believe that! More high level officials in his administration have been indicted than ever before, and Douglas is facing charges of mail fraud on campaign solicitation."

"Douglas is the Devil," Kat said as she moved to the wall of shelves and drew out tarot cards, an abstract expression turning her face to marble.

"Let's ask. Do the five-card spread." Roxy lifted the cards from their box and shuffled.

"Who will be my opponent in the senate race?"

Her palm tingled as she turned the first card: the back of a man on a hillside gazing out to sea. She noted Kat's triumphant snort as the Devil card turned up next. Quickly turning the next three, she wondered at the reappearance of the Lovers, still reversed. The fifth card featured a woman sitting in bed, head in her hands, nine swords hanging over her.

Faced with the chilling portent of the final card, Kat asked another question, motioning for Roxy to lay out another five.

"How will I suffer?"

Three of the cards in the second message were cups; the knight of cups rode at the head of the five, lovers exchanging cups were reversed at the end. The suffering would be emotional and it would have to do with a man.

"Do you think this is Winston or that someone else will die?" Roxy asked, pointing to the Death card in the middle.

"I don't know," Kat muttered as she walked mechanically toward the shower. "I don't want to think about it now."

★ ★ ★ ★ ★

Driving from the airport to the campaign office on Federal Hill, Roxy told Mario about Winston. He reacted calmly; only his tight mouth and whitened knuckles gripping the steering wheel revealed how upset he was. In all the time she had known him, Mario had been unfailingly polite, soft spoken, and in control regardless of the stress around him. She wondered if he ever got flustered or angry.

They parked in the alley behind the office for a few minutes, reviewing Kat's instructions before Mario handed her the van keys and sent her home. He planned to hit the streets and gathering spots listening for murmurings of Winston's fate.

The answering machine at the house was flashing furiously as Roxy passed through the office into the kitchen. She was not ready to talk to anyone, not even to listen to them. She wanted to spend the next hour or so in the Jacuzzi then walk on the beach. When she returned, she would consider collecting her messages. There was too much to think about first, particularly what she was going to do with Hayes, who would be in Rhode Island for the strategy meeting.

Evening brought a changed tone and deeper colors to the ocean. The water shimmered sapphire, so dark it almost looked brown. There were different people, too. Beach walkers in the morning seem more determined; dusk drew those who wanted a leisurely stroll. Some things did not change. Clouds rolled in from the west, waves and surf from the east. Several fishermen were casting from the rocks at the mouth of Narrow River exposed by low tide. Off in the distance, lights on the bridges gleamed like strings of fairy dust hovering in the air.

The phone was ringing as she returned from the beach. No need to accumulate any more messages, she decided as she answered. It was Jake.

"Obviously you just returned and haven't heard my dozen or more messages pleading to hear your voice. Where have you been?"

She scarcely mumbled a reply before Jake was onto his next thought.

"There have been so many funny encounters because of the commercials. I can't wait to tell you. Pete and I are escaping for some ocean fishing Saturday and Sunday. He's spending tomorrow preparing the boat so dinner is just you and me. I thought we could eat around here and then come back to my place and continue with our tantric teachings." Roxy smiled at the glee in Jake's tone. "I want to concentrate on taste, touch and aroma tomorrow."

"Three of my favorite senses," she replied, glad she had answered the phone.

"I'm off to plan strategy for my fight to keep Narragansett Beach free, so if I don't see you in the morning, I'll pick you up there at seven and introduce you to an incomparable Chinese restaurant only a few blocks away."

Roxy made a half-hearted mental note to ask him who or what was threatening the freedom of the beach.

★ ★ ★ ★ ★

Dawn was almost non-existent as ominous dark clouds scudded across the water, stirring up the waves, deepening their roar. Roxy was so concentrated on rehashing all that had happened in the past few days, she almost walked on the message etched in the sand obviously meant for her. Jake must have been up before dawn. She looked around but he was nowhere in sight. She read the words, smiling.

Morning Rox
Sunshine smile
Aphrodite
Tonight we eat

It took her several hours at the campaign office to return her calls and make the scheduling arrangements Mario outlined for her. Late in the morning, Jasmine called. What could she want? thought Roxy, as the press secretary's whining voice came over the line. Jasmine never called her.

"I've been trying to reach you for days. I heard you were in Washington but never came over to the office, and obviously no one taught you the basic rule of political life: always return your phone calls." Roxy said nothing as Jasmine continued, her tone a notch more irritated than when the conversation began. "What happened to Carrie? The congressional office claims she left, there's no answer at her home number, and no one here seems to know anything."

"Have you asked Hayes about it?" Roxy asked, desperately seeking a way out. She did not want to be the one to tell Jasmine they had fired Carrie, and why. Nothing to date had changed Roxy's initial paranoia about and dislike of the press secretary. Although, it could be interesting to observe Jasmine's reaction to Carrie's little jingle about her.

"I'm asking you."

"Carrie was on congressional staff. I have nothing to do with the workings of that office," Roxy stalled.

"Cut the crap! I know you know everything that goes on in this entire operation whether congressional or campaign." Jasmine's harsh voice seemed to reach out of the receiver and grab Roxy by the throat. "What happened to Carrie?"

"Mario discovered she had close ties with some big Mafia types and thought it was too dangerous to have her involved with Kat. He fired her last week. I'm surprised no one's told the Washington office about it." Roxy tried to sound casual, as if Carrie's departure was routine.

"What alleged Mafia figures was Carrie allegedly involved with?" Jasmine asked snidely.

She decided the safest course was to be truthful.

"This Mr. Coleman where she lives is supposed to be a Mafia lawyer and Mario also mentioned a Race Scarlatti whom he describes as the head criminal in the state."

Holding her breath in anticipation of Jasmine's reply, Roxy was taken aback by the press secretary's next question.

"And what about Carrie's suspicions that the congresswoman is quite smitten with that sexist pig, T.J. Stuart?"

There was a sweetly sarcastic tone in Jasmine's voice that hinted she and Carrie had discussed this before. In fact, knowing how Jasmine loathed Stuart, she probably planted the idea in Carrie's head to begin with, thinking it might drive him away from the campaign. She is a man-hater, thought Roxy. What a depressing way for a woman to live.

"Carrie's fantasy about Kat and Stuart is just that, a fantasy. She admitted to us she knew it wasn't true. Besides I just spent..." Roxy stopped herself as Jasmine interrupted. "Spent what?"

"Ahh, spent several days thinking about it and decided Carrie's a young girl with an incurably romantic nature and tendency to exaggerate."

Roxy was pleased with her recovery. She then held the phone away from her ear and flipped through the morning paper as Jasmine began to rant and rave about Carrie's loss, all the secrecy, what a disaster the campaign was, on and on. She was so detached from the conversation, it took several seconds for her to realize that Jasmine was no longer on the line.

When Mario came into her office about an hour later, Roxy could see his need to talk with someone about what was going on was as great as hers. They set off for lunch at Tony's, slipping down the back stairs so no one could ambush them and tag along. The day had become increasingly dreary, promising a storm ahead.

They sat in a booth hidden in shadows. Mario told her no whisper of Winston's affliction was on the streets although everyone seemed to know about the impending revelations that he manipulated drug approvals from the FDA.

"Street odds on Kat's victory are now in her favor," he relayed, "so our strategy to move ahead full steam in this next month will make perfect sense to everyone."

Roxy asked the question she knew must be in Mario's mind.

"Do you think Jamie was lying to us about AIDS?"

Mario shrugged his response.

"At this point it doesn't matter to anyone but Winston. The drug testing scandal should clinch this race for us. Frankly, I hope the AIDS story isn't true. I'd rather run against a fatally wounded Winston than have him retire and be faced with another opponent."

"Kat thinks it would be Douglas," Roxy added, interested to see Mario nod agreement. She half listened to his discourse on Douglas' corruption, evil nature, and the lie-filled dirty campaigns he had run in the past.

"Mario," she began as he paused to twirl some of Gloria's linguine with calamari around his fork. "What do you do about safe sex?"

She had been worrying about this at some borderline conscious level since meeting with Jamie. There had been no opportunity to discuss it with anyone since. Mario's reputation as lady-killer suggested he was an appropriate person to ask.

As he speared a ring of tomato-drenched squid on his fork and chewed its rubbery texture, Mario looked at her as if speculating on whether this was prelude to a sexual offer.

"I do what the ads tell me and wear my rubbers whenever it looks like rain."

She ignored his light tone.

"Do you always use condoms? What about spontaneous sex, or weird locales where there may not be time or opportunity to suit up?"

Several times Roxy had wondered about Hayes and their encounters. He had definitely been unsheathed each time.

"I take the threat of sexually transmitted diseases seriously. I'm always prepared. Besides, I find planned and properly executed sex much more fulfilling than a quickie bang in the back seat." Mario bent down for another forkful of linguine, missing Roxy's scarlet face.

Obviously, she and Hayes needed to discuss the issue if there was to be any more sex between them. She felt certain that Jake, as a devotee of sacramental sex, exercised proper care.

★ ★ ★ ★ ★

"The Dragon Lady is always glad to see me," Jake teased as the Chinese woman seated them, her face cold and stony.

"We'll work on taste here, with some aroma, then do touch and more scent when we go back to my place."

He was obviously delighted to see her and Roxy leaned against the chair, gratified, looking around the restaurant as he ordered without even picking up the menu.

The Ocean View was tucked away in a small shopping center on the road to Point Judith, packed with people who apparently knew it well. All were prepared with their own beer and wine. Roxy had been surprised to find many small restaurants in Rhode Island that did not have alcohol licenses. They allowed patrons to bring their own. Liz would have a fit. She insisted it was only the money she made from selling drinks that allowed her to keep the restaurant open. The Chinese clan that owned Ocean View must not have heard that money cannot be made from serving food.

As they ate the exquisite dishes Jake ordered, he guided Roxy in what he called sensory meditations.

"Tonight I want you to taste the divine from the root of your being to the tip of your tongue. These we call ears since they look like ears. Fried are better than steamed. This very hot, oily sauce is what you put on them."

He spilled it over the pork filled dumplings and began eating, motioning Roxy to do the same.

"Let the red pepper excite you, feel it rush into your sinuses. It helps clean out toxins, so eating hot foods is good for you. It's also stimulating."

Roxy agreed, she had always liked the burning lips left by peppers on the upper range of hotness.

Jake encouraged her to try and catch the rivulet of particular scent that would waft past as dishes were carried to other diners. He had chosen a table near the kitchen entrance so they could fully indulge in an often neglected sense. The effect of mingled food aromas escaping each time the door opened, cut by a focused stream of the aroma from a particular dish, was quite potent. By the time their own dinners came, she felt almost satiated by the smells alone.

They drank a refreshing ice cold white wine from a winery in Little Compton.

"They're big supporters of Kat's," he said, "and make excellent wine. This is their white nouvelle from 1989, almost too late to be drinking it, but it's my last bottle and I wanted to use it tonight to exemplify subtleness in both aroma and taste."

Jake interspersed his instruction on sensory enhancement with stories of his sudden stardom through Kat's commercials.

"Consuela is not the only woman who's expressed indignation that I never confessed to having a wife."

He looked serious for a moment.

"You may not believe this, but I try to be an anonymous man. For years I used stick-on gray dots as my logo on my art. People could easily pull them off if they wanted no trace of my identity."

"You don't think your identity is indivisible from the art you create?"

"If the viewer has the eyes to see."

Roxy began to understand his discomfort. His treasure was inner and for the discerning only. Now he was suddenly thrown before the masses and admired for his surface: his eyebrows, his twinkling eyes, his dazzling smile. She laughed.

He turned his attention to the two dishes that appeared at their table.

"This," he said with a flourish, "is crispy shrimp, truly divine with its combination of delicate crunchy texture and spicy but not overpowering taste. We never eat the broccoli," he said pointing to the bright green trim around the mounds of shrimp.

"And this is General Gao's Chicken; smell first," he directed bringing the platter filled with blackish clumps of meat up to her nose.

Roxy inhaled, tasting the distinct sweet and sour streams as the smell caressed the back of her mouth and throat. When she ate a chunk of the crispy chicken smothered in a molasses-like sauce, she recognized the exact tastes she gleaned from the aroma, but infinitely more powerful. She could feel the taste all the way down to her stomach. They ate a few of the broccoli flowers and remaining pile of rice to clean their palates. They then broke open their fortune cookies.

"Your star is rising," he read from his strip, a dismayed look furrowing his remarkable eyebrows. "At least Kat will have someone to commiserate with about one hundred percent recognition. No wonder she leaves town to get laid."

Roxy was astounded and wanted to ask him what he meant about Kat, but he had taken the cookie's fortune from her hand.

"Love makes the world go 'round. Give it a spin," he read with a broad smile.

★ ★ ★ ★ ★

Lying on a towel spread across the pillow couch, Roxy luxuriated in the latest exercise. Jake was blending touch and aroma by rubbing her down with scented oils.

"Perfumes and incenses have existed forever. The ancients knew that inhaling certain scents stimulated people. In moderation, they were stimulated spiritually; in excess, sexually. That's musk incense you smell now."

Roxy had no difficulty distinguishing the deep perfume of the musk. Jake was oiling her feet, so the aroma didn't compete with her perception of the incense.

"Musk is the ultimate sexual perfume, a revered aphrodisiac, favorite of history's most notable love goddesses from Cleopatra to the Empress Josephine. It's a glandular secretion from male musk deer, used in attracting females.

"Your skin is so willing and responsive. As I rub the sandalwood oil along your thigh, it feels like my fingertips are being caressed in return. Almond was the oil I used on your feet and I'll put jasmine on your hands. When I reach your sacred mound, I'll switch to musk."

Roxy was becoming accustomed to Jake's unusual juxtaposition of scholarly tone and information and intensely sensual hands and movements. She surrendered, conscious only of the unique flavor of each oil as it penetrated her skin.

Finishing her extremities, Jake rolled her over and began rubbing musk into the base of her spine then moved along her back.

"Feel the heat as we begin to raise the serpent power upward. Hold onto the energy and let it flow under my hand. As it pours through the channel around your spine, the oil on your body will be heated and you'll smell like a living, breathing potpourri."

Roxy was astounded to feel the heat and throbbing pulse in her back as Jake rolled her over again. She was enveloped in a delicate cloud of mingled scents and found it surprisingly easy to hold the sexual energy in check, imagining it as a glowing tube confining dancing beams of sparkling light.

"Full breasts are essential in this practice," Jake remarked as he rubbed patchouli oil around her nipples, stroking each breast upward from below, "and yours are perfect, sacred mountains for a hero to conquer."

The energy swelled but did not break as he rubbed pungent musk into her pubic hair.

"The sacrificial grass to be burned upon the sacred altar," he intoned as he pulled on it. The underlying rhythm of expansion and contraction was beginning to slip out of her control. He stroked musk oil between her eyebrows, and she was startled to see an uncoiled snake, its hooded head gazing forth at the world from her third eye.

"Don't let go Roxy," he whispered "Close the lotus at the base of your spine and let the energy stay inside to burn out all the blockages. Move it up and down, up and down, but don't let go."

His voice and hands ruled her, strengthening her will. There was an orchestra of sounds pulsing loud and soft with the beat of the energy: ocean roaring, thunder, bass drum then upward on the scale to strings and lutes and finally a constant humming, tides of passion slowly surging like molten lava along her spine.

The ringing phone shattered her concentration and the lava blew the top from her volcano. She lay moaning and quivering on the pillows from the force released and opened her eyes to see Jake looking at her, distressed.

"I'm sorry," she stammered, "I tried to hold on but the phone distracted me."

From his tentative smile, Roxy knew something else was wrong. The phone call. She sat up, instinctively pulling the ends of the towel around her. Echoes of the kundalini energy sent spasmodic pings along her nerve endings and she struggled to refocus attention away from her body.

"What's wrong? Who was that on the phone?"

"Do you know where Kat is?" Jake asked.

"Did something happen to her?" Roxy almost choked on the words. Her nerves had settled into a low humming and the heat was receding; the pounding in her head stopped and her checks no longer felt burned.

"No, don't worry." Jake's voice was soothing as he sat next to her, smoothing back a tendril of sweat soaked hair from her face.

"The call was from a friend of mine who's a cop. He just pulled Senator Winston from a car wreck at the construction near the Jamestown Bridge. He must have been blinded by the rain and not seen the detour in time. Indications are he left the road doing about ninety and plunged down into the pit smashing head on into a concrete piling. He was driving his son's Porsche. They dragged Winston out just before the car exploded. He died on impact, Fred said."

Winston was dead. Her brain sent new shock waves along her already-aroused nervous system, and she could not control the deep shivering that engulfed her, even when Jake wrapped a blanket around her and cradled her in his arms.

"When did it happen?"

"About an hour ago. Fred wasn't able to get away until now. They called Colin Proctor, Winston's chief aide and he's there taking care of things."

"Why did Fred call you?"

"He's seen the commercials. Thought Kat should know and that I could get a message to her."

Roxy's head was as clear as the twin jolts to her nerves would allow. She reached for the phone and dialed the private line at headquarters, the only one Kat would answer.

Kat was silent on the other end as Roxy relayed the tragic news.

"Mario walked in a few minutes ago, between dates I guess. I hope the next one wasn't his preference, he probably won't be seeing much more social action tonight." Kat sounded strained.

"Get some rest. The situation will change quickly and we need to be alert. Be here by nine and bring the cards. I'll talk to Max and see if we can get some answers before then."

She felt chills run up and down her spine, but not from erotic pleasure this time. It was all getting too bizarre. Her whimpered demurral brought a sharp response from Kat.

"What's the matter? Surely it's better to know calamity's true form?"

Roxy was not sure it was but said nothing as she hung up.

★ ★ ★ ★ ★

Blowing wind kept her tossing and turning all night, haunted by creaks and moans in the old house. She wondered if Winston had chosen to die. The thought, and its accompanying despair, twisted her dreams into unbearably dark and frightening shapes. As dawn seeped in the window, she gladly sat up and turned on the light. She always felt braver awake and upright.

When the phone rang, Roxy hesitated. Pre-dawn calls inevitably brought bad news. She was relieved then outraged when a female voice identified herself as Janet Gilroy from CBS News looking for comment from Kat on Winston. Roxy slammed down the phone, letting the machine answer when it rang again a few moments later. There were three more calls, undoubtedly from more diligent reporters, as Roxy showered before setting off for Providence.

She found Kat waiting for her in their shared office upstairs, several pages of notes littering the table next to the computer. Motioning Roxy to begin shuffling the cards, Kat started her questions. After each set of cards were turned, she would stare, close her eyes and ponder their pictures, make some notes, then scoop them up and ask another question. When she sat silently, eyes closed, for several minutes, Roxy assumed the questioning was complete.

"Well?" she asked. "What do we know now?"

In a voice curiously void, Kat said "the next two months are productive and positive. We will move ahead strongly. After that —" she paused and rummaged through the exposed cards and threw the Fool onto the space between them— "we step off the abyss."

This card always mystified Roxy. Showing a sex-indeterminate youth gaily dressed, holding a white rose and knapsack with a small white dog barking at her or his heels, she never knew whether the youth was about to step off the precipice which she or he did not seem to see. She never could decide whether the card was positive or not. Kat seemed to be interpreting it bleakly.

Finally, Kat smiled.

"Let's go to work. We have two months of grace."

Kat clicked alive the dark screen on her computer, closing the file she had been working on earlier and set up a blank page. Picking up the phone, she slipped a black lipstick-shaped device along the mouthpiece then set it on the desk. She handed Roxy a similar device except it had a plastic tip at one end.

"Plug this into the private line in my bedroom at the house. It checks for phone taps. I'll keep the portable one with me. No sensitive calls are to be made from any phone identifiable as ours without checking the lines first. Since my line in Narragansett will be constantly monitored by that little trinket, it can be considered permanently safe."

Roxy turned over the device several times but could identify nothing that gave a clue as to what it was—no serial number, name, nothing. It could have come from outer space.

"Where did these come from?"

"A present from Senator Stuart to the campaign. He claims tapped lines and covertly recorded phone conversations are the latest in campaign dirty tricks."

"Where did he get them?"

Kat smiled indulgently. "The boys at DARPA."

Seeing the blank look on her friend's face, she explained.

"They're a small band of civilians that create toys for the military and CIA with beneficial spin-offs like this." She rolled the black tube in her hand. "Stuart sits on the committee that approves secret funds for them. His James Bond mentality loves this stuff and they love giving it to him. Boys will be boys."

At the mention of Stuart's name, Roxy thought about the trip to Key West.

"I wonder if Rosa's husband has been released yet?"

"He has," Kat answered quickly.

"Why hasn't it been in the papers? That should be big news."

"It wasn't an official release."

"What do you mean?"

Kat looked up from her notes and said deliberately, "It was one of Stuart's personal gestures of defiance to Castro. Two Leos clashing egos. He went in with some of his Cuban exile buddies and spirited Domingo out. That's why he was flying to Key West."

Ignoring Roxy's stunned look, Kat instructed her to begin drafting a statement regarding Winston's death and the effect this would have on the campaign.

"We'll polish it when I finish talking with Max."

During the conversation with Max, Roxy glanced over and was astonished to see a block of indecipherable symbols and graphics flowing onto the screen from Kat's fingers dancing across the keyboard. Dingbats! She recognized the font with its collection of stars, geometric shapes, arrows, hearts and the like. It was designed for use in borders and decoration; she had never heard of writing in it. Suddenly Roxy understood: it was code. Anyone knowing could simply change the font and the block of gibberish would appear as words and sentences of meaning. Computer players like Max and Kat had probably built in further protection to keep it from being easily translated.

Finishing, Kat cleared the screen and placed the disk she had been using into the small, green lead-lined case in which she transported her critical data. The two women began weaving Roxy's collection of sentences and key phrases into a formal statement. They were hard at work, Kat still at the computer, Roxy stretched out on the couch snatching poignant and evocative ideas from the air and relaying them for transcription. Neither heard Hayes and Mario until they were standing in the doorway.

Roxy looked up to see Hayes smiling appreciatively down at her reclining form. All the erotic force not quite released the night before gushed through her. She scrambled to sit upright and stem the orgasm she felt being triggered. Ignoring the pulsing at the base of her spine, and praying that her look did not betray her aroused state, she dashed out of the room proclaiming a need for them all to have some coffee.

When she returned, Kat waved her to sit at the computer and they began to complete the statement, drawing on information that Hayes and Mario had picked up from dozens of calls to press and informants.

"We don't want to say anything that indicates we have information not publicly known," warned Hayes as they kept checking the *Providence Journal*'s version of the story.

"Here's an interesting tidbit," he said, reading from the lead article. "Investigators reported Winston's high rate of speed was due to a stuck gas pedal."

"You don't think that's true, do you?" asked Roxy.

"I think Colin Proctor has the situation well in hand. I wouldn't be surprised if the reports on drug test fraud were buried along with Winston, leaving the family name, and his illustrious career, intact."

There was a cynical tone in Hayes' voice indicating that in a similar situation, he would have done exactly what Proctor was doing, protect his candidate, dead or alive.

They quickly assembled a collection of comments to be mixed and matched depending on circumstances. Kat called radio stations to do actualities, Mario spoke with Rhode Island press, and Hayes took on the national media.

Picking up a copy of the remarks to fax to Jasmine for wide distribution, Hayes noticed the sheet of dingbats and picked it up also, a questioning look on his face. Kat smiled and took the sheet from him.

"Computer jokes. It's how I amused myself all night. They're great punsters, these Macs."

Gould arrived, and they settled into the front room. It was set up as a conference room, street style, as the Hose called it. There was a dining room table with a few chairs around it along one side, the rest of the space was strewn with couches and overstuffed chairs. Meetings at campaign were usually held under stressed conditions and Kat felt everyone functioned better when they could be comfortable. The Hose came barreling up the stairs, plopped himself into a worn, blue armchair next to the phone, and immediately began calling,.

"Checking the latest street talk," he explained.

As Kat motioned people to get settled, the Hose let out a roar, slammed down the phone and addressed the group.

"That was Jason Worth, president of the WASP butt-fucking club, Newport branch. They're all upset about the old boy croaking and want you to know they're solidly behind you, which means I wouldn't bend over anywhere in Newport."

There were smirks and chuckles around the room. Gould innocently asked who was in the club.

"It's a club you gotta be born into. You're a Jew, right? You aren't allowed in this club. Me either. I'm an immigrant, and a Papist," the young man hissed.

Mario and Kat grinned. They recognized the teasing underlying the Hose's snarling tone but Gould was uninitiated; he looked ready to flee as if he expected the Hose to pull a gun and start shooting.

"Every morning all these white-bread boys sit around and inspect each others' bare asses to see if there's hair on them. If there is, you're out of the club. It's a known fact that true gentlemen don't have hair on their ass." The Hose was nodding sagely at Gould who sat open-mouthed, his usually placid deameanor shattered.

"Sounds like you've studied this cultural phenomenon quite extensively," Hayes commented, barely able to control his mirth.

"You learn a lot of important stuff growing up on the streets in Providence," the Hose replied, "and one of the most important is not to trust any man with a smooth ass." Having settled the value of Worth's endorsement to his satisfaction, the Hose returned to the phone.

Kat began the meeting without ceremony.

"We can save expressions of sympathy and speculation on cause for the press and the funeral, which is scheduled for Tuesday morning, by the way. I will be going, Mario and Bruno also."

"Today, we make plans for the next two months, when the ball is exclusively in our court. Once that game plan is set, we'll review what's being said on the street," she nodded to Mario and the Hose, "and what we'll be saying in return."

She had adopted the clipped and distinct speech pattern of someone taking command.

"I am now the incumbent. No other candidate in the state for any office can match my seniority. The truth of my insistence that I am running against no one but for the U.S. Senate has been revealed."

Kat moved gracefully around the room, a halo of light surrounding her as she passed in front of the windows, as if her vibrant energy set in motion the atoms and molecules of the air around her. She wore a black wool jumpsuit adorned with a silver star around her neck that shot flashes of light as it caught a stray sunbeam or two. Sparks of light came from her earrings and her blue-black hair was writhing on her head.

"Scheduling, press, speeches—I want to be everywhere. We'll double our fundraising efforts, especially out-of-state and from groups who remained neutral because of Winston's clout and position. I am the known. The alternative is unknown. Uncertainty works in our favor," Kat said.

"All legislative activities and comments must be Senate-related."

She stopped in front of Hayes, focusing on his attentive face.

"Keep in touch with Senator Stuart. He'll know what we need to do. Previous plans to solidify environmental support during April remain unchanged except for redoubling our efforts. We have one theme: polluter pays. We play it everywhere."

Again she directed her remarks to her chief of staff.

"We exploit events surrounding the twentieth anniversary of Earth Day and schedule an award a day during the last week. By May 1, I want to be firmly enthroned as Queen of the Environment, safe from any usurper." Hayes nodded consent and Kat continued, lowering her voice.

"Now that Winston's dead, he'll become a hero. Without being ghoulish or betraying our own positions, we grab his scepter, wrap ourselves in his robe, and start highlighting our similarities. No one should question the obvious. I am his natural successor."

Resuming the tones of a general outlining tactical considerations for her troops, she turned to Gould and addressed media activities.

"Push our video more. Mario can see that it's done here but it might be beneficial to attempt some press-related distribution as part of our national blitz in the next two months. This is only a suggestion," she softened her voice and sat on the arm of Gould's chair.

"We may want to show the Aunt Helen piece soon as a way of reassuring the old folks that I'm still around to care for them."

Encouraged by his smiling nod of agreement, Kat continued.

"I have an idea for an additional spot to begin when the mourning is over and continue until mid-June. Here's a rough script." Gould looked amused as Kat handed out copies. "This is nothing new," she assured him. "I've simply adapted your premise to the changed situation."

"I'm at the Senate desk looking senatorial. Calendar pages from 1991 through '95 are torn off as headlines announcing Senator Tomasso's accomplishments."

She read from the script: "1992: Senator Tomasso Upsets Foes of Medicare. 1993: Tomasso Leads Fight in Senate Against Tax Hikes.1994: Health Care Plan Passes Senate, Tomasso Victorious. 1995: Deficit Cut Drastically, Tomasso Energy Savings Key Item, and so on. It concludes with the cut line: Kiley Tomasso, a Senator We Can Be Proud Of."

Gould loved the concept. Hayes interjected a note of caution from Sun Tzu.

"Those who are about to advance speak humbly and yet increase their preparations."

Kat considered the words.

"Point well taken. We shall be cautious of our immodesty. Conclusion: by mid-May, I want to look so formidable no worthwhile candidate will want to run against me."

"Now that you've opened that Pandora's Box," Gould speculated, "do we have a consensus on who our opponent might be?"

Before anyone could speak, Kat instructed them to write down the name of their choice and turn the paper over. As she went around the group asking each to hold up the name, she grimaced. They were unanimous. Emmett Douglas was the one.

Mario delivered a brief sketch of the governor, his low opinion of the man evident in his tone.

"Emmett Douglas is a mean-spirited man who has greased palms, bought favors and generally appealed to the basest instincts of the electorate. He is renowned for taking care of his friends, destroying his enemies, and considering no lie, no attack too vicious. We must be careful not to dismiss him lightly. He may be devoid of intelligence and integrity but he is undeniably shrewd."

"I agree with all of your assessments of the man as corrupt and useless scum. The problem is everyone knows that," Gould said, worry creasing his brow. "Polls show voters can recite his scandals from selling liquor licenses to his cronies to his current problems with mail fraud. His sins are old news and people have extremely low expectations of him. There is nothing we could do to make Emmett Douglas look worse in the eyes of the electorate. He is invulnerable to attack. Anything we say against him would only degrade us.

"Kiley, on the other hand, is extremely vulnerable to his one-weapon arsenal—that weapon being lies. She is a spotless angel in the eyes of her public, a being above reproach. It doesn't matter if the mud Douglas slings is false, even a few drops sticking at random could cause the fickle public to abandon her because she betrayed their faith. He could be our most dangerous opponent. We can allow him no ammunition. Not only must Kiley continue to act in her usual honorable fashion but we must be increasingly aware of the appearance of impropriety, no matter how innocent the truth. One slip, one doubt and Kiley's on a downward slide."

"And if you do get attacked," Hayes interjected, jabbing his finger emphatically, "you must answer immediately and decisively. Ignoring an attack means you agree it's true."

The Hose added his assessment.

"With Douglas as our opponent all we need is more cash. The only way he can win is to buy the election. We need to buy it first, or last."

"No, Bruno. We don't do it that way, no matter who the opponent." Kat's voice rang with determination.

"You and Mario are my secret weapons for the next phase. We must know exactly what the Democrats are doing so we can maximize our advantage. What do you two hear on the street?" Kat turned the meeting over to gossip and inside stories, favorites of all political operatives. Mario began.

"The general public is reacting to Winston's death as we would expect: shock, sadness, idolatry of his goodness now that he's gone. The only interesting reaction, at least to me, is that they find this a perverse indicator of Kat's destiny to be in the Senate.

"Insiders have a more cynical view. Those who know wonder about the pharmaceutical investigation and assume it will go away now. There's lots of speculation about why he was driving Sonny's Porsche and whether he was drunk and speeding. But, for the most part, all their concern is focused on what the Democrats will do. Street talk is less unanimous about Douglas being your opponent."

"Bruno?" Kat asked.

"I can give names and specific comments but Mario's said all the important stuff. We need to decide what to say back."

Kat looked around the group. "Suggestions?"

Gould spoke first.

"It's a tragic loss. You admired him greatly, always looked to him as a model. Since you never saw this as a race against Winston, your plans for presenting your qualifications to the voters of Rhode Island will proceed unchanged after a respectful period of mourning, of course."

"Which is?"

"However long it is to the next public political event you have scheduled that cannot be canceled."

★ ★ ★ ★ ★

Deciding a fundraiser in a private home was exempt from the period of mourning, Kat and Mario left headquarters. A young boy from the neighborhood ran up to them and handed Kat an envelope bearing her name. She flipped quickly through the sheaf of papers inside while Mario questioned the child about who had given him the envelope. They exchanged a worried glance when they recognized the woman he described as Carrie.

★ ★ ★ ★ ★

"That's the last change." Hayes stood at Roxy's shoulder in Kat's converted dining room as she printed the final version of Kat's statement about Winston's death. Jasmine was unreachable so Hayes had volunteered to stay and deal with media calls, persuading Roxy to help. They decided to work at the house.

She leaned back against the rosewood chair, rubbing her fingers absently across the edge of the embroidered seat. The printer hummed in the background. A rosewood breakfront that matched the antique table and chairs was strewn with folders, papers and the fax machine. Other bits and pieces of documents, clippings and handwritten notes were arranged neatly around the cherry red Oriental rug. As Hayes discussed selecting a place to eat, he massaged her tense shoulders. Their blood chemistry had not diminished, Roxy realized. If anything, Jake's instructions to pay attention made her more responsive to the feeling she got from Hayes. It took every ounce of will she could muster not to throw back the chair and jump him on the spot. But she was determined to have something more than another roll in the hay.

She moved out of the chair away from his fingers although her skin continued to feel their imprint. Her voice was shaking from the energy churning around her stomach and pressing against her throat.

"I don't want to be another feather in your cap, available whenever you have ten minutes to kill."

He had the grace to look remorseful, though she had just sprung the announcement on him without warning.

"You're right." His voice was soft and sorrowful. He tenderly ran his finger along the edge of her cheek and across her lips. Roxy could not prevent them from instinctively parting but she resisted the compulsion to throw herself into his arms. Instead she moaned and moved further away.

"I've thought of nothing but what I wanted," Hayes continued. "There's so little time for anything but the politics. When I needed you, I took you. But you do deserve more. After the election, I'll take you away to a mountain cabin or tropical beach, wherever you want, and we'll wallow in each other." His promise was exactly what she wanted to hear.

"Wait for me Roxy, don't give up."

Tears slid down her cheeks.

"What do we do now?"

"Let's go have dinner and you can tell me about your books."

★ ★ ★ ★ ★

They were both asleep in front of the late night news, Hayes stretched out on the wicker couch with his head in Roxy's lap. Waking to see Kat standing in the doorway, Roxy jumped up startled, dumping him unceremoniously on the floor. Kat laughed as she walked into the room skirting her chief of staff who was rubbing his eyes and trying to make sense of what happened. "Overreacting, Roxy?"

Kat reported that the evening's fundraiser raised several thousand dollars more in campaign contributions than predicted, an immediate impact from Winston's death.

"Two physicians who'd been playing it safe came over and signed on. Mario claims they want to protect themselves from Douglas' pressure by saying they'd come out for me before he decided to run. It's all so twisted." Contempt laced her voice.

"Speaking of twisted, we have this." She tossed an envelope onto the couch. "It's a letter of resignation from Carrie. Ten pages of perverted threats, dark warnings, and general weirdness."

As Roxy scanned the letter, Hayes stood and begged off from the discussion.

"I'm going to bed. Hopefully I'll see you for breakfast at dawn."

When the two women were alone, Kat opened the long casement window and listened to the rain.

"From the looks of things, it's good that I came along to remove temptation," she teased.

"I'd already said 'no'," Roxy declared, realizing too late what she had revealed. But Kat chose to ignore the underlying meaning.

"Thanks for indulging me. Jake's a much better choice, at least for now. After November, you're a free agent!"

The eerie sound of a foghorn blared mournfully from the dark. The same melancholy note resonated in Kat's voice as she talked about Carrie's letter.

"There is so much darkness in her. She seems drawn to it, consumed by it, and the predictable outcome has been psychic disturbance. Often when a young girl is sexually traumatized, as Carrie was...."

"If the story she told us in various versions had any truth to it," Roxy interrupted.

"She bears all the psychic scars of a sexually abused child. There must be truth somewhere in what she's told us."

The aching sorrow in Kat's voice caused her friend to check the disparaging remark she was about to make. From a dark corner of memory, Kat continued, almost talking to herself.

"It scars a girl forever when her innocence is forcefully ripped away. Carrie deserves our sympathy and understanding. Being violated before you even know what your sexuality is creates demons that take years to exorcise if the girl is fortunate enough to find her way back on the path to love and tenderness. Maybe Saint Maria Goretti had the right answer."

"Maria Goretti?" The name sounded familiar but Roxy could not remember her particular story.

"She was canonized in the late '50s, one of the modern saints for modern problems. My cousin John brought back a relic of her for me from Rome, a piece of bone encased in plastic. He told me if I prayed to her daily she would keep me pure. Unfortunately, I must not have prayed hard enough."

Carrie and her problems faded into the background. Kat was facing her own shadows, reliving the experience that caused them.

"He considered me his prize in life and when I was sixteen, he claimed me. I was drugged and beaten into submission. One of the reasons I married Jamie was to erase his mark." She laughed bitterly. "It was Max who healed me. I guess Carrie hasn't been as fortunate."

"What did you do? " Roxy could not suppress her astonished curiosity.

"As soon as I was able to move, I crept out of the room and went to his father's study where I knew there would be a gun. I found the pistol easily and returned upstairs. I was not ready to die for my virginity the way Maria Goretti did but I believed I had the right to kill my despoiler. He was coming out of the bathroom looking thoroughly pleased with himself as I stood in the doorway holding the gun on him. My bloodstained clothes hung in tatters around me. Bruises were beginning to darken my face and arms. I was trembling so hard I was afraid my shot would miss so I walked closer. He never flinched just stood smiling at me. 'You'll enjoy it more next time,' he said. I frantically willed myself to pull the trigger. But I couldn't. I couldn't kill another human being no matter how despicable and corrupt he was, no matter how much he'd hurt me. I threw down the gun and ran from the house.

"I was so ashamed. Maria Goretti was stabbed to death because she refused her fiancée's advances. Not only was I still alive, but I was unable to punish the rapist.

"Until my bruises faded I pleaded illness and stayed in my room. Fortunately, Duke was out of town on business for a few days and my mother chose to take my side. I told no one else. If I didn't have the courage to kill my violator then I couldn't ask anyone else to, and I was certain my father would kill him if he knew."

For several minutes the only sounds were rain and the regular plaintive cries of the foghorn. Dim light carved her angular face into an alien mask with no color to soften the black and white starkness. Even her gray eyes were dark pools of recollected anguish.

"Persephone is a goddess with harsh lessons to teach," Kat said, turning her thoughts back to the present. "Facing the darkness is a terrifying experience for even the strongest and most hopeful of us. There is the constant worry that we may not find our way back to the light."

A mist hovered around Kat's shoulders.

"When Persephone is dragged beneath the earth by Pluto, we are never told what happens. We know only that her mother makes a deal so she can return to the light six months each year. Maybe sinister drama draws Carrie and she looked to us, to me, as some sort of light to lead her back." Kat shook her head regretfully.

"You don't feel responsible for her craziness, do you?"

Picking up the letter, Kat read.

"'You are the brilliant light that the world needs and I am willing to sacrifice myself to the darkness that you may continue your path.' Carrie certainly wants me to feel responsible.

"The more rational we are, the more cosmic law demands a compensating level of the irrational. In some universal way that makes us responsible. More realistically, Carrie's just one among many victims of the degraded energy that fills our world. Evil is a very real force, embodied by real people, and weak souls like Carrie are prime targets for its forces of disintegration and chaos. As old patterns and rigid rules dissolve, the strong find freedom and bliss. The poor damaged children find nothing but despair. Her rage and lust for power act like a magnet drawing evil to her."

Kat read again from the letter:

" 'I feel cut off. The gulf is widening, and before I drop from sight I wanted to warn you.' Her warnings are drawn directly from her warped sexual energy. 'Trust no man, past, present, or future whether they claim to love or assist. They bring only danger and pain,'" Kat quoted. "There are corrupt and evil people around you, from past lives. I want only to shield you.' This is a disturbed adolescent speaking whatever her chronological age. Her dabbling in magic is the way she confronts the irrational."

Kat stood by the window absorbing the spatterings of rain blown by a shifting wind. Roxy strained to hear her muffled voice.

"Sudden cold depressions may arise in anyone's life. Darkness engulfs like a chill fog and we can sense the inexorable force coming to take us away, draw us out of the pain and anguish of life. Fear of darkness drew Carrie to it, like Persephone returning to Hades willingly. The same fear pushed Winston to end his life. I felt that way several times: after the rape, when my marriage to Jamie ended, and for nearly two years after my father died.

"Max taught me that madness can be avoided only by recognizing this darkness as our other half, our toxins and garbage. This is the shadow side of our moon which must be embraced and explored if we are ever to be whole."

Kat turned away from the window, closing it against the rain. The front of her dress was gleaming as light scattered off thousands of raindrops caught in the dark fabric.

"Persephone was taken to Hades by Pluto as a weak and powerless girl. She returned a woman with a woman's power gained from her embracing the darkness. When Duke died, I spent months suspended in despair, trying to understand death, its finality."

She paused and looked at Roxy.

"It's the finality of death that was so impossible to accept. Duke was gone. I would never see him, or hear his voice, or feel safe and secure in his arms. Max helped me extract wisdom from pain; joy became a treasured experience because it could disappear at any moment."

Kat stared at the diamond-flecked darkness of the window. The ancient grandfather clock struck midnight, its tones playing a melody over the foghorn's single bass.

"What brought you back after Duke's death?" Roxy asked softly.

The silence continued so long Roxy was almost ready to repeat her question when Kat faced her, a pensive smile on her lips.

"Love and magic."

Before she could pursue it further, Kat shook her head deliberately as if to drive away the gloom and began discussing the next day's schedule.

"Mario is coming with me so you can take the day off."

★ ★ ★ ★ ★

Gloom eroded Kat's spirit during the two days of rain and constant discussion of Winston's death and what it meant for her. The funeral service was held at St. Martin's. Faces and voices were a blur as Mario guided her through the crowds, murmuring names and dodging questions. They decided not go to the cemetery because of the rain. They stood under an overhang along the side of the church waiting for the endless procession of cars to follow the hearse, surrounded by State Police cars, to burial. Neither saw Jamie until he was standing directly in front of them blocking the only path of escape.

"Since I knew how important the information I sent you was in helping to understand this great tragedy, I assumed you would not renege on our deal so I returned to attend the funeral." Jamie reached over to kiss Kat but Mario stepped in the way.

"Aren't you a dutiful campaign manager, inserting yourself between your candidate and her sordid past?"

There was a sneer on his face as he stood back a few steps but not enough to let them pass.

"Or maybe it's more like filial devotion. Speaking of relatives," Jamie dodged to prevent Mario from forcing him aside, "I miss seeing my former mother-in-law. Where is Celeste? It's been months since I've heard even a whisper."

"Months?" Kat responded blankly. "You've stayed in touch with my mother?"

"Of course, my sweet. We're friends and allies from way back. Surely you remember that. In fact, my biggest mistake was selecting the daughter instead of the mother. Celeste and I are much more suited. She would have been a willing partner for all my enterprises."

His cackling laugh galvanized Kat who tried to slide around him. Jamie caught her arm and shoved her back against the wall of the church. Mario stood frozen, unwilling to create a scene by physically dragging him away from Kat.

"You two better change your attitude toward me. Things are different now that my dear uncle, who so diligently shunned negative attacks on his opponents, is no longer the candidate. Someone like Emmett Douglas might appreciate my view of history, Kat's history anyway. After all, who knows what pictures I have in my family album."

His scraggly black hair and mustache were plastered by the rain against his skull, his black suit hung limply on his skeletal frame. To Kat, he was the personification of the dark spirits that pursued her waking and sleeping dreams for days. She cried out and pushed him aside running directly into Harry Crast, almost knocking him over.

Mario was two steps behind and steadied the journalist as Kat kept running. They followed her into a small entry hall that stood empty. Most of the mourners were driving slowly along Orchard Street. Shaking off the rain, Crast spoke gently to Kat who stood in a corner, hugging her arms, eyes closed.

"I wanted to talk with you for a minute."

"She's exhausted and upset, Harry. Can't this wait until later?"

"This is personal, not political," he responded. "Your Aunt Rose was one of the kindest women I've ever known. During her illness, I promised I would watch out for you and always be fair in what I reported of your public life. I'm not sure what our worthless governor might do. Know that I'll be watching every move Emmett Douglas makes. Any underhanded attacks I discover, I'll pass on to Mario. And whenever journalistic ethics allow, I'll be in there working for you."

Kat's wan smile was grateful as she reached out and patted Crast's arm.

"Thank you, Harry. I may need your vigilance."

"I've known you most of your life, Kat honey, and I don't intend to let that corrupt scoundrel destroy you with lies and slander."

Crast's pledge of support cheered Kat as they ran into the rain to their cars.

10

Sex Magic
April

Rhode Island
Washington

Squeals of delight from volunteers stuffing and sealing another in the endless procession of fundraising appeals alerted her; Jake and Pete had arrived. Fueled by the commercials, Jake's star quotient rivaled Kat's in the eyes of the mostly young co-eds. He accepted it good-naturedly and allowed Pete free rein among the amorous girls.

Pete pulled a black book from his pocket as the three set off for Solmar's, one of his favorite Portuguese restaurants.

"I'm devoting this one strictly to the women that have fallen my way due to my buddy Jake's remarkable stardom. Someday he might change his mind and decide he wants to sample a few of his fans."

Pete waved a hand vaguely at Jake.

"I know, I know, sex is a spiritual experience and it requires the right person, the right state of mind, blah, blah, blah. But, should you choose to indulge in simple fucking, the list will be here waiting for you. I'll be happy to share."

Jake reached over and ran his hand lightly along the sensitive skin inside Roxy's arm as if to assure her that the promised delights of diversity did nothing to alter his intentions. She felt sexual energy in his touch for the first time. He must be relaxing his discipline. The full moon was only three days away.

Located in an unimposing single-story structure along the main street of East Providence, Solmar's was an elegant surprise inside with pink cloth-covered tables and gray napkins, soft lighting, and formally dressed waiters. Since the restaurant was Pete's choice, he took responsibility for ordering. Roxy had learned their pattern by now. They found several favorites—the restaurant's best efforts according to the two men—and ate only those, selecting the restaurant when they had a taste for its particular specialty. Every three or four years Pete would publish a small booklet listing his favorites from all over the state. He called it *The Best of Silver Tongue and Golden Tastebuds*, the name of his regular column.

While they waited for the various dishes to arrive, they talked about sex and love and the difference between them.

"I'm not qualified to explain their difference," objected Pete, "I've never been in love."

"Never in love? I'm always in love." Roxy was shocked. "The last time I held no flame in my heart for some man or another was for six months in 1972."

"Do you love only one man at a time or do you amass them?"

Considering that one of the two men she was currently involved with sat beside her, Roxy danced around the question.

"All my relationships have heart, are loving and intimate. I try to love the one I'm with. Looking at anyone with loving eyes tends to bring out the best in them."

The waiter interrupted, bearing a flaming pig-shaped casserole in which chourico was being grilled. He placed it on the table and left them to determine when the sausage was ready.

"This is what sex is like for me. The fire, the burn, waiting until it's done exactly right." Pete blew out the flame under the tiny grill and speared a chunk of barely charred chourico. "Then eating the tasty treat, savoring the flavor."

Jake watched him devour the sausage, grinning hugely at the look of intense pleasure on his friend's face. A squat grandmother with traces of European birth in her words shyly approached him.

"I saw you with your father on television. You're a good boy. I wish my grandsons were more like you. And the girl you talk about, Kiley, I like her, too. Is she your girlfriend?"

Jake assured her he was helping Kat because he believed she would make a good senator. He beamed when she promised to have her whole family vote for his friend.

Conversation veered to the sensual aspects of food as the waiter arrived with a platter of sweet and succulent squid, pork, little necks, and potatoes in a spicy brown sauce, and a paella overflowing with meats, seafood, and vegetables stewed in saffron-tinted rice. Muffled comments about the delectable sauce in the pork dish, how the squid melted in their mouths, and the fruity splendor of the house wine were interspersed with moans of pleasure. Each found the sensual experience of the food fulfilling, needing little intellectual commentary. They were perfect eating companions.

As their rhythm shifted to picking lightly at remaining fragments of the various foods, the trio picked up the threads of their earlier conversation.

"I'm tuned to the sensual and the intimate so the world of love and sex are my natural focus," Roxy explained. "Supposedly it's because I'm a Cancer. I love soft chairs and clothes that feel good against my skin, the perfume of flowers and fine foods. Rough and tumble is not for me, thank you. The trip to Russia I took with Kat was ideal: limos, handsome young translators, champagne and caviar. I like to know I'm going to eat and have a soft bed to sleep in, preferably not alone.

I like a life of adventure as long as those adventures are romantic. Pain, dirt and discomfort are never romantic.

"To me, love is the thrill, all the thrills: discovery, falling in love, the first time making love, and every other time." She laughed expressively. "Max always uses me as his example of the natural pagan whom he describes as an innocent user of inborn erotic talent."

"Should you ever tire of my buddy's rules and rituals, come see me. Nothing I like better before breakfast than a taste of ripe pagan juices," Pete commented, popping another clam into his mouth.

As she and Pete continued to exchange views of love and sex and the difference therein, Roxy wondered about Jake's reticence. He listened attentively, picked mushrooms, shrimp and meat tidbits from the scraps on the serving plates but said nothing.

"A sexual partner can be enjoyed without requiring love," Jake finally stated.

"Yeah," interjected Pete with a longing sigh, "you don't even need to know her name."

Jake ignored him. "And much can be found through love that does not require sex."

"I agree. Love doesn't have anything to do with sex or at least it isn't necessary. And I've learned it's better not to pretend. Counterfeit love turns sex to anger," Pete added.

Pursuing one of her favorite intellectual exercises: proving that men and women were different, Roxy asked, "Do you find a gender difference in attitudes about sex and love? Besides the obvious, of course—that men put it out and women take it in."

Pete answered immediately.

"Men are less romantic about sex and more about love while women require their sex to be romantic but are eminently practical when it comes to love. Maybe they think about relationships so much, it becomes a practical issue. Then there's the whole question of honesty. Women can fake their sexual pleasure; men's dicks never lie."

"Let's not forget the most important difference—outcome." Roxy was emphatic. "For women, sex is the magic connection to their greatest power, creation of life. They confront the potential each month in their cycles. For men the connection is more transitory. They ejaculate and then it's over. Maybe that's what makes the act of sex more compelling for a man than for a woman. It's his only opportunity to feel the life force directly."

As the waiter cleared empty plates from the table, they talked about the next day. Jake and Pete were planning to be out before dawn for one of the great Rhode Island rituals, the opening of trout season.

"Some folks only go out the first day," Pete explained. "We're going to Silver Lake. It's an incredible scene. People get there by 3 a.m. Dozens of boats line up along the shore, crashing into each other, dropping gear and bait overboard. Then at dawn, a horn is blown and trout season begins. Drive by. You can see it from Rt. 4."

"I think we're going in the other direction. Kat pledged that every day in April she was in the state, she would investigate some aspect of the environment. Tomorrow we're touring public beaches, beginning with Scarborough, where Kat's being interviewed by the *Narragansett Times* and ending with the Coast Guard lighthouse at Point Judith."

"I went to Scarborough with my family every summer as a kid," Jake told her. "We swam and fished, but mostly we ate. It was called Lido then. You graduated from one beach area to another. When I was old enough, I could walk from Lido north to Olivious. Finally, I was ready for hormone central—Scarborough Beach proper. There was a fenced-in area where beer could be consumed. It had tables, and courts for volley ball and bocchia. They're making a new area, Scarborough South. It should be ready by next summer."

After they arranged to meet the next evening for the maritime fundraiser both men helped organize for Kat, Pete pulled out his pipe, motioned ritualistically at them asking permission, drew on it and sighed, "Ah, dessert."

Roxy was not ready to abandon the topic of sex and love without some useful information. She turned to Jake.

"Since Pete claims never to have been in love, I guess this question is for you. Don't you find that love enhances sex, changes it, makes it sweeter and more profound?"

"I thought that's what pot did," Pete laughed, Jake joining in. They signaled for the check and the question went unanswered.

Roxy was giving Jake a ride home. As they headed south, she mentally reviewed and rejected several ways of approaching her earlier question. Did love make sex better, or was it a justification to soothe moral sensibilities? As if reading her mind, Jake's voice came smoothly from the dimness alongside her.

"For you, romantic love is obsessive. You feel it intensely for certain people, usually inexplicably, and then it fades. Is that a fair description?"

Roxy mumbled her agreement and he continued.

"It's chemistry. The ancient texts of tantra offer techniques for transcending it. The ultimate power of sex is the reality of energy exchange between the partners and tantra recognizes that it improves with love because the barriers are down. When sex is approached with the sacred reverence it deserves, the result is explosive and transformative."

Roxy parked in front of Jake's house. His voice was husky with feeling as he finished his discourse.

"The deepest connection between a man and woman comes through aware sex. Once that link has been made, it's impossible not to love the partner."

★ ★ ★ ★ ★

Roxy groaned as she reviewed her list of tasks. Responding to Kat's call for a high-velocity campaign, staff had jammed Earth Month, as they took to calling April, with environment-related events in Washington and Rhode Island. Endless numbers of statements, speeches, remarks and other written material were required to support all the activity. Plus Kat asked her to produce a monthly "insiders" report of the campaign gossip they wanted known. Fortunately, she did not have to worry about producing legislative testimony or press releases.

Hayes had helped put the correct political spin on the background information she had collected, but she needed to review the basic themes with Kat. The erotic fantasies his intimate tone triggered, even over the phone, often caused her to lose her train of thought. Although she suspected he was doing three other tasks while cradling the receiver against his shoulder and whispering sweet nothings in her ear, he seemed totally focused on her. She was grateful not to be continually faced with the weak-in-the-knees, wet-in-the-crotch feeling his presence induced.

"You look recovered from last weekend's gloom," Roxy commented as Kat bounded down the stairs, dressed to walk on the beach in a blue-green sweat suit and the Nikes she won annually as the fastest woman in Congress. Her hair was tied in a striking hand-painted scarf and around her neck was a dolphin, hand cast in a silver arc. It must be an amulet, thought Roxy. She remembered seeing the necklace in at least two media photos that week.

"It's working just as we hoped!" Kat's exuberant voice affirmed Roxy's observation. She described several groups asking her to substitute at meetings or speeches for Winston.

"They've concluded I'm the de facto junior senator. I even testified before the Senate Environment and Public Works committee on two pieces of legislation critical for Rhode Island. I proposed a list of beaches to be preserved, including one in Middletown slated to be developed by several of Emmett Douglas' cronies. Sharpening my sword to skewer the devil," she chuckled. "And I requested funds for a state-of-the-art joint sewer project for Cranston, Warwick and West Warwick. They're key cities to have in our vote column. Senator Stuart sits on the committee and virtually guaranteed the funds would be approved."

"I hope you're ready for 'round the clock campaigning while I'm here for Easter recess. Jasmine arrives soon to deal with all the national media who want to spend time on the campaign trail. Once Hayes gets back from his junket to Costa Rica, he'll be working on out-of-state fundraising."

Roxy had decided it was fortunate that Hayes would not come to Rhode Island during the recess. She and Jake had a date with sexual destiny on Monday. After that, she might be unwilling to share herself with another man.

"You may consider testifying in the Senate to be the high point of your week, but the campaign kids would disagree," Roxy giggled. "The picture of you being kissed by one of Hollywood's most celebrated hunks, silhouetted against the gleaming Capitol dome, is plastered all over the walls at headquarters. It made every paper in the state as well as network news. Obviously hunks are great copy."

"I hope everyone realizes the point of our appearance was to promote stricter ocean dumping regulations." They both laughed at Kat's wishful thinking.

After the walk, they met a reporter from *The Times* for a scheduled interview along the seawall. Roxy listened intently as Kat spoke. It was the best way to absorb both Kat's ideas and her cadence.

Kat described her long-time crusade to protect what she considered Rhode Island's most significant resource—the ocean and coastal waters that surrounded most of the state. She briefly outlined her well-known work with Baywatch, how she built it from a shoestring operation based in the finished room over her garage to the multi-million dollar political powerhouse she left eight years ago to run successfully for Congress.

Once in Washington, she became undisputed queen of the seas, unceasingly vigilant against attempts to use the precious waters for cheap dumpsites.

"The ocean is mother of us all! How can we poison her with our sewage?"

Kat railed as she told of battling nuclear power plants, chemical seepage, and hospital waste. Success came last year with passage of strict ocean dumping legislation. She gave an example of how meaningless political considerations were when the fate of the oceans was at stake. Horrified by Pentagon plans to base nuclear weapons underwater along the continental shelf early in her second term, she threatened to reveal plans to the public, earning her the distinction of instant removal from her seat on the Intelligence committee. The missile-basing plan was rejected.

"There's a constant theme to my environmental work," Kat told the reporter. Roxy began taking notes. This was what she needed.

"Economics. We must restructure economic indicators to account for environmental and social costs. Only in this way can the free market system actually work to protect the environment in economically feasible ways. My drive to legislate a pollution tax as a means of forcing economic consideration of the costs of polluting was defeated by a powerful senator owned by the oil companies. It's one of the key reasons I want to be in the U.S. Senate. I want to assure that polluters pay."

Kat invited the reporter to their maritime fundraiser that evening.

"You should hear about ocean pollution and what's being done to halt it from those it most affects—fishermen, many of them your readers. Without a clean bay and ocean, neither sport nor commercial fishing will survive. It was through friends who were lobster fishermen that I started Baywatch and ultimately passed the ocean dumping legislation."

SEX MAGIC

★ ★ ★ ★ ★

Roxy reviewed the list of attendees for the evening's fundraiser as Kat got dressed. She was wearing a new color of lingerie—a silvery blue satin chemise covered with delicate lace, a scant shade darker—as she sorted through the lines of clothes in her walk-in closet.

"Are you wearing black for mourning?" Roxy asked pointing to a bra and slip of jet black laying on the bed. There was a discouraged look on Kat's face as she carried a white silk dress with a spectacular blue and green marbleized silk tunic from the closet.

"There's so much to mourn. I try to concentrate on the environmental success stories but see only failure everywhere. Another generation of pollution and the biosphere will collapse and our gene pool may be permanently and tragically altered. What if we're too late?" she cried. "What if some galactic council has decided that we've gone too far and Earth must be sacrificed? Children will have to live in controlled environments on a poisoned and toxic planet or be prepared to escape into space."

The sound of despair choking Kat's pure voice moved Roxy to breath a prayer of gratitude that all she had to worry about was how to keep Jake in Rhode Island and Hayes in D.C.

"When I stand on the earth, or with the ocean lapping at my feet, I know this planet is a great being, alive and pulsing with a destiny as splendid and compelling as its form. Those ancient ones who worshipped the earth, especially as the Great Mother, are my spiritual ancestors. It's my sworn duty to protect and cherish the earth.

"Tonight I have to face all my friends who are fishermen knowing they're a dying breed. The price of lobster is so low they're selling them directly off the boats in Galilee. That hurts the wholesaler and retailer and barely keeps the fishermen alive. High quality ocean fish are virtually extinct as a commercial product because of pollution and over-fishing. We're looking to bottom feeders and bait, like squid, to support the industry.

"Boat owners who work their own boats have always been the epitome of the state's independent man—Rhode Island's cowboys. They're being replaced now by floating factories staffed with hired hands who assembly-line fish, clean and freeze all in one operation. It's my task to protect the waters so at least they can fish for sport and not lose the spirit and skill altogether."

Giving herself a final glance in the mirror, Kat changed the subject.

"I'll drive, you review the week's schedule with me."

The next day was Palm Sunday. Kat would attend Mass at her cousin's church then spend the rest of the day as she and Mario usually spent Sundays, attending to the literally hundreds of relatives, associates, and family friends from the state's Italo community who made up the unshakable core of Kat's political network.

The rest of the week was packed with constituent meetings, tree plantings, Rotary Club speeches, radio and print media interviews, and school visits. There was not an environmental group in the state, no matter how small and informal, that was not scheduled to meet with her during the month. All would hear Kat's theme that until polluters pay for everything from ocean dumping to toxic waste clean up, nothing would change.

Kat was particularly pleased with the Civil Air Patrol excursion Roxy had set up.

"They want to make you a general or something. Senator Stuart apparently ranks high on their hero list. This is at his suggestion. I knew you wanted to do a fly-by inspection of the coast and bay so I worked it out that they'll fly you around to talk about drug interdiction but you can check environmental damage."

Roxy was also pleased with this event. She knew Kat relished accomplishing more than one goal at a time. An added bonus was the fun she had working out arrangements with the air patrol representative who had an inviting twinkle in his eye.

"Good job, Rox. This will give me a chance to visit the weather station at Green Airport and announce how I've saved their facility from the ax. Have Mario try to arrange press for that and tell him to pursue an endorsement from their union. Relay the message to Stuart that this one's for him and his fellow pilots. I don't like feeling so indebted.

"By the way, I particularly like your line 'once ours were voices crying in the wilderness, now we can hardly be heard above the chorus of millions.' I want to use it every chance I get. It inspires hope and hope is the fuel we desperately need."

"Do you mind if I work at home on Monday or do you need me to drive?"

"There are dozens of people who can drive me," Kat replied. She cut off Roxy's protest that she enjoyed the task. "You can choose it as your pleasure. Occasionally I'll need you to drive, for security of one sort or another." She smiled wryly.

"Wednesday night I'm going to the town council meeting with Jake to protest beach fees."

"I know this happens every year and Jake's been in the forefront of the protest but ask him to minimize his public involvement for a while, with the commercials and all. And you behave yourself, too."

When she saw her friends blush furiously, Kat laughed.

"I meant at the meeting, not with Jake. He's exactly what you need right now."

Roxy looked at her speculatively. "Do you know that Jake practices tantric yoga?"

Kat pulled into the parking lot across from the Dutch Inn where the maritime fundraiser was being held and stared out at Galilee's Harbor of Refuge, built after a destructive hurricane. "Yes, I know."

Something in her tone spurred Roxy to continue.

"Do you practice it also?"

"Yes. It works on evolutionary development, the drive toward unity."

"With him?" Roxy asked, ignoring Kat's philosophical meanderings.

"Max and I learned the practice when we were on the road. We brought a woman back with us from Colorado who ended up moving in with Jake and becoming his teacher/partner. Jake and I shared the rituals once. We felt we had karma to finish and we did." Kat moved to get out of the car.

"Why didn't you ever talk to me about tantric yoga? You know sex is one of my fields of interest."

Kat laughed at her tone of indignation.

"It's not really girl talk. At least not our kind of girls. There are some things that can only be learned from men."

"Yeah, like what to do with a throbbing blue veiner." They both laughed as they walked into the crowded fundraiser for a night of talking fish.

★ ★ ★ ★ ★

It was the most perfect morning Roxy had seen on the beach to date. The waves rolled in with precision. Crystalline blue water broke neatly into white lace that decorated the light sand. Blues and pinks had not yet been burned from the horizon by a fully risen sun. No matter how often Roxy saw a pastel sunrise, she always recalled her childhood fascination with what she thought was an impossible color—sky blue pink. Now here it was, streaked impressionistically across the dawn sky. Gulls littered the beach as usual but there were also other birds, tiny ones whose legs scurried them across the sand like cartoon characters. The windows of the Dunes Club glowed in hot pink squares.

She had just passed the club approaching the empty dunes fringed with spiky green oat grass when she saw the sand sculpture. It was about five feet long, a remarkably detailed dragon with a coiled tail surrounded by a wall to keep away the surf. In a flame bursting from the dragon's mouth was a message: *My passion lies in wait for you tonight.*

It had to be from Jake, for her. When she returned, there was a message from him stuck to the door.

Come over at six. Don't bathe first. I have some special essences and oils.

★ ★ ★ ★ ★

She sat wrapped in a huge white towel on a handcrafted maple bench along the life-sized stained glass window that portrayed a featureless woman with long, flowing auburn hair in exactly the pose Roxy now held. Jake's bathroom was as large as most bedrooms and paneled in barn wood that was a warm brown, highly textured and streaked with rosy pink. The tub was oversized, built into a platform of the same wood and trimmed in bright Mexican tiles. Jake was pouring lavender flowers and oil into the hot water.

"Lavender is for purification," he explained, motioning her to get in. Roxy dropped her towel and slid into the water, excited by the look of anticipation on his face. She smiled as he slid into the tub facing her.

Afterwards they rubbed each other dry, "To fluff up the bioelectric currents" he said. He instructed her to anoint herself with musk oil.

"Rub it heavily into the areas you find most sexually responsive. As you touch your skin, feel the pleasure. Get in touch with your body. Love it so I can, too."

She felt the heavy waves of musk filter through her nostrils, penetrating to a back part of the brain, summoning the serpent.

"Do you rub yourself with oil?" she asked between deep breaths of the sensual fragrance.

"You're the sacred object, the divine force here. You're the anointed one."

He handed her a sheer red silk negligee to put on and wrapped himself in a deep blue cotton robe then took her hand and led her into the living room. He sat her on the platform to his left, facing a pure white china platter with various foods arranged on it. Two crystal goblets were placed by a matching pitcher of water on the right. Two hand blown wine glasses that looked like captured soap bubbles guarded a crystal decanter of wine on the left. A red and a white candle in crystal starburst holders flanked a ruby glass vase filled with red roses behind the platter. Musk incense pervaded the room. Roxy thought about the fortune strip for April she had drawn the previous morning: *That which is not celebrated, goes unnoticed.*

As they sat cross-legged, rhythmically breathing, to get in tune with each other, Jake spoke of what they were about to undertake.

"This is the secret ritual, the heart of tantric practices. Each action, each breath must be conscious. The ancient enlightened ones sought the descent of higher power and lavish enjoyment of divine bounty here on earth. They understood that the purpose of life is to infuse the physical with the divine. Sex is an ideal channel for this union of opposites.

"At this Aries full moon, the Mars-ruled sun is polarized and balanced by the Venus-ruled moon. The male Shiva cannot exist without his Shakti, his female mate. She is universal power; without her, he is a corpse. In turn, without his regulation she is blind, uncontrolled force. From their union is born everything in the universe. Because woman is divine, all intercourse with her, even the most casual, is sacramental. It's essential that you understand clearly what happens as we come together. Sharing sexual energy means we take on pieces of each other, pieces that stay with us forever. Will you accept me, Roxy?"

Struck by the solemnity of his request, she mutely nodded.

He began the ceremony uttering strange syllables while decanting, breathing, then pouring the wine. He raised his glass, motioning her to do the same. Both gazed transfixed at the shimmering red liquid suspended in invisible globes of light then drained their glasses. Jake refilled them and led Roxy through a ritual tasting of strips of grilled steak, chunks of fresh tuna, and cubes of home baked grain bread, explaining their significance in nourishing the life force. After each they drained their wine glasses. By the time they cleared their mouths with water, she was feeling lightheaded and relaxed.

"These are an offering to the love goddess," Jake said handing her a glass box streaked with purples and blues. She took out a strand of rosy quartz beads and hung it around her neck. He smiled his approval and took her hand leading her upstairs to his bed.

He directed her to remove the robe, leaving on the beads, and sat her on the edge of the bed where the violet light could shine dimly on her naked body. He looked at her with eyes filled by admiration and awe as if seeing in her the mystery of all women.

"It is this revelation of the eternal female in you that makes what we are to do sacred," he whispered as he signaled her to lie down.

He then touched her lightly at various points along her body. She understood none of the Sanskrit words he chanted softly while the tips of his fingers brushed her forehead, the hollow of her throat, ear lobes, breasts, upper arms, navel, thighs, knees, feet, seemingly summoning forth her energy. As he returned to touch her pubic area, he called its name.

"Yoni, your treasure."

Roxy liked the word. Yoni. It sounded female and sacred, better than the crass terms it was usually called.

Jake removed his robe and she got her first glimpse of the real teacher looking expectant but controlled, nothing like the shy bulb soaking in the bath. He laid on his left side, facing her, and indicated she should remain on her back. The sky god and forest deva hung suspended at the end of the room, their otherworldly images captured in the glass shimmering with the full moon's potent light.

He barely penetrated her yoni as Roxy began to think of her goddess shrine. Although Jake said nothing about whether speaking was permitted or not, she decided to wait before asking questions. She was curious to know the word for his treasure.

"We lie so joined for thirty-two minutes."

Her eyes flew open in surprise and she forgot silence.

"Thirty-two minutes!" she exclaimed.

"Try to stay relaxed but concentrated. Imagine the flow of energy you've experienced moving up and down your spine now flowing between us at the point of contact," Jake replied gently. She suppressed a giggle at the thought of their "point of contact."

After several minutes she began to notice an increasing tide of pleasure centered in her genitals as if forces there were being stimulated although neither of them moved. His breathing continued in a deep and regular fashion, his body resting against her. She could feel his firmness barely touching the soft lips of her sex.

"Can we talk during the time we're lying together?" she whispered.

"We search each other's eyes for the archetypes of male and female that we represent during this ritual. We can speak of what we see. We can share words of love and tenderness. But nothing should be said that will break our concentration otherwise there can be no surrender and we will not achieve the ultimate sensation."

Roxy gazed at him and was startled to see a flashing series of male faces, young, old, dark and pale. She told him of the American Indian she saw with black eyes and long hair that hung on his bare chest. She described the image she intuitively recognized as the God of men.

He breathed words into the hollow between her breasts as if speaking directly to her heart and recounted the delights of her skin, her silky hair, her shell pink nipples, the fragrant lotus of her soul drawing him in. He called her Aphrodite and thanked her again for choosing him.

She had no idea how much time had passed when suddenly she felt as if a rocket began to rise within her. At its tip was a blue-green orb that shone with increasing intensity as it surged past the whirlpools of sensation surrounding each chakra. Ecstatic ripples mounted and swelled as the rocket and its orb slowly rose from deep inside her belly. When it reached her heart she could scarcely breath. Both their bodies stiffened and the thought that she should try to stem her orgasm flashed past. Was the time right?

Her desire for release was unbearable causing her knees to quiver slightly. She wiggled and the energy was unleashed. The rocket hurled the glittering orb upward through her throat where it pulled her screams along on its scorching path out the crown of her head. The orb burst through, scattering a cloud of diamonds that settled like a cap on her hair. Flames shooting from the base of the rocket burned themselves into every cell of her body. She rocked with the force as wave after wave of sublime sexual pleasure swept her from head to toe.

Her last conscious act was to notice Jake holding his breath, then she felt him release and ejaculate. A fireball exploded melting all separation between them. She could taste their blended juices. They were male and female united. She knew all that had gone before was unimportant, and all that followed was the divine blessing of the goddess.

SEX MAGIC

★ ★ ★ ★ ★

They sat in the crowded Town Council chambers, a traditional New England public room with cream paneled walls and large windows. Exposed brick served as backdrop for the council seated in a semi-circle on an elevated stage at the front of the room.

"As you can hear," Jake whispered after several labored exchanges between council members and citizens, "there are four idiots and one thinker."

The issue was clear. Two members of the council were strongly pushing to fence in Narragansett Beach so the town could charge an entry fee. Fees would be in effect only during summer season but the fence would remain year round. They hastened to explain that residents would be allowed to purchase season passes at a special rate. Virtually every person in the audience opposed the idea as they had each time it had been proposed during the past several years. Jake had agreed with Kat's request to limit his involvement. A bright young woman, home on Easter break from Harvard Law School, issued the challenge that Jake usually made: to enter the beach, refuse to pay, and force a legal battle which proponents of a free beach felt certain they could win on constitutional issues.

Jake sat silent during the meeting rising only to offer his traditional reading of the constitutional section that guaranteed freedom of the beach. The attention he routinely received as a well-liked native of the area was trebled by his new celebrity status.

"Article 1 - Section 17 of the Constitution of Rhode Island and the Providence Plantations assures," he solemnly intoned, "the people shall continue to enjoy and freely exercise all the rights of the fishery and the privileges of the shore to which they have been heretofore entitled under the charter and usage of this state including but not limited to fishing from the shore, the gathering of seaweed, leaving the shore to swim in the sea and passage along the shore."

The dullest looking of the idiots on stage guaranteed Jake that people would still be able to collect seaweed since city workers regularly rake it into huge piles placed at one end of the beach. He remained silent in response.

★ ★ ★ ★ ★

"Sudden, dramatic surprises have been the stellar special of the week and I received my dose yesterday thanks to our perverse former employee Carrie. Make certain all events on my schedule are double-checked."

Roxy did not like the sound of Kat's complaint.

"What happened?"

Kat pulled a folded sheet of newspaper from her fanny pack and read, "If this is Saturday then I must be in Lincoln, or so thought Congresswoman Tomasso as she breezed in to address the small elite group of business powers in the northern part of the state who were meeting at Bryant College. Was her face red as the men showed her a letter written in response to a request from her office to speak explaining their policy of not inviting any political figures involved in current campaigns to address their group. We're certain there were a dozen other gatherings waiting to be thrown into her busy schedule."

Kat looked up from the papers. "When we called to find out how a reporter from the *Woonsocket Call* happened on this meeting, we were told our office sent a fax trumpeting the speech as a major breakthrough in garnering support from previous hold-outs in the business community. We never sent any such alert. This event barely rated a notice on our schedule. With the chaos over Winston's death and my increased activities, no one had the time or inclination to check it out."

"How do you know it was Carrie?"

"The man who wrote the letter told me his contact was Carrie. The event was also logged on in her name and all correspondence took place while she was still in the office." Roxy trotted to keep up with Kat who strode along the beach kicking at quohog shells. Roxy expressed relief that Carrie's trick did not involve black magic. Kat laughed.

"I know you're worried about her so I checked with Max."

"What did he say?"

"He claimed fear of God is the only charm a magician has against the power. Once that is lost, anyone playing at magic is bound to be destroyed by their own ego masquerading as magic power. Carrie's days are numbered if she is indeed strolling down the left-hand path."

Somehow the thought of waiting for Carrie to self-destruct was not the protection against her evil thoughts that Roxy wanted.

"Can't we do anything to help her slide into the pit quicker?"

"Mario suggested asking my Uncle Louie's oldest boy to take care of Carrie. They call him 'Sweeper' because he has the region's most extensive collection of the 12 gauge, semi-automatic revolver shotgun called the street sweeper. It's very attractive looking—a mean, black cylinder with shotgun shells in it. I liked the idea."

Alerted by her gasp, Kat chuckled and assured Roxy she was only kidding.

"People who have relatives with names like Jerry 'the Mole' and Carmine 'Big Fish' are capable of doing anything," Kat said. "There must be something in the quotation marks."

Roxy did not like murder and mayhem jokes, even directed against someone as scary as Carrie. Several of Kat's uncles and cousins terrified her. She knew it was blind ethnic stereotyping that labeled Italians as gangsters but burly members of Kat's family looked straight out of The Godfather.

"Is there anything less drastic we can do?"

"Check everything twice and hope Carrie finds a new obsession soon."

"I mean about protecting ourselves from her magic."

Kat put her hand on Roxy's shoulder.

"We have too many real problems to deal with for me to waste much time worrying about a confused young woman pretending to be a witch."

They stood facing Narrow River at the north end of the beach, the full moon creating high tides so only the rock boulders were visible in the passage.

"This is a unique body of water," Kat explained, changing the subject. "It's not really a river but rather an estuary, one of the few virgin ones in the northeast, meaning it's an opening into the ocean untouched by the hand of man." There was a queer twist to Kat's smile.

"The channel is very tricky and shifts every year. Bamboo poles are placed to mark it but still someone dies in a boating accident here almost annually. A vocal minority calls for dredging to stabilize the channel. Last year, when the *Alexander Gold* spilled its oil, we were concerned it would penetrate up the river. We moved a boom into the mouth immediately that kept most of the oil out."

She turned and they began walking back.

"Tomorrow night we're doing focus groups to test what people are thinking and saying about the senate race. It'll be interesting to see if they've picked up on our environment emphasis or not."

Roxy was looking forward both to the results of the focus group and to seeing how the process actually worked.

★ ★ ★ ★ ★

Silently, they stared through a one-way mirror at the dozen representatives of the electorate chosen to act as a focus group for Kiley Tomasso's senate campaign. The men and women of varying ages and occupations, selected by how well they matched demographics of likely voters, knew only that they were being paid fifty dollars to participate for two hours one evening in a question and answer session about a product of the advertising agency. Kat's pollster, Lila Gravely, was directing the session, seated at the head of a long conference table around which were arranged the dozen people.

While the rest of the viewers in the small room behind the mirror occasionally got up, shuffled around, and snacked from sumptuous trays of pizza and antipasto, Kat never moved. She fixed on the interaction in the next room as if she were recording every nuance, look, and word in her brain to sort through later. Roxy noted the phrases of a retired military man and a middle aged woman who worked as a nurse at the VA hospital that seemed to resonate with the others. Their opinions won the most nods of agreement from the group. She could use them in speeches. It was highly effective to repeat back to people what they were thinking.

There were few surprises. They loved Kiley, thought she was just what Rhode Island needed, could not imagine anyone but her as their next senator, although it was too bad what happened to Winston. Everyone knew of her work with the environment. "She's Miss Environment all right," said one young man who sold used cars. When another man pointed out she had the legs to be Miss anything, the group tittered and held several side discussions about Kat's dancing and the pin-up picture that had appeared on the cover of People magazine. They seemed proud.

Lila led the group in an exercise to describe various politicians she named as animals. Except for one woman who thought she looked like a black swan and a man who saw her as a half-broken young filly, every person seated around the table identified Kiley Tomasso as a cat.

When asked what they would change about Kiley, her hair, her clothes, her general appearance rated the most comments. Universally they wanted to tone her down, soften her up. Kat jerked her shoulders when a soft-spoken gray haired grandmother described her as "cold and aloof, like she's known tragedy and can't bear the pain of touching anyone again." They praised her intelligence. Several called her brilliant and visionary and felt inspired by her work.

Their sole concern was that her victory could bring a Republican-controlled Senate. Two youngish women in the room and an older man, a laborer, were terrified by what that meant for women's rights and unions. Only two of the twelve said they would not vote for her because she was a Republican.

The characteristic that most defined her in their eyes was her integrity. Each person mentioned it in various contexts. In a state where adoring voters overwhelmingly elected a convicted felon then argued whether he could hold office, Kat's impeccable honesty was a shining light. They turned to her when discouraged by the mediocre and venal mass of politicians. The more that participants spoke of Kat's honor, the more intensely Gould frowned until Roxy thought the end of his lips would curve down off his jaw.

The media advisor brightened immediately when his commercials were played. There was no doubt, even knowing they were Kiley's creations, that the focus group believed every word Jake and the other characters said about her.

To close the session, Lila took a straw poll matching Kat against several possible candidates. No one stood a chance. Her smallest margin of victory was losing four of the twelve votes to Calvin Davis, the handsome young Mayor of Bristol who was odds-on favorite in the gubernatorial primary.

Everyone in the room was elated, patting themselves on the back, popping open cans of beer to celebrate. It was only April. They had no opponent and a locked up race. Life was sweet. Kat sat apart from the group, eyes veiled, processing what she had seen and heard. Gould continued to mutter. Standing behind Roxy's chair, Jake tossed a wadded up napkin at Gould hitting him on his bald crown.

"Hal! What's the matter? We're a hit, ready for Hollywood at least."

Gould looked up, glanced at Jake then over to Kat who was once again focused in the present and waiting for his answer.

"I don't like the way everyone thinks you're uncorruptible. It's not natural. You're human, not some tinsel trimmed angel."

Kat closed her eyes and said nothing.

"I don't like people having unrealistic expectations of my candidate. One slip and you're finished. They'll hate you for not being the saint they enshrined. It's a precarious role especially when we know Emmett Douglas will spread every filthy rumor and lie he can dream up."

Kat interrupted the downward spiral of his analysis.

"Don't you think they know me well enough to give me the benefit of the doubt if some absurd allegation of dishonesty surfaces?"

"It's not that simple. Most people won't believe the lies but their faith in you will be cracked. If he can hammer away long enough at the crack, and get some unscrupulous reporter to slant the news only slightly, we may sink on the merest hint of impropriety."

"Do you consider the Press Club dance and issues over Max to be threats?" Kat asked.

Glumly, Gould shook his head.

"Well, what then? Do you know something I should know?" There was no resisting the command in Kat's voice although Gould looked pained as he stalled, searching for the right words.

"I have a couple very clandestine contacts in the Democratic camp. They agree that Douglas will be our opponent. Supposedly, he's given orders to several of his key lieutenants to keep their eyes on you."

"Did he specify any particular areas so we can be especially careful?"

Everyone looked at him expectantly. Kat insisted he tell them exactly what he knew. Squirming briefly Gould capitulated and said in an embarrassed tone, "Douglas told them to watch your bed. 'I can't imagine a cunt like her sleeps alone,' were his exact words according to my source."

"That'll be a futile watch," she laughed ruefully. "Make sure they know I sleep on the third floor. I don't want them to mix my bed up with Roxy's."

Roxy sputtered her indignation and the rest of them laughed, including Jake.

Lila Gravely came in, exuberant at the outcome of the focus group, and expressed her confidence that the upcoming poll would demonstrate the same results.

"With good numbers, comments like those we heard tonight, and no opponent, people should be beating down the door to give you money," she exclaimed.

Mario seconded her assessment, reporting that by mid-month they had achieved their April fundraising goals and money was coming in daily. Kat directed him to concentrate on raising money in the state.

"Once Douglas declares, a lot of cowards will hide their check books."

★ ★ ★ ★ ★

It was Earth Day and Kat was flying in from New York after taping Charlie Drummond's morning show on ABC. Jasmine had withdrawn her objection after being assured the environment would be the only topic. Kat was able to reiterate her theme of "polluter pays" several times. Driving back to the office, Kat told Roxy that only in the closing seconds did Charlie's lust show through.

"He hailed me as 'an apt representative for our beautiful and desirable Mother Earth.' Once the red light flashed off, Charlie was practically on his knees begging me to stay and have a private brunch with him."

As Kat twitched her disgust, Roxy thought she should turn him over to her. He was cute, and she would like to know how she rated on his list of hundreds. When two dozen red roses arrived in the office after the show was broadcast, Roxy decided Drummond must have his sights fixed firmly on Kat.

The three-day celebration of Earth Day at Roger Williams Park opened with a Speak Out for the Environment Soapbox that Baywatch was sponsoring. Kat was the first scheduled speaker and the press was there, print and television. After a pro forma recitation of her environmental accomplishments and reflections on the long road traveled since the first Earth Day twenty years ago, Kat made a pronouncement that triggered the whirring of television cameras. She pledged passage of oil spill legislation she had sponsored by the anniversary of the *Alexander Gold* spill on June 22.

"No obstacles shall stand against our crusade," she said. "I shall not rest until our waters are protected. Only through our vigilance and dedicated purpose can we realize the true meaning of Earth Day."

Before the television cameras could stop filming, she launched a blistering set of challenges to Emmett Douglas. Everyone on the campaign team had agreed that attacking Douglas while he was still governor was excellent strategy.

Kat first accused Douglas of jury-rigging state regulations to try and claim sufficient protection for the beach in Middletown she wanted to preserve while he and his partners moved to obtain backing for its development. She quickly moved on to Big River and the governor's plan to flood two thousand acres of wildlife habitat and twenty miles of cold water streams to provide a reservoir for projected development and population growth in areas where he and his cronies owned huge stretches of land.

"This destruction need not take place. Using water conservation methods readily available we could provide the same amount of water the Big River project would, at less than a quarter of the cost. The Governor and his partners could still develop their land and Rhode Island would have its first wild and scenic river."

A crowd had assembled filling the casino lawn where many had cheered Kat's announcement two months earlier. They were silent and attentive. Her final attack was an issue they first heard the previous day. Douglas closed the Kickimuit River's shell fishing beds, claiming the water was polluted by sewage. Long rated the cleanest salt water river in the state, rumor said the ban was motivated by a desire to downgrade the river from Class A to a ranking that would allow marina development.

"And who is a major partner in development firms planning these marinas?" Seeing the shock on Mario's face, Roxy realized with a sinking stomach that Kat was launching this missile on her own.

Her elegant diction contradicted the harsh words of her continued onslaught. Kat reminded people they had a choice to make in November.

"By choosing a governor who does not consider the state his personal piggy bank, we can achieve the economic prosperity that should be ours. Rhode Island has all it needs: location, trained population, modest costs, unique natural resources. Once again we face economic disaster, and for the same old reason— we're being ripped off by the state's politicians. We can no longer allow business as usual. It's up to you to throw the bums out."

Kat's closing flourish drew waves of delighted applause.

While Mario hurriedly assured journalists and television commentators that her negative comments were not in anticipation of Douglas as her senate opponent, other reporters tried to break through the crowd massing around Kat.

She faced a battery of flashing cameras, microphones and note-taking journalists with Mario by her side. She spoke determinedly before any were able to question her.

"It's Earth Day in Rhode Island. Every day should be Earth Day, and could be if political leaders were serving the public. Each of the issues I cited is deemed critical by people of this state. Each is within the power of Governor Emmett Douglas to resolve. I urge voters to exercise their power and hold elected officials responsible for their actions."

Roxy was amazed to hear Kat paraphrase the fortune strip she had drawn for March.

"If the people of Rhode Island don't use their power, someone else will."

"Do you want them to do the same in your senate race?" a female voice yelled from the notebook section.

"Absolutely!"

"Do you anticipate Emmett Douglas will name himself to the vacant U.S. Senate seat then decide to run against you?"

All three local network affiliates focused cameras on Harry Crast as he blandly asked the question they all wanted to know.

"Neither Governor Douglas nor the Democratic Party have chosen to confide their plans to me. And you know how I hate to speculate."

"Yeah, prediction's more your style isn't it Congresswoman?" Kat ignored the bearded, bespectacled young man in a Planet Earth teeshirt who spoke in a voice heard by few beyond the first row.

She turned additional questions about opponents and Douglas' plans into platforms for launching other environmental statements. She announced an inspection tour of the Kickimuit River later that afternoon, pledging quohog vessels available to take along any press who might choose to come. Roxy knew all three television stations would be there as well as several key print journalists. Her Big River expedition scheduled for the next day would also draw full media coverage.

"I'll be announcing proposals to designate Big River Rhode Island's first wild and scenic river and to establish a model ecosystem plan for the area."

Finally, the media surrendered and Kat left the park pleased with her performance.

★ ★ ★ ★ ★

Snuggling against Jake as he slept, Roxy reviewed the day, rating it a success. She had accomplished her primary goal: discovering whether all sex with Jake would be bound in ritual.

"I have a wonderful surprise," he exclaimed when they met on the beach that morning. Kat's caravan of media and University of Rhode Island student volunteers had just set off on their expedition to Big River.

"Sandy has reopened the Bait Shop in a new location, calling it Peppers, and it's only a few blocks from here. We can walk."

Jake had been devastated when the Bait Shop burned down the week of Kat's announcement and rumors spread that Sandy would retire from the restaurant business and set off to live on the beach in California.

"It's opening day and service is by invitation only." He pulled a pair of chili pepper shaped cards from his pocket. "We're invited."

They crossed behind the shopping center, waving to firemen who greeted Jake with wolf whistles and joking requests for his autograph, to a charming white frame house with a wide porch set with tables and chairs. It was a warm, sunny day so they chose a seat outside, greeting the waitress from the Bait Shop who took their order. The good food was unchanged and Roxy selected her favorite American pancakes. Jake ordered one of their many spicy omelets.

After breakfast, they returned to Jake's for his version of a naturalist adventure. He led her to the stream behind his shop and laughed as she gasped at the sight. There were thousands of small silver fish he called Buckies, clogging the stream heading up to a small lake where they spawned. Roxy could see several fisherman standing with dip nets scooping up the fish and dumping them into bushel baskets. Once a basket was full, they would leave.

"One bushel per person is the limit," explained Jake as he urged her to grab a herring from the stream with her bare hands. She did, enjoying the slippery feel of the squirming fish as she lifted them from the stream then tossed them back.

"Don't we eat them?" she asked.

"No. They taste disgusting. They're used for lobster and sport fishing bait."

The afternoon they devoted to an extended dalliance in the Jacuzzi. Stretched out on the bed, watching the afternoon light dance across the mirrors, Jake assured her that ritual sex was for special occasions. For everyday, he was quite proficient in "the old in-out" as Liz would say. Roxy agreed.

That night he introduced her to the application of tantric principles of focus and attention to various forms of oral sex. Rolling over for another hour or two of sleep before dawn, Roxy whispered her appreciation against his bare shoulder.

"You sure can do it, boy. And your tongue's no slouch either."

★ ★ ★ ★ ★

The governor's response to Kat's attacks on his environmental positions bore his trademark of overreaction. Monday morning at a State House press conference, he shocked political observers of both parties and the press by appointing himself to the vacant U.S. Senate seat, resigning as governor, and declaring himself a candidate for the Senate against Kiley Tomasso in November. The Democratic hierarchy was livid. Douglas had consulted no one before announcing his decision. Insiders everywhere mumbled their disgust. Conventional wisdom had predicted no action until early May.

Kat was furious that he upstaged her plans for a final week filled with environmental awards and group endorsements. All any reporter would want to talk about was Douglas and the race.

Roxy and Mario were closed in the private office with her, watching the tape of Douglas' announcement. Hayes was in Washington, connected by speakerphone. Kat paced the small room, screaming her rage, circling around Roxy slumped in a chair taking notes on Douglas' comments. Mario stretched out on the couch, shoes off, tie loosened, shirt collar unbuttoned. A lock of soft black hair fell almost to his liquid black eyes. Glancing over at him as Kat stopped by the foot of the couch reciting her litany of Douglas' vices, Roxy smiled. If those girls downstairs could see him now, they would be all over him, sucking him like a lollipop.

She snapped to attention hearing Hayes laugh. Had she missed some shift in the topic?

"He may be corrupt, despicable and all the other adjectives you've been tossing his way but don't underestimate his cunning." His voice sounded sharper and more defined on the phone, though its drawl was still distinguishable.

"You may hate his tactics but his strategy is a stroke of genius. He suspected you felt safe in attacking him because he was not yet a candidate, so he declared. Men who don't give a shit are formidable opponents."

"Harry Crast asked him about conflict of interest in his development activities, citing my charges."

"What did he say?"

Kat was suffused with indignation and could scarcely sputter a response.

"He laughed and said that was the way business was done in Rhode Island as I well knew, since it would be Tomasso Excavating that would land million dollar contracts building the Cranston sewer. When Harry asked if he was implying I obtained the sewer money to benefit my family's business, Douglas shrugged his shoulders and said that was the connection I'd made in my discussions of his activities."

The speakerphone was silent as Kat stood facing it, hands on her hips waiting for Hayes to respond. Her face darkened as he pointed out it had not taken long for Gould to be proven correct.

"Everyone knows he's a crook, it makes sense for him to accuse you of similar actions. Will your company build those sewers?"

"Tomasso Excavating is one of only three east coast contractors capable of installing the state-of-the-art materials and equipment to be used in this project. We are one of the most respected public works contractors in New England. We've built most of the sewers and water treatment facilities in the Providence area, will probably have the lowest bid, and have never had a cost overrun on a public project. I'd say chances are good no one in Cranston would want to do the project if it wasn't done by Tomasso." Pride in the company and reputation her father built filled Kat's voice.

Mario slipped his hand over his eyes. Kat was blind to any suggestion of impropriety by Tomasso Excavating and refused to concede others could question her faith and not be evil incarnate.

"Maybe we should hold the Cranston sewer appropriation until we're in the Senate." Kat's face tightened at his suggestion.

"Wait? And let Douglas go in and move it through the Senate now that he's our new senator?" she retorted curtly.

"The people of Cranston and Warwick are not going to vote for Emmett Douglas because of a sewer."

"We thought it would make them vote for me! Besides, even if Douglas gets the funding passed, Tomasso Excavating would still be the likely contractor."

"Kat's right," Hayes agreed. "Douglas is using this to block her charges against him. We should hold tight and ride it out."

★ ★ ★ ★ ★

The week was ruined for Kat. No matter how prestigious the award she was receiving, how important the endorsement being given, how filled with praise the words being said about her were, questions inevitably focused on the senate race and the impact of Douglas' entry. She refused to speculate on whether there would be additional Democratic candidates forcing a primary in September, or what Douglas' strategy would be. Privately she vowed never to mention Douglas' name. Sun Tzu urged indifference to opponents and focusing on one's own objectives and strategies. She intended to follow his advice.

Kat's anger soon turned to dismal flatness. She scarcely commented on poll results that showed her stature soaring with nearly 70percent of those queried unable to imagine anyone else as their senator. The rest of the campaign team danced with glee.

She sat dully as Hayes rebuked her for almost missing the presentation of a critical endorsement by Environment United, the newly established super-group, umbrella for nearly a dozen of the nation's largest citizen organizations.

"We sweat blood, create hundreds of pages of justifications, lobby everyone in sight and pull in every debt we were owed in the environmental community to get them to name you their first choice. They're opening a grass-roots campaign office in Rhode Island targeting your race as top priority. You barely muster the enthusiasm to say thank you."

There was dismay as well as irritation in his voice. He began pacing in front of her desk. "This morning, the Science committee passed your pollution prevention plan, and you cancel the press conference."

"No one would ask about the legislation anyway, so why bother?"

"Have you forgotten everything you ever knew about redirecting questions? Have you forgotten we want press talking about your senate race? Have you forgotten how remarkable this proposal is?"

Her chief of staff's indignation roused the merest spark of remorse. The pollution prevention plan was remarkable as was the strong bi-partisan support she had received for her creative suggestion to finance innovative waste prevention technology from a fund established with a percentage of the savings realized.

"Roxy wrote you a great statement. You could have read it and walked out."

Kat nodded listless agreement.

"You have a meeting with Senator Stuart late this afternoon to discuss the Cranston sewer. Maybe he can pound some sense into your head." Hayes stalked from her office, slamming the door behind him.

★ ★ ★ ★ ★

There was no trace of a despondent Kat when she stepped from the plane on Friday. Roxy drove her directly to the taping of Channel 6's Sunday news show where she delivered clear, concise, and occasionally brilliant responses and parries. She looked stunning in a royal blue silk dress with full sleeves slashed with pale green, and matching blue suede shoes with three-inch heels. In a rare display of pique, Kat used her height to intimidate a hostile questioner at the show's conclusion. He had attempted to harass her several times about her style, rumors of magicians advising her campaign, and Douglas' suggestions of conflict over the Cranston sewer. She deflected each attack serenely, sliding easily to points she chose to make. His last question was personal.

"And is there a special someone in your life?" he smirked.

Kat laughed, coquettishly tilting her head. "Are you asking me out?"

"Oh no! You're too old for me."

With his comment, the show ended and cameras shut off. Kat quickly rose from her chair, walked over to where the reporter sat, and as he stood to face her, patted his head which was about chin level and said, "I thought I was too tall."

Kat asked Roxy to drive to a weekend full of events.

"You keep me charged like a battery," was her explanation.

There was no time for beach walks. Roxy promised herself long ones once Kat returned to Washington. Watching Kat in action was compensation. Her anger and despair were gone. In her mind, there was no Douglas, no Winston, no opponent. She reaffirmed her intent to run a campaign of hope, presenting people with her vision of the future and asking their endorsement of it by electing her to the U.S. Senate. Her hopeful attitude was transmitted to the crowds they met: at town meetings where she was cheered on Big River, at St. Joseph celebrations in the streets around their Federal Hill office where hundreds of fellow Italians lined up to hug and kiss her.

"Max reminded me the campaign is another step in my process of initiation," Kat told her as they drove to their first event on Sunday. "I've resolved to accept the tests and pain as divine gifts, occasions for growth."

Roxy shook her head, once again grateful her tests were limited to decisions about sex or more sex.

"However, I wish they had warned me in candidate training about some of the real skills I needed." Kat smiled as she applied mascara to her long lashes. "Do you think they teach putting on make-up while driving in secretarial school?"

They parked beside the hulking mass of Rocky Point Palladium for a letter carriers union breakfast. Roxy recalled the president's visit and the night with Hayes that followed. He was scheduled to be in the state for the strategy meeting and planned to return to Washington the same evening. She had no intention of urging him to stay. She wanted to postpone as long as possible any choices she might be forced to make.

The cavernous hall was filled with the hum and bustle of nearly fifteen hundred letter carriers. Kat spent the twenty minutes before she was scheduled to speak shaking hands and chatting at every table along her path as she moved to the raised podium set in the center of the crowded floor. She wore a suit of the same gray-blue as postal uniforms, cut with a short jacket and more stylish skirt than any government would issue. She wore a flame-red cap that no self-respecting carrier would wear but set exactly the right note for Kat. She was one of them and they loved her for it.

Her speech was filled with personal recollections, remembrances of victories shared, and specific praise on issues of concern to the letter carriers. They left the hall, thunderous applause echoing in their ears. Douglas drove up in a black Cadillac, a well-muscled man jumping from the front seat to open his door. He brushed past Kat without a glance.

They went from the breakfast to a special environmental picnic Ben and Jerry's Ice Cream was sponsoring with all proceeds to benefit rain forest preservation. Kat was thrilled at the opportunity Mario had arranged for her to be guest of honor and chatted lightly about the Crescent Park Carousel in Riverside where the picnic was held.

"The sixty-six hand carved figures are magnificent. There's an even older one at Watch Hill created by the same artist, Charles Looff, America's premier carousel-figure maker. He established his factory in Riverside at the turn of the century. I promised myself years ago I would preserve Rhode Island's historic carousels even if I had to buy them personally."

Roxy knew seeing Douglas disturbed Kat although she tried to conceal it with her tour guide lecture. She decided to use the encounter to discuss Kat's reportedly glum behavior in Washington, and what or who relit her fire.

"I heard you weren't very upbeat this week, even at special events that should have had you dancing in the streets. I guess you worked it out. You sure seem sparkling this weekend, as soon as this small cloud from seeing Douglas the dirt-bag fades."

"Do you really sit around all day talking about how I'm feeling?"

"That can't be a serious question," Roxy said, shocked. "Of course we do! Who else would we talk about? It all depends on you, you're the product."

"Please do not refer to me as the product." Kat was decidedly cool.

"So what turned you around? I heard Senator Stuart talked to you. Did he say something that cheered you up?"

"Keeping a close watch on my schedule, eh Roxy?"

Kat changed the subject and began peppering her with questions about the May schedule which would be a main topic of consideration at the next day's meeting. The campaign needed to be rescripted now that Douglas was certain as the opponent.

★ ★ ★ ★ ★

Hayes delivered the day's bombshell to the team assembled in the conference room even before the meeting began. Emmett Douglas, Rhode Island's new senator, decided to keep Colin Proctor as his chief of staff, the position Proctor held for nearly twenty years in Winston's office.

"Douglas can't be bothered with serving in the Senate. He has a campaign to run," was Hayes' assessment. "We ignore his absence for a month or two, until the pattern is obvious to everyone, then suggest the job may be too much for him. We want to force him to be in Washington at least during the fall. He won't be here behind our backs. He'll look like a bozo in Washington because he knows nothing about functioning in the Senate. If Stuart's right and we're all trapped there with budget battles until mid-October, Douglas will be trapped with us." There was unanimous agreement. Hayes was assigned to monitor the performance of Rhode Island's real senator, Colin Proctor, a man elected by no one who had not spent more than a weekend in the state since 1956 when he graduated from Portsmouth Abbey.

The meeting began in earnest. The team immediately decided that May's plans needed no change because of Douglas' entry into the race.

"We knew he would be the opponent, it was his timing that surprised us. And I think we learned a lot from it including that Douglas is easily spooked into hasty action," Hayes noted.

A young volunteer interrupted the meeting to bring three copies of the latest *Lear* magazine featuring a photo-filled profile of Kat, headlining her as a Woman of the '90s.

Jasmine has earned her whole year's salary and tolerance of every bitchy thing she might ever do with this coup, thought Roxy as she flipped the pages. An eye-catching photo of Kat in safari shorts climbing a huge tropical tree prompted Gould to mutter, "What is it with you and legs?"

Mario told him how the campaign office opened before the previous tenant removed their sign.

"Our first week, we were identified as a L'Eggs Boutique."

"I hope Douglas doesn't have footage of that. I can see the commercial now," Gould snorted. "By the way, I heard this morning that Douglas not only is keeping Proctor on but he's also hired Winston's media firm, the thugs at Roberts & Sondhiem. They'll find Douglas their kind of candidate. He'll egg them on to ever more vicious attacks."

"There's a part of me, a big part, that wants to jeer at the idea of Douglas as a serious candidate," Mario said, detailing reaction to the positive poll numbers and public disdain of both Douglas as a candidate and his attempted smears of Kat. "Not only are most of his business deals and fund raising methods suspect, and his associates deplorable, but the man is also deeply involved in gambling: dogs, poker, sports, as well as his personal attitude. He's going to continue acting recklessly, should alienate most Democratic politicos, and will never have a positive idea to offer. But then I start remembering the lives and careers he's destroyed before with his slanders and smear campaigns. The possibility of this campaign becoming a free-fire zone and Kat being hit by some random bullet makes my blood run cold."

Kat affectionately smiled her appreciation for his concern.

"We continue as planned, " she summarized more than an hour later. " The Senator Tomasso spot goes on next week, a new Jake—Big Mac—Aunt Helen ad about taxes follows a week later. Business and the economy is the theme for the month, and my Rhode Island time is jammed with festivals, hearings, and business related speeches. We ignore Douglas until next week when we're scheduled to announce funding for the Cranston sewer with major fanfare. What do we expect?"

Kat sat back and listened as discussion flowed around the group. Her face remained peaceful and composed even as they discussed the possibility of audits, investigations and continued harassment. Mario threw the problem back into her lap.

"What do you intend to do?"

"Yield."

Her face had a mysterious glow and a slight smile touched the corners of her red lips.

"I have nothing to hide. Tomasso Excavating has nothing to hide."

Noting the cynical twist in Hayes' face, Gould's also, she elaborated.

"We'll drown them in facts, figures and testimonials. We'll anticipate every attack and question and be prepared. At best, television cameras and journalists see only a narrow sliver of the truth. They can be easily led to wrong conclusions. I will never again consider myself to be above suspicion. I will never again disagree about educating the press in our point of view.

"I'll also follow my own rules. I attacked Douglas after pledging repeatedly not to do so. What I put out, came back to me fourfold. His name will never be publicly mentioned by me again and I'll work to detach myself from any feeling towards him. No anger, disgust, hatred. Only with purity of motive can we hope to succeed, to survive the poison of his attacks. If he can rouse responding poison and evil in me, then I've lost—whatever the vote total. Emmett Douglas will be a non-person. When I look at him, the space will be blank. He will get no energy from me."

It wasn't Stuart who'd turned Kat around, Roxy realized as she listened. It was Max. That was his guidance she was citing.

11

A Conflict of Interest
May

Williamsburg, VA
Rhode Island

"We leave tomorrow afternoon for the big Williamsburg Golf Tournament," Hayes reported to Roxy in his regular close-of-the-day call. "It's a fundraiser for Republican Senate candidates at Kingspoint along the James River. If all goes well, she could raise sixty thousand dollars or more."

"Kat's going to play golf?"

"She's going to play tennis and lie around the swimming pool between schmoozing with Senatorial Trust members. At events like these, big donors meet the candidates and earmark their donations for particular ones. Senator Stuart's carrying her banner on the golf course along with the rest of his harem."

"Harem? What harem?"

"It's a joke. Better not tell Kat, she might not be flattered. Ever since Stuart took on all the female Senate candidates as his special project everyone at the committee calls them his harem."

Not flattered, that was an understatement, thought Roxy.

"Does Stuart know about this?"

"The first several times people teased him about it he would solemnly list his strategic and personal reasons." Hayes mimicked Stuart's sonorous tones: "If I'm talking about more women in the Senate, I feel duty bound to help make it happen. Women are the GOP's largest potential area for growth and the seven running in 1990 are all good candidates, slightly more progressive than the party, but that's where I can help by lending substance and conservative credentials."

Jasmine would explode if she heard that explanation. Even Roxy was slightly put off by the senator's assumption that his male patronage would automatically help the women.

"What makes him a conservative if he supports these progressive women?"

"Who knows? He calls for strong action on drugs, crime and defending the national interest. He promotes the link between political and economic freedom, and people see him as a rugged individualist with a traditional sense of duty and honor. Plus he's a man." Hayes returned to discussion of the golf fundraiser.

"Stuart told Kat there was a betting pool set up on the amount of contributions per candidate this weekend at a hundred dollars a chance. He selected her for seventy-five thousand which is impossibly high. She's pumped and determined to raise more."

"She liked the idea?"

"I wouldn't say that exactly. It motivates her. She and Stuart had what we well-bred types describe as an exchange of words over the betting and she stormed off, accusing him of treating it all like a game. He turned to me and grinned. 'She's right. I do treat it like a game and it's the best damn game there is.'" Roxy noted the near reverence that filled Hayes' voice as he talked about Stuart.

"He's flying us to Williamsburg along with Rachel Palczeski. She's the congresswoman from Maryland who's also running for Senate. I'm leaving Saturday night. Kat's staying on and flying back with them on Sunday."

"Do all incumbent senators put as much time into campaigning for their colleagues or wanna-be-colleagues as Stuart does?"

Hayes dropped his voice conspiratorially. "I think he has a master plan for revolution that includes electing a Republican Senate, having a lot of new faces indebted to him, then raiding the leadership, maybe grabbing the majority leader job. Also, I think he's slightly bored with being a senator. It doesn't provide the adrenalin rush of a campaign."

After discussing Kat's increased visibility in national media, Roxy reported Rhode Island news, starting with Dan Burkhart's long-anticipated announcement for the governor's race. That led to reminiscing about Burkhart and the president's visit, which in turn led Hayes to recall their night together.

"I'll always have a soft spot in my heart for that evening when I slid into paradise on satin sheets." His voiced slowed and the drawl became more obvious. She could almost believe that she competed with politics as his primary passion.

His next call came late Sunday morning.

"Kat's arriving this evening, the exact time and flight number are in the computer. Will you pick her up?"

Roxy agreed and pumped Hayes for stories about the golf tournament.

"I don't know what happened after I left, but Kat said nothing this morning when I spoke with her so I suppose no blood was shed."

"What? Did something terrible happen?"

Hayes described an action-packed two days. Kat spent Friday afternoon at the resort's heated swimming pool where most of the non-golfers assembled in an elaborate tropical bar.

"It's fortunate this event is off-limits to the press because she had eyes popping all weekend. Stuart was outraged when he saw her bathing suit. He made me swear I wouldn't let her out of my sight unless I knew he was on guard duty.

He was concerned some of the money boys might think their check would buy more than a thank-you call from the candidate."

This did not sound at all like Kat, Roxy worried.

"Kat worked the crowd. At the pool, during cocktails, and at dinner." No fashion aficionado, Hayes could only describe her attire on Friday by its general color, length and acceptability.

"Stuart's shipyard friend Beckham showed up with a limo and plans for a night at some local club with a band. He kept telling Kat the five thousand dollars he sent the night of the Press Club show was nothing compared to what he'd pay to have Kat go out dancing. Stuart and I went with them."

The scene Hayes described had Rozy's head reeling.

"We caught everyone's attention when we pulled the limo into the parking lot of a honky tonk blasting country music. They got really stirred up when they saw Kat. We guys blended in perfectly—jeans, shirts and boots. The girls inside all looked like extras from a grade-B biker movie: long frizzy blonde hair, red lipstick, tight jeans and ruffled blouses. Kat was dressed for an evening out on some planet that has a green sky and triple moons rising every night."

Roxy solicited as much detail on Kat's costume as Hayes could provide.

"She had on those shiny tights in hot pink with purple satin running shorts, a skinny top in bright yellow with a tie-dyed see-through shirt over it. She had the same stuff as the shirt around her head. No jewelry except for gold hoop earrings and a wrapped scarf knotted tight around her throat with a big gold hoop in it."

"What?" Roxy exclaimed. "You let her go out in public like that?"

"Stuart tried to stop her before we left the resort but she refused to change into something that approached normal. Beckham backed her up. He was infatuated with the comic book Amazon look. She looked weird and she acted weird."

"What do you mean, weird?" Roxy was growing more concerned.

"She said almost nothing, obviously wanting to dance. Beckham wanted to watch her dance and Stuart was ignoring her. He sat, drinking his own brand sparkling water and lime, occasionally nodding at a remark Beckham made. We didn't dare let her loose on the general population so I was nominated."

"I didn't know you were a fan of dancing?"

"It's one of Kat's unwritten rules, some ancient saying about never giving a sword to a man who can't dance. I've heard she and Mario are famous for their disco routines. When she was ready to offer me the job as chief of staff she arranged to be at a function where we could dance. We finished the dance. She offered me the job. Friday night, we danced through the first set and returned to the table where Beckham had polished off several more bourbon and waters."

"Was Kat drinking?"

She had seldom seen Kat do more than sip at a glass of white wine. Except for chocolate and pasta, Kat seemed oblivious to addictions taken orally. Roxy had addictions to endless items that fit in the mouth and tasted good.

"Beckham was buying her champagne as he proclaimed how much he adored her, how beautiful, wonderful she was. How he was ready to leave everything and run away with her, on and on. Stuart said nothing, just sat and listened, no expression on his face. I was trying to rest up in case I had to dance another set with her. Kat sipped champagne, smiled at Beckham and occasionally patted his hand saying 'you don't really mean that' in this coy voice I'd never heard before.

"When the band returned, they announced a series of sweet and slows to get the love back in life. Kat listened for a few minutes then turned to Stuart and asked him to dance. He scowled at her and refused."

"He refused or said he didn't dance?"

"He refused. Beckham said he never danced but Stuart out and out refused. She glared at him then said in this indignant tone 'Earl will leave his wife and kids for me and you won't even dance.' There was this tense silence as if she'd slapped him. I couldn't see his face, only his clenched fist. Whatever she saw was enough to bring her to her senses. She sat back down, talked a while more to Beckham then announced she had to make a presentation the next morning and was ready to go home. Beckham was sloshed so he made little protest. Back at the resort, after sending Beckham off with the driver, Stuart warned her that the breakfast presentation was her opportunity to look and behave senatorial and he hoped she could manage it. He walked away, she stomped back to her room, and we all slept alone as far as I know."

There was no time to digest this remarkable tale before Hayes continued.

"Saturday was more of the same. Kat was perfect at breakfast, precise and controlled. A little lacking in her usual glow but subdued was best for this crowd. She talked about the future direction of the GOP and development of candidates and voter bases. She discussed economics and education and how to turn America's resources to global opportunities."

Who cared about political content? Roxy interrupted. "How did she look?"

"She was close to the edge of being too stylish. She did wear a navy pinstripe suit."

Roxy recalled the article he sent her. Republican Members of Congress all wore blue suits in their official photographs. Democrats also showed up in blue suits but there were grays, browns, and charcoals as well.

"Her blouse was glaring white with an exaggerated wing tip collar and big cuffs that showed, and a big, droopy red polka dot tie. Her hair was restrained."

"Sounds like Senator Stuart in drag," Roxy laughed. T.J. Stuart was notorious for the white shirt, conservative image he maintained in public.

"Maybe she was mocking him, now that you mention it. The jacket was fitted, the skirt short and tight, and she had on a pair of those backless high heels Gould calls fuck-me shoes, in red no less. Stuart seemed content although they pointedly avoided speaking to each other. He was playing golf so I was charged with babysitting. Kat and I worked a few more donors after breakfast and scored about ten thousand dollars, then she went to change for tennis. She and Senator Cartwright were scheduled to play doubles with two major donors, a tax attorney and the CEO of a big California asset management firm. Kat and her partner, the California guy, beat Cartwright and the lawyer in straight sets. Cartwright was not happy and during lunch he must have challenged her to play singles. She beat him again. A crowd gathered during the last two sets, making bets, watching the action and wanting to see Kat's tennis outfit."

Roxy groaned. It must be the weather, or something perverse in the stars. Max claimed that as an Aquarian with a full moon, Kat was prone to bouts of erratic behavior. She asked Hayes about the tennis clothes.

"I know I'm a traditionalist and whites are not required for tennis anymore but Kat was breaking new ground."

He described a short red dress with ruffles and a bow in back, a low cut neck, and glittery silver panties. Her red tennis shoes had big silver stars on them and they sparkled.

"By the time Stuart finished his round of golf, Kat and Cartwright had moved into a small bar area with a pool table. He was apparently determined to beat her at something. They were playing nine ball and betting big money on each game. So was everyone else who'd come in to watch. You know Kat's not my taste in women. Too angular, dark and unusual for me. I like my girls to be built like females with angelic faces and long blonde hair that feels soft when it brushes across my arm. Your golden eyes are a nice touch."

Roxy luxuriated in the intimate change of pace. She was rudely surprised by his next remark.

"But bending over that pool table with her long legs and silver butt in the air, I was almost tempted. She's a remarkable pool player. She made rail shots I would've sworn were impossible and set up at least three combinations that won her the respective games after fewer than five balls were sunk. Kat had almost seven hundred dollars from Cartwright. Each time he'd pay, she would snap the bills, fold them and slip them down the front of her dress. Some drunk Texan kept offering ever increasing check amounts if she would let him make the deposit for her. Cartwright proposed one more game—five hundred dollars—and Kat agreed.

"Just then Stuart walked in and leaned against the wall next to the cue rack. Kat ran her fingers up and down the end of the cue she'd been using and announced she wanted a new stick for the last game. 'This one seems too small, not adequate for the challenge.' She walked over, picked out a cue, and as she was running her fingers around the edge of it looked straight at Stuart, smiled and said 'this one seems bigger, much better.'"

Roxy groaned at the image. She was not a pool buff so she did not understand his amazement as he described Kat's break shot which knocked three balls into pockets and set up a combination that she took with her second shot. It kissed the one ball then spun down the table, sinking the nine in a corner pocket.

"She won again. Cartwright never got a shot," Hayes let some pride show in his voice. "She walked over and took the money from his hand, smiled and said 'It's a good thing you're not running against me.' He turned purple but she just breezed on, and threw several bills on the bar telling the bartender to buy a round for the house and keep the change. She never looked at either Stuart or me as she walked out.

"We stood around for a few minutes while the bartender poured everyone a drink on Kat. Cartwright tried get someone to join him in bad-mouthing her. Stuart was getting ready to go over and calm him down when Cartwright stormed out of the pool room and headed down the hall. It wasn't hard to guess where he was going. Stuart and I followed him."

By this point in Hayes' story, Rozy had a small mountain of shredded paper in front of her.

"What happened?"

"We could hear banging and turned the corner in time to see Kat open the door to her room. She must've tried to shut it when she saw who it was because Cartwright roared and threw himself against it. He had Kat backed against a wall and was pulling on her robe when Stuart yanked him away and tossed him into the hall."

"Cartwright laid on the floor a minute or two, cursing, then got up and headed toward his room. I could hear him yelling, 'Is that the way it is, Stuart, she's yours? Aren't you taking this shepherding too far?' There was a moment or two of silence then Stuart answered, cool as ice.

"He said, 'My goal is a Republican Senate, not a piece of ass. I would like to think you share that goal. You need to save your energy for fighting the Democrats, especially considering the weakness of your poll numbers.' The next thing we heard was a door slamming.

"Kat was sitting on the bed clutching her robe when Stuart came back in. He was agitated and asked if she was all right. She said yes then thanked him for intervening. He just looked at her, never smiled, and said that he didn't mind rescuing beautiful ladies in distress but it was bad policy to make unnecessary enemies in Washington. He walked out and Kat burst into tears waving me to get out, too.

"Stuart and I waited in the lobby to take Kat to dinner. He assured me he would be her shadow and would call me Sunday night with a final count of contributions made that weekend, and the result of the pool. She appeared looking like an angel in a white flowered dress and some type of sparkling stuff in her hair. She was gracious and calm when Stuart dragged Cartwright over so he could apologize. Then I left. You'll have to get the rest of the story out of Kat."

A CONFLICT OF INTEREST

Getting any part of the story out of Kat was not easy, Roxy discovered on their ride south to the beach. She insisted on driving, and driving fast, a sure fire sign she was tense. She talked about everything but the weekend. They laughed about Gould's fax when the photo of her in running shorts winning the Nike race in Washington appeared in *The Washington Daily* and several Rhode Island papers. More legs! Is this what happens when women run for office?

Kat announced they had a final date in June for Marge Jamison, the president's popular wife, to visit Rhode Island for a major fundraiser. The goal was two hundred and fifty thousand dollars. Claiming the field organization was crucially important because in off-year elections local concerns were paramount, she grilled Roxy on applicants for the four field staff jobs and on organizing the volunteer crew.

Roxy explained that Mario's mother, Yola, was taking the volunteer operation in hand and that Kat was scheduled to meet with field staff finalists.

"We'll be able to hire by midweek."

"Good," said Kat. "This month is all rallies and festivals so we need to be up to full strength."

They were speeding down the highway, almost to Narragansett, when Roxy asked about the weekend. She did not want Kat to discover her close communication with Hayes so she pretended to know nothing. From Kat's description, she and Hayes had attended different events. She never mentioned the hassle with Cartwright, the night at the honky tonk, or squabbling with Stuart. Her only mention of Stuart at all was to report that he had won three thousand dollars by selecting her in the betting pool.

Roxy was prepared to extract more details when a siren screamed behind them. A cute young trooper pulled them over and approached the van. He was smiling.

"I'm a big supporter of yours, Congresswoman. I wanted to warn you about how fast you were going. No one in Rhode Island wants anything to happen to you."

"I was speeding, officer, and I insist you give me a ticket. I should know better."

Adoration gleaming in his blue eyes, he refused.

"I appreciate your support and hope I have your vote. But for now, for both our sakes, please give me the ticket I deserve."

★ ★ ★ ★ ★

Two figures moved off the porch and waved as Kat and Roxy pulled into the circular drive.

Max twisted his hand behind his back then brought it forward holding a bouquet of exotic tropical flowers. He must have come directly from Key West. Roxy led him and Jake into the bamboo-papered TV room with its jungle of plants and wicker furniture to wait for Kat to change clothes. Prodded by her questions, Max explained he was there to celebrate Buddha's birthday. "Legend claims he returns to Earth each year at the Taurus full moon to convey blessings on humanity for the upcoming year. It's called the Wesak festival."

Max described how ritual based on natural phenomena like the full moon was true organic living, helping keep humans in touch with the greater whole.

"D.H. Lawrence was concerned about humans becoming disconnected from cosmic rhythms too," Jake added. Max chuckled.

"You must be absorbed in your tantric practices again if you're quoting Lawrence."

Roxy's round cheeks burned a deep rose but Jake was undaunted.

"He claimed that humans needed to submit to the eternal revolutions of the cosmos and instead were given bank holidays and political celebrations. Such total abstraction from the great cosmic rhythms 'is neither bliss nor liberation but nullity', he said."

"Roxy, you watch him tonight. The eve of Wesak is a powerful time for all natural energies and Jake will be promoting sex as the 'great unifier' if I may quote a bit of Lawrence myself." Max's words had Jake blushing too. "Not that I disagree," he continued. "There's little doubt that sex raises the vibration level of matter to where it can reach the spirit."

Lawrence was right about sex, Roxy thought later, delicately tracing shadows cast by brilliant moonlight on Jake's lean body as they lay on pillows in front of his wall of windows. She had gone home with Jake, not only because she did not want to miss a night of powerful energies, but also to leave Kat and Max alone for whatever rituals they would perform—hopefully rituals as satisfying as those she and Jake had completed.

"We aim to lose ourselves to the greater power that explodes as we come together, and from this union, we are reborn more complete," Jake explained as he introduced her to what the French called "the small death," the loss of self that can derive from orgasm. Roxy was not sure the feeling she had was completion but it was certainly satisfying. She did feel far more in touch with every nook and cranny of her body as the lava of sensual pleasure ebbed and flowed along her muscles and nerves.

Jake was up early dragging her out of bed so they could get to the beach for sunrise. They walked along the sand watching the palette of color shift as the sun climbed from the ocean.

"Sunrise has always been an important ritual for me, evoking all the transcendent emotions the poets and gurus praise: renewal, hope, joy. I'll never forget how shocked I was on my first visit to California when, after a lifetime of worshipping at east coast sunrises, I saw the sun plunge into the ocean instead of climbing out of it. A big revelation for a swamp Yankee like me. The horror and despair I felt watching the sun drown itself in the Pacific eventually drove me back here. I couldn't bear the thought of being condemned to attend this death night after night with never the possibility of seeing it born from the waves the next morning.

"My devotion to the ocean taught me about natural rhythms. For me, its patterns are as cosmic as Max's dance of the stars and the moon. I love the rituals Max does around the natural patterns. He makes it theater. Worship of the divine should be ripe and juicy, calling the body to exultation as well as the soul."

They reached the estuary at the end of the beach and found Kat standing on the furthest spit of sand facing Max. He was perched atop the biggest of the boulder family that guarded the river entrance, his loose fitting pants and jacket flapping in the wind. Low tide uncovered a path of scattered rocks from the shore to the boulder where Max stood. At high tide, the river mouth was treacherous and impassable.

"Max is preparing for both the ritual and some extensive campaign forecasting," Kat explained as they watched him jump from rock to rock back to the shore. "Years ago, he selected this particular spot where water, land and air meet as a magic one. He stands on the highest boulder which remains nameless. The ones on either side he calls Boaz and Jachin, the pillars of light and darkness that guard the Temple of Solomon. He works always from the middle."

Later that afternoon, the four assembled in Kat's library. Roxy never entered the darkly paneled room without recalling how Max described it as representative of Kat's brilliant mind. It was lined with locked cabinets, secret panels, and floor to ceiling shelves filled with books, sacred objects and art. The odor of leather mingled with incense, and aromatic herbs hung in pots in front of the turret windows.

Following Max's direction, Roxy sat in the heart at the center of the patterned carpet, Kat at the apex of the pentagram that encased it, facing her friend. Max and Jake were at diagonal corners of the square that lay within the pentagram.

"We'll take a quick peek at the future, then move on to wish Buddha a happy birthday," said Max spreading a deck of cards face up in front of Roxy. It was a different deck, with pictures she had never before seen.

"Since this is obviously a goddess motivated campaign, I thought the goddess tarot might be an appropriate oracle to use. We'll begin with just the twenty-two major arcana, the named cards. It is in these that myth resides, that the destiny of the soul can be glimpsed. The cards are unused and still in order. I want you to look at them, notice the ones that draw you and tell me what you see." Max's voice was hypnotic.

Roxy picked up the first two cards—the Magician and the High Priestess—cards she always thought represented Max and Kat. Looking at the new images she was surprised to hear herself describe them as a unit representing two sides of magic, with Kat obvious in both. There was a crouched pre-historic shaman surrounded by ancient magic: runes, a unicorn, a wolf emerging from a flame, Stonehenge. The high priestess, her naked body visible through a transparent robe, was far more sensual than in the deck they usually consulted. Next, Roxy picked up the Emperor card and showed it to Kat.

"Senator Stuart. It looks just like him, leaning on his throne, in robes and armor looking regal." As Kat examined the card, Roxy felt her attention pulled further. It was the Lovers. Never before had cards spoken to her. She said words that came from nowhere. She had no idea what would be next. She did know that the cards she held—laying them down one by one as if revealing a poker hand—had a single message.

"The Lovers must find mastery and strength," she intoned.

Mastery and Strength were the names of the next two cards she pulled. They featured the pair seen previously as the Lovers. The man on the Mastery card was shown crowned and in armor, driving a chariot pulled by four magical steeds. Strength showed the woman of the pair riding naked on the back of a lion, twisted snakes of sexual energy held as a wand in her hand. "And though they have the guidance of a Wise One, their ultimate fate lay with chance." Roxy handed the next card to Max, so obviously depicted as the white haired man with magic spilling from his robe.

A wheel of fortune ended the first set.

As Roxy gathered her focus to continue, Kat interrupted.

"For a newly developed deck, these cards reflect a rather antique version of what our heroes and goddesses should look like. All fair, light-haired women, no dark curling beards on the men or Oriental cast, no racial or ethnic image at all."

Roxy disagreed. She liked the cards. Not only did they speak to her but all the lovely ladies, either naked or in diaphanous gowns, matched her image of the goddess. It was disappointing that the male figures were mostly clothed, and even when they were naked there was no genitalia shown. Max claimed the cards had been developed by a group of witches. Obviously, the danger of not having men in a group was the danger of forgetting their most salient feature. Feeling the pull of the cards again, Roxy picked up another pair and stared. The Guide and Temptation, new words.

The fourteen and fifteen cards were called something else in the former deck. She asked Max what.

"Temperance and the Devil," he replied. These new pictures seemed much clearer to Roxy.

"They represent the two sides of sex," she recited. "It's being sanctified by the angel in the Guide card; Temptation shows seduction in a forest." The words were barely out of her mouth when she realized the pair was for her. She dropped them as if they were live coals. This was the choice she would have to make.

A CONFLICT OF INTEREST

Two final cards drew her interest. Both showed female figures she knew represented Kat although, as she had complained, both were blonde.

"This Star is most appropriate for Kat, pouring water from conch shells, and representing her science with the astrolabe and observatory. The beautiful lady surrounded by stars in the World is Kat's goal: the high priestess initiated as goddess, completing the task."

Roxy stopped speaking and was trying to reorient to her normal state when Kat grabbed up the cards and announced, "We can work on this new deck later. Max, do you have any predictions we need to know?"

Max shifted them around, taking his place at the northeast corner on a side tip of the hexagram where it intersected the circle filled with magic symbols that defined the specially woven pattern of the library rug. He arranged Jake, Kat and Roxy in an arc facing him, seated along the inner circumference of the circle.

At his request, they all wore orange. Max wore an orange silk shirt almost to his knees over white pants. He was wrapped and hung with a variety of magic symbols and cords. Kat wore an embroidered white robe bound with an orange scarf, a matching one around her head. She had no jewelry except for several rings of various crystals and gems. Roxy had on orange silk pants and a glowing yellow shirt while Jake contented himself with an orange teeshirt that read JOY across the chest in black letters.

"On the global level I see turmoil and chaos, maybe even war. An Islamic uprising could occur before the end of summer. In the U.S., illusion and deception continue to surround all discussion of the economy. Expect nothing cataclysmic before '92, although Rhode Island will hit the stone wall head-on before then.

"Attacks will continue as part of the campaign. Why the surprise?" Max responded to Kat's groan of dismay. "We all know this campaign is more than material success. It's a quest that will move us closer to enlightenment. And as each individual inches a little closer, the whole of mankind is uplifted.

"Maybe you'll feel better with some magic help. I created special amulets for us to carry."

One by one he pulled four small ovals of plastic from the air and laid them on the yin / yang symbol woven into the rug. He pulled two more and placed them in his pouch. "All the amulets are tuned to Kat's purpose, represented by the star etched on each. Her destiny rules this magic. In each is sealed a piece of white paper inscribed with a single symbol representing the specific quality or virtue each of us needs to fulfill our part of the drama.

"Before I invoke their power by sounding the name of each, I want to warn you about words, their power, and the evil we will confront from them during the campaign. The truth that words clothe thought has been expressed from the Great Singer of the Hindus whose song is the universe, to the Bible's message that the word was God. When words are spoken, the thought takes form. Wrong speech, lies, and distortions produce malignant forms. This is the danger we face in Emmett Douglas. Once loose, the evil can be used by anyone, or by chance."

"How can we protect ourselves?" Kat tried to conceal her trepidation.

"Prayer, luck, preparing our defenses, and using magic." Max handed her an amulet. "For you Kat, hope."

He handed one to Jake. "For you, fortitude."

Another to Roxy, "And for you, prudence."

All three nodded in agreement with his choice.

"I get faith."

"What about the other two?" asked Roxy, curious.

"One is for Liz and reads charity." She snickered at his choice.

"And Stuart's reads justice."

Roxy howled in disbelief.

"How can you give one to him? This is weird magic. He'll think we're crazier than he probably already does."

She could imagine Hayes' reaction if he discovered Max giving Senator Stuart amulets to help Kat's election. Max answered, unconcerned.

"Believe it or not, Roxy, he's a great soul. From what I foresee, only he can provide the protection that will keep Kat from harm." Before she recovered sufficiently from his endorsement to question Max further, he signaled it was time to begin the Wesak ritual.

Starting them on breathing exercises to calm and focus, Max prepared the room with incense and ringing bells. He moved a bench-sized carved wooden turtle into place, setting a gleaming crystal bowl of water on its back. On the floor in front of the bench he set three objects explaining that they represented the three Great Lords who would act on behalf of humanity receiving the blessings from Buddha.

"Here is the Christ, most familiar to us." Max set down a small, painted statue of the baby Jesus that must have been a remnant from Kat's Roman Catholic youth. "Here, representing the Lord of living forms known as Manu, is a jade tree." Max placed it to the right of the statue. "And on the left, the Lord of Civilization, represented by this book."

"We are celebrating a heavenly event that actually occurs somewhere in the Himalayas because the aspiring hearts of humanity demand it, and because at this one point during the year those in charge of Earth's evolution are listening most carefully. Thousands attend annually. By doing this, we agree to transmit the forces of peace and goodwill bestowed on us today to the rest of humanity. Both the Buddha and the Christ collaborate in this unique celebration.

"Ancient patterns can be dissolved through the blessings we will receive, and new ones can be established. There is a great Life forming near our Earth and it is breaking down the walls that engender selfishness in individuals and nationalism in countries. It creates new forms of unity. We can help by directing our thoughts and aspirations along the same path, the path of love."

A CONFLICT OF INTEREST

Roxy was slow to switch her attention from worrying about Stuart's increasing importance in the campaign to Max's recitation of the Wesak legend. She took notice when he began speaking of the Buddha's appearance in the northeast and a tiny green light appeared shimmering in his hand.

Shining particles streamed towards him from everywhere in the room. Max arose and began a series of ritual movements accompanied by chanted mantras. The cloud of illuminated particles intensified around him and the spark of green light moved to the left. He signaled them to stand and join him in chanting a single sacred syllable. As waves from their intonations filled the room, the cloud of light swept around the pulsing green spark and coalesced into a glowing image of the Buddha hovering over the crystal bowl of water.

In a few moments the Buddha disappeared and they sat in silence to absorb the blessings. Max rang a small silver bell and filled an ornately cut crystal goblet with water from the bowl. "This is the communion of Aquarius, the sacred water ceremony of a new age. So says the ancient legend." Max closed the ritual.

★ ★ ★ ★ ★

Kat wore a red wool shirtdress belted in red suede with an elaborately cast lion's head belt buckle. The mid-calf skirt covered the tops of her black leather boots. A navy silk turtleneck peeked from the open collared dress and a jacquard print, three-quarter sleeved jacket quilted with fantastic floral shapes protected her from the cold. Her hair was loose and blew wildly in the wind as they waited near the outside platform from which she and other dignitaries would speak, announcing funding for the much anticipated sewer project.

Standing off to the side, she stared out over the mountainous and bleak terrain of the Cranston landfill that would serve as backdrop for the ceremony. They were assembled in the parking lot of a nondescript government office building. Television crews set up with their backs to the building entrance. All three of the affected mayors had greeted her effusively when they first arrived but left her alone when it became obvious she would not engage in small talk. Mario acted as her intermediary. Kat felt like a warrior queen ready to meet any challenge. She blocked any softness or yielding from her attitude. Even the normally insensitive members of the press corps noticed her mood and kept their distance.

When the newly-promoted governor arrived, a brief twinge of annoyance flashed across Kat's face. He was a burly, bear-like man with a gray beard and longish gray hair. A typical party hack relegated to a pointless job, no one thought he would ever serve in the state house, even for the few months left to this term. But who imagined the much-despised elected governor would elevate himself to the U.S. Senate over the corpse of his predecessor? His booming voice repeated the observation—funny when they heard it for the first time, deadly on its twentieth repetition—that if the wind shifted they would really understand the need for new sewers. Kat shook her head and resumed gazing at the landfill.

Her posture was tense. Max had imparted a "morning pearl of wisdom" as she left, warning that the event was momentous.

"It is sometimes necessary to give them what they want so they can learn the price of wrong desire," he advised, holding her hand.

She twisted her mouth in a bitter smile. More than fifty other guests at the ceremony huddled around the platform.

The announcement ceremony proceeded without incident. Nearly an hour of speeches repeated the need for the facility, thanks to those who obtained the funds, and visions of a glorious future promised by its completion. Judging from the extravagant adjectives and grandiose promises, this was far more than a waste water treatment plant designed to clean up the dirtiest river in the state. The involvement of three municipalities with almost indistinguishable boundaries was elevated to a political accomplishment only slightly less impossible than an Israeli-Palestinian peace deal.

Kat spoke simply, explaining how government had the obligation to help communities meet its stringent and necessary sewage treatment regulations. She briefly acknowledged her five year effort to obtain Federal assistance for the project. As the press scuffled for position in the question period that followed the ceremony, the air began to prickle. Whatever was expected to happen, Kat knew that now was the time.

Harry Crast lumbered to a microphone placed in the press area.

"Congresswoman, you are here today announcing a laudatory accomplishment. None will deny the value of this sewer project, nor the major role you played in getting it underway. Yet, Senator Douglas has stated that your motives for undertaking this project were less than altruistic and include a desire to personally benefit your construction firm through contracts on the sewer. What is your response to his allegations?"

Kat began in a low, modulated tone that cut through the wind. She recited her now standard reply outlining briefly the unique technical requirements of the project, Tomasso's capacity to meet those, and the company's exemplary reputation built in concrete throughout the state. Then her voice changed and took on a deepening that was almost an echo as she shifted topics. The television crews got the message and all three network affiliates turned on their cameras.

"It is an unfortunate reality in today's political arena, driven by the demands of public and media, that even a wrongly-created appearance of impropriety is enough to command total attention. Enough to create obstacles to effective work. The political choices we must make in November are too important to be sidetracked by quibbling over alleged financial conflicts. I refuse to participate in actions that will distract from discussion of what really matters—Rhode Island's future and by whom it can best be served. Having reviewed the situation with members of Tomasso Excavating, and regretting the losses to workers and residents this decision will incur, I am forced to announce that we will submit no bids to work on any aspect of the Cranston sewer project. There must be no occasion for conflict of interest."

Kat's concluding words were drowned out by the shouts and protests of the three mayors and several environmental officials who ran toward the podium. Her friend Mike Zagarella, Mayor of Cranston, reached her first. He wrenched the microphone towards him and said her decision was unacceptable and he felt certain he was speaking for everyone when he said they would not undertake the project unless she agreed Tomasso would build it, given the proper process. Mayors from the other two cities involved strongly echoed Zagarella's statement, although both were Democrats.

Kat stepped away from the fray and stood looking out over the landfill, hiding her delight behind a detached expression. The remainder of the press conference was given over to escalating protests by involved officials. Everything had unfolded as she planned. Kat left before the conclusion to return to Washington.

★ ★ ★ ★ ★

Two days of aggravation started the next morning just after dawn. Some excavating company, not Tomasso, began digging up the street in front of Kat's house. Jackhammers screaming against resisting road surface greeted Roxy as she walked out to the beach. The piercing beeping of huge yellow Komatsu digger machines clashed with mournful fog horns. There were piles of giant concrete sewer pipes at the end of the street.

Roxy cut short her walk on the beach as a second day of cold wind lashed her face with salt spray and blowing sand. The day went downhill when she arrived at headquarters. Every time she walked near a phone it would ring. The radio call-in talk shows were consumed with the task of persuading Kat to reverse her decision. Hundreds of callers swore they never doubted her integrity.

Kathy from Bristol said she never imagined Kat would "steal like the rest of these politicians."

Mario flinched and muttered, "I can't believe she's even talking about stealing in the same breath as Kat."

Newspaper headlines screamed about Douglas' deliberate lies and television crews tripped over each other chronicling successful Tomasso construction projects throughout the state. Kat's brother Frankie, who ran the company, appeared on television both days. Looking handsome and assured, he reminded people that the controversy was about more than Kat. It affected the lives of thousands of Rhode Islanders who worked for the company or its suppliers.

Kat remained out of sight in Washington, refusing all comment until she returned to the state. A press conference was set for noon on Friday at Green Airport. It would be broadcast live on the three television stations.

Hayes reported she had immersed herself in plans for the next week's Capital Links broadcast with the Soviets which anticipated Gorbachev's upcoming visit to America. The show was also linked to a Washington Summit of Soviet Women. Participants would be featured on the show.

"She wants you to come down for the show and other Soviet related festivities. I want you here for two nights so you can't avoid me." Roxy felt a tingle sweep upward from her toes as he hesitated for a few seconds then added, "I'll leave you to imagine my current state of acute need to see you."

Reporters, crew, radio commentators and photographers floated around Kat like schools of bat fish, attaching themselves as she walked with purposeful grace from the airline gate down the long hall. She was elegant in a rich purple crepe suit with an asymmetrical jacket, button-trimmed sleeves, and a narrow skirt. A pale blue silk camisole peeped from the close in the jacket and a square-cut blue topaz set in a curved shape of gold hung from a gold chain around her slender neck. She smiled pleasantly, greeting by name every press person she knew, but she refused all questions. Mario walked ahead, clearing her path. He reminded the crowd they were on the way to a press conference. All their questions would be answered.

Roxy met Kat at the lounge door and watched as she quickly brushed out her hair and freshened her make-up. There was a satisfied turn to her full mouth as she applied a red lipstick that had enough blue in it to work with the outfit.

"Does your pleased look mean, I hope, you're going to announce Tomasso will bid on the Cranston sewer so the phones will stop ringing and people will talk about something else?"

Kat smiled broadly at her friend's reflection in the mirror and spread her hands in surrender.

"How can I do otherwise when all of Rhode Island is begging?"

★ ★ ★ ★ ★

Slumping onto the wicker lounge, Roxy idly flipped through Sunday's paper, half listening to CNN on television. She was relieved when Kat offered to drive herself to the airport. They attended so many ethnic festivals, rallies and clubs she felt like a world tour had been completed in two days. She was ready for a rest. There was a photo in the *Journal* of Kat at the Cambodian rally at Rocky Point Palladium, towering over the tiny Asians who had been thrilled to see her.

Roxy was developing a sentimental attachment to the faded glory of the huge, amusement park hall in Warwick. Saturday's visit was an object lesson in the gradations of immigrants in this state that lived its varied ethnic heritage more than any other in the nation.

In one door of the Palladium streamed the Twenty-five Week Club of St. John's parish, some mysterious assemblage of old nuns, fat ladies and men in polyester, and young pregnant Italian couples. Kat entered the other door where a sign announced the Cambodian Day of Peace in pictographs and English.

Hundreds of young Asians were lined up to pass through police barriers and enter the cavernous hall already filling up with their countrymen and women. Roxy thought their shiny black hair was made to be punk cut and teased. Black lace stockings, rhinestones, and draped pants for the men seemed styles created to enhance their small, delicate bodies.

Kat energetically wound her way through crowded tables, escorted by awed community leaders. Roxy hung out in the lobby talking with a couple cute cops. She asked why there were so many of them at this Day of Peace celebration.

One with red hair and freckles all over his obviously Irish face explained how the previous year's celebration was held in a club far too small for the crowd.

"People couldn't get in so they hung out in the parking lot. There were dozens of fights and a near riot. So we're here this year to keep order." He pulled out his billy club slapping it against his hand, telling her in a tone meant to impress, "I spent four days in school learning to use this."

He went on to inform Roxy that Asians, particularly Cambodians and Hmongs, made up nearly ten percent of Providence's population.

"For some reason, these folks have become the target of violence by blacks and whites. I don't understand it. They look nice enough to me."

She noticed there was not a Cambodian in the place that the solidly built young cop could not have broken in half with one hand. There was more ethnic diversity that evening when they attended a low-dollar fundraiser at Club Mendonsa in Central Falls where a mixture of Portuguese, Hispanic and French Canadian supporters assembled. Kat danced with several of the men while Roxy listened to a stout, older lady instruct her on the intricacies of class consciousness among ethnics.

"If the wrong people are seen supporting her, she could be ruined."

She gestured toward Kat spinning around the floor with a portly gentleman who barely reached her shoulder. Roxy was certain this lady considered herself the ultimate arbiter of who were "the wrong people."

The May breakfasts, church fairs and craft festivals that completed their whirlwind weekend faded into a single blur. Roxy was repeatedly struck by Kat's capacity to remember names, faces, and histories for hundreds of people they met, all whom felt they knew her personally and expected her to respond.

Two of their new field staff accompanied them on Saturday and Kat was effusive in her praise of their efforts. Both, on the job for only a few days, produced several volunteers who tagged along handing out brochures and lapel stickers with an enthusiasm Roxy lost months ago. All were dressed in the newly-established Kat uniform of light pants or skirts and Kiley for Senate shirts, giant blue stars printed on the front.

When she finally motivated herself to go out on the beach after Kat left, Roxy found the weather gremlins had struck and summer arrived without warning in mid-May. It was warm and sunny, promising to be hot by afternoon. The city was gearing up for the season, which would open officially in two weeks. Signs announced no dogs on the beach after May 15. Gigantic white chairs that served as lifeguard stations were standing in place, or rather in six places, along the shore. As she stood looking up at the wide seat of the chair nearly seven feet above her head, she vowed that someday she would climb the ladder and see the view.

★ ★ ★ ★ ★

Roxy awoke to Jake's tickling fingers moving from the soles of her feet to the tender flesh behind her knees.

"I've come to carry you off. I was fishing from the pier when the ocean started steaming and boiling. I knew you were thinking of me. We've enough time to do some sketching and eating, then I have a special treat for late tonight."

As he moved his fingers back to her instep, she noticed it was dark outside. She must have slept through the afternoon.

They went first to the studio where she admired the final panel of what had developed into a beautiful six-piece series of flower devas—all variations of Roxy's softly rounded face and form. Rose, trillium, peach, gardenia, and violet were each depicted in their own piece. A radiant sunflower, featuring Roxy's long golden hair streaming around her face like petals, completed the set.

Back at the house, Jake drew intently although he claimed he had no specific project in mind.

"For the past week, I've had brief dream flashes that leave the same afterfeel: expectancy, inspiration not yet close enough to grasp. I know only that you're involved and I want to be prepared."

She was surprised when he pulled two sketches from his pad. They were the two cards from the goddess tarot deck that she described as representing the dual aspects of sex.

"These are another clue to the process, part of the expectancy. I remembered your words: sanctified and seductive. I see them made as windows. This one, the sanctified, I'll keep. The seduction window belongs to someone else."

As he cast a questioning look at her, Roxy felt a flush creep over her face and she quickly glanced down at the drawings. For several seconds there was only breathing.

A CONFLICT OF INTEREST

"When the correct point is reached in the work we're doing, we'll talk about fidelity and the tantra," he said, tightness hovering around the edge of his smooth voice.

The rest of the night progressed amiably. Jake was pleased with several poses he finished, his favorite being one of Roxy standing with her arms held high above her head. She liked it too, the sleek line it gave her. They sat down just before midnight to a steamed lobster feast he prepared. More than an hour later, they parked at Kat's and walked down the beach. Roxy assumed there was sex involved in the expedition since there had been none yet.

They saw no one on deserted streets. Ocean Drive was cleared of even parked cars. The beach was also empty. Jake led her to a particularly dark area south of the Dunes Club and stopped, blanket thrown over his arm, at the base of one of the large lifeguard chairs. Roxy needed no urging when he signaled for her to follow him up the ladder. Score another fantastic sex location, she thought, as they settled on the broad chair seat and leaned against the back. The ocean looked almost chocolate at night, with scattered diamonds of light along the horizon. Behind them, the white stucco fairy castle a noted business magnate called home, gleamed softly. Its red-roofed turrets seemed carved from shadows. A bright light in the cupola of the Dunes Club shone across the waves.

"It's perfect timing," explained Jake. "The chairs were placed on the beach yesterday. College kids haven't discovered it happened yet. And it's an exceptionally warm night."

He slipped out of his clothes, laying them carefully across the arm of the chair. He motioned Roxy to do the same. They sat side by side, hands entwined as Jake explained his purpose.

"You notice when we do the ritual sex, sitting motionless and still, natural pulses develop based on heartbeat and breath. It's the intensification of these pulses building ultimately into a crescendo that completes the ritual. The ocean is a massive, more complex version of the same rhythmic pattern. Before light, there was sound. I want you to listen to the ocean, hear its life pulse. It's the mother of all our beating hearts. The surf's roar is the most basic, plenary sound of sex. You and I have chosen the path of developing feeling to the utmost, of conquering the senses not by shrinking from them but through experiencing them fully. Tonight, we work to potentize our force by immersing ourselves in the ocean's voice and inviting it to expand our ecstasy."

He positioned her kneeling over his outstretched legs, facing him, her back to the crashing waves. Lowering her to enfold his rigid phallus, he duplicated her breathing rate, attuning their minds through the mirroring of their breath. After a while, as they sat connected, she could feel his thoughts filtering through her mind. She could see and feel and understand the ocean as he did, with a profound and unquenchable attachment.

If I could not feel the rhythm of the surf and tide, I would die.

She concentrated on the sound of the ocean as he expanded to fill her. The roaring started with the waves breaking, then dipped into the next roar as waves turned to surf creeping up the sand, silenced by entropy. The shattering blow of each wave activated an ebb and flow around the base of her spine that moved from her to Jake and back through their most intimate connection. The ocean's percussive chords dominated their sexual symphony. Energy continued to build and Roxy could hear sobs as the waves crashed and an intake of breath as they reluctantly left the shore. She could not distinguish whose noises these were.

There was no need for speaking or further touching. Jake placed his mouth against the hollow at the base of her throat and she could feel a common pulse pounding. They became a single fluid unit and when the orgasm came, it swept through with the force of a tidal wave, backed by all the life that swelled the ocean.

Jake was murmuring in her ear, his voice filled with wonder and excitement as she regained a sense of her own separateness, slightly saddened by the shrinking.

"I saw her. I saw the goddess. I know what I have to do." He was gentle but deliberate as he lifted her off his lap and put on his pants, pulling her to follow him down the chair's ladder. "Take the blanket to wrap around you, but don't put on clothes. I need to see you naked against the surf."

Her body still felt so attuned to the breaking waves she barely noticed the water's chill as Jake posed her in the foaming surf, motioning her to walk towards him.

"You are truly Aphrodite, born of the foam," he said, his eyes gleaming, seawater drops shining on the blanket he draped around his neck. "I'll immortalize you in sacred charms of love."

He dropped to his knees on the wet sand, grabbed her soft ass, pulling her toward him, and pressed his lips against the triangle of her sex. A cool breeze brushed across her wet body and she shivered.

★ ★ ★ ★ ★

Two days after the sanctification, Roxy faced the temptation.

She had surrendered to the demands of her blood the moment she saw Hayes coming toward her. He turned her away from Kat's office and steered her down the hall.

"We have to be at a meeting in Senator Stuart's office in half an hour. I want to spend it walking there with you on this lovely spring day. Kat's on the Floor voting. She'll meet us there."

Roxy felt in her pocket for May's fortune strip and suppressed a moan of dismay. She had convinced herself the sex with Jake would alter her reaction to Hayes. Wrong again. If anything, the burn was worse. Nothing was left but to arrange where and when.

Let your doubts be consumed in the flames of delight, the strip read.

They crossed to the Senate side, strolling across acres of the green-shaded plaza on the east front of the Capitol, beneath the colorful pink canopy of blossoming crab apple trees. Warm breezes carried the low humming of an empire being run as players in the congressional world moved past. The blended perfume of flowering trees and fresh mown grass hung in the soft air. Whenever a particularly sweet fragrance would stream past, she thought of fairies and spirits, wondering if these smells were their jet trails. By the time they reached the ugly, ultra-modern Hart building where Stuart had his office, they agreed that Hayes would meet up with her late in the evening. Roxy stared up at the giant black Calder mobile dangling five stories from the ceiling in the open center of the building. It looked like a rogue space station, its top platform slowly rotating.

"I was working for Senator Hsu when that was first hung. We spent hours tossing wads of paper onto the winglike areas, betting on who would get closest to some pre-determined spot," Hayes told her.

She examined it from eye level when they reached Stuart's glass-walled offices on the sixth floor, then shuddered as her eyes scanned the stark, metallic and cold white marble interior of Hart. Seeing her instinctive shrinking, Hayes nodded his agreement.

"Not only is this an aesthetic horror but it's also one of those 'sick' buildings where every virus and germ in the place gets shared with everyone because it's hermetically sealed. No open windows or fresh air in here. It's like those medieval physicians who insisted night air could kill."

When they walked through large glass doors into the expansive reception area of Stuart's Senate offices, Roxy recognized a benefit of being promoted to the upper house: more room for more than twice the staff. Both receptionists were on the phone so they examined the wall of photos that seemed prerequisite for congressional offices.

Stuart's array in this public area included none of the usual vanity shots of him with world leaders and celebrities. Instead the wall was covered with photos of real people in various poses, many of them autographed to Stuart, interspersed with pictures of Roanoke, the mountains, and the water bottling operation.

An aide emerged from behind book-laden wooden walls and directed them to await the Senator in his personal office. Although nothing could ease the barren feel of the building, Stuart had tried. Virginia was everywhere in maps, photos, posters and ornaments. A magnificently framed portrait of Thomas Jefferson hung between the windows. Green leather couches and chairs were scattered in several groups around remarkable handcrafted wood tables while a massive cherry roll top desk dominated one corner, a computer sitting incongruously on a small cherry table placed alongside. One of the walls was covered completely in a detailed map of the world, another lined floor to ceiling with overflowing bookcases.

While they waited, Roxy reviewed media coverage of the Cranston sewer conflict following Kat's announcement that, yielding to overwhelming public pressure, Tomasso would bid on the job. Hayes was pleased the topic had not been discussed on radio, TV or in the papers the past two days.

"It was a big gamble but Kat insisted on taking it, and she was right. I predict we'll hear no more from Douglas on this."

Stuart threw open the door and scarcely greeted them before beginning his tirade against another budget vote that added more millions to the federal deficit. He directed their attention to the view of the Capitol and downtown that stretched beneath his window.

"This government was founded on my state's tradition of personal freedom and now it's a monster, bloated beyond recognition on taxes, regulations, guidelines and economic parasites that live off the public dollar. A magnificent planned city of parks, fountains and marble monuments to democracy and freedom now thrives on the tyranny of the bureaucrat and the lawyer. Jefferson would shed tears of blood at the sight so far distant from his cherished notion of gentleman farmers and merchants setting aside a few years of their life to serve their nation."

He was preparing to launch another harangue when Kat arrived looking breathless and flushed. They talked issues, or rather Stuart lectured them on issues.

"The Republicans plan an all-nighter in both houses on drugs and crime. Let's talk about how Kiley can fit in and how we can use whatever she does against Douglas. He's a crook. How tough can he be on crime?"

"I don't plan to spend all night on the floor of the House trashing the Fourth Amendment and begging for establishment of a police state. I find the hysteria generated by this war on drugs, the money spent with absolutely no return in decreased use or lessened drug-related crime, to be almost as destructive as any imaginable drug use. Besides, my ex-husband is a known cocaine user and suspected dealer," Kat blazed.

"That should encourage you to all-out support the death penalty for drug kingpins."

Roxy giggled involuntarily, recalling the encounter with Jamie she had shared with Stuart. Kat scowled at her and the senator shrugged his shoulders in surrender.

"OK, you're a conscientious objector in the war on drugs. Let's lash out at crime. Since I'm certain that increased police power and tougher jail sentences are off limits as considerations, how do you feel about victims' rights? It's a major concern among the older women who are your softest support, and an issue that lends itself perfectly to your style."

Kat stiffened, but responded.

"Street thugs are nothing but modern barbarians. On the large scale we need to alter the mainstream culture of war that produces the weapons, training, and attitudes they use. On the personal level, I think vengeance is a victim's right. Rape victims should have the right to execute their rapist, but only by their own hand."

Both men stared with the same question in their eyes. Only Roxy understood the personal roots of Kat's position. Stuart broke the silence as it became uncomfortable.

"A little harsh, but direct and effective. That should allow us to say you support the death penalty, another popular position." He waved aside her protests. "You can qualify your support to the victim as executioner after you're elected."

He dropped a folder on the couch next to her.

"Here are some bills you might consider signing on to. Several are related to increased protection of women and children. Try a Floor Statement or two, some visits with local police and a talk with the Federal Attorney for Rhode Island. That should cover you on drugs and crime. We can expect a modest silence from your opponent."

The phone rang and Stuart mumbled a few words then hung up.

"All this talk about issues was a ploy. I lured you over here to make a special presentation."

The door opened and four young men walked in, each carrying a long, narrow package wrapped in plain brown paper. They leaned them in a row along the map wall then left as Stuart waved them out. Standing next to the brown rectangles, a slight smile twisted up the edges of his lips. He explained to the bemused trio that these were his contribution to the myth of the campaign. Ripping paper off the first rectangle he announced, "Miss Yankee Doodle" then moved down the line, exposing each poster-size photo in succession. "Miss Jungle Bunny, Miss Nike, and finally, a private peek at Miss Moneybags."

Kat bounded from her chair and stood facing Stuart, exasperated.

"You're crazy! Whatever possessed you to do this?"

She flung her hand at the posters almost life-size blow-ups of her dancing at the Press Club, climbing a tree from *Lear's* magazine profile, the Nike road race winning picture, and one in a bathing suit from the Williamsburg trip.

"You'll find the work of a senator is often tedious; little jokes help sustain us. Levity balances gravity. It's one of those parallel laws you like so much." The glee in his voice left little doubt that his gesture was having exactly the response he wanted.

Kat did not relax her disapproving stance. Stuart shrugged.

"How about this excuse: I thought they'd help me recollect your finest assets while I'm out there raising money for you."

"How did you get into the U.S. Senate?" Kat shouted in disgust.

"Makes you wonder whether all your efforts are worth it, doesn't it?" Stuart laughed as she jerked open the door and stormed out, Hayes and Roxy following in her wake.

★ ★ ★ ★ ★

Roxy trotted along the high-ceilinged Senate halls, their cream walls bound with gold carved moldings, careful not to slip on the tiled floors patterned with blue diamonds. Nodding to the guard, she skipped down the east side stairs, looking for Hayes. He was leaning against a rosy marble pillar under one of the Parisian-style green streetlights with large globes.

"You look like a gilded angel," Hayes greeted her. The light turned her hair and face to shining gold. They walked hand in hand, gazing up at the Capitol dome which gleamed white against a blue-black sky.

"It makes my heart skip a beat even after I've seen it a couple thousand times. This is my temple," Hayes said, stroking her hair.

Resting in his arms, bathed in dim light that streamed into the bedroom from outside, the difference with Jake seemed clear. Hayes needed her. He told her that as he fondled her body stretched out on his bed.

"There's nothing soft in my life, nothing undemanding and accepting. It's all competition, jockeying for position, watching my back. You don't compete. It's difficult to perform with a woman who's trying to one-up me. Everything is simple with you, no hidden agendas or dishonest motives. You're light and laughing and playful. When I need to feel refreshed and have only a moment, you're there. I can lose myself in you and reemerge ready for battle again. It's easy and for that I'm eternally grateful."

She started to feel indignant until he turned his full attention to stroking her body. She had a great weakness for caresses and his ignited her with an intensity she could not explain. She stretched expectantly and insinuated her body against his hand, urging him to continue. He dipped his finger in the glass of bourbon by his elbow and touched her nipple. The tip became hard and red.

"Your nipples are a lovely soft pink and see how they blush when I stroke them."

He bent to lick the alcohol from her full breasts as he pushed them up. Roxy whimpered, pleasure rippling through her. She lifted herself to face him and rubbed her stiffened nipples teasingly across his chest.

A gasp of unspeakable pleasure escaped as he entered her. It was always a miraculous moment that made Roxy feel like her secret treasure had been revealed to a worshipping seeker. Hayes plunged himself into her again and again. She could feel his demand for release, comfort, caring, and it thrilled her. His tension and obsession with power and control poured into her like molten lava until it detonated in a blinding flash that carried them both away.

Rolling off her body, he flashed her a sign, making a V with his fingers.

"Vulva? Venus?" she whispered, a pleased smile on her face.

"Victory, which it is." He lowered his lips to the topic of their attention—her vulva, his victory. He rotated his arm beneath her shoulder enough to see his watch then sat up in bed and turned on a light, kissing her quickly.

"I have a few calls to make before it gets too late." He picked up a stack of yellow message pages and pulled the phone onto the bed.

"Don't go yet," he pleaded as Rosy moved to get up. "This will be so much more pleasant if I have you here to look at and touch."

She only hesitated a moment before settling back down under his raised hand. He looked satisfied as he began a series of calls, rubbing his fingers distractedly over her breasts.

★ ★ ★ ★ ★

Roxy spent all morning checking guest lists and arranging seating for the Capital Links broadcast that night. She liked working with Cheryl, ABC's project director, and hanging out with the crew. Their huge trucks, packed with equipment and food, parked for days outside the Rayburn building before each broadcast. By the time she returned to the congressional office to begin a round of Soviet-related events with Kat, she was dreading another late night. It would be the second night in a row that she had not gotten to sleep until after two a.m. She was getting too old for such hours. Hayes handed her the schedule as Kat hurried her from the office.

First stop was the Capitol Hilton. Kat was addressing the closing session of the Soviet Women's Summit. They would walk from there a half block to the Soviet Embassy where ABC was hosting a small, private reception. Ambassador Shafirov was leaving the post soon and this would be his final opportunity to preside over the unique program he had been so instrumental in creating. There was an hour or so break after the reception before Kat was expected back in the Foreign Affairs committee room on the Hill where the show was staged.

The white-coated doorman jumped to open Kat's door as she squealed the red Triumph to a stop beneath the portico at the Capitol Hilton. A second doorman, lacking the gold braid and white conductor's cap of the first, helped Roxy from the passenger side. Roxy trotted behind Kat through the elegant wood-paneled lobby, up the wide expanse of carpeted stairs, and across the open balcony to the Senate Room. It was an appropriate omen, thought Roxy. The closing session of the Soviet Women's Summit was about to begin, and the director was delighted to see the main speaker arrive.

Most Soviet women thought glamour was having the peroxide blonde hair that had not been seen in the U.S. since 1958. Kat was dressed to demonstrate how power and sex appeal could be harmonized. She wore the wine-colored knit dress and sleeveless vest ensemble and added several gold chains to the garnets set in gold she usually wore with the dress. Her hair was restrained in a neat bun at the nape of her neck. Once again, she was color-coordinated with her background, a pale gray draped curtain behind the speakers' table.

Although she wrote the speech, Roxy stayed to listen. She wanted assurance that the inspirational mode Kat preferred sounded natural and worked on the audience. The Soviet women already had worship in their eyes for her stunning appearance. Wait until they hear her ideas, thought Roxy.

Kat opened with the famous Tom Paine quote, only mildly altered.

"These are the times that try women's souls. The harder the conflict, the more glorious the triumph." Roxy knew the direction from there: discussion of dramatic changes in the Soviet Union, the stress it put on the women, their need to continue with devotion and courage during this profound moment of history. Then came Kat's personal call to revolution.

"You have shown as a people that you have outgrown your institutions. They no longer serve you. There is no going back, you can move only forward, no matter how terrifying and chaotic the unknown, the uncharted, may seem. You have spoken often during these several days of the economic changes necessary. Far more than that is required. You must engage in free enterprise on the life level. In the course of the past year, you have been well ahead of your government. Keep moving. Leave the failed attempts behind. Forgive but don't forget!

"There is nothing to be gained for you in business as usual. Your land, and the planet as a whole, can endure no more trends that threaten human extinction. Women have been awarded the divine task of producing the bodies and souls of the future. If the food is poisoned and the air is poisoned then our wombs are poisoned, and the future offers little purpose and less duration."

Having created an evocative picture of the evil that threatened, Kat offered hope in the form of several clear and understandable courses of action for critical problems. She handed the Summit director a packet of papers that included contacts and preliminary agreements for cooperation on the actions she proposed. It never ceased to amaze Roxy how Kat's speeches inevitably triggered realizations. Eyes widened. People leaned forward, intent upon hearing every word. These women were enthralled almost to a person, but then glamorous heroines were in short supply in the Soviet Union these days.

On their way across the street to the Embassy, Roxy noticed the street sign identifying those few dozen feet of Sixteenth Street as Sakharov Plaza, an irritant left from the Cold War. Few remnants of pre-*glasnost* security remained as they easily walked into the Soviet Embassy past a single uniformed D.C. cop. They all probably belong to the University Club next door now, thought Roxy. They're ready to get rich and vote Republican like the Supreme Soviet member who had recently offered to campaign for Kat.

They were escorted by a stolid young man into a white-trimmed private parlor with gilded gold carvings. He wore the type of cheap suit that seemed the universal costume of under-echelon Soviet staff. ABC and Capital Links executives were waiting with the dashing white-haired ambassador beneath the painting of an ethereal troika skimming across the snow.

Several gracious speeches were made, thanking the departing ambassador for his invaluable help and assistance in developing the broadcast series. Kat was as surprised as Shafirov when ABC's news director brought out two boxes, presenting one to each. The ambassador gallantly indicated Kat should go first, and she gasped with delight as she pulled an Emmy from the wrapping.

"Although the academy gave the award to ABC we wanted both of you to have one also. Without you, this influential and unique series would never have been created," the news director explained. The ABC photographer immortalized the moment. Roxy could see Kat calculating column inches of press.

★ ★ ★ ★ ★

Carrie slid into a booth in the dingy bar less than a block off Atwells Avenue on Federal Hill, dreading the report she had to present.

"I've been monitoring all calls in and out of Kat's campaign headquarters. They've managed to clear the private line she has in her office."

She handed over a folder of items she thought would interest him. Tossing it aside, he leaned forward out of the shadows. His thin brown hair was pulled back and bound in a long ponytail, beady dark eyes magnified by small, wire framed glasses. Thin lips barely closed over yellowed reptile teeth as he softly hissed his reply.

"Get me someone on the inside."

"They'll never hire anyone now who's not thoroughly checked. Once they discovered my ties to you, I was history."

"You spoiled it by indulging in gossip."

Carrie never engaged in arguments. Let Race think what he wanted.

"And you weren't delighted to know your precious virgin queen may be planning to combine her leap to the Senate with a leap into a senator's bed?" She was pleased when her deliberate jibe drew a bitter scowl from Scarlatti.

"I want someone on the inside. Recruit a person already there."

Carrie had already decided who her slave would be. She had been casting binding spells for weeks. She pretended to be considering the problem as Race sank back into the shadows, motioning for the dark woman behind the bar to bring him another glass of his habitual drink, iced anisette with lemon. The thought of more than a taste of the sweet licorice-flavored liquor was enough to turn her stomach.

"Jasmine," she said snapping her fingers as if the thought just occurred to her. He stared blankly.

"Jasmine Elliott is Kat's press secretary in Washington," she explained.

"Why should she be willing to entertain betrayal?"

"First of all, she hates Senator Stuart and is convinced he's having an affair with Kat. Since she's madly in love with the congresswoman herself, she sees Stuart as a dangerous threat. Besides, he's quite a man I hear, and that's not Jasmine's cup of tea." A flash of hatred crossed Scarlatti's face as she praised Stuart. Carrie chalked up another direct hit.

"Secondly, we hook into her major vice. She gambles. Her rich daddy keeps a stable of horses in Middleburg and they spend weekends there racing and riding. Apparently a lot of money changes hands on those occasions, not only betting on the races but in all-night poker games above the tack shop in town. Since she knows horse racing, she'll think she's an expert on dogs. She's scheduled to be in Rhode Island over Memorial Day. We'll go to Lincoln Park. We set her up with some early wins, then take her for a bundle. Maybe we throw in a card game or two as a way to recoup. She'll need to lose at least a hundred thousand dollars before she'll begin to worry about where to find it. Once she starts worrying, I recommend she see you. We keep it up in Washington. Aren't you a junior partner in the action there?"

Scarlatti's hand cut her off.

"I don't want to see her. You handle it all. If you think Washington help is necessary, let me know. I only want a reliable source from her. You know the information I need."

The venom in his soft and deliberate voice did nothing to dissuade her.

"You want to know if she whispers your name when Stuart fucks her," she replied with the barest tinge of spite.

Scarlatti slid from the booth seat and leaned across the end of the table. He looked like the sac human beings come in, surrounded by an aura that Carrie swore was shit brown. She wondered where the blood came from to fuel his frequent nosebleeds.

"I'll kill any man who tries to take her away. I've waited long enough. It's time for me to claim my prize. If election to the Senate drives her to another man, then she cannot be elected."

Carrie sat for nearly an hour after he left, reviewing her plan. All the pieces were falling into place. She was not sorry to have been fired from Kat's office. She had much more freedom working for Race. For more than a year she searched for the perfect test of her power. Now it was almost ready. She designated herself the Spider Queen when a deck of animal cards indicated that was the creature that ruled her destiny. Carrie sought magic power so she could weave the web of fate in people's lives.

Four of the people were selected. Kat was both bait and prize. Race, Jasmine and Stuart were all competing for her. Carrie needed a fifth to create the pattern she wanted, a magic pentagram. Roxy or Mario? Which one would it be? Roxy, she decided. She was weaker, more susceptible, and Carrie enjoyed being in her head. It was like a high-quality X-rated movie. She cackled and the woman behind the bar looked over to see if she wanted something. Carrie shook her head.

Yes, Roxy was exactly the right addition. Since learning to do black magic, she understood it was lust not love or money that made the world go 'round. All that sexual energy was out there waiting for someone like her to put it to use.

★ ★ ★ ★ ★

Roxy spent the week preceding Memorial Day immersed in heritage, both Kat's and Rhode Island's. Much of her research was done in Kat's library at the house. Almost a quarter of the third-floor space was enclosed within its bookcase-lined walls. Roxy settled into the large squishy red leather armchair that shared the turret end of the room with a plain walnut trestle table ideal for laying out books and notes. Before long, she was enveloped by the strange array of scents unique to the library. Expected odors of books, leather and wood were embellished by exotic incenses, oils and other substances Kat stored in locked cabinets disguised as wood panels. Kat's early history was preserved in a series of binders, identified by calendar year, which Duke had painstakingly assembled, filling them with the personal and public triumphs of his daughter. After he died, Kat removed them from his study and brought them to her library. Her mother had seen the packed boxes, insisted on knowing what they contained, and unleashed a tirade of abuse when she saw the books. She claimed never to have seen or known about the collection. When Kat asked if she was upset because she had done the same, Celeste simply pursed her lips and glared.

The illustrious Miss Williams School for Girls invited Kat to be the graduation speaker at her high school alma mater. It was a singular honor, and important to the campaign since many of the state's opinion leaders and financial donors had children at the school. Roxy was determined the speech would be perfect, inspirational to the graduating seniors and filled with nuggets of truth and wisdom drawn from Kat's experiences at Williams.

Celeste demanded Kat's transfer from the neighborhood parochial school at Holy Ghost for years. Finally, Duke relented. By begging favors from numerous alumna within her family, Celeste was able to enroll her daughter at Miss Williams in seventh grade. Roxy examined the photo taken the year Kat first participated in Field Day exercises, purple crepe paper on her arm, marking her team. Her inclusion on the dominant purple team was because all Kat's aunts and cousins had been purples. In the photo, Kat stood at the very end of a "W" the girls were spelling out on the field. At twelve, her legs looked ungainly and impossibly thin, her hair was cut short in what undoubtedly was called a poodle.

Kat sang in the Glee Club, another demand of Celeste's, so she could participate in joint productions with boys at St. Mark's and Portsmouth Abbey. A news clipping showed a photo of her winning a statewide science competition, posed with the headmaster. Roxy giggled. Where did they ever find a man who so perfectly looked the part? He was tall and lanky, with a kind but determined face, a scattering of sandy brown hair, horn rimmed glasses and a bow tie.

Thumbing through a special volume devoted to events surrounding Kat's own graduation in 1966, Roxy examined the class photo. An elitist crowd, she observed. Only Kat looked remotely foreign or exotic. She rebelled against Celeste sufficiently that her hair was long and wildly curled. Roxy was intrigued by the tradition of the school giving each graduating girl fifty dollars to purchase a book, any book, which would then be embossed with the traditional flame, her name and date, and the adage *The spirit giveth life*. She trailed her finger down the column listing the book titles each girl selected to find Kat's. *The Essays of Ralph Waldo Emerson*. She made a note to ask if she should use any particular Emerson quotes.

Grazing through Kat's well-packed shelves of Rhode Island history books, Roxy spent two solid days assembling a timeline of events. She decided to choose an economic thread for the speech that Kat was giving to commemorate the state's 200th Anniversary.

She would include a special mention of both ethnic heritage and its contribution to contemporary life, and her favorite character, Anne Hutchinson. Roxy drew up an outline to prove her point: traditionally Rhode Island found economic well-being in its ingenuity. Merchant grandees at Newport and Providence were early symbols of the American success myth. Claims that the mills of the state introduced the Industrial Revolution to America were easy to support. Through various phases of its economic history, the state's population had shown remarkable skill in adapting to changes. A quarter of the work force were seamen in the 18th century.

When the economy shifted to manufacturing in the mid-19th century, immigration was encouraged as a source of cheap labor needed in the mills and factories. Textiles developed in the state for two reasons. There were swift running rivers to power the mills, and climatic conditions produced just the right amount of moisture to keep threads from drying out and snapping in fast-moving machines.

Political backwardness kept the majority of immigrant workers in the cities subservient to a minority group of small-town Yankees who controlled the legislature into the 20th century. They sustained power by ignoring violent rebellion against their corruption. Balanced against this was the progressive thread of religious freedom expressed by America's first Baptist church established by Roger Williams; Touro Synagogue, one of the nation's first; and the country's first industrial strike at Slater's Mill in Pawtucket. That's where the 200th Anniversary celebration would be held.

★ ★ ★ ★ ★

Thursday afternoon Kat arrived with Treasury Secretary Magnuson in tow. He looked as a man who was responsible for the largest economy in the world should look. He had sharply cut salt and pepper hair, a chiseled profile and strong jaw, and a pearl gray designer suit that modestly flattered his athletic body. Tennis was his game and he was teasing Kat about humiliating Senator Cartwright in Williamsburg when Roxy fell in step behind them at the door of Citizen Bank's elegant penthouse boardroom. Sitting around the highly polished chestnut table were almost two dozen men and a few women whose clothes alone were worth more than the forty thousand dollars the campaign raised from this private briefing.

The press conference that followed inaugurated a five-day orgy of media worship. Even Kat was satisfied that concern with substance was finally taking hold. Stories surrounding Secretary Magnuson's visit stressed her position on economic issues, the several tax awards she had received during the past few weeks, and her ardent support of budget reform as an alternative to increased taxes. Douglas was neither seen nor heard. At parades and holiday events, Democrat officeholders scrambled to be seen shaking her hand.

The weather was as worshipful as the press coverage. Every day was glorious, bright and shiny with hot sun and cool breezes wafting flowered scents. If a season can be predicted by its first holiday weekend, thought Roxy, then Memorial Day 1990 presaged a spectacular Rhode Island summer.

Kat was on the third floor of the campaign office resting her feet between parades. She had dazzled thousands of shorts-clad citizens and children clutching balloons who lined the prosperous streets of Barrington from the high school to the picture-perfect Town Hall. The bright and casual colors of summer splashed through the panorama. Dozens of young Kiley for Senate volunteers contributed to the sparkle with their white shorts and blue starred shirts. They ran along the curb ahead of her position in the parade, handing out Kiley for Senate stickers to endless questing hands.

The candidate strode along tall and striking, waving enthusiastically, blowing kisses from side to side. Red high heels did nothing to slow her progress. Her hair fell in loose twists, loving the humidity-free breezes. A blue star-filled scarf held it off her face. Blue stars were scattered on the full skirt of her sundress. Its white halter top was covered modestly with a sleeveless red jacket. Harry Crast stood on his shaded front lawn, his wife by his side. He waved and smiled broadly as he noted Kiley once again taking his advice to wrap herself in the flag.

While Kat rested in a back bedroom, Roxy corralled Mario into reviewing the speech she was finishing for the mammoth Rhode Island birthday celebration on Tuesday. Kat was the prime force finding private funding for the celebration when then-Governor Douglas chose to ignore the 200th anniversary of statehood. She had always been on the program, but was quickly elevated to keynote speaker when Senator Winston was killed. Douglas' protests were easy to ignore. Not only had he disparaged the celebration but organizers insisted they wanted a native to deliver the address. Douglas was a carpetbagger from Maryland who married a New Yorker and settled in her family's Newport summer home.

Lying on the couch, shoes off, in a Kiley for Senate teeshirt, Mario looked like someone's sweet little brother. Yet his insights into ethnic and group connections and disconnections, were as clear and calculating as any of the cigar-eating street bosses twice his age who hung out in the card room of the Garibaldi Club.

"There's little melting pot activity in Rhode Island. Groups have remained fairly distinct. Even in exceptions like Kat, you can see the separation," he explained to Roxy.

"Here's a line I picked up somewhere that seems to fit what you're describing: 'a salad bowl of hyphenateds.'"

"That's good. Use it. Who said it?"

Roxy shrugged.

"Who knows? I must have skimmed more than twenty books collecting ideas. It comes from being a novelist. Stealing phrases, anecdotes and personal histories is what writing fiction is all about. How about if I say: 'one historian describes Rhode Island as....'"

Mario nodded his agreement. Suddenly, the Hose charged through the door waving a photograph.

"Hot scoop, guys! Guess whose press secretary turns out to be a big dog lover?" He tossed the photo on the desk in front of Roxy. Mario swung himself off the couch and came over to look. It was Jasmine all right, and Carrie was with her!

"Tightening her hold on Jasmine," Mario muttered. Roxy nodded. She knew they were both thinking about Carrie's weird rhyme aimed at the press secretary. She almost felt sorry for Jasmine.

"Where did you get this?" Roxy asked, inspecting the two seedy men standing with the women. "Do you know who these guys are?"

The Hose smirked.

"A lucky coincidence."

Pointing at the picture, he identified the two men as members of Race Scarlatti's organization.

"The short weasel with bushy blonde hair lives at the dog track. The tall, skinny one is the best card sharp around."

They agreed to investigate further but not tell Kat.

"When are you going to tell me Scarlatti's story?" Roxy asked.

Mario's charming smile could not hide the reluctance in his eyes.

"When I can't avoid it any longer. Take my advice, Roxy, don't ask Kat."

★ ★ ★ ★ ★

Kat went to the Williams graduation exercise alone. She wanted no one to observe her conflicted feelings about the event. As academically and athletically successful as she had been at the school, she was never allowed to forget she was there because of her mother's family. Her Italian blood prevented her from being a true Williams girl.

Duke was proud of every honor she earned, saving news clippings, event programs, report cards, even her essays and papers. Her mother was concerned solely with her making the right friends and connections, areas in which Kat proved continually inadequate. Every time a teacher, administrator, or mother-informed classmate snubbed Duke, disparaged or insulted him by word, action, or disinterest, Kat was wounded. All those scars tingled as she sat in a seat of honor with the headmaster in the gorgeous, cavernous church on Angel Street where the impressive Williams commencement exercises always began. She cordially greeted classmates who were there. One now taught at Williams, another was head of alumni giving for the school and was watching her own daughter graduate.

The kilted bagpiper led the single-file procession of white-clad girls from the headmaster's backyard into the church. The organ played, and two student leaders who traditionally led the procession stood and faced the girls as they filed into the front pews. Kat's heart tore and she pushed down tears as she remembered the ethnic insult Sally Haines whispered to her as she filed by on her own graduation day almost twenty-five years ago. Sally was now president of the Rhode Island State Women's Club and Kat was certain her old classmate was costing her at least a few points of support among older women.

Kat's treatment at Miss Williams pushed her natural fairness to a level of compulsion when it came to representing those excluded for whatever reasons: race, gender, ethnic origin, economics, or general gracelessness. As each girl received her book and diploma from the headmaster, Kat recollected her choice of Emerson. At the time, he was her philosophic ideal. She would read the essays like daily lessons. She chose from "Self Reliance," "Heroism," " Illusions," or a score of others based on the quality she was drawn to that day. She remembered how vindicated she felt years later when Max revealed the mystical roots of Emerson's profound thoughts, his eagerness to make the leap from the natural to the supernatural. Although Emerson disparaged quotations, instead urging to "tell me what you know," she felt he would approve of her quoting him in her speech.

Kat mentally checked her attire before standing to address the assembled graduates, families and friends. She knew Roxy was exasperated as they stood in front of the jam-packed closet while she bemoaned having nothing to wear. Finally they agreed on a deep rose silk top with a matching straight skirt. She wore the famous three-strand Albright pearls her mother had given her in a fit of tradition on Kat's wedding day. Celeste had tried to get them back with great regularity over the years. Her hair was caught back with a braided gold clasp, only a few rebellious tendrils escaping to trail along her neck and cheeks.

Roxy had drafted a speech that captured both Kat's personal Williams experience, and the single idea she wanted to convey. Once again, Kat blessed fate for her friend and made a mental note to thank her, something she didn't do often enough.

Mobilizing her intent, allowing her gaze to slowly scan the faces sitting before her—several were dark or foreign, she was delighted to see—Kat consciously summoned spirit and directed it to her audience. She wanted them to understand the pain of separateness. To value diversity and uniqueness, not demean and threaten it.

"To believe your own thought, to believe that what is true for you in your private heart is true for all men—that is genius," she began, citing Emerson's praise of self-reliance.

12

The Tower
June/July

Rhode Island

"What do we know about this Charboneau I'm having dinner with," Kat glanced at her watch, "ten minutes ago?" She was at the computer scrolling through details of her weekend schedule.

The couch in the office was piled with crime reports, education studies, notes from the U.S. Attorney for the state, clippings and position papers. Mario shook his head at Roxy's research techniques and sank into the pink chair by the window.

"He bought ten tickets to the First Lady's lunch and got pictures for his wife, daughters and secretaries. Carolyn thought he might be a productive new member for your finance committee and wanted you to meet him. When she approached Charboneau, he suggested assembling a group of other men who were willing to donate to the campaign and arranged the dinner. I think there's a note on the schedule outlining what we know about him personally."

As he talked, Mario scanned his copy. There was not much. Charboneau owned a restaurant and some real estate near Smithfield. Carolyn dealt with him only on the phone. She had no idea who else he might be bringing to dinner.

Kat called a contact in the northern end of the state. There was no answer.

"I'm already late. Fortunately, I only have to go down the block to The Venice. Hereafter, I'd like more information on people I'm trying to hustle for money. It helps me slant my pitch."

Her plane had been delayed in leaving Washington. There was no time to do much more than brush out her hair and paint her lips. She repinned the wildly printed shawl over the shoulder of her deep gold dress. Her blue-black hair was loose and her color still high from outdoor events the previous weekend. Except for gray eyes, she could have passed for a gypsy anywhere.

Kat loved Federal Hill on warm evenings. Old men on stoops greeted her as she walked by. Everyone in the neighborhood called her Kat. It was their right. She grew up on their streets. She seldom patronized The Venice, which was owned by a questionable branch of the Merola family. She followed the tuxedo-clad waiter up wide carpeted stairs to a private dining room.

"I'll send up the other guests when they arrive," he announced.

He nudged her into a dimly lit room with deep red velvet curtains and white statuary goddesses standing on several columned pedestals around the wall. A small table was set for two, champagne bucket standing beside it. The waiter must have brought her to the wrong room. She turned to leave and found the door locked from the outside.

A man slowly moved from the shadows near one of the statues, greeting her cordially in a soft voice. She expelled her breath in a startled gasp. She was locked in a room with Race Scarlatti.

Horrifying images of the last time he locked her in a room flooded her mind and froze her heart. Kat remembered struggling futilely against ropes tying her hands to the bedposts as his arm rose and fell repeatedly against her body, bruises rising beneath his clenched fist. There was blood everywhere—from her, from his chronic nosebleeds. Her frantic screams were muffled by a cloth stuffed into her mouth. His hands pushed up her dress and wrenched apart her clenched legs..

Mortified by fear, she choked back sobs and tried to banish the nightmare memories to concentrate on reality. Her eyes darted around the room like a hunted animal looking for a way to escape. He was speaking to her but all she could hear was a dull pounding battering her brain. It was her heartbeat. How did this happen? What could he want?

Kat straightened her graceful dancer's body and willed herself strength. She directed her attention at Race.

"What do you want?" Years of voice training worked, disguising the fear.

"There's only one thing I've ever wanted." He seemed to be swaying slightly and spoke in measured, hushed tones. His lips slid back from his teeth in what she assumed was a smile. He raised a full glass of champagne to her. "I want you."

Kat clapped her hands to her mouth and stifled a cry. This was insane. Why now? Why all this trouble to get her alone? She had spoken to him fewer than a half dozen times since that night more than twenty-five years ago, and then only when it was completely unavoidable. Although his obsession with her continued, he left her alone. They had spoken last at Duke's funeral.

That day, Race hid in a corner of a back parlor waiting until most of the mourners were gone. Finding Kat alone by the side of her father's casket, he slithered up behind her and whispered hoarsely in her ear.

"Don't mourn. Time and space mean nothing to real love."

She screamed when his arm snaked along her shoulder and she saw the possessive madness that filled his half-closed eyes. Then he was gone and her uncles were leading her away from the casket. For weeks after, she would wake up terrified by nightmares where Race dragged her kicking and screaming down into the pit of Hell.

He sat calmly at the white-clothed table. Candles cast flickering shadows on his pasty face and silk shirt. He graciously waved her to the place set across from him.

A clear, elegant voice in her head repeated the passage she read from Sun Tzu only that morning about knowing the opponent. Maybe she was turning into a politician after all.

Misreading her ironic smile, Race more ardently urged her to the table pouring a second glass of champagne.

Kat relaxed slightly. He could not keep her in the room indefinitely, he did not seem to be armed, and she felt certain she could give him a good fight hand to hand. Sun Tzu was right: having no information about an opponent was a great disadvantage. She decided to sit down.

He looked at her intently, barely blinking his eyes, sipping champagne in silence for several minutes. Kat strengthened her resolve and stared back, assessing the man she had blocked from her mind for decades. His eyes pulled her in. She was horrified to confront a cold, dead void. She dropped her gaze to the champagne glass, lifting it to her lips.

Race apologized for locking the door, the barest modulation in his tone.

"You would not have offered me the opportunity to talk with you if I had not made it impossible for you to leave."

She could not raise her eyes to acknowledge his words. Even without seeing him, she felt repelled. She suppressed a frantic need to scream, or throw up, or run away. He acknowledged his brutal rape of her in an almost inaudible voice that made her skin crawl.

"I'm sorry it had to be that way. We've lost a lot of time suffering apart because I acted impatiently. I was young. My empire was just beginning, but I could see its form and you were at its center. We would join the families. We would heal the wound your father created when he refused to work together. You were my prize. I was only taking what was mine. I know now, I should have asked."

Kat shrank back in horror as he reached toward her.

"I told you that night, it will be better the next time."

She pushed herself away from the table and stumbled to the door desperately trying the knob again. It was still locked.

"I have the key."

She looked over as he held an old gold key up then slipped it in his hand-stitched leather shoe.

"I've paid them well to hear nothing. Sit down. I have something to show you. A gift. Then you may leave."

His sinuous movements, the toneless quality of his voice mesmerized her. She returned to the table. What else could she do?

He rolled an old style videotape machine from behind a column and placed a small portable television set beside it. Quickly he threaded a tape from one reel to another. He turned on both machines without starting the tape.

Kat shuddered as he fixed his gaze on her, occasionally taking a sip of champagne then flicking his tongue quickly across his lips. She tried to be watchful but succeeded only in growing increasingly tense as the silence continued. She almost thanked him when he finally spoke.

"For weeks I've searched for something I could do, something I could give you that would help you understand the depth of my love. Then, in a flash of genius, I came up with the perfect gesture. I would return your purity, give up the intimate part of you I alone possess."

She felt drawn against her will as she wondered what he meant.

"Before he married you, Jamie Caldwell was an important client of mine. I supplied him with drugs, women for his movies, protection. He liked me, invited me to watch his filming, sample the girls if I so chose. I was the first, and only, person he showed the tape he'd secretly made of his new wife being instructed by him in the joys of oral sex. He never knew that you belonged to me. I made certain there was only one copy then I took the tape. I told him I would give him whatever money he asked, and swore he would die a slow and tortuous death if he ever turned another camera on you. I did it to protect you.

"Caldwell didn't care. He said you were flat and uninteresting on tape then asked for ten thousand dollars. I want to give you the tape. It's better if you have it."

Gasping for her voice, Kat asked, "I'm to believe there are no other copies?"

"There are no copies and no other tapes."

He slid from the chair and moved to the tape machine.

"Before I give this to you, I want you to watch it so you'll know it's what I claim it to be. It was done on early video tape. The machines are no longer available."

"No!" Kat jumped up. "I can't watch."

"You're quite lovely regardless of what Caldwell said. I've watched it thousands of times and I never tire of your beautiful body, your serious and intent expression as you followed his instructions. You wanted so much to please."

His oozing voice made her feel unclean. Horrible possibilities splattered her thoughts.

"There was a time that I watched the tape daily. You were not here and I couldn't arrange to see you on the streets or in public places. I used up a lot of women taking out my frustrations."

"Who else …. Who else have you shown this to?"

"No one. I would never share you with anyone. You must remain untouched to be a worthy prize. It's your purity and light I want to possess." He turned on the tape and returned to his chair.

She watched in horror as she and Jamie were shown naked in the black master bedroom of her house. Lights were dim and flashing against the mirrors. There was strange music playing. Jamie's slurred voice was telling her to tighten her lips, flick her tongue as he wrapped his hands in her mane of hair and pushed her head up and down in his lap. In a few seconds, Kat descended from rage to disgust to humiliation as she heard Race's heavy breathing and saw the gleaming light in his eyes.

Tears streamed down her cheeks and she ran again to the door and began sobbing and beating on it. She jumped away as he came up behind and slid his hand under her shawl and around her arm.

"Take this with you," he said. "No one ever needs to see it again."

He unlocked the door and Kat fled, clutching the tape against her chest.

★ ★ ★ ★ ★

There were times Roxy wondered if she knew Kat at all. The news all weekend was spectacular. An independent poll showed her at seventy-five percent with scarcely twenty percent of the electorate admitting they would vote for Douglas. Almost no one was undecided. They sold their allocated forty photographs with the First Lady and moved the luncheon to a larger room to accommodate everyone who wanted a ticket. Her ride in a Pawtucket police cruiser Saturday night had been covered in depth by one of the television stations while another was scheduled to follow her on a statewide tour of drug treatment centers the following weekend.

Roxy had worked diligently to summarize Kat's claim that drugs, crime, family disintegration and failures in education were linked problems with common solutions. She had been disappointed when Kat read it through in a lifeless voice, declared herself satisfied and filed it away.

All the other good news was received with no more enthusiasm than Roxy's speech material.

Brown University was taking the unprecedented step of presenting Mikhail Gorbachev with an honorary degree if he would come to Rhode Island during his visit to the U.S. Mario's report that she would be part of the official reception committee failed to spark more than a mild "Good job." It was like a vacuum had sucked Kat's spirit and left her a shell, moving on automatic pilot.

Sunday night, Roxy made her regular check-in call to Liz who wanted to be certain she was up-to-date on all the doings of the campaign.

"When I arrive in August, there'll be no time to fill me in," Liz said, justifying her thirst for gossip.

"For example, it's important that I know the most critical problem in the state is the tripling of fees for vanity license plates. That's because they solved the crisis of poor cable television reception for several daytime soaps."

Roxy cut short Liz's monologue on the absurdity of Rhode Island politics.

"Kat's been acting spooky all weekend. I can't figure out why. Everything I know about looks great."

Willingly shifting gears, Liz suggested they attack the mystery as if it were a plot in one of Roxy's novels. She agreed.

"Since this is new behavior, we eliminate her long standing weirdnesses," Liz began the analysis. "We know it's unnatural for any over-forty woman who has more money than she could ever spend and is still beautiful—although a little bony for my taste—to waste her time running for the U.S. Senate when she could be spending some of that dough on a friendly playmate or two. We also know she needs to get laid, bad."

"Liz, that's ridiculous. She's in the middle of a campaign against a man who would smear her with anything and everything he could. She certainly can't go out and pick up some stud in a bar. Or place a personal. I can see it now, in the back of Washingtonian. Its readers would love this: 'Tall, beautiful, very intelligent, WSF running for U.S. Senate. Needs to get laid, no conversation necessary. Call my scheduler.'"

"Actually I have a man in mind."

"Unless Max is your suggestion, I think we're wasting our time discussing this." Roxy was exasperated.

"I've been watching C-Span all day, every day at the bar. I'm driving everyone crazy but I want to be informed about this whole scene before I come up for the campaign. Anyway, mostly I'm unimpressed but I have been watching our favorite senator, T.J. Stuart, when he appears. He's hot."

"Liz, are you going to suggest that, instead of worrying about Kat getting involved with Stuart, we encourage it?"

"Exactly! If they're not having an affair—and I believe you when you say they're not—then they should be. We can help make it happen. It's ideal! He's already around a lot helping with the campaign, so it wouldn't look suspicious. He would want to keep it a secret as much as Kat would. They have the same interests, and he's tall enough. What more could she want?"

"Well, there is the minor detail of his wife."

"That makes it better. No chance for long-term involvement which would mess up her plans to change the world, and more reason for him not to get reckless and expose them. No one needs to fall in love. We don't want a world class romance here, just some gritty sex. He looks capable. I wouldn't throw him out of my bed. We tell him if this seat is so important to his plans then he needs to screw the candidate regularly so she can be kept acceptably sane until after the election. After that, we can work on finding her Mr. Right!"

Arguing with Liz was hopeless when she had a course of action thought out and ready to go. Roxy decided the best strategy was to ignore it. Hopefully, by the time Liz arrived in Rhode Island, she would have forgotten her insane plan for mating Kat and Stuart.

She did take Liz's advice about solving the mystery of Kat's despondent behavior and concluded it began after the Charboneau dinner on Thursday night. She would inquire about the dinner when she drove Kat to the airport later in the morning.

A squall appeared from nowhere as she passed the Dunes Club on the return leg of her walk. Rain fell in silver sheets. Wind whipped waves into towering fonts of surf. It receded as quickly as it began, leaving the remnants of nature's fury scattered across the beach. Trash barrels had blown over and bottles, bags, and cups were everywhere. Darkened clouds promised more rain. Turbulence and violation seemed keynotes of the day.

Roxy's arms were aching from the effort of holding the van steady against the force of blowing rain and speeding traffic. Concentrating on the road, she ignored Kat, who blankly stared out the window. Interrogation about the source of her withdrawal was put on hold while Roxy drove.

Suddenly, a large black car was bearing down on them. Roxy caught its approach in the rear view mirror and quickly pulled into the right hand lane to let it pass. She gripped the wheel tightly when a heavy spray of water from the passing Lincoln hit her door, causing the van to swerve.

Fighting to keep control, she managed only a glance at the speeding car's license. Fortunately Rhode Island's penchant for vanity plates made one glimpse enough.

"RACE" she read from the rear tag. "Must be some idiot who thinks he's racing at the Indy 500."

With the van steady once more, Roxy noticed Kat straining forward, watching the black Lincoln speed out of sight. She looked dreadful. Knowing they were early for a flight that would almost certainly be delayed, Roxy quickly pulled off at the East Greenwich exit, parked at the empty end of a shopping center lot, and faced Kat who was still staring out the window.

"What's the matter? Is it my driving? We have time to wait here until the rain lets up."

Kat's face was a pale death mask, dark circles seeming to spread beneath her eyes as Roxy watched.

"That was Race Scarlatti," Kat whispered hoarsely.

In a flash, she knew Kat's turmoil was about more than highway rudeness or rainy weather. Race Scarlatti was somehow connected to her strange loss of spirit.

"Who is this Scarlatti, anyway? Mario would only tell me he was the head gangster in the state and an admirer of yours. That doesn't make any sense." Roxy's eyes widened as she watched a terrible expression ravage Kat's face and her gray eyes cloud until they were almost black.

"Remember the night we read Carrie's letter, and I told you I could understand her madness because I had been raped as a virgin also? It was Race. He was the boy who raped me. I should have killed him." Kat's voice dripped pain as if a razor had sliced her heart to ribbons. When she recited the events of the fraudulent dinner at the Venice the other night, Roxy's horror grew. By the time she told of running from the restaurant with the tape, her voice had been bled dry. Kat sat silently crying, tears streaming down her face and dropping onto her tightly clutched hands.

"Did you watch any of this tape?"

"Yes."

"And it was a tape of you and…. and Jamie?"

"Yes."

Roxy groaned. This was unbelievable.

"You had no idea he'd ever filmed you?"

"Until Thursday night when Race turned on the tape, I knew nothing. I suspected nothing. I was totally unprepared for something so awful."

"So, now what?"

"We trust Race Scarlatti and say nothing. What else can I do?" Kat asked, anguished.

★ ★ ★ ★ ★

Kat remained in Washington rewriting, twisting arms, and counting votes, keeping her word to have oil spill legislation in place by the June anniversary of the *Alexander Gold* tanker disaster. Stuart introduced her bill in the Senate and was working hard to move it along there.

Roxy used the free time in Rhode Island to concentrate on writing. When Kat was in the state campaigning in high gear, there was none of the quiet, formless time she needed to think and write.

She needed a theme for drug symposiums planned at two high schools and a day of town meetings related to drug problems, all scheduled for the next weekend Kat was home. Facts and statistics were provided by legislative staff. Recent excursions gave Kat abundant anecdotal material. Roxy needed a hook. More than that, she needed an answer.

She made a mental note to ask Mario what actually happened the night the *Alexander Gold* spilled nearly half a million gallons of number two heating oil in Narragansett Bay and how Kat was involved. Tying her hair into two tails, she pulled on a pale pink Magnolia's sweatshirt and headed for a long, contemplative return to her favorite muse.

It was a beautiful spring day and fragrance filled her nostrils as she walked to the seawall. Cloud-shaped masses of blue-green foliage and drooping clusters of the locust trees' cream white flowers dominated the street. Their heavy, languid smell overpowered the delicate fragrance of white lilacs and baby breath that she managed to catch in random wafts. White banks of flowers were broken by hot pink azaleas hidden against stone walls and old foundations. She was almost reluctant to leave the tree-shaded street to set out on the beach. The sea goddess included no floral scents in her perfume.

Roxy waited for a single idea to emerge from the varied topics, a single note around which she could improvise.

Jake was perched on top of the seawall, smiling delightedly, his brown eyes sparkling. Busy with Kat, she had seen him only briefly since returning from Washington and Hayes. Being with Jake was smooth and easy. No plunging stomach, tight loins or weak knees, just feeling happy and appreciated. It was a treat knowing her comfort and pleasure were important concerns to him. Maybe great sex with a good man and no obsession was the right choice. But how to keep the obsession from ever happening again was her recurring problem.

"I want to talk to you about true love."

Roxy tore herself away from her own speculations to pay attention to what Jake was saying. Could he have been reading her mind?

"She's the first in the Aphrodite series. I've decided to do various faces of the goddess: art, beauty, grace, intimacy, pleasure, ecstasy."

"Do you think those are separate qualities?"

"I think you wear a different face for each." His voice was soft as he stopped, brushed a few stray strands of golden hair from her cheeks and lightly kissed her.

"There's a dice throw named for the goddess where each of the four dice show a different face."

To avoid other walkers on the beach they moved on, Jake kicking at the long brown streamers of seaweed washed up by the storm.

"It looks like whole wheat lasagna," Roxy commented, remembering she had not eaten a real meal in several days.

"Sushi," he responded. "It's why I can't eat sushi. I've seen enough seaweed and raw fish to know I don't want to eat them."

Back at Jake's shop, Roxy praised the Aphrodite panel. Like the legend, she was portrayed rising from foaming surf, pieces of the multicolored globes set as churning water. The body of the goddess was cut from creamy, almost opaque glass swirled with muted tones of gold and rose. She was alluringly draped in blue. Her golden hair streamed like a curving halo around her head. It was the delicately painted features of the face that stirred Roxy. She knew if her face ever glowed like that, it would be true love. Somehow Jake captured that look from her. There was no doubt who the model was.

"I'm a bit rusty on my goddess history. Did Aphrodite have a husband?" Roxy could scarcely imagine what the goddess of love would do with one, but those Olympians had strange notions of family structure and relationships.

"She had two, actually." Jake smiled, causing her to blush.

"Mars, the god of war, and Hephaestus or Vulcan, who was the celestial artist. Always the choice for a man: to become the warrior and ruler or the one who grows food, builds homes and creates beauty."

"Always the choice for women, too," Roxy muttered.

"Both types of men are drawn to Aphrodite's gifts," Jake continued, not hearing her comment.

"There's no doubt she understands what her man needs. Aphrodite inspires creativity in me. More importantly she helps me project it into reality. All this art," he waved his hand around the shop filled with jewels and sparkles of crystallized color and light in the glass, "has come from you.

"Teaching you the tantra has allowed me to relive the joys and wonder of my initial discovery. You've become the unfailing mirror for the beauty and harmony and joy I find in myself, that I can make into my glass. You've lured me back to my soul.

"That's what Aphrodite does for me, what you do for me, what I want to capture in these pieces."

Roxy was overwhelmed by the emotion in his voice. She decided to avoid considering its meaning by pursuing the story of the goddess. They moved outside, settling comfortably into a worn wooden bench with a curved back alongside the stream. The rain turned everything a sparkling green. Blooming trees and bushes perfumed the light air.

"The Romans called her Venus but she is more potent, more complete a goddess as the Greek Aphrodite. Although, if potency was the main criteria, I should be worshipping Ishtar. Scorned as the Whore of Babylon by the ancient Jewish prophets, she was a powerful and complete representation of the sexuality of the Great Mother goddess before she got sliced into different personas." Jake continued his lecture, his voice alluring as the goddess deserved.

"There are many culprits in the degradation of Aphrodite's gifts from the ancient prophets of Israel and lawgivers of Christianity to the vultures of television advertising. Her sacred dimension is lost to the legions obsessed with only her physical charms. For the truth is—as Lawrence wrote to prove—sexuality is a sacred gift, not a commodity to be exploited. Beauty is sacred as is the civilizing influence love has on brute male energy. And what can be more sacred than the connection that comes through love, through the exchange of pleasure and the encouragement of intimacy?

"It's no surprise that our goddess of love and beauty figures prominently in many legends. Love is an art and can create the pure and intense emotion that a great piece of music does. Obsessed love produces the most dramatic and sublime of madnesses.

"An ancient legend tells of Aphrodite winning the golden apple of beauty from Paris. Hera had promised the youth power and riches if he chose her. Athena offered him glory and renown in war. Aphrodite knew her man. She won by offering him the fairest of women for his wife. I'm Libran, ruled by the planet Venus. Like Paris, I chose the goddess of beauty and love."

The brushing of his breath past her ear as he spoke of the goddess and her lovers, his gently but consciously caressing hands soon had Roxy ready to stop talking about Aphrodite and do a little hands-on worshipping.

But Jake had more foreplay in mind. He arranged her reclining on the bench while he stood looking at her and continuing his recital of Aphrodite's attributes.

"The essence of her energy is sensual. In practicing the tantra, we worship in her chosen way. Troubadors of twelfth century France created the world of chivalry inspired by their remarkable Queen, Eleanor of Aquitaine. They were practitioners of a secret discipline of love that had tantric principles at its heart." He reached down and reverently undressed her.

"They would gaze rapturously at the naked body of their beloved so as to awaken slumbering forces in her. Their accolades to feminine beauty recognized its power to rejuvenate."

He ran his hand along the curve of her body from her soft, round shoulder around the globe of her breast into the turn of her waist then flared out along her hip, gazing at her intently.

"You have the most beautiful skin. It's a cruel and ugly world that requires it to be covered with inferior materials and shallow colors." He bent and kissed her in the hollow beneath her breasts then rose and began to sketch.

As the spring breezes played across her skin, Roxy stretched voluptuously and thought it an easy choice: Vulcan who was at home prepared to love while Mars was off playing at war. Or, in this case, politics.

Quickly finishing the lines he wanted to capture, Jake set aside his sketch book, laid beside her and whispered as he lowered his lips to her breast.

"You should honor Aphrodite in all your rituals, Roxy, for she has clearly chosen you as a favorite and assigned you the supreme mission for a woman—to be loved."

Later, Roxy searched out several books of myth in Kat's library. After reading enough of Aphrodite to know she belonged in her temple, she explored further. The story Kat had told of her dreams about Race after her father's death tickled a memory. She skimmed through *Bullfinch's Mythology,* easily finding the legend she was seeking: Persephone, goddess of the underworld, darkness and magic. She was kidnapped and ravished as a young girl by Pluto who took her for his mate. Through various interventions, her mother, Demeter, managed an arrangement where Persephone could spend at least part of each year in the world.

The legend disturbed Roxy's naturally sunny outlook. She recalled Kat's most recent bout with the gray and formless cloud of depression when Winston died. She hoped there would always be a guardian figure to protect Kat during those periods when her own energy seemed to withdraw.

Goddesses dominated her dreams that night. Just before dawn she awoke in a state of erotic arousal, a great insight flushing her further with excitement. She dreamt of being a handmaiden of Ishtar, lying on a mat in Babylonian temple, draped in a simple white cloth as men passed by and examined her as a possible choice. Somehow she knew this was a first visit. The hair was long, black, and curly like Kat's but the body was hers, the one she had now. Her dream face wore a look of profound anticipation mingled with flashes of terror.

Men passed her by with scarcely a look. Most were older, looking for an hour of pleasure with an experienced woman, hopefully one highborn and usually unreachable. None wanted a virgin ignorant of the goddess' skills no matter how lovely she was. Then a man stood before her, neither young nor old and not of her land. He was compact and finely built, fair skinned with reddish hair and pale eyes. This was the man she wanted! There was a matching spark in his eyes and he stepped into her cubicle drawing the curtains behind him. As he removed his sword and began speaking words she could not understand in a melodious voice that soothed her fears and awakened love in her heart, she woke up. It was so clear, as dreams before dawn often are. She could still feel the thrill of recognition and discovery. She knew she continually searched for this man.

★ ★ ★ ★ ★

Roxy's conversations with Hayes were brief and to the point. Bringing the oil spill legislation to the Floor for a vote was an arduous process that required almost total focus. He called mid-week with a curt message to watch Senator Stuart on C-Span that afternoon. "I know you've been searching for an overriding theme for Kat's statements this month. Stuart's talking about flag burning today. He might have something to say that would help."

How flag burning connected with drugs and oil spills was a mystery, but she was drawing a blank in her own ruminations and decided to give the senator a chance.

She briefly wondered how Hayes found time to concern himself with Stuart's Senate speeches. He probably saw the senator from Virginia as the shining light in his future. It was no surprise. She already identified Hayes as Mars with politics his chosen battlefield. There would always be another election, another campaign luring him. Love would never be more than an escape, the pause that refreshes.

Roxy watched the Senate debate in the big room at campaign headquarters along with a dozen or so mostly female volunteers who were addressing invitations for yet another fundraising house party, this one in wealthy East Greenwich. She observed that the big winners in a political campaign were the U.S. Post Office, phone company, and television stations.

Kat's volunteers responded positively to Stuart. He looked like a U.S. Senator. His navy pinstripe suit was impeccably tailored to fit his well-muscled frame. His trademark white shirt gleamed. Stuart's intensity commanded the camera's attention. In a strong, unadorned voice, he briefly outlined the Supreme Court's decision in a flag burning incident the previous year that had generated calls for a constitutional amendment banning the act.

He heightened the drama, tightening his face muscles, deepening his voice. Not much difference between acting and politics, Roxy thought, not for the first time. She watched the faces of the volunteers brighten as he described what he saw when he looked at the American flag, "golden light, a sunny day, people having a chance."

He proclaimed America a country of last chances, whether for boat people or his ancestors fleeing harsh English landlords. He described the flag as a symbol of the hope and liberty embodied in the nation's founding principles. He objected to its desecration.

"I object to the act of flag burning as I do to all desecration, for that is the greater issue. Burning a flag is meant to be a slap in the face of those who hold it a sacred symbol—and that's assault. I will listen to any person's opinion, any person's argument. I will not succumb to any person's assault. Violence is against the law, all law, God's law. There is no need to amend the Constitution to address this issue. Unfortunately, good taste and respect for others cannot be legislated."

The epiphany Stuart's words triggered was sweet. Her fortune strip for June had promised that inspiration would lend her mind wings. The thread for Kat's diverse statements was a desperate need for the sacred in contemporary life where so little was respected and virtually nothing but money revered. The sacred was not limited to symbols like the flag. Roxy recalled June 1989 when the flag burning issue emerged. There were also several major oil spills causing enormous ecological damage and Chinese students were shot for their devotion to liberty in Tiananmen Square. All were violations of the sacred.

Roxy scribbled down the theme as it unfolded in her mind. She caught only fragments of Stuart's speech and the resulting praise by the others watching. Learning and knowledge were no longer sacred so schools were crumbling, education unfocused and libraries wilting on the vine. There was nothing sacred in families and relationships, so the societal structures built on them were disintegrating. Drug use was another symptom of growing spiritual hunger, the search for something beyond the self.

She wrote that a sense of the sacred cannot be instilled by spending more money. Kat routinely rejected the notion of separation between the sacred and the mundane, and contended it was the separation between environmental concern and economics that made degradation of the earth possible.

SENATE MAGIC

★ ★ ★ ★ ★

The smash of Jake's new commercial dubbed "Why do you think they call it dope?" exceeded Gould's most optimistic predictions, although he claimed to have known all along the commercials would have major impact. Press anticipation of a new Kiley Tomasso commercial exceeded that for network television's fall schedule or the Christmas movie releases. Relaxed and attentive, Kat asked probing questions during the weekend's town meetings, seeking ways to apply her prevention techniques to drug use among children, her most pressing concern.

She described an enlightening meeting with the U.S. Attorney for the state.

"He identified the distribution of illegal drugs as our most serious crime problem, pinpointing coastal smuggling and proximity to key markets in Boston and New York as reasons. State efforts in this area are woefully inadequate with no encouragement from our former governor, now my unworthy opponent."

Roxy smiled, knowing Kat considered Douglas an insult as contender for the senate seat. She totally ignored the fact that Douglas was now the official junior senator from Rhode Island.

"What shocked me was his claim that cocaine and heroin distribution are currently the almost exclusive domain of several Hispanic groups, primarily Colombians and Dominicans, many of whom are illegal aliens. It appears that Scarlatti's organization is almost out of the drug business and long-time dealers like my ex-husband stay involved primarily to keep themselves and their friends supplied."

With the drug message unfolding on its own, Roxy directed her efforts to the speech for the *Alexander Gold* anniversary. A press conference announcing Kat's oil spill legislation was scheduled after a tanker cruise around the Bay. She had the mythic theme—to respect the sacred earth. It was facts she needed to weave around it, history to go with the content of the legislation and what it would mean for future protection.

The perfect occasion for in-depth research arose when Tony called to say the restaurant had a limited special of homemade ravioli and bracciole. Scooping up Mario and the Hose, Roxy dragged them to eat while she questioned them about the night of the oil spill. The Hose claimed to know nothing about what happened in the bay. Instead, he ate his way through two platters of the delicate cheese-filled pastas and stuffed meat rolls while Mario told the story.

"The spill happened shortly after midnight on June 22. The *Alexander Gold* was a Greek-flag oil tanker that had sped past the pilot station near Brenton Lighttower and headed unguided toward Newport. Almost immediately it crashed on the rocks at Brenton Reef. One of Kat's pilot boat buddies called her and she sped over to Goat Island where he had a boat waiting. They beat the

Coast Guard to the scene. Given the location and state of the wind and sea that night, they realized that a spill of any measurable size posed a direct threat to Narragansett Beach, particularly the estuary of Narrow River and Mackerel Cove on Jamestown. According to the boat captain who took Kat out, she began immediately working the radio, talking to the Coast Guard, then me."

Mario paused and a wistful smile curved his lips.

"Kat's interruption caught me in the flames of passion, as the expression goes, and my partner was rather disturbed. I never saw her again after that."

"Wasn't that when you were doing it to that gas station broad from Newport?" the Hose asked between bites.

"You 'do it' to gas station attendants, I entertain heiresses to oil company billions, and this one did not find being distracted by an oil spill even remotely entertaining." Roxy smiled as Mario added dejectedly, "She stopped contributing to Kat's campaign, too.

"The upshot of the story is that our esteemed then-Governor Emmett Douglas refused to be rousted from bed by the Coast Guard to make any decisions. Early reports estimated a spill of two million gallons, a huge disaster. Kat was on the Coast Guard ship, freaking out over the potential scale of the spill. She called the governor and threatened to drag him from bed in rather strong and colorful language. He hung up. Kat then called some Tomasso connections and had a private crane in place before dawn to protect the estuary. Needless to say, she was the heroine of the hour and the Federal government eventually picked up the cost of the crane she ordered when Douglas refused state payment.

"Nearly every environmental group related to the bay honored her last year because of what the press termed her 'resolute action.' There were several other oil spills that week elsewhere in the country. She mobilized the delegations from all those areas and drafted the oil spill legislation. She'll get to announce passage of it just one year later." They applauded and cheered as Mario finished the story with a flourish.

There was Roxy's theme: Kat, the crusading angel, protecting the body of her goddess, Earth.

★ ★ ★ ★ ★

Roxy liked being hooked in from home to conference call strategy sessions so she could watch television, do her nails or work on the computer while listening to the political geniuses calculate. Hayes kept the congressional world in top condition while Kat's legislation moved forward.

Gould was so pleased with the success of his media strategy, especially since it was being touted in trade columns and journals everywhere, that he would entertain no suggestions for change, not that anyone really had any. Money was pouring in, Kat's national press coverage was gratifying, and Mario had few qualms about campaign activities in the state.

There was only one gnawing concern: what was their opponent up to? Since Tomasso contract accusations were laid to rest, Douglas had been the invisible man. Kat claimed this was because she refused to speak his name or think about him as more than a vague presence on the other column of the ballot. But she confessed to Roxy she was tense, just waiting for the next inevitable attack.

It was a gorgeous, sunny day, and Roxy took the conference call on the cordless phone. She settled herself on the manicured lawn under one of the large peony bushes interspersed with rhododendron trees around the edge of the porch. The exotic smell of the frilly, lush white flowers blended with Hayes' drawl. Her erotic temperature skyrocketed. As she sat listening to the different voices arguing, cajoling, reasoning their positions, she switched to examining the various stages of the rhododendron's hot pink blossoms. There was a tight cone that was a solid green bud. Next to it, a slightly more advanced flower sported flashes of hot pink peeking from the green like a silk hanky in a lapel pocket. Finally, there were hundreds of mature flowers—several blossoms emerging from a single bud. Those were trumpet flares of hot pink, smelling sweet and light.

When Gould repeated his warning that Douglas had no issues but Kiley's missteps, a sudden terror gripped Roxy's stomach and mashed it as she mashed the pink blossom she held in her hand. The tape. They were forced to take Race Scarlatti's word that Kat now had the only copy of her tape, and that he would keep silent. Jamie surely remembered this tape existed. His reliability was a given. He had none.

Hayes did not know about the tape, and urged the start of an assault on Douglas' continued absence in the Senate. He was sure Douglas wouldn't bother to attend the upcoming vote on the oil spill legislation. That would be the trigger.

"Sun Tzu advises to confront when the opponent is idle, and take the initiative so others do not." Everyone agreed.

Roxy perked up her ears when Jasmine suggested the direction she thought Douglas might attack.

"He has no positions, everyone knows he's a corrupt and useless swine, his attack on Kiley's honesty backfired, so all that's left to him is to oppose her on emotional issues. I think he's going to declare himself pro-life." She could envision Mario, sitting at headquarters raising his eyebrows and thinking the same thing: this did not sound like a guess but a certainty. They never told anyone about Jasmine and Carrie at the dog track. She wondered if Jasmine was playing both sides of this game and whose side was uppermost in her affections.

Kat was back in Rhode Island two days later, oil spill legislation in hand, preparing for a hectic week that included both the *Alexander Gold* anniversary and the First Lady's lunch. There were more hints of upheaval and attacks to come. It was Summer Solstice and Kat had Roxy read the cards as a brief seasonal preview. She insisted on using their standard Waite deck, continuing to ignore the goddess cards. She directed Roxy in a layout created particularly for seasonal readings.

Three cards were arranged in a triangle moving from the top point down to the right. Then four cards were arranged in a surrounding square. The inner triangle, which Kat claimed represented the flow and rhythm of energy, was clear even to Roxy's non-interpreting eye. The familiar Death card appeared, once again reversed. The red heart pierced with three swords that defined the starting point of the summer's energy gave no consolation. The cards of the outer square, which described the external events of the season, were not obscure either. Although the Lovers were not present, a similar card showed a handsome couple drinking from each other's cup. Roxy was pleased by the beautiful Empress card. She was a golden haired lady seated in an abundantly blooming garden. There must be something about the Empress that she did not get. Kat frowned severely at the sight of it.

"Max was right. Our two months of grace are nearly over. Chaos, upheaval and betrayal are about to begin." Kat's summary was curt and invited no discussion.

Summer was but a few hours old when the forces the cards depicted began to unfold. They were reviewing the salient points of Kat's oil spill legislation and watching the debate in the Senate, its vote on the bill scheduled for that evening or the next morning. Hayes had called earlier, elated that there was no sign of Douglas in Washington; he would miss the oil spill vote and they would have a sharpened sword to use against him.

Assembling facts for the speech, Roxy was impressed with how comprehensive the bill was, and how much Kat managed for Rhode Island. The legislation was built on two key tenets of Kat's faith: prevention and polluter pays. There were increased safety provisions, a requirement for double-hulled tankers, substantial penalties for violation of piloting regulations, and a tanker-free zone established in several sensitive areas including the Montauk Point–Block Island channel visible from the house. At Hayes' suggestion, the bill created a demonstration project, a five-year study of damage from the *Alexander Gold* spill that would release its findings in time for her re-election to the Senate.

The oil spill legislation was a major victory for Kiley Tomasso, U.S. Senate candidate. The stage of the *Alexander Gold* anniversary offered maximum media exposure. Kat was worrying aloud about mentioning Douglas' absence from the Senate on this vote when the phone rang. Mario answered, his face growing strained as he silently made notes.

"That was a friend at Channel 6. They're assembling a special show for the *Alexander Gold* anniversary tomorrow." His tone indicated the call was not an invitation for Kat to participate. "Today they received, anonymously, an audio tape from the night of the oil spill. You were expressing derogatory opinions of Governor Douglas' manhood in rather explicit language. It's too profane for them to use on the air but everyone at the station has heard it, repeatedly it seems. They wanted you to know it was out there."

Kat laughed defensively and threw up her hands.

"I thought two million gallons of oil were being spilled into Narragansett Bay while the governor was refusing to get out of bed and make some essential decisions. Whatever I said was well deserved under the circumstances."

Hostility crept into her voice as she paced the small room.

"Why should I care if the conversation is made known? I was acting to save the bay, Douglas was home in bed. He's the one who would look bad."

Mario calmly reminded her that a five minute, obscenity-filled screeching harangue at the state's elected governor was not exactly senatorial.

"Based on what I know about some of my august future colleagues, it's probably the most senatorial thing I've done to date," Kat retorted.

"The point is not whether you were right in what you said. People consider the U.S. Senate to be America's House of Lords. If they send you there, they want to be certain you won't embarrass them," he admonished.

"I know, I know. It isn't something the elegant Grace Langley of New Jersey would do, and she should be my model."

Whatever happened, Roxy hoped Mario could score a copy of the tape. She wanted to hear Kat shred Douglas.

Hours of phone calls, conversations, and wordsmithing later, Kat was prepared. She ignored Gould's suggestion and dressed for the three-hour boat trip from Bretton Point to Providence harbor aboard a tanker, not the press conference afterwards. She looked right at home in a thick knit fisherman's sweater over jeans and sneakers, her hair tied back in a red bandanna, a yellow slicker tossed over the stool behind her. The politicians in suits were the ones who looked out of place at the harbor.

A grossly overweight stringer from a Boston newspaper brought up the taped conversation with the governor. The evening news on all three network affiliates carried the resulting exchange in total.

A wry smile touched the corners of Kat's lips, and her voice held the slightest hint of apology as she answered his question.

"It was two o'clock in the morning. I was in the middle of Narragansett Bay wondering how it could survive the massive amounts of oil we thought were being spilled. The Coast Guard officer in charge was having no luck in persuading the governor to leave his bed and assist in the crisis. Who knows what I said trying to change his mind?"

Her smile increased almost imperceptibly, her eyes twinkled, and a sly note was added to her tone.

"I must apologize however for the content of my remarks. I work diligently to speak only from reliable sources and first-hand experience. In this case, I admit to violating my standards and using common rumors as my source. I have no first-hand knowledge of Governor Douglas' manhood or parentage."

Thousands all over the state joined those watching at campaign headquarters in cheering Kat's response.

She quickly selected another questioner whose hand shot up. He probed further about her abuse of Douglas. Ignoring his specific question, she launched her attack.

"Action, or in this case inaction, always speaks louder than words. This was not an isolated incident where public responsibilities were ignored." She reached into the pocket of her jeans and read from a yellow page she pulled out.

"Less than one hour ago, the United States Senate voted to pass oil spill legislation that will go far toward preventing the type of tragedy we are mourning today. There was only one vote for the bill from the state of Rhode Island; our other vote was listed absent. The vote that would have been Senator Winston's proud 'yes' to protect our precious bay was not cast. Rhode Island deserves its two votes in the U.S. Senate. Rhode Island needs them."

★ ★ ★ ★ ★

The state's large French-Canadian population celebrated its heritage on St. Jean Baptiste Day with special Masses, feasts and activities. Compounding the usual high spirits was news that Quebec separatists were celebrating the defeat of Canadian moves to weaken their ethnic identity. Contact with the Quebec homeland was strong among French Canadians, especially in Woonsocket. Even after three generations, some still spoke of returning to Canada.

Kat was scheduled to speak at St. Marie's Church. Her local coordinators were standing nervously by the curb in front of the church as Kat and Roxy drove up. Bishop O'Reagan was across the plaza behind a hedge of microphones and reporters at the entrance of the Union St. Jean Baptiste, social and cultural center of Woonsocket. Although Douglas was nowhere to be seen, Jasmine appeared to be right—choice would be his next attack and the bishop was his ally.

Kat immediately called Mario on her phone and frowned as he told her they received notifications less than ten minutes ago that her speech was relocated to the Union plaza. He had been tracking down the reason why. The result of his search was verified as the bishop began speaking. He announced Cardinal Wolfe in Chicago publicly supported his position that Catholic legislators be excommunicated from their church if they supported what he described as "the heinous crime of abortion." A letter was being sent to the Holy See in Rome for authority to implement their position.

As his tirade continued, Kat moved slowly and deliberately through the crowd toward the stage area, shaking hands and greeting people as she went. Fear streaked many faces and some turned away. Everyone in the plaza knew who Bishop O'Reagan was attacking. She reached the stage as he concluded. He gave no indication he saw her ascend the platform. As he turned to step down, Kat moved quickly to take his place at the microphone. Although she was scheduled several speakers later, no one moved to prevent her from speaking.

She was radiant in a white silk suit with ankle-length skirt and long, fitted jacket. The large jeweled cross she wore pinned to the lacy throat of her blouse was as magnificent as the bishop's. Another Duke legacy, Roxy guessed. She wondered what Kat's father would have done to any mere bishop who threatened to excommunicate his daughter. Kat's hair was primly rolled at the nape of her neck and bound in white webbing. Her blazing eyes belonged to an avenging angel.

Kat opposed the bishop's right as a spiritual leader to punish her for a political decision.

"He has no more right to prescribe my political actions than legislatures and governments have the right to prescribe what a woman may do with her body. Should he attempt to excommunicate me for representing the views of my constituents who support a woman's choice more than two to one, I will contest his action to Rome and beyond. Should the Supreme Court remove a woman's right to choice, I will contest that to the U.S. Senate and beyond."

Ignoring shouts of both support and opposition, Kat delivered her prepared speech celebrating the French-Canadian heritage in the state with its strong family and community bonds. She described a future guided by the rich traditions of the past. She slipped quickly from the stage when finished, refusing both press questions and pro-life hecklers. Her position had been clearly spelled out numerous times, further debate or explanation would serve no purpose. Kat realized there were few minds to be changed on the question of choice.

They watched phase two on a news brief. Douglas arrived at the plaza only moments after Kat left. Posing with his new best friend, the Roman Catholic bishop, he proclaimed himself strongly in support of the pro-life position and Bishop O'Reagan's right to censure dissenting politicians. Mario wondered aloud how Douglas would explain his approval of funds for state-run abortion clinics while he was governor.

The worst was yet to come.

Roxy was on the beach before dawn the next day so she could walk before driving Kat to a final meeting of the First Lady's luncheon steering committee. She should jog, it went so much faster than walking. The litter-strewn sand moved her to complain under her breath about summer tourists ruining the beach. If she came later on Monday mornings, she might avoid evidence of the spoilage. City employees were out picking up the trash, and several people combed the beach with metal detectors looking for lost change, watches, and jewelry. Returning to the house disgruntled at the human capacity to trash beauty, she was surprised to find Kat glued to the TV.

A small crowd of pro-life demonstrators picketed the women's clinic in North Providence that was one of Kat's special projects. Reporters were asking their opinions on Bishop O'Reagan's excommunication threat and Douglas' new support of their position. A tall, gawky young man with a prominent Adam's apple announced the protesters' next move and Kat moaned. They had called the White House insisting the First Lady cancel her planned fundraising activity for Kat the next day and swore they would stage massive protests around the Biltmore Hotel where the luncheon was scheduled. It was a difficult position for the First Lady. However true the rumors that she was pro-choice in her heart, the public fact was that she supported her husband's pro-life stance.

★ ★ ★ ★ ★

Roxy and Mario slumped dejectedly, blankly watching the final few minutes of a network sitcom with the sound muted as Kat picked at the remains of a huge antipasto from Tony. Every minute she was not on the phone pleading with various White House and GOP functionaries not to cancel the First Lady's visit, she was confirming to press and ticket holders that the event would proceed as planned.

Kat tried to steel herself for the late news broadcasts which would turn the White House's no comment and her continued assurances that the First Lady was coming, into the truth: the White House could not decide whether it was worth the political heat and she had no idea whether the First Lady was coming or not.

She was about to pick up the phone and call someone, anyone, who could tell her anything before the news went on when it rang under her hand, startling her. Mario jumped up and answered it before it rang a second time. He handed it to her with an anxious look, "Senator Stuart."

She uttered less than a syllable before he began.

"The First Lady is coming as planned."

"Thank you, thank you, thank you…." Kat crooned softly as Stuart continued talking.

"I had to call in some big favors and remind them just how valuable a Republican Senate would be as well as make several promises for you. You cannot mention the subject of choice to the First Lady or in any remarks at the luncheon. No harassment by picketers or proponents of either side. Security must be so tight that she sees no one from airport to hotel and back that is not a paying guest. No press anywhere. And Kiley, you need to control the security—not local or state authorities. Let De Palma and your uncles handle it, they'll know what to do. Agreed?"

"Anything, I'll agree to anything. Can I call the press and tell them before eleven?"

"Yep."

"No changing their minds tomorrow?"

"Nope. She's coming."

Kat could barely choke out her thanks, she was so filled with appreciation.

"This one was easy," Stuart replied quickly, "I agree with you. It should be a woman's choice to bear a child or not. The government should have no part in it although it would be nice if the contributing male could be consulted." The irony hung in his voice for an instant before he concluded. "Details on security needs will be faxed to your office by morning. Be nice to Marge Jamison. Not only is she a lovely lady but she admires you greatly. She was the one who prevailed with the president; I only helped with a few minor arguments."

Kat leaned her head against the receiver for a few seconds after he hung up, flooded with relief. Roxy and Mario whooped gleefully when she told them of Stuart's assurance that Mrs. Jamison was coming. They called each of the television stations to report the good news.

★ ★ ★ ★ ★

Afraid the exposure would decrease his credibility in the commercials, Gould banned Jake from official Kiley for Senate functions. He did not object. The effects of recognition were beginning to wear on him. He was stretched on the porch swing waiting for her when she finally arrived after the First Lady's lunch.

"Kat flew back to Washington with Mrs. Jamison. A huge coup, I might add," Roxy said proudly as she joined him on the swing.

"Kat looked great and so did Mrs. Jamison. Almost everyone else, especially me, looked short posed for pictures between the two of them. Mrs. Jamison is a true grande dame, elegant on the outside, shrewd on the inside. Everyone says she's the motive force behind the president. She's as attractive in person as she is in pictures and on television, with the most gorgeous white hair ever. It just sweeps back off her face into these soft wings. Her eyes are sparkling green, very shocking when you first see them. She wore a green designer suit today which probably made them even more noticeable. I hope I have skin half as smooth and clear when I'm her age.

"She and Kat seemed to genuinely like each other, and as I said, they made a great picture. Kat was in a sophisticated silk print dress with her hair pulled back in a cascade by two beautifully carved ivory combs shaped as butterflies. She wore a necklace and matching earrings of angel coral mounted in gold."

Jake was grinning as he interrupted her fashion report.

"What color was her underwear?"

Roxy laughed. He loved the story of Kat's underwear colors and made her promise to keep him posted as soon as she noticed a change. He insisted by plotting out the changes and analyzing the colors, they could provide Kat with amazing insights into parts of herself otherwise unknown.

"She's still in the April phase of black and light blue; she had on a pale blue teddy today." She continued with her event report.

"Security was our greatest concern and it worked perfectly. The Hose pulled strings and masses of Providence police were there keeping demonstrators well in hand, same with the Warwick police at the airport. There were no problems at lunch although the sight of some of Kat's uncles and cousins on guard duty probably unnerved the general population of upscale, Republican women who came to lunch with their First Lady. By the end of the event, some of the younger guys were copying the practiced stance of Mrs. Jamison's Secret Service contingent and lusting after a looping wire behind the ear.

"With all due immodesty as the author, Kat's speech was marvelous, and Mrs. Jamison was very attentive, even took a few notes. She seemed taken with Kat's vision of future libraries as community information centers that could be expanded to self-taught adult education and retraining programs. The Friends of the Library were delighted with the five thousand plus they made raffling off the luncheon tickets we gave them and not one of them stayed away because of the controversy. In fact, Carolyn claims we surpassed our most optimistic projections for both attendance and money raised.

"When Mrs. Jamison swept Kat off to Washington with her, they looked like the best of friends. If we hurry, we can catch the evening news and see how the media reported a First Lady's visit they never saw." Roxy got up to go inside and watch the news, but Jake pulled her back onto the swing.

"Enough business," he said nuzzling her neck, "I'm ready for some pleasure."

She could not agree more. The past week had been an enormous strain and nothing restored her happy attitude about life more than immersion in pleasure.

"Let me catch the news, then my work will be done and I can abandon myself completely to whatever pleasuring you have in mind."

Roxy looked plaintive. Jake proposed that they turn on the television and make out until the segment on Kat came on, watch it, then escalate their fun.

Television thrives on action and the First Lady's visit provided none. Coverage was satisfyingly low key. There was footage of Mrs. Jamison and Kat waving from the car as they turned onto a cordoned-off street. Interviews with the few demonstrators who appeared at the hotel portrayed them as disagreeable fanatics. Gushing remarks by prominent Republican women who attended the lunch universally reported Mrs. Jamison's strong support of Kat. Radical feminist groups had been persuaded by Kat that confrontation with either Mrs. Jamison or any possible pro-life demonstrators would be counter-productive.

Jake took her to his shop, stopping by the outdoor grill to turn the heat on under a giant pot of water.

"Tonight we begin a summer orgy of lobster eating. Prices are so sinfully low—unfortunately for all my lobstermen buddies—we can't afford not to eat out several nights a week. In fact, Pete begged us to accompany him on a tour of lobster eating in Galilee on Friday. I accepted. But tonight, we're at home and the eating will be more sensually consuming."

As Jake pulled her against him for a deep kiss, she wondered whether his longing was from her absence for the past couple days or if there was something more behind it.

"This is Aphrodite as beauty, and here, as ecstasy."

The look in his eyes as he displayed his newest work told her what had inspired his ardor. The goddess as pleasure was a hand mirror with a gracefully curved naked female body as the handle, her raised arm, profiled face and flowing hair cradling the oval mirror along one side. There was the briefest tinge of sadness as Roxy accepted she could never be as beautiful as Jake created her with his artist's vision. Ecstasy, on the other hand, was a height to which she could aspire.

They carried their lobsters to a secluded area of the yard under a gigantic old willow tree that hugged the stream bank. Eating like errant children with no adult watching, they tore apart the large crustaceans, pulling out sweet parcels of tender white flesh from the shell, dipping it in melted butter and stuffing it in their mouths, laughing as lobster juices and butter dripped down their faces and hands. Jake pulled a bottle of white wine from where it was chilling in the stream. Bowing formally over her hand, he opened the wine and poured it dramatically into one of his beautiful crystal glasses.

"Another Sakonnet treasure, this one a blend of Chardonnay, Vidal and Seyval grapes with just a hint of oak—the tree from which Hercules' club was reputedly made and believed to give fortitude. Max recommended it to me."

He dropped a juicy ripe strawberry in each glass. She finished the first claw, a glass of wine, and several strawberries, then paused to delicately lick her fingers clean and take off her shirt. Oil stains from melted butter were impossible to remove from some fabrics. Jake immediately followed suit, smiling appreciatively at her bare breasts. They merrily ate lobster topless in the still light of evening. She felt a sensory cloud envelop her. The air fumed with the fresh smell of grasses and leafing trees and a wet aroma from the stream. Pungent butter and the lobsters' ocean fragrance blended into birds and tree frogs singing and rippling water and the smooth slide of warm butter down the outside of her throat and along the valley of her breasts. Jake leaned towards her, stuffing a butter-soaked chunk of sweet flesh into her mouth.

She laid on the blanket and sighed in pleasure as he continued to dunk choice morsels into the butter then slide them between her parted lips, deliberately dripping on her chest. When he rubbed the butter and juices across her skin, then licked them off, Roxy reciprocated and they were soon engaged in a variation on the tantric practice of oiling the partner that was designed for a midsummer revel by the sea when all restrictions on chastity are lifted.

It was dark when they settled into the pillows, squeaky clean. Offered the choice of washing down in the ice cold stream or steaming hot shower, Roxy showed her true colors and unhesitatingly selected the shower. She felt decidedly energized, especially wrapped in the red silk robe Jake insisted she wear. He wore a similar one in blue. She wondered aloud if her increased energy was related to practicing tantric yoga.

Jake's delighted smile transfigured his face when she went on to ask if there were ways they could use the sexual energy they were generating.

"There are, and now that you've asked, I can teach you."

His voice changed and she had an eerie feeling of stepping into another room of his being. Then the door closed and he was once again a scholar explaining his field.

"There are two levels of energy use possible. The first automatically follows tantric yoga, as you've noticed. It increases vitality in youth and restores it in old age, making sex the only true potion for eternal youth known to humanity. Physicists would categorize the transformation that comes from sex as bioelectric, the exchange of energy between a physical negative and a physical positive. You know what electricity can do."

As he ran his finger lightly along the inside of her thigh, she decided she was more on the bio side than the electrical. The pulse in her oozed rather than flashed.

Jake sat up and pulled her into a more decorous position beside him.

"The second level is conscious and requires intense focus as well as pure motives to be undertaken safely. The tantric energy we raise through the sex we have together can be used to materialize an object or a condition."

Roxy stared at him wondering if he meant what he said literally or if this was some sophist twist where the so-called materialization occurred on a non-physical level, meaning it did not really happen at all.

"We could work to produce massive amounts of energy through frequent tantric sex and direct it to Kat winning the senate race," Jake said simply.

"Do you think we could really do that?" Roxy was incredulous.

"I've never attempted anything on this scale before, or that involved any reality but my own. Theoretically it should work. And we'd have a great time trying."

They deliberated about what they would specifically create and finally decided to work on two hundred and fifty thousand people voting for Kat in November. That would be enough for her to win and seemed to fit the parameters of what they could manifest. Roxy begged Jake to explain the process so they could start immediately.

"Before we do sex magic, there's something we need to discuss." Jake took her face in his hands and looked deeply into her eyes, saying nothing. Then he dropped his hands and began.

"Using sexual energy to create something is extremely powerful magic. That's how babies are made you know." Roxy smiled with him, relieving a portion of the tension she felt building.

"I don't want to own you or possess you except as you offer yourself to me."

To illustrate the treasure he wanted, he slid his hand between her legs; they instinctively parted.

"When we started this work, I taught you principles that would help you enhance the energy you already had. Now, we're going beyond that into practices that assume serious responsibility on our parts, and frankly, require that neither of us pollute what we're creating with someone else's energy."

She looked at him perplexed, not really understanding what he was saying. Jake continued.

"D.H. Lawrence says 'the instinct of fidelity is the deepest instinct in the great complex we call sex. Where there is real sex, there is the underlying passion for fidelity.' The potency of tantric sex magic requires exclusiveness both for success and the safety of the participants. If we decide to undertake a project of directing the sexual energy we generate towards Kat's election, we must be sexually involved only with each other. I'm prepared to pledge my fidelity to you and teach you the technique. Are you willing in return?"

She examined Jake's face as he waited for her response. This was not a man pleading from burning desire or consuming jealousy. He was a scientist asking her to wash her hands before undertaking a delicate experiment. Well, maybe not quite as simple a request but Roxy was ready to trade a few quick fucks with Hayes to guarantee Kat's victory. It was only a few months. If Hayes was as obsessed with the campaign as he seemed, she was sure he would support her decision.

"What exactly does fidelity entail?" she asked, uncertain that she could give up thinking about sex with Hayes.

"Good question," Jake laughed. "The tantra describes eight levels of sexual intercourse that range from thinking and discussing it to intimate conversations and finally, actual copulation. I think for the purpose of the magic we're doing, we can define fidelity by physical copulation only. You can flirt all you want."

She could do that, she agreed. They began the first attempt at sex magic on the campaign trail.

Breathing in unison, they sat face to face. Each placed their hands over the pulsing center in the solar plexus and imagined a small brilliant tongue of flame corkscrewing ever larger as they fanned it with their breath until it glowed white hot. Then each substituted the agreed upon image of the vote count for the flame. They visualized two hundred and fifty thousand written next to Kat's name in a newspaper report of the election. For two minutes they pumped their breath in staccato bursts strongly willing the vote count to materialize. Holding the image they lowered and raised their heads breathing accordingly.

Jake pulled Roxy towards him and pushed into her, sending a spurt of flame up her spine. Their shared image of the vote count was blasted by the raging fire through the crown of their heads into objective form.

What a way to influence the votes, thought Roxy as she felt bliss rocketing though her body for the second time that night.

★ ★ ★ ★ ★

Light slowly faded and giant oak trees, more than a century old, became shadowy Titans, then disappeared as the four friends sat quietly in the curved room-size space that defined the east end of Kat's impressive porch. Piazza, thought Roxy. Kat had corrected her last week when she was describing one of the house's more remarkable features. Only the beating surf and lonely cry of the fog horn disputed the silence as each pondered their own inner script.

So much happened in any single day on the campaign that Roxy ceased trying to impose any linear order to her memories. Out of sequence or not, dramatic events retained clarity in her mind. The latest crisis was about money, or the lack thereof. Although Congress had been in recess for the Fourth of July since Friday, Kat returned to the state only the previous day.

She spent the four days in and around Washington raising money at small dinner parties and a large picnic Senator Stuart arranged among his supporters in northern Virginia. With money raised at these events, and the continued flow from the Senate committee, there was enough to soften the impact of in-state funds drying-up. Kat appeared unfazed, reminding her finance people she had predicted in May that Douglas would scare away donors. Mario was less sanguine, convinced the trickle of small checks was a direct result of Douglas' sniping at Kat. He was terrified that hesitance to give money would translate into lost votes. However, regular spot polls showed no lessening of Kat's huge lead.

Earlier that day, Mario practiced delivering his fundraising report to her while Kat was having lunch with their Volunteer of the Month, a wild and crazy middle aged woman from Wakefield. She was one of Kat's favorite drivers since she ignored speed limits as blithely as Kat did. Roxy was so disturbed by Mario's gloom that she immediately offered to stop taking any salary.

"I never wanted any money from the campaign. I don't need it, but Kat insisted," she explained as she pulled out her checkbook and offered to make a thousand dollar contribution if necessary. Her strong reaction shocked Mario into modifying his presentation. No need to add to Kat's already tightly-stretched nerves.

"We'll know better how we're doing in comparison to Douglas when the quarterly FEC reports come out listing all campaign donors and expenditures. Of course, we'll have to consider that he ignores rigid campaign funding rules. I've heard not only most of his payroll but even some purchases of advertising time and space are being paid for in cash."

Roxy's eyes widened in surprise. Cash was poison in Federal campaigns. Carolyn always panicked when people insisted on donating even small amounts in cash. No doubt Douglas was receiving his in brown paper bags from men in ill-fitting suits. Any large cash donation was suspect. Either the source of the money or the amount being given were illegal. Mario confirmed both were true in this case.

"Most of it's gambling money. Douglas was one of the silent partners in Narragansett Park, a horse-racing track that's now defunct. His interests in jai alai and the Lincoln dog track are well known. That's how he's connected with Scarlatti."

"Does that mean Scarlatti would work against Kat?" she asked, concerned.

"If he's giving cash to Douglas, it'll be like a lot of others who always pay both candidates. It's a more delicate task now that new campaign finance laws require listing all donors. In this race they can donate the two thousand dollar limit to Kat openly then give Douglas cash. He won't turn it down or report it."

Judging from Mario's matter-of-fact tone and his answer, she decided he knew nothing of either Kat's recent encounter with Race or the tape he had given her.

Campaign contributions were a minor concern compared to a corrupt man with ties to their sleazy opponent holding a destructive secret over Kat's head. It worried her that she and Kat seemed to be the only ones who knew.

Drifting back to the present on a summer breeze laden with heavy flower smells and salty sea air, she focused on Max's bulky shadow across the circle. It was good to have him there even if he was leaving before dawn. She was slightly envious. Watching Kat march in the Barrington parade, the oldest July 4th parade in the nation, could not compensate for missing the extravagant parade and picnic back home in Morgan Springs.

Velvety darkness wrapped their safe circle, aglow with twinkling fireflies that previewed the next night's fireworks. Kat announced she was going to catch some and grabbed a jar stashed against the piazza column.

"Are you going to do the wishing ritual?" Max asked, as she walked out on the lawn.

THE TOWER

"What's the wishing ritual?" Roxy snuggled closer to Jake on the cushioned settee they shared.

"Fireflies hold in them the remarkable mystery of cold fire. What is the source of their light? Why do they glow primarily when ascending? Why are they around mostly in early summer?"

Whatever stage personas he assumed through the years, Max's voice always sounded most authentic when he was being the wise teacher.

"Kat could answer the scientific questions better than I. To me, it's magic!"

Kat's vague shape moved silently in front of the rhododendron, regularly opening and closing the jar lid as she captured glowing insects. Her neon pink playsuit flickered in the light from the jar.

"Just before dawn, I'll release the fireflies, whispering a wish that they'll carry to Heaven for me." Kat's voice rang out from the dark lawn. A scattering of far-off pops announced impatient celebrators with their firecrackers.

"They have to be released before dawn so they can carry out their own purposes before the sun snuffs them out."

Satisfied with her assemblage of fireflies, Kat came back on the porch and hoisted herself onto the railing, settling against a smooth column.

"How about a miracle story or two, a quick peek behind the veil of the future, and then off to bed," she said to Max. "We have to be up early for a big day tomorrow."

Max leaned against the chair and his powerful voice emerged from the shadows.

"There is a well-worn legend about a fiery-voiced stranger who suddenly appeared among delegates in the Philadelphia State House as they were debating a document that would rock the world. It was July 4, 1776 and the document was the Declaration of Independence. His rhetoric inflamed them. Crying 'God has given America to be free!' he disappeared as delegates rushed to sign their names."

"Some believe this was the same mysterious man, described as a professor, who joined the committee of six authorized to design a flag for this new nation. The group included among its members both George Washington and Benjamin Franklin. Reportedly, this unnamed professor was well known to them and when he suggested a magical design for the flag, it was unanimously accepted." Max pointed to the flag hanging from the house.

"I could lecture for hours about the impressive mystical implications of the stars and stripes but all of you would benefit from your own meditations on it. It's easy to notice the uniquely striking design when you look at a page of photos of flags of the world. It's simple yet profoundly complex, blending the cosmic and the mundane, mixing colors with boldness. Graphically perfect, there's much to be seen in Old Glory."

Max's interest in the flag was a scenic centerpiece of his Fourth of July party when he proudly displayed a collection that numbered almost a hundred, including a large, wool flag with forty-five stars and a battalion size one that took three men and several ladders to attach to the barn each year.

"The magical symbols are more obvious in the Great Seal of the United States with its phoenix masquerading as an eagle, the unfinished pyramid and all-seeing eye, and the motto which reads Novus Ordo Seclorum—the new order of the ages. Many have spoken of America as the New Atlantis, including Nostradamus and the great 16th century thinker, Francis Bacon, a partner in the Virginia Company that established some of our earliest settlements. Some claim the mythical Temple of the Sun that was the heart of Atlantean genius was located on Manhattan Island near the spot where today the Statue of Liberty stands."

Roxy felt a chill up her spine and goosebumps on her arm as Max talked of profound destiny. What happened if they failed, if America failed in its purpose as Atlantis apparently had?

"Another America-related miracle story features George Washington, one of the great advanced souls of humanity."

Max had accumulated a wealth of George Washington stories when he created a one-man show years ago for the Morgan Springs Museum. George had used the hot springs in their small town as a summer retreat for nearly fifty years, making him both a tourist attraction and subject of local historical interest.

"While at Valley Forge in that terrible winter of 1777, Washington reportedly was visited by the Goddess of Liberty who afforded him visions of three trials his nation would face. The first showed a cloud gathering in Europe, enveloping America, then sweeping away to reveal towns and cities springing up across the continent.

"The second presaged the Civil War with a dark angel showing scenes of brother fighting brother, then a reconciliation announced by a bright angel wearing a crown with the word Union emblazoned on it.

"The final trial began with thick black clouds issuing forth from Europe, Asia and Africa, explosions of dark red light flashing. Armies marched to America in this cloud and devastated the land, slaughtering citizens and burning cities. As the population sank to its knees in defeat, the angel of light once again appeared, leading a legion of its fellows to drive out the invaders. Once victorious, the angel planted an azure standard in the ground that said. While the stars remain and the heavens send down dew upon the earth, so long shall the Union last. Before leaving, the Goddess told Washington the final trial was not yet set and would be held at bay while we worked out our destiny.

"It is said that a nation lives when it stays true to its founding ideals and dies when it varies. That's why I believe a Soviet Union founded on the principles of communism, as warped and twisted as they became in the hands of demons like Stalin, will cease to exist when communism is finally rejected."

"I saw Gorbachev three weeks ago when he was in Washington."

Kat was gazing out towards the darkness as she began to speak. Her voice sounded distant.

"Even though it was the briefest of exchanges, I was so moved by the encounter I had to leave the hall."

There were several moments of silence before she continued.

"I knew clearly his was the same advanced soul who was Abraham Lincoln, the blood marked wound on his head identifying him. This time his task was to maintain union without war." She turned to face them.

"Perhaps it's his work in changing the communist world that is holding the destruction at bay until America can achieve its destiny. I've always felt the greatest lesson our system of government had to offer the world was the balance of power between central and local."

"I'm convinced the critical events of 1993-94 will determine America's fate and with it the direction of the world development for decades to come. That's why I believe it's essential for you to be running for the Senate now. We'll desperately need enlightened vision to take us through the mutation," said Max.

Roxy got up and poured herself some lemonade, asking all around. Sometimes the speculations and prognostications lost her completely. Gorbachev as Lincoln and global mutations. She shook her head in disbelief.

"The point of magical stories about the U.S., or any country for that matter, is to aid its people in realizing they have a destiny to fulfill, a purpose for which their nation was founded. Rhode Island's Roger Williams declared America's purpose to be 'soul liberty.' Esotericists speak of lighting the world. Of course, American work in electricity is accomplishing that on the physical plane with great efficiency," Max laughed. "Supposedly, the peculiar destiny of the United States is encoded in a trestle board on the reverse side of the Great Seals' pyramid."

Jake's voice drew her back to the settee as he asked Max what could prevent America from its purpose.

"Where shall I begin?" Max laughed again. "The United States has several great conflicts to resolve. One is the love of freedom that amounts almost to license and irresponsibility. It must be resolved into willing world service. Our obsession with material well-being while most of the world is hungry and ignorant is another. A third is racial, the lack of harmony among separate groups. This incredible blend of cultures and races is what marks the U.S. as an ancient soul. Our new task is to blend the differences without diluting the special gifts that arose from them. We're in charge of developing a prototype for global humanity and a pattern for right relations. Finally, there is a lack of understanding as to the ultimate ideal of government."

"Which is?" Kat asked from her perch.

"The true purpose of any government must be to allow—indeed encourage—the maximum amount of individual self-government. Our current democracy is only a stage to aid in developing free will. Someday we'll have what took form imperfectly in past times as oligarchy—rule by an elite. Only in our ideal future, this elite would be obvious and drawn from the highest, most spiritual, most illumined minds."

Kat swung her legs down off the ledge and faced Max excitedly.

"That's what I want to say about selecting a senator. The U.S. Senate should be composed of the one hundred most enlightened beings willing to serve. That would easily exclude the insult to the seat who is running against me."

"And probably most of your potential colleagues," Max added.

Kat jumped down from the railing and walked over, picking up his bag and setting it on the table.

"Do we have the future in here?" she asked, obviously ready to get down to practical business.

He waved her to a chair.

"We'll cast the runes in a bit but first I want to say a few words about this mythic experience. You are Hercules, the greatest hero of all, facing each test, learning from it then progressing onward. There are no shortcuts. No matter how other people arrive in the U.S. Senate, there is only one way for you—enduring. You have to face every fear, examine every action, purify every desire.

"Remember basic physics. Overcoming obstacles is but part of the task. The rest requires establishing balance among the forces set in motion. Every action produces a reaction, as you experienced in attacking Douglas."

Max took a white candle from his bag, set it on the table and lit it. Then he reached in again and drew out a small marble statue and handed it to Kat. It was a strongly built man with a club over one shoulder, a lion skin hanging from his other hand.

"It's Hercules and he is you—and the hero you seek."

He shook his bag of runes, letting three of the carved stones fall onto the table before him. He picked them up and moved them across his knuckles like coins, palming them, making them vanish then pulling them into sight again. He arranged them in a line, face down, their long oval shape upright.

"These are an ancient magic script, like Sanskrit, with power in the symbol. Utter the magic words and they become manifest." He offered the bag to Kat who gingerly reached in and drew a stone. She laid the rune she held in her hand on the table, turned over the other three, and stiffened as she recognized the meaning. Before Max could say anything, she ran into the house and up the stairs, her sobs carrying through the silence on the porch. With a sad expression, Max quickly examined then gathered the carved stones, snuffed the candle and rose to follow Kat. "What do they say?" Roxy asked, frantically grabbing his shirt.

"They say the gates of Hell are opening at her feet and she will not emerge unscathed."

"No wonder Liz calls them nasty little stones," Roxy called to his retreating back.

13

The White House Barbecue
July

Washington
Rhode Island

Ten days later they descended through the ever-lowering circles of Hell, flames increasing as they turned downward. Kat absently bit into a donut from the campaign's limitless supply and continued to scroll through the AP wire on her computer. Mario was busily scanning a selection of the state's daily papers while Roxy watched CNN. Their stream of consciousness dialogue focused on the audacity of Washington's mayor whose cocaine use had been documented in an FBI video set up by his former girlfriend. He was neither resigning from office nor removing himself from consideration as a candidate in November's mayoral election.

Kat tore herself away from the reported testimony of mayoral sidekicks in the white powder snorting game when she heard her chief of staff's voice on the speaker phone.

"I have bad news and good news. How do you want it?" Before she could give her standard reply, Hayes continued.

"Senator Stuart received a call from a contact of his in the South Florida Attorney General's office. It seems there was a major drug investigation that recently climaxed in more than five hundred arrests. One of the small fish caught in their net was your ex-husband."

She stared transfixed at the small speaker from which Hayes' voice was emitting.

"Jamie apparently tried to plea bargain his way out by spilling his guts. Not only did he offer them names of other drug dealers but also juicy gossip about Senator Winston and AIDS, and boxes of pornographic films he'd made including some starring his former wife."

Her heart plummeted to her knees, the blood from her face following it. Kat tightened her lips and claimed with an assurance she prayed was well founded.

"That's ridiculous."

Hayes kept talking. "The contact knew Stuart was involved in your race and called him."

"I suppose you're going to tell me the good news is Stuart's taken care of this?"

"Yep."

"Hayes, may I remind you that T.J. Stuart is not the candidate, he is not the campaign manager, he's not even a political consultant on this campaign. I make the decisions, not him." Kat's voice was tense as she fought to control her anger.

"I know you're infatuated with his political genius but haven't you gotten a glimmer yet? There are occasions on which he is a certifiable lunatic. He thinks this is 1853 and senators are fighting duels and carrying pistols onto the Senate floor."

"He didn't shoot anybody."

"I guess we can be grateful for small favors. When did this happen?"

"Last weekend."

"Last weekend, and I'm hearing about it now?"

"Stuart only told me late last night."

"I'll kill that crazy son of a bitch! It must be all the carbonated water he drinks or those ridiculous spy novels he reads." Her head was pounding and small flashes of light burst behind her eyes. She was winding up for a full blown tantrum.

"Doesn't he know obstructing justice is a felony, and not one of those nice felonies ignored for U.S. senators? What exactly did he do?"

"He arranged for bail, then spirited Jamie out of the country. Apparently the case can be delayed until after November. The boxes of film are locked away in some police vault where they, too, can disappear until after the election."

There was no mistaking the satisfaction in Hayes' voice. He was certain Stuart's actions were absolutely correct.

Breathing heavily, fighting to regain a semblance of composure, Kat disabused him of the notion that she considered Stuart a hero in this action.

"First of all, there are no films of me from which I need to be protected. I'm delighted Jamie was busted, it's long overdue. I think he should rot in jail. Finally, the only real danger I now face comes from Stuart's swashbuckling escapade. If someone contacted him about this, why shouldn't we assume Douglas was also contacted? And what do we say when it's discovered that a Republican senator assisted a known criminal to jump bail? Why do we expect Jamie to keep quiet about this? Or has the mastermind fixed it so Jamie will never be a problem again?"

She was screaming as she hit full stride in her tirade. "We can't even call Stuart off! It's too late! He's going to have to sit on Jamie wherever he has him stashed. We have to pray that no one ever discovers his interference.

"And Hayes, the new commercial showing Jake and Aunt Helen talking about crime, fear, drugs, and the future—don't put it on the air."

The tight ball of tension in her stomach was pushing so hard against her lungs that she knew she would stop breathing if she did not get out of the room and into fresh air. She jumped up from the chair, cut the phone connection and ran down the back stairs into the small garden behind the office. She gasped for air and prayed for strength to the worn statue of Saint Francis that had been a favorite of her father's. When she returned several minutes later, the office was empty.

She picked up the phone, buzzing Mario on the intercom.

"Where do I call Race Scarlatti?" Irritated when he questioned her, she rudely cut him off, demanding simply a phone number which she immediately dialed.

"Scarlatti here."

Briefly startled that he answered his own phone, she began talking. He recognized her voice at once and told her Jamie had called him the first night trying to trade purported additional films of her for Race's help in getting him out of jail.

"I told him I knew he was lying. He had nothing to offer me. There were no additional films and if he tried to trade my name for release he'd be dead in an hour. He agreed. He laughed and said he was going to approach Douglas. He wasn't as smart as I was, and besides, the rumor of porno films starring his popular opponent would be almost as valuable as actual footage."

"You're certain there are no other films, no copies of the one I have?"

"None. Whatever my follies in the past, you may be assured that I will never lie to you." His flat, mild voice slithered along her nerves as she shook uncontrollably.

"What's happened to my friend Jamie? I never bothered to check and see if Douglas was able to spring him."

"I don't know what happened," she floundered, and quickly hung up.

★ ★ ★ ★ ★

Carrie smiled as she rubbed her fingers across the blood-soaked handkerchief that marked Scarlatti's place on her board. She had witnessed one of his routine nosebleeds. Later she stole the handkerchief he used to stop it. Having his blood gave the spells extra potency.

Race was furious on the phone. He discovered that Kat's ex-husband was released from custody through Senator Stuart's intervention. Now Jamie had disappeared and Race was certain it was more of Stuart's doing. He ordered her to pass the information on to Jasmine and have the press secretary find out anything more she could.

Having assigned the task, Race lost control and began raving about doors that had slammed in his face as he tracked Jamie.

"I will tolerate no rivals. I will allow none to stand in my way and keep me from my rightful prize. He must be stopped," he screamed, slamming down the phone.

Carrie stared at the special board she made to represent the web she was weaving. She, as the Spider Queen, reigned at the center. Kat was directly overhead in the point of the pentagram. A broken end from one of her long fingernails still coated with red polish was encased in a silver box.

Jasmine and Roxy occupied points on the pentagram's outstretched arms. Scarlatti and Stuart were the legs. She had a physical hook into each of the participants except Stuart.

She smiled, recalling how she had gotten each piece. With Kat and Race, she had been lucky—in the right place at the right time and able to collect physical tidbits. It took her nearly a month of shadowing Roxy to collect enough hair from her brush. That blonde bimbo must glue her hair into place, Carrie snarled, tapping the wooden box. Jasmine was almost as trying. Another weak soul chained to the senseless demands of her body, thought Carrie. But, she admitted, the soaked silk panties that resulted from their little pleasure romp made a powerful charm.

She would arrange to get something of Senator Stuart's when he came to Rhode Island. It would be the most challenging task of all.

★ ★ ★ ★ ★

Roxy arrived in Washington the following week to find Stuart in the office with Kat and Hayes.

"I guess she didn't have him killed" she muttered to Maggie, who looked confused but waved her towards the door.

Her senses were assaulted by the palpable tension in the room as she tried to slip invisibly onto the couch next to Hayes. Kat managed a weak smile in her direction and Hayes barely nodded. Only Stuart looked at ease as he leaned against the bookcases, arms folded. He flashed her an impudent grin. Maybe this was the first opportunity Kat had to harangue him about interfering in Jamie's arrest, Roxy thought in dismay. She did not want to witness any bloodshed and desperately searched for an excuse to run out of the office and climb on a plane back to the ocean.

"How well could you have covered your tracks if my press secretary knows?" Kat continued the argument interrupted by Roxy's entrance.

"What makes you think she knows?" Stuart replied, straightening slightly.

"She handed me a list of questions this morning she thinks might be asked during the interviews and television shows I'm scheduled to do later this week."

Kat picked up a sheet of paper and began reading. "It's rumored that the Republican Party intervened to have drug charges dropped against your ex-husband recently."

Glaring at Stuart she concluded, "It sounds like she knows to me."

"Too bad you don't have a press secretary you can trust."

"This is not about Jasmine and whether I can trust her or not."

"Maybe it should be."

They stood, eyes locked, battling wills, then Stuart smiled.

"You can answer that question easily. You have no influence over the Attorney General in Florida, and no one at the Senate committee said anything to you about your ex-husband's arrest. Then you can disavow your marriage to him as a brief folly of youth. I'm more concerned about toughening up your responses on other issues we know can be a problem."

"Such as?"

"Drugs, magic, your ex-husband's pornography collection, your obvious lack of respect for your opponent, ex-communication, construction contracts for your family's firm. It's an impressive list for a lady who is ranked among the archangels by her adoring constituents."

"At least no one can accuse me of obstructing justice, kidnapping, and whatever other criminal tactics you employ so blithely." Kat's gray eyes flashed darkly. Veins stood out in her neck. Loose hair twisted wildly as she hurled words, like poisoned darts, at the senator.

Stuart relaxed into a chair in front of Kat's desk, loosened the knot of his tie and unbuttoned the collar of his gleaming white shirt. His suit jacket was already flung over the arm of another chair.

"Let's start with your position on drug use. I've never heard your justification for opposing harsh measures."

Taking her cue from his control, Kat sat back in her chair and put on her serenity mask. She pulled back her hair and deftly clamped it in place with a jeweled barrette. Only tight lines at the corners of her lips revealed how great an effort the calmness required.

"Try as I can, it is impossible for me to reach any conclusion beside the obvious, that war is not the way to defeat the threat of dangerous illegal drugs. So far, the government has done little but lie, spend money, trash personal liberty and force up drug profits so that few can afford to say no. They destroy peoples' lives for smoking a weed no one has ever proven dangerous while dealing cocaine for arms.

"I understand there are grave dangers in the use of mind altering substances. It has always been so from the ancient alchemists and initiates who drank magic potions believing as Paracelsus said, 'we shall be as gods,' to more recent magicians who have duplicated LSD trips of the late '60s in complex computer programs. Those who are unprepared, weak, or driven by base motives fall by the wayside."

"So the candidate who cares promotes legalizing drugs and too bad for those too puny to handle their glorious potential—they can die in some gutter?"asked Stuart. "You welcome the random genetic engineering of crack babies? That seems a little cruel and shortsighted."

"There are destructive substances being peddled everywhere from crack cocaine to DDT, all inducing who knows what mutations. I think they all should be stopped. They were created by men, they're being fought against by men, they are all part of the cult of death men worship."

Roxy and Hayes gaped at the hysterical edge to her voice, the randomness of her arguments. Stuart managed a weak smile.

"You can't say that, even if you do believe it," he grunted, a rare uncertainty echoing in his voice.

Kat's smile broadened at his tone, the crazed glitter in her eyes calmed.

"Of course not. The price of truth in this arena is still too high, but it won't be for long if drug-related murder and mayhem continue to escalate in major cities." She cut off his argument with a slash of her hand. "For now I can speak of meeting the need in other ways, offer paths other than drugs. Drugs are about a hunger for the sacred. I can talk about the flag with you."

Stuart begrudgingly moved on.

"It's rumored you use various arcane devices like astrology and tarot cards to plot the strategy and timing of your campaign. Is this true?"

"It's true."

His look remained one of mild interest. "Explain it to me."

Kat primly folded her hands and began her recitation in a bland voice that belied the ever-increasing tension coursing between them.

"I'm a scientist. I've mastered the methods and understand the need to measure physical reality, to pick things apart and subject them to rigorous and objective analysis. Science is ideal when you're seeking the what, when, and how questions. It does not tell why. It often harbors contempt for the natural order. Seeking meaning in this natural order is my quest, discovering the why of evolution. With the magic of vision or intuition a whole field of facts can be illuminated and the underlying meaning instantly exposed. In recognizing parallel laws, magic is often more efficient than science.

"Astrology is a mathematically based analytic and predictive system that is capable of enormous expansion through its symbolic nature. It is both art and science. Max is master of that system, I know only enough to ask the right questions. The Tao instructs 'in action, watch the timing.' That is how I use astrology.

"The tarot operates in a slightly different manner, less intellectual but equally informative. I use it as a way of seeing the inner truth."

Kat took a long pause, looking out the window towards the Capitol. Her voice was almost trance-like when she continued.

"I had a dream, years ago, just before ending my marriage. I was dressed in a white robe, standing on the edge of a pit whose bottom was lost from view. Suddenly a ladder appeared and I began to climb down. As I descended ever lower through heavy darkness, a voice kept crying out 'here perish all fools who covet knowledge and power.' At the bottom a magician opened an ornately carved door into a long gallery where twenty-two pictures were lit by oil wicks. He took my hand and led me through, explaining each picture.

"I forgot the dream but felt an intense sense of déjà vu the night I discovered Jamie had been making pornographic films. I ran down a stone stairway in the fraternity house that was the one in my dream, and there I found Max. He was with me constantly during the chaotic days that followed. We were leaving the student union at Cornell one day, and as he opened the large wooden door from the reading room, the whole dream flashed into my mind. I told him and we went back to the house where he pulled out a deck of cards and selected twenty-two that he laid on a table."

She turned her gaze on Stuart, her voice becoming more animated.

"I was astounded. They were the pictures from my dreams! I'd never seen tarot cards before. Considering my fragile emotional state at the time, it's not surprising that I became obsessed. Soon I found I could manipulate the cards. They became useless to me until I met Roxy. She's a very clear channel and serves to ground the psychic energy so I can't twist it."

Both of them shifted their gaze for a moment and looked at Roxy. It was like a volley of lightning bolts hit her and she slumped back against the couch hoping Kat would keep talking. Turning back to Stuart, Kat leaned forward across her desk, and changed from Sphinx to Cheshire Cat.

"Do you think I should give this explanation on the television show or use it in the newspaper interview where I'm certain they'll capture it more accurately?"

When he said nothing, Kat sharpened her tone.

"You do an excellent job pretending to be the media, interested only in the irrelevant. Don't you want to hear my positions on health care, economic restructuring, Capital Links and what to do with nuclear weapons if the Soviet Union crumbles? How about the application of chaos theory to the evolution of social systems?"

Stuart's face was unchanged as he crossed his legs and leaned forward, adopting the challenging rhythm of the best tabloid reporters.

"I only report what people want to know, lady. They care about stories, about scandal, about sensation. They don't want to think, and I'm not about to make them. Now, what about the porno films?"

Kat jerked upright and two spots of pink brightened her pale face. Her eyes seemed to spin like metallic pinwheels shooting off sparks. Roxy was shocked when she glanced over at Hayes and saw him watching as if this were a championship boxing match and he had money on both contestants. He was there purely for blood sport.

A bitter shadow crept across Kat's voice.

"When I discovered early in our marriage that my husband made pornographic films, I divorced him. I never knew about the films. I never participated."

"Could there have been surreptitious films made of you, without your knowledge or consent?"

Kat looked chiseled from fine white marble. Her mouth was red slash across her face, her eyes almost closed, the thick black lashes throwing the slightest of shadows across her smooth cheeks. The alien chill in her eyes when she opened them was matched by the icy tone in her voice.

"Yes. There could have been."

Roxy could almost hear Hayes panting next to her, obviously urging Stuart on in his mind. He wanted to know. He wanted to be titillated. Stuart's estimation of what the public wanted was accurate.

"Were there?" Stuart asked bluntly.

Kat's control wavered and she looked visibly upset, gripping the edge of her desk, ridges in her knuckles visible through taut skin. With a tangible imposition of will, her face became once again a blank mask of serenity and she quietly answered his question.

"Yes. One. The sole copy is now in my possession."

Stuart's eyebrows shot up and his eyes widened. He stood and moved against the bookcases again.

"How do you know you have the only copy?"

Kat repeated the story of the tape and the painful circumstances by which she came to have it while somehow remaining cool and collected.

"Have you watched this purported tape of you to make certain it's pornographic?"

"I have," she answered, tightness appearing in her controlled voice.

"Too bad. I would have been honored to volunteer for the task."

Roxy could almost hear a high-pitched whine as Stuart's sick humor snapped Kat's control.

It all happened in slow motion. Long-buried memories of Kat's peculiar system for releasing explosive energy surfaced as she reached alongside her chair and opened the bottom drawer of her desk. Oh no, Roxy muttered to herself, recalling Kat smashing nearly a dozen glasses against the brick wall of some building in downtown Ithaca.

"It's a madness valve," she told Roxy that night.

Glass in hand, Kat stood behind the desk, quickly scanned the room then hurled it at the wall to her left. As the glass hit the edge of a bronze Oriental goddess on a nearby shelf, it exploded. The force of impact catapulted a piece back, slicing her cheek and drawing blood.

Penitent horror flooded Stuart's face. Kat stood immobile, blood dripping through the hand she held against her cheek. By the time Roxy got around the other side of the desk, Stuart was holding her, pressing his handkerchief on the wound.

"Go get whatever first aid kit you have and some water to wash out the cut," he ordered. "Thank God it wasn't her eye."

Kat swayed against him, pale faced, shaking, pupils enlarged. Roxy knew she was in shock.

"Where's your arnica?" she asked, pulling Kat's hand. She motioned to the center drawer. Roxy found the tiny tube of white pellets and slipped one into Kat's mouth. Hayes came back into the room with a pitcher of water and two kits. By the time the senator carried her to the couch, her color returned to normal, her breathing steadied and the ravages of shock were defeated.

Stuart was gently washing out the wound, bright red blood spattered over the front of his shirt. Kat opened her eyes. The demon in them was gone and she looked sane again.

"Get some calendula salve on the cut. Then staphysagria for when self-expression comes back and bites you in the ass."

"There should be no scar to mar your face," Stuart explained as he carefully taped bandages over the salve-covered cut.

"Why not? I can explain I earned it defending my honor." Kat's kind tone brought a sparkle to Stuart's eyes that could have been mistaken for tears.

He stood and backed away as she sat up on the couch. Bowing slightly, he apologized for his crude remark and acknowledged it was unforgivable. Kat smiled.

"You were right. It is too bad you didn't have the opportunity to view Jamie's tape. You would have been pleased to see me turn away his offer of cocaine. We could have used it to prove I'm tough on drugs."

There was the briefest flash of irony on his face.

"All that's left for both of us is to beg for mercy," he said, once more in control. Opening the door to leave, he faced Kat again.

"You shouldn't have to look deep into your magic cards to explain what was behind all this." Walking out, he ignored the stunned looks from staff as they saw the bloodstained shirt disappear beneath his jacket.

★ ★ ★ ★ ★

She had avoided being alone with him knowing what would happen. Hayes would slide her into some corner, look into her eyes, and tell her how desperately he needed her in that stroking tone that ravished her body. Roxy could never muster up the will to say "no" once he set her heart pounding, no matter how much she thought about Jake and her promise and ruining the work they were doing. Kat obviously was going to need all the help she could get to win this race and Roxy was terrified her surrender could pollute the magic and cause Kat to lose. The only solution was to keep away from Hayes; avoid the occasion of sin as the good nuns back in high school warned.

She decided to tag along with Kat to the evening's regular schedule of receptions. The next night was the White House barbecue and then she would be safely flying back to Rhode Island, probably guilty of all degrees of sexual intercourse with Hayes except the ultimate which she had pledged to Jake.

It was the end of the day and Maggie and the interns were gone. She was leafing through magazines while Kat reviewed the next day's schedule with Hayes when a messenger arrived with two boxes addressed to Kiley Tomasso. Roxy held the smaller one lightly as she signed the manifest. The larger was so heavy she immediately set it down on the divider.

Kat picked up the larger box and tore off the wrapping. It was a beautifully lacquered treasure chest filled with at least five pounds of dark chocolate exquisitely molded into flowers. A look of sublime sensual pleasure softened Kat's face which bore the signs of the morning's stress in more than just the bandage on her cheek. Dark chocolate was one of the few vices she allowed in her disciplined life.

Reading the card, she offered the chest to both Roxy and Hayes, each of whom took a candy and remarked on the excellence of its quality.

"The note says these are to share."

"Who are they from?" Roxy asked as Kat unwrapped the smaller box.

"Who do we know should be sending peace offerings?" Kat replied. She opened the box and lifted out a green silk bag.

That Senator Stuart was the penitent sender was confirmed when Kat eased a magnificently carved jade pendant out of the silk bag.

"It's the same goddess you have in your office, the one you threw the glass at," Roxy exclaimed.

"This is Kuan Yin, Chinese goddess of mercy whose name means she who hears the weeping world and I did not throw the glass at her. It was quirk in my aim that landed it in her hands."

"Whatever happened, Senator Stuart gets an A+ in the art of groveling for forgiveness in my book," laughed Roxy as she took another chocolate, arguably the best she had ever tasted. "I wonder where he found this candy?"

Hayes looked ready to contradict her assessment of Stuart's gesture as groveling when Kat smiled and read the card that accompanied the goddess.

"You may be able to forgive me, but only she can provide the level of mercy you will need.' He's truly a master at groveling."

A twist in Kat's smile accompanied her ironic tone as she swept up the chocolates and went into her office, closing the door deliberately behind her. It was a moment before Roxy realized she was alone with Hayes.

THE WHITE HOUSE BARBECUE

★ ★ ★ ★ ★

They sat in what passed for a dark corner of the outside patio at Tortilla Coast. It was the usual sultry Washington weather with trees and shrubs baked by the heat, only landscaped blossoms remaining. Congress was cranking full tilt so it could recess and go home to mend fences and campaign in August. Capitol Hill traffic was studded with political stars enjoying the summer night. Hayes could not resist muttering their names and pithy observations as they walked by, interrupting her explanation of why Kat's victory depended on them not sleeping together and how she knew that was his primary goal.

"Not if I have to give up sex with you to do it," was his heated rejoinder as he handed her another frozen strawberry margarita, her new favorite drink. They tasted like fruit slushes at the beach. She was not sure they were making her explanation any clearer but it was lots easier on her.

"It would only be until November."

There was no mistaking the look in his eyes: November! What about now? What he said was worthy of his professional stature.

"Now let me summarize what you've been telling me. You and our commercial star Jake are using sex magic to create an attitude where two hundred and fifty thousand people in Rhode Island will vote for Kat in November."

She nodded dumbly.

"You and I cannot have sex because my energy could pollute the process and lose the election. Is that accurate?"

It sounded weird laid out like that but Roxy could not argue its accuracy.

Hayes leaned back in the metal chair, nodded at two men walking into the American Café next door, then turned back to her, mustache outlining his smiling lips, blue eyes glittering.

"That's a great line. I'll have to remember it."

He sprang forward and grabbed her hand, looking at her intently. Roxy almost swooned from the hot tremors that pulsed through her body.

"Assuming the sex magic is possible, doesn't it seem strange to you that someone equally focused on the same goal could pollute the process?"

He kissed her palm and then the pulse spot on her wrist, his stiff mustache tingling the skin and setting her blood racing.

"Do you think our making love has polluted you?" he whispered smoothly against her hand, his eyes still fixed on hers.

"No." Roxy was barely able to speak she felt herself so pulled by his will. "But I promised Jake, no copulation."

He sat back suddenly and looked surprised. "The ban is that specific?"

Roxy nodded. "He said there are eight levels of sexual intercourse and I could

311

do all of them up to the last which is actual copulation. I can desire you, I can even determine to indulge, I just can't actually fuck you."

Almost hysterical with the longing she felt, it took a moment for her to decipher his satisfied grin and the solution he was proposing.

"How about a blow job? You won't get polluted with my energy, none of the magic will be upset, and I'll get the inspiration I desperately need to return to the fray fighting for the same cause we all hold so dear."

★ ★ ★ ★ ★

Kat was changing clothes for the White House barbecue in her office. Roxy had come to work dressed for the occasion in a long tiered skirt and romantic ruffled top that could be pushed off-the-shoulder. She loved how soft and rounded her bare shoulders looked.

She noted different underwear colors as Kat slipped her dress on over champagne lace bikinis with scalloped edges that cut high on her leg. There was a matching lace underwire bra although her high molded breasts scarcely needed the help.

"What's the other color?" Roxy asked, wondering if Kat actually plotted out the pattern of color selections.

Kat backed over for assistance in zipping up her dress which was tightly fit in the bodice. "Red. This color is called champagne. I felt I needed to be hot and fizzy all summer. So far it hasn't worked out quite the way I had in mind," she concluded ruefully and walked over to the mirror to start working on her hair and make-up.

"You look pretty effervescent," Roxy commented.

"And sufficiently down-home to satisfy the main street standards of Congress," Kat laughed. The bodice and short sleeves of her dress were bright green covered with large white polka dots and continued to a pointed hem below the waist that hugged a very full white skirt. The wide sash that tied in the back was the same green polka dot and reached in long streamers below the hem of the short skirt.

"Are those crinolines you have under that?"

Grinning, Kat nodded. "They're sewed into the skirt. I haven't worn crinolines since elementary school when we tried to persuade the nuns the circle skirts of our blue jumpers looked better all puffed out. It was the ugliest look in the world but we loved it."

Hayes knocked on the door and Kat gestured for Roxy to let him in. Embarrassed by her ready surrender the previous night, she slipped over to the door positioning herself to be hidden when it opened. There was no need to worry. Hayes was all business and more concerned with Kat's appearance than hers.

THE WHITE HOUSE BARBECUE

Kat finished tying up her curls with a matching polka dot bow. They were even more tangled and unruly in Washington's infamous summer humidity. She spun around smiling to show off her outfit.

"Am I appropriately attired for a backyard barbecue at the White House?" she teased her chief of staff.

"It makes it difficult to suppress speculation about you in sex films when you look like a figure on top of a birthday cake that every man wants to take off and lick clean of frosting." Ignoring the disgusted tone in his voice, Kat smiled.

"Why that's the most flattering thing you've ever said to me, as a woman."

She planted a kiss on his cheek engraving it with the perfect outline of her freshly painted lips. Both women laughed as he scowled and turned toward the door, not touching the lipstick mark.

"Senator Stuart asked that you be at the barbecue by 7:30. He's arranged a brief private meeting with the president for you. He said to bring your wish list."

"Stuart's certainly generous in his groveling," Kat laughed to Roxy as she sprayed them both with perfume, the door closing behind a disgruntled Hayes. Linking arms they strolled out to wow the boys at the White House.

It was a perfect evening, almost cool for Washington in July. They stood in line on the barricaded East Executive Avenue waiting to be checked by security and passed through to the White House lawn. Concrete bunkers disguised as planters and filled with flowers attempted security from car-driving terrorists. Roxy wondered if there were also elevating metal panels in the roadway as there were behind the Capitol. The guard found both their names on the list, checked identification and badges then waved them on, the expression on his face remaining neutral but alert through the whole process.

This is how it should be thought Roxy as she gazed around the meticulous but not ornately landscaped vibrant green lawn with its rolling mounds and clusters of huge trees. It was a photo of the ideal. The curved portico of the White House gleamed against its surrounding foliage, more than half the nation's Congress sat at scattered tables or wandered the lawns with the one guest they were allowed to bring to this annual event. Looking away from the mansion, she could see a natural raised area to the right crowned with a stage. The Washington Monument peeped white and phallic through a cluster of trees, completing the picture.

Kat received admiring looks from several men standing with Senator Stuart as they walked over to him. The president was visible over his shoulder at the end of the high hedge, surrounded as usual by his phalanx of Secret Service. Even here in his own yard, thought Roxy shuddering. What a price to pay.

Stuart hung back, still contrite until he noticed Kat wearing the jade pendant. He quickly hustled the two women away from the others.

"I ordered this weather in your honor. Yesterday it was hot, burnt grass, dingy sky—today it's perfect, good enough to serve as your backdrop. The president's preparing to leave. We'll walk in with him. Roxy can wait for us over by the food tables, we won't be long." He coached Kat on what she could conceivably request from the president on behalf of her campaign as they walked toward the White House.

The food tables were disguised as chuck wagons, piled with beans, huge hunks of beef and pork being carved, salads and rolls. Roxy noticed two men standing watching the carver. They did not look like either members of Congress or guests. As the tall, skinny one with a flaming red mustache and cowboy hat turned towards her, Roxy recognized them as the band. Of course, who else but the perennial best country band, known simply as Kentucky, would be entertaining at the White House barbecue? Smiling, she walked over. She could easily amuse herself while Kat played politics and Hayes sat home with instant replays of the previous night.

★ ★ ★ ★ ★

Stuart was visibly unhappy as they approached the food tables, stopping just short of Roxy and the two musicians.

"If you lose, he's the man who'll see that you do or do not get a job with the administration," he chided Kat about her antagonistic attitude to the president's chief advisor.

"I am not going to lose and I decidedly do not want a job in the administration. I do want them concerned about polluted air and water and that big toad is standing in the way." Kat pointedly tossed her head and walked over to join Roxy, Stuart following.

After introductions revealed the musicians both knew and admired the senator from their neighboring state, the red-haired one named Marty, who played mandolin and wrote most of the band's hit songs, pulled off his hat and stared at Kat.

"I'm not meanin' to be forward, ma'am but you look very familiar. I know you're a congresswoman and runnin' for the Senate and all, but I mean from before. I knew you someplace a long time ago but you were not called Kiley, it was somethin' else. "

"Kat," supplied Roxy.

"That's it! Kat. It was a little bar in Gardiner at the north entrance to Yellowstone. There'd just been a big full moon beer party down by the hot pools along the river and we were all back at this local joint playin' music. You were with some big guy with long white hair in braids like an Indian. He had nine fingers I remember, and played the harmonica."

Kat's eyes widened.

"Max," she said. "I do remember that night. Incredible hot pools and people body sliding down the rapids of the ice cold river. But I don't remember you."

"I wouldn't expect you to. I was just a kid learnin' to pick a guitar. I sat against the wall and watched, listenin' to your pure, silvery voice. I fell in love and carried your image in my heart for a long time after that. You know our big hit, "Angel in My Heart"? I wrote that to you. I've had two dreams since I wrote that song. One was that I could someday sing it to you and the second, that you would sing it with me. This seems the perfect night for both."

Moved by the intensity of his devotion and sincerity of the request, Kat readily agreed. Marty nodded toward her bandaged cheek.

"If some ornery man did that to you, I'd be happy to run him off."

"Oh no, the lady is far too independent. She did that herself," Stuart said.

Kat scowled and walked off with the mandolin player. Roxy conferred briefly with the slight blonde drummer, arranging to party with the band later, then turned to the senator who was staring quizzically at Kat's vanishing form.

"We should go stake out a good spot. I don't want to miss Kat's performance," Roxy said, assuming he would decline and she could slip off alone. He smiled as if the idea that this could be fun had never occurred to him before, and agreed.

By the time they reached a good spot in front of the stage, the band started to play. Kat could have stepped off the cover of the sheet music for "Angel in My Heart" as she sat on a stool being serenaded by its composer, her white skirt spread around her.

"Is there press here?" Roxy whispered to Stuart, worried. He shook his head and she relaxed. Hayes would not be happy to have that picture in the local papers no matter how appealing it was in real life.

Kat's expressive voice worked perfect harmony with the soulful mandolin in a classic country duet of unrequited love.

"It's easy to believe he wrote it for her," Roxy observed. The ardor in the mandolin player's voice was evident. It was a beautiful love song and Stuart admitted it had always been a favorite of his.

"I had no idea......," he muttered looking as wistful as a man of steel could.

Marty called on the audience to back him up with applause, and persuaded Kat to remain on stage for another song. They ended their performance with a rousing round of clog dancing. Stuart was clapping as wildly as anyone when Kat finished.

"If she keeps this up, people will wonder why she's wasting her time with politics," he laughed.

As the band continued the set, Kat rejoined them in the audience, flushed and breathless from both excitement and exertion. Damp ringlets escaped from her bow and struggled sweetly down the back of her neck and in front of her ears. They moved toward the edge of the crowd and Roxy told Kat she was planning to party later with the band.

"They really want you to come, too," she added.

"You certainly should go and have a good time. I don't want my lovestruck friend to misunderstand so I think I'll go home. You keep the car."

Overhearing their exchange, Stuart offered Kat a ride home after the Senate vote which was scheduled in less than an hour. As she smiled absently and agreed, several other members swept her away to applaud her performance and discuss some committee legislation. Roxy found herself alone again with Senator Stuart and examined him speculatively. Maybe Liz was right, she thought. Kat was glowing from all the love her admiring mandolin player had focused on her. Sex might be even better.

Feeling her stare, Stuart turned and looked back. Roxy was so mesmerized by his intense gaze that she heard herself describing Liz's plan to him before she could stop to think.

"She's convinced that Kat will flip out if she doesn't get… ah, have, ah… you know, find someone to sleep with." His eyes compelled her to continue although Roxy knew she had gone too far already. "Liz thinks you're the man for the job," she finished up with a rush, feeling color flooding her face.

She almost sank to the grass in relief when he smiled.

"Liz is a wise woman. I totally agree. Unfortunately, our favorite lady candidate doesn't."

Watching them leave the barbecue soon after, Roxy wondered if Stuart was not wrong. Kat certainly seemed to be pleased with his company as she linked her arm through his and strolled across the White House lawn.

★ ★ ★ ★ ★

Roxy tried to shake the dull roaring from her head. She was not in Narragansett, it was not the ocean she heard. Her eyes opened to narrow slits and she focused on the bright red satin. The other color was indeed red, she thought, and it did make Kat look hot.

"Jake called last night. Nothing urgent. He wanted to know when you'd be coming back," Kat said, noticing Roxy's half-opened eyes. "I told him you were leaving about noon. He'll be at the airport to meet you."

"You talked to Jake? What time?"

"About ten, I guess. Soon after I got home."

Even in her muddled condition Roxy knew that meant Stuart had taken her directly home after the vote. Kat was brushing her hair with short, choppy strokes that did not look like the calm motions of a woman who was soothed and relaxed from a great night of sex. Score zero for matchmaking.

"Was Senator Stuart here with you?" Roxy asked, thinking aloud.

Kat turned and faced her, eyebrows raised suspiciously.

"Why would Senator Stuart be here, Roxy?"

An icy knife plunged through her already confused stomach. From Kat's sarcastic tone there was no doubt in Roxy's mind that Stuart for some unknown reason had repeated her suggestion. Kat must be enraged. She hated when people interfered in her personal life. She considered it the ultimate in blind arrogance that anyone believed they could direct the flow of life better than fate.

Her mind was too tangled to answer the question coherently, or to construct an excuse. What if Stuart put the moves on Kat and when she shot him down told her Roxy had said it was the thing to do. She moaned audibly and Kat bent over, shaking a small white pellet into her hand.

"Nux vomica. The best way to drive out the demons of over indulgence."

Taking it gratefully, Roxy waited for what she knew would be its almost immediate effect. She silently blessed Samuel Hahnemann for his development of homeopathy although he probably did not have hangover cures in mind. Seeing Kat clasp the jade pendant Stuart gave her around her neck, Roxy wondered if maybe she had not rejected him after all. She decided to confess the plan she and Liz had.

"You seem so tense, I thought a good man might help."

"That's your solution, not mine."

"But you're wearing the pendant he gave you again."

Kat looked Gothic with her hair pulled away from the austere line of her face. Her voice had the ring that came when she was talking about serious matters.

"I'm wearing the goddess so I can continually petition her for mercy. I don't need you to pimp for me, Roxy. When the right man comes along, I won't let him get away."

★ ★ ★ ★ ★

Everything but the awful reality of an interview with the unfriendly New England correspondent of the *National* was driven from their minds. Kat was testing potential answers out on Roxy when the door to her office burst open and Jasmine rushed in, clearly outraged. She began screaming at Kat.

"How could you? How could you betray your ideals like that? It's every man's fantasy that no woman is beyond reach. I thought you understood. I thought you were above all that—that simpering and coyness. And how could you yield to him? Full-blown manhood at its worst!"

Roxy was glad to see Kat appeared as mystified at Jasmine's outburst as she was.

"I saw you last night. I saw him pull the bow from your hair and kiss you. Parked in that hillbilly truck of his like a couple of sex-crazed teenagers."

Emotions flashed across Kat's face like flipping through channels on television. Surprise, embarrassment, anger and finally, curiosity.

"Exactly what do you have against Stuart?"

Roxy gaped. This was not the enraged denial she expected. Maybe something was going on after all.

"I don't like the way he looks at you." Jasmine was indignant.

"Which is how?"

"Like he's a great white hunter who sees you as the prize trophy missing from his wall, the trophy he deserves because he's a man!"

Kat jumped up from behind her desk and glared back at Jasmine.

"That's ridiculous! And what were you doing spying on me anyway?"

Roxy wanted to jump in and explain: it's personal, she loves you, Kat. She sees Stuart, or any man, as a threat. Then she remembered Carrie and Scarlatti's men in the picture with Jasmine and her stomach knotted. What if Jasmine were spying? What if she told Carrie?

"I wasn't spying. I was driving home and saw you in the truck, parked along some back street. I thought you might be in trouble so I stopped. When I saw it was Stuart with you ...I ... I ... and then when he kissed you....."

"It was probably just a friendly kiss good-night, Jasmine." Roxy tried to intervene hoping to deflect her attacks. "After all, he is married."

Cruelty twisted Jasmine's pinched face and laced her voice as she spun around to face Roxy.

"Married? Not any more."

Stereo gasps greeted Jasmine's gloating revelation.

"What do you mean, not any more?" Kat asked her press secretary coldly.

For an instant, Jasmine looked disconcerted.

"Don't tell me you don't know." There was arsenic in her sugary tone.

"In Virginia, a year's separation is grounds for divorce. If it's uncontested, the parties may file after six months. Then in three to four months, the divorce is final. Clarice Stuart filed divorce papers in Richmond at the end of April. Rumor has it she's set her cap for a judge on the Virginia Supreme Court, a man who'll live in Richmond. Conveniently, by election day our favorite senator will be a free man. Maybe he wants to be certain you win before he marries you."

Jasmine delighted in the look of betrayal that shaded Kat's eyes. She should know better than to trust some man. Buoyed by her success, she turned back to Roxy.

"Shall I describe last night's touching scene in all its erotic detail for you? I'm sure someone with your taste for sexual adventure would love it. This was no chaste peck on the cheek between colleagues. First of all they were parked several blocks away from Kat's house."

The shock of hearing about Stuart's divorce seemed to have paralyzed Kat. She did nothing to deter Jasmine's recital.

"They were sitting there gazing into each other's eyes. He would stroke her cheek and run his fingers along the back of her neck. He kissed her a couple of times and then with this huge smile on his face he pulled the bow from her hair like he was opening a Christmas package. They both sat there laughing as her hair tumbled down and he wrapped it around his fingers. Then he pulled her against him hard and kissed her, passionately I might add, probably swallowing her tongue and doing who knows what with his hands."

"That's enough!" Kat shouted. "I'm sure you followed us home and noticed he dropped me at the door and if you were crazed enough to sit there watching all night, I'm sure you noticed no one entered the house but Roxy."

Kat's guess hit home and Jasmine's eyes flickered uncertainly for a moment.

"I don't know which of you is worse with their romantic fantasies. But I'm going to tell you both this just once and then I don't want to hear anymore about it. I am being brutalized in this campaign, in ways none of us would have imagined. Every day I pray for the strength and energy to make it through another twenty-four hours. T.J. Stuart has provided invaluable assistance, not because he's trying to seduce me but because I hold the key to his ambitions. He wants a Republican Senate and mine is the seat he needs.

"I am not sleeping with him. I do not intend on sleeping with him. I can make it through this nightmare without some man as a pacifier." She glared at Roxy with this last remark.

"In less than three hours I have a critically important interview with a journalist who may want to fuck me but only in print and I don't consider this little exchange the least bit constructive in preparing me for that." Kat's voice was reaching maximum volume. "So, get out Jasmine! Go pump your sources and check your files or whatever you do and come back in here with something helpful for this interview or you're history on this campaign. Have I made myself clear?"

Roxy shrank against the couch at the blaze of hate in Jasmine's eyes as she pursed her lips and spun on her heel, walking out of the office slamming the door behind her. Kat dropped her head onto the desk and began crying.

★ ★ ★ ★ ★

Hayes caught up with her in the bunker-like Rayburn garage as she was swinging her bag out of Kat's Triumph.

"I don't have time for your acrobatics today. Besides, the car's a little too small, even for you." Roxy tried to push past but he blocked her way.

"What happened just now? Jasmine tore out snarling and grabbing her hair. Kat's locked in her office and only sobs over the intercom, and you're trying to steal away without even saying good-bye."

Daunted by the accusing look in his eyes Roxy related Jasmine's claims about seeing Kat and Stuart.

"I thought she was with you?"

When Roxy confessed she had gone out with the band he began generically fuming. She could not tell whose behavior disturbed him most: hers by going out, Jasmine's spying, or Stuart's with Kat. As she described the photos of Jasmine and Carrie they had seen, Hayes focused all his frustration on her.

"Who did you and Mario think you were protecting by not telling me or Kat?" he raged.

She cried all the way to National Airport on the Metro, then redoubled her tears on the plane after calling Jake and begging off from seeing him, pleading campaign chaos that she would explain later. In all the recent furor, she had forgotten about feeling guilty for betraying her promise to him. By the time she reached Rhode Island, she was crying mostly in anticipation of how irritated Mario would be that she told Hayes about the photos of Jasmine.

★ ★ ★ ★ ★

Her eyes burned, red and puffy from several hours of tears as she drove towards Narragansett, sniffing for her first scent of the ocean. Mario had been too distressed to harass Roxy. Kat's interview was calamitous. She peremptorily ended it when the journalist revealed knowledge of Jamie's porno films and persisted in questioning her involvement in them.

Roxy stopped along Ocean Drive by the Towers before heading home and sat on the seawall, picking at the wild roses that covered the stones. As their delicate petals fell away, they revealed voluptuous pink rose hips trimmed in spiky fringe. The humidity was high since the wind was blowing from the east but like a true water nymph she loved the way it made her skin feel as soft and luxurious as if she had stepped out of a bath filled with oils. Fog horns mounted on lighthouses south along the coast sounded at regular intervals as the spray broke against the wall and coated her face. She was so happy to be back at the ocean again.

Max's voice on the answering machine ended her bliss as he reported a psychic weather bulletin for her. Sometimes Roxy wished Max would keep his information to himself. He warned there was an eclipse the next night, it was in Cancer and would affect her. Rocky emotional weather was his warning.

"What a surprise," she addressed the machine sarcastically.

★ ★ ★ ★ ★

Not wanting to meet Jake on the beach or have him come to the house as he often did if she did not appear for a morning walk, Roxy left early and waited for Kat in the passenger lounge, anxiously scanning the *National* to see if the previous day's aborted interview was reported. She panicked when she saw the flashy, bordered photo and story. It was the notorious Yankee Doodle showgirl picture, in color no less, with a two column story headlined by, she groaned "Is There More to See?" Who taught these people journalism anyway? Roxy cursed as she read the lead:

"The GOPs most promising challenger in the race to win control of the U.S. Senate repeatedly denied rumors of interfering in her ex-husband's recent drug arrest. Further, Congresswoman Kiley Tomasso also denies reports that she was featured in her husband's extensive collection of pornographic films."

Roxy crushed the paper. Maybe Kat had seen it in Washington. She did not want to be the one to present this hand grenade. Smoothing it out again, she scanned the story, noting mention of the Press Club dance, Winston's death, and conflict of interest charges. The story closed with one sentence of substance: Ms. Tomasso is a popular and noted environmentalist and speaks out often for women's rights.

The glow on Kat's radiant face as she walked off the plane laughing and chatting with constituents told Roxy immediately that she was the messenger risking death. Whatever pumped her up hopefully will sustain her through this, thought Roxy as they walked out to the van, Kat waving and shaking hands as people called to her and approached. In a pale green suit with reverse appliqué on its broad, scalloped lapels, she was a living image of the jade goddess she once again wore. Her hair was tightly bound on top of her head and carved jade flowers curved up the edge of her ears. Roxy did not have much faith in this goddess. Kat seemed to be getting no mercy at all from the cosmic forces.

As they set out for the television station where Kat was taping another Sunday interview show, she excitedly told Roxy she had a response for questions about Jamie's films, "Should anyone here even have heard the rumor."

"Oh, they've heard the rumor," Roxy replied, tossing her the crumpled newspaper, knowing it could well be her last act alive.

Kat read the article. All the strain lines around her mouth and eyes re-appeared and the scar from her glass throwing glowed an angry red as the color drained from her face. Calmly closing the paper, she sat silent, obviously thinking, occasionally jotting down a word or phrase. Nothing could have torn a sound from Roxy's throat. Mario would be at the station, he could deal with preparing her for the interview.

Kat's magic answer when the interviewer almost immediately brought up the *National* article, was to firmly deny any knowledge of or participation in Jamie's films. She explained she had contacted the authorities holding films and arranged for a designated panel of people to view them and certify that she was not involved. Aghast, the interviewer merely sputtered as Kat continued.

"I've asked your admired and respected colleague at the *Providence Journal,*

Harry Krast, to oversee selection and operation of the panel." The grin on Mario's face as they sat in a small room outside the studio monitoring the taping indicated he knew and approved of this response.

For the remainder of the half-hour show, Kat refused to be drawn into further comment on the subject and determinedly used each denied response as time to insert information on oil spill legislation, heath care proposals, and social security cuts.

Although the show she taped was for broadcast on Sunday, the station used her startling proposal as a newsbreak immediately following the taping. They added the information that there were literally thousands of hours of film, much of it on twenty-year-old outmoded video tape, and verified Harry Crast's designation. By late afternoon, Kat had repeated her statement and nothing more to countless media outlets and questioners. She banished the several dozen red roses that appeared in mid-afternoon to the downstairs campaign office. Roxy was now certain Stuart was the rose sender. Hayes confirmed he had passed on Mario's report of the interview to Stuart who admitted the notion of reviewing the films was his. It figures, thought Roxy. He probably volunteered to serve on the panel hoping to discover a nubile Kat hidden among the reels of tape.

Roxy could not imagine where Kat found the energy to be planning an evening of political calls in Providence with the Hose. She was ready for a nice, quiet padded cell, having helped field calls all afternoon, her patient manner invaluable when dealing with crazed callers. Mario was convinced the most rabid attacks were plants from Douglas' campaign and told Roxy to ignore them. She managed to put off Jake again, her actual state of advanced emotional disorder evident. They arranged to meet Sunday on the beach.

★ ★ ★ ★ ★

The Hose and Kat were leaving campaign headquarters on Federal Hill when the black Lincoln pulled up and a back window silently opened. Race Scarlatti leaned his sleek head out of the shadows and gestured for Kat to get in. An armed gorilla in a cheap human suit jumped from the front and opened the door for her. As she climbed into the backseat facing Race, the gorilla spoke, barring the Hose from following Kat.

"You wait out here Capaldi. They ain't goin' nowhere."

"I spoke with Jamie," his voice sounded hoarse and strained. She had to lean forward to hear him and he noticed her surprise.

"You didn't know he was back in Key West explaining he was on a pleasure cruise and had forgotten to tell the authorities? He has agreed to support your claim that there were never any films of you. It appears I was not the only one persuading him of this."

Race examined her face which was unmoving.

"You look lovely, almost glowing in fact. How surprising considering the stress you must be under from these rumors. Your tactic of offering viewing of the films was brilliant although it of course relies entirely on your trust in my word. I admit I am touched by your faith in my devotion."

Kat shrank back as he brushed his fingers against the palm of her hand. Cold sweat beaded her brow and turned her skin clammy. A cord of tension palpitated from her palm to her heart. Then he tightened his grip and pulled her toward him snarling, his thin lips invisible against his identically shaped teeth.

"If Stuart ever touches you again, he will beg to die, to end the unspeakable torture I will inflict upon his puny form." The door suddenly opened and he pushed her out.

Stumbling into the Hose's arms, Kat followed him up the stairs to her office as the black Lincoln roared away from the curb. She was shaking with rage and fear as she told Mario and the Hose what Scarlatti said about Jamie and Stuart. She omitted mentioning the tape she had; too many people already knew it existed. When Mario explained about the photo of Jasmine and Carrie, Kat knew why Scarlatti had targeted Stuart as a rival.

Suddenly the Hose jumped up, slamming his hands against each other.

"She's watching us. Scarlatti has her out there somewhere close watching us, and probably listening too."

He charged out of the room yelling. "I'm going to find that ugly witch if I have to search every building on the block."

★ ★ ★ ★ ★

Scarlatti hissed into his car phone.

"Get a picture of Stuart. Send it to this address."

He gave a Post Office box number in Washington, D.C.

"Is there a message?" Carrie replied.

"He'll know what I expect."

"He's coming to campaign with Kat in August. I just saw the schedule," she reported. He snarled to get him dates and exact itinerary, then hung up.

Carrie was pleased. All the threads of her plots were coming together nicely, woven into a dazzling pattern of illusion, betrayal and sexual obsession.

14

Walking the State
August

Rhode Island

It was past ten when Roxy awoke to a flagrantly sunny day after more hours of continuous sleep than she had had in years. There was a note pinned to the intricately carved pillar at the top of the stairs:

"I'll be back late Sunday. Direct all questions to Mario. I'll need a ride to the airport early Monday morning. K.A.T." She tossed the note on the floor, promising to add it to her list of concerns when she worked her way through the ones she now had.

Passing through the hushed and shaded space beneath the Towers arching over the road and sidewalk, Roxy emerged to find the beach already crowded, countless splashes of moving color strewn across the light sands, sparkling blue waves crashing on surfers and small children. Cars were streaming alongside her through the Towers and parking everywhere along the seawall, the hum of their engines overwhelming the relentless roaring of the ocean. The choking smell of carbon monoxide almost obliterated the pungent salty odor of the sea. It was all too much, too noisy, too crowded, too bright. Summer! All these people cluttering up her beach. Feeling somehow betrayed, Roxy abandoned her walk and returned to the house.

Glumly, she sat in a wicker chair in the TV room, and turned on the news, muting the sound so she could call Mario.

"She's with her friend Ellen on a boat somewhere. Our agreement was that she would call every twelve hours and return before midnight on Sunday. She claimed she had nothing additional to say to anyone, especially the press."

Mario explained they cleared Kat's schedule the previous evening after her harrowing encounter with Scarlatti, an account that sent shivers up Roxy's spine. Sensing his relief at talking with someone from whom he did not have to hide the truth, she encouraged him to speculate on Jasmine's role in all this.

Mario's view was that innocently or not, Jasmine was talking to Carrie, who they knew was working for Scarlatti. Early that morning, the Hose traced ownership of a building across the street to a known associate of Race's. The back entrance on the top floor apartment was visibly guarded by two thugs. As the Hose walked away, he swore he saw Carrie standing in a window, giving him the finger. He spent the morning on the phone trying to find a way in.

Intent on his crusade to "get" Carrie, whatever that meant, the Hose outlined her position in the Scarlatti organization, describing her as part of his collection operation. Reportedly, she was so adept at inflicting psychological terror in pursuit of protection payoffs, gambling debts, and general loan shark operations that she usually worked without any back-up muscle. All the Hose's contact knew was that Scarlatti had pulled her from routine operations to work on some special project. Unhappily, they agreed the project must be Kat.

Neither could guess why Jasmine was still on staff and decided the recent scene would push Kat to firing her once Congress recessed for the summer.

Roxy pieced together Kat's history with Scarlatti from the recent stories she heard. She pumped Mario for information on who he was in general, and why he was called Race.

Mario began his story with the name. Julius Scarlatti, Race's father, was a two-bit thug who started out in the auto body repair business, chasing accidents and scamming insurance companies. He shrewdly graduated to car theft and other transportation related crimes and invested heavily in junkyards and slums. From there he branched out. His current empire included trash hauling, teamsters, taxis and other odds and ends. His sole heir and son, Julius, was known to all as Race.

The street legend claimed that Race was banished from parochial school at age seven for selling sacramental wine and betting on CYO basketball games. He escaped the notice of authorities for almost a year before they caught up with him and condemned him to public school. During that formative year, young Julius hawked horse racing forms at Narragansett Park. Gamblers soon used him to phone in their bets to local bookies summoning him by shouting "race." He decided it was a designation far more appropriate to his character than either Julius or Junior, so Race he became.

His criminal career progressed easily from its early beginnings. While still a teen-ager, he had almost total control of illegal sports gambling and bookmaking operations in the state. By the time the "numbers" racket was legalized to become a foundation of state revenue, Scarlatti had diversified into several legitimate fields including trading in precious metals, an occupation that required handling enormous amounts of cash. When anyone needed quick cash with no questions asked, they went to Race. His success brought him to the attention of crime bosses in New York who considered Rhode Island part of their empire. He was a model for the new generation of mobsters and soon became a partner.

Mario explained that according to family stories, Race's obsession with Kat began in childhood. Mafia-linked organized crime became public in the late

'50s, culminating in several shooting deaths at Smith's Restaurant not far from campaign headquarters. Duke led public denunciation of Italo involvement and refused to do business with anyone so connected. Julius Scarlatti Sr. was one of Duke's primary targets. At the time, Race was about fourteen and already had grandiose plans for a life of crime. Kat was a pivotal player in his dreams for creating what he described as "Roman ascendancy" in the state. He would marry her, unite the Italo community and use her to breed the sons who would carry on his empire. It was the myth of the horrible monster under the bridge who demands the beautiful princess as his bride in return for not committing murder and mayhem.

"Needless to say, both Kat and Duke considered the notion insane," Mario concluded.

"Is he dangerous?" Roxy asked.

"He's smart, ruthless and very powerful. I think he's more drawn to Carrie's brand of psychological terror than physical violence although I'm certain he never hesitated to order death and destruction when necessary. Scarlatti's a sick and twisted soul. I've always imagined him smiling and softly chatting with his prisoners as he watched them dismembered on his orders."

Adding Race to Jamie, she wondered what in Kat drew creatures of the darkness who wanted to drag her down with them. Too much Persephone, Roxy concluded.

Sworn to secrecy, Mario did not tell her of Scarlatti's threat against Senator Stuart and how serious it was, although he hoped Kat would at least tell Stuart.

After she called Mario back with all the messages, Roxy slumped dejectedly onto the wicker lounge. She had been disturbed by the number of calls volunteering to screen Jamie's films no matter how long it took; most were obscene. All this sexual energy, where was it coming from? She remembered Max explaining how sex, magic, and politics were all the same basic power. Why was it being so sexual in this case? It really was not Kat's usual direction, it was more....Roxy sat up shocked at the thought. It was more her style! Was all this random sexual energy careening around because of her, the same way she channeled energy for the tarot cards? Was it out of hand because of the sex magic she was doing with Jake? Or because she had polluted it with Hayes?

Max was better than any weather man. It was rocky emotional weather, as he predicted, and right on schedule. Roxy was desolate. She hated being responsible for causing anyone problems, especially people she loved like Kat. What could she do? She could leave but somehow that did not seem like a solution. Vaguely she recalled Max saying that she was part of the pattern, she had lessons to learn in this experience, too. There was only one thing to do. Roxy spent the rest of the day cleaning the house in anticipation of Liz's arrival on Tuesday.

By dark she was bored and set out in her reliable Volvo for a summer Saturday night in Newport. She wanted to be incognito, no campaign van. She fought her way through Narragansett, jammed with kids. Cars were parked for blocks around the beach. At the Coast Guard House, young men and women swarmed around plastic white tables on an outside deck overlooking the bay, searching for the right warm body. Younger teens clumped around the seawall at the stairs leading down to the beach. They postured, mostly ignoring the opposite sex. A few concentrated on their bikes, skateboards and basketballs. Surfers bobbed like black seals in chocolate streaked water, and a neon glow-in-the-dark dragon kite fluttered from the arm of a lifeguard chair over the waves. Roxy averted her eyes. She did not want to see her beach being violated.

The crowd in Newport was slightly older and more upscale than across the bay, and far more numerous. Roxy finally found a parking place on a steep side street and trudged down Prospect Hill to the bright, glittery waterfront vibrating with activity. Picking up a fruit drink at a stall on Bannister Wharf, she settled on the shadowed porch of a geode shop at the Wharf's entry.

People-watching was a favorite sport and this was a four-star location. She was amazed at how blatantly enticing many of the women were dressed. One bleached blonde paraded by in a short black and white spandex dress with non-attached tubes posing as sleeves on her upper arms. As she strutted along the sidewalk Roxy saw a straight young couple, probably tourists, coming in the opposite direction. The "Strumpet" as Roxy termed her, refused to move and bumped right into the man who also did not yield. He definitely did it on purpose and probably copped a quick feel while he was at it.

Two sleazy couples next caught her eye. They were dressed up for a slick night out. One of the women had a decided Eurotrash look with a tight black skirt slit to her ass in the back, dark fitted jacket over a black tube, chopped black hair. She grabbed her partner's jacket and started to move off. He called her back then began to follow her as she teased him along. Nice ass, Roxy noticed as his tight bottom passed by.

The bars on the wharf were too crowded to wade through and most of the patrons too young for her. Then she saw a group of middle-age couples, accountant genre, walking up the wharf tearing Douglas stickers from their lapels. Judging from the snips of conversation she heard as they passed, they had been at a fundraiser. She wandered back into the crowd in the direction from which they came, idly wondering where the fundraiser was. She found nothing. She decided to go home and prepare for seeing Jake the next day. She had wrestled with her guilt through bathroom and kitchen cleaning, vacuuming, dusting, and putting sheets on Liz's bed. She still had no idea what she was going to say.

She stood at the concrete barrier that divided America's Cup Avenue as this section of Thames Street near the wharf entrance was called. Right or left? The street where she was parked was accessible either way. She randomly chose left and headed back towards her street. From the corner of her eye, she noticed the Morgan Springs naked lady logo on the bumper of Max's van. Amazed, Roxy approached the driver's side where Max was sitting. A streetlight cast a halo around his white spiked hair and bounced off the sparkles sewn in magical patterns on his purple shirt.

She recognized the hand of fate when it pinched her. She jumped into the passenger seat, immediately pelting him with a disordered recital of the week's insane events, Kat's strange behavior, and her rampant guilt about creating sexual chaos around the campaign.

"You need to activate your prudence amulet in self-defense," Max said. "You can't do anything about the type of energy that gets generated when people chase power. Sex, magic, politics, they're all Scorpio. The issue is the same for each: seeking power. I can assure you the sex magic you're learning from Jake is not the source of the problem.

"As far as polluting sex magic with other sexual relationships—Jake always was a purist, although it may be a wise prohibition in this case. You are undertaking a rather spectacular effect." Max smiled at the thought of two hundred and fifty thousand voters being swept by a tide of sexual frenzy to vote for Kat.

"Let me understand clearly what happened with Hayes. You explained your pledge to avoid copulation but agreed to his suggestion that a blow-job would not violate the letter of the pledge, although it seems to me the spirit would be seriously mangled."

Roxy frowned. She wanted Max to tell her Jake was being excessive even though she had agreed, fully understanding what he was asking.

"You engaged in this act, decidedly sexual, although questionable as to its inclusion in the definition of copulation. At the last minute, confronted with an alluringly straight and strong prick staring you in the eye as it were, your resolve wavered and you jumped aboard for the final steam into the station."

Roxy looked like a boiled lobster as Max finished his revealing summary of her night with Hayes. How could she be so...so...easy?

"Regardless of how rigid I may believe Jake's standards are, you did agree. If you don't tell him what happened, you will poison the energy you generate together. It could be dangerous but mostly to you." Max's tone did not invite negotiation.

"I know you work hard to maintain your role as an observer of life, dabbling enough to satisfy your sensual nature but mostly functioning as the recording angel, not as an actor. This time you're a player in the drama. You're almost forty. I won't bore you with the astrological details but generic issues pop up now that compel examination of what is essentially the first half of life. The urgent question is what is missing. The urgent quest is to find it.

"No matter how reluctant you are, this is a time of choice. Right or wrong is not fatal, indecision is for it removes life from your control."

"What do you think the choice is?"

"You defined it when you looked at those goddess cards, remember?"

"And you think Jake is the sanctifier and Hayes is the seducer?"

Max shrugged. "Your path is clear: to explore sensual pleasure. Only you can decide what is sacred and what is temptation."

Roxy felt her mouth turn into a pout that seeped through her whole attitude. She hated difficult situations. She especially hated making choices. If she chose, someone would lose and she would face a road not taken. She remembered the difficulty Paris got into when he was forced to choose among the three goddesses.

"There's a man you should meet, study with actually....."

"I don't need any more men," Roxy exclaimed. "I don't need to meet anyone. I already have more phone numbers than in my whole life. There are numbers for car phones, FAX machines, offices, homes, press—I dream about lines of numbers parading over me."

Max ignored her outburst. "He's going to be teaching a course at Brown this fall called Erotic Literature. I'm sure I could get you enrolled. If you're ever to write myths, you have to understand their sexual basis. His name is Robert Christopher and I'll send you his number before the class starts. Don't neglect any of the opportunities for growth this adventure provides.

"But don't neglect Kat either. She's the main reason you're here."

Roxy nodded. She agreed. Kat was her first priority.

"Whether by choice or chance, Kat has a demanding destiny. She's driven by her daimon to seek balance on a scale that will engrave it in human consciousness, to embody it in a myth. That's why her life is filled with seeming incongruities," Max continued.

"When you seek balance, much of the time is, by necessity and physics, spent in imbalance.

"Kat apprenticed herself to the Great Ones in their various guises long ago, a path that exacts a high price. The obstacles of this current quest will show if she has the capacity to continue struggling while keeping love intact.

"I have a theory that the quest of a particular soul is defined in a question, or questions, that must be answered. Kat claims hers are two. What is the truth? And what is my duty? I think she must add a third—what saith my heart?"

"What's my question?"

Max smiled at her. "That's easy. How can I extract from each moment of life all the joy and pleasure it holds?"

Roxy laughed with him and they sat staring at the blazing waterfront, listening to the dull humming of thousands of celebrating voices. Thoughtfully, Max returned to talking about Kat. "She's not like you. She resists the idea that she must seek balance outside herself, in an opposite, a man. She's afraid it's weakness to be complete only in relationship with another."

"Is that why the Lovers card keeps turning up?"

"Possibly." When it was obvious Max would say no more on the subject, Roxy asked "how about Death? Does there have to be all the suffering and chaos the cards keep predicting?"

"Mythic quests require challenges; the seeker must earn the prize. You know what the ancient philosophers said, there ain't no such thing as a free lunch! This senate race is like one of Hercules' labors, another step along her path. She spent many years accomplishing the preliminary work, grounding herself in the laws of nature. Her public life provided tests for courage requiring her to face external obstacles and overcome her fears. This episode leads to the most difficult test of all: humility, yielding humbly to fate.

"It will be a strenuous test, yielding to a greater will. Kat thinks she's done this many times over but in reality she hasn't. She has great faith in her ability to influence events."

"Doesn't it frighten you to see the future?"

"Only when I can't see it clearly."

Roxy wondered if the strain of knowing etched the deep lines that scored his face. "Do you have hope Max? Not just for Kat or the campaign, but for humanity, for evolution in general?"

"Of course."

He waved his hand vaguely at the waterfront that lay before them with its thousands of lights illuminating the sky.

"Five hundred years ago, life was ruled by the sun, otherwise the world was dark. The expanded mind of humanity is symbolized by this now timeless light."

★ ★ ★ ★ ★

The first shy colors of dawn were making their way across the sky, tinting the calm waters with lilac and pink and a clear soft blue, zones of color flowing with the waves. A long band of some nameless hue wrapped the horizon like glittering trim, the colors of the waters reflected above it in the lightening sky.

Roxy set out early hoping to walk for a while and clear her head before meeting Jake but all that filled her mind were unconnected observations about the impact of summer. The hordes of visitors and tourists that jammed the sand the previous day were not yet a reality. The air was still tangy and clear. The empty beach displayed unavoidable signs of their presence. Volleyball nets were up. Trash was scattered around, crews just beginning to clean the beach. She danced away from the huge lumbering machine that raked and waffled the sand south of the Dunes Club each morning.

The giant white lifeguard chairs were out. Empty beer cans and a shirt stuffed into the back corner of the seat of one reminded Roxy of the night she and Jake worshipped Aphrodite here and how the goddess inspired him for his reverence.

Thinking of relevant divinities, she admired Apollo's chariot as it popped up from the horizon, a glowing ball of crimson and gold, and began its race across the sky.

With the tide out, a large sandbar extended into Narrow River from the hidden cove which she still had not explored. It was separated from the beach by only a few feet of water. Staring at boulders in the estuary mouth, she considered walking out on the sandbar. Then she noticed a starfish at her feet, another and still another leading in a path. They drew her along the edges of the dunes. As she rounded the dune and looked along the previously hidden curved shore, a hand suddenly grabbed her ankle and tumbled her onto the sand. It was Jake, sitting in an arc of starfish grinning at her.

"I knew I could get you to fall for me."

He attributed her hesitant response to concern about the campaign and began commiserating.

"People seem confused and a little disinterested. Corruption is not new in this state. We've been called Rogue's Island and the Licentious Republic. There was even a famous Supreme Court decision in the 1840s involving Rhode Island that declared the people could not replace a duly elected government even if it was unrepresentative and corrupt. Daniel Webster argued the people's case. A few decades later, vote buying was so flagrant that two U.S. Senate committees were established to examine election fraud here. Of course, nothing happened to change things. For decades everyone's known the pinnacle of most political careers in the state was criminal indictment.

"They've always believed Kat was different." He quickly leaned over and kissed her as she began to protest that Kat was indeed different.

"And she is, I know. But Gould was right. All the lies and attacks are causing tiny little cracks, almost unconscious doubts. What makes it doubly dangerous is that the attacks don't seem to be coming from Douglas."

Jake's matter of fact assessment of the campaign's current state of crisis did not relieve her anxiety but it did displace the cause. He jumped to his feet, pulling her up and into his arms.

"So that means we need to get to work on influencing those voters."

He kissed her again, this time slowly and deliberately, drawing her gently in to him. Roxy vowed she would tell him about Hayes, later, and kissed him back.

Dressed in Kiley for Senate teeshirts, they went out and "made friends" as Jake called it, spending the day indulging in Sunday activities around South County. Reading the newspaper while eating breakfast on the porch at Peppers, the Charlestown flea market, yard sales, local festivals. By the time they arrived at Jake's, Roxy was exhausted and focused on sorting through the reactions they had observed in their travels.

On the surface, nothing had changed. People smiled at them, indicated their support in various ways, and shyly approached Jake like he was a celebrity, which in a way he was. Through the commercials, he had probably accumulated as much TV time as Kat recently. But there was something beneath the smiles, a quick looking away, a furtive glance in some eyes. Several punks gathered around the edge of one of the festivals wanted to know where they could sign up to review Jamie's film collection. Roxy hoped wherever Kat was, she was thinking about how to defuse this issue.

"It looks like we have our work cut out for us. But not to worry, I feel up to the task. Let's start with a shower." Jake led her into his roomy bathroom and began undressing her. Once in the shower, steam everywhere, his hands sliding over her soaped up body, Roxy felt her anxiety washing away. Maybe she did not have to tell him about Hayes. It was only a single slip. She would resolve never to let it happen again. They had just begun the sex magic anyway. Maybe it was not able to be ruined so early in the process. Or being good from now on would compensate.

As Jake rubbed her dry with his oversized, rough towels she felt her mood lifting. Feeling guilty and depressed would certainly affect whatever magic they would do now. She resolved to make the sacrifice, for Kat, and yielded to Jake's effort as he led her to the pillow couch and began brushing her hair. It was one of the most mutually satisfying aspects of their lovemaking. Jake loved brushing her thick, golden hair over his hands, running his fingers through it.

"It's so like sunshine, streaming out from your sweet face, lighting up everything around you. Soft and silky..."

He buried his face in the still damp handful he held and the rest of his words were lost but Roxy understood. She loved the stroking. There was plenty of stroking this day.

"I've missed seeing you," he whispered as he slowly examined her with his fingertips, occasionally bending closer to brush his lips along a particularly treasured curve or hollow.

Roxy drifted, knowing he wanted no response from her in this stage. He worked delicately to stir the sexual energy in her with light touches and the force of his gazing. He was soon successful. Her pulse pounded under the surface of her skin pulled like iron fillings by the magnet of his fingertips.

As he lay down beside her, matching his breathing to hers, he kept his hand lightly resting on her stomach, directly below her breasts on the chakra used in magnetizing power and desire. Roxy felt the shimmering blue-green orb she first experienced during her initiation into tantric yoga slowly rise along the central core of her lower torso, settling in the area beneath Jake's hand. "See the flame," he whispered and she did. It flickered and swayed, growing ever larger. From the corner of her almost closed eyes, Roxy could see his fully erect penis—lingyan, she corrected herself, much preferring the Sanskrit word—swaying and swelling like the flame.

"You must want this too," he said softly, bringing her back into her head from drifting bliss as he rolled onto his back and pulled her towards him.

"Lower yourself onto me, then sit quietly."

Following his instructions, she sat lightly, her legs bent beneath her, feeling him fill her with throbbing hardness. His hands stroked her breasts, following their curve and ending always in the pulsing chakra centered beneath them.

"Hold the image of the votes," were the last words she heard him say before his force shot up through her and swept the hovering blue-green orb up through her heart and out the crown to the heavens, carrying their wish for two hundred and fifty thousand votes along with it, as Kat's fireflies had carried her wish to the gods.

Jake lay beside her limp and satisfied, resting his hand on her hip. A series of sporadic muscle spasms twitched and jolted his body like electric shocks. She was astounded and wondered if something terrible was happening. What if Jake was reacting to the pollution he said someone else's sexual energy would cause? Fear swept through her still stimulated nervous system followed quickly by guilt. Then she looked at his face and it was radiant. He was smiling broadly. Moans of pleasure were coming from his throat as each spasm rocked his body. As she watched, he finally stopped and opened his eyes to look at her.

Lifting his finger to her lips and pushing their corners up to induce a smile, he spoke to the concern her face showed.

"It's nothing to worry about. It's electrical. Part of equalizing the charge that built up between us. It's never been so powerful before."

Roxy blushed as her guilt pushed to the front of her mind. She shoed it away and prodded Jake for more explanation.

"A blaze of heat bursts all through the core of my body. As it pulses electricity through my nerves and escapes through my skin, the intense waves of pleasure trigger a new round of heat and pulse. All I know for certain is that the impulse is electrical and it happens on every square inch of my body. Sexual aftertaste is how I think of it, and the aftertaste from your honeyed juices is the most delectable of all."

Tears leaked out the corners of her tightly closed eyes as Roxy sat up and hunched herself into a ball. She had to tell him, confess and swear to go and sin no more. This was magic and she did not want to destroy it. Besides, she would have to be crazy not to prefer this wonderful man whose intensity was focused on the pleasure they could find in each other to one who had answered the ringing phone while she was "pleasuring" him the other night and seemed a bit put out when at the climax she changed her mind and insisted on participating.

Before her resolve weakened, Roxy faced Jake.

"Bless me father for I have sinned. I copulated," she mumbled.

She could not open her eyes and watch the hurt and disappointment she was sure would be there. When nothing happened, nothing was said, she peeked through her lashes and was amazed to find Jake smiling gently at her. She was so startled by his calm reaction to what she considered a major offense that she did what she had learned years ago never to do, she discussed one lover with another.

She told him everything—about Hayes, his arguments over polluting the magic, the compulsion she felt for him and how she had experienced this obsessive blood magnetism before. Through it all she cried and Jake held her lovingly, occasionally brushing a strand of hair from her wet cheeks, pulling it from between her lips where it got caught up during her impassioned recital.

"And when I saw you just now, I was terrified that my weakness polluted you, that you would be hurt—physically hurt because I broke my promise. I'm sorry, really and truly sorry, and I'll never do it again."

As she took a deep breath in preparation for continuing her self-abnegation, Jake lightly kissed her.

"It's OK, Roxy. We'll work with what's possible. I haven't met Hayes yet but everything I've heard of him indicates his argument with my ban was well-taken. He's totally focused on the same goal we are and who am I to deny him the solace of the goddess of love if that's what he needs to make this victory possible. Magic only works when it flows with natural forces, not against them."

Roxy collapsed into his arms, sobbing in relief. Whatever she had done to deserve this man, she hoped it was enough to keep him around for a while.

She knew the fates had chosen their champion when she found her fortune strip for July the next morning, stuffed in a corner of her jewelry case. *Your secret shame has been forgiven*, she read, astonished.

★ ★ ★ ★ ★

It was a toss-up whether Saddam Hussein invading Kuwait and stirring up war fever or Liz arriving in the state changed the campaign more. Since she appeared on the horizon first and influenced daily life so dramatically, Roxy threw her vote to Liz.

Less than forty-eight hours after she arrived, Liz was on the strategy conference call re-arranging plans for campaigning during Kat's month-long recess. Setting aside all the drama, the major concern of both Kat and campaign staff was what to do during the five weeks she was home. She refused to consider either official junkets or a vacation, insisting this was the only large bloc of time she had before the election. She agreed with Stuart's assessment that Congress would be mired in budget issues well into October. Yet she was frustrated, knowing from a lifetime of Rhode Island summers how useless it was to focus people's attention on a political campaign when their main goal was accumulating beach time.

"No one cares about issues, no one but us cares about the campaign, and we're paid to feel that way. We're hustling for money no one wants to spend on political ads no matter how wonderful they are, and I agree, Hal, they are wonderful, because they know that no one is watching TV. All people have seen of me recently is denying some degrading accusation or another. Now you tell me a syndicate of Douglas cronies have brought up a group of small local newspapers and are launching a statewide semi-weekly with regional sections." Kat paused for breath to grasp the enormity of the information Mario just announced to the connected campaign team.

A Douglas-friendly legitimate press outlet could print lies and misinformation and send it out over networks nationwide that publicize anything tantalizing or scandalous. As for impact within the state—their collective horror at the implications was reflected in the lengthening silence. He was calling it the *Ocean Beacon* and claiming it would print the truth now denied expression in the dominant statewide *Journal*. They assumed that meant unfounded attacks on Kiley Tomasso and her senate candidacy.

Roxy was startled when Liz jumped into the dead space and announced with the absolute certainty experience taught her to dread.

"I have the answer," Liz said.

The mystified group waited. Except for Kat, they had been introduced to Liz by phone only moments before.

"You need two hundred fifty thousand votes to win, I've been told. You need to reach those folks especially now when they have all these doubts about what they once thought was absolutely true. You can't seem to be hiding. You claim we can't get to them by TV or newspapers, and we know that nobody goes to meetings in August so what do we do? It's simple! We go where they are. Outside. Kat walks the state!"

Before anyone could react Liz steamed on, outlining the benefits of her plan.

"Mario and Bruno both agree it can be done in the time we have. You actually walk the shortest path we can map out from Westerly to Little Compton, and zig zag back and forth on side trips by car. You could do it in twenty days averaging ten miles a day."

Mario jumped in with details about locations, key people, potential press coverage and logistical considerations.

Kat loved the idea. It answered every need and handled correctly could be a media bonanza. It did mean exposing herself relentlessly to the public, but she accepted that. She began reminiscing with Mario and the Hose about 1982 when they campaigned on the beaches. At least two men on the call shouted "no bathing suits" into the phones in response.

In her most sarcastic tone Liz responded, "I don't want to be along the day they make you walk Narragansett Beach in those three-inch heels and nylons." Kat laughed in appreciation and assigned the Rhode Island group basic responsibility for drafting a detailed itinerary and faxing it to everyone before a Monday conference call.

"I have a solution for the second part of the problem," Kat continued. "Roxy, you and I are going to develop an issues book. I want one-sheet statements on every issue we think people care about written as clearly and simply as possible. We can distribute them on the walk, release one each day. We'll work those details out."

They concluded by deciding to postpone decisions on paid media until mid-August when the team would meet face-to-face in Rhode Island for the first time in months. Some quicky phone polling would be done before then.

★ ★ ★ ★ ★

By the end of her first week, Liz's structure was firmly in place. The Narragansett house became headquarters for initial planning since the walk would begin at the carousel in Watch Hill. Most of the first week would be spent on the southern half of the mainland.

Mario and the Hose—who Liz, like Kat, insisted on calling Bruno—provided the content. They knew where and what everything was, they knew who the key people were in each area and what their concerns were. Liz directed the process by asking basic questions and keeping them from getting "too deep," as she would say, dropping her voice to a rumbling bass. And she fed everyone.

Roxy scribed. She created the walk plan on paper as Mario and the Hose unfolded it from the maps. Liz was so enchanted with how it looked she insisted Roxy be neat and use good paper.

"We'll hang it around the walls at headquarters and add clippings, photos, general memorabilia we collect as it happens. It'll be art! The press will love it, and we can fold it up as a memory book for Kat when we're done. She can save it for her museum and add it to all those stars she collects."

Liz thought everyone should collect something.

"It helps focus one's acquisitive instinct. I myself, collect real estate; Roxy collects men."

"Do you know that Roxy has an album with pictures of every male she's ever loved—or maybe it's kissed—anyway, she's on volume six?" Liz told Mario and the Hose.

She brought Kat a foot-high neon star mounted on a base. Kat decided to use it as an indicator that she was "in" at the campaign office.

Much to Roxy's dismay, Liz intercepted a call from Jake and arranged that he and Pete would join them for Liz's first feast Friday night. They proved naturals for walk planning and begged to work on it all weekend. Jake knew everything about South County and Pete proposed paralleling the walk, "by car of course," with a series on restaurants he would visit and review along the way.

Dinner was the triumphant event Liz planned. She asked no one about their food preferences. Liz was impatient with weird dietary requirements.

"People need to concern themselves more with what comes out of their mouth than what goes into it," was her justification. When she discovered lobster abundant at two dollars a pound, she vowed to eat it daily.

That night, she steamed lobster and served a tasty pasta salad filled with oil-dried black olives she was thrilled to find in almost every market. But it was the crusty French bread hot from the oven that was the biggest hit. When she set out shallow bowls of olive oil spiced with fresh chopped basil and garlic for bread dipping, Roxy marveled to see four men fall instantly in love.

Liz immediately recognized that Mario and the Hose were the foundation on which Kat's empire was built and that there was nothing she needed to know that one or the other could not find out. Perched on a kitchen stool, waiting for pasta to cook, her ever-present giant glass of iced tea in hand, Liz explained her theory to Roxy.

"They're most valuable because they're always there for Kat. She can count on them for anything. You can buy skill and talent but loyalty has no price."

She went on to sing Mario's praises beginning with his cherub face and puppy dog eyes and concluding with his accomplishments as a political advisor.

"When I first saw him I thought just another pretty face who majored in women and took a few classes in political science. Then I asked him about one of the voting districts in Westerly and he rattled off a perfect summary comparing it to the other five hundred odd districts in the state and gave me a count of how many swing votes there were and how we could swing them almost name by name."

"No wonder all those political groupies throw themselves at him, he's a B-cubed."

When Roxy looked mystified, Liz explained, "Brains, beauty and balls! The perfect formula."

She championed Jake's cause, describing him as the man of honor Roxy needed. She was initially wary of Pete being a "professional customer" as she described him, relenting when he declared himself her slave for life if only she would throw him occasional scraps of her bread. By the end of their first feast, she was offering advice on the restaurant chain he was planning called Fast Food Fettucinis.

They saw Kat sporadically on Saturday as she went from the Blessing of the Fleet in Galilee to a suffragette rally organized by NOW in Newport then back across the bay again for a huge South County clambake. She would breeze through the house, snatch at tidbits of food Liz left around for her, and ask acute questions that always left the planners more focused. She was ecstatic about the walk and how it was coming together.

WALKING THE STATE

"Max decided Friday was the best day to begin an unusual and revolutionary journey. He said the runes described movement and progress. The image he used was the primitive search for totem magic. I told him I hoped it would not turn into forty days wandering in the desert," she told Roxy on one pass-through.

A chain of papers outlining every day of the walk snaked across the rosewood table, breakfront, mantle and several chairs in the dining room. All morning, Roxy scribed for Mario, Jake and their field organizer for South County, listing names, contacts, organizations, media, suggested side trips, issues. They could walk to Ninigret Pond the first day, making downtown Westerly a side trip. Saturday they would greet dawn at the wildlife refuge and walk along what would be clogged roads to the beach, ending up among the fishermen of Galilee. Trekking north along the bay beaches, on Sunday they would march triumphantly into Narragansett as thousands were leaving to return home.

Liz baked blueberry muffins, kept them supplied in lemonade and tea, and coerced Pete into cleaning cooked meat from more lobster so she could make limitless bowls of lobster salad. They talked restaurants as he outlined the food tour he would be having while Kat walked. Liz had cut her mane of frosted hair and modified her showgirl make-up to look like she belonged awake in the daytime.

People drifted in and out all day with information about various sections of the state. They planned a side trip to walk around Jamestown Island the first week, and considered various options for hitting the northern cities and scattered settlements in the western section. As Roxy wrote down all decisions and tried to keep her walk charts neat, she had to keep reminding herself that driving time for the area Kat would walk from one end of the state to the other was less than three hours.

Sunday, Liz solidified her internal empire by joining forces with Yola, Mario's mother, who fulfilled Roxy's prediction by brilliantly running campaign headquarters and the office volunteers.

Mario was hosting a One Hundred Days Until the Election party at Duke's compound, as it was commonly known. He lived in a separate apartment attached to his parents' house across an open courtyard from the mansion in which Kat grew up. Her brother Frankie, sole male heir to the Tomasso name, now lived in the pink marble house with his two lovely but unfortunately female children. Liz had worked feeding the troops all day alongside "the aunts," as Duke's four sisters and Yola were collectively known, although Mario's mother was not a Tomasso blood relative. There were more than fifty congressional and campaign staff, volunteers and interns partying on the lawn and around the swimming pool.

When Kat arrived at the party after dark, having spent another day shaking hands at fairs and festivals, she was delighted to see how much of the month-long extravaganza was in place. Mario had used the afternoon and evening to extract information about areas of the walk route from everyone there, including "the aunts."

The *Ocean Beacon* newspaper chain was not yet in print and they blessed their good fortune in having the rest of the state's press once again fade away in the face of Kat's clear responses to various attacks. She insisted the weekend of campaigning had presented her with no real hostility. She was returning early the next morning to Washington for the final few hectic days before Congress recessed. Since her brother and his family were at their beach house for the summer, Kat opted to stay at the compound only a few miles from the airport.

"The aunts told me everything about the family, Kat's mother, everything," Liz informed Roxy as they drove back to Narragansett late that night. "I'll tell you in the morning," she promised and promptly fell asleep.

★ ★ ★ ★ ★

Roxy had not walked on the beach since Liz arrived, partly because of hectic schedules, partly because of what seemed like weeks of rain and gray skies. Monday morning it was bright and sunny and she skipped down the backstairs at dawn to gulp some juice before walking. She was stunned to find Liz in the kitchen waiting for her.

"Normally I consider dawn the end of my day, but I decided I'd see how it felt as a beginning."

The ocean was wonderful, the walk terrible. The weather boys had finally designated the storm hanging off the Atlantic coast a hurricane. It still showed around the edges of the horizon as hints of gray clouds out to sea and surf that was both active and of respectable size. Liz commented on everything: the walkers they met on the beach, the ones who walked on the sidewalks, the gulls, shells, waves, trash.

"Do you think those tiny little round stones started out like the huge boulders over there and were worn down by the waves, or does the state truck them in each season?"

They had scarcely reached the Dunes Club before she started nattering about the distance. Once back in the kitchen, she swore she would never walk with Roxy on the beach again.

"Only refugees in desperate flight walk that far. Even if my car broke down and I was out of beer I wouldn't walk that far. You have to understand, I'm still waiting for riding vacuum cleaners. All my years of cultivating sensuous flab could be ruined. I could actually develop muscles or at least, tone," she sputtered.

Roxy assumed Liz would not be walking around the state with Kat.

They were sitting around the beautiful kitchen table, handcrafted from calcified logs with matching cushioned chairs. Historic concerns had no place in Kat's kitchen any more than they had when she created the glass-enclosed conservatory for her Jacuzzi. Roxy never understood why the kitchen was so elaborate. Except for visits to her pasta-cooking relatives, she never knew Kat to either cook or eat with any seriousness. There was a separate butler's kitchen hung with glass-doored cabinets, and a well-stocked pantry. The floor was highly polished wide board walnut with large hand woven rugs scattered around. In the brief time Liz was there, the kitchen had been transformed from a corridor leading to the Jacuzzi to the central gathering place and operating heart of Liz's empire.

She was cooking cheese omelets for breakfast, filling the bright room with the fragrance of melted butter and fresh tomatoes. She popped a couple bagels in the toaster then laid it all on the table and began complaining about Kat.

"She looks terrible, she's entirely too thin, and her hair is a disaster. The other night she was pacing around at three a.m. I'll bet she hasn't slept through the night in weeks." Liz leaned on her arms and squinted her heavily lashed blue eyes at Roxy, who was devouring the delicious breakfast. "And I know just what to do."

Slathering strawberry jam brought from Liz's personal stash, Roxy sighed. Now what?

"First, I'll feed her. Yola says she's always been a picky eater but she does love pasta. I'm going to start keeping a pot of sauce always simmering on the stove so I can cook up spaghetti and meatballs in a moment's notice. I'll start making her breakfast, too. By the time she's here for a month, I'll have her nice and fattened up, just like me. She'll come to appreciate the effort it takes to maintain this dynamic dirigible shape. Next, I'm going to cut and style that tangled mane so she doesn't need to carry around a hay rake to comb it."

Roxy snorted at that. It was a constant battle to get Kat to keep her wild mop neatly trimmed at shoulder length, anything shorter was considered butchery.

"And for the stress and sleeplessness," Liz continued, unabashed by the lack of encouragement, "The oldest and most effective remedy of all—a good fuck."

She cringed. She knew this was coming when Liz spotted the schedule notation that Senator Stuart would soon be in the state overnight to campaign for Kat. Roxy had been racking her brain to find a way to keep Liz away from Stuart. She concealed the events at the White House barbecue which indicated he would be a willing participant in any plan to relieve Kat's sexual tension. Knowing Kat was resisting would only add to Liz's resolve.

Unable to deter Liz with reminders that a massively publicized visit by Senator Stuart to campaign was probably not the best circumstance for an illicit and secret rendezvous, she retreated and absorbed a few more moments of fantasy before steering the conversation onto the topic of what "the aunts" had revealed at the party.

Liz's face lit up and she settled against the back of her chair.

"Family gossip, direct from the source. There's nothing more juicy and full of life. It was great! All of us up to our elbows in tomato sauce, chicken, lobster, bread, olive oil. Cutting, stirring, tasting, grilling. All the smells. They all yell. No one talks in a normal tone of voice so to be heard you have to yell. Five of them, and me." Liz tossed her head and puffed herself up, saying in a pleased-with-herself girly voice, "I could out-yell them all. They were impressed."

Roxy laughed. She had heard Liz shout down a packed bar and blow out amps when she was really singing, and she had noticed an incredible noise level in the kitchen the previous day.

"When they start to tell the inside stuff they talk real quiet, so 'the men' can't hear.

"Let's start with Kat's mother, Celeste. She is universally hated and despised by the aunts and probably by the uncles and cousins, too. To all of them, family means tribe. Tribal loyalty means you find jobs, do favors and lend money to your tribal members. Celeste hated all of it."

Roxy nodded, wondering what Duke's tribe would think if they knew about Celeste's confession regarding their chief's death. They probably would not be surprised in the least.

Celeste Albright belonged to an undistinguished branch of a family that traced its roots back to the earliest days of Providence Plantation. Her mother died when she was young. Her father Henry was a weak and easily dominated man who squandered away what fortune they had before Celeste was able to use it to launch herself into society and find a rich and suitably aristocratic husband. She found herself at nineteen embittered, with little useful education, few saleable skills and no desire at all to earn a living like the common girls from Providence she always scorned.

Tomasso legend painted Duke, the only son among five children, as a young demigod who at twenty-eight had built a major excavation and construction firm with trucks and crews everywhere in the state. Even then it was accepted wisdom that Tomasso involvement in any construction project insured its successful conclusion, usually under cost. Duke accumulated a fortune, found his sisters good husbands who worked in the business, built his parents a wonderful house, employed dozens of cousins and paisans, and generally sacrificed himself for the good of his family and broader clan. He was a hands-on owner who could work every machine and knew every job in the business. It was a family mystery how Duke met Celeste and what possessed her to give a second glance to a man she consistently berated, often in front of family, as a "dago laborer."

Celeste was beautiful in a cold, New England way with her shining platinum blonde hair, sleek figure, and elegant manners. As an Albright, even as an undistinguished one, there were doors open to her forever closed to Duke.

"There was a big argument, obviously well-rehearsed," Liz explained, "over why Duke and Celeste got married, aside from the obvious one of our favorite candidate's conception. Yola claimed Celeste went after Duke for money, pure and simple, but the real aunts, Duke's sisters, had another story. The oldest sister Tillie was the one who did most of the talking. She said Duke realized all the money he could make wouldn't get him inside certain Yankee houses, not that he cared, but he wanted this for whatever children he would have. As much as Kat's father loved his heritage—'the hot Italian lifeblood that revived the Yankee corpse of Rhode Island' was what he termed it—he wanted his children to have opportunities that couldn't be found in the tribal devotion of his ethnic family.

"Whoever was doing the manipulating, the upshot of the two versions was the same. Celeste Albright got pregnant and married Duke Tomasso. Not long after, Kat was born and her brother followed two years later. Celeste was never interested in either of her children and that's how Yola came to be part of 'the aunts.' She was the daughter of a long time associate of Duke's father and needed a job. She became the live-in babysitter." Roxy once again was amazed at how Liz was able to cajole everyone into telling her their deepest secrets. In all her years with Kat, she never heard any of this.

"When Yola took over telling the story, things got juicy. She claimed they fought all the time. Celeste was always reminding Duke that her father loathed him and warned her not to marry a cheap gangster. She blamed him for her father's death soon after they were married, insisting he died of a broken heart, and regularly called him a murderer."

Ironic, thought Roxy, considering what later happened.

"The small inheritance she received when her father died, she kept in a special account, never even telling Duke where it was.

"Everyone agreed that while Celeste would alternately spoil and ignore Frankie, she always resented Kat. Duke considered his daughter the most precious jewel in his life, even more important than the son who bore his name and the responsibility for keeping the Tomasso dynasty alive, which is very strange in Italian culture. Their close relationship infuriated Celeste, who was pointedly excluded.

"Duke always treated his wife with elaborate politeness, giving her a generous allowance but no independent finances. She had her interests: charities and clubs based primarily in Newport. Neither Duke nor any of his family were ever invited along. Although they never came right out and said it, 'the aunts' made it clear that Duke never slept with Celeste again after Frankie was conceived. When I asked them what they thought was going on since I was sure their brother was as remarkable and virile as they described, they hemmed and hawed then explained that divorce was unthinkable in Italian families of Duke's generation. Besides, divorcing Celeste would lose Duke the one thing he wanted, entry into Yankee society especially for Kat.

"Apparently Duke and his cronies, maybe even some of 'the aunts' husbands, obeyed strict rules about marriage and what was permissible or not. The boys had a string of girlfriends. They may have even passed them around, according to one aunt—the short one named Carmella. They would go out on Friday night to clubs where they would never have taken their wives. It was the boys and their bimbos. None of it ever came home. There were no threatening phone calls, no throwing over of family life for some sweet young thing. Everyone knew the rules.

"Now here's where it gets real interesting," Liz lowered her voice although they were alone in the house. "When Kat and Frankie were old enough not to need a live-in babysitter, Duke married Yola off to one of his childhood friends, Joey De Palma, and built them that house in the compound.

"Did you notice how the kitchen and large family eating room are in Yola's house, not Duke's mansion? And how the two houses open onto a single court-yard?" Liz paused knowingly. Roxy admitted the few times over the years she had been in attendance at Tomasso family events it was so tumultuous and con-fusing she had no idea where in the compound she was. Liz gave no further indication of what she considered implications of the architecture, continuing with the story.

"Joey came back from Vietnam in a wheelchair and Duke sent him to ac-counting school, then set him up as Tomasso Excavating's chief finance officer. Not long after they were married, Yola had Mario and asked Kat, who was about fourteen at the time, to be his godmother. They grew up as one big happy family."

Roxy did find this interesting. It was remarkable how seldom adult friends ever discussed family matters and childhood.

"Apparently all this tribal behavior pushed Celeste over the edge and she de-manded that Duke buy her a house in Newport, in her name. For all intents and purposes she lived there, seeing Kat and Frankie through their schools and on summer trips to Europe."

"Kat spent summers in Europe with her mother?" Roxy asked astonished. Although she knew Kat had traveled widely, she always assumed it was as an adult on her own or with Max, never with her mother.

"I don't know the details of how often Kat actually went along. We'll have to ask her that. Anyway, that's not what's important. What's important is that it all fits."

"What fits? What are you thinking in that twisted and deviant mind?"

"C'mon."

Liz jumped up from her chair and grabbed Roxy dragging her to the front of the house. They went into the living room and stood in front of the portrait of Duke hanging over the fireplace.

"Mario's a beautiful young man, literally beautiful, especially those liquid brown eyes. He doesn't get those from Yola. Have you ever met Joey De Palma?" Roxy nodded but could not have described his eyes.

"I knew a lot of those boys who came back from the war with mine damage.

They didn't go around fathering children within weeks of their arriving home wounded." She looked up again at the portrait of Duke.

"I think this is Mario's father and that Duke replaced Celeste with Yola as the wife of his heart. Do you know anything about his will?"

Roxy gaped at her. This was too bizarre to even consider.

Liz gave her a disdainful look from under her long lashes.

"Obviously this never occurred to you."

"Why should it? Why should I assume that Kat's campaign manager is really her illegitimate brother and that her father built a house so his girlfriend could live there with her family next to him and his wife and kids? That's crazy! Stuff like that only happens in soap operas."

"Sorry, Miss-sophisticated-writer-of-virginal-teenage-novels, but you should have spent more time behind the bar with your ol' auntie Liz because then you would know how many children grow up believing some totally unrelated person is their parent. Remember your biology. Only the mother is guaranteed, fathers are always open to speculation. Not everyone is as faithful to their sexual partner as you are, Roxy." Liz smirked then added, "I think we need to investigate this further."

"What do you mean, investigate?" Roxy shouted.

Liz began muttering to herself as she wandered back to the kitchen.

"I'll bet Kat doesn't know or even suspect. I wonder if Mario knows? Yola obviously knows."

"You can't be serious about this," Roxy followed her.

"Not only am I serious, I'm so certain I'm right I'll bet you a hundred dollars! I think Kat doesn't know and, what's more, doesn't want to know." Liz looked shrewdly at her. "She and Mario couldn't be any closer than they are now. He obviously adores her and the feeling seems to be mutual. Finding out he was her brother wouldn't make much difference unless, of course, she was planning to release her sexual tension with him."

Roxy howled in disbelief.

"Only kidding," Liz grinned.

★ ★ ★ ★ ★

Kat was counting the hours until she could escape the oppressive heat and humidity of Washington and get back to the ocean. This was the result of allowing Virginians to choose the location of the nation's capital. Here she was, arguably in the center of the world, and it was a steaming swamp. During these tense stretches she realized how essential the tide and sea were in regulating her naturally erratic rhythms. The ocean was her pulse as much as it was Rhode Island's.

She had been at the Capitol since dawn, blessing Roxy as she changed a few words then printed out the several speeches and statements her friend had prepared. Scrolling through the AP wire, she heard noise in the outside office and felt a tight band settling around her head as she rose to summon her press secretary for the early morning meeting she requested.

Jasmine had to be confronted with her treachery although Kat was prepared to offer her a final chance to work with, not against, the campaign. She owed the woman that much.

No one else knew of the debt she felt and Kat prayed there would never be a need to tell them. She would not forget the emotional solace Jasmine provided her when they met at a weekend workshop soon after Duke died. She regretted it had gone as far as it did but she was desperate for a loving connection. She felt terribly betrayed by her father when he died suddenly, leaving her alone and unprotected. Kat was too raw with pain to allow any man near her.

Almost four years later, Hayes recruited Jasmine with her impeccable credentials and impressive skills for the job of Kat's press secretary. He knew nothing of their prior relationship. During the interview Jasmine offered to withdraw from consideration but Kat brushed aside her reluctance. She felt no threat, believed her preferences were clearly understood. She admired both the quality of the woman's work and strength of her devotion to shared causes—particularly with regards to empowering women in the political field. She had no misgivings until T.J. Stuart became involved in the campaign and her press secretary began acting like a jealous lover.

Now Jasmine was enmeshed in moral betrayal if not political sabotage and Kat found herself struggling with a vague sense of guilt. She composed her face, transformed herself into a true New Englander, willing irrelevant emotions into a back corner of her mind. She called Jasmine into her office. Her only hope for saving the woman was to confront her with the truth. She believed villains were created and given power by cowardice, by denying truth and seeking blindness.

A calm alertness settled her mind as she weighed the cold, wary look in Jasmine's dark eyes peering over her glasses, the tight frown on her narrow face. Kat knew this was a liberating choice. She would present Jasmine with the truth, offer her the chance to redirect her loyalties back to the campaign, and if she failed, cut her off with no regrets.

"I know about your relationship with Carrie, that you talk with her about activities here and on the campaign. I know you told her about seeing me with Senator Stuart. She works for Race Scarlatti and reports everything you tell her to him. In case you don't know, he's a major crime boss in New England. I know he's holding almost fifty thousand dollars in gambling IOUs from you." She waved away the denial Jasmine began to make. "Whomever you think that money is owed to, it is actually Scarlatti. And don't deny you gamble. I know about the horse races, the poker games in Middleburg and Georgetown.

"I cannot have Race Scarlatti own my press secretary. He is a corrupt and dangerous man. Your loyalty must be only to me and this campaign or you must leave. I want your promise that you will no longer compromise the campaign by contacting Carrie in any way. And you must become free of Scarlatti."

Kat handed her a piece of paper.

"Gamblers Anonymous. Get help. If you need money to pay off your debts, I would consider loaning it to you. I'll go with you to tell your father, if you want." Kat's voice softened and she looked steadily at Jasmine whose pinched face and thin body contorted with conflicting emotions too powerful for her to voice.

"I know what's behind this, Jasmine. I don't believe you want to sabotage the campaign or my election to the Senate. I need your help now more than ever. Rhode Island and the Senate need your help." As she read the agreement, the shame on Jasmine's face, she made her final point. It had to be spoken.

"Because of what you told Carrie about Stuart, Scarlatti has threatened to kill him. Race does not make idle threats. Having a U.S. senator executed because you think he lusts after me is not beneficial to anyone's cause. Stop lashing out at men through Senator Stuart. Leave him alone."

"He wants to own you, to make you a diversion for his ego. He has no respect for your power and accomplishments," Jasmine attacked.

Kat shook her head sadly, pity welling in her gray eyes.

"I'm sorry you've been embittered by your wounds. But the reality is that a free woman is not defined by her relationship to a man. Independence makes her devotion to him a valuable gift. Humans are divided into two categories and great miracles arise when the two halves come freely together."

"What are you saying?" Jasmine screamed. "You think you're going to stroll hand-in-hand into the glowing sunset with that wild man, the master manipulator, and not end up on your knees—or your back—as his slave."

Eyes blazing, Kat moved from behind her desk and stood facing her press secretary. She could see the dark gleam in Jasmine's eyes. The Maenads, she thought, female cannibals who devoured men to protect themselves. There was no way Jasmine could ever appreciate the grandeur that drew her to Stuart. She fought back a primitive urge to reach out and choke her.

"You want to turn me over to Race Scarlatti to be truly owned and exploited in a manner that surpasses even your most degraded idea."

As Jasmine attempted to sputter a denial, Kat pushed her onto the couch, stood over her threateningly and waved her silent. In a voice that built to a chilling anger, Kat told her the graphic details of her encounters with Race. She spared none of the brutal horror or her own feelings of shame and violation. Jasmine was shaking uncontrollably, sobbing on the couch when Kat finished.

"That's what you condemn me to if you plot with Carrie, owe huge debts to Race, and incite them against Stuart." Her whisper raked Jasmine's nerves with its barely restrained rage.

"I need Stuart. He is strong and often hard but he has honor and a clear mind. Leave him alone. It's non-negotiable. He is no threat to my independence either politically or personally."

She pulled the woman to her feet and shoved her toward the door.

"Those are my demands. Agree or get out." Her voice was as harsh and bleak as her emotionless face. "No more contact with Carrie. Free yourself from any debt to Scarlatti. And leave Stuart alone!"

Jasmine fled from the office, slamming the door behind her. Kat slumped against it, squeezing her eyes closed, watching brilliant flashes in her head. She had to remind herself that the power in darkness and rage was authentic, another face of the goddess. It was the power of Kali—chaos—dancing with the lord until the world would shake itself to pieces.

★ ★ ★ ★ ★

The issues project gave Roxy reason for reinstituting daily phone conversations with Hayes. Although she felt no weakening in her resolve to devote herself to Jake and the sex magic, she was not one to willingly limit her options when it came to men. She wanted to talk about Superfund toxic waste sites in South County. Hayes was totally absorbed in Iraq's invasion of Kuwait.

"She almost blew it on this one, he explained in exasperation. "Fortunately Senator Stuart managed to drag her back from the edge."

According to her chief of staff, Kat returned from a Republican House-Members-only briefing on the invasion raging about the perverse blindness of the past two administrations in developing a national energy policy that now put the U.S. in the position of having to defend a corrupt royal family because they sat on a sizeable percentage of the world's oil supply. She added attacks on the hypocrisy of policy makers who built Iraq's forces as a bulwark against the Iranian religious crazies, then used as their justification for alarm at the invasion the fact that Iraq, by some mysterious means, had become the fourth largest army in the world.

"I was upset because I knew this was a repeat performance. She'd probably voiced those same criticisms at the briefing. The Republican leadership was still miffed at her for refusing to support the Panama invasion. Stuart arrived as she was preparing to return a stack of press calls. He was not a happy man. He pushed Kat into her office and indicated I should join them, I assume so he would be restrained from slapping her silly. I stayed for the first couple rounds then Stuart asked me to leave. You'll have to find out from Kat what went on then."

Roxy added this to her ever-growing list of Kat mysteries that she despaired of ever solving. In the past several months, Kat had become expert at dodging questions. Persistence only earned a sharp rebuke. Roxy had given up probing. Of course with Liz, master interrogator, now on the scene, the situation could change.

Hayes summarized Stuart's arguments.

"He began by insisting we could not stand by and allow such naked aggression, that the Saudis could be the next to fall, and that an Iraq on the move could stir the Israelis to apocalyptic actions. He had her almost convinced until he stated his basic principle of foreign policy, that other countries must believe if they do something evil we will step on them, big or small. That triggered one of her random skips of logic and she launched into a speech on how world service does not mean being everyone's policeman.

"Stuart glared at her for about three sentences worth of polemics, then walked over and grabbed her arm, hard. When he finally let go I could see the imprint of his hand. She was so shocked she stopped in mid-sentence and he began talking, very deliberately as if he were warning some ten-year old in mid-tantrum to stop and behave or else." As Hayes turned away to answer a quick question to someone on his end, Roxy wiggled in her seat.

"Now where was I?"

"What did he say?"

"Oh yes. Stuart had hold of her arm and he reminded her the Senate committee had almost a million dollars invested in her race and that he was there to protect it. She was expected as a Republican running for the U.S. Senate to show some respect to her president and her party. She claimed to be a scientist, she should wait until there was more information before proclaiming her theory.

"Kat snapped back at him. 'I heard them this morning. I know what our recent history has been. I understand the politics of oil. I have the information I need.' Then he let go of her arm and stepped back asking her pointedly: 'Do you?'

"At this point he politely asked me to leave. 'I have some classified information to share with the congresswoman.'

"Whatever he told her changed her mind. When he came out he called me into the hall and said she had agreed to wait for more information before making any statements on the invasion. 'The deal is, she has no position but wait and see, give the President a chance, so on and so on, until I come to Rhode Island. That's less than two weeks. I want you to be certain she lives up to that deal. If anything in Kuwait changes drastically, I'll contact you. I'll be out-of-pocket until then.'"

"Out-of-pocket? What does that mean?" Roxy interrupted.

"Unreachable."

"Where's he going?"

"I don't know. He offered no explanation and I asked for none but if I had to guess, I'd say the Middle East.

"Kat came out a few minutes after he left and essentially told me the same thing. Then she left for your doorstep where she'll be arriving in about half an hour. I sure hope she was organized and packed last night; she looked lucky to know where her hands and feet were when she left here."

Roxy was trying to absorb all this when Hayes dropped another bomb.

"Our big strategy session is being scheduled to coincide with Stuart's visit to Rhode Island. I'll be flying up with him and probably stay through the next day. Pencil me in, Roxy. I won't accept no for an answer."

He was spending entirely too much time with Senator Stuart she thought, as her mind raced over the endless possibilities for conflict from having Hayes in the state.

★ ★ ★ ★ ★

Since she was planning to walk with Kat the first day, Roxy only stood by the seawall and checked the ocean for portents. All she saw was seaweed strewn everywhere on the beach, torn up from reefs and ocean floors by the hurricane and swept onto shore. Legions of seagulls were feeding on the noodle-like, brown vegetation. Crews were out raking up the southern end of the beach, massing the seaweed into huge ten foot piles, free for the taking just as the City Council said.

She walked from Watch Hill to Narragansett with Kat, the four-day excursion being enough to give her the flavor she needed. When even heavy doses of homeopathy did not relieve her strained muscles, she willingly accepted Kat's direction to stay in Narragansett and base the operation with Liz. The issue papers had been well-received and Kat wanted more.

Liz had also organized two support activities for the walk: flooding phone-in radio talk shows with pro-Kat calls, and generating dozens of letters which would be given to field organizers who then passed them on to letter writing circles of volunteers. Liz would eventually receive a dated copy of the letter with the sender's name so she could track them; the average turn-over was two days. Roxy called in to the radio shows until the day Jake recognized her voice, though she identified herself as Ramona from Warren. He called in immediately after praising her profusely and wanting to know how he could meet such an astute lady. After that, she stuck to writing letters.

Time mattered to those who worked only some of it. Time lost all meaning for Roxy when she worked around the clock. It was the mode in which she wrote her novels. She would emerge every so often and peer around, blinking, wondering what month it was, what kind of day: a Monday, a Thursday? Liz fit into the grueling schedule easily. A restaurant was continual work, divided into critical hours and busy times but unrelated to starting on Monday morning and ending Friday afternoon.

Liz elevated Kat's cousin Diane, a fourteen-year-old fussbudget, to keeper of the walk record.

"She's a worker," Liz proclaimed vehemently. "Not one of those blister kids who shows up when the hard work is done."

Dozens of news clippings, all with photos, spread out from the walk plan as it snaked along the wall at headquarters. No scrap of memorabilia or publicity escaped being transfigured into art.

The *Ocean Beacon* newspaper chain was off to a slow start, so press still flowed in Kat's favor. When the *Beacon* did cover her walk with unflattering photographs, there was no way to hide the large crowds. Interviews with disgruntled voters sounded contrived. Kat learned the truth in the conventional wisdom that it is more difficult to hit a moving target. Dodging tough questions was easier when the reporter had to run to keep up with her long strides. The quick answers they had developed for attacks, and the simple statements from Roxy's issue papers were ideal.

Seemingly released from any urge to fairness by what they perceived as the Douglas inspired bias of the *Beacon* against Kat, the remaining press was soon treating the walk as a triumphant march. Responding to the tide they saw flowing clearly in their direction, Kat's team threw in all their cute ideas and gimmicks. Who knew when the bloodletting would start and there would be no room for fun?

They took to sitting around the kitchen table early morning and late night when it was just the three of them. "Three hearts beating as one" as Kat had promised the previous winter. Once the business of the day was complete, mostly finalizing and reviewing walk segments, they would engage in more far-ranging discussions usually prodded by Liz's speculations and fueled by the food treats she always had available.

"Why do you do all this?" Liz asked Kat one night.

"Sometimes I feel I live in more than one time. History was my academic framework, but it's the future that draws me, it's the era in which I would choose to live. Since I can see the shape of the ideal future, I feel a duty and obligation to do the work necessary to accomplish it. It's not a philosophy that can be easily explained. Wanting to change the world is how people describe it. But that's not completely accurate. I'm not looking simply to change things. I seek the satisfaction of uncovering the pattern, seeing it emerge perfectly because I'm playing the part I should play, completing my section of the design. Duke would tell me repeatedly that I was a lucky little girl. 'You've been gifted by the angels' he would say as he held me on his lap. 'And you'll be expected to make good use of those gifts.'"

Another night they talked about men. Roxy was terrorized by the whole topic since she knew Liz was accumulating information to plan her assault on Kat regarding Stuart. Plus she had taken to staging a major campaign against Hayes.

"I gave him a pop quiz and he failed," she claimed mysteriously soon after arriving.

"All he really wants is a pocket pussy, and you should be shooting for something better than that." Liz would watch while Roxy talked with him on the phone and if she saw the parted lips and glazed eyes she claimed Roxy assumed when he was sweet-talking her, she would slip in the tape of all Jake's commercials and start playing them.

"What a job I have this weekend," she told Roxy that afternoon. "Keeping you in Jake's bed and out of Hayes' and trying to get Kat into Stuart's."

Roxy would do anything to disappear Liz, just for the weekend.

"Let's start with Roxy. She's had more hands up her skirt than the Muppets. But when you insist on your lovers coming in pairs, the numbers add up fast. Roxy's never learned she doesn't have to sleep with every man who gives her a wide-on."

"I don't, unless they ask."

"Of course, to you a raised eyebrow or a wink is asking. Men are lust, Roxy. It's an instinct. They don't expect continual satisfaction."

She glowered at Liz, hoping Kat would not wonder what two men she was consorting with now. Of course, she could honestly affirm that there were no two men at this moment. Who knows what the situation would be when Hayes arrived?

"I have to marvel at the fact that Roxy seems so easily able to find the men she needs particularly since her standards are so high. They have to have moist in their voice. Actually, if my observations are accurate, only one of the pair has to meet that requirement, the other serves as her shield. Roxy likes to hedge her bets."

"That's not true, Liz. You're exaggerating," Roxy snorted.

"OK, OK, whatever you say. So you tell us. What do you want in a man?"

"I want them to stay interesting longer."

"Or just plain stay longer?" Liz joked.

"No, I'm always ready for them to go."

"Go? Who are you kidding? They don't go anywhere. You get more Valentines than anyone I've ever known and that includes Patsy Shunney who was the cutest girl in my second grade class." Liz loved to harass her. Roxy ignored it and plowed ahead.

"I don't want to be a madonna or a sex toy. I don't want to be a servant or prized possession. I want to be all those things and more at different times. In my case that seems to mean different men. Fundamentally, I'm polygamous. I prefer an erotic smorgasbord. Today's lax divorce laws are moving us towards serial polygamy which is a step in the right direction. It would be more honest simply to promise 'til completion do us part' than to lie in marriage vows and suffer the consequent torture of divorce when all expectations of forever are shattered."

"If you consider marriage useless, how come you're so moral about married men?"

Roxy was surprised at Kat's question.

"I don't like men who lie," she answered quickly.

Liz did not want to dwell on the subject of romantic ethics.

"What about you Kat? What do you want in a man?"

There was a serious expression on Kat's face as she answered.

"I want one who is not afraid of my completeness, who sees it as worthy and equal to his own. With a whole man, I can be a whole woman and see myself reflected in him. I want to be honored as well as loved, and I want to honor and love in return. There must be both self-reliance, which can be a lonely state, and mutuality. I want to exchange and fuse with him knowing I can give and receive in equal measure. This is the only plausible goal of sex in a world with two genders."

"Well, I'm glad to hear you mention that dread three-letter word. I was beginning to think politics had turned you into a nun."

Kat laughed.

"For the record Liz, sex is a critical factor in my choice of a man. Like Homer's ancient legend about the marriage of the god and goddess, I want to lay in my beloved's arms in a bower of flowers covered by a golden cloud from which a glistening rain of dewdrops falls."

"That's great unless you have hay fever," Liz responded as they all laughed. "As for me, I want a man who says please and leaves money on top of the dresser. One who considers it a gourmet meal when I cook in a black garter belt and high heels."

It was the night before the Back Room interview, a legendary weekly press conference with a political figure conducted in the seedy back room of Bert's Lunch and Tap in Providence. The three women talked about how they looked and what they were wearing that summer.

"I brought several of these sleeveless knit tank dresses in bright colors for me and Roxy to wear. We'll be twins all summer. Actually we'll be triplets since I make two of Roxy."

Liz had a plan for something, it showed in her eyes as she watched Kat. She praised the uniform Kat had created for the walk at Gould's suggestion. Begging favors from fabric artists she knew, Kat had several off-white cotton dresses silk screened with varying versions of her Kiley for Senate blue star logo. She wore them daily. The official volunteers they recruited, who by now composed the merest fringe on the huge crowds that accompanied the walk, wore the basic Kiley shirts.

The next day's interview was critical. It would be one of the few times Kat was not in motion and could be pinned down. Pro-Douglas reporters from the *Beacon* would be there en masse. Mario expected an attack but had no idea of the direction from which it would come.

"I think it's extremely important how you look." Liz launched her idea. "No more innocent angel, we need to toughen you up. You need to look like a sharp career woman able to whip those boys in Washington into shape. You need a haircut, and I have just the thing in mind."

Before Kat could protest, Liz hauled a large bag from under the table and handed Kat her oversized hand mirror as she began brushing through the mass of curls.

"I can't believe how much hair you have. A little tough and wiry, but the right cut will help that. It certainly has that live and shining look that only natural color hair has. I'd have them lined up at the beauty shop if I could produce black this dark and still keep those blue tones when the sun shines on it. That's how you can tell when black hair is dyed: flat color, no tones."

Kat looked at herself in the small mirror.

"It's an inheritance from my father. He barbered his hair so there would be no curls but it was so thick he could easily carry around pencils in it. And his hair was 'black as ravens wings' he would say. He claimed it was a color found only in certain gene pools clustered around the Mediterranean."

"I used to have nice thick hair, too, when I was younger. My mom would have me kneel in front of her big red chair every night and she would wind my hair into huge sausage curls. Once I got control, I did all kinds of strange stuff to it and now look what I'm stuck with." Liz pulled at her over-teased and frosted hair.

"If I'd known I was going to live this long, I would've taken better care of myself."

While Kat was laughing, Liz began snipping at her hair.

"Roxy, of course, is Goldilocks. Her hair is perfect and all she does is let it hang there. Occasionally I have to drag her in and trim the ends but that's all she allows. The original drip-dry kid. For someone who's so interested in getting laid, she puts little time and effort into paint and powder. I suppose that's wise. All it would do is come off on the sheets, when she uses sheets, or even beds."

Roxy ignored Liz's jibes. She had become used to it ages ago and knew it was meant as affectionate idle conversation. Kat seemed oblivious to the pile of pitch black coils accumulating on the floor around her chair. When Liz finally finished, she picked up the hand mirror again and stared into it. The same amazed expression reflected on three faces. She looked chic, stylish, and—no denying it—beautiful.

Liz thinned and cut her hair so it was full and bouncy on the top, with tapered curls scattered across her broad forehead and hanging demurely along her cheeks. The back was razor cut short along her neck, leaving several shy tails streaming across her shoulders. With the mass of hair removed, her magnificent gray eyes dominated her face. The lines of her angular cheeks were softened by the curls and the absence of the dark cloud of hair that cast her pale skin in such contrast.

She gingerly shook her head.

"I feel so light. So unburdened."

She fluffed up the top fullness and smoothed her hand across the short back. Finally, she smiled at Liz and handed her the mirror.

"Thank you. It's perfect. And thanks for just going ahead and doing it. I would never have agreed."

"Now hopefully, we won't have to listen to complaints about your hair anymore, or politely accept everyone's suggestions for a good hairdresser," Roxy crowed with glee.

★ ★ ★ ★ ★

The Back Room interview was scheduled to be broadcast live on Wednesday. Kat planned to use the occasion to declare the walk a success.

Liz dressed and made her up for the interview. Roxy never caught her at it but she was certain Liz was conspiring with Gould on Kat's "senatorial" look. Her lipstick was a soft rose, subtle shading around her eyes made them appear even more luminous. She wore a soft blue shantung dress with a narrow skirt and stand-up collar. The impressionistic blue and green print of the swingy, semi-fitted, yoked jacket with long sleeves contrasted perfectly. A delicately carved cameo was pinned at her throat. No one recognized her when she walked into Bert's.

After brushing off the host journalist's comments about her changed image with the response that walking the state in the heat of summer required a short and easy haircut, she launched into proclaiming the walk a success, inviting everyone to join her somewhere along the route. One by one she defused the standard gossip questions that seemed to be the prime concern of both the media and the public they served. Mario claimed political gossip was an addictive substance for people in the small state.

"It intoxicates them," he declared. "And because they all feel they know you personally, they believe it's their right to talk about you in the most intimate terms."

She gave her agreed-upon response to Iraq's actions then took the first question on the recently nominated Supreme Court Justice. As a senator, she would vote on such nominations.

"As with Iraq, I plan to wait for more information before venturing an opinion, particularly since in the case of the Supreme Court nomination, I am not able now to vote on the matter. However, my support would require his recognition of the Bill of Rights as absolute protection for privacy and the integrity of the individual."

There were no journalists left with questions except for the *Beacon*'s chief hatchet man. The aroma of frying onions and sausage was beginning to work on Kat's stomach. She hoped his questions would be brief so she could eat before moving to her next event.

"Congresswoman Tomasso, you've never dealt with charges that you employ rather questionable scheduling techniques in your campaign, consulting with an astrologer and magician." Roxy felt her heart stop as she remembered how Kat responded when Stuart asked this question the day that ended with the glass-throwing. She quickly looked around and saw no glasses within Kat's reach.

Totally ignoring the gray haired man with a scarred face who asked the question, Kat leaned over to the host, the state's most popular local television anchor, and said in a stage whisper, "What if I admitted I can see the future?"

Recovering instantly, he quipped, "I'd ask you who was going to win the World Series?"

Kat sat back in the chrome framed chair looking pleased.

"Not the New York Yankees," she said.

Several moments of silence filled the packed room as the zen lesson dawned on slow wits. Seeing a few glimmers of realization, Kat looked directly into the camera.

"Everyone wants their fortune told, wants to know about themselves and their future. Everyone is superstitious, no matter how sophisticated they pretend to be."

The gray-haired man followed up.

"You don't find it unusual to have a U.S. Senate candidate who uses fortune telling techniques?"

"Obviously, the only unusual aspect is my acknowledging it."

Magic became another dead issue and the anchor made jokes that evening on the news calling her Glenda after the good witch in the *Wizard of Oz*.

The *Beacon* man was not finished yet.

"Do you have plans to debate Senator Douglas so we can have a full understanding of your stance on the issues?"

Kat's mouth tightened. She bit back her true reason: debating Douglas would acknowledge him as an equal candidate, a position that would degrade both her and the race she was running. Instead, she smiled sweetly.

"It would be a boring debate since my candidate seems to have nothing to talk about but me."

She stared at the reporter as if daring him to probe the subject further but he had other directions in mind. When the attack came, in the final question of the day, it was surprising because it was so obvious. The reporter prefaced his question with promising a racist chairing Judiciary, a hawk on Foreign Relations, and an oil man heading up Environment. As he rambled on in this vein pointing out the fundraising assistance she was receiving from the Senate committee and speculating if this were linked to her silence on U.S. plans for Kuwait, Kat began to wonder what the punch line was.

"And now we discover you're bringing in to campaign for you one of the most radically conservative members of the U.S. Senate and a man devoted to pre-eminence of the Republican Party regardless of cost."

Kat almost laughed. They were attacking her on Stuart. She began to make a flip remark then became wary when she thought about Jasmine and Scarlatti and if this was more than political.

"Republican senators pride themselves on their willingness to campaign for promising candidates. Senator Stuart is particularly interested in electing more women to the U.S. Senate. He has been enormously helpful in my campaign without making any demands related to my political positions. My independence is well-known among members of my party including our esteemed president. Senator Stuart and the others who are concerned about counting Republicans and Democrats know that when it comes to the final count, I am an automatic vote in no one's column but Rhode Island's."

She allowed herself a controlled smile.

"I believe there are lists demonstrating that I have consistently voted against the president more than any other House Republican and all but three Democrats. And I do so, not from a spirit of rebellion, but because I am in Washington to represent the people of this state, not one or another political party. I will not waste our final few minutes reciting the many issues on which I feel both free to and justified in opposing the administration although environmental and women's concerns lead the list. The task of Rhode Island voters, as well as those throughout the nation, is to elect the one hundred best people to the U.S. Senate, regardless of party.

"In regards to Senator Stuart of Virginia, I think you might be surprised by some of his ideas and invite all of you to see for yourself. He'll be having a press conference on Thursday when he arrives at Green Airport. Our full campaign schedule will be available to you tomorrow."

Kat smiled into the camera as the director indicated time was up. She would have to warn Stuart he was their current target, and pray that he saw fit to behave.

★ ★ ★ ★ ★

The strangest aspect of this new phase of the campaign came in her dreams. It was but the vaguest of feelings, a wisp of memory when she awoke. Roxy began regularly to dream that there was someone, or several someones, involved in the campaign that she knew nothing about. And they were important. The feeling was so real she found herself one day at campaign headquarters checking over finance reports to make sure no one new had been added to the staff. These are dreams, she reminded herself. They are not to be taken literally.

15

The Knight of Swords
August

Rhode Island

It was the type of coincidence that happens in mythic tales, not in real life. There was a major crisis at Magnolia's. It was one of the biggest weekends of the resort season in Morgan Springs, and hours of frantic phone calls back and forth had convinced an adamantly resistant Liz that she had to fly there the next day.

"This is all your doing, Roxy, I know it is. You don't fool me with that innocent face and those whiskey-colored eyes. You pretend that you're only indulging Max and Kat when you play at magic but you're probably the biggest witch of all. You don't want me here this weekend watching you, keeping you away from ol' horny Hayes. Horny Hayes ruttin' Roxy. I'm turning into a poet, it must be the company. Maybe I can use it in a song."

As Liz began belting out a plaintive whiner of a country tune, playing air guitar while gyrating her abundant body, Roxy cut more melon into a bowl. It was easier to keep the pleased expression off her face when she was eating.

"You know I had nothing to do with this. Don't you believe the crisis is real?"

Liz stomped and huffed around the kitchen, checking the bread she was baking so Roxy and Kat would not starve while she was gone.

"Oh, it's real all right. I knew they couldn't get through a month without calling me back. In fact, I won five hundred dollars in the pool my bar manager set up on how long they could go on without me. I picked thirteen days. No one else wanted it, they thought it was unlucky. Guess I fooled them. Thirteen days practically to the hour." A smug tone crept into her voice and she batted her long lashes, rolling her eyes upward.

"See, you probably did this yourself by picking thirteen days."

There was only a pair of hearts beating. Kat went immediately to bed when she arrived back at the house. The next day would be a hard and busy stretch of walk from East Greenwich to the Warwick mall. And then there was the weekend. Roxy's tiny mouth was barely visible as she again suppressed a smile. Not that Liz's absence solved the problem of Hayes being in Rhode Island, but it did remove a substantial irritant.

"I expect you to carry on in my place getting Kat together with Stuart," Liz ordered.

Roxy rolled her eyes and picked at the ever-present bowl of lobster salad.

Liz grilled her about the schedule for Friday and Saturday, the days Stuart was to be campaigning in the state.

"This is a very detailed schedule from his press conference at the airport to the fundraiser at the winery," she said, waving the printed schedule. "But it doesn't say anywhere where the principals are sleeping Friday night. When I asked Mario, he claimed Gretta was taking care of the senator's arrangements."

Gretta was Stuart's aunt who ran both his Senate office and Capitol Hill house.

"Then he said Hayes could stay with him unless he preferred to stay here." Liz shot her an accusing stare.

"Believe it or not Liz, I'm not interested in having temptation flaunted in my face. I asked Mario to let Hayes stay with him. And I don't know where Stuart is staying. I haven't asked Kat and she's said nothing to me. Somehow I can't imagine anyone would think it was appropriate for him to stay here. Anyone but you, that is.

"I keep telling you Kat is not interested in a lover, she has a senate campaign to run," Roxy insisted.

"Really? Then why was she sitting in his pick-up truck letting Stuart lick her?"

"Who told you that?" Roxy snapped.

"Obviously not you!" Liz retorted.

The next morning Roxy was at the table as Liz caught Kat breezing through the kitchen to grab a quick glass of juice. She passed up fresh-from-the-oven peach coffee cake pleading a schedule of stops at breakfast places in East Greenwich. Kat expressed disappointment that Liz would miss meeting Senator Stuart and assured her that she understood Magnolia's had first claim on her time.

"I feel guilty sometimes that I'm pulling you away from your own business. You can't know how appreciative and glad I am that you're here. The idea of the walk alone puts me eternally in your debt, not to mention my haircut and all the fun we've had."

Kat wrote out a check for the airfare.

"The least I can do," she said.

Roxy caught Liz's eye and they realized simultaneously whose magic had manipulated events and sent her out of the way. A look of respect crept into Liz's face. She had always considered Kat naïve and easy to chump. Roxy wondered why Kat wanted Liz in Morgan Springs.

"She's too wrapped up in this silly political race to see what's best for her," Liz exploded after Kat left. "She doesn't want me here pushing her into Stuart's arms."

Roxy tried to be reasonable.

"Even if you're right and they should be together, given all the scandals and everyone watching don't you think it might be wise to wait just a couple more months? If you think Kat has to be tricked into all this then obviously it's not so compelling a drive that it can't be postponed."

"Projecting Roxy? The situation is not quite the same. Just because you're limiting your choice of flavors for a while doesn't prevent you from getting laid regularly. Besides, who knows what could happen in a couple months. Did Kat get some kind of letter saying it was guaranteed that she'd be alive and well the day after the election?" Liz's voice turned serious. "Didn't you read your fortune strip?"

She tossed the pale pink paper over to Roxy who had opened it the previous night and recited, "Some moments in time are too precious to lose."

Driving to the airport, she tuned out Liz's continuous stream of directions, hints, cajoling, and insistences that she take seriously the encouraging of romance between Kat and Stuart. Painted and primped to return to her role of Queen of Magnolia's, she tossed a final threat to Roxy.

"I'm going to call you Friday night and I'd better find out that you're sleeping alone and Kat's not."

★ ★ ★ ★ ★

It was the first time Kat walked on the beach with her in weeks. Roxy felt the difference. Kat had a psychic weight that somehow magnetized people like particles around her. Considering Liz's departure, she wondered if Kat was able to magnetize and rearrange particles of destiny into waves and patterns of her own choosing. She shivered when Kat began talking about magnetism.

"The water is negative and magnetic, the sand positive and electrical. Walking along an ocean shore is the ideal way to develop perfect electrical balance," she said as if resolving a profound discussion. "It reverses the damage caused by city tension which is all electric and positive. It also keeps the spine flexible."

Roxy confined herself to random observations on the gulls swooping around scavenging the beach, or the pair of small birds that soared and dove, barely skimming the sand in front of them. After several days of misty mornings with coastal fog often lasting until noon, it was a clear enough sky that Stuart would be able to fly in easily. When they reached the sand dunes past the club, Kat spoke about plans for the weekend.

"I've asked Yola to fix rooms for Hayes and Senator Stuart in the wing I keep at Frankie's house. I think that's acceptable and proper. They'll be far more comfortable there than in a hotel. Mario will meet us at the ball in Newport tonight and take them back with him. You and I can drive home to Narragansett. You can take Hayes to the airport the next morning while Mario and I go to Mass."

Roxy grabbed onto Kat's final statement as the easiest inquiry.

"Why are you going to Mass tomorrow? Is there a holy day I've somehow forgotten? It's not the Assumption is it?"

"It's the anniversary of Duke's death. My cousin John always says a special Mass for him at Holy Ghost."

Emptiness echoed through her voice and Roxy kept the silence as they walked back. Kat had offered her a way out of her quandary with Hayes and she was not about to ask any questions. At least Liz would have one of her conditions met. Roxy would be sleeping alone.

★ ★ ★ ★ ★

A battery of television cameras and crews, journalists and photographers filled the lounge area of the small Dynair terminal where private planes tied up at Green Airport. An aggressive young woman representing the *Ocean Beacon* ran onto the tarmac with her photographer to ambush Senator Stuart as he walked to the terminal from his plane. He laughed with Hayes, nodding to the approaching press, slipped on his jacket and tightened his tie. Two of Kat's volunteers brought up the rear carrying their bags.

Stuart was inundating the reporter with meaningless flight data as they walked through the terminal door. Totally absorbed in watching Hayes, Roxy noticed the look on his face first then saw it reflected in Stuart's. It took a moment for her to realize they were shocked at Kat's hair. And Kat was nervously watching them in return. In a split second Stuart was once again a man in control, kissed Kat's cheek lightly in greeting, then taking her arm, swept into the lounge to engage the press.

With a few easy quips and sharp answers, the senator had the initially suspicious audience eating out of his hand. When he revealed, in answer to a question from the *Beacon* reporter, that he had just returned from the Middle East, the men in the audience relaxed and seemed ready to trust him as an expert. The look in the women's eyes screamed hero.

Hayes slid alongside her, whispering his greetings and brushing his lips lightly along her cheek as he did.

"I have a present for you," he said, handing her a box. It took several minutes before Roxy could once again hear the press conference over the beating of her heart. This was going to be far more difficult than she thought.

Stuart shared his observations about the situation in Kuwait and his trust in the path the president was taking. Then he responded to a question attacking the notion of a Republican-controlled Senate.

"Look who the committee chairmen are now. We have a man under investigation for accepting illegal contributions heading up Banking, and one who sleeps through most hearings chairing Labor and Human Resources. This latter paragon of liberal causes is the main reason no child care bill has been reported from his committee in almost two years. I think your congresswoman is correct when she calls on the people of Rhode Island, and voters throughout the country, to elect to the U.S. Senate the hundred best legislators."

Stuart gestured to Kat. Her neat and stylishly cropped hair and trim seersucker suit with its shaped and fitted short jacket and slightly flared lower calf-length skirt gave her a crisp and professional air.

"The voters in Rhode Island are fortunate to have a choice in November that goes beyond the usual one of which disease to die of. You could have no finer senator than Kiley Tomasso."

They both answered a few more questions while the television crews were packing up. They had their sound bites: Stuart on Kuwait, on a Republican Senate, and calling Douglas a disease. Meanwhile, Roxy noted his line about no finer senator.

As she sat behind the wheel of the car, waiting for Hayes to finish loading their bags in the trunk, Roxy noticed Stuart in the back seat tentatively touch Kat's hair.

"At the advice of your media advisor, I assume. To make you look more 'senatorial'?"

Kat bridled and pulled at the tails of hair along her collar.

"Do you think it does? Make me look more 'senatorial'?"

"I liked the wildness. It was elemental. Your hair always looked uncontrollable or at best barely restrained. It's important to keep that spirit alive and remember we're mountain lions not sheep. Conformity is a harsh master. It's the same with legislation. The urge today is to control everything, and it's dangerous. People think new laws will improve their situation. They expect too much of both laws and the men and women who make them."

"Then why are we legislators?"

"I'm there to put my finger in the dike, to protect whatever individual freedom I can. I'm trying to reverse the trend of Americans being overregulated and under inspired."

"But you supported stringent ocean dumping regulations."

"I have as much coastline unable to protect itself as you do. There's a fine line between allowing license and limiting freedom. It's called responsibility and I'll work to legislate it properly if man's foolish behavior so requires. I want the question of whose freedom and whose responsibility answered wisely."

"Why are you a legislator?" he asked in return.

She looked at him searchingly, then said with a tinge of resignation, "The Earth needed my help, more help than I was able to give at Baywatch. Fortune swept me into Congress. I do my best."

"I'm glad to see the wildness isn't gone from your mind. I'll warn you though. The world hates a mind that thinks differently than its own and often destroys it in self-protection. You're a history scholar, remember Hypatia. I'd hate to find you sliced to ribbons at the bottom of a pile of seashells for refusing to compromise your clear vision. The limited view of an ignorant public can be fatal to brilliant philosophers."

Roxy felt the same shiver along her nerves as when Max made one of his oracular pronouncements.

★ ★ ★ ★ ★

Senator Stuart impressed the crowded dining room of the Turks Head Club filled with businessmen who had paid two hundred dollars to eat lunch with him. They were assured by his tailored navy suit and snowy white shirt, and by his personal success in business. First-hand observations on Kuwait launched him as a hero in their eyes as surely as it had with the press. He spent most of the speech lauding Kat for her various economic initiatives, emphasizing all the right points from Duke's business empire to her understanding of the links between environmental costs and economic measures. He turned a thoroughly convinced group over to Kat with the phrase he seemed to have chosen as his slogan: "Rhode Island could have no finer senator than Kiley Tomasso."

As they drove to headquarters for the long-awaited strategy session, the senator handed Kat several business cards explaining how much each had pledged him for her campaign.

"You should invite me more often."

Seeing the bemused expression on Kat's face, Roxy wondered how long she could tolerate Stuart upstaging her. Hayes obviously considered the senator the star of the weekend and Kat lucky to have him willing to lend her his shine. If the evening television news and papers portrayed that same attitude, Roxy shuddered to think of Kat's reaction.

★ ★ ★ ★ ★

While Kat was reviewing the impact of the walk by exhibiting the wall art that marked its progress, Roxy slipped upstairs to open her present. She felt her blood flash to the outermost edges of her skin as she ran her fingers across the soft folds of an emerald green cashmere sweater, the exact shade of green to match the flecks in her eyes. It was sleeveless with a deep-cut V neckline. She quickly pulled off her blouse and sighed as the supple knit tickled her skin. It was almost indecent and Roxy half-heartedly cursed Hayes for tempting her as she threw propriety to the wind and decided to wear it to the meeting. The gold heart locket she wore fit perfectly into the point of the V. Let him appreciate the view his gift created, she thought with a pleased smile. And sweat the fact that he could not touch.

She nearly collided with him as she darted toward the front meeting room. The harsh look on his face faded as he saw his gift so flatteringly displayed and he reached out to stroke her. Roxy danced away from his hand, and teased, "Eyes only, no touching."

The frown returned and he steered her back around the corner away from the assembling team.

"Why are we sleeping in different cities tonight?"

"It was Kat's idea," Roxy stumbled.

"Then we'll just have to find a few minutes to slip off while she and Stuart schmooze with all those rich socialites at the ball in Newport. I would've preferred the comfort and convenience of a bed, but…." he finished his comments by fondling her breasts in their new, soft fur and leaning down to kiss her.

Summoning all her will, Roxy slipped out of his arms and scurried down the hall to the meeting room. She was flushed and panting as she slid into a chair along the side wall then looked around the room to assure herself no one noticed her disordered entry. Her heart stopped when she saw Jake at the table with Gould, smiling at her. What was he doing here? Her brain numbed and nothing but static filled her ears as Hayes stalked in scowling. Life as she knew it was over. She was trapped. There was no way out. And then Kat began the meeting.

Kat yielded to Stuart her usual posture of pacing around the room and sat demurely at the table with Lila Gravely and her poll reports on her left. Introducing Jake, Kat nodded to Gould who explained his presence.

"Jake's become more than just a face and voice. Many of the ideas we're proposing for our second phase media are his and I thought he should be here to answer any questions. Kiley assured me Roxy keeps him up to speed on campaign strategy so he won't slow us down."

Disconcerted, Roxy pretended to examine the papers in her hands, peeking under her lashes only enough to catch Jake's pleased smile and the raised eyebrow Stuart gave her. Hayes must be bragging about his amorous adventures to his hero, Roxy thought dismayed. Now who knows what the senator would think?

Kat instructed Lila to begin with the poll numbers which had been assembled on the plane. No one on the team had even a hint although Stuart stood by the window flipping through the printed charts while Lila reviewed the trend beginning with their numbers against Winston last fall. Roxy knew something was amiss when she saw Stuart furrow his brow at the pages he held, then quickly look over at Kat, concern reflected on his face. He was only moments ahead of the rest of the team as Lila presented the bad news.

The numbers were down. For the first time since she announced, the trend reversed. Although Lila provided clear explanations of the causes and minimized the scale of change in attempted reassurance, Kat was clearly distressed.

"I've seen thousands of people in this past week, I've seen their faces, heard their voices. They love me," she exclaimed in disbelief. "They're in the streets, walking along the beaches with us, calling, writing letters. We've deflected every attack, turning some to our advantage. If the numbers are going down under these circumstances, what can we do to reverse the trend? How could we be doing more, or better? And how can I trust numbers that don't reflect what I'm feeling when I'm out there?"

Stuart interrupted Lila's response.

"Let me share a bit of wisdom I learned from my legendary predecessor about voters and love." He had that tone good storytellers project to get their audiences to settle in and listen up.

"I'd been working for him about a year and knew enough to realize he knew everything there was to know about masses of people and their behavior. We'd finished working the crowd at a large breakfast for state workers in Richmond. They loved him. He'd been their senator for years. It was obvious in the way they greeted him, they loved him. Thinking to impress him with my astute observation, I commented on how much they loved him. He pulled me aside so we could watch the passage of his opponent through the room. Although he was no threat to the senator's reign, he was on the ballot. They loved him. The same people who had pounded the senator's back pounded his opponent's with the same admiring smile. He put his arm around my shoulder and said, 'Well, Tommy Jeff'— he always called me Tommy Jeff in true southern fashion—'I'd say they loved him. Our job, boy, is to see that they vote for me.'"

He paused for effect, and to collect appreciative smiles, then sat down facing Kat. He spoke to directly to her, his voice low and thoughtful.

"The point is to take the love of a voter with a grain of salt. Take your polls the same way. Lila's explanations are right. You were impossibly high at seventy plus percent. There's no way to sustain such idolatry. You've taken some hits. Eggs thrown against a stone wall as your favorite Chinese general would say, but messy nonetheless.

"Plus, you and the other lady senate candidates I'm overseeing have been dealt a wild card. The impending war will drive every other concern off the front page. As I told you months ago, people may be prepared to trust protecting their families and the environment to you, but some of them will not follow Athena into battle, Maggie Thatcher and the Falklands aside. Especially not an Athena reluctant to brandish her sword. It's too bad I'm not running this year. But it doesn't matter. You have plenty of room to yield a few votes to ex-tank gunner Douglas. Of course, we could toughen up your position on Iraq a little."

Several heads that had been nodding and agreeing with Stuart's analysis stopped at this point. Mario and Jake agreed with Kat: a key part of the campaign was doing it differently. No altering positions because of a passing public whim. They were inspired by Kat's notion of transforming people's attitudes about politics by presenting a transformed candidate, one for whom getting out the right message was as determining a factor as winning. The pros in the room—Lila, Gould and Hayes—agreed with Stuart. Redirecting the message could regain those few lost points. For them, votes were the only thing that counted.

Kat's concern over dropping poll numbers slowly changed to irritation. She checked herself, masked her face with polite interest, and addressed the senator.

"Everyone else in the state seems enthralled with your views on the Middle East. Go ahead, let's hear your suggestions about what I should do."

Before Stuart could reply Hayes jumped in.

"It's important to understand how the local press and people in the state are seeing Senator Stuart so we can maximize the benefit and possibly pick up a few pointers."

Kat arched her eyebrows and shifted her gaze for the first time from Stuart to fix on her chief of staff with a calculating expression. Roxy flinched. Hayes was treading on thin ice. Kat agreed with Liz's assessment that loyalty was all-important.

"Besides his obvious personal charisma," Kat's eyebrows rose higher and the corner of one side of her mouth tilted slightly, "people here are attracted by the fact that he's a senator, a real senator acting like one. They have no senator right now. Winston's gone, Douglas has not yet shown up in Washington, and Morrison is one of those long-dead patrician ancients Rhode Islanders so love and haven't the heart to vote out. Stuart's fresh from the mysterious desert bringing them word on a conflict they've only begun to recognize as possibly dangerous to them. I'll bet they think he has clout."

Kat stiffened in reproach. The polls said that people ranked her lowest in having clout. "I appreciate Redcliffe's flattering analysis," Stuart chuckled, preparing to take back the floor. At the sound of his voice, Kat turned and her eyes blazed frustration and anger at him.

"If you could get that indignant about Saddam Hussein," he remarked, returning her look steadily, "We wouldn't have to be concerned about dropping poll numbers."

He directed his words to the group.

"I don't want to waste too much time hashing over Kuwait. Kiley's heard me say everything that should be said to the public. For your information, but not to leave this room, it's likely there will be no active conflict involving U.S. troops until after the election. Active conflict soon after is virtually guaranteed."

"That's what Max said in the spring. No war until after the election."

As soon as Roxy interrupted, she regretted it. Hayes looked like he wanted to reach over and clamp her mouth closed.

"Max predicted war last spring?" Stuart asked surprised.

Roxy nodded agreement.

"But he thought it was a preposterous idea. He did say no war until after November."

"I should find Max a place in the Pentagon or CIA. They could use his help, and his sources."

Kat's frustration burst out.

"I don't understand why we're talking about war. All you boys can think of is fighting. This conflict about oil has none of the nobility of the dissolution of the Berlin Wall and that came down without a shot. Is it so difficult to absorb the lesson that there are no winners in war games, that the only way to win is not to play?

"This isn't about the warrior ethic either. There are accountants in the Pentagon figuring out how we can make money fighting this war; what other countries we can get to pay us for defending the oil. We all know it's about oil, and I think there are other ways to deal with that issue. Energy efficiency for one. No one was interested when I talked about eco-security and the dangers of dependency on certain natural resources."

"It's not exciting, my dear," Stuart replied. "It has no flash, no sex, no adrenalin. Give a guy a choice between a Patriot missile to launch and replacing his car with a bicycle and he'll choose the missile every time. It's the flaw in human nature, original sin. Inevitably the masses are more attracted by vice than virtue. They choose consuming over saving. It takes a developed will and some luck to turn your back on vice. I'm sure I don't have to tell you that the world is not filled with lucky people and even fewer have a firm will."

"I don't believe that. The biggest news story connected to Kuwait is not whether or not we're going to war but how high the price of gasoline has jumped since the invasion. That's what I want to talk about." She jabbed her finger emphatically.

Stuart smiled as he leaned on his arms toward her. He had rolled up his shirt sleeves and removed his tie.

"The public has a very short memory. By November, the price will either have dropped or they'll be used to it. The only way a gas hike will help you win a vote is if it jumps fifty cents the weekend before the election. But come election day when there are legions of troops and equipment massed in the desert waiting for word to strike, people are going to be concerned about their leaders and whether they have the balls to face down some petty thug."

"And I, by definition, don't."

He smiled indulgently.

"Having balls of steel would not add to your charm."

There was a mocking tone in Kat's voice as she responded.

"Maybe it's time we tried charm instead of swords." She puckered her lips and batted her eyes at him.

"Try flirting with Saddam, I'm sure he'd be delighted to lay Kuwait at your feet."

Stuart leaned back in his chair looking satisfied. Kat's brief flash of softness vanished, replaced by the Furies. She stood up, trembling slightly from the force of her anger, demanding he take her seriously.

"I don't want war because it makes governments into monsters. Authority, male authority, is worshipped and domination becomes the standard mode. I don't want to see one-man-rule in this country and that's what war accelerates."

Stuart interrupted her to laugh.

"Not to worry. With all five hundred plus members of Congress and most of the fifty governors considering themselves potentates, there's little chance of a king emerging in the White House or on the battlefield."

Kat scowled at his interruption and resumed her tirade.

"I don't trust the men," she underlined the word men as her tone toughened, "to get the right point in this conflict. They're caught up in ancient blood feuds they don't understand. They're retreading their Crusader ancestors of a millennium ago, only this time it's a Holy Land of oil refineries and pipelines at stake."

Smiling benignly, and tilting his chair back so he could look up at her, Stuart responded.

"Please invite me to your perfect world once you get it underway. You'll need the excitement. I promise I'll leave my weapons at the door. Until then however, I'll keep my sword, thank you, and urge you most strongly to do the same."

Roxy could not imagine that Stuart's patronizing attitude could be doing anything to win Kat over. She either had to abandon Liz's romantic notion altogether or whisper some advice in his ear. She would remind him that when she asked him to fuck Kat, she meant he should do it lovingly.

The senator rocked the chair forward again and gestured for Kat to sit down. His voice was low and calm and he watched her intently.

"I know you believe in your heart that good triumphs because it's good. That's not how it works. Men like Saddam, and your enemies here in Rhode Island, know nothing of love. They cannot be dealt with in that way. They mistake it for weakness and increase their assault. They must be met with unshakable will and stern resolve. Evil often has great power and can be matched and overcome only with greater power, or luck.

"Don't let your compassion, your marvelous and inspired vision of what our best can be, blind you to what we are now, and the real obstacles we face. Let me try to cast this in terms you might understand. There is an ancient and colossal evil massed behind Saddam Hussein. You're right. This is an old battle. For whatever historical reason, we in this blessed land are now charged with the task of facing down this evil. We have no choice. We cannot, for our own development, shirk this role. You're right about the Berlin Wall, but it took thirty years to come down without a shot. If we can see what needs to be done, why is it a problem to make it happen quickly? Remember, it's you who describes the ultimate goal as one where many fossilized points must be broken and destroyed so a newer unity can be born."

Kat suddenly grinned.

"Would it be more appropriate if I opposed the war because fighting in the desert does nothing to encourage building submarines, our main share in the military-industrial economy?"

He did not smile in response, instead nodded towards Hayes with a serious expression. "It may hurt more than you expect. Our two states have been competing for an important submarine related contract from Israel." Kat indicated her agreement.

"We've both lost. The decision was just made to give the contract to a German bidder. The Israelis are furious at German complicity in arming Iraq. As restitution they demanded, and got, an impossibly low bid on the submarine systems. Everyone's happy but Rhode Island and Virginia."

Kat stared, unbelieving. For all her idealism, she realized the state's economy was in shambles and people were most concerned about keeping jobs. Electric Boat losing a big contract to the Germans would raise everyone's anxiety level even higher.

Hayes moved toward redemption by changing the subject and soliciting Stuart's agreement with Kat's position that Douglas was beneath her notice and there should be no debates. He added an acute analysis of their opponent.

"He has no positions. That makes him invulnerable to planning or spying against him. His only strategy is to watch you like a shark and move in when he smells blood somewhere. Since you can plan nothing against him, it's best to do what you're doing—pretend he doesn't exist. But don't underestimate him. He's a natural tactician understanding the rules instinctively. He's the most dangerous kind of opponent one who cares about nothing."

Stuart once again addressed Kat.

"There is an obligation that comes with power, the obligation to serve with your best, your all."

"Are you inferring that I fail to understand this? That I fall short in doing my duty?" Kat interrupted curtly.

"On the contrary, you're the ideal. It's your opponent who hasn't a clue. Your concept of serving the people of Rhode Island in the Senate is alien to him. He does possess several of the key characteristics found in those who achieve the high station you seek—present company excluded, of course—while you do not."

A tight but tolerant smile curved Kat's lips as she waited for Stuart to continue.

"You have neither the intrinsic hypocrisy nor the dedication to exploit anything and everything in pursuit of a political objective. You do have a brilliant mind, devoted to truth. For this to be a strength not a handicap you must be able to distinguish truth from reality; sometimes they're the same, sometimes not. What people believe is often far more important than what is true.

"Once again I warn you about the cruelty and blindness of the world. You are one of those rare and much feared politicians who run in front of people, leading, who want to change the world from altruistic motives. The public trusts only self-interest and doesn't want to hear truth. Those who insist on speaking it are often thought to be eccentric if not actually mad. They may fall victim to humanity's cherished illusion that truth can be destroyed by murdering the truthsayer."

Roxy felt chills. She wished Stuart would stop suggesting such threatening circumstances.

At Kat's request, they moved onto economics, the need to convince people of an optimistic future and her capacity to lead them there. Stuart lectured her on the sublime perfection of free market forces and they started off in agreement, both having lived with successful personal businesses of the sort that defined a purist's view of capitalism. Neither could imagine a true entrepreneur who did not value efficiency above all else. They even agreed that unless the true costs for environmental degradation and structural disruptions of the social system were added in, the market forces could never work. When Stuart proclaimed he was a conservative because he understood delayed gratification, Kat smiled. Then she introduced her notion about the next step in the evolution of economic structures.

"I call it Economics in the Fourth Dimension and I want to use it as my major theme this fall. It will coincide with the budget debates in......"

Stuart interrupted her with a quizzical look.

"Pardon me? Economics in the Fourth Dimension? Where are we here? You want to introduce that into this senate campaign, here on Planet Earth?"

Her face betrayed not a spark of her rage; her voice was so controlled as to be metallic. "The fourth dimension is where the others interconnect. We need to develop a system of economic analysis that utilizes the concept of unity so we can make correct choices."

"Can we talk about this in December?"

"It's a concept we need." The sword in Kat's voice was audible.

"I told you earlier, the world hates a wise guy."

Kat stood, drew herself up to full height, and glared at him in best high priestess fashion. Roxy would have been terrified to be the target but Stuart sat, unruffled, watching her with just the slightest turn of amusement to his lips.

"There are several arguments I have with your notion of market forces. Of course since none are economic you may choose to dismiss them outright." Her voice sliced the air. Mario and Roxy cringed. They had seen this mode before. Kat was about to make an impassioned speech fueled by the wrath of an aroused spirit.

"Economics is like science. Sometimes a value judgement is required. The underlying values of the current operating system have been corrupted. Consuming has become paramount. Making money, not turning out a worthwhile quality product, is the overriding goal. Every opportunity to make money must be seized or you're considered out-of-step. Production is not concerned with need or improvement, its aim is pleasure, intensifying pleasure. The market forces you worship are undermining the traditional morality you claim you also revere so they can make more and more money. How do you confront the conflict?" she asked rhetorically then sped on.

"I know you understand moral corruption in various aspects of life. But like Jefferson you're blinded by the ideal of your own situation from seeing its failure elsewhere. You claim I envision a fantasy world—yours is equally unreal."

She paused for breath and shook her head at his delighted face.

"Stop looking at me as if you're amazed to discover I have a brain," she said abruptly.

"You misunderstand. I've always found your intellect almost irresistible."

"And I happen to agree with your outrage. Foolishly, America has elevated money and wealth as the measure of a person's worth. It's foolish because any thief or despoiler can accumulate a fortune. When the common mind with its obsession with money rises to power, nobility is doomed and so is any pretense of civilization. What we need to do is reinstitute nobility, democratically of course, as an ideal behavior."

Mario finally intervened in what he considered an unnecessary diversion and suggested a short break to collect the newspapers and make a few radio press calls. He was calm and soothing, showing his honest admiration for Stuart while reassuring Kat that she was his sole concern. He set a reconvening time for fifteen minutes, handed Hayes a list of calls for Stuart and sent them downstairs. He led Kat off to her private office.

Roxy was alone in the room when Jake reappeared and sat next to her.

"A sweater that alluring should be banned anywhere but in a bedroom. Speaking of which, I asked Kat if I could tag along with you tomorrow and take some photographs. Gould insists I have a great eye and should develop it more. I want to take some pictures of you. I can use them for future goddesses. Afterwards, we can slip off and work on our vote count. I don't want sexual tension turning you into a nervous wreck like Kat."

Roxy looked at him sharply.

"Why do you think sexual tension is what's making Kat nervous?"

She read volumes into the quirk Jake gave his expressive eyebrows and knew her reaction was irrational as she attacked him but did not care.

"Oh, I forgot. You two were lovers once, you would know."

She jumped up and moved to sit across the room. The whole situation was getting too crazy for her.

The meeting reconvened, Mario adding another defused confrontation to his score. Directing the group to a hopefully productive exchange of views, he turned the meeting over to a discussion of media. Gould jumped in, beaming at Kat.

"In case I haven't told you a dozen or more times already, you look gorgeous. I don't know who to thank for this, but the image is perfect—elegant, intelligent, strong yet feminine. I think it's time to put you on TV."

Kat was cheered by his enthusiastic presentation of spots using her.

"We tout you as homegrown, display you in familiar Rhode Island scenes, stress the key qualities the polls tell us people want and that they think you have: courage, integrity, intelligence, vision."

"People have been chanting 'she's one of us' along the walk route," Mario reported, "and I've been suggesting 'she leads us onward' as a slogan to the press as often as I can."

Gould arranged to send a crew to get some footage of the walk and its chanting crowds then reviewed the next series of commercials using his now famous stars.

"We have one more issue spot to air in September with all three characters. Jake and Big Mac are working on a car while Aunt Helen talks about her friend Gladys who's facing all these unnecessary doctor bills because she doesn't take care of herself. They call for a preventive approach to health care and assure each other that with Kiley in the Senate it will happen. 'We won't go broke paying for it' is their key line.

"In October we reap the rewards of our brilliant strategy and shamelessly exploit the credibility we developed for these characters. Jake, Aunt Helen and Big Mac do endorsements for the generic groups they represent with Jake being our prime pitch man. It's his job to defend your virtue, in the abstract of course, and clear up any residue of the lies Douglas keeps slinging and we keep knocking out of the park."

Gould was practically crowing with glee as he finished and was rewarded with a resounding kiss on his bald pate from Kat, a hand slap from Jake, and applause all around. Stuart had nothing but praise for the plan and seemed much subdued from the earlier session. He and Kat had switched positions. She paced the room, perching on tables and chair arms while he sat relaxed in a large green leather armchair.

"I have some information about your opponent's media plans." Stuart spoke as Gould wound down his presentation. All eyes swung to him intensely interested.

"Douglas fired Roberts and Sondheim, media muggers. It seems they were too restrained in their tactics for him. They insisted on at least a shred of truth in any accusation they made. He's now a free agent."

Mario reported there were long standing rumors that Douglas was the evil genius behind most of the smear campaigns he had run in the past, and all agreed that technical skill was readily available for the right price. The meeting became a jumble of questions and answers about when, what it meant for their campaign, and how did Stuart know.

"Is there a reason you waited so long to tell us?" Kat asked accusingly, speaking to him for the first time since the meeting reconvened.

"This seemed to be my first opportunity. I couldn't find a way to use it in casual conversation." He smiled blandly at her.

They concluded the meeting in time to see the six o'clock news which led off with Stuart's comments on Iraq. The coverage was glowing and Kat was not too disturbed that the senator received the lion's share of quotes. She looked wonderful in all the visuals.

"I guess they loved you, Tommy Jeff," she said mockingly as they finished watching. "Just remember, the job is getting them to vote for me."

★ ★ ★ ★ ★

Mario dropped Stuart and Hayes in Narragansett, arranging to meet them later at the Beaux Arts Ball. He had his own series of events to attend.

They were standing in the living room archway examining Duke's portrait on the wall. Roxy paused for a moment in the landing midway down the dramatic stairway of Kat's house. She loved making entrances to the accompaniment of admiring male eyes and wanted to give the pair time to notice her. She flipped her blonde hair back across her shoulders, bare except for a thin strip of black ribbon pretending to hold up her softly fitted black dress. Her tactics were rewarded and they greeted her with flattering comments. She began laughing and talking about how handsome they both looked in their tuxedos as she hit the bottom step, hoping to keep Hayes at a respectable distance so Stuart would not have any first hand verification of their relationship. She need not have worried. Stuart had no eyes for anyone but Kat who appeared at the top of the stairs.

She was spectacular, like a magazine layout come to life. Her hair looked as vital and alive as when it was a mane and her long sparkling earrings peeked through the tendrils dangling on her cheeks. She had a matching jeweled collar that Roxy knew, along with the earrings, were not rhinestones. These were real diamonds that were kept locked, along with other precious gems, in one of the secret cabinets in Kat's library. It was the Givenchy dress that substantiated the oft-whispered claim that Kat was among Washington's few glamorous women, and the only one in the notoriously dowdy society of government.

A deep, vibrant blue satin, the dress was strategically shirred to fit like a second skin. A large ruffle in richly contrasting green ran across the strapless bodice and down the front to the above knee hem. Her high heeled sling-back shoes matched the blue satin. She gracefully offered Stuart her hand as if he were her favorite courtier and she a queen he had bowed to many times. He kissed it expertly.

Roxy caught her breath as she turned into the circular drive at the dazzlingly lit entrance to Highlawn-by-the-Sea, one of Newport's newest mansions-turned-private-clubs, and the scene of the year's gala Beaux Arts summer ball. The quickly gathering fog turned the naturally lovely scene into a dreamscape. A white liveried young man jumped from the portico and took the car as Hayes and Roxy followed Senator Stuart and Kat into the elegant lobby.

It was a grander version of Kat's house in Narragansett, displaying many of the vernacular characteristics of turn-of-the-century architecture including large, comfortable rooms, open halls, and the shingle exterior popular in the Ocean State. Wood paneling was everywhere as were embossed sheet metal ceilings recessed into carved walnut beams. The walls that were not paneled glowed a delicate pale blue with elegant accents of gilding and gold tracery; elaborately decorated curved panels defined their junction with the ceiling.

The large expanse of interconnected downstairs rooms was filled with gaily dressed women and their darkly elegant escorts. Kat and Stuart were immediately swept up by swirling clusters of admirers who flowed into ever-changing configurations around them. Since this was not a crowd that staff could work, Roxy yielded to Hayes' pleas and followed him onto the polished wood dance floor. Once in his arms, feeling his warm breath along the side of her cheek, her knees and other more intimate parts of her anatomy turned to jelly. When he talked to her in that knowing tone she never heard him use to anyone else, Roxy resigned herself to being seduced. She hoped they could either find an acceptably comfortable and secluded spot here, or less likely, that Stuart could be sufficiently ingratiating and charming to overcome Kat's chaste sleeping plans.

When he maneuvered her past the embroidered peacock blue velvet curtains and onto the sweeping porch that faced elaborately landscaped grounds and beach beyond, Roxy knew Hayes was not waiting for accommodation arrangements to change. It was a balmy summer night. Now-thick fog obscured all but the closest landscape, plaintive fog horns blowing through the roar of the invisible surf.

They wandered along a slate path following the sound of the waves, veering away the only time they heard voices. Roxy loved the moist heaviness of the fog against her skin. It felt as rich and soft as an exotic body lotion, one perfumed with pungent salty smells. Even when Hayes pulled her into his arms and she could feel his lips and mustache pressing against her throat and down to her breasts, she could make out little but his outline.

He began pulling off his shoes as they stepped from the path onto the beach. Waves crashed in front of them. Faint sounds of music and the excited hum of voices from the ball filled the gaps. She had her shoes and stockings off and was setting them on a bench beside the path when Hayes came up behind her, unzipped her dress, and slipped it off. As he unhooked her bra and pushed her slip and panties down over her hips, she was shocked by the thrill she felt at being so exposed. She turned to face him. He was unbuttoning his formal dress shirt and laid it on top of his jacket and her pile of clothes. As he finished undressing, Roxy could feel his intent gaze on her although she could scarcely see his face. A faceless man staring at her naked on the beach surrounded by a dense fog, the thought inflamed the sensations spreading from her loins through every part of her body.

She lost herself for a brief moment in the thermal melody the light breeze was playing on her stimulated skin. First a stream of warm moist air, then a colder current followed once again by warmth, the tempo increasing as she ran to keep up with the man pulling her along the edge where the manicured lawns met soft sand. She imagined they were hurling themselves into the abyss of the fog-shrouded beach like the tarot's Fool card with its sublimely innocent expression.

They slipped back onto a dark end of the porch and into a side hall where they separated. Roxy desperately wanted to repair herself before finding Kat. The crowd had thinned. It must be time to leave. Using her slip, Hayes had cleaned most of the sand off before she put on her dress. Recalling the feathery touches of the silky fabric as it brushed clean her gritty body made her knees weak enough that she was forced to stop and lean against the high wainscoat of oak.

She stared with blank interest at the exotic carved flowers that topped the wood paneling trying to remember where in the house she was, and where there was a ladies room. She located her destination and was mobilizing for the final dash to safety when she saw Senator Stuart watching her from the ballroom. Kat's back was facing her from the same group. She was still beet red when she reached the haven of the lounge, remembering the barely perceptible raised brow and smile he gave her before redirecting his attention to the group around him.

Meeting at the campaign van, they efficiently sorted out keys and vehicles, checking details of the next day's schedule. Mario had arrived while Hayes and Roxy were on the beach. He was driving the two men back to Cranston to stay at Duke's compound. Stuart allowed himself a few good-humored shots at Kat for making the boys sleep in one city and the girls in another—obviously he and Hayes had been rehearsing this, thought Roxy—but yielded gracefully to the inevitable.

They crossed both bridges across the bay slowly, headlights breaking only a few feet ahead into the fog, streetlights the merest shine, and were approaching the still torn up construction site where Winston died. Kat broke the silence. She was driving and did not turn her eyes from the confusing detour—even more hazardous in the fog—that brought them onto Ocean Drive.

"I saw you leave with Hayes. I was starting to follow you when Stuart stopped me. He said someone should have some fun tonight."

Searching madly for some plausible defense, Roxy stared at her dimly lit profile able to read no expression but attention to the barely visible road. She was relieved when Kat continued onto another subject.

"Tomorrow's his birthday."

"Whose?"

"Tommy Jeff's," she drawled sarcastically and they both laughed. "It's weird that Duke died on his birthday."

★ ★ ★ ★ ★

There were three messages on the machine from Liz, each more suggestive than the one before. When faced with calling and waking Liz to tell her the previous night was a failure all around or walking on the beach, Roxy walked. The thick fog remaining from the previous night blanketed the other end of the passage. Nothing was visible.

As she walked along the very edge of the surf all she could see was a lacy skirt of white emerge from formless gray and break up at her feet. On her other side, the beach faded back into the same void. She jumped, startled when Jake did an about-face from nowhere and began walking alongside. She could not imagine how he found her.

"It should burn off by noon so we'll have a beautiful day for the ride to Little Compton. Kat asked me to meet you at Duke's compound before noon."

Jake's voice sounded as tenuous as the fog and Roxy was flooded with the guilt she had been repressing. She should have chosen to call Liz.

She reached out and took his hand. He deserved no pain from her. He did not need her confessing further sexual weakness.

"I'm glad you're coming today. Maybe you can show Senator Stuart how to be a little more sensitive to Kat."

She repeated Liz's matchmaking scheme. Her usual buoyant spirits returned as she lost herself in trivial chatter. Jake revealed Liz had called him last night when she could not reach Roxy and begged his assistance with Stuart.

"What did you say?" Roxy asked, curious.

"I told her I was always ready to champion the cause of true love, not to mention much-needed sex."

★ ★ ★ ★ ★

Turning off Dean Parkway, onto East Hill Drive, Roxy parked the campaign van in front of the Italianate pink marble palace Duke had built for his family. No wonder Kat felt like a princess growing up in a mansion like this, thought Roxy as she admired the mosaic sunburst floor in the arched doorway. She walked back to the courtyard where she could hear someone diving into the pool.

She felt fortunate to have sent Hayes off with no more than a few deep kisses and some minor fondling after reminding him they were in the campaign van. She refused his suggestion to park the van in a deserted service alley behind the strip mall next to the airport for a few minutes so they could say a proper good-bye. When he dropped his bomb, she wanted to roll him out the door while the van was still in motion.

"I bought a stained glass window from Jake yesterday. He had photos of it at the meeting. Said he thought I should have it and offered to give it to me. I insisted on buying it."

She stewed about the two of them buying and selling her all the way back from the airport. He had paid eight hundred dollars for the Temptation window that was the pair to the one of Sanctification that Jake now had mounted alongside his bed. She could not believe Jake deliberately offering the window to Hayes. Men! She was thoroughly disgusted with male creatures when she found herself approaching the pool as Stuart was lifting himself out. Great, she thought. Ten minutes with him should eliminate any remaining doubts about the monster nature of men.

Before Stuart had time to do more than graciously accept her birthday greetings, Mario appeared from Yola's house and joined them at the table by the pool. He set down a pitcher of juice and five glasses.

"My mother is bringing some coffee to tide us over until Jake arrives. She refuses to serve breakfast without him. He's her absolute favorite, hers and virtually all my cousins, surpassing all known movie stars and sports figures. When they found out you were dating him, Roxy, it was civil war. Half of them were delighted someone they knew had him, the other half were insanely jealous."

Roxy blushed furiously as Stuart smirked at her and quipped, "Exactly what kind of novels do you write?"

She quickly changed the subject.

"Where's Kat?" she asked Mario.

"She wanted to change clothes for the afternoon of festivals and barbecues, and have a few minutes alone. This is always a difficult day for her although it's a lot better now than the first couple of years when darkness seemed to hover around her."

"How did her father die?" Stuart asked.

Recalling Celeste's revelation about her role in Duke's death, Roxy wondered what Mario would say, whether he now knew the truth.

"The doctors said it was a massive cerebral hemorrhage killing him instantly. It was an incredible shock to everyone. Duke had never been sick a day in his life.

My mother found him in his study. Kat was in Washington and no one wanted her to find out by phone so I flew down to tell her. It was the hardest thing I've ever done. She was berserk. Max came and gave her something that calmed her sufficiently to get her on a plane back here. When she found out her mother had been at the house on one of her rare visits from Newport, she flipped out all over again, convinced that Celeste's presence had something to do with her father's death and that she was at fault for not being here.

"For months it was a scene from hell. Duke's will established Kat as sole heir, leaving everything in her control with explicit instructions on allocating his resources. Frankie was installed as CEO of Tomasso Excavating although Kat held title to the business. He rose to the occasion and the transition was seamless. Later, when she was rational again, Kat restructured ownership providing Frankie and most long-time employees the opportunity to receive stock in the company. She also gave her brother the house with the exception of the kid's wing. She kept that part of the house where her and Frankie's childhood rooms were, where you and Hayes slept last night. She also kept Duke's study untouched which drives Frankie's wife crazy. Connie'd love her own house but Frankie refuses to leave the compound.

"Early on, Kat settled a monthly payment on her mother and essentially banished her to Europe, demanding that she make her summer visits permanent. I'm not certain Celeste has been back since."

Roxy was relieved that Mario had no idea Kat had seen her mother in February and discovered her blind accusations about Duke's death were indeed true.

Stuart's interest in the saga was obvious and Roxy remembered his story of paternal desertion.

"How long did the mourning continue?"

"Too long. She won the '86 election, just a few weeks after he died, without campaigning a single day. We spliced together footage we had from past campaigns and Washington, put a few commercials on the air and counted on everyone knowing how traumatic Duke's death was for her. It was almost two years before Kat started functioning with any consistency, not breaking down in tears or just drifting off to some black hole. I guess time finally healed her."

"She told me recently it was love and magic," Roxy commented, wondering about the strange look on Stuart's face as she said it.

"I don't know about that," Mario responded. "Max was with her most of the first few months but she wasn't very responsive to his efforts. She went through a stage of violent anger, convinced Duke had betrayed her by dying without saying good-bye and transferred her feelings to all men. She kept claiming they inevitably betrayed the women who love them. He finally turned her over to some women they both knew who worked on the type of healing Kat needed."

"Did she move into her house in Narragansett once her father died?" Stuart asked Mario.

"She's lived there almost as long as I can remember. According to family stories, Kat hated using her mother's house in Newport when she wanted to sail or go to the beach, so Duke gave her the place in Narragansett as reward for winning the state science prize when she was entering her senior year at Miss Williams. He said a brilliant scientist like Kat should be adult enough to have her own space. Of course, he bought another house around the corner for the aunts so she wouldn't be afraid," said Mario

"Afraid?" Stuart sounded surprised. "I thought she was fearless."

Shooting him a piercing glance, Mario decided the senator could be trusted.

"She was not yet eighteen and it was about the time that Race Scarlatti was determined he was going to marry her. He's the only person I've known Kat to fear and at that time, she was reportedly terrified of what he would do. I'm not sure Duke or anyone else knew Race was the specific cause of her fear. Duke considered protection one of the realities in life. Until the summer she and Jamie were married and lived in that house, I don't know that she ever stayed there without Frankie or one of her cousins."

Stuart began to ask more about Scarlatti when Kat came out of the house, Jake in tow. Mario greeted them then went to tell Yola she could start breakfast. Her hero had arrived.

★ ★ ★ ★ ★

Watching Kat and the senator charming the ladies of Saint Bernard's who staffed the booths at the church fair in Tiverton, Roxy attributed their high spirits to the gorgeous weather. The fog had burned off as Jake promised and the sky was a dazzling blue scattered with a few puffy white clouds. It was sunny and warm and Kat was dressed for a holiday outing in a below-the-knee, white skirt topped with a fitted green check jacket with cap sleeves and a shaped hem that grazed the top of her hip. She was wearing the jade Kuan Yin from Stuart.

He even looked ready for a relaxed afternoon in the sun in a white linen suit that Roxy thought southern senators wore only in the movies, and—shocking to consider—a pale blue shirt. He gave Roxy his jacket to hold as he followed Kat, shaking hands and kissing cheeks. She and Jake looked like twins in their Kiley teeshirts and blue shorts. Jake tried to stay out of sight, hoping not to be recognized as he took pictures of Kat campaigning and Roxy perusing the quilts and cookies.

Impressed at the number of Kiley stickers people at the fair were sporting, Stuart praised the work of her advance team as they headed south along the peninsula to Little Compton. Kat directed Roxy to pull in at the Evans Farm Inn just outside of Tiverton, claiming she wanted to get something quick to eat.

Considering the huge breakfast Yola fed them less than two hours ago, Roxy could not imagine what Kat had in mind. It must be Liz's influence, she decided. Liz could not exist for more than a few minutes without something in her mouth. She drove Roxy crazy carrying around one of those huge plastic glasses with a permanently attached straw that was continually filled with some beverage or another.

They sat on the veranda looking out over the glassy blue ocean lapping against the rocks below them and the waiter brought out a birthday cake, putting it before Stuart. Astonished, he beamed at Kat in pleasure that increased to ecstasy when she presented him with a beautifully wrapped box. She warned him it could not be opened until they were outside the restaurant.

Jake was poised to capture the moment of revelation on film as they stood by the car and Stuart tore open his gift like a little kid. Obviously expecting a trinket the value of which was in the giving, he was visibly shocked when he opened the box and saw the pistol. Gratitude flashed in the senator's eyes as he stared at Kat, the clicking of Jake's shutter echoing around them.

"It's a .45 long Colt single-action," Stuart said, awed.

Kat nodded agreement. "An original, made for the army in 1873. Duke was serious about his guns."

To Roxy it looked like the familiar revolver that hung on every cowboy hero's hip.

"There are bullets in the bag." Kat reached over and lifted them from the box.

Suddenly Stuart's eyes gleamed and he looked at Jake. "Are they here? "

"Parked in the corner, just over your right shoulder," Jake answered not in the least mystified by the question. Roxy was though, and she saw the same perplexed look on Kat's face. Was who here?

Before she could examine the parking lot to determine who they were talking about, her attention was captured by Stuart's antics. Turning slightly sideways, he began posturing with the gun, holding it up to the sky, aiming it at some gulls flying overhead, opening the chamber and snapping it closed with a flourish. Then he deliberately took the bag of ammunition from Kat's hands and pantomimed placing bullets in the empty gun. Nodding to Jake who seemed to understand what was happening, he spun around and leveled the pistol at a maroon sedan parked along the front edge of the lot with two men sitting in it. He was snarling and holding the pistol with both hands, crouching slightly like cop shows on TV. He and Jake laughed as the car wheeled out of the parking lot and onto the highway heading back towards Tiverton.

By this point, Kat was livid.

"Are you crazy?" she screamed as Stuart and Jake exchanged a delighted look. "What's going on?"

"Jake noticed that car following us as we went into the last town. They watched us work the church fair."

"I got some pictures that should help us identify the driver," Jake interjected. "I recognized the thug riding shotgun." Anticipating Kat's question, he said, "It was Mike Bassion." Recognition widened her eyes.

"He's one of Scarlatti's men," he explained to Stuart who did not look pleased at the information.

"Does your boyfriend always send his thugs on your excursions?"

Kat shot him a scathing glance and flounced into the car refusing to answer any of his questions as they sped off.

Roxy knew the answer though. This was a special occasion brought on by the television coverage and newspaper pictures of Kat with Senator Stuart. She shuddered thinking of how ineffectual Duke's protection of his daughter had been, how much more powerful Race was now, and how much more vulnerable Kat was.

Just when she thought the beautiful day could be ruined no further, Roxy found herself staring error in the face. She was standing at the edge of a crowd gathered around Stuart who was delightedly playing hero, slapping a huge mallet on a pad that sent a marker careening to the top of an upright where it rang a bell. Catching a whiff of a slightly noxious odor that cut through the smell of burning charcoal and scorched chicken slathered with sauce, she turned and saw Carrie looming beside her.

"What are you doing here?"

"I wouldn't miss barbecue in Little Compton for anything. I didn't realize that being run off the campaign meant I was also banished from any public event at which our esteemed congresswoman might appear."

"What's that supposed to mean?"

Gesturing towards Stuart who was winding up another whack, she explained, contemptuous.

"I assume by now even you can see the obvious. You do realize he was the one sending her the roses, exactly as I said." Carrie was beginning to give Roxy the creeps but when she started to move away, Carrie stopped her.

"The congresswoman better watch her step if she wants her boyfriend to stay alive. Race has no intention of sharing his prize."

Roxy snapped her attention back to Stuart. He had rung the bell twice on his first two tries and the crowd was screaming for more. Jake looked over, winked and waved at her. Automatically, she waved back.

"Our favorite TV spokesperson," said Carrie sarcastically, noticing their exchange.

"I heard he was poking you. Mr. Southern Charisma in Washington was not enough, eh Miss Hot Pants?"

A flash of insight burned through Roxy's rage as she realized why Carrie was here. She was back-up for Scarlatti's men that Stuart had run off. When she turned to scream at Carrie, she had already slipped away through the crowd as if she recognized the light dawning in Roxy's brain. Stuart rang the bell a third time. He bowed repeatedly to the crowd and posed, hammer on shoulder, jacket hanging from the fingers of one hand, looking for all the world like the statue of Hercules on Kat's desk.

Noticing that Carrie's trajectory would take her directly past him, Roxy tried to intercept her, arriving too late to do more than catch her final words.

"No princess comes cheap. This one might cost your life. Sleeping in separate cities hardly makes it worthwhile." Then she was gone and Stuart stood looking after her, confused.

★ ★ ★ ★ ★

After forcing Roxy to describe every moment of the weekend, Liz declared her verdict. Senator Stuart was the undisputed hero, Hayes a blackguard and Roxy a dimwitted slut. Kat earned countless headshakings and mutterings about what a fool she was. She wove endless plots that involved mobilizing Bruno's legions to sweep the state clean of Carrie, Scarlatti and their corrupt minions.

Life around Kasa Kat, as she called the Narragansett house, was soon back to normal, meaning Liz running everyone's life, feeding Kat, and deciding sleeping arrangements. Even when the walk moved to the northern part of the state and along East Bay, the house remained action central, housing several members of the Washington staff who came to spend their recess time working on the campaign.

Liz managed to find time to invade campaign headquarters, placing herself under Yola's direction as they churned out endless mailings. Since the mid-July cut-off of franked bulk mail from the congressional office, the campaign had been generating target issue mail as well as their usual fundraising appeals. The rhythm of the volunteers was hypnotic. Pick up the invitation, stuff a return card, put them in the envelope. The next person would draw from the pile, seal the envelope and affix the stamp. A third crew sorted and packaged bulk mail. Liz set the pace, keeping the engine running with a constant steam of upbeat campaign gossip, irreverent commentary and comic abuse from the stool she straddled like she was once again a saloon queen.

By mid-August she knew everyone on Atwell's Avenue, from the Vietnamese grocer to Mrs. Angostino, who swept the sidewalk in front of her religious artifacts store at least a dozen times a day. She pestered Mario to change the office address to #39 Not-a-Public-Thoroughfare, claiming that was the actual designation of the ten-foot alley that ran alongside the headquarters building to a mini-neighborhood behind it. Discovering the white-coated young people who congregated in Garabaldi Park were trainees at a nearby beauty academy,

Liz was soon giving impromptu master classes in fingernail art or envisioning ideal haircuts. When not in the office, she camped at Tony's, teaching Gloria the intricacies of California cuisine in return for secrets of gnocchis and handmade pasta.

The first weekend Liz was back, festivals were the main focus. On Saturday evening they staffed a Kiley for Senate booth at a block party in Woonsocket. The drive north on I-295 wound through miles of rock outcroppings and empty landscape that looked more at home in the west than in the nation's most densely populated state. The main street, curving through the old commercial district of the former milltown, was closed to traffic and filled with food booths, sound stages for continual entertainment, and people. Every political candidate who could possibly need a Woonsocket vote was there in force with volunteers, balloons, sticker brigades, posters and brochures.

Liz was entranced by the event. She loved the line of old people parked in their lawn chairs along the curb in front of an old mill now converted to senior citizen housing. Fascinated, she watched as one politician after another moved along the rows shaking hands, putting their stickers on worn sweaters and cotton dresses. Then the next would appear and the same thing would happen. Soon the old folks were covered with stickers. They were mostly non-partisan, refusing to remove one candidate's sticker for another's. When Roxy told her Stuart's story about the same phenomenon, Liz clapped her hands in glee.

"I told you, he's a genius. Does Kat think men like that grow on trees?"

"No, just swing from them."

Liz derided the cluster of balding men in suits handing out Douglas stickers, claiming no one would support a candidate with such a nerdy team. Then she would fluff up the covey of cute young girls in Kiley shirts and shorts who returned for more stickers and send them out again. Kat was Miss High Energy Senate candidate, beaming as people reached out to touch her and tell her they loved seeing her on television. The Prudhomme boys had done their job well and virtually every vendor or storekeeper on the street was wearing only one sticker: Kiley for Senate.

The main event however, was dinner at Chan's, part of the restaurant tour that was Pete's version of Kat's walk. Jake was there, too, and the four of them experienced what Pete described as "one of Rhode Island's most memorable dishes, mussels in black bean sauce." They had lost count of the platters when Liz let out a huge belch and announced "this is the last mussel I'll eat to live. The rest," she pulled a half empty platter to her, "I'll eat for pleasure."

The next day they were walking through the Towers to examine a small arts fair that was set up on the village green in Narragansett. Believing in round-the-clock attention to whatever business she was conducting, Liz insisted they dress in matching Kiley teeshirts.

"Of course, Roxy, mine's a tent and yours is a postage stamp, but otherwise, we're identical, don't you think?"

As they emerged from the shadows of the arch and waited to cross the traffic-clogged street to the park, Liz clamped a vise-like grip on her arm. Roxy turned to shake her off. Three young people faced them, the center one an astoundingly ugly, dark haired, olive skinned gargoyle who was pointing to their shirts and mouthing obscenities about Kat. Following Liz's horrified stare, she saw the giant black snake wrapped around the woman's neck and hanging off her shoulders.

"Well, you can't expect much sense from someone who walks around with a snake," Liz shouted, leaping into the stopped traffic dragging Roxy with her.

They walked up and down the small collection of booths at least twice before Liz calmed down. They were sitting at the base of the no-neck Indian statue that faced the ocean eating some fried dough, one of Liz's favorite Rhode Island treats, as she babbled about the meaning of their terrifying encounter.

"I hate snakes. I can't tell you how much I hate snakes. I hate snakes so much I don't even like shoelaces. How disgusting to be walking around with one like that. And to not like Kat." She became slightly more coherent. "Max says nothing's too insignificant to be regarded as a clue to guide us."

"From your reaction, I wouldn't call this insignificant," Roxy observed.

Liz stared at her for a moment then began muttering again.

"Snakes, snakes, what do they mean besides terror?"

"Kat says she keeps snakes on the payroll," said Roxy. "They attack mice that eat book-bindings." Liz stopped in mid breath. "That better not mean Kat has pet snakes at the house," she snarled then returned to her hysteria.

Roxy burst out laughing. She knew what snakes meant.

"You need to take your own advice Liz, and find a man."

Roxy seldom had the capacity to render Liz speechless so she took full advantage, chanting "Lizzie needs a boyfriend, Lizzie needs a boyfriend," like a sugar-high eight year old. Then she began making a list of possibilities including all of Liz's pet volunteers who changed almost daily. "How about Bobby, he's…"

Liz cut her short with a yelp.

"You're a genius Roxy. You're absolutely right. I know exactly what to do."

She refused to discuss the topic any further and dragged Roxy to her feet, in control again and ready to shake every hand at the fair.

After recruiting the seller to volunteer for Kat, Liz acquired four hermit crabs in a plastic case. Pets. Roxy added a new anxiety to her growing list. It made her nervous to watch Liz drag them out in their borrowed shells twice a day and spray them with water. She let them wander, claiming they needed their exercise. Roxy began whining about her cavalier attitude towards the uncaged crabs, and the possibility of them ending up in her bed, nibbling on her toes.

"Roxy thinks everything wants to end up in her bed," she told Kat one night as they sat around the kitchen table.

Then she began harassing Roxy about Jake. Somehow, she found out about the tantric yoga they were doing which was a secret Roxy had planned to keep from Liz until the grave. The teasing made her nervous because she was certain Liz would slip one time and let Kat know about using sex magic to influence votes, or worse yet, reveal her relationship with Hayes.

Roxy decided to deflect her with a stream of detailed information on the non-sexual aspects of the work they were doing. She told them about smells.

"Jake says each person has their own distinctive odor and that people who do tantric work for a long time develop such an acute sense of smell they can immediately identify who's been in a room by the aroma they leave behind."

"I know men who can sniff out an unhappy wife looking for a good time," Liz offered.

"You both have very different natural fragrances," she told them. "They're easy to recognize because neither of you wear additional perfumes regularly." At their urging, she tried to describe the subtle smell of each. "Kat smells like ozone, clear and sharp as if there are lightning bolts exploding in a rainless sky all around her. And Liz smells mostly like bread or more accurately, like the aroma of fresh baking."

"Roxy smells like a flower ready to pollinate," Liz added.

Ignoring the barb, Roxy became serious.

"There's a slightly putrid odor I've noticed recently. It's barely a wisp when I quickly turn a corner or walk into a closed space. I've noticed it mostly at campaign headquarters although a couple days ago I could have sworn I caught of whiff of it on the front porch. It's familiar. When I smelled it for the first time at campaign, I knew it was a particular stink I'd experienced before. I still can't place it, though."

Liz rambled on for a few minutes, making up appropriate odors for staff kids and volunteers based on her analysis of their characters.

"Too bad I'll never meet Jasmine. I wonder if she smells like her name or if she has that special dyke essence that warns men away."

Kat frowned at Liz's crude assessment and responded tartly.

"For all her apparent wealth and social position, Jasmine has not had an easy life. Her mother died before she was a teen-ager and she grew up worshipping her father. He was not at all interested in her as a child and drove her to grow up as soon as possible so he could have her as a stable companion with whom to discuss his numerous female conquests, a role her mother apparently played for years. He would show her obscene photos he took of his dates and pushed her to begin sleeping around once she was in high school. At the same time he gave her every material object she wanted. Her father owned her. Still does, in fact. She hates men because she can't bring herself to hate her father."

As Liz looked interested but not the least abashed by the story, Kat asked why she thought she would not be meeting Jasmine.

"After all that Roxy's told me about her association with Carrie and how she hates Senator Stuart, I assumed you'd fired her. She's friends with the enemy and she knows too much."

"I did confront her with her disloyalty and we dealt with it. I chose to give her one more chance. If she betrays me again, I'll fire her with no compunction."

Liz did not let the rebuke in Kat's voice deter her.

"You have no idea how to confront evil people. You have to throw the fear of God into them. That's even in the Bible, let alone every how-to book from your hero, Sun Tzu's to the Garden of Eden's user guide. I've written it in my training manual. I'll give you a copy. Employees have to believe it's your way or nothing. I have no intention of trusting that bitch and plan to watch her and that looney-tune Carrie like a hawk."

Roxy felt her stomach knot again. She had not told Kat about her encounter with Carrie in Little Compton although Liz knew. From Kat's silence on the episode, Roxy assumed Stuart had not mentioned it either.

A few days later when the walk was moving through Providence, Liz and Roxy met Pete and Jake for dinner at Amsterdam's. Near the financial district, it was filled with, "Richard-heads. Those are dick-heads in suits and ties," explained Liz.

Eating with a professional restaurant critic and a super-chef was always chancy but this night both were pleased. Liz was impressed by the black-shirted waiter and his skilled recitation of the intricate specials. She and Pete thoroughly examined the gigantic open spit in the middle of the dining room where whole chickens were grilled over flames of various exotic woods. A variety of sauces and garnishes came with the chickens.

Two margaritas and some beer made Roxy sufficiently daring to kid Liz about the snakes and her need to find a man.

"Maybe Pete could fit you into his busy schedule."

"Pete and I discussed that," Liz said demurely, "but when he took me back to his bedroom and I saw the handcuffs hanging behind the door, I began to have second thoughts. Then there were all the body parts he had strewn around, arms holding his shirts, pants folded over a leg stuck out from the wall. He had several female torsos that seemed to be used for nothing but stroking. I didn't see any heads."

"Pete likes the silent type better," Jake joked.

"I will admit," Pete added, laughing, "Liz has changed my notion of feminine pulchritude. I'm more appreciative of the succulent aspect of womanhood."

"Now he measures it with his stomach not just his eyes," Liz derided.

"The other obstacle with Pete is his insistence that his women shave their legs from top to bottom every day. This comes from a man who has hair all over his face."

The clambake in Warren was another high point. Clambakes happened weekly during the summer all over the state, used as fundraisers for a variety of groups. They were fair game for campaigning politicians and Kat loved them. She walked up and down the long rows of tables under a pavilion where several hundred people sat waiting to be served, shaking hands, acknowledging support and listening to concerns. Roxy trailed behind handing out stickers and brochures. Liz enrolled herself in a bliztkrieg apprenticeship to the food crew. The baking was done in a giant pit lined with seaweed. More seaweed was packed around containers of food under huge tarps—clams, sausage, stuffing, fish, corn, potatoes. Liz talked about it for days after.

"Did you see those boys running up and down those rows serving that food so fast it was a blur?" She made Roxy write down plans for conducting them in Morgan Springs.

"But there're no clams or seaweed there," Roxy protested.

"We'll improvise."

One evening towards the closing days of the walk when planning was an easier chore than in the early days, Liz decided she was prepared to give walking on the beach another chance. Roxy felt a twinge of concern about what might happen. No doubt about it, Liz's beach karma sucked.

It was different walking on the beach at night. It was not one of Roxy's favorite times. There were no gulls, foghorns blew out of the dark and white surf was all that was visible in high contrast against the shiny black sea. There were shapes in the ocean, kids playing in the waves and surfers bobbing like black seals. Kids were also sitting in groups everywhere along the seawall, parading up and down the sidewalks, making out on benches along the wall or in the high chairs on the beach.

They stopped where a small crowd had gathered around one of the shorter white lifeguard chairs. The seat was filled with the corpse of a huge sea creature. It had no tail and looked more like a fat ray than a fish.

"Good thing you and Jake did it right the night you were out here or the goddess could have turned you into that," Liz observed. When they returned to the house, she renewed her pledge to never walk on the beach again. "What if it hadn't crawled up to the chair to die? I could have stepped on it," she squealed.

Liz's dissatisfaction with the walk spilled over into her monologues that night as the three of them sat around the kitchen. They bordered on abusive and Kat finally clamped down.

"As you said Liz, I have to learn to confront evil. No more ethnic slurs, jokes, or what you consider humorous observations."

Shocked, Liz nodded.

"I keep forgetting, you're one of them. Sorry. No more side-by-each Woonsocket dialogue, big-hair jokes, or trashing St. Rocco, patron of bookies and loan sharks."

Liz had been ruminating on the stop they made at the gargantuan St. Rocco's church festival in Johnston the previous weekend. It was a parish composed of mostly long-time Italian families and did not match up with the white-bread groups around Morgan Springs, mostly Germans and Scotch-Irish. She also mocked the silver haired men with their white pants and green silk shirts loaded with gold and manicured to the hilt who packed a fundraiser one of Kat's rich Ferrarie cousins in Lincoln threw.

"I don't know what you're so upset about. I love your family. I want to take all the aunts home with me. I could build a restaurant empire on them. But these guys were phonies trying to buy their way to identities that are no better than the ones they have."

"You have to understand, Liz, immigrants have been exploited and discriminated against in this state forever. They couldn't even vote until the '30s. Because there are so many different groups competing in a small area, they've stayed distinct longer than in most places."

"Seeing you, Kat, they should realize how hybridization helps evolution. Mixing gene pools creates some extraordinary effects. In my neck of the woods inbreeding is the social pattern and we get collections of biological wonders like the boys in Skin Dirty Hollow."

The walk ended with August. They made a triumphal entry into Little Compton where Kat's local network set up a cookies and punch reception in the downtown triangle near the picturesque Meeting Hall. Everyone in town must have been there, as well as hundreds of walk groupies, volunteers, and staff. Dozens of press representatives rounded out the crowd. Kat spoke, sharing anecdotes of people and places along the walk. Her strong voice and the clear, precise diction she learned at Miss Williams seemed to make her ideas easier to grasp.

A pair of eyes on the left would light up, then another in the center and one in the back. Recognition would deepen the light and they would begin to move forward. Roxy had seen this happen before when Kat spoke from the heart. People would approach afterwards and want to touch her, affirming her inspiration and pledging their support. This must have been what it was like to recruit for the Crusades.

Summer was about to take a fast train out of town, Roxy observed as she walked along the beach one morning just before Labor Day. The sky, cloudless for several days, was now streaked with a few long white streamers of cirrus reaching from the south. She hoped the weather would hold through the weekend. She meandered along, kicking at the waves. Thoughts jumbled through her brain with equal disorder.

She thought about Max's suggestion to use the ocean as an oracle, her oracle. Miles of walks had turned into months of data and she had to admit it seemed to work. Pastel skies and crystalline water presaged days with rosy meetings and placid exchanges. Fog on the beach usually meant confusion ahead. However it happened, on whatever magic level, the ever-changing ocean defined the day.

"Let's do a close of season reading with the cards," Kat suggested when Roxy returned from the beach. "We haven't looked at them in weeks."

Liz busied herself flipping pancakes and heating maple syrup as Kat went upstairs to get her magic toys.

"I hope you do better handling Jake than you're doing with those cards," Liz commented as Roxy struggled to hold and shuffle the oversized cards.

"Max said they're made too big so people can't do card tricks with them."

Liz turned her attention to Kat. "Doesn't all your science training make it hard for you to believe that stuff?"

"As a scientist, I must be objective. I can't reject observations simply because the underlying mechanism has not been satisfactorily explained. In simple terms, it works so I use it."

"I admire your courage, Kat. They burned women around here a couple centuries ago for trusting their inner powers."

"The oracles play many roles. Sometimes they're sacred games designed to teach us needed skills or send a particular message. Other times they're road maps to the future. We're in a time where old forms are dissolving so we're free to create our own maps, and anything can be used. Roxy uses the ocean. The oracles just focus the energy. Discovery often requires only new eyes."

Roxy signaled she was ready, and Kat directed her to lay the cards in the Celtic cross.

As Liz and Roxy examined the colorful pictures spread before them without understanding the meanings buried in their details, they were chilled by the look of distress on Kat's face.

"Maybe we can bargain with the cards, rough the stars up a little so they'll tell us what we want to hear," Liz suggested.

Kat smiled ironically. "Pythagoras warned never to threaten the stars. And I can assure you magic allows no compromise. It cares nothing for diplomacy. Truth must be served without adjustment."

"Read the cards, Kat. We want to know what they say, too."

Speak for yourself, Liz, Roxy thought.

There was a noticeable silence as Kat appeared to be listening to voices only she could hear. Liz pulled out a bottle of Mezcal, the first Roxy had seen since that night in Washington when Hayes licked her hand and she let him follow her home. She set out salt and a dish of limes then poured the golden liquid for the two of them, a small glass of Dos Equis beer for herself. Each licked their salty hand then bolted down the shot; each wore a different expression. It was the willing of courage on Kat's face that disturbed Roxy most. Liz looked only expectant.

Kat smiled bitterly as she lifted the first card.

"This is me. Bound and tied to my destiny. There's no escape now." Roxy shuddered at the picture of the blindfolded dark haired woman standing in front of eight upright swords. "This sly fellow running off with several swords is my unworthy opponent. He's the obstacle." Both nodded in agreement.

Picking up the card that lay below the first two, Kat explained.

"This is the root of the matter. The moon. Scavenging creatures eating away my soul. This is the deception that putrifies around us. And this is our old friend

Death, set in the place that represents the past. However, it's reversed indicating in this case that there is more death to come."

Kat's voice sounded almost hollow as she recited her bleak interpretation. Roxy's stomach knotted. Who else would die? It was too much to expect it would be Douglas. If that happened Kat could stop worrying. No one would ever risk running against her again.

"Here, at the top of the spread we see the energy that overshadows it all, the Hanged Man. He represents what seers call the reverse point of view. That which you see when you rise to the next level, where human concerns fade into the pattern set by destiny. Things look very different from that perspective, winning may be losing and vice versa."

Liz and Roxy merely stared in silence as Kat continued, her voice sounding more abstract by the word as if she needed to distance herself from the messages that were aimed directly at her. This was her path that was being plotted and as the opening card said, there was no way out but through.

"This sturdy young man, rod in hand, battling invisible foes, is what the future holds in store." She smiled bleakly. "I hope you have another walk idea or two up your sleeve, Liz, we may need them."

"Now for the final line. This bottom card depicts my fears."

No explanation was needed for the picture of a woman sitting up in bed sobbing, nine swords lined up on the wall behind her.

"The Empress is how the world sees me."

Roxy noticed Kat said nothing about the beautiful lady's reverse position. She would check the guide book later. Her voice lightened a bit as she picked up the next card named The World.

"This is one of my favorite cards, it signifies completion and it is placed in the spot representing my hopes."

Her lips twisted into a smile as she picked up the final card.

"This is the outcome. The Emperor."

Roxy started. In the goddess deck which Kat still ignored, this card looked just like Senator Stuart. Here the Emperor was old with a long white beard. She wondered what it meant. Did Stuart hold the outcome of the race in his control? She hoped that was true. She knew what his goal was. He wanted a Republican Senate.

"What about the timing?"

Neither woman believed Kat's face could look more strained until it did.

"The Fall Equinox marks a dramatic week of upheavals and illusions."

"I don't know that I like any of this. Can we try something else? How about those little stones? Maybe they'll be more polite." There was a rare quaver in Liz's voice.

Kat shrugged in resignation.

"You can't hear bad news too many ways." She reached into her sequined studded bag and pulled out a smaller velvet bag embroidered with the Egyptian Eye of Horus.

"Pick five" she said, holding the bag in front of Liz.

She shook her head. "Not me. Roxy's the aluminum tube around here."

Roxy reached in and pulled out five engraved stones, one by one, laying them face down in a vertical line. Kat began with the one closest to Roxy, turning it over with the abstract air of concentration a reader used when describing destiny to a stranger.

"This gives us an overview of the situation."

It looked like a graphic arrow, point to the sky. "It is the rune of the warrior and counsels perseverance, courage and dedication. Vikings would paint this glyph on their shields before battle."

Turning over the second stone, Kat chuckled darkly.

"This," she pointed to what looked like an H, "warns of disruption by forces beyond control. It is the challenge, helping us to grow."

The third one looked like an F and designated the course of action. Kat smiled.

"This one is Loki, the ancient trickster of the god of the Norsemen. He brings wisdom in his messages, if we are able to recognize it."

"The sacrifice is reversed, the glyph which looks like the sign indicating greater than in mathematics calls for giving up the old gladly. It mimics the Death card that seems glued to our path."

Kat hesitated a moment before turning over the final stone.

"Finally, we have the evolved situation. Where we are at the end."

When she saw the squared off infinity sign that was called Dagaz, she laughed, a short sharp bark.

"This rune marks the conclusion of the cycle of initiation. It announces a major shift in attitude, a total transformation, one that introduces a period of achievement and success."

Liz patted the bag of stones smiling.

"That doesn't sound bad. I guess these stones aren't so nasty after all."

Kat smiled at her.

"Spoken with the courage of one who does not have to face the darkness."

16

Dunes Club
September

Rhode Island

"They're yellow and navy blue," Roxy informed him.

"What are?"

"Kat's current underwear colors."

Jake chuckled. "Did she explain the choice?"

"She said the yellow was for wisdom, the navy to remind her she was a Republican."

Jake had pilfered one of the Dunes Club's green tablecloths and spread it on a corner of the raised lawn that lined the beach side of the weathered gray shingle building. They were sitting, bathed in full moon light. The oracle had not lied. It had been a perfect evening since the moment Jake arrived to escort Kat and Roxy to the end-of-season ball at Narragansett's premier club.

The ocean oracle shouted its prediction that morning when she walked along the shore. The promise of paradise was obvious in the colors, the scents, the scenes. Roxy had never known there were so many blues in the world—sky, clouds, waves. No wonder people came to the beach to paint, it was a challenge both to discern and duplicate the range of tones. The ocean was dotted with boats. The Block Island Ferry was making its way across the Bay to the south. There was enough of a breeze to excite the ocean though the day was warm. Waves rolled in as parallel white stripes of surf, barely kissing the sand before another stripe rolled to oblivion atop its predecessor. Since the weekend was just beginning, carbon monoxide had not yet polluted the fresh sea air.

The fates obviously considered Roxy too dense to guess the style of the day from glorious sunshine and gleaming sea. They provided additional hints. She passed a shiny black limo in the lot of the Coast Guard House, an adorable, blond chauffeur in black tie leaning against the car looking out over the rocks. Massachusetts tags. Town would be jammed with tourists for this final weekend of summer.

As they turned off Ocean Drive that night, past the turreted gray stucco guard house and along the curved driveway lined with the ubiquitous beach foliage of sand pines and rose hips, she realized it would be her first view of the club exterior that did not front on the beach not to mention her first time inside. It was the fiftieth anniversary of something related to the club, so the theme for the annual black tie event was 1940 and most guests came in period clothes. Jake had borrowed a vintage Cadillac convertible to compliment his Depression-era tails acquired in a Newport antique shop years ago.

The Dunes Club was the province of the rich, mostly from out-of-state. There were a few legacies like Jake. He inherited his club membership from a great-uncle who emigrated to New York while a young man and made a fortune in banking. The uncle loved summering in Rhode Island and considered Jake the only one in the family who looked the part of Dunes Club member. Kat's plan was to work the crowd for campaign donations. There was little chance that anyone would outshine her star.

She wore a pale yellow slinky satin dress that softly skimmed her hips and hung to the floor. There was little that could be termed a back and the plunging neckline in front was equally dramatic. It did have long sleeves, one of which was embroidered in tiny seed pearls. A long rope of creamy pearls knotted at the lowest point in her neckline, and tiny pearl clusters studded her ears. Liz's diet was working. Kat appeared less gaunt and strained; her body seemed softer and rounder.

Out-of-state or not, Kat's admirers were everywhere and swept her up as Jake led them into the silvery-white entry hall.

Since few of the guests watched Rhode Island television, Jake enjoyed anonymity except for generally admiring glances, leaving Roxy the delighted recipient of his undivided attention. They amused themselves exploring the club, watching the people and dancing. Green was the predominant color of club décor. They examined an enormous oil painting of the Narragansett Towers and their missing casino that hung in the large ballroom now crowded with white-clothed tables and green chairs. Black overhead fans kept the cool ocean breezes circulating along with an array of fabulous perfumes on both men and women that would have dazzled the most extravagant Eastern potentate.

Roxy slipped a few of the small white napkins printed with DC and a green light tower that were the Club's logo into Jake's pocket.

"For my memory book," she responded to his cocked eyebrow.

"Let's work on some real memories," he said leading her onto the dance floor where he intoxicated her with compliments. She wore a dress her mother had danced in fifty years ago. Babs Holland was a saver; she never got rid of anything. Her father, Bert, insisted they had to retire to a hundred acre farm with three barns and a full basement to store her life collections. This night, Roxy appreciated her mother's quirk. They were similar in figure and coloring. The green crepe chiffon full skirted dress with its criss-cross draped bodice and tight waist accentuated all her best features. The intensity of Jake's admiring gaze reinforced her satisfaction.

Dancing with Jake was unlike the night she danced with Hayes at the ball in Newport when he was simply killing time until he could drag her off for sex. Gliding across the floor in Jake's arms, she convinced herself that his reverence was more arousing than Hayes' lust.

They sat at a small table in a narrow room that extended from the inner lobby to the ocean. From this vantage, they could see everyone arriving and departing as well as passing from bar to ballroom. Kat worked the crowd diligently. Roxy watched her several times receive a business card from some formally dressed couple, jot a few notes and slip it into her beaded evening bag with a smile. The room's glass doors were open to a magnificent view of the ocean, the lights of Newport sparkling to the east. Crashing surf blended with the tinkling sound of a metallic fish sculpture that rotated in the ocean breeze over their heads.

At Jake's urging they moved out to the lawn, the ball echoing behind them. Moonlight was so bright Roxy could distinguish every hair in his remarkable eyebrows. As she reached over impulsively to stroke them, he took her hand and kissed the palm tenderly.

"Remind me to thank Kat once again for turning me on to you," he said ardently.

"What do you mean?"

"She's never mentioned it to you?" he asked, apprehensively.

"Mentioned what?" When he seemed reluctant to explain, Roxy became insistent. "What did Kat do? Tell me."

"It wasn't anything important."

"Then why do you feel the need to thank her—again? Tell me what she did."

"It was nothing for you to be upset about, Roxy."

Another reassuring phrase that flashed warning lights to her.

"Tell me."

Jake sighed in resignation.

"She called and asked if I would meet her friend who would be here for the campaign."

"Meet? She asked you to come meet me? Nothing more?"

"Well, actually she asked me to … ah, to … she suggested I could do with a good relationship, that you were worth my time and that I could both teach you things and learn from you."

The blow to her pride, located somewhere under the tight midriff of her dress, pushed her to her feet.

"When did this happen?"

"About a week before I met you that day on the beach."

"You knew who I was?"

"Kat sent me a picture."

She was horrified as the implications of Jake's confession dawned on her. He was babysitting, keeping her out of trouble and away from Hayes at Kat's request. And she had begun to convince herself that the feeling with Jake was better than blood chemistry. What a trick! She would never again ignore her gut feeling—or more accurately, loin feeling—in dealing with a man. She knew there was no spark from Jake when they first met. Now she knew why. He was just doing this for Kat. What a chump she was torturing herself with guilt about Hayes. He wanted her in spite of Kat's prohibitions.

Sobbing, she ran from the lawn, through the glass doors and out the front entrance, catching a glimpse of Kat's surprised face as they almost collided. Roxy did not stop running until she broke a heel just after passing an abandoned weathered wood guard house about halfway up the driveway. She removed both shoes, peeled off her panty hose, and walked barefoot the rest of the way home, too blinded by tears and humiliation to notice the concerned glances from people she passed along the way.

Sprawled on her bed, she sobbed for hours over what she saw as Kat's betrayal, not to mention Jake's, before falling asleep.

Jake appeared in the lobby in time to see Roxy run past Kat and out the door.

"What's wrong?" Kat asked when he moved to her side. Frowning at his explanation, Kat agreed to his request not to follow her.

"I don't want Roxy hurt. How do you feel about her?"

Flashing his now famous look of total sincerity, he replied, "Love is sweetest when you come on it unexpectedly."

★ ★ ★ ★ ★

She must have slept at some point because her eyelids were stuck together. They felt so filled with sand and grit she could almost believe she slept on the beach. Open, her eyes burned so she rolled out of bed and into the bathroom peering through tolerable slits. She kept her eyes closed as she finished brushing her hair although that made them burn even worse. She could not bear looking at herself in any of the mirrors. The room was filled with reflections of red ringed eyes and puffy lids. Everywhere she turned she was confronted with the evidence of a miserable, tearful night caused, as usual, by some man. It had been such a perfect day. Why had the ocean oracle not warned her it would end up in grief?

Months ago she told Max she did not want to be involved with any men during the campaign. Even though Hayes was honest about using her like sexual water softener, she could not kid herself into believing it was love or even romance. But that Jake had moved from the prince category to selfish user as well was disillusioning. She wondered what Kat had offered him—were the television commercials a payoff? Don't be stupid, she chided herself, you turned Gould on to Jake and Jake's presence made him a hit, and once a hit no personal recommendations were needed. She had been right in her initial impulse to give up men! Even the best of them ended up using her because she made it so easy.

She sat on the edge of the bed, pressing a wet, cold cloth to her eyes, trying to soothe them enough so she could see to walk on the beach. Sanity began to return. Her time with Jake had been wonderful. He taught her so much, admired her in a way she never before experienced. He was not the villain in this drama. He did a favor for a friend, it turned out well, and he was expressing his gratitude. Simple! She should be angry at Kat.

Rushing from her room to get out on the beach before tourists began spreading their blankets, she fell against the wicker chaise that was stretched across the hall. Jake pulled her onto it and into his arms before her tortured eyelids could open enough to see where she was going. It was not in her nature to struggle against a man holding her but she gave it a thought before surrendering to the calm that poured into her heart from his fingers placed between her breasts. He brushed his fingertips across her swollen eyes and looked pained. Cupping her face in his hands, he lightly kissed her eyes, her cheeks and finally her lips.

"Love is sweetest when you find it unexpectedly," he said.

"Did you lie out here last night thinking that up?"

"I've known it for a while. I wanted it to be the first thought spoken to you this morning."

"Why didn't you follow me and tell me that last night?"

"You wouldn't have heard it then."

Her lacerated eyes could tolerate no more tears. Annoyance faded quickly as she snuggled into his arms and allowed him to cajole her into forgiveness.

★ ★ ★ ★ ★

They spent a wonderful day at Jake's avoiding holiday traffic and thoughts of the campaign. Roxy was not yet ready to confront how she felt about Kat's role in the matchmaking.

Over the past hectic month of the campaign, she found little opportunity to see his work. The door of his shop now opened to the heartbeat rhythms of Ravel. The walls, windows and benches were covered with adoring images of her in various poses and mediums from intricate sketches and water colors to half completed glass. They made love for hours on the enfolding cushions of the hand-me-down couch infusing each image with the essence of the goddess of love according to Jake. She indulged herself in more loving atonement from a man than she thought possible.

Later, they walked on the beach, the bright full moonlight casting shadows everywhere: sharp and precise, dancing and frisking by their sides, slipping behind or scurrying on ahead. They sat on the beach, leaning against the retaining wall that held the Dunes Club lawn where they sat the previous night. For a long time they were silent. Nothing had been said about what Roxy still thought of as betrayal and she did not want to be the first to introduce it. She was ready to completely forgive but wanted at least to have a spoken acknowledgement. The silence continued as they wandered alone in their reflections, thoughts tossing like the moonbeams sparkling on the waves.

Jake finally broke the silence.

"Does it really matter how we came together?"

When she did not respond, he answered his own question.

"It doesn't for me. Not any more. Not now that I love you."

Rolling onto his stomach, Jake took her hand and concentrated the full force of his sincere, brow wrinkled gaze on her face.

"Can I tell you why I love you?"

She nodded mutely.

He made himself comfortable, still holding her hand and looking into her eyes.

"This may take a while," he said with a smile.

"To you, life is never dull. I love your sudden impulses, your joy in every moment, how even the simplest of experiences can satisfy you. Expressing yourself so freely through your body, you live in the world I seek—sensation. I like how you stretch and curl under my strokes, how you hug back.

"I love how you give appreciation freely and treasure it as a rare gift when its given to you. I love the laugh that's always lurking in your voice and the pout that's there when the world insists on being unpleasant. There's no doubt that faced with a choice, I could count on you to always urge the most enjoyable path. I love it that you've chosen to serve pleasure rather than pain.

"Is all this adulation bothering you?"

"It makes me afraid. I understand desire and lust. I know how to satisfy them in a man, but love? I'm not certain I know how to satisfy that."

"It's my love, freely given to you. You don't owe me anything for it. I love you right this moment for what you are, nothing about you needs to change now that you know I love you."

She laid in his arms and cried as the rhythm of the waves beat inside her and the burning returned to her eyes.

★ ★ ★ ★ ★

Arranging with Jake to pick her up around noon for the Tomasso company picnic, Roxy spent the night at home hoping to encounter Kat. She could easily forgive Jake. He saw Kat's gesture as the gift of a lifetime. How could she be irritated at that? Kat's motives still needed to be resolved as far as she was concerned.

When she came down the next morning to a kitchen filled with delectable smells, she found only Liz bustling away making food for the picnic. Halfway through her monologue on the day's events, Roxy interrupted.

"Have you seen Kat?"

"She stayed at Duke's compound last night. She had a full day of festivals yesterday and wanted to be up at dawn to help prepare for the picnic. She said last year they used five huge trucks to cart all the food, beer, soda, games, tables and other paraphernalia to the park for this shindig. As soon as my pies are done, I'm meeting up with Yola and the aunts to set up the food operation. Do you know they expect to feed seven hundred people? Thank heavens, it's going to be a perfect day. In fact, I just phoned in my order for two months of today, beginning now and running through the election. I don't care what the weather is like once I leave."

Closing the oven on her final batch of blueberry pies, Liz noted the pensive look on Roxy's face.

"Are you having an unpleasant thought, or is it indigestion? What's the matter?"

Roxy shrugged and whimpered. Liz ignored her and went on with her recitation.

"Kat asked if you would meet up with her around four to go over the final draft of her speech. This is apparently a major public address although the audience is limited to Tomasso employees and families with some special suppliers and customers thrown in. We, of course, are now considered family."

Knowing that Kat was expecting her usual devotion having done nothing to find out how she was feeling, made Roxy angry.

"I found out that Kat asked Jake to start seeing me so she wouldn't have to worry about me messing around Hayes."

"Oh. And you're upset because you can't think of a sufficiently lavish gift of appreciation to give her for this."

Roxy growled. Why did she ever expect Liz to take her side?

"Are you pouting? The number one draft choice of half the women in this state chooses to lavish his sweet love on a dim witted slut like you, and all you can think about is being annoyed at Kat for being a good enough friend that she pushed him in your direction. You're an idiot, Roxy."

"I guess I don't like it that Kat feels I can't pick a good man by myself. That somehow, I need help in choosing well."

"Of course she feels that, you dumb blonde. It's true! You make terrible choices. This is a prince. Don't toss him aside because you like kissing frogs."

"But she manipulated me, and it wasn't because she thought it was time for me to find a good man. She just wanted me safe so I wouldn't mess up her campaign."

Liz sat down at the table and poured Roxy a glass of juice.

"Kat's a woman with a mission. Everything that does not contribute to that mission is an obstacle that must be overcome. She never questions the basic premise of whether the mission is worth it or not, and in great part that's her charm and power.

"Because I'm a good friend, I won't remind you that you did the same to her. You asked Senator Stuart to fuck our favorite congresswoman."

Roxy shrieked indignantly.

"I did it because you told me to. And how do you know about that anyway?"

Liz ignored her outburst and moved to the back stairs.

"I have to go get dressed. I'm leaving as soon as those pies are done."

★ ★ ★ ★ ★

There was a strong wind blowing along the shore, stirring up the waves and making walking a strain. But Roxy was determined to have her solitary walk before subjecting herself to the madness of the most enormous family picnic in the state.

The sky was cloudless and bright promising a perfect day. Surprisingly, the water was dark, not the usual iridescent blue of sunny days. She wondered if this were an omen of difficulties ahead. She still had to face Kat even if only to clear the air. By this point she realized everyone was right. Kat had done her a favor and, grateful or not, it was petty to be angry.

Briefly, she worried about the sail boat she saw sitting empty about a hundred feet off-shore. Then she spotted the buoy and assumed it had been anchored there probably as transport to a larger boat. Once on the sand beach, she let the strains of the past few days, and the weeks to come, sift through her mind. She almost stumbled over the sand sculpture that lay near the steps to the Dunes Club. It was an incredibly complex castle with inner and outer courtyards, different sets of walls, and numerous buildings. A white feather was stuck atop the highest of its five towers. In the courtyard, there was a message scratched in the sand. R. You reign in the castle of my heart. J.

Everyone was right about Jake, too. He was a prince and she was a fool to let anyone else interfere.

★ ★ ★ ★ ★

They drove into a small park along the Scituate Reservoir. Duke had given it to the town with the understanding that Tomasso Excavating would have exclusive rights to it on Labor Day, in perpetuity. It was perfectly maintained waterfront property with pavilions, ballfields, swimming and boat docks, playground, picnic tables scattered through several groves, and a specially-constructed clam steamer.

By the time Jake and Roxy arrived, softball was in full swing, the beer truck was strategically placed, the steamer was cranking, and several tables were laden with pre-dinner snacks. Liz was right, there were hundreds of people there, most dressed in the special tee shirts distributed each year. The current edition was navy printed with a white grinning steam shovel taking a bite out of a map of the state. Roxy was a stand-out in her strapless red polka dot sundress. She had her hair pulled back and tied in a perky red polka-dot bow. Jake immediately changed into his Tomasso teeshirt and resigned himself to spending the day being surrounded by adoring teen-agers. Roxy waved him off to the softball field and wandered over to hang out by the food.

It was after four when Kat finally led her to a secluded table overlooking the reservoir. Roxy had butterflies in her stomach as they sat side by side, reviewing Kat's recent additions to the text she had written on work and family.

"I'm feeling particularly inspired today. Would you make notes on anything spontaneous I may say that we could use in the future? I'll be speaking to the AFL-CIO convention in a couple weeks, and want to hit labor and the economics of work as a special theme all month. I'm going on the offensive with critical issues."

Kat's focus on the campaign inflamed Roxy's irritation over the matter of Jake. Did she not realize they had unfinished personal business to resolve? Of course not, she was a woman with a mission as Liz said, and that was all that mattered, Roxy chided herself. Then she remembered her fortune strip for September which she belatedly opened that morning: *Know the truth then act in love.*

It was several moments before Roxy realized Kat was silently staring at her.

"You seem to have forgiven Jake. Can't you forgive me too?"

After a few moments of silence, Kat continued. "I understand how you feel and I'm sorry. As William Blake said, 'I was angry with my friend; I told my wrath, my wrath did end.'"

"I was irate that you saw the need to push me into Jake's arms."

"I know. I felt the same way when you tried to do that to me with Stuart."

Roxy perked up at Kat's tone. There was something different in how she was talking about the senator.

"What about you and Stuart anyway?"

Kat looked at the players on the nearby ballfield so long without responding, Roxy was sure she was once again avoiding the question.

"Sometimes T.J. Stuart is a hero beyond my wildest imaginings. Sometimes he is completely insufferable," she answered with a sigh.

She quickly changed the subject reaching over to affectionately pull on a strand of Roxy's hair that had escaped its bow.

"Your hair is so soft and pretty, not like my bailing wire corkscrews. It's been true all through history: it's better to be blond. Do you know how often I look at you with an attitude that can only be described as awe? It's not because of your many talents, which I do appreciate, but because of your good nature. Everyone always wants you around, not because of what you can do or produce but because life is more fun when you're there. You're easy to be with. It's not like that for me." Kat waved away Roxy's protests.

"I'm aware of my flaws and weaknesses. I know that people respect and admire me, some naïve ones worship me. I've even been loved on occasion. But I don't think it's easy for people to like me the way they do you. I don't know how much they would forgive me based on affection. I'm valued for what I accomplish, for what I have. No one seeks me out for my warmth and charm."

Roxy had to agree. Kat's nature was austere and aloof. It did not inspire love. Still, she objected.

"But you're on a mission, a soul-defining quest. There's no time for you to be nice and easy. That's your destiny, and mine is to help you."

"Thank you for doing this with me. Having you as a friend has been such a blessing. You're always smiling and laughing. When people come to you with complaints or a hard-luck story you don't rush around frantically trying to fix it. You just listen, make no judgements, then soothe and sympathize. When you agree with my vision, when you translate it into words everyone can hear, it lessens my uncertainty. It's easier for me to trust destiny, to be confident in my path, when you're around.

"Don't think I take you for granted, dear friend, because I often skip the amenities. It's as if you're a part of me. Understand clearly, I appreciate and value your loyalty and support more than I can ever say.

"When I called Jake to meet you, I was thinking of the campaign and your obvious infatuation with Hayes, but I was also thinking of you. I don't know a better man than Jake Hansen, and I can't think of someone who deserves a good man like him more than you. Love him, Roxy—it will be the best thing you've ever done."

Kat's speech to her assembled tribal family was as heartfelt and moving as her speech to Roxy. She was dressed in jeans and the same Tomasso teeshirt as most of the crowd, a red bandana wrapped around her forehead. Rays from the setting sun colored her aura with rainbows as she stood on a flatbed truck, microphone in hand.

She had the crowd in tears with her reminiscences about Duke and how they all loved him, sharing anecdotes from her childhood, family stories about the early days of the business. As she talked about Duke she was also talking about work, about family, about duties and responsibilities. Roxy took notes. Kat was right. She was inspired and there was much they could use in the weeks ahead.

Jake was standing by her side as they said their good-byes to Yola and the aunts who were sitting around the food tables preparing to dissect the event and share the stories they collected. Roxy caught the noxious stench that was now as distinct in her olfactory memory as the lavender she kept in her dresser drawers but still unidentified. As they moved off she mentioned it to Jake who agreed he could discern the stink. She struggled to remember when she had first smelled it.

★ ★ ★ ★ ★

All the tourists left with summer on Labor Day. Fall arrived with the opening of school. Even the weather demons knew. No waiting until the equinox for them. By mid-week, walking on the beach was once again private and calm. The boat she had seen on Labor Day appeared filled with water and washed ashore. Then it was gone. Roxy saw the spry old man she passed daily, usually near the now empty flagpole in front of the Dunes Club. She guessed she would never again see the several flags that hung from the poles all summer, nor discover what two of them meant. One had an elongated diamond printed on it, the other was white emblazoned with a gold anchor and the word Hope.

There were winds whipping up whitecaps and the big white lifeguard chairs were already removed. She was disappointed, having anticipated a replay with Jake of their spring night on the beach while it was still warm. She smiled as two rascally looking mutts peered through a gap in the storm fence lining the beach then scooted onto the sand heading north. Even the unescorted dogs had returned although the ban was theoretically in force through mid-September.

With the primary less than two weeks away, and Kat's candidacy uncontested, the campaign adopted a strange rhythm of watch, wait and plan. From Mario down to the most junior volunteer, everyone was relieved that activities could slow long enough to catch breath and gear up for the final seven weeks. August's walk through the state, although the undisputed success of the year, had pushed them all to exhaustion.

Douglas too had no opposition in the primary yet he remained in the state campaigning. He seemed unaffected by Stuart's daily attacks from the Senate floor noting that Rhode Island's self-appointed senator had yet to appear in Washington.

The *Ocean Beacon* newspaper focused on the primary, endorsing the strongest Democratic candidate in local races. The stronger the overall ticket, the greater benefit to Douglas. Whatever his agenda in the primary, Kat's campaign rejoiced that Douglas was ignoring her.

Although there were dozens of house parties and other fundraisers on the schedule in September and October, no one believed in-state money could provide even a third of the million dollars they needed to raise. The decision had been made: Kat would spend the next two weeks fundraising among PACs in Washington. There were trips scheduled throughout the month to Chicago, Atlanta, Dallas, Aspen, Seattle and San Francisco, all to raise money from rich Republicans, devoted environmentalists and ardent supporters of more women in the U.S. Senate. A southern tour ending in a huge Miami fundraiser had been organized by Senator Stuart and featured all seven of the Republican female senate candidates. If successful, there were tentative plans for a similar tour with the women that would take them to Kansas City, Denver, Las Vegas, and Los Angeles. A final gift from the Senatorial committee was a fundraising breakfast with the president in Washington that would guarantee at least another hundred thousand from PACs.

With the walk over, Liz moved lock, stock and barrel into campaign headquarters. Mario assigned her a desk alongside Yola's so they could motivate the volunteer corps. They immersed themselves in mail, yard signs, and planning a day-long celebration for the grand openings of four regional campaign offices. Liz also staked out a project that utilized her trenchant wit to the fullest. Knowing she could never disguise her distinctive voice, she created the character of Dolly from Nooseneck and set out to trash Douglas relentlessly on the call-in radio shows that served as favorite daytime entertainment for thousands of Rhode Islanders. Within a few days, she was well-known and anticipated by talk show hosts and regular callers. Liz felt her strategy was a success when Dolly from Nooseneck's description of Douglas was quoted in the *Journal*'s weekly political notes column: "He's what's was left when a spiritual vacuum sucks everything out of a human being."

Senatorial sent Paul Reilly to supervise a special series of mailings funded by committee money funneled through the state Republican party. Roxy could not wait to see the encounter between Liz and Reilly. They would hate each other on sight.

She was content with her assignments. Kat was determined to ignore any further attacks from Douglas or the Democrats. She staked out the economy, the budget, and jobs as the issues she would focus on for the rest of the campaign and drove everyone crazy developing and scheduling speaking opportunities in the state. Roxy was working on several major speeches as well as preparing the issue statements from the walk for publication in early October as a small book. Kat resolved to ignore the build-up of troops and tensions in the Middle East, believing Senator Stuart's prediction and Max's pronouncement that there would be no war until after the election.

As part of her tasks, Roxy spoke several times a day with Hayes who never allowed a call to end without a brief sample of his intimate tone. That sugared drawl still moistened her panties. She also spoke daily to Kat who, by the beginning of the second week, was bemoaning her exile from Indian summer in Rhode Island and her ardent longing for crisp fall walks on the beach.

The slow pace of the campaign allowed social time to flourish. Pete was using his restaurant tour as core of a new book and was rounding out the menu with Providence. He saw Liz as a golden opportunity and invited her as well as Jake and Roxy to accompany him on his rounds.

Liz provided entertainment as well as expert analysis of the food and restaurant operations. One night at Café Roscoe on Hope Street they ate superlative regional Italian food and listened to an Armenian jazz trio from the Soviet Union, another benefit of *glasnost*.

Liz was describing life in the campaign office and snorted, "Don't you think we should have staff old enough to vote? Douglas at least has adults working for him."

"How do you know that?" Roxy asked suspiciously as she beat Jake off from stealing her next-to-last chunk of lobster drenched in a tomato sauce and strewn along with mussels over fat pasta.

"I visited Douglas headquarters today," Liz replied off-handedly.

"What! Does anyone know you did this?" Roxy could imagine what Hayes would think of Liz conducting reconnaissance missions in the enemy's camp.

"I told Bruno and Mario as soon as I came back. They loved it. It was an accident, really. I didn't go out spying. I was trying to find my way back from one of our satellite office sites and got lost. Lo and behold, there I was at Davol Square, a huge Douglas sign staring from the building. I stumbled onto a back elevator, chatted with this fresh-faced staffer who was going to the fourth floor and followed her off. We cruised by a well-coiffed gray-head sitting at the fancy reception desk. Since I was obviously with what's-her-name, the dragon guarding the entry never gave me a second look. Also it was the staff, not public, entrance. The roster posted for messages listed almost fifty names! Do you think that's how he's going to get votes, by hiring them as staff?"

Liz steamed on.

"I told my staffer that I needed bumper stickers and brochures and followed her as we went looking. The halls were carpeted, walls neatly hung with signs, all very professional. They have two whole floors with fancy offices, dividers, desks, machines everywhere. Definitely not the fraternity house party room décor we have. She couldn't find any stickers so took me downstairs to the third floor. It was marked Field and there were at least a dozen cubicles labeled with different areas of the state. And here we are with four field staff. After she delivered the stickers, she sent me back out unescorted so I nosed around, picked up several schedules and field organization lists. I gave them to the boys to sniff out but there is an interesting tidbit for you."

Before Roxy could ask, Liz said gloatingly, "Our friend Carrie's name was on the list for Woonsocket."

"Carrie! Do you think Race Scarlatti is supporting Douglas?"

"Maybe he's trying to sabotage the man by sending him Carrie." Liz laughed. "You boys know everybody in the state. Either of you have anything to contribute about our friend the gangster?"

"All my stories are second-hand but Jake had a close personal encounter with Race."

They all turned as he nodded agreement and began to tell the story.

"Actually I owe Race Scarlatti my career as an artist because he effectively destroyed my career as an athlete. It was my senior year in high school and I was ranked the number one guard in the state. South County High, which was my school, was playing Bayview in the state basketball finals. Race came to me about throwing the game. He was in the throes of solidifying his hold on illegal sports gambling in the state. Manipulating this game was his big break. He offered me a lot of money, told me refusing would hurt only me because someone would agree if I didn't. When I continued to reject his offer he turned ugly and threatened to make me sorry. 'You'll never play ball again,' were his exact words. He was right. I didn't. The next day my motorcycle was hit broadside by a woman who ran a stop sign. My ankle was shattered and my arm broken. Three operations and more than a year in casts later, I could walk but would never run again."

"Did you go to the police?" Roxy asked, stunned by his recital.

"Without me, South County lost. No connection was ever found between Scarlatti and the driver of the car that hit me. Race effectively owned whatever part of the law enforcement system was concerned with illegal gambling. A couple of my father's buddies who were on the force in Providence and Cranston came to see me in the hospital and urged me to consider the real danger to my life and possibly my parents. I decided they were right."

He paused for several moments while the other three considered his story.

"But I haven't forgotten. Nothing would satisfy me more than helping to rid this state, this planet, of Race Scarlatti."

Roxy shivered. She hoped she would never hear that tone or see that harsh look on Jake's face again.

★ ★ ★ ★ ★

About two days after Liz's penetration of the enemy camp, a Democratic spy wandered into Kat's campaign headquarters on Atwell's Avenue. Liz's bar-owner radar immediately picked up a dissonant blip and she intercepted the young man before he could walk beyond the first table filled with volunteers addressing envelopes. As soon as she spotted the donkey-tail watch he wore, she started inching him out the door, nodding politely at his tale of being from North Carolina and lost looking for Brown University. Once gone, she nattered around for a while wondering if his appearance was a coincidence or had her reconnaissance been detected by Douglas workers.

Roxy wandered downstairs, taking a break from the computer and the long list of floor statements she was drafting from Kat's issue sheets. Liz pounced immediately, relating her successful detection of the spy, then dragged Roxy into a dark corner in the back of the storage room. "This is where I do my magic," she said waving her hand at several posters. Roxy examined them. "This is my Carrie sighting chart. Every day someone sees her, or hears about her, or has an unidentified encounter that we suspect may be Carrie, it's listed on here. It was Bruno's idea. He's convinced Carrie is shadowing us round the clock." Seeing all the entries on the chart, Roxy was inclined to agree.

"And this is my Douglas voodoo."

Liz pointed to a Douglas poster, one of the huge, grinning ones. She had divided it into a hundred squares, each representing one percent of the vote.

"Each day I work to slice a square off. I just started so there's only about ten percent missing. But I started with his brain," she pointed to several squares gone from his forehead. "I figured I'd start easy, with parts he won't notice are missing. By the election, I'll have him whittled down to thirty percent. I haven't decided what features I'll leave yet. Maybe just his neck so we can string him up."

★ ★ ★ ★ ★

The first Saturday Kat was away, Roxy and Liz were scheduled to join Pete and Jake at Newport's Taste of Rhode Island. Pete was, of course, an honored guest with free tickets for them all. Jake and Roxy were dressed in Kiley for Senate sweatshirts and jeans, laden with Kiley stickers and brochures. Liz staunchly refused to wear any campaign garb.

"I look enough like a billboard as is, advertising would clinch it," she insisted. "If I appeared in a Kiley sweatshirt, they'd vote me into the Glamour Magazine Fashion Don'ts hall of fame."

The Taste celebration began with a parade of chefs, resplendent in white hats and jackets, marching along America's Cup Avenue from the visitor's center to the wharf where the food bazaar was being held. Pete seemed to know them all, and they waved to him as they passed, most offering a thumbs up sign when they spotted the Kiley sweatshirt standing by his side.

Liz never left Pete. Each of the fifty plus restaurants that participated by selling their specialties from booths to the public offered him free samples. The four stopped and ate their treasure trove more than a dozen times, each break signaling a change in content for Liz's commentary. After lobster rolls, stuffed quohogs, and fried squid from a block of seafood restaurants, Liz began talking diet.

"This campaign has not been the least bit mind-expanding," she claimed, "but it sure has been waist-expanding. I'm considering starting the Colombian diet tomorrow."

As usual, Roxy played her straight man. "What's the Colombian diet?"

"That's what you eat when you're in Colombia and it's guaranteed to have you thin as a rail in weeks. In a way it's macrobiotic. You eat only what's natural to the environment. In the case of Colombia that's coffee and cocaine. It's tough to eat three meals a day on this diet. No thanks, no lunch for me, I haven't come down from breakfast yet.

"Of course, conventional wisdom claims the best way to lose weight is to fall in love. We know that's not true by looking at Roxy. If it were, she'd be a skeleton."

During their stop to sample a range of Oriental treats they collected, Liz began badgering Jake.

"Why don't you make me a goddess like Roxy? I have tits as big as hers. I could be Earth Mother or something."

"I'd love to photograph you and see what we could develop," Jake replied sincerely.

"No photographs!" Liz insisted. "Cameras don't lie, artists do. Truth doesn't look good in my size."

After losing themselves in a tray full of desserts, Roxy decided to harass Liz again about finding a man. She pointed out how much time the four of them had been spending together and what fun they had.

"Are you reconsidering Pete as a potential date, Liz?" she teased.

"Now I know I should be kind to a man who's managed to feed me from more restaurants in an hour than we have in a fifty mile radius of Morgan Springs, but truth must be served. So, don't take this personally, sweetie." Liz patted his hand. "All men come into the world between some woman's legs. Pete's one of the multitude who devote their lives trying to return. This man has fondled more breasts and thighs than Colonel Sanders. Pete's a social disease. I like my men to be loveys: wanting to please me, reliable, faithful, and sweet. This man's a lovey," she leaned over and pinched Jake's cheek. Pete laughed then turned to Roxy.

"I've been meaning to ask how you deal with sex in your books. They're written for teen-age girls aren't they?"

Before she could finish the cream puff she was eating, Liz answered for her.

"Roxy never addresses sex in her books, partly because she can't decide what words to use in addressing it. I remember her telling me once how disturbing it was to apply filthy names to the precious jewels of men and women's sexual organs. I quoted you right, didn't I?" she said, turning to the blushing Roxy.

True though Liz's statement was, Roxy decided to ignore it.

"The need for educating teenagers in the proper reverence for sex does concern me," she began seriously.

"Well you're certainly the one to do that," Liz interjected. "You've bent your knee and given lip service to more erect penises than anyone I know."

Losing her train of thought, Roxy responded impulsively.

"I didn't even know what an erection was until I read about it in some sex-education book when I was fifteen. I was an avid reader and consumed dozens of my mother's books. But it was pre-sexual revolution and the sex in mainstream fiction was vague, no technical details allowed."

Jake interceded hoping to prevent a food fight.

"Speaking of books, Roxy and I started our Erotic Literature course Thursday night." Before he could provide any further details, Liz pounced.

"Erotic Literature? You're taking a course in that, Roxy? Why? Planning to write your autobiography?"

When Roxy stuck out her cream coated tongue, Liz continued.

"Are you going to include the charming vignette about your introduction to the word fuck? That'll convince everyone you're an innocent at heart, " Liz teased.

Rolling her eyes, Roxy told the tale of how she was hanging out in the woods once day with a couple male playmates when they used the word. She had never heard it before but somehow knew it was sexual although she barely knew at that time what sex was.

"I guess we were about ten. Of course, today, most ten year olds use the word fuck in casual conversation. Anyway, I badgered them about what it meant and they refused to tell me. I remember them laughing hysterically when I asked if it was like tickling."

Jake sat grinning. For all his devotion to the sacredness of sex, he never felt ribald conversation detracted. Then Liz turned her attention to him.

"How come if you're such a student of erotica, all of your Aphrodites are draped ladies, not a pubic hair visible among the lot?"

"I guess I wanted to keep that part of my model for myself alone."

Roxy almost pushed a slice of strawberry cheesecake into Liz's face as she laughed uproariously.

"It's a little late for that, bud."

★ ★ ★ ★ ★

To everyone's amazement, Liz decided Paul Reilly was a genius.

"His ethics are a pile of cavalry litter, as Barney would say, but he always recognizes the straightest line between two points. And he's disrespectful. I like that in a tool."

The top of his thinly-haired head barely skimmed her shoulder. She would affectionately hug him as he peered up at her over his thick glasses.

"Doesn't he remind you of one of those worker gnomes, all snarled up but really a softie inside. Rumplestiltskin. That's who he is. Reilly Rumplestiltskin. I'll call him Rump!"

She gave him a squeeze and a smile and "Rump" was born, although no one but Liz ever called him that to his face. Roxy always wondered what she really had in mind.

His reaction was as mystifying as her adopting of him as her pet. He loved it. He beamed. He treasured Liz's screams for "Rump."

The day of the primary, Liz called Roxy over to the desk she and Reilly had strewn with papers and announced, "The Senate Race Game." She pointed to a mock game board lined with squares that snaked in a pattern of mazes, describing how the game was fueled by money with rolls of the dice deciding fundraising success. There were cards and events represented by squares on the board at which the candidate arrived through buying moves. They had selected six candidate characters including Kat and Stuart. Roxy was impressed as they talked of press hit cards and special moves for Opponent Scandal Leaked, Debate, and Endorsement.

"We're going to use a part of our millions to have a big campaign reunion party at Magnolia's every year. Maybe we can do one in Rhode Island, too," Liz said.

In turn, Reilly enlisted the admiring Liz in his mailing scheme and together they plotted a saturation campaign for money and information that included dunning donors with Special Delivery letters. In a memorable strategy conference call prior to the primary, Kat vetoed that technique.

"There's a minor profit and the potential for maximum damage. You don't understand. If a letter from me drags people down to their Post Office, heart beating with anxiety over the contents of a Special Delivery message, they'll take it personally and I'll hear about it forever. It's not worth it.

"I'm unhappy about a whole list of other things," Kat harangued, beginning with an attack on the president for focusing total attention on foreign affairs and Iraq, ignoring mounting domestic problems. She went on to call the budget talks a farce.

"If I ever escape from this prison and get back to the state, I want to go on all the radio talk shows and ask people to call me with their suggestions for budget cuts."

Several voices were heard to bemoan Kat's proposal but that did not deter her. She lashed out at Gould when he asked about the debates.

"No debates. I thought that was clear. You all think Senator Stuart walks on water and he agrees I should not stoop to debating that worm."

Mario reported that several polls commissioned by various Democratic candidates were asking deliberately skewed questions about her.

"They ask whether finding out you made pornographic films, lobbied for state contracts for your family business, or supported Republican senators who opposed environmental regulations or rights for women would change their vote."

The stream of obscenity she unleashed before disconnecting herself from the conference call surprised all the participants. They had never heard such language from Kat before.

Hayes agreed with Mario's assessment that Kat's current erratic state precluded them taking much advantage of Douglas' distraction with the primary.

"All the polls, ours and others, show the same thing. We're still twenty points ahead but our weakest point is Republicans. It doesn't help that Kat seems to be galloping wildly to the left of Mao Tse Tung. When I pointed this strange fact out to her she insisted she was not moving left but above where all things are clear. Fortunately, she seems able to control herself when she's out begging for money."

Reilly jumped in to add his pet peeve about Kat's independence.

"She's berserk that Burkhart might siphon off a few dollars. She doesn't get the fact that a strong Republican party effort will only help her. She doesn't care about the GOP. She's a party unto herself and likes it that way. Somehow we have to convince her it's the Democratic machine that could have us on the ropes."

Roxy was concerned to see both Mario and Bruno nod their heads in agreement as they listened on phones within view of each other. Most discouraging was the resounding cheer Liz received when she closed the phone call by offering thanks for plans to keep Kat in Washington and on the road raising money.

★ ★ ★ ★ ★

Wanting not to alienate any Republican in the few contests that involved them, Kat's campaign staff took primary day off and stayed home to watch results on television. It was the strength of the Democratic ticket that interested them most.

Roxy watched the returns at Jake's allowing him to attempt distracting her by massaging her body with a specially blended musk-based oil.

"The woman who sold me this swore that the aroma alone would make me irresistible." She was more than ready to agree as Jake's practiced hands fondled her favorite erotic spots. Months of tantric practice had developed her capacity to hold a state of almost total sexual frenzy for long periods of time before releasing it in ever more intense orgasms. She could feel every nerve ending in her body screaming for the final push as she took her turn rubbing the love oil into Jake's almost hairless body admiring his flat stomach, rippled back and adorably tight ass.

As diligent as they were in working on their goal of directing the sexual energy they generated toward achieving two hundred and fifty thousand votes for Kat, they were unable to manage sex more than five times a week. After the frantic conference call with Kat, Roxy was worried that they needed to pump more energy into their vote project.

"Is there a way we can work on the vote totals in addition to the energy from having sex? Something we can do alone, or in public?"

"Now that we've developed the power initially through sex, there is," Jake responded. "You can raise the same power, and direct it as well, by breathing through both nostrils."

"That's all it takes?"

"That's all it takes for us. Consciously breathing through both nostrils is extremely powerful. I can make wishes or curses come true. It's also dangerous in that it controls destiny, time, and death."

Vowing that she would start breathing through both nostrils and concentrating on the vote totals as she walked on the beach each morning, Roxy returned her full attention to the pulsing she was feeling under her skin as Jake moved to impale her.

She was almost embarrassed as she felt her pounding climax sweep her mind to oblivion just as Rhode Island's premier news anchor announced the results of the Democratic gubernatorial primary. Getting off during the news she was becoming a true political junkie.

Watching the now familiar aftershocks sweep Jake's body, Roxy worried aloud about Liz.

"I feel guilty having all this fun with you while Liz is sitting home alone and unloved."

She was astonished as Jake laughed, starting a new series of muscle spasms.

"Don't worry about Liz," he said when he stopped twitching and began gently stroking what he termed his favorite stretch of terrain, the curve of her torso from breast to indented waist and back out again over her hip and around the globe of her ass.

"She's working on her own vote count."

Roxy sat up and stared. "What do you mean?"

"You don't know?"

There was an irritated pout on her lips, as she shook her head.

Jake laughed again as she began pounding on his back.

"Know what? Tell me, you brute. What do you know that I don't?"

"Ask Liz," he responded. "Ask Liz why they call Bruno 'the Hose.'" Jake collapsed into a pile of belly laughs as Roxy gasped. Bruno!

★ ★ ★ ★ ★

"He's Mario's age!" Roxy cried indignantly as she confronted Liz at breakfast the next morning.

"That may be. But I don't think they really work as a couple." She continued making pancakes filling Roxy's plate and ignoring her stream of reasons why this was all too improbable.

"I don't know what you're complaining about," Liz finally retorted. "Finding a man for me was your suggestion. You didn't have anyone specific in mind I assume?"

Roxy stared at her.

"I tell you Roxy, he won my heart with his manly hydraulics. When he sucked up his stomach, shook it and said, 'All this turns to dick for you, baby,' I knew he was the one. He's a good worker, notices everything, knows what he doesn't know, and follows direction well. His momma raised him to open doors and carry packages. Finally, the man can eat. That's the real reason he's called 'the Hose.' How much more can you ask in a man?"

Not pausing for an answer, Liz continued.

"I like them young and Catholic. When I drive away all that useless guilt they're so appreciative I can train them the way I like 'em."

Roxy limited her conversation for the rest of the meal to compliments on the pancakes.

★ ★ ★ ★ ★

The Democrats emerged from the primary with a strong slate of young, attractive, popular and ethically clean candidates. Douglas, who repelled even his own party members, seemed less of an anchor as war fever built. He would visit a Legion post or VFW hall, ramble about his days in Germany as a tank gunner, and walk away with a few more votes. It did not take long for the Democratic Senate leadership in Washington to realize their sole hope for holding onto the Rhode Island Senate seat lay in voting a straight ticket. They began lavishly distributing money among state and congressional candidates as well as to the state party. The theme: trash the Republicans, even if that meant trashing Kat, a longtime ally of many of the state's most progressive Democrats. A few refused to play the game; most succumbed to calls for party solidarity.

Senate Democrats managed to get Douglas to Washington. Colin Proctor, the aide who would be senator, worked diligently to keep him off the Senate floor where Senator Stuart continued daily assaults.

Kat's decision to discuss economic issues including housing and health care made her sound like a radical progressive. Douglas meanwhile spent his time waving the flag and posing with pro-life groups who flooded his Washington office. The strange positioning became so obvious that even Harry Crast was forced to comment in his weekly column. Trying to urge ticket splitting without appearing too obvious in his support of Kat, he wrote that Washington analysts had called, chiding him about the Humpty Dumpty race in Rhode Island.

"A normal senate race is but an illusion here," he wrote. "The Republican is defining the edge of possibility for a progressive 21st century, while the Democrat stakes out the high ground of the far right last held by Ferdinand Marcos. It does make it difficult to wave the specter of a Republican Senate filled with reactionary committee chairman when everyone knows it's our current self-appointed senator who agrees most with the bogey men he conjures up."

Yet no one was too anxious to challenge Douglas' obviously exploitative positions. Kat railed at their cowardice as Mario tried to justify it or at least explain its roots.

"I know, I know," she responded. "A half a dozen of my former friends have waffled around before admitting they're scared shitless. One of them drove me past a cemetery claiming all the tombstones marked graves of political careers ended by Douglas' lies. They agree there's virtually no one in the state who does not believe that I'm the ideal person to send to the Senate. In the next breath they wonder if I can win against a man whom they feel is prepared to lie, steal, bribe, and if necessary, kill without compunction to stay in the Senate."

When Reilly discovered Kat refused to return to the state until the third weekend in September to start the final phase of the campaign because the stars were not right, he flipped. When he discovered the massive volunteer rallies and headquarter openings were scheduled the same way, he revolted, pushed the designers and printers and insisted on sending out the first mailing of seventy-five thousand pieces to registered Republicans on a day Kat had described as confused. He told no one of the rescheduling until it was too late. They all paid the price.

From its inception, the mailing program had flaws. Senatorial was paying for it and election rules required substantial volunteer input which was interpreted by those who watched such things, as a volunteer touching each piece of mail. Reilly refused to believe Liz and Yola could turn out that much mail as quickly as he wanted it, so he chose subterfuge over the objections of everyone who knew better. Already miffed at having their messages spurned by some human twerp, the gods took their revenge.

After staff spent four days chasing bags of hijacked mail around the state, eluding reporters, and trying to pin criminal intent on Douglas, they dragged a full confession out of Reilly. Notified by phone, Kat furiously swore she was prepared to throw Reilly and the Senatorial committee to the wolves if she was accused of any campaign rule violations.

"Kat said Mercury was retrograde, nothing moving works, but you wouldn't listen." Liz kept muttering, as the tale of the debacle unfolded. Reilly threatened to leave and never confess all the machinations if she did not shut up. Liz subsided.

The edited version printed out in Roxy's mind as Reilly spun his tale of intrigue. All the mail was to be sent from the fabricators in Oklahoma, labeled, sorted, bundled and ready to go. Bags and bags of it would be flown to Boston where it would be sent by pre-arranged truck to the basement of the Hose's liquor store. A few bags would be brought to campaign, unpacked and checked by volunteers, photos taken, hours logged, and substantial volunteer input substantiated. Then the remaining bags would be collected from their basement hiding place, taken all together to the Post Office and mailed out. No one would ever be the wiser.

What actually happened was a textbook definition of star crossed.

Reilly got the first whiff of disaster late Friday afternoon when the truckers called saying there was no mail waiting at Logan Airport. He and the direct mail house frantically traced the bags of mail through re-routing, mislaid manifests, and delivery screw-ups to Chicago where supposedly an alert shipping employee saw it was mail and sent it to the Providence Post Office. A weekend of calls to personal friends and political allies in various offices of the postal service uncovered the chilling fact that officially, seventy-five thousand pieces of bulk mail from the state Republican party never arrived. One anonymous source claimed to have seen it.

Roxy discovered the message on the computer Sunday afternoon.

"Looking for mail, or is it male? Call 555-1111 and ask for Butch."

A quick huddle decided to call. The party claimed to be disinterested in the political ramifications and asked instead for a monetary ransom giving detailed instructions for making a drop and finding the missing bags of mail. Reilly, Mario and the state Republican party chief who would be held liable for any violations, set out to pay the ransom. The Hose smelled a rat and initiated his own quest. He was convinced Carrie was behind the mailnapping.

After criss-crossing the state several times on wild goose chases, the trio had given up by Monday afternoon and were prepared to break the news to Kat who had been skipping around Florida, fundraising all weekend. The Hose saved the day by parading into headquarters with a line of cousins, volunteers, and general supporters all carrying bags of the missing mail. He waited until each piece had literally been touched by a volunteer then carried to the Providence Post Office and delivered into the hands of a bosom buddy before he confessed to breaking and entering. Carrie engineered the hijacking and false ransom call. She stashed the bags in the mysterious building next to Mrs. Angostino's Religious Supplies store across the street. The Hose had enough. He and several accomplices overpowered the guards to the upstairs apartment, broke in and liberated the mail. Miraculously, no press ever got wind of the caper.

When Kat was filled in at the adventure's successful conclusion, she said little. Quietly, she threatened to personally vivisect any person involved with her campaign in any way who questioned her decisions on timing. Liz presented Bruno with the situational ethics medal of honor, declared Reilly mental midget of the month, and revoked his rights in the Senate Race game. Everyone pledged all future mailings would be handled by the book and at Kat's choice of times.

They were breaking up the final torture session and heading over to Tony's when Roxy caught the noxious stench from one of the mail bags left behind. She knew in an inexplicable flash where she had smelled it before. Little Compton. Carrie. The real crisis of the mailings was how much access Carrie had to the campaign. The key question: how to stop her.

★ ★ ★ ★ ★

She had been so involved in the mail caper, Roxy had not seen Jake for several days. She knew he would be on the beach hoping to intercept her so she waited by the stairs leading down to the sand. At first the beach seemed unusually empty of sea gulls, then a few appeared. She stared at a large dead fish laying on the sand, eaten away and covered with gull feathers like an Indian prayer stick. Impatient, she decided to start walking. She would intersect Jake at some point. The tide was out and the beach seemed to extend infinitely to the surf. When she completed her stroll to the Dunes Club and back, she found him waiting at the curve of the seawall.

"Could you recognize that stink I brought to your attention at the picnic if you smelled it again?" she asked as they headed back to the house passing under the Towers. When he agreed he could, Roxy shared her speculations.

"You told me that doing tantric practices would enhance my sense of smell, that each person has a specific scent I could learn to distinguish. And you said that evil exudes its own smell too." Jake nodded. "That stink is Carrie. I remember the first time I smelled it, the day we were in Little Compton with Kat and Stuart and I ran into her, remember? I've been trying to recollect all the other places I've smelled it." She ticked off locations on her fingers. "The campaign office, at the Tomasso picnic, and here." They stopped to stare up at Kat's house before going in. "I want you to walk around the place with me and see if we smell her stink."

Surprisingly, Liz was totally supportive and agreed to cook nothing until they completed their search. They split up and moved through all the rooms independently. When they returned to the kitchen and compared notes, Roxy felt a chill run up her spine. They agreed on every scenting. Carrie had been here and they could detail her trail. Her scent was traceable in the dining room-now-office, in Roxy's room and in Kat's bedroom. The porches reeked of her stink now that they were attuned to it, and they found traces in the Jacuzzi-sun porch as well. Kat's library door had an elaborate lock on it. As Roxy opened it to enter, she knew immediately that Carrie had been unable to penetrate the magic Kat used to protect her sacred space.

When they arrived at campaign to tell Mario about their conclusions, they found no doubters. Carrie had struck again, logging onto computers sometime before dawn that morning, making subtle changes in timing and details for the volunteer rallies and headquarters openings planned for that coming Saturday. None of her changes were meaningful. The real point was that she could do it. Roxy and Jake detected her stink everywhere, including Kat's private office.

With everyone in concurrence, Roxy called Kat on the cleared line and proposed her solution. Kat agreed. Saturday's schedule was too complicated to change so they would continue as planned, keeping their eyes peeled for minor disturbances or signs of Carrie or Scarlatti.

"She may simply be letting us know she's got us covered," Kat said, echoing the Hose's tirades that the bitch was playing with them. She also agreed with part two of Roxy's plan. Max would be invited to set up protective shields that would keep her from penetrating again.

"What I don't understand is why," Kat said puzzled, "although I suppose there's no doubt Race is behind it."

"What do the stars say?" Roxy asked.

"It's a notable week, filled with critical aspects, which is why I wanted us to keep a low profile. The message is the usual one we enjoy so much. The time is replete with illusion, deception, karma and the possible emergence of progressive forces to balance the old ways."

★ ★ ★ ★ ★

The day before the volunteer rallies, every telephone pole for blocks around each of Kat's headquarters was plastered with Douglas posters. Sign laws were violated and Mario sprang into action calling allies in the Transportation Department and mobilizing supporters to flood the talk shows and local newspapers with complaints about the unsightly and ecologically disturbing mess. When public response overwhelmingly opposed Douglas' action his campaign manager gallantly blamed over-enthusiastic volunteers and pledg,ed to have the posters down by nightfall.

The Hose detailed special crews to comb each area after dark to remove any signs Douglas' troops may have missed. They returned to Atwells Avenue about midnight with stacks of the posters. The Hose burned them in the parking lot across from campaign headquarters, shouting imprecations at Carrie, whom he swore was watching out an upstairs window.

Discounting anxiety and constant surveillance, the day of rallies unfolded perfectly. Roxy was not surprised. She left the house for her walk as dawn broke and a hot pink sunball announced an ideal day. She felt no unsettling vibrations as she briefly entered and exited the world of darkness under the Towers arch. The sapphire ocean was calm and placid with many out fishing. She felt a slight twinge of sadness walking past the boarded up windows at the Dunes Club. The feeling deepened as a line of geese flying south passed overhead. Soon her morning walk outfit would be sweats.

The only hint of disturbance came in Woonsocket where they were opening headquarters in a small storefront next to the Prudhomme brothers' family hardware store. The brothers, Paul and Martin, assembled throngs of relatives, friends, and Kat's supporters for the early afternoon rally. The rallies also served to launch a massive voter registration drive. The Prudhommes had been signing up voters at the new headquarters since dawn. Not long before Kat was scheduled to arrive in a full motorcade, Paul began assembling his troops for raucous welcome. There were more than a two hundred folks of all ages and sizes, carrying Kiley for Senate signs and practicing their screams and chants. Paul had a bullhorn and was leading them through the ritual he planned.

Suddenly a smaller but equally loud group began marching down the old curved main street carrying Douglas posters. They stopped about twenty feet away from the assembled Kat supporters. A shouting match began with Paul and his bullhorn, proving more than the Douglas crew could overcome.

While his brother engaged in verbal artillery fire, Martin had the presence of mind to call and warn the motorcade to delay briefly and see if the opposing crowd would yield. Kat declared she was coming through regardless. The Prudhommes encircled the small Douglas group with their much larger contingent shouting them down and keeping them pinned in place for the half hour that Kat was there. Liz counted it a blazing victory as she leapt in Roxy's car to speed back to Providence and the final rally in the parking lot across from their Atwells Avenue headquarters.

Roxy was traveling with Kat's motorcade. They started in Newport that morning, sped across the southern coast of the state to a pancake-breakfast-in-the-street rally in Westerly then up the Interstate to Woonsocket. While each event reflected the subtly different character of the locale, none could compare to the scene at their main headquarters. Federal Hill was a giant carnival. A huge striped tent covered the parking lot and Kiley-sweatshirted people were spilling out of it in all directions. Music was blasting, beer was flowing, and hot dogs were being grilled by the thousands. A never-ending parade of pizza platters wound their way down the block from Tony's. The Hose bribed a tribe of street urchins to stand by the helium tanks blowing up balloons. They occasionally sucked a burst of the gas so they could dash around squeaking like cartoon characters. Liz was most proud of the Del's Lemonade truck she commandeered. She declared unequivocally on endless occasions that it was Del's Lemonade and cheap lobster that would forever be linked with Rhode Island in her memory.

Standing by the lemonade truck waiting for the motorcade to scream into sight, Liz regaled her once again with Del's story.

"Can you believe they started all this almost a hundred and fifty years ago in Italy? It belongs to the DeLucia family...Del's. They brought their discovery to the shores of Rhode Island at the turn of the century. Somewhere along the line they invented and built a machine that perfected the technique of making this nectar from fresh lemons. I love it! I love the trucks! And I especially love their idea of setting up alongside crowded highways to the beach each weekend in summer. I'm trying to come up with a way of adopting it all to Morgan Springs."

Roxy barely listened as she nodded agreement. Del's was one of the state's icons, along with quohogs and vanity license plates.

The party was still in full swing when Kat assembled a quick assessment meeting. She was cheered by reports of hundreds of volunteers recruited and hundreds more new voters registered in all four corners of the state. She had drilled her field organizers relentlessly in targeting their voter registration efforts to young and youngish women, particularly those not working in professional jobs.

"They are underrepresented in the voting public and they're the ones who need me out there fighting for them most. Tell them about my stand on day care, equal pay, and credit fairness," she lectured. "Remind them that no man will be as faithful to them as I'll be."

That pledge always brought a howl from Liz, who insisted it was a coded appeal to the state's gay community.

Flattering television coverage picked up the "are you frustrated with.....?" theme her speeches stressed. They filled in the blank with mostly economic concerns targeted for the crowd and locale. Once the rhetoric was complete, the punch line was "Then vote Kiley for U.S. Senate."

Roxy made the issues simple and emotional. Kat found easy response among a public swept with anxious, fearful, frustrated energy as troops were shipped daily to the desert for who knew what outcome. Television caught it all and verified the day was as successful as they rated it. Hayes called warning of possible House votes early Sunday. Success in hand, Kat decided to catch the last plane back to Washington.

Liz also felt buoyed by the television coverage. She adopted the prevalent public attitude of TV junkies that truth was defined by what television news reported.

"If it isn't broadcast on TV, as far as the general public is concerned, it didn't happen," she claimed.

Gould egged her into making the pronouncement on every conference call as he urged Kat to film a final series of commercials using their fictional characters, portrayed by Jake, Big Mac, and Aunt Helen in adulatory endorsements. She continued to reject the notion as false advertising.

★ ★ ★ ★ ★

Kat's decision to return to Washington left Roxy with a free Sunday, or at least one that started later than dawn. She heard him whistle before she saw him walking toward her across the sand. Then he called her name and she waved.

"I heard you when you whistled."

"I know, but I'm just raising some hell out here." Jake began talking about the fishing. "I've been out for a couple hours indulging myself in one of the great rites of fall: catching blues. Almost every other day from September through November small blues cross the Bay, bringing out legions of fair weather fishermen, the ones who emerge when the going is easy. I was out on that stretch of rock as dawn broke," he motioned to a spit extending beyond the pier much further south along the shore than Roxy ever walked. "I've been spending most of my time unhooking fish from my line. Throw anything in the water then pull out a fish. I was fishing so hard I didn't notice the tide come in and found myself stranded on the rocks. I had to get wet to get back. But sometimes it's worth getting your feet wet."

They reached the house and Jake stopped his fishing monologue long enough to give Roxy a searching glance before he kissed her. Bliss was short lived as he changed topics.

"I drove by on my way to fish this morning to see if you were up yet, and noticed a strange car parked in the driveway. It was your friend from the darkside, Carrie."

Roxy stared at him amazed. Carrie was here watching the house. Kat's decision to fly to Washington last night was made at the last minute and showed up nowhere on any schedule. Whatever they planned must have been for this morning. Roxy felt inordinately pleased that Kat's impulsive decision foiled Scarlatti's plans. Or was it impulsive?

Jake repeated his story as they sat around the kitchen table indulging themselves in what Liz termed a breakfast for real men. There were fried potatoes, scrambled eggs, homemade muffins, bowls of fruit salad, broiled ham slices, "and because we're here in Rhode Island, a tray of raw clams. It's like having sex before breakfast," she explained as she slurped one of the slimy masses from its opened shell.

"Some people claim that raw clams remind them of female genitals. Having never had my face in any woman's pussy, and being unable to bend over far enough to smell my own, I can't comment on the truth of the statement. What do you think, Jake?"

"I think I'll miss you when the campaign is over," he replied diplomatically, ignoring Roxy's scowl and concentrating on another helping of Liz's potatoes.

She accelerated to acute paranoia, harassing Roxy about when Max was coming to protect the house from Carrie, how she was going to grill all the workmen on the street crew Monday morning about whether they had seen her around before, and what Bruno would do when he learned of this latest Carrie sighting.

"It's probably some weird spell she cast that had Kat walking the floors."

When Roxy pushed her for more information, Liz claimed she heard Kat moving around between two and four every morning she was in the house.

"She's beginning to look like she never sleeps and I know without me around to force her, she never eats. All my efforts to fatten her up will be in vain."

"Did you say anything to Kat about not sleeping?" Roxy was almost afraid to hear the answer.

"Of course. And she agreed. Said she was having a lot of weird dreams but that it was only to be expected. Then she gave me this long speech about some planet or another standing around in the sky right now making extra dream energy. As if that was not spooky enough, she felt the need to share with me some of these dreams."

Roxy giggled. Liz had dreams that were boring, mundane, and only in black and white. When one of the self-analysis books she read by the boxful postulated Technicolor, surrealistic dreams as key to a rich inner life, Liz rebelled and dismissed dreaming as meaningless. She recently found an article by some scientist who described dreaming as brain backfire.

"Tell us," Roxy insisted.

"First of all, Kat claimed she was walking around in the middle of the night trying to sort out what was real and what was a dream, as if any of the nutty stuff she dreamt could ever be real. She dreamt one night that everyone was harassing her because they believed she'd shot Stuart and she woke up trying to remember the last time she'd seen him, wondering if maybe she had shot him. Then there was one where hundreds of people she'd known at various times in her life were lined up on bleachers down by the beach waiting for her to perform but she didn't know what to do. Finally, she had these recurring dreams about people in the house, always dressed in black, always melting through doors and standing over her bed."

Liz stopped suddenly in her recital and looked at Roxy.

"Maybe those aren't dreams. Maybe it's Carrie, or her spirit, or that first senator's spirit, what was his name?"

"Reynolds Winston," Jake told her.

"That's him. Reynolds Winston. In fact, I think Kat mentioned that she felt his ghost was around." Liz sat down heavily and stared dramatically at Roxy.

"This is getting too weird for me. You know how I hate ghosts and spooky stuff. I won't even go out on Halloween. When did you say Max was coming?"

Roxy had not said but she promised another phone call to Morgan Springs to find out.

They knew for several weeks that Douglas planned a copycat rally the day after Kat's series of headquarter openings. Liz had immediately volunteered to spy. She left Roxy and Jake considering plans of action against Carrie as they finished breakfast and set off for Kennedy Plaza in the heart of Providence. Two of Bruno's protégées were meeting her there.

Liz returned as they watched the evening news that night and caught reports of Douglas' performance. Her ranting about the event practically drowned out the television but Jake and Roxy got the idea. Emmett Douglas was playing fundamentalist preacher enraged about moral and ethical corruption in the nation's capital. He insisted on the rightness of his decision not to go there and claimed his two weeks on the Senate floor taught him how a strong voice from outside the good old boys network was desperately needed.

"And he's calling Kat the ultimate insider," Liz said. "He's pointing to the president's visit, all the other Members praising her work, how often she's mentioned in national press. And those stiffs the Democrats dragged down there were cheering as if he were exposing a murderer."

Roxy knew the *Beacon* papers would resound with these attacks and others in the same vein, Douglas would accelerate his slanders, other press would comment on it, and issues would once again slide beneath the surface. She was as frustrated as Kat with the inability of both press and public to sustain interest in much beyond sordid political gossip. Who would quote Kat on the need to protect Rhode Island educations from being technically obsolete or strategies for keeping American entrepreneurial skills competitive in a global market when they could demand her reaction to Douglas' pointless and twisted attacks?

"The upshot of all this is that the jerk announced he's not going back to Washington until the people of Rhode Island elect him to clean it up."

"At least there was a smirk on the reporter's face when he quoted that," Jake said, trying to pacify Liz.

★ ★ ★ ★ ★

She wished he would choose somewhere other than this dingy corner bar to meet. At least he was never late. It was one of Race Scarlatti's most notable attributes and afforded him incalculable advantages. He arrived early and always controlled the turf. She did not care. He was not doing such a great job as far as she could see. Besides, she knew her magic web gave her the ultimate advantage, one that did not rely on mundane factors like time and space. She managed to rub a handkerchief against Stuart's sweating arm in Little Compton and her pentagram of lives was now locked in place. She worked daily on twisting and tightening the entanglements.

"You lost Jasmine with your grandstanding threats." She decided to land the first blow. "For weeks she refused to answer my calls or letters. I went to Washington to confront her in person. It was an interesting encounter."

She pilfered another pair of panties hoping fresh juice would strengthen her hold on the press secretary. Carrie's face took on a cunning look and she smiled thinly.

"She may not be lost forever."

"While I was there, I decided to check on your plans for our friend Senator Stuart."

A twinge of distress slithered across his puffy face.

On second thought, she was glad he chose a dingy spot. She was able to see much in auras and his always looked coated with a slimy film. In the light it was truly gruesome.

"I see my report of failure doesn't surprise you. I was told a burned-out junkie was sent on a street hit and Stuart used him as a punching bag. Jasmine gave no indication that Stuart considered it anything but random violence.

"Jasmine refuses to talk about Kat or the campaign but she was responsive to attacks on your rival."

She lobbed the last two words at him deliberately. He focused his fixed stare on her in retaliation. Carrie knew too much about what could be seen in unveiled eyes and dropped her gaze.

"I suppose you have a better way to handle him," he hissed slowly.

"Actually, I did some checking while I was in Washington," she began smugly, "and discovered the senator maintains quite a cache of firepower in his Capitol Hill house. Apparently he likes playing war games with his Cuban buddies and spends a lot of time in Miami. It should be much easier to find a professional assassin there and get the job done right with little chance of even Kat suspecting you.

"Speaking of the object of your obsession, what do we do about her?"

"Your job is surveillance not harassment. I do not want Kat disturbed."

He waved his hand dismissively.

"As long as she stays away from him, she can have whatever pleases her, including the senate seat. Your only concern is to keep me informed on everything that goes on in her life."

"Especially any intimate moments she might spend with her dashing hero."

Carrie could outwait anyone.

"And have you found any?" Race was finally driven by the silence to ask.

She glimpsed Stuart on her Washington mission but stayed away from Kat, not wanting her suspicions aroused.

"No," she answered, not countering the absence of any discernable contact between them while she was watching with her certainty that the two were lovers and had been for quite a while. If they were not, the web she was weaving certainly would drive them together.

Satisfied, Scarlatti slid from the booth and slumped out through the shadows.

17

Death Card II
September/October

Rhode Island
Washington

The death of the vice president of the United States in a freak golf cart accident had less impact on the frazzled nerves of Kat's campaign staff than the string of accidents in their own backyard. Roxy was frantic. Max was in Manhattan performing at a place called the Cosmic Egg and would not arrive in Rhode Island until Friday.

The screen he sent for Kat's bedroom, on loan from the castle, arrived in a large crate. She and Liz uncrated it, wrestled it to the third floor and set it up along one side of the bay window. Light illuminated the three linen panels embroidered in wool, silk and gold thread strung between mahogany uprights. The same woman, with long curling hair, appeared in a different heroic pose on each panel.

"How come Kat gets an Amazon with a sword and Max tells us to drink aspen and rock rose tea?"

Liz's indignant comment did nothing to relieve Roxy's fears. Having Max do protection charms against Carrie was her idea, but it still made her shiver that such precautions would even be thinkable let alone necessary.

Her twice daily calls to Max relating the latest manifestation of what Liz described as a jinx on the campaign proceeded like a well-rehearsed play. Max would advise her to encircle herself with light and keep drinking the tea mixture he created for them to deal with fears both known and unknown. She would whimper and protest that she wanted something more powerful for her terror, that Carrie was practicing black magic on them according to Liz, and that he was leaving them alone and unprotected.

"Only your magic can keep her away," she wailed repeatedly.

He would reiterate his advice, murmur soothingly and conclude by promising he would be there Friday. Another call for help would end, leaving her nervously speculating on what the next calamity would be.

The reign of terror started at Republican Party headquarters in a restored brick school building on Smith Street. A gas leak forced evacuation but not before several of Burkhart's campaign underlings were overcome by fumes. The attorney general chose to interpret the accident as an assault on his faltering campaign for governor and called out his official investigative forces to unearth the perpetrator. For a few hours Kat's campaign believed Burkhart was a paranoid nutcase.

Then Monday night the Hose was hurt in a car accident. His vehicle looked like a crushed beer can. Liz freaked out just seeing the car. As befit a man of the Hose's outlaw nature, he was spared major injury by not wearing his seat belt. The force of the impact on the driver's door slammed him into the passenger seat and relative safety. He was bruised and battered but Liz was maintaining a vigil at his bed along with his mother, pumping him full of homeopathy to heal his bruised ribs. She dragged a cooperative chiropractor over to his house daily. The most difficult part of the nursing, she reported, was that Bruno was ready to be up and around and hot on the trail of what he insisted were his assailants.

Tuesday morning there was another gas leak, this time at Kat's Woonsocket headquarters. The ever-alert Prudhomme brothers were able to avert any replay of fume-poisoned personnel but their report of obvious tampering behind the building launched Mario into a frenzy of phone calls to the entire Tomasso network. He even consulted Burkhart although the pompous number two man on the ticket refused to believe the attacks could be aimed at anyone but him.

Roxy took to driving the old Volvo, hoping her father's protection charms would keep her safe. That notion was shattered along with her composure when she backed out of a small parking lot and heard a sharp crash. She jumped, thinking she had been shot, looked around frantically and saw her entire back window was smashed where she had blindly backed into the corner of a parked tractor-trailer body.

She called Jake and insisted he come stay with her in Narragansett since Liz was camped out at the Atwells Avenue headquarters working all-nighters on mailings and checking on Bruno. Before going to bed and upon awakening, she coerced him into accompanying her on a thorough sniff of the house to make sure Carrie was not lurking around.

The Rhode Island staff agreed before the conference call on Wednesday, to tell Kat nothing about the weird happenings until they could offer some responsible explanation other than the universal belief that Carrie was behind it all. They need not have worried. Business was brief and consisted mostly of Kat raving about the lurid headlines the pro-Douglas *Beacon* papers were running.

Tomasso Excavating started work on the Cranston sewer project the previous day. The *Ocean State Beacon* reported: "What's that stink?" Insinuations about Kat's manipulating government contracts for personal benefit were rehashed. News stories were run about Senate and House races in other states featuring racist and sexist Republican candidates that Kat would no more support than most Democrats would support a crook like Douglas. With true tabloid distortion, the *Beacon* reported that the commission appointed to examine Jamie's collection of films "has not yet located footage featuring our own Kiley Tomasso." Several other articles quoted Douglas accusing Kat of virtually every illegal or corrupt act he had committed in the past thirty years.

When Kat calmed sufficiently to change the subject, her pollster, Lila Gravely said that the nightly phone canvassing they began on Monday showed her substantial lead remaining with little indication of softening.

"We'll know better about trends with a few more nights of data," she concluded. Everyone muttered appreciatively. Gould repeated his pitch to begin filming the final round of commercials as celebrity endorsements from their created characters. Kat once again brushed his plan aside.

"Why don't you put me on the air?" she asked indignantly.

There was a moment of silence while the media advisor ran through and rejected a variety of responses settling on a slice of truth sprinkled with flakes of flattery.

"You've been an appealing heroine to the people of this state for so long and still look wonderful in the photos and news stories. Voters seem to be shrugging off the negative attacks. My concern is that the present strain you're feeling will show in your face and more so in your voice. It will make them begin to question. We'll have existing footage of you in each of the spots I've proposed, but for now, I'd like not to film anymore."

Mario interceded with good news: several Democrats found their integrity after primary defeats blamed on Douglas' attacks. They approached him very surreptitiously about supporting Kat.

"The ones in Providence we need most, and they're the ones we can check out and watch the closest."

His enthusiasm was contagious as he reported mail and phone calls were both voluminous and positive, small contributions were flowing in from the direct mail pieces at an encouraging rate, and press—other than the *Beacon*—were reporting her activities fairly. Kat's mood was buoyed and even Roxy began to feel better. With no mention being made of the accidents, she found them drifting to the back of her mind.

Uncharacteristically, Lila concluded the call with a choice bit of first-hand gossip. She had been playing golf with Vice President Daley on Monday when the fatal accident occurred. She filled them in on details. Most media coverage was devoted to political speculation about how the tragedy would affect the 1992 presidential campaign since the Republican establishment had been grooming the now-dead Bill Daley as heir apparent for more than a decade.

"We were playing at the Mount Vernon Country Club—we being a half dozen senators, the vice president, a consultant or two, and me as their token woman. Plus the usual battalion of Secret Service agents. I don't think I've ever seen so many blue blazers on a golf course before. The course was closed to the public so we were playing through pretty quickly. I'd just teed off at the ninth hole. It's a long hole, almost five hundred feet, with a dog-leg to the left and out of bounds on the right. There's a small creek below at the base of a brush-filled hill with trees everywhere. I was watching Daley ride up with a blue blazer on one side of him and another perched on back of the white electric golf cart. They just kept coming and were so close I could see the look of shocked surprise on the agent's face when the cart wouldn't stop. He jumped out pushing the vice president to the other side trying to knock him out of the cart. But the poor man just hung there half in and half out. Later we found out his foot had jammed. Just as the cart catapulted over the hill towards the creek, the agent on the back flung himself to the floor and wrenched Daley's foot free. Unfortunately, as he fell away, the cart tilted and crashed on top of him. The agent tumbled out and was found unconscious against a tree. When they got to the vice president he was dead, his neck broken on impact."

"Chaos really broke out then. All the blue blazers were either standing around looking menacing as if they expected armed Iraqis to come bursting through the woods or were babbling on their earplug radios. Calls were made to everyone— the White House, Daley's wife, the FBI, local police, even the Army Corps of Engineers. They're in charge of the golf course stream. I was one of the few people on the course not frantically calling someone."

Kat signed off soon after Lila finished her story, most of the others following suit. Roxy hung up as Hayes and Mario launched into a detailed analysis of how the vice president's death affected the chances of the senate majority leader. David Clanton was touted as the Democrats' prime contender for regaining control of the White House sometime before the end of the century.

For some reason a tragedy visited upon a Republican not connected in any way with Kat's campaign lifted Roxy's spirits. Vice President Daley had not come to Rhode Island to campaign nor had he ever attended one of their Washington fundraisers. Maybe Burkhart was right and the accidents were aimed at Republicans not at Kat. She would have to ask Paul Reilly if Senatorial had reports of other campaigns suffering bizarre events. Her secure feeling lasted only until dark that evening.

Jake was sprawled on the Oriental rug, finishing a sketch of Liz as the primal Mother goddess. Roxy was proofreading bluelines for Kat's issues book.

"She may be the most complete goddess model of all," Jake said as he showed her the drawing that captured Liz's round face and confident Wonder Woman expression perfectly. "She's a throw-back to the primal Mother before she was divided up and weakened. Liz is right. Her large spirit requires a large body."

"But does it require false eyelashes?" Roxy teased, laughing at one of Liz's most distinctive characteristics. No matter how unprimped she claimed to be, she was never seen without luxurious eyelashes firmly attached over her large blue eyes.

The three pops were loud enough to disrupt their laughing as the room plunged into darkness. Jake pulled her from the chair and into the lit kitchen where they spotted the blood dripping between his fingers from a wound on her arm. As she sat holding a towel against it to stop the bleeding, he grabbed a flashlight and returned to the dining room where they had been working.

"Nearly as I can tell, three light bulbs exploded, a fragment of glass from one cutting your arm. I couldn't find a trace of any outside source or that anything else was damaged. Too much psychic energy, I guess." He returned to Roxy still sitting in the kitchen nursing her arm. "Better take some of Max's shock remedy."

Restored to a semblance of calm, Roxy allowed him to wash and bandage the small cut then lead her upstairs to bed. Her final thoughts as she fell asleep cradled in his arms were of Jake and how comforting it was to know he was there keeping her safe.

★ ★ ★ ★ ★

The ocean's pulse was as erratic as the series of accidents. Not that Roxy was surprised. Oracles were supposed to indicate the bad as well as the good.

Each morning the water was a churning lead gray mass. Pounding surf strewed the sand with an apron woven from the whitish-yellow sudsy scum of pollution. Gulls fought hard to fly against the wind and settled for hanging almost stationary while being buffeted by turbulent currents. Gyrating wind demons would burst onto the beach, whip sand particles into funnels that stood a foot or so high, and then dart off. Thursday morning she had been hopeful.

Jake woke her with tickling lips on her arm.

"I was kissing it to make it better," he said, seeing her eyes open.

"It hurts all over," she moaned, suspended between waking and sleeping.

She surrendered to Jake's cure as he kissed comfort and soothing into her soft skin and across her nerves. They finished their lovemaking in the Jacuzzi room. Jake rubbed her with tangible solace in the form of a special cherry blossom oil he blended to relax her and bring her peace. They reclined on a pile of pillows striped with soft green light and shadows cast by the jungle of plants that lined the windows. The aromatic white blooms of a shelf-full of some bizarre succulent wrapped them in a tropically sweet cloud of fragrance.

The walk began later than usual under a sky washed out by the still visible sun. Wind blew up already high surf ,spattering them with flecks. Rain was obviously on the agenda for later that day. The sound was also blown up, surf roaring then clicking as it retreated from the stone beaches on the south side of the Coast Guard House.

"This was all called Narragansett Pier," he explained waving his hand along the curved shoreline.

"Oh, now I understand why all the stained glass windows in the church next door are dedicated to people who died at Narragansett Pier. I wondered if there had been some natural disaster or something involving a pier."

He chuckled.

"At least you noticed the windows. It wasn't until I'd returned from California as a stained glass artist that I realized the treasure trove here in my own backyard. St. Peter's Church is filled with original Tiffany glass windows. I felt reaffirmed in my artistic purpose when I discovered they were here."

She was shocked by the pain in his voice when he called her at campaign headquarters later that morning.

"Three of my Aphrodite glass pieces were shattered. Nothing in the house was touched but I could detect her stink everywhere."

Galvanized by Jake's loss, Roxy called Kat. Maybe she would have a solution. Besides, if innocent people were suffering because of her, she should at least know it. Only the exploding lights and broken glass art were news to Kat.

"Tell Jake how terribly sorry I am." Her voice was laden with fatigue and despair.

"I'm devastated by all these accidents. Even though Max keeps reminding me that the tension of impending war is bound to cause an increase in anger everywhere, I'm still walking the floors every night riddled with guilt over putting other people in danger. If the planetary indicators are accurate, the period should soon be over."

This was not reassuring. Roxy wanted the period over yesterday.

"I don't have any solutions to suggest other than swilling Max's anti-terror juice by the gallon."

★ ★ ★ ★ ★

Roxy's additional tales of woe eroded the small amount of courage Kat had left. She agreed: white light and anti-terror flower remedies did not seem to be effective tools for battling a dark spirit like Carrie's. She had no other suggestions at the moment and dropped her head wearily into her hands.

Even her clothes felt fragile. She had searched through her jammed closet that morning searching for something to give her strength. With no corresponding inner force she could not put on any of her power clothes. No reds or purples for her, no shoulder pads or tight skirts. Her puny compromise was a long silk blazer in a wine color. Her hip stitched pleated skirt was beige and her softly shaped camisole with its button front and thin straps was a slate blue. A strong hand could rip it all away. Only the cast silver ram's head she wore on a heavy silver chain possessed any power.

Hayes poked his head in to ask if she was ready to meet with him and Jasmine to plan press strategy. Kat waved him away begging ten more minutes. It was her will that fueled this office, this campaign, and she struggled to squeeze out a few more drops from some reserve buried deep in her heart. She picked up the onyx frame with her father's photo in it and rubbed her fingertips across his face. It was a precious talisman. But today, instead of inspiring her, it dredged up remnants of old resentment. Why had her father died and left her here alone? None of this would have happened if Duke were still alive. No petty crook like Emmett Douglas would have dared attack her. No handmaiden of Race Scarlatti's would have been terrorizing her friends.

I'm tired of doing it all alone, she sobbed inwardly, I'm tired of doing it all.

Kat's will to fight began to feel revived as she reviewed the physical evidence of Douglas' absurd attacks on her with her chief of staff and press secretary. As she ranted her frustration at hearing his nonsense parroted by people on the call-in radio shows or when they met her on the street, the office door opened and Senator Stuart walked in.

She stopped in mid-sentence. Catching the exchanged look between Stuart and Hayes, she knew her chief of staff had summoned him. To the rescue, she thought, indignant. Well, let's see if the great political guru has a solution.

Kat continued her diatribe.

"His puppet newspapers keep repeating the same tawdry lies. He spends a few days in Washington, his first appearance in the Senate, comes back and begins attacking me as a corrupt insider." Flaring up, she barely noticed Stuart moving closer to her, an almost menacing look on his face. She felt frustration building as she described the press analysis and commentary. "They know the truth! Why do they allow him to continue his lies?"

Stuart was within arm's reach and she had to consciously will herself not to move away. What was wrong with him? She wanted to hide behind her chair. Out of the corner of her eye she saw a matching concern on Jasmine's face.

"I'm tired of being a target for mindless mud slinging," she exclaimed, feeling frustration turn to anger. She jumped from her chair and faced Stuart who nudged her arm sharply.

"I don't know what to do! I want to talk about real issues, he wants to slander me." Stuart nudged her harder almost knocking her off-balance. His face was stony; he had said nothing since entering the room.

"What do I do? What do I do?" she cried, slamming her fist on the desk.

He raised his hand, poised to hit her.

"No! Stop!" she screamed, grabbing his hand and forcing it away, eyes flashing, her body shaking with rage.

He smiled at her, a glint in his brown eyes.

"Now you know what to do."

Gracefully lifting her hand on his wrist to his lips, he kissed it.

"As Goethe said, 'you are either the anvil or the hammer.'" He walked out of the room.

She blinked, perplexed for a moment, then turned to Hayes who was holding a struggling Jasmine back from flinging herself at the departing senator.

"Please leave," she said with assurance. "I have work to do."

He certainly focused the warrior in me, Kat thought, as she listed the phone calls she needed to make. We'll see how silly and naïve I am to keep my anger under control if he finds himself swept away in the flames. Then she cursed her chief of staff, knowing he considered Stuart a hero with his little Zen lesson.

Her first call was to her media advisor telling him to film the television spots using Jake and the others endorsing her.

"Make them as hard hitting and direct as possible," she said, encouraged when he promised a finished product on the air by mid-October. There was a questioning note in Gould's voice as he wondered, but did not ask, what had changed her mind.

Mario was her second call and he sounded delighted to hear the steel edge in her tone. Her instructions to him were brief and pointed.

"I want to toughen my image in all future direct mail pieces. I want to know every possible way we can hit Douglas without it seeming to come from me. And I want to have dinner with my friend Sal Pascucci at the Garabaldi Club Saturday night."

Her final demands were of Race Scarlatti. She would wait until she arrived in Rhode Island so he could see her face and know she was cowed no longer.

★ ★ ★ ★ ★

Roxy volunteered to pick Kat up at the airport and drive her to the press conference scheduled for their Newport office. She wanted to lobby her about dealing with the accidents before someone was seriously injured.

"That is not a Tomasso project," Kat said emphatically, pointing to the steel and concrete skeleton of a second span rising from the bay they drove across the Jamestown bridge.

"It's years behind schedule and grossly over-budget. People should run Douglas out of the state on the strength of this fiasco alone."

They headed south on Broadway in unusually heavy traffic that slowed their progress to barely a crawl. Kat's nonchalance faded when they ground to halt. She sprang out to discover the problem and whether they would have to desert the van and jog the remaining few blocks. There had been no movement in the line of cars when Kat returned, a haunted look once more in her eyes.

"A truck carrying a liquid they think may be toxic overturned near our office. The police have cordoned off both ends of the street. We can pick our way on foot through the back alley but no press conference. Every camera and reporter around is absorbed in the disaster."

There was no need to spell out the obvious.

Roxy turned the van around and parked then waited for Kat to return from her incursion to the disaster site. If the press could not come to her, she would go to them and talk about the crisis of the moment, the ever-present potential for disaster in disposing of waste.

Kat's brave demeanor faded as they headed back to Narragansett where Max was scheduled to arrive by noon.

They found him slowly walking around the perimeter of the large house sporadically brushing aside a bush or peering along the foundation. After a brief conference he sent Kat to rest and gave Roxy a list of tasks.

"We'll meet back here by four. That'll give me time to purge the house. Bring Liz and the four of us will complete the protection rituals. I'll also require photographs or sketches of the other places we need to safeguard. Plus, I'd like a picture of Carrie. It may be most efficient to simply stop her."

Roxy stared at him.

"Stop her? You mean banish her, or kill her, or something?"

"I was thinking of a slightly less dramatic approach than death and destruction, but rendering her impotent is the goal. I'll be working in Kat's library. Don't return before four and bring no one but Liz." He stopped at the bay seat halfway up the imposing staircase.

"Is there anything of Carrie's in this house?"

Roxy reviewed the times Carrie had been an invited guest. It had been months ago and the house had been thoroughly cleaned several times since. She was ready to answer no, then recollected the first conversation she had with Carrie about a Christmas present for Kat.

"The stand-up mirror in Kat's bedroom. It's not Carrie's exactly, but she did buy it as a gift for Kat from the Rhode Island staff. Does that count?"

★ ★ ★ ★ ★

Max was stretched on the bay window seat rolling a single silver dollar across his knuckles when Kat awoke. She sat up as he tossed a small metal device to her.

"It's a microphone. I found it secreted in one of the curlicues in the mirror frame, a surprise from your friend Carrie. I assume it has you hotwired direct to Scarlatti."

Kat frowned as she examined it.

433

"Was there a camera, too?"

Max shook his head and grinned wolfishly.

"They couldn't see your impassioned midnight liaisons, only hear the heavy breathing. I screamed a few profound obscenities into it and then crushed the mechanism. Pass it on to Stuart. He'll enjoy fooling with it."

"He came to see me yesterday promoting his solution to all crises—power flexing."

"Don't underestimate Stuart. He sees clearly. Right use of power is the contest and you can't win if you don't play the game."

Max waved away her protests. "I know how you feel about power and control but there's no way to reach the gold at the end of the rainbow without engaging in this test. I can't do it for you, nor can Stuart, hero though he is."

"Heroes are not the safest men to have around. Hercules killed a friend or two if I remember. After all, a hero is questing man not perfected man," Kat argued.

"Don't get all superior. Goddesses suffer from flawed divinity. Ambiguity is rampant in their feminine descendants." He reached into a worn leather satchel. "I have a few ritual items in addition to the screen," he nodded at the triplet of sword bearing women glowing from the screen leaning against the wall. "They'll help whip your warrior into fighting fettle. Athena would be proud."

She laughed as he unfurled a large, glossy poster of a pneumatic, bare breasted Viking warrior queen, horned helmet on streaming blonde hair, mounted on a snarling polar bear, upraised sword in hand. It was an advertisement for peppermint schnapps.

"Courtesy of Liz's liquor distributor. Hang it on your wall for inspiration."

"What will it inspire me to?" Kat asked still smiling. "Pumped up breasts or dyeing my hair blonde? Aren't any of these Amazons ever brunettes?"

He tossed a video tape on the bed. "Sigourney Weaver in *Aliens*. She's a brunette and warrior first class. Watch it daily."

Kat looked bemused as he pulled a tiny red velvet bag from his pocket.

"This is why I couldn't be here until today. Having a magic charm made takes time. Luckily I was in Manhattan which made the process easier."

He sat on the side of the bed and took her left hand, slipping a ring onto the middle finger.

"This is for strength. If it won't ruin your high fashion look, I suggest you wear it constantly."

Curious, she examined the shining silver colored ring. It was huge and heavy, its domed top mounted with a dark stone that seemed to have a splattering of light in its heart.

"It's polished steel," Max explained. Then he reached over and opened the dome. Kat gasped as she saw the bizarre interior.

"The eye of a wolf," he said. Kat grunted.

"Is it real?"

"Yes, but don't be concerned, it had a meaningful death." He removed the ring and held it open to the light. "This is a star garnet."

She could see the white rays cutting through the dark red stone from a center point of whiteness. He snapped closed the dome and slipped it back on her finger.

"When you fire up your warrior energy, the wolf's eye will gleam and the star in the garnet will be illuminated by it. That's how you'll know you're ready for battle."

The tarot card he threw onto the dramatically embroidered crazy quilt that covered her bed offered another upraised arm with a sword, this time a knight in armor astride a galloping horse.

"An image for you."

"I thought that was my hero."

"I thought you told me you didn't need a hero."

They stared at each other in silence for several moments each knowing what the other knew.

"Do you need to brush-up on any breathing exercises or ritual movements, or can you train for this bout yourself?" Max broke the silence.

"Will it come to open confrontation at some point?"

"Doesn't every political contest? Someone wins, someone loses."

Kat responded thoughtfully. "It doesn't seem as simple as me against Douglas. There would be no contest. I feel other forces massed against me as well, and a much larger battle raging."

"All the more reason for gladiator training to go into effect. You're in the phase where intelligence may be of less use than will and endurance."

Casting her thoughts toward the outcome, Kat asked about consulting the oracles for more specifics.

Another two coins appeared in Max's fist as he returned to sit on the window seat.

"As soon as Roxy gets back with Liz and we finish with the house, then we'll ask some questions. Speaking of 'the girls', I want to discourage their thinking that black magic is involved. However," Kat stiffened as the coins began to spin faster across his knuckles, "you know how easily the power can be misused, especially by someone as naturally bent as Carrie. Take her threat seriously. Evil is a real force and she's got it. She only looks mild and stupid. The price of misusing occult power the way she does is high, but a lot of damage can be done before the bill comes due."

★ ★ ★ ★ ★

Max assigned them to ring bells as he paraded them through the house. They were supposed to imagine spheres of protection expanding into every nook and cranny as the bells sounded. Liz was an enthusiastic participant. She would hurl herself into a room, madly ring the foot-tall brass bell she carried, and scream for Carrie to keep her useless body away from them. "You're lower than slug slime," she shouted into the hall. "Step across this line and I'll ring your bell, you black-hearted bitch," was her cry from the small balcony off Kat's bedroom. Max would grin, keep chanting and ringing his silver bell mounted with a falcon's head, then lead them snaking into another room in the huge house. They finished the ding-dong rampage, as Liz termed it, in Kat's library. Liz required no more than a stern glance to recognize that subdued was the proper demeanor for entry.

Max took a position to the west, outside the magic pattern that was woven into the rug. He motioned for Roxy to sit again in the heart. Mirroring Kat to the south, Liz sat on the point of the star's northern arm. He pointed to the cards laying in front of Roxy and gestured for her to begin shuffling.

"Well, girls. Interested in the initials of the man you'll marry?"

"Yeh! Let's start with Kat," Liz responded.

"I appreciate your concern for my female needs, but it seems it's the warrior I have to be summoning, not the concubine."

"Great! A cat fight. Always my faves. We have one a week in the bar. They're worse than any of the men. I can stop men fighting by stepping between them and speaking sternly. With women, they're as likely to pull me into it as not."

"Listen to Liz," Max said to Kat. "She understands that being a warrior does not require murder and mayhem but rather a stance of alert watchfulness. For everyone's information, I plan to take care of Carrie myself."

"Evil witch combats wise magician, ringside seats still available," Liz crowed.

"All I want to do is hasten the inevitable," Max replied enigmatically.

Roxy's eyes kept opening wider with fear.

"I'm glad you're taking on Carrie. I'm afraid. I don't want anyone fighting or killing. I thought we were on the goddess path. How come all we've been talking about is being a warrior?"

"Don't be fooled into thinking all the faces of the goddess are kind and loving. There's a dark side as well, the point of chaos in women that balances the rigid cyclic order of their bodies. It's the Indian goddess Kali, the destroyer. She holds swords in her hands and dismembered bodies strung on her necklace and earrings. Face Kali and you will face your own terror. Once understood she releases you from fear," Max told them.

Liz looked thoughtful then turned to Kat.

"Kali. It sounds the same as the way Senator Stuart says your name."

How did Liz know? She hadn't met Stuart yet.

"Can we do the cards?" Kat's voice was strained.

Max nodded. "Do the Celtic cross, Roxy. Tell us about the campaign."

She laid out the familiar pattern, not surprised when the first card, indicating Kat, was the Empress. Once again she promised herself she would look at the card in the goddess deck. She was getting so accustomed to the same cards repeating she barely flinched when the Devil turned up next, as the obstacle the Empress must overcome. Liz howled when she saw the furry, horned demon with chained humans at its taloned feet.

"Carrie and black magic, right?" she asked Max who reluctantly agreed.

The ace of wands appeared as the card underlying the remaining action. Liz laughed at the white hand emerging from a cloud, holding an erect rod from which leaves were sprouting.

"I guess the only mystery is whose shaft that is."

Roxy kept turning the cards, Kat growing more edgy as each card was displayed. She croaked "Race" as the King of Cups was reversed. Liz pounded on the card laid atop the structure showing a man stealing away with an armful of swords.

"Bruno was right! That says Douglas will try to steal the election, doesn't it?"

There was a twitch of surprise as Max nodded again. She picked up the next card and held it up to Max.

"A boy with a talking fish in a cup?"

"It promises betrayal and lies in the near future," he answered attempting to keep his voice emotionless, fooling none of the women.

"Jasmine!" proclaimed Liz. "My prime choice as betrayer."

The gasp was in stereo, or quadraphonic, to be more accurate. Roxy turned up the Death card in the bottom place of the final line.

"Why are we surprised?" Kat asked of no one in particular. "Death always comes in threes."

They all looked at her, trying to guess how many she thought there had been to date. Judging from the fear on her face, no more than two.

A group of youth fighting was the next card and again needed no explanation to any of the four: attacks would continue. Roxy laid the final two cards in a rush and was rewarded with delighted looks from both Max and Kat. Even Liz smiled, the pictures were so encouraging. There was Justice, promising that good would be rewarded, and the beautiful Star card as the completion.

"Great and lasting love, given and received," Max concluded.

Liz was bursting with probing questions. Kat cut off further speculation by asking Max to add his reading of the stars to the message the cards sent.

"The campaign will find itself enmired in ever increasing amounts of Scorpio manipulations of power, magic and deceit. The same force will impact you personally," he nodded at Kat. There was a noticeable pause as Max considered his next words, glancing at the women sitting to Kat's right.

"The hidden flame of your body will challenge the ambition of your soul."

"And the outcome?" Kat asked, as if she believed there was no answer.

Max picked up the Star card that concluded the tarot spread.

"A foot in each world. There will be no victory. The two forces will learn to co-exist."

★ ★ ★ ★ ★

The weather demons either read her mood or decided to take pity on a frail mortal. The ocean was calm and shining, the sky a vibrant sapphire once the madcap streaks of pinks, purples, and reds disappeared. Sunshine streamed down, forming golden pods that caught her hair and danced beneath her feet. Even the gulls looked picturesque standing along the curve of the beach outlining the river's edge. Though Jake was back at home, Roxy slept soundly knowing Max was there along with Kat and Liz. Even Carrie would not challenge such a formidable line-up.

She was so absorbed in working out Kat's speech for the AFL-CIO convention the following night, Roxy barely noticed the car driving along the fence as she walked up the stairs from the beach. The back door was being held open by the man driving. Her heart froze for a moment. Was this a kidnapping? One of Scarlatti's men? Then she realized it was Pete and Jake. Pete was working and they came to take her to Pepper's for breakfast.

★ ★ ★ ★ ★

She sat in a soft chair outside the conference room where Kat was meeting with the editorial board of the Newport paper to determine whether the publication would endorse her for the U.S. Senate or not. Roxy wanted to be able to doze after her filling breakfast. Turning her head slightly, she could see Newport, the bay, the bridge stretching across it, islands with lighthouses. The views alone were worth spending time in Rhode Island.

No printers ink and noisy machines for the world of modern journalism. A fax machine sat in the corner, overflowing with press releases from Burkhart, Douglas, and the other political candidates. Jasmine does her job, Roxy thought grudgingly as she gauged an equal number of Kiley for Senate releases.

The door was open so she could hear everything and see Kat sitting at the end of the table nearest her.

Thanks to Liz's deft hand, Kat's make-up was subtle, her hair neat and controlled with an escaped curl or two attesting to her feminine charm. She wore a slate gray pinstripe flannel suit, swingy jacket to mid-thigh over a softly draped above-the-knee skirt. A white silk wrap blouse framed her long neck; a jeweled scimitar pin decorated her jacket. On her finger she wore the wolf's eye talisman.

The force Kat directed at the three men who were the editorial board was almost as visible in her focused gaze as it was audible in her rich voice. She presented a clear and plausible vision of a golden future for Rhode Island that Roxy could not imagine anyone resisting. It was a virtuoso performance and Kat dazzled them with her wit, her unabashed brilliance, her dedication to serving the state. Her voice remained elegant and ladylike but the message shifted and she became the lurid poster on her bedroom door, an Amazon who devoured her lovers.

"Emmett Douglas is a petty, corrupt man who should be a convicted felon. Instead he's a candidate for U.S. Senate. He is attacking me with a series of lies and false accusations that have distracted the attention of the public, robbing them of any opportunity to hear intelligent discussion of critical issues. You, the press, have exhibited the integrity of moldy cheese. If my father were still alive, you would be unhappy men. I have devoted my life to proving there are other ways, cooperative ways of achieving what's best for all. Don't make me lose faith. Don't force me to prove my father's way best."

★ ★ ★ ★ ★

"Pout," Liz ordered as she painted Kat's lips her usual red. "You look like a smoldering Madonna, as ordered." She fluffed up Kat's hair, pulling wisps loose along the back of her neck and her cheeks. "An ancient Roman cameo of Venus. Is there a reason you're not wearing anything around your neck?"

Kat's crimson knit dress of angora and silk had a romantic sweetheart neckline and bodice that clung to her torso then flared from a drop waist to mid-calf.

"My dinner escort asked that I not wear a necklace." She allowed Liz's imagination to churn for a moment before explaining.

"Sal Pascucci owns an exclusive jewelry manufacturing firm. He and Duke were best friends from first grade on. Sal and his wife never had children so they considered Frankie and me substitutes. He's showered me with jewels for decades. Duke would have him stockpile particularly fine gemstones and Sal's been making them into pieces for me a few at a time."

"I assume you're not having dinner with him tonight just to collect a present?"

"No. I have to impress the Italo community with my need for their support. The Garabaldi Club's Saturday night dinner is the only time they allow women on the premises. It's the ideal place and Sal the ideal patron. I can't do any overt campaigning; the rule is no talking business. But I'll be visible and Sal can harvest the contacts for me later."

Kat's estimate of the opportunity available for political benefit was not exaggerated. The older men of the club guarded her jealousy, each seeing themselves acting for Duke. The younger ones wondered how accessible she was. Sal was delighted to subtly receive pledges of support and equally pleased by the sensation the ruby necklace he created for her was making.

She was standing near the carved fireplace waiting for Sal to finish with a group of four men seated at a linen-clothed table. She felt a hand on her arm. It was one of Tomasso's plumbing suppliers and he was grinning up at her broadly.

"Ya look great kid. Your old man would be proud. Listen, I want to warn you about your boyfriend."

"Boyfriend? I don't have a boyfriend."

"Yeh, the senator. You know, the one who came up here. I saw the pictures."

"He's not my boyfriend!" Kat said firmly.

"OK, OK, whatever you say. Anyway, it's not what I think matters. It's what Scarlatti thinks. Someone told me he's hired some street trash in Washington to hurt your boyfriend. You should warn him."

Kat's stomach tightened as the little man kept talking earnestly. There was no doubt he saw this as a favor.

"Is he here?"

"Who? Scarlatti? Nah! We'd never let that gangster in no matter how much money or guns he has. Ya gotta have some standards. He gives us all a bad name. Not that most of the guys in this place don't do business with him when necessary, if ya know what I mean."

★ ★ ★ ★ ★

Roxy was waiting outside the Biltmore's ballroom with the final copy of Kat's speech to the labor convention. It was the same room where they hosted lunch with the First Lady in June, which seemed like years ago. Hundreds of union members were squeezed around tables. Banners announcing Health Care Now and member unions draped the walls. Young politicos from various camps stood in the ballroom foyer with rolls of stickers, slapping them on the lapels of carpenters, electricians, transport workers and other union professions. Delegates looked like walking billboards advertising the Democratic ticket. Kiley for Senate was the only Republican message shown. Knowing the formidable presence the Democrats would have at this event, Mario and the Hose plus a few of their street politics protégées replaced the usual college girls handing out Kat's stickers.

DEATH CARD II

Applause was polite for the Republican seeking Kat's vacated House seat and non-existent for Attorney General Burkhart who was recognized as no friend to labor. Mario praised his courage in showing up at the convention at all. Kat appeared only moments before she was scheduled to be introduced and brushed aside the speech Roxy attempted to hand her.

There was no uncertainty in Kat as she faced what any Republican would consider a hostile crowd. She knew it was filled with men and women who had been friends of her father's and known her all her life. A sense of expectancy built as she stood with graceful dignity, scanning the room touching familiar eyes and allowing her face to relax into an ever-broadening smile.

She spoke softly, touching the masterpiece around her neck. The square cut ruby was mounted on a diamond-encrusted heart. She announced she would talk to them tonight from the heart. They were her friends, her family.

She began by singling out key union and political leaders in the room by name and sharing childhood anecdotes with them.

"There's Mikey Campagna who would always slip me an extra twenty dollars for my prom dress or that special angora sweater. And Carol Martinez who brought me home bags of costume jewelry for favors at my twelfth birthday party."

As Kat continued, faces changed, hearts melted. This was not a Republican challenging the Democratic machine. This was Duke Tomasso's little girl running against a corrupt outsider who never did a day's labor in his life and who could not remember the names of delegates who turned out party line votes for him in the past. She reminded the assembled crowed of who she was, talking about Duke and her grandfather, who did so much to make the state a union stronghold. She described what she had learned from her father, from her friends seated before her.

"My father taught me the value of work. He taught me about creating jobs and being loyal to your workers." She recalled her unswerving support during her years in the House of Representatives opposing her party to fight for just wages and benefits.

"When I am in the U.S. Senate I will continue to fight for family leave policies, health care plans, better training and more jobs. My background guarantees my votes are right regardless of my political party."

"I don't care that the CEO of Weyland Industries won't give me ten thousand dollars from his political action committee if I support guaranteed health care. I care that James Reed's wife can afford to have the operation she needs, and Johnny McGarvey will not be bankrupted by his cancer treatments."

She filled the room with her perfect voice and precise words.

"We deserve more than money for our work. We deserve respect and the opportunity to build our skills, we deserve a secure old age. The American workingman and woman will not become obsolete if I am in the U.S. Senate. I will fight to guarantee a skilled and employed workforce well into the 21st century so America will be able to produce the wealth of the future."

She paused as if deciding what next to say.

"Many of you in this room are Democrats. I ask you to look beyond the narrow confines of a political party when you vote next month. Look into your hearts, into what you know about me. Frankly my friends, Rhode Island and the U.S. Senate do not need another Republican or another Democrat. They need a leader, a person who is not afraid to ask the hard questions and give the hard answers. But most of all, they need a person who knows which is the working end of a shovel."

The crowd roared its delight recalling a recent photograph of Douglas holding a groundbreaking shovel upside down.

When she finished there was absolute quiet in the ballroom except for a few muffled sobs. Then the applause began. Ralph Toramenci of the bricklayers union stood and began pounding his hands together and whistling. Others followed: rough men who had held her on their knees, who had come to her father for a loan or a job. She was calling in her debts and they knew it. Soon the whole ballroom was standing cheering the beautiful young woman who truly was one of them.

Kat's gray eyes filled with tears as she stepped off the speaker's platform and made her way through the tables. Hands reached out to touch her as she went by. People tried to hand her money as they did when the Civita Madonna was carried through the streets of Knightsville each July. Mario was beaming as she reached the door. No one but Kat could have gained unconditional surrender from this crowd.

They shouldered their way into the hall, Kat smiling, shaking hands with the people who clustered around her, nodding at her opponent's operatives who looked away or gave her frozen glances. Then they began the round of parties, visiting suites of the more prominent unions or those who were particular allies of hers.

Bulky ethnic men filled the firefighters' small suite so tightly there was scarcely air to breathe.

Another longtime Duke friend wrapped her in a bear hug and shouted her praises to whomever was close enough to hear.

"Look at her boys. Isn't she a knock-out? I've known her since she was born. She's the best."

Then he pulled Kat aside and told her how much he admired her.

"I never heard anything so beautiful as that speech you gave at your father's funeral. I cried. I was proud to know I'd helped you grow up."

The older man had not been in the ballroom. He did not know she reran her father's eulogy in her mind and borrowed heavily from it in her conquest of the forces of labor. Max was right. Being a warrior did not necessarily mean murder and mayhem.

★ ★ ★ ★ ★

Roxy grabbed her arm as they crossed the entry drive in front of the Biltmore and headed toward the campaign van parked along Kennedy Plaza.

"It's Race Scarlatti," she whispered pointing to the black Lincoln with its vanity tag.

Kat instinctively veered away, but caught herself. After almost twenty-five years of avoiding him as if he were a communicable disease, she was pleased that her psychic energy was able to call him up on cue.

"Good. I have something I need to say to his face."

Seeing her approach, he slowly emerged from the rear seat of the car. She stood facing him under a street light mesmerized by his unblinking gaze behind rimless glasses and the deliberate sliding of his thin lips across his small, even teeth. She supposed he was smiling.

"Wonderful speech. I almost shed a tear for Duke myself. May I offer you a ride somewhere?"

Kat shuddered, recalling the last time she sat in a car with him and how he had threatened to kill Stuart. The warning she heard earlier in the evening told her Race had not forgotten his vendetta. As she shook her head, declining the offer, she also shook off the paralysis of her will that he seemed to induce.

"When you returned to me the tape that Jamie made, you did me a great favor. I understand that and appreciate it. You claimed you did it as a gesture to demonstrate your … your … your feelings about me. I want something more from you."

Nothing altered in his expression. His eyes remained dark, dead pools. His face was smooth and formless as if there were no bones beneath the pasty skin.

She willed herself to continue, rubbing the domed top of her wolf eye, imagining a flaming sword in her hand.

"Carrie has been terrorizing my friends, violating my home, and generally harassing my campaign. I know she's your tool. Order her to stop. And that's not all. I want Douglas gagged, his lying tongue put to rest, the same with his friends' newspapers."

He stared so long in silence, she began to feel her resolve drip away.

"What do I get in return?" he finally asked.

"No deals. No trades. I want this done. All I guarantee is that we will talk after the election."

"I think we will talk before then."

Kat frowned. "What do you mean?"

"Next week my organization will help many nursing home residents, non-English speaking citizens and others to vote absentee. They sign, we fill in the ballot later. In a close election, my five thousand votes could be decisive." His deliberate voice strained to escape between unmoving lips.

"I consider the money this cost me to be a most effective campaign contribution."

She imagined her flaming sword aimed at his throat and vowed this election would never be close enough that his fraud would decide it.

His rasping voice once again broke the silence.

"Carrie will present no further problems. Douglas, I have no control over. I'm not certain anyone does."

"Talk with him. He'll listen. Threaten him. Isn't that your usual and most successful tactic?" She was gratified to feel her anger continue to build, verified by a gleam on her left hand.

Finally he blinked, once.

"My sources tell me there have been no intimate meetings."

Kat was furious. He was tailing Stuart. Then she felt afraid.

"Senator Stuart is not the issue."

"Wrong. He's my issue."

"I have no control over Stuart," she said.

"We each have a mad dog for whom someone wants to hold us responsible. I know how to take care of mad dogs—shoot them!"

The ring was blazing.

"Forget Stuart. Call off Carrie. Do what you can with Douglas." She spun on her heel and plunged into the traffic dragging Roxy behind her.

★ ★ ★ ★ ★

They gathered at Tony's to eat and drink while they watched the incredible news on television and shared the comments they each had been collecting all day. At 10 a.m. eastern daylight time—the announcers kept repeating the time as if they still could not believe what had happened—President Sam Jamison nominated Virginia's junior Senator Thomas Jefferson Stuart to fill out the term of the late Vice President William Daley.

Roxy had been on the phone talking with Hayes about Kat's unusual behavior two days earlier. She had been missing all morning, arriving without explanation only after a vote called her to the House floor.

"She missed a fundraising breakfast which is definitely not like her. Fortunately Senator Stuart was there and covered for her. When I walked into her office later to try and find out what was going on, she was starting blankly out the window. I called her name about three times before she turned and gave me a beatific smile then seemed to snap out of whatever other world she was in and looked at me perplexed. I never did get an explanation of where she had been."

Before she could extract any further information, the announcement of Stuart's sudden ascendancy to the near pinnacle of power was broadcast. Hayes called back hours later. Roxy's first question was about Kat's reaction to the news.

"Do you think she was surprised?"

"She was alone in her office when the press conference started. No one expected it to be an announcement of a vice president. The rumored hot news was supposed to be about breakthroughs in negotiations with Iraq. I didn't hear any shrieks coming out of her office but that's probably because Jasmine was wailing in my ear. By the time I saw Kat she seemed quite content with the whole idea. If she knew before the news this morning she was probably the only person in Washington besides Stuart and the president who did. My contacts at the White House claim it was a shock to everyone there including the omnipotent Bud Swearman, their most despised chief of staff. Apparently the president made this decision on his own."

At that point, Mario jumped on the call.

"Will he be confirmed?"

Hayes' thrilled response suggested that he already saw himself enthroned on the vice president's staff and considered the upcoming nomination hearing as far more exciting than the senate race.

"They don't like his attitude, his independence but they can't reject him on that. Unless there's some scandal, and knowing Stuart I can't imagine there is, he'll be vice president before the end of the year."

Reaction in Rhode Island was indicative of how personally politics was taken in the smallest of states. Everyone was delighted, treating Stuart as if he were a favorite son because of his recent visit. He had come to Rhode Island just a few weeks ago, now he was the most talked about man in America and they basked in some strange sort of reflected glory.

Later that night Liz and Roxy were sitting around the kitchen before going up to bed, rehashing the stunning notion of Stuart as vice president of the United States.

"Well, I guess this ends our plans for romance," Roxy commented.

"Why?" asked Liz. "Is sex banned for vice presidents?"

"Sex with a U.S. Senate candidate for a not-yet-divorced man who is being considered for vice president and has some powerful opponents is definitely a no-no."

"Who do you think really cares?" Liz was not giving up her fantasy.

"Let's see. There's Jasmine, Race Scarlatti and Carrie, Douglas….."

"Oh yeah, him."

"…… and the *Ocean Beacon* newspapers. Plus all the people in Rhode Island who thrive on political gossip and scandal which, as we know, is everyone over age ten. And if I understood everything Hayes and Mario were saying about how both Democrats and Republicans don't want Stuart that close to the White House, I could extend the list even further."

"Lots of people are sleeping together and no one cares except maybe their mates and in this case there are no mates to care. At least we can assume Stuart's wife won't care in the final weeks of her divorce."

"This is politics, not real life," Roxy exclaimed. "Anything can cost votes. Last year there were probably as many people who voted against Senator what's-his-face because they believed he didn't fuck the beauty queen as those who voted against him because they believed he did."

★ ★ ★ ★ ★

It was after midnight when Carrie returned home to find a message from Jasmine on her answering machine. She followed instructions, ignored the time, and returned the call, holding the panties from her magic pentagram in her hand. She knew exactly what was on Jasmine's mind.

"I heard about Senator Stuart's promotion," she said once they exchanged protestations about how it had been too long since they had spoken, both knowing why the silence. "I guess a man who's vice president can have any woman he wants, and we know who he wants," Carrie added maliciously.

"Plus he'll be free soon to have her. It doesn't give you too much time to save your heroine from falling into the clutches of a primitive who wants her as a bed toy."

She continued to goad the press secretary, allowing Jasmine to sporadically interrupt and curse Stuart ever more vehemently. Race had ordered her to stop harassing Kat but she was certain he would consider any priming of Jasmine for use as a tool against Stuart to be acceptable. She could scarcely wait for her meeting with Race in the morning so she could goad him as well. Sexual obsessions, jealousy, emotional entanglements were ugly but effective threads in the pattern she was weaving. What a gift to be free of such humiliating addictions. Better to be weaving the web than caught in it, she observed.

The black Lincoln was waiting for her the next morning. Climbing into the back seat with Race, she smiled secretly. Having a weapon that could cause him pain was exhilarating.

"Looks like you missed your chance to eliminate Stuart. Now that he's been named vice president he'll be surrounded by Secret Service. You don't know anyone smart enough to get by them." Carrie watched him sitting against the seat, eyes closed lifelessly. She had to lean closer to hear his words.

"I will never give up. This is vendetta, the path of honor. It is in my blood. If I allow him to steal my prize, I can no longer call myself a man."

Carrie smirked. She almost found herself cheering for Stuart. Of course, her web had no victors in it but her, the Spider Queen.

"All the scrutiny of the hearings will probably keep him away from her bed. That gives you a little more time to win her heart. Maybe once he's vice president and she's a senator they'll have to separate, nepotism rules or something."

At her last sentence, his eyes snapped open and he stared at her hopefully.

"Do you think if I see that she wins the senate seat she will turn to me?"

He was pathetic, Carrie thought disgustedly. She wondered if it were her spell that made him so.

★ ★ ★ ★ ★

They heard the story of how Stuart came to be named vice president directly from Kat when she managed to escape from Congress and futile votes on what she termed a criminal budget. She was in the state only overnight, long enough to march in the Columbus Day parade on Federal Hill, which was in fact a tribute to the Italo community.

"It was the endless procession of Italians marching in the 1910 parade that first made the powers-that-be sit up and take notice of a new group to be reckoned with," she explained. Kat would have missed votes to walk in the parade.

They were once again three hearts beating as one, eating spicy, hot apple dumplings Liz had just pulled from the oven.

"The Apple Butter Festival is happening in Morgan Springs," she reported. "I make thousands of these critters every year for that weekend. It would throw off my internal calendar if I neglected the task even though I'm marooned in some flat fingernail of land barely big enough to measure."

Neither Kat nor Roxy cared about Liz's reasons. They were happy to feast on the product. Pouring herself a glass of milk while waiting for her second dumpling to cool, Kat told them the story of how America was getting a vice president who defined "unprecedented."

Jamison was governor of Texas when Stuart first started working for the Virginia senator he eventually succeeded. The senator and the governor were longtime friends and Jamison took the senator's successor under his wing. Not too long after Stuart was elected to the Senate in his own right, Jamison's son was killed in a plane crash in the Caribbean during Air Force maneuvers. Stuart reminded the Jamisons of their son and for a couple of years they mutually adopted each other as surrogate family. When Jamison stumbled into the White House, Stuart studiously avoided capitalizing on their personal relationship for any political favors. But the president, and especially his wife, valued his honesty in opinions on both policy and presidential advisors. Marge Jamison also treasured Stuart because he never treated her husband like an idiot, which most of the White House staff, leftovers from his predecessor, did.

"Jamison is not the political ninny his advisors consider him to be," Kat explained. "According to Stuart's humble assessment, Jamison saw his chance to introduce a wild card into the poker game of American politics. He also saw this as a way of spiting his handlers. He knew that every time Bud Swearman looked across the cabinet table and saw T.J. Stuart facing him, it would stick in his craw. Given enough time, Swearman might choke on it."

"Does Stuart have presidential aspirations?"

"He claims he doesn't," Kat responded, sounding unconvinced. "And in some ways, I believe him. Power is such a natural aspect of his character he doesn't lust for it. He has several excuses for accepting the job. He said the president begged him to, showing him the list of nominees acceptable to both his chief of staff and the senate minority leader. They both gagged on the selection and the president promised one of them would be chosen if Stuart declined. With a Republican governor in Virginia, the party won't lose a senate seat when Stuart steps down and he'll be in place in case of a tied Senate. With a single tie-breaking vote, he can accomplish his goal of Republican control. And he can hardly wait to drive crazy the 'non-elected stuffed shirts who think they run the country from their cubicles in the West Wing' as he describes the top echelon White House staff. He said to tell Liz they're all Richard-heads."

Liz tried looking nonchalant as both Kat and Roxy watched her load another tray of dumplings into the oven.

"I meant to ask you the other day when Max was here how you knew what my name sounded like when Stuart said it."

Fruitlessly, Kat waited for a response.

"Have you been plotting with him behind my back?"

"Phone sex only. Nothing to worry about," Liz replied, obviously disinclined to discuss the subject of her contacts with Stuart. Roxy was amazed they had any contact at all.

★ ★ ★ ★ ★

Roxy and Liz sat in lawn chairs in front of headquarters handing out campaign brochures and selling Kiley for Senate artifacts. They ignored most of the Columbus Day parade of parochial school bands, marching collections of Knights of Columbus resplendent in their tri-corner hats and gleaming ceremonial swords, and other politicians. Liz was excited when she saw a school bus covered with a huge American flag, a line of kids in school uniforms marching along either side holding the ends of the flag.

"I guess that's an informational float," she quipped, "demonstrating how to flag down a bus."

Liz maintained color commentary on the parade and activities surrounding it, making Roxy laugh out loud.

"See all those sacrificial altars set up?" She motioned to wooden booths where Italian sausages and fried dough were being prepared.

"They burn a special oil to thank St. Christopher, you know, the one who found America—not that it was ever lost. The ritual oil is called Crisco and we'll probably have to scrape the fumes off our windows tomorrow."

She was also enthralled with all the vendors selling the state's famous costume jewelry. "They're all selling that twisted horn. Columbus must have worn one."

"Max says Columbus was steeped in astrology and claimed he was guided to America in fulfillment of a prophecy."

"It must have been quite a prophecy, Roxy. Led him right to some dinky island in the Caribbean crawling with cannibals that he thought was India."

They were on their feet screaming with the rest of the thousands lining the sidewalks of Atwells Avenue when Kat walked by. Even the baby-faced mayor who had grown up on these same streets did not get the reception she did. Kat looked as colorful as the Knights of Columbus who preceded her in the parade. It was easy to imagine her with raised sword leading soldiers into battle against injustice as she strode confidently along, waving and smiling enthusiastically at cheering fans. She wore a blazer of velvet patchwork embroidered with exotic symbols that Roxy was certain she never learned about in parochial school. Her sage green skirt flared out just below the tops of her green suede boots. A jeweled gold cross hung around her neck announcing her birthright to a place in this parade.

Mario waited with a car beneath the pigna arch at the end of the parade route, picked up Kat and raced her to the airport so she could get back to Washington for more votes. They were both frustrated by the daily loss of campaign days while Congress dallied on useless budget proposals.

★ ★ ★ ★ ★

Jasmine threw the newspaper down on her desk, rage rendering her speechless for the moment. All she could do was snarl at the huge picture of Vice President-designate T.J. Stuart grinning at them from above the fold.

"This pandering is the most fraudulent excuse for journalism I've ever seen.

And I thought this woman had professional standards. You can practically see her drooling over him." Kat shot her press secretary a look of irritation that caused Jasmine to flinch but not to stop.

"Look at this headline—'V.P.T.J.? Or Should We Call Him Tommy Jeff?' I can't believe the whole country's gone gaga over this hillbilly."

She snatched back the paper and began reading ignoring Kat's deepening scowl.

"Listen to this drivel: 'He is one of those beloved of the fates. He has heart, guts, brains and a streak of insolence to challenge and delight those same fates, to overcome any obstacles.'"

She jumped to another paragraph, disgust filling her voice.

"'He is one of those rare individuals able to blend the natural popular instincts of a politician with a profound and brilliant mind and irrepressible daring.'"

Kat sat back and began to enjoy the pained look on her press secretary's face as she continued reading the laudatory article about Stuart.

"'There is little doubt that he is certain in himself, his own attitudes and ideas. He is a man who will act on principle without thought of the personal cost.'" She crumbled the paper and started to throw it on the couch. "There're two full pages of this nonsense. And in the *Post* Style section no less. I cannot believe they can't see through him."

Jasmine glared at her, then once more opened the paper.

"Perhaps you'll find this nauseating detail amusing." Kat's eyes tightened at the mean gloating in her voice.

"'The best news yet about our soon-to-be vice president is that he's single, or at least he will be any day now. Word has it that there is no special lady in his life but that won't last long if we know the hero-starved women of the nation's capital. Line up, girls. T.J. Stuart is a certified heart throb.' I wonder if she fucked him before or after writing her closing paragraph."

Jasmine's victory was brief. There was barely time to absorb the annoyance in Kat's voice before the congresswoman snatched the paper from her hands and ordered her out of the office and back to work.

"Regardless of Stuart's good fortune, which I'm sure you don't begrudge him, we have a senate race to run."

★ ★ ★ ★ ★

The conference call was not scheduled until eleven so they began working on the final direct mail piece. Roxy was sorting through piles of photos looking for ones that said it best, showed Kat in the right poses: listening at the center surrounded by regular folks, looking bold and courageous. Liz poured over contact sheets, turning them this way and that, doing the same.

Inspired by Kat's new crusading spirit, Liz announced her bumper sticker pledge.

"It's war and we have to let the world know we're winning. Bumper stickers are our most effective weapon. Every day this week that you don't see a Kiley bumper sticker, not including our staff cars, you have to find someone and put one on their car. Next week, you have to see two bumper stickers before you're off the hook." She dropped her voice several registers and glared. "Swear!"

The entire staff took the pledge.

There was a similar martial air to the conference call. First order of business was Lila's report on the nightly telephone canvassing which showed what she claimed was an unprecedented pattern.

"Your support is solidifying, apparently a reaction against Douglas' attacks. But there are too may undecideds for this point in the campaign, and they're growing daily."

Lila blamed some of the uncertainty on general concern about the possibility of war, some on disgust with budget delays.

"I'd say large segments of the voting public are being alienated from the process." Mario agreed.

"Our strategy at the beginning was geared to corralling these people and getting them to vote because they wanted to vote for Kat. I'm not certain we can do that anymore. No matter how false all the allegations are, they seem to involve her in the same murky politics that turned them off initially."

Taking advantage of a lull in the analysis, Roxy asked Lila to translate the percentages into actual numbers of votes.

"I estimate we'd have two hundred and twenty thousand votes if the election were held today."

The number satisfied everyone but Roxy, who frowned and promised herself a visit to Jake that night. In the meantime, she began breathing through both nostrils.

Mario added peripheral observations about increasingly ardent defense of Kat on radio call-in shows, other than Dolly from Nooseneck. Liz snorted her delight. She abandoned the character after Mario warned that the political ears were convinced she was a Kiley plant. But just last week, someone calling into Carole Ann's morning show referred to Dolly's description of a Douglas brainstorm as barely able to produce a drizzle.

"Letter columns are also flooded with support and Roxy claims authorship of no more than a few. The grass roots network is humming. Town captains have lists of all those we're identifying in our canvassing as undecideds and are calling them with persuasive messages about getting off the fence and into Kat's camp.

We're going to hammer them with paper and calls until they surrender. They also have lists of supporters so we can turn them out on election day."

"What do we know about Douglas' activities?" Kat's frustration at being trapped in Washington seeped through her voice.

"We see him nowhere," Mario answered.

"Well, he's not here," Hayes interrupted.

"Oh, we know he's in the state. He's just keeping out of sight, in some sewer probably."

"Yeh, checking on Tomasso work results." Kat's voice was bitter but at least she was making jokes. Mario continued.

"Apparently the Democratic Senate leadership got to him. They've hired Roberts and Sondheim back as media advisors. The strategy is to push the Democratic ticket and pretend Douglas is not a part of it. My sources tell me Douglas is meeting privately with key people offering deals and making threats. We should be prepared for a final surge of poisonous direct mail feeding each individual the exact single aspect they don't like about Kat.

"The Democratic machine is geared up to the max, more than in years. They smell blood on every level, including ours. I've heard they believe they can sweep the state and I'm not certain they aren't correct, except for you, of course."

"Do you think they really want to elect Douglas? The ones in Rhode Island I mean?" Kat asked reproachfully. "I know David Clanton would elect a man-eating plant if it was counted as a Democrat and kept him majority leader."

"I think they'll elect him, then indict him after the two-year limit that allows the governor to appoint a replacement. Any sooner than that and they would face you again in a special election and it would be a sure thing—for you. They appoint who they want getting your House seat as a bonus this election. Only you lose. The ones who think or even care about you assume you'll stay and work for Rhode Island anyway."

The aftershocks of harsh truth made a pinging sound as they spread along phone lines, Roxy noticed.

"Unfortunately, Douglas' vanishing act is a little late for us to escape unscathed. He's gotten the media so hooked on his attacks that tabloid politics is the new wave in Rhode Island. I get calls daily from journalists I used to respect asking me convoluted questions about innocent actions, desperately looking for a way to twist it into something sordid."

Gould then commandeered the phone-linked group's attention.

"Our new theme is that this is an important choice, it makes a difference. Jake is our pitch man. We start filming tomorrow, in Washington. We'll frame Jake against the Capitol dome saying words to the effect of 'I came to Washington to see how our senator works and what did I find? An empty seat!' He concludes with the message: 'Our future deserves Rhode Island's best.'"

Roxy caught her breath. Jake was going to Washington tomorrow to film commercials. He had not mentioned it to her. But then he had been totally absorbed for the past few days in the annual feeding frenzy of blackback flounder in Narrow River. They were supposed to meet on the beach that morning but something kept them apart. She looked everywhere for him, expecting him to appear from behind a dune, or be dropped at her feet by seagulls. There was a message for her when she arrived at the office from him claiming to have been there looking for her as well. Then her breathing really slowed when Gould added: "Roxy, I need you to work on the rough draft of the script today, then you should come along with Jake so you can finalize it here."

Kat seconded the invitation adding that there was a presidential fundraising breakfast for her at the Mayflower the day the filming was scheduled and that she and Jake should plan to stay for that as well.

"I owe Jake a special treat for being such a public and successful champion."

Tricky ramifications of the situation emerged later in the call when Hayes began talking about political machinations. Roxy ignored the details but noted how the sound of his liquid drawl, which seemed much sweeter than his usual public tone, revived memories of his hands, lips, pressing body; memories she had been resisting for weeks. What would she do in Washington with both of them? She unrolled her fortune strip for October that she opened only that morning: *Desire comes in two types—shallow and profound.*

★ ★ ★ ★ ★

Jake was fishing off the seawall on the northern side of the Towers. He looked sporty in black pants and windbreaker slashed with blue and gray racing stripes.

"What are you fishing for?" Roxy asked, approaching.

"I didn't have anything better to do while I was waiting for you."

She laughed as they walked down to the beach, noticing the continuous circles of splashes that marked the presence of an enthusiastic school of fish, the ones Jake had been stalking. They were not flying out until noon. They had plenty of time.

"Come help me choose my wardrobe for the filming, plus I have a new tantric technique to try." Roxy agreed. She was packed and ready. Spending time bonding with Jake would strengthen her resolve to avoid Hayes while they were in Washington.

There was a line of exercise mats stretched across the atrium in Jake's house. He led her over and they sat facing each other in the center.

"Tantra claims that once the channel is opened between a couple, they can experience union without touching."

"No contact at all?" Roxy was incredulous.

"None, although it is a rare experience. There are other positions that only approximate the ultimate, meaning there is some contact. There's one I've always wanted to try."

Jake gestured for her to stretch out on her back along one half of the line of mats. He began massaging her bare feet, rubbing them with an oil called India Bouquet.

"It's a secret and exotic blend that magnetizes on the physical plane. It will help draw energy to the soles of our feet."

Stretched alongside her, his feet at about her chest, Jake indicated she should rub the oil on his feet as well.

"Make sure you get the bottoms," he murmured, enjoying the sensual touch.

He sat up and finished explaining the practice.

"We'll lie end to end, connected only by the soles of our feet. The image we'll work from is one of the sexual flame being lit and energy passing downward to the soles of our feet and flowing into the other person at the same point. Once we have the energy connected in that way then we can allow it to flow up the spinal column, through the crown and in an arc reaching to the other person's crown. Ultimately, we should be encased in a circular stream of ecstasy. This position is called Sole to Sole. That's a pun not a joke," he added quickly. "Are you ready to try?"

Sounded fine to her.

"But, when do we think about the votes?" Roxy asked.

He laughed. "As soon as the energy starts spinning."

Roxy had experienced relative timelessness before. When she would be writing and rewriting and really cranking, she would suddenly notice three or four hours had passed. But never anything like this.

Igniting her own sexual energy had never been difficult, tantric practice made it as easy as snapping the flame wand she had for starting the gas stove. Moving energy downward was a little tricky, but she soon felt a pulsing in the soles of her feet where they touched Jake. His energy magnetized hers. Then it all happened in a rush that lasted for hours, minutes, days? She had no idea. She watched through closed eyelids. The energy was spinning around and around them. She could feel it soaring through her body, rocking her rhythmically. She could hear it in the repetitious humming she knew was coming from her own throat. It was indescribable. Not the usual orgasmic bursting plasma and rushes of heat, but a continuous almost droning charge of sexual energy everywhere in her body. She knew it was only the binding force of skin that kept her molecules from deserting her skeleton to leap into the brilliant wheel whirling and whirling, endless, like the perfect wave or the streaming of stars through the universe. Safe sex is not so bad, she thought, losing herself in rapt contemplation of the sparkling stream flowing through her.

DEATH CARD II

★ ★ ★ ★ ★

Her feet tingled during the plane ride to Washington and she almost screamed in pain when she first walked on the hard concrete of the city's sidewalks. By the time they arrived in Kat's congressional office, most of the stimulated nerves had calmed. If she had known how long her feet would remain aroused, she would have worn sneakers.

Jake was immediately gathered up by Maggie and taken into the back office to meet the Washington staff, most of whom knew him only as a face on the screen. Roxy quickly nodded to Hayes as she escaped into Kat's office. It was empty.

"She's in a special briefing on Iraq and won't be back for an hour or so."

Roxy's resolve was melted wax as Hayes finished. He closed the door behind him and had her in his arms before she could avoid him. Halfway down to the couch, she felt the burning return to her feet and remembered what was happening. She dodged away, leaving Hayes off balance as he fell against the cushions.

"I better find out what Jake and I are supposed to do," she babbled nervously, heading for the door.

"I have that information."

She turned to face him, waiting.

"Come and sit down and I'll tell you." His voice was so ravishing she felt herself pulled to it like ants to honey. She perched primly on the edge of the chair next to the couch. looking at her hands, afraid to lose herself in his blue eyes.

"Maggie is taking Jake over to the Capitol to meet with Gould and the cameraman. They're to lay out shots for filming tomorrow morning after the presidential breakfast. We're to review the script here, put on finishing touches and have it ready for some rehearsal in Kat's presence by five. After that, who knows? Maybe Jake and I can draw straws. Although I must admit, it seems selfish of him to demand your presence here when he has you all the time in Rhode Island."

Roxy was annoyed that Hayes would think he and Jake could decide her fate.

He leaned back, smiling lightly under his mustache, his ginger colored eyebrows drawn together over his slightly flared nostrils.

"Read me the script."

She described the scene haltingly, gaining control as she began reading the words. Peeking up through her thick lashes, she could see him watching. There was no other word but lust for the hungry look on his face. She dropped her hand to her thigh hoping to stop the spasms of yearning she was feeling. When she came to the message line: Our future deserves Rhode Island's best, Hayes' voice suddenly had a tone of irritation instead of its usual seduction.

"Is he really Rhode Island's best?"

She knew in a flash that she could resist him. As she said "No," she wondered about the pleased smile on his face. Then she realized she was answering a question he hadn't asked, not the one about Jake's talents in bed

"I mean yes, he is the best, and no, I won't sleep with you again." She stalked out to find Jake, scoring one in her column for will.

★ ★ ★ ★ ★

After leaving the remaining staff to finish their night of drinking at the Hawk and Dove, Jake and Roxy strolled along the brick sidewalks of Capitol Hill, green trees arching over narrow streets. They were meeting up with Kat at Café Berlin. She insisted on taking them to dinner.

They peeked into open windows admiring the renovation and decorating jobs that raised many of the high-stooped, brick row houses to a never-before experienced elegance, or at least tastefulness. Sitting in the outside café section of the restaurant on a perfect Indian summer night, chatting casually about the campaign, the next day's filming, and Jake's excitement at meeting the president, Roxy wondered what this dinner was all about. Kat claimed she had a desire for meat and wanted gourmet barbarians to share her blood lust. Jake was pleased, explaining he had never tasted authentic German food before as he hungrily attacked the admittedly delicious veal and doughy noodles that were the evening's special.

She had almost given up on finding any but the most innocent of motives when she caught a glance from Kat. Inexplicably she knew. Kat wanted to be certain she was in Jake's hands for this visit, not slipping off with her chief of staff.

★ ★ ★ ★ ★

They passed through two portable security gates to the Mayflower Hotel's elegant drawing room, which was almost filled with the PAC representatives and Washington or New York supporters of Kat's who were delighted to pay more thousands for the opportunity to have their photo taken with the president. Rumors that the new vice president-designate would also put in an appearance had increased attendance to the point of overcrowding.

Press were barred from the fundraising event but a clutch of regional and Rhode Island journalists were hanging out beyond the security gates, waiting to pounce on notable guests entering and departing. Roxy stood by the remarkable array of breakfast food that filled two long tables.

Kat wore a rust wool Lagerfeld suit. A loose fitting jacket fell above her hip. The skirt was tapered, ending just below the knee, with a long back slit. The dipped hem of the jacket and the rows of buttons curving precisely along the line of her waist certainly accentuated her ass, thought Roxy.

"Sure would catch my eye if I was following her up the Capitol steps," a familiar male voice said as Kat walked away from them across the room.

Roxy was shocked to see Stuart standing next to her, popping a danish into his mouth.

"I thought I'd leave the dramatic entrance to the president, and of course our favorite senate candidate. Me and my boys slipped in a back way." he said, nodding to a pair of blue blazers standing nearby, the tell-tale coiled wire draped from their ear.

They chatted for a few more minutes as the president's entry distracted anyone from noticing Stuart was there. Then Jake spotted them and walked over.

"BYO for you? Don't you think we have any male talent here in Washington?" Stuart commented before he reached them.

"He's filming an endorsement commercial for Kat," she responded, blushing.

Knowing their period of anonymity was almost over, Stuart invited them both to come visit his vice presidential office in the Capitol when they finished filming.

"Bring the candidate along," he said, almost as an afterthought. "Three p.m." Then he was surrounded by senators and powerful lobbyists all looking for a receptive ear.

★ ★ ★ ★ ★

"Television loves sincere," Gould crowed about Jake's filming. "And this boy is the prince of sincere."

The crew packed up their cameras and equipment as Kat steered Jake and Roxy around the block of junior high students in matching jackets who posed for pictures with their congressman on the marble steps of the Capitol. Still in her suit from the presidential breakfast, she collected admiring glances from men who followed them through the mid-Victorian gold and mosaic embellished halls of the Capitol.

They stopped outside the official office of the vice president and Kat asked, with a casualness that screamed fake, whether Stuart had given any indication of why he wanted to see them.

"He was just being friendly, I think," Roxy replied. "Probably wants to show off his office like any kid with a new toy."

★ ★ ★ ★ ★

Kat could find no reason to dispute Roxy's assessment of Stuart's motives. He met them in the outer public lobby of his official office with its magnificent mosaic tiled floor, and led them into his private office unmarked and hidden among a series of identical doors in a corridor that led directly into the Senate chamber, next to the Senate library.

"These are all the vice presidents from my predecessor's state." He waved his hand at the half dozen portraits decorating the walls of the ornate office with its marble fireplace and impressive crystal chandelier. "I'm going to hang the portraits of every vice president from Virginia who became president, starting with my namesake of course. That'll make all those boys who don't like me sweat."

He casually talked about the price of being vice president: the loss of privacy and almost obsessive concern about his safety.

"The Secret Service detail is probably the most unexpected thing about the job, at least so far. They could make a suspicious man out of a saint. They have a process called enemy training where they alert all the men of my detail to any potential enemies. They use pictures, descriptions of habits, that kind of thing. I was amazed at how many enemies they included. Of course, most of them are generic. Foreign spies, kooks who have it in for any vice president. My real enemies are other political figures who would not be included by the Secret Service. Surprisingly, a few personal enemies showed up."

Kat's heart sank. She knew what this was all about and wondered if he was going to berate her in front of Roxy and Jake.

His face remained a charming mask; the vice president talking with important constituents. But Kat knew he knew. When she returned from Rhode Island after her meeting with Race, she approached the head of Stuart's Secret Service detail secretly. She gave him a picture of Race, described his position as the head of organized crime in Rhode Island, and insisted they be on the watch for him or his henchmen around Stuart. When the man asked her why, she waved aside the question and mumbled that it was personal but serious. She should have known he would go right to Stuart.

He pushed himself away from the desk he had been leaning against and politely asked Jake and Roxy to wait in the hall.

"I have an appointment in three minutes but I need a moment alone with the Congresswoman. I want to rebuke her and prefer not to do it in front of her friends. I'd like to leave her a shred of pride."

Kat watched despairingly as Jake and Roxy quickly left the office. As she began to stutter an explanation Stuart motioned for her to be silent, nudged her out of the chair and over to a door that cut off the back corner of the room.

"The only place I feel alone is in the bathroom. Let me show you the one here." He opened it and pushed her into the corner that had been completely tiled in pale green and turned into a bathroom. He cut off her protest.

"This is the only spot without cameras or listening devices."

Gripping her wrist, he spoke very softly with the barest hint of anger.

"I am besieged by enemies as I'm sure you know. Every part of my life is under investigation by people determined to find something that will rid them of me. There are two groups of agents tailing me in addition to the Secret Service. I'm a little edgy so please excuse what may seem to be unnecessary roughness.

"Why didn't you tell me Scarlatti threatened to kill me, that he's made attempts in fact, that he told you this directly? Were you protecting him?"

"Don't be absurd," she said, trying to wriggle free of his grip. It was an impossible task. He had her pinned against the small sink, the commode effectively blocking her way out.

"I just didn't want anything to happen to you."

"Did you think I was going to go after him, guns blazing?"

She said nothing, quelled by the force in his voice and foolishness of her position.

"You did, didn't you? I appreciate the high regard in which you hold my judgement." Before she could protest he continued.

"No more secrets, Kiley. Do you understand? No more secrets or I'll have to ransack your brain to find out what I need to know."

His voice was a threatening growl as he flung open the door to the bathroom and directed her to the door, his firm hold on her arm a reminder that there were eyes and ears in the room. She walked wordlessly into the corridor where Jake and Roxy stood along with several Republican senators who were Stuart's next visitors, a sharp tear of agony ripping her chest.

18

The Inquisition
October

Washington
Rhode Island

"The thought of spending another evening watching his smug face on television or reading more puffed up drivel in some newspaper was more than I could bear. No one is investigating anything or asking any hard questions. The *Los Angeles Times* actually described him as a twentieth century version of his namesake Thomas Jefferson with a touch of Clint Eastwood thrown in. Can you believe such fawning tripe? I hope the Democrats mangle him during the hearings." Jasmine nearly choked on her rage and disgust.

Marina was a well-preserved Dutch fabric designer who had been Jasmine's sexual mentor years ago. They had arranged to meet for dinner at the Inn at Little Washington. Hopefully the elegant Victorian décor, gourmet food, and her friend's placid wisdom would soothe her sensibilities.

They sat at a small table in the front corner of the dining room, several white shirted, black vested waiters poised around them. The setting sun cast a pink glow outside that was mirrored inside by the shirred and gathered soft pink lampshaded light at each table. Jasmine took a break from deploring Stuart's ascendancy in the political world to concentrate on her delicately flavored crab and spinach mousse appetizer and the crisp white wine that hovered in an exquisite crystal globe at her left hand.

Midway through an appreciative comment on the succulent firmness of the crab chunks, she stopped. The majority staff director of the Senate Rules committee was escorted to a table set up in a long narrow hall opening through a wall of windows onto the Inn's charming interior garden. Why was he here? The vice presidential hearings were starting in two days. He should be too swamped with preparations to be driving an hour into the mountains of Virginia for dinner. Everyone in Washington knew the hearings were the first shot in the '92 campaign, a shot no one anticipated a month ago. She could not imagine the Democrats fumbling the opportunity to hack away at Stuart, weakening him as a potential

461

presidential candidate in two years. She wanted the Democrats to be doing their job, exposing the designee as the arrogant male pig that he was.

Two waiters appeared bringing more bread and fluted glasses for the champagne. A third brought a small tumbler of creamed dill soup for them to taste. The food was delicious, Jasmine admitted, as she stared at the weeping Japanese crab apple tree with its little red berries scattered along the stone walk of the garden. Another man was escorted across her line of sight to the private dining hall. She was stunned to recognize the Rules committee's minority staff director.

Random bits of information fell into place, spelling out intrigue. Stuart had several political enemies among Democrats on the committee, not surprising considering his radical views and ardent partisanship. Jasmine concluded rumors were true about ruffled Republican feathers, especially among those senators who considered themselves far more appropriate candidates than Stuart.

She bent to examine the flowers in a porcelain swan that decorated their table, averting her face so the minority staff director, a long time acquaintance, could not see her. Jasmine's racing mind blocked all but bits and shreds of Marina's report on her recent visit to several groups in Sri Lanka who manufactured Belgian lace as a village craft.

A stir among the multitudinous serving staff caught her interest and she asked the young blond waiter about it when he returned with their entrees. He eagerly explained that someone was coming for dinner from Washington by helicopter.

"One of the staff was dispatched to Rappahannock Park just down the road to pick them up. I'd heard people occasionally did this but this is the first time since I've been here."

When Jasmine asked if he knew who it was arriving in such style, he smiled ingenuously, pushed his shell glasses up on his nose and looked around. He leaned over and whispered loudly, "Supposedly it's the White House."

Forewarned, she recognized the slight, ferret-faced man with slicked back red hair as he furtively joined the senate staffers: one of the notorious White House "mice" as Swearman's loyal forces were derisively known in political circles.

"While we're waiting for dessert," Jasmine said abruptly, interrupting her companion's chatter, "I want to examine that pyrantha they have espaliered along the stone wall in the garden before the light completely vanishes. I've been trying to get one in my garden to do that."

She invited Marina to accompany her knowing she would refuse. The older woman almost never ventured into fresh air, claiming the pollutants in it counteracted the rejuvenation treatments she received annually in some exclusive Swiss clinic.

Jasmine studiously ignored the three men clearly visible through the glass doors. With a fixed price dinner cost of seventy dollars per person, and an almost full main dining room, serious strings must have been pulled to insure their privacy. Four tables sat empty alongside them. One of the attentive serving staff accompanied her into the garden, explaining the process of training the shrub along the lattice. When she recognized the fourth man who joined the group as Gene Undahl from the *Washington Daily,* she allowed him to see her and waved casually in recognition. Feigning a sudden impulse, she walked over and greeted Undahl, whom she knew well, nodding to the minority staff director. The two men she did not know looked decidedly uncomfortable.

"Planning an assassination, boys?" she asked cheerfully, watching their expressions. The minority staff director showed no reaction, the majority staff director blinked quickly several times and ferret-face looked like he had caught his tail in a trap and could not decide whether he could bear to chew it off and escape. Undahl laughed maliciously. He knew her feelings about Stuart from previous conversations.

"Want to help?" he responded. "Since both press and public seem infatuated with the second string political hit man our esteemed president chose to foist on them—a man more discriminating judges," he nodded at his co-conspirators, "find disturbing—we're open to suggestion about effective weapons."

"Isn't your boss one of his adoring harem?" interjected the minority staffer suspiciously. Piqued by his remark, Jasmine saw a sword shining in the dark clouds that had gathered around her since Stuart's nomination.

"Fatal weaknesses are often another version of gleaming strengths. If I were searching for the chinks in this hero's armor, I would investigate his vaunted manliness. Women, guns, Cubans, his divorce, VMI—there could be something juicy in any of those topics."

Pleased with herself, Jasmine started to walk away.

"Who's Race Scarlatti?" the Democrat asked quickly.

"Why?" Jasmine responded, consciously keeping her face composed.

"He's got thugs watching our subject around the clock."

She shrugged, searching for a way to extricate herself without involving Kat any further. "Maybe he has something to do with the Cubans or drugs. Our favorite designee is a noted anti-drug crusader." She smiled tightly.

"Or maybe he's working for the Majority Leader."

As the Democrat scowled, she made her escape back to Marina and a helping of Chocolate Seven Ways, one of the Inn's exceedingly rich desserts.

So, Scarlatti was trailing Stuart. She would have to quiz Carrie about that, Jasmine thought as she allowed the delicate white chocolate shavings to melt on her tongue, satisfied with the serpent she had loosed in Eden.

★ ★ ★ ★ ★

The president had taken a few hard rights to the jaw from brutal confirmation hearings during his truncated first term. He inherited the office when his predecessor, a popular ex-astronaut, was fatally wounded by a crazed Iranian claiming terrorist ties. Determined that his choice for vice president would not meet the fate of his nominees for secretary of state and attorney general, Sam Jamison moved fast.

He claimed that a vacancy in the vice presidency while war with Iraq seemed imminent presented a dangerous national security situation. Demanding the Senate and House convene hearings immediately, he announced he would call Congress back after the election for final approval. Distracted by the crucial senate elections, the press were willing participants in a masterful media blitz regularly citing "high White House sources" in their praise of Stuart.

He was a colorful and eminently quotable figure in a field that was increasingly boring and homogenized. T.J. Stuart was a new face, a new story. They highlighted his independence portraying him as a wild man capable of driving Bud Swearman and his pack of political vultures from their pinnacle of usurped power. Swearman had stiffed the press too many times. They would cheer on anyone who challenged him, who refused to be handled. The president had learned from bitter experience that it was the press who approved or refused a nominee. Much to his delight, they became his staunchest allies.

Pledging to Kat that he would not neglect her during the chaotic final days of the congressional session, Hayes gleefully accepted Stuart's request to serve on his "murder board," the small group of political strategists he assembled to help prepare for the various confirmation hearings. Kat and her staff were kept fully informed in the strategies and maneuvers of the process by her chief of staff.

Her first priority was concluding congressional business so she could return to Rhode Island. She was frantic about missing campaign appearances while trapped in Washington and increasingly impatient over Hayes' preoccupation with Stuart and the hearings. He assured her the session would be over by Thursday, Friday at the latest, allowing her little more than two weeks to campaign.

"We're ready for anything,"

Hayes predicted confidently about Stuart's nomination hearings when he finished reviewing the remaining votes of the session with Kat.

"All the financial disclosure material, tax records and medical history have been sent to both Senate Rules and House Judiciary committee staff and they've indicated all is moving on schedule. The FBI investigation is nearly complete and the preliminary reports we've seen are glowing. Except for terrified Democrats who plan a presidential bid in '92 and disgruntled Republicans who think they should have been the designee, no one has anything but kind words for Stuart."

Hayes ignored Kat's obvious irritation with his obsession and continued his recital.

"There's so little precedence for this process, no one is quite sure what protocol requires. Ford and Rockefeller went through it during Watergate years but that was a bizarre situation. Stuart decided to follow the practice of Cabinet nominees paying courtesy calls on committee members in both houses. The House committee is easy. This is the only confirmation hearing in which they can participate so they're rather inexperienced. The Senate presents a more difficult case."

"Why is the Senate a problem?" Kat asked. "Except for obvious political opponents, shouldn't we expect they would easily approve one of their own?"

"Normally, that would be true. But in this case, there are intense political rivalries. This is higher stakes than any Cabinet post or even the Supreme Court, at least in the eyes of potential presidential candidates. Matt Steele of California is chairman of the Rules committee and he definitely has his eye on the race for gold in '92. He's a pompous and arrogant bastard who's proud of being labeled the senate bully. The Democratic front runner is our friend David Clanton and he has a loyal slave in the next senior Democrat on the committee, Charlie Alexander of Louisiana. I'm certain these two will find a way to set aside their own potential rivalry to try and fatally wound Stuart. Although I have no concrete reason for believing this, I suspect that Andrew Cartwright, the senior Republican on the committee, is no friend of Stuart's. But his own tight race should keep his opposition inconsequential, if it even exists."

Kat readily agreed that Cartwright was a foe.

"With all due immodesty, he's assembled a great team," Hayes continued. "There are no handlers from the White House. Whenever we need anything from them, Stuart speaks directly, and exclusively, to the president. We have briefing books prepared on every imaginable subject. It's like condensing a presidential campaign into a few days of questioning.

"Stuart is a dream to brief. He knows everything but appreciates our advice and differing views. He's writing his own formal statement to be entered in the record and planning to speak without notes for his opening. He claims the secret for winning the all-important game of milking the press is to master the form. They care nothing about content and Stuart is a genius at speaking in thirty-second sound bites. Since cool is the way to score on television, he's been working on his look."

"His look?" she asked archly.

Hayes smiled. "He's switched from his trademark white shirts to pale blue. He claims the white ones stimulate the cameras too much. And no red ties."

Kat returned his smile. She was glad to see it was not only the female members of Congress who had to worry about wardrobe.

★ ★ ★ ★ ★

The Democrat from California gaveled the Senate hearing open. A string of television lights suspended from the ceiling behind the magnificent crystal chandelier shone on the marble walls and heightened the effect of Steele's dissipated complexion.

The cavernous Senate Caucus Room was filled to overcapacity with press seated at long tables running perpendicular to the table of committee members stretching across the front of the room.

Stuart sat alone at a small table facing the panel. A pitcher of ice, a glass, and several bottles of his own Crystal Springs Water were arranged to the left of the ubiquitous pair of microphones: one for television, the other for the internal public address system. He had no papers, only a blank yellow lined pad. Seated in the row of chairs directly behind him was a smiling man Hayes identified to the assembled staff watching in Kat's office as Stuart's best friend and key advisor, a quick thinking, slow talking attorney from Richmond. Next to him sat Gretta representing Stuart's family. During the introductions Stuart explained his mother was too frail to travel and his Uncle Gordon was involved in complex international negotiations regarding new water markets.

Speaking with the exaggerated cadence he inherited from his namesake matinee idol father, Senator Matt Steele introduced the Rules committee members in order of seniority. The essence of the hearings as round one of the '92 presidential campaign became apparent in the brief statements made by each senator as they were introduced. The Democrats unanimously attacked Stuart's conservative views while Republican Senator Cartwright, a presumed supporter and the man expected to carry the White House's arguments, sounded as hostile as he could without risking an open challenge.

Stuart's extemporaneous opening statement was a modest and succinct introduction of his personal background and political career that created a believable and engaging portrait of the American dream come true. A few eloquent phrases about growing up in the mountains of Virginia indelibly cast him in the American public's mind as the quintessential frontier hero. A few more phrases and they knew he was a hands-on businessman who understood firsthand their complaints about too much paperwork and too many taxes.

"To paraphrase my namesake, I hold these truths to be universal and self-evident. The land and the individual are sacred. Freedom must be earned through a capacity for taking personal responsibility. Honor is found in a noble character, useful work and the love of friends and family.

"My values have traditional names like duty, self-discipline, fairness, and honesty. Yet I believe they are as essential and relevant to a global society as that of a village."

He ticked off the key tenets of his political philosophy that defined him as a conservative, "The only label besides Virginian and American I bear proudly.

"I have found that political and economic freedom go hand in hand. That humans require challenges and responsibilities to thrive. That there is no such thing as a free lunch. I firmly believe the American people are overregulated and under inspired."

As his clear and simple vision resounded in his deep voice, Stuart never took his eyes off the camera. He knew where his audience was and it was not in the Senate Caucus Room seated behind green felt covered tables. Looking cool, contained, and assured, he offered America the leader they had been desperately seeking for more than two decades, one they could safely trust with their lives and their dreams.

Once Stuart concluded his opening statement and the acid hints of political rivalries faded, boredom reigned as the predominant emotion. The exodus of Stuart and the panel twice during the proceedings for votes on the Senate floor was the most exciting activity of the morning session. When Senator Steele, who had been an All-American quarterback at UCLA, asked whether he had participated in high school or collegiate team sports, Stuart stared at him briefly as if wondering whether this could possibly be a relevant question to ask a potential vice president.

"I was too busy playing real life to have time for team sports. I did wrestle in college however, earning this profile honestly," he answered in a tone filled with levity.

On cue, the cameras focused on Stuart's slightly bent nose and he claimed another victory in the elusive war of images.

At the third call for a vote, Steele bowed to the inevitable and ordered the hearings reconvened at two p.m. Stuart eased his way across the worn red carpet along the single-file path through the crowded hearing room out to the lobby and rotunda where hundreds of cameras and reporters were waiting. He quipped that the proceedings so far had the atmosphere of a twentieth high school reunion where catching up on life since graduation was the prime topic.

Gnashing her teeth at the ineptitude of Stuart's questioners, Jasmine called Undahl at the *Washington Daily* and berated him for the love fest tone of the proceedings.

"I guess you boys didn't take my suggestions seriously. Everyone's going to cave in and allow this clown to walk off with the White House. I assume you are all astute enough to realize that is what this appointment is all about."

Undahl chuckled. "Your leads have been followed up, fruitfully, I might add. You'll be hearing about Cuba this afternoon and VMI tomorrow."

"What about his divorce?"

"We drew a blank there. His wife refuses to speak personally to the media. She released a brief statement claiming that she filed for divorce months ago and plans to marry a Virginia Supreme Court justice at Christmas which will allow her to remain in her beloved Richmond. She has nothing but good to say about Stuart. No children, no property disputes, no infidelities."

Jasmine was furious. She was not ready to betray Kat by sharing her suspicions with Undahl. Besides, she had no proof.

Charlie Alexander carried Majority Leader David Clanton's standard into battle during the afternoon session which was dominated by foreign affairs. Stuart was obviously pleased to be discussing a topic with more meat on the bone. When Alexander concluded his rambling speech on the need to proceed with caution, economic sanctions and negotiations in Iraq, Stuart quoted Sun Tzu in response, much to Kat's amazement.

"I'm a believer in the fiery attack. Overwhelm the opponent with pre-emptive displays of power and end the conflict quickly. It's both humane and cost effective. There are far more serious problems being masked by the current conflict in the Middle East, long term economic problems for America originating in Germany and planned European unity.

"Although it is more than two decades of German and French technological assistance that has created Iraq as a horrifying threat armed with nuclear, chemical and biological weapons, I am not suggesting deliberate German mischief in stirring up the Iraqis and thus distracting the world's attention from reunification."

His response was so matter of fact that it was several seconds before the press realized how dramatic his veiled accusation was. Senator Alexander missed it completely, moving to the next question on a sheet obviously prepared by Clanton and not understood by his puppet.

Another rambling and disconnected speech seemed to focus on the single-handed establishment of world peace by Soviet President Mikhail Gorbachev and the misguided efforts of a decade of Republican defense build-ups. Pointing out that Gorbachev had recently been awarded the Nobel Peace Prize for his efforts, Alexander asked Stuart his opinion of Gorbachev's work.

"There is no denying that Soviet President Gorbachev had the vision and courage to end his nation's seventy years of relentless attempts to overrun the globe. However, I believe that pressure from the American commitment to defend ourselves with all the technology and wealth at our disposal created fissures in Soviet society that permitted Gorbachev to act."

Then Stuart allowed his slightly crooked grin to briefly appear, indicating to those who knew him well that he was about to skewer Alexander.

"Perhaps the Democrats should approach Mr. Gorbachev about being their nominee for the presidency in 1992. Of course, we'll probably discover when the dust settles in the Soviet Union that all those Russians are really Republicans at heart."

Grimacing, Senator Steele gaveled down the laughter that erupted from the press.

Too dense to understand Stuart could outgun him on foreign affairs and defense issues, Alexander persisted.

"America is on the verge of moral and financial bankruptcy, most of it attributable to bloated Pentagon budgets and hard-line attitudes towards Communism. Can you honestly claim it was worth the cost to put the Soviets out of business?"

The flash in Stuart's eyes was obvious to millions watching the exchange.

"Can there be too high a price for a world where communism and the threat of nuclear holocaust has virtually disappeared?" he responded.

"So you believe the SDI, with its multi-billion dollar price tag, is a plausible method for assuring world peace?"

Stuart hesitated only briefly before presenting what all America knew was an honest response.

"No one ever believed SDI would be built. It was a bluff and we won. It scared the living daylights out of the Russians because they knew we had both the technology and money to make it happen. It was the will of Republican administrations in promoting the notion that convinced them we would build it if necessary. Inner strength matched outer strength and the Soviets threw in their hand."

Again Stuart paused as if considering what piece of his vision should be offered in this forum.

"We are emerging into an era where the threat no longer comes from an equal opposing force but from random handfuls of warheads scattered in unstable locations all over the globe. Until we are able to dismantle the entire nuclear arsenal, some form of SDI continues to make sense as global protection under international control."

He was met by blank stares. Obviously none of the senators on the panel had considered the next step in nuclear proliferation or protection.

It was during Alexander's disjointed discussion of Cuba that Stuart's attitude changed. Kat swore she could hear his epiphany like a piano wire finally tuned to its proper note. Later Hayes verified that during the question Stuart realized he was all that stood between the America he loved and the various nonentities, mediocrities and out-and-out dangerous men who were striving to be her president.

"He realized this was not a trivial game. None of the men facing him, nor the candidates for whom they were stalking, were capable or deserving of the job."

Seeing the trump card of Cuba being wasted, Senator Steele made a fatal mistake. Violating all rules of senate protocol, he tore the questioning away from the fumbling Alexander and began grilling Stuart. Using the vice president's traditional designation as head of the National Security Council for justification, Steele attacked Stuart's associations with exiled Cubans in Miami. He detailed a long list of meetings and trips to Florida asking snidely at one point whether Stuart was thinking of replacing his Republican colleague as the Sunshine State's senator.

Stuart sat cooly during Steele's increasingly strident diatribe, only his unwavering stare and tightening mouth indicating his growing rage. Finally afforded the opportunity to respond, his voice was a lethal spear of ice propelled by heartfelt sentiment.

"While the esteemed Senator from California was sharing Christmas cigars and aged brandy with the world's sole remaining communist dictator, a man even his former Soviet masters have disowned, I was indeed in Miami. I was consorting with Cuban exiles, friends of freedom who are willing to die for the same dream that motivated my namesake Thomas Jefferson and his contemporaries. The right to self-determination. The opportunity to improve their lives and those of their families and descendants. The right to think and speak and dream without fear of being thrown in some stinking prison or condemned to a lifetime of slave labor on a sugar plantation.

"I admire these men and women. I cheer with them when they promise next year in Havana. I am proud to be considered their friend and willing to help however I am able."

"And does that include secret incursions into Cuba and plotting to overthrow the government?" Steele interjected in fury.

"Are you one of those pushing the CIA to assassinate Castro?"

The only sound that broke the absolute silence in the packed hearing room was Steele's rasping breath. Stuart had turned to stone. As the silence became almost excruciating, he spoke calmly.

"In 1961 a Democrat in the White House abandoned fourteen hundred patriots to be slaughtered or captured on the beaches of Cuba. My friends bear those scars. Since innocent lives could be at stake discussing these issues, I request that we continue this line of questioning behind closed doors."

"There will be no hiding behind closed doors as long as I'm chairing these hearings," Steele exploded.

Stuart nodded.

"Then I refuse to discuss it further except to say my personal preference would be to meet Castro mano a mano, knights on a field of honor."

"I'll bet phone lines to Miami will be clogged for hours," Hayes observed as Steele closed the proceedings for the day. "I hope Stuart's pals know how to keep their mouths shut and their smoking guns locked in some closet."

★ ★ ★ ★ ★

It was surrogate week in Rhode Island. Staff and key supporters were farmed out to dozens of speeches, forums, and meetings that had been arranged for Kat in anticipation of Congress being in recess well before the third week in October. Roxy flatly refused to speak in public, so she was assigned to monitor the vice presidential hearings and keep the campaign office under control.

THE INQUISITION

When questioning began about Cuba, she wondered if they would find out about Rosa's husband and his mysterious release from Castro's jail. She did not know exactly how outside witnesses were selected but hoped no one would ask her about the trip to Key West. She decided she had no recourse but to lie, not that she knew anything concrete about Stuart's activities while she was meeting with Jamie. But she had seen enough courtroom dramas on television to know how much can be inferred from circumstantial evidence. She arrived at the same conclusion Stuart had. Whatever his flaws, none of the alternative candidates for president were acceptable. Roxy was amazed at how easy it was for public and press to grasp the fact that the vice presidency was a secondary issue. It was the selection of a president that was really emerging. The one thought she continually suppressed as she watched the hours of testimony was what this meant for Kat.

Liz burst into the upstairs office thrilled about her just concluded appearance before the United Women's Clubs of Aquidneck.

"There were almost two hundred women there and they loved me. I told them I was Kat the Fat. They kept asking why I wasn't running for office. I told them it would take a square block of closets to hold all my skeletons. When they found out I was the one who'd cut her hair they wanted to crown me queen on the spot. Listen to this great bit I developed on why we need more women running the government. I asked them to consider who balances the checkbook and handles the finances in their family. You should have seen the light bulbs going off in their heads. I had two women come up to me afterwards and tell me that comment clinched their vote for Kat.

"Maybe I should consider running for office. I could get Stuart to have me appointed to his seat when he becomes vice president. Then Kat and I could be senators together. She could learn a lot from me."

Roxy stared flabbergasted as Liz continued posturing around the room.

"Mostly I let them ask questions. They all wanted to know about Stuart. I told them they should be very supportive of his appointment, it could do Rhode Island a lot of good. I assured them he and Kat were good friends." As she winked broadly, exaggerating the final two words, Roxy paled. "I told them to call Congress in support of Stuart."

"We're supposed to be working for Kat's election not Stuart's," Roxy rebuked.

"If she becomes Mrs. Vice President who cares whether she's in the Senate or not."

It took Roxy a few moments to catch her breath. Liz said it as if Kat had wedding invitations in the mail.

"Why would you even suggest such a thing? What makes you think either of them would be interested in marrying the other?"

Liz turned and glared.

"For someone who pretends to be the personification of the goddess of love, you sure are dumb about matters of the heart, as we sophisticates like to say."

She turned up the sound on the television and plopped herself onto the couch.

"Now, leave me alone. I want to watch my main man take America by storm."

★ ★ ★ ★ ★

The second day of hearings was devoted to domestic issues. Hayes claimed they received word late the previous night that all trails to Cuban connections mysteriously vanished. Approached by the majority leader about providing files on their monitoring of Cuban activities, the CIA stonewalled the Democrat.

"They can't imagine anyone they would rather have in the White House than T.J. Stuart."

"Do you really think this is all about the presidency? Do you think Stuart wants to be president?" Kat asked.

Hayes answered quickly, sounding surprised that she would ask.

"Stuart knows exactly what this is about. I don't think he ever had the White House in mind before the president offered it to him on a silver platter. He's as devoted to this country as anyone I've known and perceptive enough to realize most of those in power are mediocre at best. In many ways he's as much a visionary as you are and not about to turn aside the opportunity to project his vision on the closing days of the 20th century. When the time comes, he'll run for president."

They turned their attention back to the screen as Stuart walked through the crowds three deep at the dark wood double-doored entry into the Senate Caucus Room.

Battle lines solidified overnight. Senator Steele had coerced the other Democrats into ceding him their speaking time and Senator Cartwright sat silent. Stuart's most effective Republican support came from the junior member of the committee, the energetic young first-term senator from Montana and from Grace Langley, the gentlewoman from New Jersey. Stuart looked fresh and relaxed, obviously pleased with overnight polls and press coverage that barely stopped short of hailing him as the last great hope for America's future.

The domestic political agenda of the '92 election unfolded in the morning's questions. Senator Steele considered himself the savior of working class America with his promises of comprehensive national health insurance for everyone living and breathing. Stuart had attacked the plan often on the Senate floor insisting nothing could be added until means for paying the cost were found. Given an opportunity during Steele's speechmaking to outline his own thoughts, Stuart laid out a radical plan that made preventive care freely available, guaranteed choice in caregiver, provided for low cost home care and refused coverage for illnesses caused by willful persistence in health damaging lifestyle choices.

"I believe people should be free to smoke but not to bill me for the damage," was the sound bite most favored in coverage of that particular debate.

They battled over tax policy and budget restraint.

"I'm no fan of big ticket spending programs. Money is not the solution for all problems, and the only question that government is the answer to is what do we have too much of. Individuals are responsible for their own lives and I want to encourage them to be more not less so. At best, government should help people help themselves, workfare and training rather than welfare. That includes foreign aid and development loans as well. No more hand-outs."

The newspapers loved that quote.

They skirmished on initiatives taken to halt the spread of drugs and crime. Finally Stuart was exasperated with a debate that had less to do with his qualifications for the job than with Steele's desire to display his political platform.

"The senator from California is not a candidate for this nomination. I do not see why I should compete with his political philosophy. I read everywhere in the press that these hearings are really about who should be president in 1992. My visionary colleague may be thinking that far in the future. I will be satisfied to complete these procedures and serve as vice president."

"Why do you want this job?" Steele shouted the question, again violating the Senate's unspoken rules.

Stuart leaned back in his chair and smiled slightly watching Steele's face become dangerously red.

"My president asked me to serve my country. Once I determined I could do the job, it seemed my duty to accept. I planned to step down from the Senate at the end of my term anyway."

The stunned looks and sharp intakes of breath by panel members at Stuart's casual announcement of retirement was matched in Kat's office.

Answering the question written on every face, Stuart explained.

"I have long proposed limited terms for Members of Congress, twelve years for senators, ten for representatives. How could I propose something without abiding by it myself?"

When his ally from Montana finally earned the time for questions, he asked Stuart about his vision for the future.

"The most critical need is low cost, high quality information. The most significant rights for the American people are the opportunity and skills to use this information. Power to the people is more than a retrofitted '60s slogan. It's the path to the 21st century. And the world needs a path, an ideology. Everywhere change is obvious; nowhere is the thought behind the change apparent."

Two breaks for votes later and Senator Steele was once again questioning the nominee, his color a more characteristic dull brick. Kat returned from the Senate floor in time to see Hayes' political hackles raised as Steele began probing Stuart's record on women's issues.

"Your alma mater, Virginia Military Institute, is currently involved in litigation regarding the admission of women to the school. How do you feel about their adamant refusal to do so particularly in light of your alleged efforts to see more women in positions of power?"

It was apparent from Hayes' intent posture that this was one avenue of questioning they had not anticipated. Stuart scarcely blinked as he answered.

"Frankly Senator, my personal experience has convinced me beyond any doubt that males and females are different, a biological and psychological reality I applaud. I support making available to each individual—without limitation due to generic characteristics such as race or sex—whatever resources they require to develop themselves to the fullest. I cannot imagine the VMI I attended providing a positive opportunity for any female. Should the decision of the courts require the school to open its doors to women, I would strongly urge them, as a proud alumni, to alter their program to suit the altered student body."

★ ★ ★ ★ ★

Kat was furious. If there was one area where she felt Stuart was invulnerable to attack it was his attitude toward women. All the Republican senators added together could not approach what he had done single-handed in campaigning for the party's seven female senate candidates. And he was insistent that his purpose was to elect more women to the Senate not simply more Republicans. It took only a few calls to assemble a bi-partisan group of more than twenty female members of Congress to plan a rebuttal to the unfair attack. The fact that Matt Steele led the attack made support even easier to galvanize. He was a noted despoiler of teenage female senate pages.

It was quickly decided that the women would hold a press conference at 4 p.m. where they would announce their support of T.J. Stuart and his actions on behalf of women. They would also insist on testifying before the committee.

"There's historic precedence for this," laughed the congresswoman from New York. "Among the Seneca Indians, the women of the tribe would gather to choose a man to be the chief."

"We should speak with a single voice," said Rachel Palcezski, the diminutive Republican senate candidate from Maryland who was currently Baltimore County's representative in the House. She urged Kat to accept the role. "You're our superstar, Kiley. Besides this rally was your idea."

Kat flushed as she declined the honor.

"It can't be me. I have to be back in Rhode Island. Rachel is really the ideal choice. She's right here in the area and would be much more convincing on this subject."

They protested, insisting she was the one.

"I cannot. It would be too damaging to Stuart if I acted as spokesperson," Kat bluntly refused.

The tone in her voice ended attempts at persuasion although a few shrewd glances were exchanged among the women in the room who were part of Stuart's senate candidate harem.

"I'll be happy to act as spokesperson, if everyone agrees," said Rachel to the unanimous nods of the other women. "But you should be the one to tell Stuart. It was your idea."

Kat escaped to the powder room when the meeting broke up. She did not hear Rachel come in until it was too late to hide the strain in her face. Reading the look in the tiny woman's eyes, she hastily tried to explain her reluctance to speak on his behalf, blushing furiously.

"It's OK honey, you don't need to explain. We all feel a little weak in the knees about Stuart."

She stood alongside Kat, who was seated on a stool in front of the mirror and lifted up her face, meeting her tear-filled eyes.

"I raised six daughters and I recognize this look. It's more than a schoolgirl crush, isn't it?"

★ ★ ★ ★ ★

Since the Senate was still voting, Kat sought out Stuart in the vice president's office outside the Senate Chamber. As she approached its ornate lobby, she saw Senator Cartwright walking out with Stuart. She had been outraged at Cartwright's hands-off attitude on the nomination, and blamed herself and their encounter at the Williamsburg Golf Tournament in June for his animosity towards Stuart. When Cartwright refused to look her in the eye and scuttled down the hall, she knew her guess was right.

"Come to tell me some secrets?" Stuart smiled as he directed her to his private office. "I'm sorry about being so rough on you the other day. Being targeted by hit men and protected by my own squad of bodyguards had me slightly off-balance."

"You were right to scold me. I was wrong not to have told you months ago when I first found out. I'm sorry." Kat was preternaturally aware of the listening devices Stuart had warned were in the room. She was shocked when he closed the door and held out his arms to her.

"Well then, let's kiss and make up." He laughed at the horrified expression on her face. "It didn't take long for my friends at DARPA to construct a system to block the devices in this office. They agreed with me that the vice president deserved a modicum of privacy."

"I don't trust Cartwright," she said moving away from him.

"Neither do I."

Smoothing the lace ruffles that brushed the back of her hand, Kat plunged into her task. "Your ah, harem…" blushing she stumbled and paused as he raised an eyebrow, amused. "I mean, a large group of female members of both parties, selected me to tell you we plan to hold a press conference in about an hour, and request time to testify in your behalf."

"To what end?" he asked, folding his arms and cocking his eyebrow even further.

"To affirm your support of us as women."

He smiled. "I appreciate that. Are you also the press spokesperson?"

She shook her head.

"Good."

He stopped her as she reached the door.

"Recess is scheduled to begin tomorrow afternoon. Are you leaving immediately?"

"I'm desperate to get back to the campaign."

"I'd hoped to get back for another day of campaigning for you, but," he shrugged, "things change. I will be there election night. So remember, Darlin', save the last dance for me."

★ ★ ★ ★ ★

When Jasmine heard about the impending press conference by the women to support Stuart, she abruptly left the office and ran from the building. She called Gene Undahl at the *Washington Daily* from the first public phone she found, and described the fundraiser when Stuart read the note about needing more babes in the Senate.

"I don't care what those shrews say, he has no real respect for them. The man looks at every women as fondling material."

"Too much competition for you, Jaz?"

She cursed and harangued him about doing his job, giving him the names of three women from political groups who complained about the event when it happened.

★ ★ ★ ★ ★

Kat escaped the mob scene that surrounded Rachel Palcezski and several of the other women members following their press conference in the lobby outside the Senate Caucus Room where the hearings were held. She was still smiling at Rachel's closing answer.

"Just because women are inoculated by experience from earliest childhood to withstand the constant barrage of sexually humiliating actions and words from men doesn't keep us from recognizing true appreciation of our female qualities when it occurs. I have never felt demeaned as a woman by my interactions with Senator Stuart, rather, I've felt exalted."

The reporter from the *Washington Daily* trailed by a cable network camera blocked her escape across the rotunda floor.

"Congresswoman, you joined with other female members of Congress to affirm what you claim is Senator Stuart's exemplary attitude towards women. How do you explain this support in light of comments he made about wanting 'more babes in the Senate,' referring rather baldly to your scanty dance costume the night of the Press Club Review? I understand his remarks provoked a storm of protest from your supporters among national women's groups."

In the brief moment she had to compose an answer while the camera whirred, Kat flashed on strangling Jasmine with her bare hands. There was no doubt her press secretary had once again betrayed her.

"The senator was delivering the message of a constituent. A message accompanied by a substantial check for the fundraiser we were attending that evening."

"And would you characterize his presentation as simply passing on a message?"

"Senator Stuart occasionally has a dramatic bent to his wit." She paused expectantly, looked directly at the still filming camera and added with a coy smile, "You can hardly blame the man for having a good eye."

She turned gracefully and began walking deliberately towards the door, knowing the male cameraman would follow her departure. She blessed the stars for the short skirt and high heels she had worn that day.

★ ★ ★ ★ ★

That night's Evening News was the biggest hit of the week in Kat's campaign headquarters. The assembled staff, led by Liz, cheered for Rachel Palcezski's statement and Kat's dazzling leg shot, which was prominently featured on every network. But the biggest applause was for Stuart's comment on the day's events.

"I was raised in a house with a grandmother, a mother, an aunt and four sisters. There's not a man alive who appreciates the remarkable qualities of the female sex more than I."

SENATE MAGIC

★ ★ ★ ★ ★

Kat's strategy was fully planned when she summoned her press secretary the following morning. Max was both her inspiration and her enforcer. He sat quietly on the couch in her office. Hayes was in a chair near her desk.

The two women faced each other tensely. A night of little sleep and great stress was advertised by the strain on both their faces. Jasmine cracked first and attempted an apology. Kat cut her off before she finished the first sentence.

"Save your breath. No apology is possible. You have betrayed me, my trust and your own values. Such behavior nullifies the worth of any apology."

"I never wanted to hurt you. It was Stuart." Jasmine's voice was shrill, her hands clenched tightly.

Kat cut her off harshly. "You are too dangerous—to me, to Stuart, to the country. You must be removed."

Jasmine's eyes widened and she sputtered incoherently.

"With your father in South America, and most of your friends expecting you to be busy with the campaign for the next two weeks, you will not be missed."

Jasmine's moans intensified and the blood drained from her face. She followed Kat's gesture towards Max, staring as if he were a monster arising from the circles of hell.

"Max will take you to an isolated mountain health resort run by some trusted friends. There are no phones and you will be watched constantly. When the election is over, you may return to Washington. I must warn you, I will do my best to see you never work in politics again."

"No! No!" Jasmine gasped, holding her stomach. "I'll tell you everything. All the plots against Stuart. Scarlatti's thugs. The White House and Cartwright. Everything. Please don't send me away. The campaign needs me. I want you to win. I do. Please."

Tiny white bulbs flashed around the rim of the clock and a buzzer announced another vote. Jasmine slumped into a chair as Kat moved tensely toward the door.

"You can make your confession to Hayes. He will see the information is passed on to the vice president. Then Max will drive you home to pack. You'll be at Cool Pines tonight." Her severe tone left no doubt that compassion was not high on her list of emotions in the current situation. Kat's final words were punctuated by the door she slammed behind her.

"I hope I never see you again."

★ ★ ★ ★ ★

THE INQUISITION

Proving that no one is more obtuse than a man driven by ambition, Matt Steele continued his attacks on Stuart's attitude towards women during the next morning's hearings. As he read from Gene Undahl's report in the *Washington Daily* detailing Stuart's remarks about Kat, Senator Grace Langley did the unthinkable. For the first time in her genteel existence, she rudely interrupted another human being.

"I object to the honorable chairman's line of questions. I was in attendance at the fundraiser being discussed and witnessed the exchange. In my opinion it was not sexist but admiring and I'm certain the congresswoman from Rhode Island agreed. I'm afraid I must insist that the chair cease this fatuous questioning."

Being the recipient of Senator Langley's uncharacteristic public rebuke so chagrined Senator Steele that he halted all questions. Before he could gavel the hearings to an embarrassed close, Stuart made a final comment.

"As CBS News announced this morning, my friend Earl Beckham of Norfolk Steel and Shipyard rightfully, and I might add proudly, claimed authorship of the note to Congresswoman Tomasso. Let me clearly state for the record that I am prepared to withdraw my name from consideration as vice president. I do not want to be part of any government that considers respectful appreciation of a beautiful woman as a disqualification for holding public office."

Sam Jamison beamed like a proud father who now had his favorite son beside him in the family business. For all intents and purposes, the hearings on Thomas Jefferson Stuart's nomination as vice president of the United States had reached a successful conclusion.

★ ★ ★ ★ ★

Daylight savings time had a few more days left so Roxy's morning walks began in the dark. A sliver moon and a few remaining stars hung in the dark blue veil that was both sky and calm seas. The horizon appeared outlined with a hot pink stripe beginning the changes that marked her progress along the beach. Once she reached the halfway point at the estuary, the sky was lightened and washed with routine pastels of dawn. Cool, crisp air and bright sun traced streaks of green along the tops of waves that announced fall.

She had been anxious to get on the beach that morning. The past few days of stormy weather made walking impossible. She saw few opportunities for empty stretches of time once Kat returned later that day and the campaign geared up for the home stretch. The storm left the beach littered along the surf line with what could be considered the seaside equivalent of piles of dead leaves, countless quohog shells and shiny black mussels that crunched beneath her feet.

Roxy finished her walk at the seawall where it led down to the sand beach.

She decided the light was perfect when the sun was less than three inches above the horizon, a measurement taken by holding her outstretched fingers up to her eye. At this stage, romantic shadows were cast on the buildings lining the beach, especially the red-roofed white stucco castle that was her favorite. Noting the gate to the beach from the parking lot was open and there were tire marks on the sand, she knew for certain the season was ended.

A sense of autumn intensified as they drove north to Providence. Even Liz was impressed at how appropriate the New England scenery looked with the blazing reds and golds of changing leaves, Halloween decorations everywhere.

★ ★ ★ ★ ★

Though she looked exhausted with never-before-seen lines marring her smooth white skin, Kat vetoed suggestions to rest. She attended the carnival-like staff dinner at Jack's planned for the evening she arrived. It was the group's final taste of partying until the big one election night. Roxy breathed a sigh of relief. Most of the Washington staff were scheduled to arrive after the weekend, giving her a few more days to decide what to do about Hayes.

They arranged themselves on both sides of the U-shaped tables that lined the walls of the tiny private dining room Victor reserved for them. Liz took over orchestration of the feast, using Pete's regimen for eating at Jack's. Soon waitresses were hauling pitchers of beer and a parade of sea treasures cooked in every way imaginable from the kitchen to their tables. About every tenth dish, one or another waitress would announce the next one was a bonus from Victor. Other patrons in the packed restaurant shyly strolled by the wide arched doorway and waved at Kat, giving her the thumbs-up sign. Even Jack emerged in his stained and smelly apron to pay a quick tribute.

The high point of the boisterous dinner was the game Liz inaugurated, demanding they create a list of words that caught the essence of the campaign. Roxy was designated scribe and recorded the list on a moderately soiled paper placemat.

"Legs," was the first word shouted to the accompaniment of whistles and cheers. Seated on the outside perimeter, Kat stood and treated them to a much-appreciated view of the limbs in question.

"This lifetime I'm working on building character," shouted Liz. "But next life I'm coming back gorgeous and I'm making a special request for legs like those, ones with space between the thighs."

Words began flying around the table, shouted from one to another, accompanied by brief explanations or longer anecdotes. Roxy could barely keep up. There were a string of epithets directed at their opponent ranging from slug slime to crook and felon.

"It's ironic that Douglas is promoting himself as pro-life, he's the perfect advertisement for abortion on demand," insisted Kat's young scheduler.

Mention of the vice president drew a chorus of sighs from various women, a series of words that all embodied the notion of hero, and uncomfortable squirming from Kat. Planning to preserve the list as part of the memory book she was assembling, Roxy added a few words of her own, not sharing them outloud. Death card headed her private list.

"Sewer, quohogs, magic," came from various sections of the table. Maggie slyly added "red roses."

"Witch, mobster, spy," the Hose cried with venomous delight introducing Carrie and Scarlatti to the list. The game ended with the word they all cheered. "Victory" chanted a couple dozen ecstatic voices.

"More beer!" Liz commanded as an encore.

★ ★ ★ ★ ★

For Roxy, the week that followed Kat's return to the state was a blur of frantic activity. Only a few events retained any specificity in her recollection. Chief among them was the final focus group session. Added to results of their nightly phone canvassing, a portrait emerged that even Lila found indecipherable.

"Nationally, polls are showing most of the same trends we see here. The budget fiasco lowered everyone's opinion of Congress, tension is increasing over our military build-up against Iraq, and the number of people planning not to vote in November is growing by leaps and bounds. It's weird how Stuart's nomination as vice president plays in this whole chaotic mess. The public loves him, adores him, considers him the biggest hero in American politics since JFK. At the same time, the fact that they're getting this paragon of political virtue outside the normal electoral process has subtly reinforced their opinion that the electoral process is hopelessly corrupt and meaningless. The minor brickbats thrown at him during the confirmation hearings are nothing compared to the smears of most political campaigns and they seem to like having an idol who has not been dragged through the mud or done any dragging himself."

"What about my race, Lila?" Kat asked with a tinge of irritation.

"All our numbers, and the focus group last night, say the same thing. The race is won. You can only lose it at this point."

Roxy wondered why a haunted look flashed across Kat's face.

"Our opponent has become the invisible man," Mario reported. "I don't know whether it's Scarlatti's intercession or the realization of his handlers that Douglas loses votes every time he appears in public. I think we can counteract the only bad news from the focus group by having you everywhere in the state."

Although the standard vote taken at the end of the session overwhelmingly favored her, Kat was horrified at some of the comments made by people during the discussion. For the first time, participants cited ways in which she and Douglas were alike. Tears sparkled in her eyes when several focus group members felt the need to defend her integrity and one older woman actually said, as justification of her vote, "at least she won't steal our money down to the last dollar the way he does." Once again the electorate saw their choices—as Jake had claimed months ago—of one disease rather than another.

When several of those who finally voted for her, muttered it did not really matter who won, Kat was unable to prevent a few muffled sobs. Gould had been right. They thought she was perfect but Douglas' lie-filled attacks raised doubts in the public's mind. These doubts were not strong enough to move people to vote for the man they knew was corrupt and incompetent but they did seem sufficient to discourage them from voting at all.

Gould outlined the final two weeks of media.

"We focus on women through cable and radio, especially in the morning. We'll continue the endorsement spots on television and put you on the radio both in paid spots and on talk shows. They need to hear your voice but I'd rather they see you only in person so they can have the full 'pow!' effect. Coverage of your grass roots campaigning and celebrity visits will keep you on television where most people think reality occurs, and Mario's been circulating the video again."

He paused for breath then asked Kat if she had any idea what she was going to do with the television time they had election eve. She gave no answer.

Mario added to his plan.

"You need to relight their fire and that will happen when they see you and touch you. It's back to the old laying-on-of-hands technique."

He had coined the image years ago, claiming that once Kat physically touched someone, they were hers forever.

"We have a full schedule planned for the next two weeks that will take you to all the swing areas and bring you in contact with every targeted group."

Judging from the past weekend's activities, Roxy thought they had already touched most of the ethnic groups. Accompanied by an ever-changing cast of volunteers and civic leaders, they ate baklava at a Greek festival and spicy sausage at a Portuguese church feast. No matter what the polls said, people loved her in person.

Liz was a superstar that weekend. She sang Gaelic lullabies with the band at the Irish Festival in Lincoln and insisted the television crews capture Kat in a dazzling Irish jig with the Democratic leader of the state senate. She assured that by the time they left any place all the food servers and preparers were converted to ardent supporters. Jake also played celebrity, cheerfully pasting Kiley for Senate stickers on hundreds of smiling people.

"This is why I never went to Nashville to become a superstar," commented

Liz as they fought their way through the crowds that surged around the candidate.

"This is worse, though. When you're a famous singer you can blow people off. As a politician, Kat has to be nice and listen to everyone."

Driving from town to town, Liz indulged in her color commentary.

"Now that Harvest Fest was quite an event. All the people in Hedgesville pull out some old card tables, set them up on a central strip of dirt and lay out their trash, with price tags. They must be fans of your recycling plans. If I owned a house in Hedgesville, I'd rent it out and move up to Hell."

She also pointed out every one of the Kiley for Senate signs they passed. Kat was impressed at how many there were, especially in the solidly Democratic section of Warwick.

"Ducky, King of Warwick," Liz explained. "He loves you, even if you are a Republican. He's twisted arms, called in debts, probably made threats. You have the best locations in town. A couple Republicans called us to try and piggy-back on your sign spots but we referred them to Ducky. He turned them down flat. This is a devoted man. Somehow after the primary all the losing Democrats' signs came down and yours went up in the same locations. Another convert to your recycling crusade, I guess."

The evening events were cross-cultural, providing endless material for Liz's routines. They worked two huge family-style dinner parties at Portuguese clubs in Central Falls and Pawtucket.

"These are my kind of men," sighed Liz as she returned from dancing with the president of one of the clubs. Kat had taken a twirl around the floor with his father who had been one of her early political sponsors. "Big, burly, bristly black hair, and don't you love his red Hawaiian shirt. Just the right touch for his light brown leisure suit."

When Jake laughed, Roxy wondered if he had a secret method for knowing when Liz was kidding and when she was reveling in her self-proclaimed tacky taste.

Liz proclaimed the Miss Latino Rhode Island pageant Saturday night high point of the weekend. She huddled with pageant organizers commenting on hair and make-up while Kat toured the packed ballroom with the reigning queen, a stunning brunette who could have been her slightly tanned cousin. Discovering they were short of contestants, Liz scoured the room, primped up a couple lovely young girls she discovered at a back table, and added them to the line-up.

"Can't you imagine the boys at Buck's dressing like that for a dance at the Legion?"

She nodded to a covey of graceful young men who sported identical pencil thin black mustaches, short jackets, blousy pants, and pounds of gold medallions and chains. Roxy was more fascinated with the glittering, off-the-shoulder, bow-trimmed dresses of the young women.

"Most of the Latinos in the state are Puerto Rican or Dominican and they're devoted to Kat," Liz pronounced as they waited for the candidate to shake the final few hands and escape. "Adia Mercurious, the event organizer, whispered she thought with a little more flash and sparkle Kat could pass as Latin." Roxy rolled her eyes. They were constantly worried about toning her down.

"I know we saw ten thousand people," Liz said Monday morning as she announced success to Kat and Roxy. "Some guy from Middletown tried to pass himself off to me twice but I caught him."

Every weeknight was devoted to raising money at a collage of elegant and beautiful homes from Barrington to Westerly. Roxy's memories mixed and matched a collection of tea sets in a nineteenth century faculty home at the University of Rhode Island with an unseasonable warm night standing on the deck of a splendid modern house in Anawan Cliffs looking at the lights on the bridges to Newport. She did note that marble floors in kitchens seemed a trademark of upscale homes.

Liz kept track of all the food so they could discuss the varying merits of the Oriental chicken they had in East Greenwich, flaky creampuffs drizzled with lemon sauce in Cranston, and crab stuffed mushrooms on Providence's East Side. One night they packed almost five hundred Young Republicans on a boat for a dockside party in Newport that featured what Liz confidently declared the best stuffies she had ever eaten.

The demand for money appeared infinite and Roxy assumed most was being spent on daily mailings that numbered in the thousands. Boxes were filled to overflowing with notated voter lists and canvassing cards. They had stacks of letters, with slightly different texts, ready to go out the next day to undecideds contacted and categorized during the previous night's canvassing calls. Seniors were becoming confused, middle class workers were concerned about the economy, and Republicans were showing greater support in light of increased partisan attacks from Democrats. Yola claimed she would be qualified to be postmaster general should Kat ever become president.

Printing material for the continual leafleting was another major expense, and Roxy shuddered to even contemplate the thousands being spent daily on television and radio time. More than anything, she admired Kat's composure in the process of raising and spending more than three million dollars. She often wondered what people thought they were getting for their money.

As general interest in the campaign dripped and sputtered away, Kat's supporters became more fervent. The field staff had literally hundreds of volunteers out daily leafleting shift changes at factories and hospitals, shopping centers, football games, bus terminals and neighborhoods. Roxy occasionally thought the Hose was right. It was cheaper and more effective to just out and out purchase a vote. She knew it would be a lot less work.

In Jasmine's health-related absence—a story that lasted about five minutes before vanishing in the flames of truth—Roxy was drafted to handle the writing part of the press secretary's job.

Mario became Kat's full-time spokesperson and all calls and contacts went through him. With the efficient team of press assistants Mario already trained, Roxy found it easy to crank out the necessary releases and accompanying paper and still travel some with Kat. She learned how easy it was to get bored saying the same thing over and over. Kat had a basic message to get out; she had no choice but repetition. Filling it with the necessary passion on the fiftieth saying took more energy than Roxy thought she would ever be able to muster.

Celebrity visits highlighted the period. The senator from Montana had emerged from the hearings and his defense of Stuart as a popular campaigner. He dropped by for a couple hours before jetting off to other stops in Massachusetts and New York. There were crowds of volunteers at the airport press conference wildly waving Kiley for Senate signs. A banner-draped caravan snaked through Cranston to the Arcade in the heart of Providence where Kat and the visiting senator mingled with the tightly packed lunchtime crowds. An historic monument billed as America's first indoor mall, the Arcade boasted granite pillars quarried in Westerly and dragged by oxen over bridges built especially for their weighty passage. Two television networks were there to cover the activities, increasing the general clutter with their equipment and reporters. Kiley for Senate supporters encircled both entrances and presented a solid sea of waving posters when cameras followed the pair outside.

Kat motorcaded off to the airport with the senator, and Liz made an executive decision. Rounding up the scores of volunteers with their posters, she marched them into and around Kennedy Plaza where they waved at buses coming and going and the lunchtime crowds sitting on benches and around the fountains and monuments. Everyone they encountered on foot or in cars was leafleted. Circling past the Biltmore Hotel on one side of the Plaza and the Fleet Center with its shops and restaurants on the other, she led them across the interstate and up Atwells Avenue promising everyone pizza on Federal Hill. Roxy went on ahead to rouse Tony to the task of feeding the hordes.

Liz was invaluable in keeping Kat looking senatorial yet feminine every day. Kat vetoed any further trims to her hair, so Liz worked diligently to capture her wayward curls and coerce them into varying demure poses. She kept her makeup in the subdued rose range that Gould preferred to Kat's tendency for more dramatic shades that emphasized her pale skin and contrastingly black hair.

Roxy was called in for daily color mixing consultations and noted that Kat's underwear remained the yellow and navy she first noticed around Labor Day. She and Jake later speculated on whether Kat would switch colors for the final week of the campaign. He proposed red and purple.

"Red, her signature color, to motivate people to vote. Victorious purple for election night."

★ ★ ★ ★ ★

Kat appeared so focused and wired with energy, so joyful in her approach to the people she met that Roxy was shocked the night they talked about dreams.

"I'm exhausted every night from constant dreaming," Kat said, refilling her cup of hot chocolate which she always drank from a silver goblet—like the Mayans, she explained once.

"I can't begin to remember them all distinctly. I've filled a small notebook with dream images in the past three weeks alone. Some feature people working on the campaign whom I do not know, some wake me with a compelling sense that I have to be at a meeting or an event. Two nights ago, I was down here at two a.m. checking copies of my schedule to make sure I really didn't have a press conference at that hour.

"In one I was a prince in hiding, trying to escape from an enemy who had a gun. My eyes wouldn't focus so I couldn't see the person chasing me. Last night, I was a soldier involved in the American Revolution, walking along the streets of some city with other soldiers, picking up a series of newspapers printed in Russian. I couldn't read them but I knew they were Russian. I kept thinking: what revolution is this?

"Another one that really gave me the creeps was about black snakes. I was terrorized when I saw them slithering up the porch. I knew if one bit me I would be impregnated. I was frozen in place and one did bite me. Within an instant I could feel a nest of tiny black snakes inside me.

"I know the numbers are creeping up, response in the streets is wonderful, money is somehow still coming, Douglas has disappeared, there's no real reason for me to worry. But there's this seed of terror inside me that...."

Kat stopped abruptly and looked at them both as if she were suddenly aware of something she could not say.

"I don't know why I'm afraid, but I am," she concluded lamely.

Friday morning was the worst. She drew Roxy aside and told her she had a nightmare about Anne Hutchinson.

"She died sometime in October," Roxy reminded her.

"How?" Kat asked, gripping her friend's arm. "From that malignant pregnancy you described?"

Roxy shook her head.

"No. It was about six years later and she was murdered by Indians. Some historians suggest they were hired by the church fathers who had driven her out of Massachusetts."

Kat's question was disturbing. Roxy was certain she told her before about Anne's death.

THE INQUISITION

★ ★ ★ ★ ★

The most memorable indicator of time passing for Roxy came from her men.

Finding herself each morning refreshed and ready for another twenty-hour workday was a miracle Roxy attributed to the energizing effects of tantric yoga. Coupled with her concern about the alienated attitude that Lila claimed was infecting the state, she felt justified in insisting that she and Jake work on vote totals daily. It took heroic logistical maneuvering but they managed.

She badgered Mario into breaking out the votes they needed by town. Dividing up the thirty-nine towns by the roughly ten days left, Roxy decided they could achieve maximum effectiveness by focusing on four towns each day. That would leave a day or two free at the end to concentrate on particular problem areas. Jake sat smiling as she handed him the alphabetical list of town in groups of four with the vote totals written by each town.

"Should we plan an orgasm for each individual town, meaning four a day, or just one that we focus on the four towns of the day?" he asked. "And what about the fact that the vote counts are not equal for every group of four?"

"I don't think I have time for four orgasms a day," Roxy said.

"Catherine the Great insisted six a day was best," Jake pointed out, an amused gleam in his eye.

"When did she find the time, or strength, to run Russia?" Roxy huffed at Jake's flippant attitude.

He shrugged. "Months ago I told you I would be your campaign slave. Do with me what you will."

"Good! Just remember this beats leafleting construction sites at dawn. I think it will work best if I yell out the towns and totals just before we peak."

Jake laughed uncontrollably at the thought.

"I've always wanted to do it for… let's see … Barrington, Bristol, Burrillville and Central Falls. That should be the first four."

Roxy scowled as he rolled her over onto the bed and worked on votes.

Jake exacted what he considered a small price for his co-operation. He insisted on spending at least a part of their time together talking about something other than the campaign. "We'll talk about the only hobby in Rhode Island that rivals politics. I'll tell you fish stories." Roxy was able to later distinguish the days by the changing stories.

One day he told her about a sunny spring afternoon when he was fishing off the docks in Galilee.

"No one had gotten a bite all day. I laid down my rod for a minute to get a beer from the cooler and along comes a fish that snaps my hook and races off with my rod and reel. I figured my luck is changing, hurried to Wakefield and bought a new rod, then stopped at home for another reel. In less than an hour

I was back at my spot on the docks. The phantom fish was the only bite anyone had that day."

Another day he talked about an hour-long fight he had landing an eight-pound false albacore.

"Somehow the hook was in its side rather than its mouth so I had no control. I got two big fillets out of that baby."

"What do you do all those hours you're out there waiting for a bite?"

"We mumble to each other about never catching anything. Having any luck? Yesterday a big one got away. You know, the usual stuff.

"You watch for the birds. Stand around any beach where guys are fishing and you'll see the birds. Birds move with the fish, guys run to their trucks, several sitting on the tailgates as they race down to where the birds are. Some follow on foot. Then of course, the fish move, the birds move and the whole routine starts again."

Hayes' midweek appearance in Rhode Island complicated logistics. Roxy was determined his still alluring presence would not distract her from the work at hand, which included Jake and sex magic.

He was staying with Mario and took over many of the in-office press contact tasks the young campaign manager had been handling. Mario was thrilled to be free to stalk editors in their lairs, make deals, and walk the streets with the Hose. Roxy struggled to avoid any occasion for intimate encounters but Hayes made that impossible as long as she was around campaign headquarters. He claimed he had to use the safe phone in the private upstairs office for his daily calls to Stuart who was involved in now perfunctory hearings before the House Judiciary committee. These calls served as entry to what Roxy considered her hideout and he used them well. Each day he brought her another gift.

The first day it was a heart-shaped antique locket. When he snapped it open she read "November 6" on one side, "I'll be waiting" on the other. As he hung the locket on its chain around her neck, she allowed his fingers to linger, stroking the hollow at the base of her throat and sliding along the soft, swelling skin of her breasts.

There were stolen kisses that reminded her how little it took for this man to make her desperate for more, and more presents that extended the moments of fondling on the couch each day. He brought her books and a hand-crafted box with secret compartments, each containing the words of another message announcing his intent to carry her off when the election was over. She refused to yield however and was increasingly pleased with her devotion to Jake and their daily work on the vote counts.

The afternoon she unwrapped a scandalously sheer lace trimmed nightgown in pale peach was almost her undoing. When she came to her senses, laying on the couch, her bra unhooked, her sweater pushed up around her neck, and Hayes' lips delicately caressing her breast, she panicked. Pushing him away, she jumped to her feet, horrified at what would have happened had someone walked in. That was the day she discovered he had been carefully locking the door whenever they were alone in the office. Fortunately Liz was spending most of her time in the field. She would have handcuffed Roxy to her side had she known what was going on.

Her final thought as she sat at the computer to draft a series of releases on Kat's accomplishments in the field of low cost housing, was how fortunate she was to be doing the tantric yoga with Jake. Once Hayes touched her skin, any thought of towns or vote counts dissolved into flames.

He did keep her posted on Stuart's triumphant adventures in Washington and the unfolding undercover campaign Douglas was now running. Samples of scurrilous letters were filtering in from horrified voters, letters rehashing in vivid detail all the distorted and false accusations Douglas had been making about Kat. The anti-Republican message also included assaults on Stuart ,painting him as an unrepentant Cold War zealot who wanted to use the build-up in Iraq to start a global war against anyone he could find. Hayes assured her their own direct mail campaign as well as their mass media could counteract Douglas' shabby attacks.

★ ★ ★ ★ ★

At least Race had not shot up any more televisions since the hearings concluded in the Senate. The House Judiciary hearings were boring discussions of voting records and Virginia politics. The cameras caught Stuart's expression of yearning to be doing something more exciting than listening to an Ohio representative mangle his position on environmental costs and market forces. From the look of rapt hatred projected from Race's face as Stuart blandly nodded, she would have sworn the vice president had suddenly announced he was personally going to skin Race Scarlatti alive and nail his hide to the Capitol door. Carrie found Race's increasing obsession with Kat and Stuart to be most gratifying.

She focused most of her attention on spells aimed at Race, new spells taken from books she found in a Haitian shop on Manhattan's lower West Side. She covertly fed him ground periwinkle which supposedly induced obsessive love when used with proper word charms spelling out the object to be loved. She monitored him daily, intrigued to see what critical mass would be in his obsession with Kat.

Race had instructed her to use the periwinkle spell on Kat to induce obsessive love in her for him. She had not been able to get close enough to Kat and her food before that useless cunt Roxy started smelling her and told everyone. The periwinkle would carry her stench and Kat would never eat it.

She told Scarlatti the periwinkle charm would not work. It was the first time he used the gun on her. It was self-protection that forced her to use magic against him directly.

One of the first spells was to render the gun useless against her. She heard whispered rumors from other members of his so-called organization about a partially-loaded .38 Colt Race always kept with him. No one knew how many bullets there were. When he became particularly enraged, he would draw the gun and shoot it. Sometimes the chamber was loaded, sometimes it was not. Reportedly, people had been killed. Her own brief experience included an empty chamber expended against her and three shot up television sets to Stuart's credit.

Once she neutralized the gun, she worked to bring Race to a breaking point. In addition to increasing the dosage of periwinkle, she suspended feathers from a blackbird's right wing with a piece of red thread just outside his bedroom window to prevent him from sleeping. With luck, the new piece of information she had could bring him to melt-down instantly.

Once Max closed the house and office to her, Carrie was forced to resort to public encounters to know what was going on. She had just deliberately bumped into the candidate during a crowded visit to the Arcade. Kat smelled her immediately and spun away but she was trapped by crowds and cameras. Carrie was able to look her directly in the eye for a split second before Mario spotted her and she had to run away. It was long enough to discover Kat's little secret. The best part, Carrie thought, was that in the same split second Kat knew she knew.

★ ★ ★ ★ ★

Roxy came home after she and Jake did Gloucester, Hopkinton, Jamestown, and Johnston, the four towns of the day. She had a light schedule the next day and wanted to spend the morning doing essential chores like laundry. They arranged to spend the afternoon campaigning among South County fishermen. Kat was scheduled to make an appearance at Jake's high school reunion that night, followed by a gala Countdown to Victory fundraiser at the Capital Grille featuring a traveling team of three Republican senators. It was Hayes' big event, one they hoped would provide funds for an intensive final week of media advertising. The Republicans saw Kat's race as their one sure win and were not going to blow it for want of a few hundred thousand dollars.

Roxy was pleased at the resulting logistics. She would get to attend Jake's reunion briefly, leave him there, then go on with Kat. She could hang out with Hayes at the fundraiser and be on the inside of the high level political maneuvering and gossip that would go on there. Having the two men in the same place at the same time would be postponed.

Feeling a twinge of guilt at her pleasure in having her cake and eating it too,

Roxy pulled out the goddess deck of tarot cards. She removed them from Kat's library earlier in the week, waiting for a few spare moments to examine them. She began by looking at the cards of her dilemma, the two pairs of lovers called Temptation and The Guide. Further examination reinforced her original impression that the cards referred to Jake and Hayes.

Jake had readily described what he saw in the card that she attributed to him when he made it into a window. Flowing water and clear light, the man tenderly holding the woman at the feet of a shining angel with tantric symbols on its robes. Both were naked but pure. He crafted vaguer images hovering over the couple on the card into the principle of male and female.

"This is the essence of sexual love, the union of opposites in a sacred task: to make each more than they could be alone. I always think of it with the word you first used to describe the card—sanctification."

She never asked him about the window he sold Hayes. Looking at the card propped up on her fur-covered bed, she knew it caught their relationship as perfectly as the other expressed how it was with Jake. In the Temptation card the couple was clothed. The graceful sandy haired man leaned carelessly against a tree, the woman's hand held against his cheek. They were surrounded by wild growth, snakes and lightning bolts. In the foreground a fox stared from the card. The seductive and compelling force of raw sensation was obvious in the images.

It was so easy to see when she was alone or even when she was with Jake. It was Hayes who clouded the picture. More accurately, it was the need for making a choice that clouded the picture. Max told her once it was her Gemini ascendant. Whatever the technical reason, she never understood why she could not have both of any two sides.

Of course, in ten days she would not have to see either of them again.

Shaking herself free of speculation she did not want to continue, Roxy sorted through the cards until she found the Empress. The shock of recognizing what she saw in the card immobilized her momentarily. There was no interpretive book to check but the picture was clear enough.

She found Liz trading quips with Arsenio Hall on television and someone on the phone while slicing up apples at the kitchen table for a week's worth of pies. Muting Arsenio, Roxy motioned Liz to finish her conversation while she sat stiffly clutching the Empress tarot card.

Before Liz could loose a barrage of comments and questions, Roxy slapped the card on the table in front of her.

"What do you see in this card?" she asked abruptly.

Liz glanced at the card. "A pregnant lady, with a crown."

19

The Empress
October 27–29

Rhode Island
Paris

Her heart skipped a beat as the phone rang. It was nearly midnight, it must be him.

"They cannot protect him from my vendetta."

The hoarse whisper froze her blood that moments before was pounding in anticipation of hearing—not Race, not this chilling tone. A metallic taste of fear registered against the back of her mouth.

"What do you want?" Kat blocked from her tone the terror she felt, and brushed her hand along the sword held aloft by the woman in the first panel of Max's embroidered screen.

"When they find his bullet-riddled corpse you will know it was me."

No amount of imagining or willing could drive out the demons that were strangling her voice. When she once again asked "What do you want?" they both knew she was asking his price.

"You will meet me at the Jamestown Bridge. You know the place, the blood of your former opponent marks it well. At midnight. We'll talk."

The call ended. No response was possible.

She could barely make the drive by midnight. Grabbing a pair of jeans stuffed in a corner of the closet she pulled them on. She cursed, breaking a nail as she struggled to zip the pants closed. She almost cried in frustration. Nothing fit anymore. Yanking off the jeans, she pawed through a pile of clothes on the floor to find a pair of sweat pants. Her clothes didn't fit, her ideas did not fit with reality, even her hopes and dreams seemed not to fit. There was so much more to consider.

Gray. She would wrap herself in gray like Ripley in *Aliens*. Max had been right about the film. It was an apt representation of the whole goddess. She remembered Ripley's face, outlined in flames, set with resolve as she faced the monster. Ripley would save the child. She was the Mother.

Kat prepared for combat wrapping a red headband around her black hair. The wolf's eye ring slipped on her finger and she worked to feel energy pulse into it from her heart then back, lighting the white star in the garnet's center. She rubbed her hand slowly along the smooth leather holster that hung from her dressing mirror. It held a small automatic pistol that Stuart insisted she take the night he came to tell her about being offered the vice presidency.

"There are probably several of these in your father's collection but I want to be certain it gets into your hands. The palace guard I now have forced one on me."

Assured that she could shoot a gun, he directed her to carry it everywhere. She pulled her hand away. She could not carry death with her, not now.

At the bottom of the narrow metal stairs that led from the third floor down the outside of the house, she peered into the lit kitchen. Liz and Roxy were huddled over the table. She slipped off into the shadows confident they would not hear the car.

Kat's hands did not begin to shake until she passed Bonnet Shores. She would be there by midnight. She would do whatever it took to call Race off. She would tell Stuart later.

The dead end parking area where she left her car was dimly lit by passing headlights. She picked her way through chopped up rock and gravel. It always amazed her how much rock there was in the ground layer of Rhode Island, cheek to jowl with the sand. Not a hundred feet from the bay and she was standing on thirty-foot rock cliffs. She could see from the edge of the parking area over an embankment to the abutment Senator Winston met head-on. Random bolts of jagged energy shot along her nerves. She felt him in the shadows behind her, and spun around, her boots crunching on the loose shale.

The smooth, rounded form of his head was broken by the peak of a baseball cap; his ponytail tucked under it. His eyes were hidden, his mouth a narrow slit that slowly stretched into something more—not a smile, a grimace of greeting. Fear filtered into her throat and threatened once again to choke her. She opened the ring and rubbed the wolf's eye.

"What do you want?"

This time she was opening the bargaining.

"You could have had it all." His measured tone chilled her more than screams or threats. "I could have given you the Senate. I still can. You never asked me. You went to him and now he's ruined you."

He pulled a pair of navy blue panties from his sleeve, waving them at her.

"I smell milady's secret."

It was no paranoid delusion. Somehow Carrie could see. In some dark cavern of her mind she could see what was not to be seen, and there was nothing Kat could do to deny it. She must have told Race and he was going to exact his revenge.

He moved closer and she flung her arm back to a large outcropping of rock. Her hand close around a jagged piece.

"There is an ancient superstition that the first man who takes a woman can claim her soul. You belong to me. It's in our blood. I can save you, purify your body of its shame, make things as they were before."

He reached into his pocket, pulled out a small metal case and flicked open the top.

Carrie! She could smell her. Her eyes widened as Race reached out, dark goo dripping from his hand. Poison! She sensed the evil and smashed a rock into his face. As she struck, his hand swiped at her and she felt a burning where the sticky substance rubbed against her cheek. She sprang away and stumbled, trying to keep her balance on the unstable rock surface.

Falling, Race threw his body against her, knocking her off her feet and down the embankment. Kat clutched desperately at rocks that came loose in her hand, clattering down behind her. A sharp edge slammed into her back and she twisted her body to a stop. Bruised and battered, pain shot through her pulling a veil of fear across her eyes. No! No! She couldn't let him win. She lay still.

When she finally gathered enough strength to limp back up to her car, there was no trace of her assailant. Kat picked up the rock, stained with his blood. Clutching her belly, she took a few grains of arnica and prayed she could make it home.

★ ★ ★ ★ ★

It was noon by the time Roxy took Mario's frantic message from the machine. Kat had missed both her morning appointments. If Roxy knew where she was, Mario would be at campaign headquarters until two. She had a strange feeling. She heard thumping from Kat's room sometime in the middle of the night and assumed she was once again unable to sleep. Roxy ran up two flights of stairs and threw open the door to the bedroom.

She screamed. Kat was sitting on the floor slumped against her bed, a dark pool collecting beneath her. She looked up dully, a wet, blood soaked mass in her hands. Roxy shuddered and knelt beside her.

"Oh God, what is it? Are you dying?" she blurted, hysterically.

"The other night I had a dream. I was in an operating room and all these people in white gloves and masks were surrounding me with pieces of bloody liver in their hands, waving them in front of my face." Kat's voice was a monotone.

Roxy shrieked. "Is that your liver? How could that be? Livers don't just fall out."

Kat's eyes were glassy with shock as she smiled up at Roxy.

"Have you called the ambulance yet?"

★ ★ ★ ★ ★

Roxy was frightened. Kat's black hair cut a streak between the white pillow-case and her equally pale face. She felt like someone had punched a hole in her stomach and all her strength and courage leaked out. As Kat's eyelids fluttered open, Roxy bent over to hear what she wanted. There were no words, only the barest of smiles.

"I cleaned away all the blood and … and stuff before the ambulance came. I told them you had fallen. They believed me. You're covered with bruises." The words tumbled out, panic-filled.

"The doctor in the emergency room said it was a miscarriage. I was hysterical and argued with him. Then I came to my senses and begged him to keep quiet about this. He's convinced you're a battered woman. For now, your entry papers read 'severe contusions, possible internal bleeding: accidental.'

"Who should I call? Mario's been looking for you everywhere. Should we tell him? What if the press finds out?" Roxy's anguished voice kept on, words, questions shoving their way between quivering lips. Finally she got to the question that was foremost in her mind. "Who is it Kat? Should we call him? The father, I mean." She finished up in a rush then stood tensely awaiting a response.

The darkened room was silent, the metallic humming and mechanical whistle of hospital sounds seeping through the door. Roxy hated the smell of hospitals, the disinfectant mixed with organic odors she assumed meant death and disease. She wondered if working among all the people dressed in white there were healers who could diagnose malfunctions through smell.

"Kat, are you awake?"

As she moved to lift herself up on the pillows, Roxy leaned over to help.

"Should I call Max?" she asked. Kat smiled weakly.

"Max was planning to arrive tomorrow for the last week of the campaign. Hopefully, I'll be out of here and home by then. He needs to know but Roxy, he's not the father."

"Then who, Kat?"

Anger began to drive out fear as Roxy waited impatiently for an answer. All the hard work, all the people who cared about changing the politics of the state and saw Kat as the light that would lead them out of the darkness, all that gone unless they could keep this out of the press.

"You do know who the father is, don't you?" she asked petulantly.

Kat's voice was very soft. "Yes, Roxy, I do know who the father is. And you're right, I should call him. As for your next question," Roxy snapped her lips closed, "he doesn't know I was pregnant with his child."

Reaching over for her bag on the night table, she flinched from quick stabs of pain.

"He may not be easy to find," she said pulling out her calendar. "Call Gretta."

Kat scribbled out a number. "She'll be able to reach the vice president. I think he's in New York stumping for the would-be governor."

She barely noticed taking the paper from Kat and getting up to make the call. She was astounded. Stuart! She felt most irritated about Liz who would be gloating. If they aren't sleeping together they should be, was her incessant cry. Roxy was dumbfounded. How could this have happened without her knowing?

"Use the public phone," Kat said. "Less chance of tracing it back to me should we manage to keep my condition out of the press." She did not sound very hopeful.

"What about Mario, and tomorrow's schedule"

"Go call Stuart. I'll think about the rest while you're gone. Tell him to go to the house and call us from there. I don't want him busting in here until we've had a chance to figure out what to do."

Kat seemed calm as she outlined plans.

"Let Liz know something's up, but no details over the phone. She may need to pick him up at some airport. We can be grateful for small favors, at least Jasmine's out of the way."

Roxy knew Stuart would be in his plane in minutes once she reached him, evading his Secret Service and causing havoc. But not near as much havoc as would be caused if word leaked out as to why he was here.

★ ★ ★ ★ ★

Talking with Stuart was easy once she tracked him down. He was at a hotel in Albany scheduled to speak in twenty minutes. Roxy tried to remain calm as she told him Kat needed him in Rhode Island as soon as possible and in absolute secret. When he asked what was wrong she started crying.

"I can be there by dark." As soon as he began speaking, Roxy quieted down. "Is there someone you can trust to pick me up at the airport and bring me to Kiley?"

"Yes. Liz," replied Roxy, glad he was taking charge and not hassling her with a lot of questions she could not answer on the phone.

"Where are you?"

Without thinking, Roxy told him they were at South County Hospital, about ten minutes from Narragansett. He caught his breath, then continued with instructions.

"The Naval Air Station near Charlestown is abandoned, only ultralights use it now. I've landed there before. It's on roadmaps so whoever is meeting me should be able to find it. Have them be there early, about six p.m. And tell them to park at the water end of the westernmost landing strip; there are three. I'll circle once then they turn their headlights on to light the strip. I can fly from here to there without having to make contact with anyone official. And have them bring whatever clothes you think I'll need to slip undetected into the hospital."

Stuart's voice was raw with pain.

"Will she be alive when I get there?"

"Oh yes, yes! She's not hurt like that. Please get here fast, and remember no one can know you're here," Roxy warned as he hung up the phone.

She made a quick call to cancel her plans with Jake promising she would see him in the morning and explain. She could postpone it no longer. Her next call was to Liz. Roxy called campaign headquarters earlier to alert both Liz and Mario that she had found Kat in her room too ill to make the Countdown to Victory reception that evening. She was deliberately vague about what was wrong and where they were. Mario knew better than to ask questions on the phone. She was forced to hang up on Liz.

As soon as Liz heard her voice she started. "Where are you? What's going on? Everyone is absolutely berserk. Hayes can't believe Kat is sick enough to justify standing up three U.S. senators and a couple hundred big donors. What do I tell them?"

By this point Roxy had worked up enough energy to shut Liz up.

"There's something you need to do right now and then meet up with us."

She could hear contentment in Liz's sigh. She hated not being in the midst of the action solving problems with both hands.

"But you can't say anything. This has to be top secret. I can't tell you what's happening on the phone." She stopped short. "In fact I don't want to say anything more on this phone. Go upstairs to the private office and use the phone there. It's safe. I'll call you on that number in two minutes. Hurry."

Roxy hung up before Liz could do more than sputter. Five minutes later she was giving directions to the airstrip and about clothes.

"If you don't tell me who I'm picking up and disguising how am I supposed to know what to bring to disguise him, or her?" Liz replied.

She conceded the point but refused to tell Liz anything more than it was a male, over six feet tall, well built and very recognizable.

"Get that fishing slicker Jake keeps in the garage," Roxy said, inspired. "With a knit hat and that, he should be able to sneak in."

"And exactly where are we sneaking in to?" Liz asked with growing irritation.

"South County Hospital, room 236. Head east from the airstrip along Route 1 to the Salt Pond exit. Follow the hospital signs and drive around past the emergency entrance. There are back stairs right near the room. If you come in and call when you get here, I'll go down and open a side door. Don't let him come in until I let you know it's safe."

Roxy was beginning to think more clearly. This was the thought process she used in plotting out her novels. Of course then she was totally in control and events occurred only as she planned.

★ ★ ★ ★ ★

She returned to the room after making the calls. Collapsing into the chair next to Kat's bed, she closed her eyes. It was no use. All she could see was the pool of blood and a pile of what looked like raw meat. She got up and walked over to the window. Kat spoke softly.

"I'm sorry Roxy. You've worked so hard, you don't deserve this."

"Why didn't you tell me before?" Roxy said, her voice hard with fear and worry as she came to stand by the bed.

"How could you do this?" She couldn't shout what should be shouted. How could you be so stupid? How could you ignore rule #1 for the modern woman: no matter what everyone says, no one is responsible for what happens in your body but you.

She saw Kat's gray eyes gleam.

"You've been immortalized as Aphrodite, don't you know the answer? No woman would commit such follies," Kat smiled poignantly, "without being in love, a slave to that goddess' twisted sense of duty. She's a powerful lady, that Aphrodite, her empire knows no bounds. Poor Athena pales in comparison. The instant she demonstrated her power, I surrendered."

Kat's voice drifted, became abstract. Roxy sat in the chair, in shadows. Kat was talking to her soul, she would listen.

"I adored my father. My childhood was spent reading myths and fairy tales where the hero was always Duke. When it was time for my prince to come, I knew he would be like Duke.

"Race destroyed sex for me. Jamie reinforced my horror. I withdrew from physical intimacy. Max understood. We knew our work together was not as lovers although we drew on that energy when necessary. We learned ritual sex primarily as a way of healing me. Romance survived only in my mind. Love remained intact, sacred, in the care of my father. When he died without a good-bye, just vanished in an instant, I gave up love too. I couldn't stand the pain. Just like sex, I couldn't stand the pain.

"I hoped the continual pain would eventually numb my heart and I wouldn't feel it but instead it became more sensitive.

"Then in a blinding flash of light," Kat's lips twisted ironically, "there was T.J. Stuart. I should have known when I saw that bloodied sword in his hand in Harpers Ferry that this wouldn't be easy."

Kat was silent so long, Roxy was ready to prod her with another question. Then she began speaking again.

"Ol' Tommy Jeff, a truly remarkable man. He's everything Duke would have wanted for me. It's not a mistake for me to love him, Roxy, I know it isn't. Although I have to admit, the man does have a knack for making me wish I'd never laid eyes on him. When I discovered I was pregnant, it was unbelievable. Suddenly I realized I wanted to have his child more than anything in the world. I just blew it on the timing. Uranus must have been in the spaghetti, as Liz would say. Remember the fortune strip I received at the Magic Circle? By year's end I would know my heart's desire." Kat's voice broke. "I know my heart's desire and now I can't have it. Now there'll be nothing—no baby, maybe no victory."

Roxy rushed over and grabbed her hand, cutting off Kat's lament.

"Don't say that! No one need ever know. What happened here has nothing to do with how great a senator you'll be. We can keep it out of the press, I know we can. And you'll win next Tuesday. Rhode Island can't afford you not to win."

Tears were streaming down her cheeks as Kat squeezed her hand.

"Thank you, Roxy. You'll never know how much your support and love has meant to me during the past year. More than anyone else, I can say I couldn't have done it without you."

A few more sniffs and Roxy was ready to change the subject. They had a couple hours before Liz would be here with Stuart. She planned to find out how all this happened without her knowing. And she was not ready to let Kat off the hook completely. All the while she was harassing Roxy about Hayes, she was violating her own rules, big time.

"I assume all this happened long before Liz started promoting Stuart as tension release." Roxy was startled to hear the sharp tone in her own voice. But it was deserved. No matter when it started, Kat lied to them.

"I didn't plot to keep it a secret from you, it just happened. In the beginning it was necessary for us to hide from the world. I did every magic trick I knew to build an invisible shield. Whenever anyone else was around, or could be around, we played roles, any roles but lovers. We became expert at disguising how attuned we were to each other. Max could see us, and strangely enough so could Carrie. She told me at Little Compton that she knew and it was so reaffirming somehow. Her vision acknowledged this love existed on a mythic level as part of the great conflict between good and evil."

"But he was married, and a senator, and now he's the vice president and you're…." Roxy sputtered, unable to finish. Then another thought hit her.

"How could you not tell Stuart about being pregnant?"

"I was going to tell him, truly I was. I was trying to find a way to see him without Jasmine or Race's thugs seeing us. I was terrified someone would expose us and his wife would stop the divorce, or delay it, or make it messy. Then fate stepped in and suddenly he was the vice president. No Congress would approve a man with a resistant wife and pregnant mistress running for the U.S. Senate. There's no room in politics for anything out of the ordinary."

Roxy considered that one of the great understatements. She did not want to be diverted from her primary purpose though.

"So when did all this start?" She hoped her voice did not convey the annoyance she was feeling.

Kat settled her head deeper into the pillows. Roxy could feel her vision shift. "I guess the real beginning was in Paris, April 1989."

"Paris? Paris? I was with you in Paris. We were on our way back from Moscow, Capital Links and all that. Remember? I was there." Her outrage building, Roxy fumed.

Kat sounded amused. "You left on Friday. A meeting with your editor, I believe. I wasn't scheduled to leave until Sunday afternoon."

Roxy harrumphed and snorted a few times but she was not letting pride stand in the way of getting this story.

"OK, OK, you win. Tell me what happened in Paris."

★ ★ ★ ★ ★

Kat began hesitantly but soon she was there, in Paris, on a beautiful April morning. April in Paris was everything the song says. Love certainly seemed to be the perfume of the day.

Kat decided to stop at the environment conference, see who was on the schedule, make some quick connections, then stroll around for more sightseeing. As she looked over the meeting list, Senator Stuart walked out of a room trailed by three or four conference speakers. Their eyes met and he seemed surprised. Kat had not seen him except in passing, since Harpers Ferry.

He walked over and introduced her to the men as one of leaders in Congress on their topic, ocean dumping. He told Kat how sorry he was to have missed her presentation and invited her to join him on the next panel.

Kat stammered some excuse, flattered at Stuart's nod to her expertise. She followed the men into the panel and pretended to listen. She was mesmerized by his performance, thinking that the stage lost a great actor when Thomas Jefferson Stuart decided to follow his namesake into government.

After the panel, Stuart escaped the cluster of people around him, took Kat's arm and steered her out of the room, through the lobby, and into a dazzling Paris noontime, proposing they have lunch. They crossed to a café and were seated in a secluded corner. Later they spent the afternoon exploring the city.

Stuart was impressed by the giant oranges that decorated nearly every corner and dispensed fresh pressed orange juice. He compared them to the soda machines on every block in America. The people running the oranges were unemployed and receiving welfare. Placed in these jobs by the government, they were allowed to put out signs announcing they were looking for work and what type. He remarked that in Washington or Richmond or Philadelphia those same people would be on a street corner dealing drugs or running numbers.

They walked for miles along Paris streets, swept up in the Easter week crowds. They rode up and down the Eiffel Tower then crossed to the Trocadero and watched kids on roller skates doing fancy jumps up steps and skateboarders weaving in and out of beer cans set up along one of the walkways. Pretending to be Parisians, they gnawed on the ends of fresh baked French loaves wrapped only in a small piece of paper.

Stuart talked about the heroic French spirit as it flowered in its kings from Charlemagne to Napoleon. He pointed out landmarks of the Revolution, comparing it unfavorably with America's. He lectured on architecture and art and traffic flow in great cities.

They stopped at an outdoor café just off St. Germain as the warm dusk crept along the streets, choosing a small table on a corner where four streets came together at an odd angle. Kat slipped shoes off her aching feet, sipped a wonderful red wine and began to examine Stuart. Out of nowhere a skinhead teenager dressed all in black with blood pouring from his scalp came running up the street directly at the café. Several other kids were chasing him, clubs in hand. He hurled himself over the low barrier and landed on their table, scattering glasses and bottles.

Stuart grabbed Kat and lifted her over the barrier. Following, he pushed her into a doorway where they could see what was going on. They began sneezing and gasping from some sort of gas. He pulled out his handkerchief and put it across her nose and mouth, holding an end up to his own. Waiters were grabbing at the kids, police sirens were sounding and people were fleeing down the street.

Kat was barefoot in the doorway holding tightly onto Stuart. Gagging, she cried that she could not run without her shoes. He pulled them from his pocket and dropped them on the ground at her feet. Brushing aside the handkerchief, he kissed her.

"Now that I've found you," he said, "'I'll never let anything harm you. I promise."

The scene on the street was quickly back to normal. They walked away, looking in shop windows as if nothing had happened.

"Everything changed in that moment, Roxy. For awhile I called it an emotional mutation," Kat laughed. "You would have recognized it immediately. I was in love."

There was no discussion when they walked into her hotel. As the door closed behind them, Kat panicked, overcome by the old feeling of being trapped, caged. She knew that there was more pain from feeling too much than from feeling nothing. When Kat looked up and saw Stuart smiling at her, she realized the pattern was unfolding perfectly. She could almost see Aphrodite checking Kat off her things to do list.

They made love for hours that night and there was no pain, only bliss. All the tantric forms and practices Kat learned with Max were now fueled by a consuming passion. The edge disappeared. They became pure continuum exploring possession from every angle, looking out the window at the Paris streets and rooftops with a single eye. In a single voice they talked about everything and anything. They dozed off then woke to love each other more.

Stuart was captivated by her hair, wrapping it endlessly around his fingers, watching it curl and uncurl. He grabbed handfuls and rubbed it across his body, laughing that he could feel her pulse flowing through it like electricity.

In Kat's enraptured mind he became Hercules, and Saladin, and Lancelot, and every hero in shining armor she had ever read and dreamt about. He was a man like Duke was a man and she was his woman to cherish and protect. It was Paris, the goddess had set her destiny and Kat surrendered. Who was she to argue?

Kat woke up soon after dawn. His face half buried in the pillow beside her was innocent and vulnerable. A voice spoke inside her head so loudly she was sure it would wake him up. *I served this prince before.* She shook her head, stunned. What could it possibly mean? Voices and visions of dead warriors. Panic returned and she decided to think somewhere out of his aura. She slipped quietly out of bed, put on running clothes and went across to the Jardin du Plantes.

She ran for awhile past the greenhouses then returned to the small gazebo near the entrance. She stood looking at the flowers, some beginning to bloom, and anguished over what to do. Suddenly she heard a sound and turned. Stuart was standing there.

In a disconnected flash, she wondered what to call him. T.J. was not who he was to her. She did not want to call him Stuart like everyone else. She had to know who he was. Before he could say anything, Kat asked him what the people of his heart called him.

He said that his grandmother claimed she loved him better than anyone in the world except his grandpa. He was long dead and he was a Beauregard. She always called him her little Beau.

Kat flung herself into his arms and they returned to the hotel for more hours of what Stuart called "worshipping at the temple of her body." Eventually they went downstairs to the hotel's little street café, devoured croissants and sipped café au lait.

Kat related bits and pieces of memories she had from that day. They walked from the hotel over to the Seine along the river walk to Notre Dame. Inside they marveled at the magnificent windows and she told him about the church next door to her house in Narragansett with its Tiffany glass.

Standing in the center of the great cathedral, Kat was gripped with an over-

powering feeling. She was back in her childhood when First Friday meant praying for the conversion of Russia as directed by the Fatima prophecies. It came together for her in that instant. The incredible soul of Russia that she experienced
the week before praying in the Church of the Assumption, packed with people
on Palm Sunday in Vladimir. The realization that the prophecy was coming true
and Americans needed to reach out to the positive soul energy of the Soviet
Union. She told this all to Stuart outside the cathedral.

He waited until she finished then reached over and stroked her cheek.

"I hope nothing ever extinguishes those stars in your eyes," he said. After a
pause, he continued, "It's a good thing you're running in Rhode Island, though I
wager you're going to hate being a Republican Senator."

The day was a blur of marketplaces full of flowers, street cleaners and trash
men in spiffy blue or bright green jumpsuits, street performers and other lovers
walking along the sunny streets. There were vendors out selling everything from
antique postcards to rare coins. Kat bought him red and white striped suspend-
ers and he bought her an incredible outfit he insisted she wear that night.

On Stuart's instructions, Kat stood outside her hotel at 10 p.m. Passers by
gave appreciative glances to her black polka dot short ruffled skirt and sheer
black body suit. She had several chains of tiny white and black stars hung around
her neck and from her ears. Her hair was tied back with a white bow. Soft suede
ankle boots completed the look. Not very senatorial but extremely Parisian.

Stuart roared up on a huge black and chrome Harley. He wore a Harley
teeshirt, a sleeveless jacket strewn with decals, motorcycle boots, and a black
scarf printed with skulls tied around his head. Kat climbed on and they rode
around most of the night, drinking mineral water and doing lewd street dances
in dingy bars draped with black leather and chains. Kat never discovered where
Stuart found the bike, clothes and list of the ten best biker bars on the Left Bank
that apparently came in the jacket

Just before dawn, they parked near the rocks at Chaumont Parc. Kat wrapped
in his arms, sitting on the bike watching the night vanish over the skyline of Paris. Stuart began talking about Plato and an ancient creation myth in one of his
dialogues. A four-handed, four-footed primordial beast was sliced in half by an
avenging deity. Forever the halves searched for the other. He described souls like
that. When they find their twin flame the two are struck by a sense of belonging
to one another. The original Thomas Jefferson never found his twin flame.

"How fortunate am I to have found mine," Stuart declared as he kissed her.

Sounds of rolling food carts along the hall and the clattering of trays as aides
brought them into the rooms, returned them to the present. When the young
woman left, Kat lifted the metal lids on the plates, sniffed at the unappetizing
fare, then continued to talk, ignoring the food.

"I could never decide whether the goddess was being merciful or not when
we had tickets on the same plane back."

They were approaching the long transatlantic part of the flight when Kat got up her nerve and asked Stuart about his wife.

He related the story without expression. His wife's name is Clarice and her father is the king of Virginia politics. Stuart took no time at VMI for social life and graduated to running his family's various businesses. He was almost thirty, his mother was hounding him to get married, and Clarice was going through a difficult time. Stuart took her on as a project like he had taken on his mother, sisters, and the businesses. Within six months of the wedding, there was no doubt that the marriage was a big mistake. Clarice was nervous and timid around anyone but her family. She wanted to stay in Richmond and keep caring for her father's house and office. Sex was her wifely duty but it was kept to a formal minimum.

She was happy because Stuart was her father's protégé, extending her father's wise rule to Washington. She had no intention of ever leaving Richmond. Campaigns, political fights, and one thing or another always got in the way of divorce. Stuart lifted Kat's hand, turned it over and kissed her palm .

"Until now I never had a reason to care," he said. " The original T.J. once remarked he liked the dreams of the future better than the history of the past. I agree."

It was nearly two weeks after they landed at Dulles that afternoon before Kat heard from Stuart on a night they were voting late. Kat knew then how desperately she wanted to touch him. For the rest of that spring and through the summer they would snatch a private moment here or there.

When Congress returned in September, Kat had a conversation with Senator Winston that convinced her he was going to run and she would face an almost impossible fight. There was no way she could run the kind of campaign needed and have a high risk love affair with a very visible Republican senator.

Stuart came to watch the Capital Links show on the environment. They returned to Kat's office afterwards. It was about two a.m. and the building was deserted. Kat was still wired from the performance, and from trying to beat back Charlie Drummond, who was one of the commentators. No matter how close to incoherent she was, she knew she had to end it with Stuart.

He sat on the couch and focused all his attention on Kat as she paced the room ranting and raving about the senate race and the personal demands. They could not continue, there was too much risk. There were too many people invested in her success, too much at stake, including his desire for a Republican Senate.

Stuart stood up and took her in his arms.

"Once the election is over, it won't matter. What's a year in an eternal romantic quest? A blink of time to wait. I would willingly agree to a lifetime, or more, spent in pursuit of this particular grail.

"I don't want to try and influence your decision but we could continue being lovers and take extra care. Remember, Joan of Arc perished on the repressed fires of her sex," he warned.

Kat insisted it had to be over and he graciously yielded, outlining all they could do for her campaign. He pledged to be her guardian angel, with her in spirit if not in body. Kat had hoped for more protest. She babbled about needing to find another man, an eligible man to guarantee there would be no rumors.

"Kiley, it doesn't matter if you find yourself a dozen boyfriends. I'll be there election night and I don't plan to leave without you." He kissed her. "Save the last dance for me, Darlin," he said, and walked out of the office.

"I cried myself to sleep on the couch."

Kat stopped talking for several minutes and Roxy got up to switch on the light. She stretched and asked Kat if she wanted anything from outside to eat, happy when Kat shook her head. Roxy was starved but she did not want to leave and miss the opportunity to hear the rest of the story.

"That was nearly a year ago, Kat. Obviously it didn't end that night."

"No. It didn't end that night. He became Stuart to me when we saw each other professionally which was the only time we met. He was Beau only in my relentless reliving of our times together. He seemed to have no difficulty accepting a ban on intimacy. He was always circumspect and formal even if we happened to be alone. He would occasionally release himself in manic behavior like with the roses.

"For me it was horrible; withdrawal from an addictive drug. There had been this secret romantic dream world where I had the perfect love. Suddenly that was all gone. I was amazed at how strongly my body missed him. I hung on for a while, then it was as if the electrical tension built to such a point it started shattering the walls of my reality. I went to him the night you came back from Key West with the news about Winston."

"Did Max know about—Beau?" Roxy interrupted.

"The instant they met in Key West. Ask Max to tell you about it. It was quite remarkable. The upshot was Max could see me clearly, standing in Beau's aura. And, by the way, I think he should remain Stuart to you." Kat quickly moved on.

"The news about Winston was devastating. He knew about it so I rationalized that I needed to talk with him, needed his guidance. The moment I walked into his house I knew what a lie that was. I needed his force, his energy shot into me. There was no price too high for that fix. That was the night all the foretelling became clear. By going to him I gave up the control I had over the outcome of my senate race. I threw it all into the hands of fate as the price of—it wasn't his love. I had that. I knew he would be there at the end as he'd promised. It was the connection with him I needed, the sex. And I needed it in the present.

"Lying in his arms that night, I knew I couldn't stay away no matter how dangerous discovery would be. Of course, I believed I was smart enough and sufficiently in control to avoid detection. I'm forty-one years old. I never considered I might get pregnant." Kat snorted in disgust.

"After that night, the strain increased. Our personal exchanges had a hidden layer of intimacy. I don't know how to describe what he would do. I guess it was teasing, in code. I knew he was making love to me; no one else did.

"Once Douglas entered the race and dirty tricks became standard opposition tactics, I thought it would be impossible to see him. There was no more sex until we flew back from the golf tournament in Williamsburg. All the craziness we went through that weekend made it clear there was almost as much danger from not having sex. There was even a time in his hideaway office in the Capitol, the day after the White House barbecue."

Roxy was horrified. She thought about Hayes and how guilty she felt that afternoon in the Rayburn garage. And here was Kat, fucking a U.S. Senator behind the Senate chamber, risking everything. She felt embarrassed, betrayed. Kat had been her ideal. No weak knees whenever a man crooked his finger. She could say no. Another illusion shattered.

Calculating quickly, Roxy decided Kat must have gotten pregnant sometime in August, when Stuart was —

"When did you get pregnant?" Roxy interrupted.

Kat seemed unperturbed by either the question or Roxy's preemptory tone. She smiled serenely.

"It was on his birthday, the anniversary of Duke's death. We made love that morning in the bedroom I had as a girl. As Beau so delicately put it—my prince had come."

Roxy flinched as Kat laughed lightly. She did not see much in this whole situation that was funny.

★ ★ ★ ★ ★

She was nodding off in the chair when the door opened and the doctor from the emergency room came in. She jumped up and faced him. Kat was sleeping.

"My shift is over. I wanted to see how the congresswoman was doing before I left," he said.

"She's asleep now," Roxy began, then Kat sat up against the pillows and told her it was OK.

"Thank you, doctor, for caring for me today. I'm anxious to hear what you found."

The doctor was a young Indian and he bobbed up and down in small bows as he approached the bed.

"Dr. Panjit. I am happy to meet you. If I were your physician I would advise a D&C to scrape away whatever tissue may be left. But you seem to have no fever and I found no reason for concern in my examination of you. However, you must rest for several days. A miscarriage is much like a birth in the damage it can do to delicate organs. You have lost a good deal of blood and suffered considerable internal bruising, not to mention the shock of the ordeal."

"Doctor, I fell down a rock embankment last night. Can I assume this caused the miscarriage?"

"My examination indicates the fetus was abnormal. It would have been terminated naturally before the third month regardless of the fall. Your accident merely hastened the inevitable."

Kat thanked him and promised she would call her gynecologist in the morning when she returned home.

"I can leave tomorrow can't I?" The doctor repeated his warning about rest. "But you can do that at home. There is no medical reason for you to remain."

"Doctor, I know my friend explained to you how sensitive this accident is under the circumstances."

He held up his hand to stop her. "Not to worry. I spoke with my cousin Dr. Rastogi. He is a big man in the Indian community. He told me you were a fine lady, important to our people. Whatever I could do to help you would be a favor to him. I owe much to Rastogi. Your records will read as your friend told me, a fall that caused internal bleeding."

As the door closed behind him, Roxy ran over and hugged Kat.

"We can do it. I know we can. If he doesn't say anything, and the records read an accidental fall, we can keep this quiet. No one but us will know."

Roxy was babbling, she was so relieved. In the back of her mind, a question darted past. When did Kat fall, and where?

★ ★ ★ ★ ★

The next time the door opened, Roxy woke up to find Liz standing over her.

"Come on, I need you to take me to the ladies room," Liz said in her stage whisper as Roxy blinked up at her. Dragged from the chair and pushed through the door into the dimly lit hall, Roxy caught a glimpse of Stuart standing by the bed. There was another person standing outside the door. Probably Secret Service considering Stuart's new status.

"This is Terrence Shanley," Liz said, smiling at the red-haired giant who moved over to block the door. "He's our hero's main muscle. Not your type, though. This is Roxy," she said to the man. "What are you doing here?" Roxy hissed, almost in tears as she followed Liz to the lounge at the end of the corridor. "You were supposed to call me so I could sneak you in the back door. Now everything will be ruined and just when we were beginning to work it out."

Liz pushed her onto the couches.

"Here I am sitting in the dark along some abandoned airstrip looking for all the world like a courier waiting for a drug flight when who should land but our friend in there. Donald Trump, right? I would recognize him anywhere from his pictures."

Roxy started to protest but Liz was in gear and rolled right over her.

"We discussed the situation briefly. Fortunately for you he had no more information than I did. We had a disguise for our famous friend since everyone would wonder what Donald Trump was doing here. We knew the room number so we just walked on in. No problem." Liz glared at Roxy sitting scrunched in the corner of the couch. "A lot less risky than opening some back door that probably had an ear splitting alarm on it which could have gotten us caught and then where would we be? Trying to explain why Donald Trump was sneaking into South County Hospital could be tricky." Liz paused for breath.

"Stop saying that! Stop calling him Donald Trump! That's ridiculous. And what are we doing out here? We need to plan." She jumped up from the couch. "We need to decide how to keep this quiet and what to tell the press and...."

"We need to give them some time alone," Liz said, suddenly serious. "He's got it bad for the c-woman and doesn't know whether she's going to live or die. Come to think of it, neither do I."

She pushed Roxy back onto the couch and sat next to her.

"So while they're working it out in there why don't you tell old Aunt Lizzie exactly what's going on."

★ ★ ★ ★ ★

She had been dodging in and out of the shadows for what seemed an eternity. She must be wounded, she could feel the pain. The doctor sent them in to give her medication. She protested but they insisted she needed to rest. Occasionally the darkness faded and she could see Roxy sitting there watching her, looking concerned.

Then came a dream, so vivid it woke her up. She was dreaming about Beau holding her, comforting her, driving away the fearsome forms woven from the shadows. The dream did not vanish. He was there, standing next to the bed. A streetlamp outside the window bathed his face in soft light and she could see pain etched in every line as he looked down at her. Kat cried out, it hurt so much to see him suffering.

In an instant, he was with her, clasping her hands, kissing her hair and face, holding her tightly. She thought it was her tears wetting her cheeks until she heard him sob.

"I'll be all right," she said, pulling up his face to look at her. Relief flooded his eyes, and he tenderly kissed her palm whispering thanks. "But I've lost our child."

It was remarkable to see the emotions, each a conquering army obliterating the one previous. Tremendous shock, incredible joy, ineffable sadness as he realized their loss. A subdued joy returned. He assured her there would be time for more children, however many she wanted. She sighed, leaning back against the pillows, knowing she would be safe now that he was there.

"As long as I could remember, my grandmother never laughed."

Kat could feel his words as well as hear them, his breath brushing against her cheek. "She was a good and kind woman and she would smile but never laugh. When I asked she told me her laugh had died with her Beau, my grandfather. They had a story book love that ended with his tragic death when he was far too young. I admired her devotion but couldn't understand it until tonight. When I was flying here I knew that if you died, I would never laugh again either."

He buried his face in her hair, his lips slipping along her wet cheek. Nothing more was said as she burrowed into his arms.

★ ★ ★ ★ ★

They were still entwined when Liz and Roxy came back into the room. Seeing the couple, the women started to back out but Stuart waved them to say. He turned to Kat, kissing her tenderly and placed her back onto the pillows.

"We have some talking to do, ladies."

Stuart insisted whatever they do, Hayes and Mario had to know the truth.

"It's much easier to lie plausibly when you know what the truth is," he said as if this were some rule written in a book of political wisdom.

"Exactly what truth should they know?" asked Roxy.

Ticking off the points, Stuart recited, "Kiley had a miscarriage. It's safely listed in all records as whatever you worked out with that doctor."

He paused then asked Kat whether she felt Panjit could be trusted to keep quiet if approached by Douglas waving cash or making threats.

"Rastogi's word is law in the Indian community," Kat answered, "especially when family ties are involved. And Rastogi loves me. He's been a strong supporter from the beginning."

Satisfied, Stuart continued. "A couple days rest…."

"I have an election in a week in case you've forgotten," Kat interrupted.

"I want you alive on November 7. I have a promise to keep to you."

Liz pinched Roxy's arm as they watched the exchange continue as if they were not in the room. The air sparkled between them.

"I'm not going to die, Beau. This is not a fatal disease we're talking about." Kat smiled tolerantly.

"Women do die from miscarriages, Darlin'. Especially when they treat the situation lightly, ignoring it for the sake of their work." There was no arguing with the tone in his voice. "The campaign can go on without you being on your feet shaking hands and giving speeches twenty hours a day, at least for a couple of days. When Redcliffe gets here we can work out a strategy where you can spend at least the next two days on the phone while surrogates go out and press the flesh."

He turned to Liz. "Call Redcliffe. Get him and De Palma here right away. We need to start thinking about statements to the press." Then he looked at Kat. "And make sure that worthless bitch Jasmine knows as little as possible."

"She's safely out of the way," Kat responded quietly, offering no further explanation as Stuart's eyebrows rose creating ripples in his smooth, broad forehead. He reached over and turned on another light by the bed so Liz could use the phone, and noticed the cuts and bruises on Kat's arm and face. Gingerly, he pulled aside a corner of the sheet exposing her bruise-covered leg. Hard lines set around his mouth and eyes.

"What happened?"

Kat leaned back, her face ashen. "I can't talk about this now." She was barely able to speak.

Liz escaped to use the phone in the hall. Roxy wanted to find out about the bruises. She fit herself into a darkened corner where she could watch their faces.

There was no indication in his calm voice of the anger she could almost see radiating from him.

"Your body has no secrets from me. Don't hide any in your mind. What happened? How did you get these bruises?"

"I fell."

Roxy had no idea silence could be so loud. She could almost hear Kat's will surrender. Then she saw fear brighten her eyes and strain her face even further.

"Now that I've known life with you, I can't bear the thought of it without you." She strained to hear Kat's whispered words, not that hearing them mattered. She did not have a clue what they meant. Stuart obviously did though.

"Scarlatti! He did this to you, didn't he? Answer me Kiley. Did Scarlatti.....?" The awful truth dawned on him and he stepped back as if hit.

"It's not what you think. Ask Roxy. She heard the doctor."

Her words tumbled out in disorder. She grabbed at his hand, pulling him back towards the bed.

"The fall only hastened the inevitable, he said. There would have been a miscarriage anyway. Race's pushing me over the embankment did not kill our baby. I had to talk to him, to try and keep him from killing you. I'm so afraid you'll go after him and then you'll be gone, dead like my father and I'll be alone again. This time the blackness would never end. I can't lose you, too. You have to understand."

Kat was so distraught, Roxy was afraid they would have to call a nurse. Everything would be exposed, the press would find out, and who knows what would happen then.

Stuart sat on the bed and gathered the hysterical woman into his arms, stroking her hair, assuring her he would be safe.

"There's no shame in being afraid but it's often our duty to carry on in spite of our fear. We'll go on Kiley. I told you before not to worry. We'll die in each other's arms, I promise. I'll never leave you."

If she could have slipped out of the room, she would have. Mesmerized by the intensity, Roxy could not move. Just then Liz came back and announced Hayes and Mario were on their way.

Kat was resting quietly in Stuart's arms and he laid her back onto the pillows.

"I have no intention of putting a well-deserved bullet in Scarlatti's head, or giving him a shot at me. I'm the vice president of the United States." There was a touch of amusement in his voice.

"When the IRS and Justice Department get finished with your friend Race, all we'll need to do is toss a few shovels of dirt on his coffin."

★ ★ ★ ★ ★

It was fortunate Kat slept through most of the strategy session, she would never have forgiven Stuart. Assured that Kat was safe and Scarlatti planned for, the master political strategist replaced the worried lover and Stuart focused on Kat's senate race. His goal was unchanged. Get her elected and he would have his Republican Senate.

He brushed off the concern Hayes voiced about his own vulnerability.

"Congress won't be back to vote on my confirmation until after the election. By then, we can be married and no one will care. Our problems are here in Rhode Island for the next week. Even the most adoring public can be unmerciful. I don't want her hurt any more."

They reviewed all the possibilities, what was recorded fact, like the ambulance pick-up, and what they could expect from Scarlatti and Carrie. Everyone was grateful Max had insisted they reserve television time on election eve.

"At least we can have the final word," was Stuart's summation. "She can go on statewide television, confess her sins and...."

Roxy was outraged and interrupted him sputtering, "Sins? What sins? Adultery, lust, stupidity, bad taste in men, or just unlucky timing? At least she could have waited another week. That's what you're all concerned about really."

Stuart looked contrite as Roxy slumped into a chair and sniffled. She was so exhausted. Poor Kat. She glared at Hayes. There was no doubt in her mind that he would put political considerations first if she were lying there instead of Kat.

In a moment the three men were back to sketching out damage control. Their greatest concern was rumors.

"It's not the open attacks that are dangerous, it's the whispering campaign," Hayes explained to Roxy and Liz. "We'll need to watch the *Beacon* newspapers and the mail. Direct mail seems to be his new weapon of choice."

"I must be missing something here." Liz sounded impatient. It was the middle of the night and coffee cups were piled everywhere. For hours she had whined about there being no bar in the hospital.

She walked over to Stuart.

"Is your divorce final?" When he nodded yes, she shrugged. "Well then, why don't you just marry her and let the people of Rhode Island vote her into the Senate as a wedding present. We could probably call her uncle and do it right now."

Before anyone could respond, an anguished cry came from Kat.

"No! I won't marry him like that. I won't be forced. I won't sneak off in the middle of the night."

Stuart was at her bedside in a moment, promising they would get married whenever and however she wanted.

"The White House, a cathedral, a deserted island, whatever you want," he said soothingly. "But Darlin', once I'm vice president for real, you have to marry me if you ever want to see me alone again."

Dawn was still a couple of hours away when Terence Shanley quietly slipped into the room and reminded the vice president he needed to return the plane they commandeered and continue his schedule which began with breakfast in Saratoga at nine. Mario and Hayes left soon after to catch a few hours sleep before beginning the strategy they worked out. Roxy insisted she was staying with Kat.

"She'll be released by noon and you can come back and get us," she told Liz.

★ ★ ★ ★ ★

Max carried her up the stairs and moved the maple rocker next to the bed prepared to take up a vigil. Kat fought to stay awake long enough to ask some questions. She knew she had to return and struggle on but first she had to know why this had happened. Why had she been wounded? She felt certain Max could tell her.

The late afternoon sun lit his hair into a shimmering cap of white. The amber-glassed lamp that sat on the table beside him looked like the lantern in the tarot card depicting the seeker. Called the Wise One in the goddess deck, the man looked exactly like Max. Roxy had been right. Stuart was the Emperor and the Empress was pregnant. Kat realized the card had appeared in a reading well before she.... There was only emptiness now. She had scarcely adjusted to the idea of carrying another life inside her when it was gone, over, not to be.

She moaned and called Max. He asked a few brief questions about how she felt, administered several homeopathic remedies, then sat back down.

"Why?" Kat asked. "Why was the time so wrong?"

"Everyone has something they want from Time. Fortunately, or unfortunately depending on your point of view, cosmic scheduling has priority. The time was not yet but you and Stuart are impatient people and you command significant force, too much force to resist.

"The mythic experience owes nothing to reason. Balance is your quest and he's your polarity. The hero and the goddess reenact their mythic union in the Mystical Marriage of the alchemists. You haven't found the balance yet so you were unprepared for the test and paid the price: death.

"It's only a matter of awaiting the right time. A path has been set in motion by your joining that will lead to rebirth, not just the child you want but a world. What are you willing to pay to change the world?"

Kat stared at him silently, absorbing his words.

"Where is the balance we need?"

"In surrender. Both of you must surrender."

"Max, I can't surrender my place in the world. I've worked too hard. Duke gave me his heart, his dreams, his ideals. But I had to make my own place. As much as he loved me, he never believed I could be his successor. Even in his will he left everything to me but named Frankie to follow in his footsteps. You know how hard I struggled to find my own power when he died. I can't surrender to Stuart no matter how much I love him."

"Love is an equal favor which two lovers exchange. You won't surrender your power to him, you'll give it lovingly when he needs it, as he does to you. Truly great women recognize that men are fragile, needing bolstering and uplifting in their purposes. That's why men love Roxy, she always sees them through worshipful eyes. It's balance and completion you're seeking, not dominance."

"Do you think Stuart needs me to be complete?"

"No. He's complete, so are you. You need each other to be more. This experience with Stuart has brought you to full power. Once you face the demands of the flesh and senses, you're better able to understand fully the demands of the spirit. Don't forget, there's a body that goes with that mind. The senator and the slut."

"I'm not a senator yet," she smiled ironically.

She felt like they had been talking only a short while but the light was much dimmer in the room, the amber glow much stronger. She must have slept. It was tension that woke her and she began to cry.

"How did this all become so harsh? Why did the campaign turn from the elegant strategic dance of Sun Tzu to guerilla war in the streets, no rule but sur-vival?"

Max was standing looking out into the twilight, straining to see the gleaming water.

"It's in the air, in the time. Forces of separation and division are rampant. It's all part of the predicted end-of-the-millennium jihad, the holy war as the Age of Pisces passes. It's been predicted forever."

He turned to face her. "In order to strengthen the forces of light you must stay above it, Kat, while still obeying the basic rules of preserving your skin."

"Does change always require such chaos, loss, death?"

"You know the process, Kat. Initiation. Coal into diamonds. It's easier to im-print a mind with radical new ideas when it's vulnerable from defeat or confu-sion.

"By loving, having the life of child within you no matter how briefly, by los-ing that life, you learned about being a woman. And your love for Stuart was profoundly changed. There was a moment when it was sublime and took root in your womb."

She began crying. "But it died. And it's my fault. I rejected my own mother. All I am I took from my father. I ignored the virtues of Demeter, the mother goddess. This is my punishment."

She clutched at Max's hand. "Find her. Bring my mother here. Maybe if I can heal my wounds from her, I can have a child."

Max promised he would track down Celeste in the morning.

"Will I have a child? Can you see it? Can we ask the cards? Call Roxy." Agitat-ed, she pulled on Max's hand, desperate to know.

"We don't need the cards. You'll know. At this point you've stepped off into the abyss. All you can do is hope, and rest. Let go of your fear. Stuart is a great warrior. Trust his courage, his ability to protect you and the force that's in your care."

Max picked up the amulet he had given her in the spring and put it in her hand. "Hope, Kat. Hold on to your hope."

She fell asleep clutching the amulet.

★ ★ ★ ★ ★

Kat's state of mind seemed to improve with hourly visits Roxy made to her room, bringing her and Max tea, juices and fruit. By late evening, she was fo-cused and ready to discuss the campaign.

As she repeated the schedule for the next day, Roxy marveled at how good

Kat looked. She was sitting up in bed, resting against a mound of pillows. Her red flannel gown reflected a glow on her pale face. The complex geometric patterns embroidered on its yoke suggested a sense of order and precision. Her hair had some life in it and curled around her cheeks like a Victorian belle. She took notes as Roxy talked and handed her a list of assignments when she finished. She wanted lists of calls she should be making and insisted Roxy do phone bank calling from the house as well. Her final instruction was to schedule a strategy meeting at the house the next night, conferencing in Lila and Gould.

When she assured Kat there was no hint of question over the story that she had fallen down the outside stairs, and no trace of Race or Carrie, her demeanor relaxed and she fell asleep while Roxy was reporting the other news of the day. Turning out the light and leaving Kat to sleep, Roxy wondered why she never mentioned Stuart. Hayes reportedly talked to him hourly.

She returned to the group sitting around the kitchen and passed on Kat's comments. Before Hayes could maneuver her into some dark corner, Roxy announced she would go tell Jake, promising to have him at campaign headquarters the next morning by eight. As Hayes got up to follow her, she heard Liz call him back.

"This is Rhode Island, it's the home team's advantage." She did not hear what Hayes replied, after he laughed.

★ ★ ★ ★ ★

They shared the spinach pies Liz brought home from Providence, reveling in the abundant mozzarella, black olives, and chunks of pepperoni. Roxy waited until they finished and were settled comfortably upstairs in Jake's bed, the nearly full moon illuminating the heroic faces in the stained glass panels.

In no rush to begin her story, she asked Jake about the Erotic Lit class she missed that night.

"You would have liked it," he replied, tracing a slow spiral up and down the sensitive skin on her arm's underside. "It was cross-cultural sex. Christopher read from Chinese pillow books, exquisitely poetic pornography. You would especially like the genital names."

He slid his hand under the covers and gently tugged on the sensitive bud between her legs.

"This is called the pearl on the jade step." She sighed and rubbed herself against his hand. "And this," he guided her hand to his crotch, "is the jade stem."

Roxy felt his jade stem harden under her ministering fingers. As the lava began to melt in the center at the base of her spine, she remembered she had a message to deliver first. She would need Jake more later. He looked at her quizzically as she removed her hand and began relaying the events of the past two days. When she told him the true reason for Kat's convalescence, he was outraged.

"Are you upset that she was sleeping with Stuart and got pregnant?" Roxy asked, amazed at his reaction.

Jake laughed. "You're the only one who didn't know they were lovers. I guess I would've expected them to be more careful, but," he shrugged, "love will be served. Sometimes the goddess takes radical action to get her way."

His voice became serious.

"I hate the idea of Kat being hurt. I'm sure losing the baby devastated her, not to mention what it means to the campaign. But mostly I'm frustrated! I'm still powerless to stop Race Scarlatti from destroying something good."

Jake got out of bed and walked over to stand facing the sky god, his naked form glowing in the moonlight.

"Max was right to give me an amulet for fortitude. I don't have the courage Stuart has. Whatever is restraining him from ripping Scarlatti to pieces with his bare hands, it's not lack of courage."

He turned around to face her, fists clenched, arms rigid at his side.

"Race Scarlatti deserves to be crushed. I should have done it years ago when he almost killed me. I should do it now but I don't think I can."

Roxy almost choked on her heart skittering up her throat. She knew how Kat felt the previous night when she was afraid Stuart would set off, guns blazing. Race Scarlatti was a killer and she did not want Jake to die. Where would she ever find such a good man to love her the way he did?

"You can't go after Race! You're too good. You have rules and honor. He doesn't. Those guys always win. I couldn't bear to have something happen to you, to lose you. Please don't think about revenge."

Tears were streaming down her face as she realized how desolate she would be without him. She went over and wrapped her arms around him, burying her wet cheek against his shoulder. Distracted by his thoughts, he lightly brushed her hair. Then his focus shifted to the present and he moved his hands down her back pulling her closer. Heat rose as he stroked the cleft at the base of her spine. She felt his jade stem push between her bare legs and flashed on the cases of ivory colored carved jade with its delicate threads of golden yellow at the Smithsonian. She wondered how realistic the Chinese were in their naming. She stepped away from his embrace, holding the now erect object in question gently in her hand and knelt to examine it more closely in the moonlight. She wondered if there was rosy jade as she took it into her mouth to see if it tasted like jade.

She did not know if this was acceptable tantric practice, but it probably fit Liz's category of "muffing him around" as a way of finding better use for all that male energy. Jake wound his fingers into her hair pulling her face tighter against him.

Later they worked on vote counts for the next four cities: Lincoln, Little

Compton, Middletown and Narragansett. Jake insisted doing it for their home-town deserved an extra special hit and they agreed to shout the name of Narra-gansett in unison. As their simultaneous orgasm hit, Roxy was laughing so hard she was afraid she would black-out before the thousand little tongues of flame stopped tickling her.

★ ★ ★ ★ ★

The meeting with Race was quite satisfactory. As soon as she returned to her little fortress, Carrie opened the black snakeskin book on the table in front of the fireplace to the section entitled Attack and Vengeance. She found in the spells listed exactly what she wanted both for Race and for her own purposes.

He was toxic with anger and infection from the gash Kat inflicted on him Saturday night. Once Carrie pointed out how successful the mission must have been considering what the hospital records showed, the storm clouds around him seemed to lessen. Then she described what she saw as the bonus.

"Guaranteed, her white knight will try to be at her side as much as possible. That could cause quite a scandal if done openly so he'll have to be sneaking around." Race flared at the thought of Stuart with Kat. "And sneaking around means much less security, a much easier target, here on your turf."

She was rewarded with a display of reptile teeth that must have been a smile then dismissed.

"I will kill him. You keep watch in your black mirror and let me know when he comes."

Inside her stone house she felt safe to formulate her own plans. The only threat she could see was Max. He was not part of the pentagram web she was weaving. She would have to deal with him separately. It would not be difficult. She was sure he suffered from the fatal flaw of all ex-hippies; believing only white magic was acceptable in their new age.

She selected a binding spell for Stuart that would tie his hands, shear the hero's locks. She would create a Tanglewood charm of knotted rope. She settled in happily to torment the mythic lovers.

It was midnight by the time she set up the magic space needed for casting the spell. A circle was outlined in marble graveyard chips and pieces of bone. In the center was spread a newspaper clipping of Stuart with a large picture. She placed a black candle on the picture, a length of rope across the bottom. Then she sat in the center of her magic pentagram web to summon her demons.

Carrie was adept at rummaging through the darkest corners of her mind to call forth all the hate and rage she carried for everyone in the world who had it better than she, and that was almost everyone. As she felt the violent force pounding in her stomach, she arose and began moving counterclockwise around the circle. She chanted the jingle she made up to hold the spell. "You can't see her, you can't hear her, you can't touch her, you can't reach her."

She sat back in the pentagram, scattered some dust from an eighteenth century church graveyard and began casting the spell. She never stopped chanting her jingle as she lit the black candle and watched it sputter and burn, dripping black wax on Stuart's face. She imagined him bound in Washington, phone calls not being connected, messages misunderstood, lost in fog. As each picture flashed in her mind she tied another knot in the length of rope until there were nine. She laughed at the idea of the multiple frustration. Stuart could not get to Kat and Race would not have his target.

To complete the spell, she took the rope to a raised bed near the pond and buried it. Looking at the nearly full moon, she wondered if this stuff really worked.

20

Shellshocked
October 30–November 3

Rhode Island

Each day was so intense. Each hour was a turning point until the next hour provided another one. Roxy could not wait for the campaign to be over. She had Jake drop her off at the beach even though there was no time for a walk. She strolled along the seawall back to the house savoring a few minutes of peace and solitude.

Weather held to an almost balmy Indian summer pattern. The usual line-up of weekday folks hung out along the shore, mostly in their cars and trucks. The pick-ups were empty, their drivers out tossing a few lines in the surf hoping to hook a quick fish before heading off to work. Cars held office workers sipping their coffee and reading their papers while listening to the ocean. Off-season weekend wall hangers were mostly men, always watching the traffic not the water, sometimes on motorcycles. She wondered if they actually thought they could pick someone up that way.

After passing through the Towers with the twinge of lust she always got in memory, she stopped along the wall to stare at the stone beach. The huge boulders sat immobile. Every gradation of rock on down to the tiniest pebble was polished by the incessant pounding of the waves. Was this evolution or devolution being displayed for all the world to note? Her farewell glance before walking back to the house under trees naked of their leaves, was of the long, glittering curve of coastline with its necklace of sea-smoothed rocks and empty bottles. Is Kat's pain and anguish worth it when even the beaches can't be kept clean? She wondered.

★ ★ ★ ★ ★

She ran up and down stairs to the third floor library a dozen times during the day bringing messages, papers, drinks and food to Kat. Each time she walked into the impressive room, she wondered which face of the goddess she would see. The day began with Athena, efficient and in control. Kat moved through her calls reporting positive responses from most. Late in the morning the goddess of love arrived. Roxy found her sitting by the bay window on the deep-seated leather chair gazing at a newspaper photo of Stuart, tears filling her eyes.

"Why hasn't he called me?" she asked plaintively.

Roxy was amazed. She knew Hayes was speaking with Stuart regularly. She could not believe he had not contacted Kat.

"I've tried to call him but we never connect." Her voice sounded wounded.

Two hours later she was Demeter and told how she sent Max on a mission to bring her mother to the house. Roxy gaped, her mouth dropping wider as Kat explained she needed to accept her own mother before she could be one herself. Asked the obvious question, Kat's whole being glowed.

"Oh yes! I want to get pregnant again as soon as possible. Beau will be such a wonderful father."

Light was dimming when she went up the next time and Persephone met her straight from the depths of Hades. Kat was draped on the worn leather hassock, her head laying on the arm of the chair. She was crying, utterly desolate.

Roxy prodded her to go to bed and try to sleep so she could be functional for the strategy meeting they had scheduled that evening. Mario, Hayes, Liz and she would be at the house with Kat. Lila and Gould would be connected in by phone. As far as she knew, there was no plan to fill in the two consultants on the real truth. They would know nothing about Stuart.

She left Kat tucked in bed, unplugging the phone so she could sleep, and went down to take a shower. Roxy questioned if creating a new unified goddess from the different traditional ones required such suffering. If so, she thought she would stick with Aphrodite and concentrate only on love.

Checking the mirror for evidence of the waist-expanding properties of being Liz's captive culinary audience, Roxy heard Kat scream. When a gunshot and the shattering of glass immediately followed, her heart froze. Throwing on a robe, she raced up the stairs and into Kat's room.

Kat spun around, pointing the pistol at her.

"It's me, Roxy! Don't shoot!" She shook with terror. She never had a gun pointed at her before, and she did not like it. Especially when the person with their finger on the trigger had eyes blazing with madness.

Shock flashed on Kat's tear streaked face and she threw the gun into a pile of clothes. Gasping and sobbing she flung herself on the bed. Roxy staggered over to the window seeing nothing but pieces of glass where Kat shot out the pane. She moved to the bed and, putting her hand gingerly around Kat's shoulder, sat beside her.

Facing the barrel of a gun was no more terrifying than seeing Kat's crazed and twisted face as she cried, "It was Carrie! I saw her face in the window. She was laughing. It was horrible. And then she held up a knotted rope and laughed again."

Max warned about possible hysteria from the grief and told her to give Kat the Ignatia he left by the bed, should it occur. Roxy followed his instructions and soon had Kat soothed and back in bed. She returned to the office on the first floor and began feverishly writing. It was obvious Kat could not be counted on for extemporaneous brilliance at the speech she was determined to do the next afternoon. Roxy would need to have it letter perfect and hope Kat could focus enough to read it. She also hoped Max would get back soon, with or without Celeste. This brush with Carrie was too much for her to digest.

★ ★ ★ ★ ★

Kat was coherent during the call, assuring Lila and Gould that her injuries were minor and she would be on the campaign trail with a major speech the next day. They accepted her at her word and reviewed the nightly tracking numbers which showed steady improvement over the past week.

"No mention of your accident showed up in comments during last night's calling," reported Lila, "not that we would expect them to," she added. "Unless you commit mass murder in the next week, our new vice president will have you to thank for giving him a Republican Senate." Everyone on phones at the house saw Kat flinch at the mention of Stuart.

"My sources tell me Douglas is crumbling and only the massive Democratic effort for the whole ticket is keeping him afloat," Gould said.

When he received assurances from Mario that word in Rhode Island was the same, he began to wax eloquent about positive response to the final spot which began airing the previous week.

"You look like everyone's dream senator: calm, serene and wise. No one could say no when you give them that angelic gaze and ask for their vote."

Roxy felt her own eyes mist as she watched a tear or two trickle down Kat's cheek. Before her world had been turned upside down, Kat thought this was her best appearance ever. She once again wore the rose suit she had posed in for Gould's original senate picture. In the current version, she wore a necklace of interlacing hearts intricately carved from rosy quartz. Intuitively Roxy knew it was a gift from Stuart.

With Jasmine's departure, Gould took over the task of hustling national press and announced interviews scheduled for the final weekend with both a Boston paper read by many in the state, and *The Sunday National* read by everyone in the country. Kat silently withdrew from the conference call as it turned to detailed discussion of media buys of television and radio time. She idly flipped through the pile of daily news clippings. The conference call had just ended when she pulled a clipping from the file and waved it at Hayes.

"He's in Chicago," she said.

Hayes nodded and looked perplexed. "Didn't you know?"

There was a stricken look on Kat's face.

"I haven't spoken with him since…" She flung her hands over her mouth, her eyes saddening, and ran from the room.

Looking at Roxy, Hayes asked, "What's going on? Why isn't she talking to Stuart? I know he's tried to call dozens of times and for some reason or another couldn't reach her."

Chills ran along her spine. This had something to do with Carrie, she knew it. Hopefully Max would appear soon. Roxy shrugged and told Hayes she did not know why they were unable to connect. He promised he would try to arrange a call sometime the next day although it could be difficult since Stuart was plane hopping to campaigns all over the Midwest.

They began an endless round of speculation and concern about Kat's capacity to appear in public, especially considering the intense press scrutiny expected. When Hayes announced Stuart asked him to move to the Narragansett house for the remainder of the campaign so the three women would not be there alone, Liz barked "Ha!" and Roxy blushed furiously.

"I'd better get that speech perfect," she said poised to escape. "I'll have it ready for you and Mario to read in the morning." Roxy quickly said good night and fled up the curved stairs.

★ ★ ★ ★ ★

"We cannot afford to lose the skills of our senior citizens. We cannot ask them to work for slave wages simply to comply with a social security cap."

Roxy was reading from the next day's speech to a statewide assembly of senior citizens, posturing in front of her favorite ornately carved and gilded mirror, when Hayes quietly slipped into the room, closing the door behind him. She stood immobile as he walked over.

"I thought we could work on the speech together," he said in his most camellia-drenched accent. Roxy was certain the three fingers of space between them did not qualify as professional distance. She exerted all her will not to reach out and unbutton his blue shirt that exactly matched his eyes as he stood smiling at her. When he reached under the collar of her robe and slid it off her shoulder following his fingers with his lips, Roxy knew she was doomed.

"I missed seeing my favorite room in the house," he whispered against her skin. "It has so many delicious memories." He buried his face in her throat then slid to her breasts, dragging his tongue along the soft skin.

The knock sounded like a shot and Roxy screamed. Hayes jumped away and she pulled closed her robe as Liz walked in.

"I'm glad I knocked. It gave you time to practice those guilty looks. I'm not the safe sex police. Max is on the phone and I knew you wanted to talk to him." Roxy ran downstairs to take the call, wondering whether she should curse or bless the fates.

He was concerned about the incident with Carrie and promised to speak with Stuart. "There's angelica root incense to burn throughout the house. It will dispel any psychic evil that's around—in this case, Carrie. I also left a small jar of powdered herbs in Kat's library. It's marked Carrie and was blended to protect against her magic outside the house. Put a little in Kat's juice tomorrow before you go out. If you're going with her, you should take some too. I'll be there by six tomorrow evening, with Celeste."

★ ★ ★ ★ ★

Finishing her make-up, Liz took the towel from around Kat's shoulders. Roxy frowned when she saw Kat's bra was black. It was undecorated, not a touch of lace or ribbon.

"There's not much I can do to soften you up," Liz said as Kat put on a short red fitted jacked. "You're all black and white." Liz had tried to brush some color in Kat's angular cheeks but it only highlighted her lack of sparkle.

Panic flashed in Kat's eyes when Roxy insisted they all drink Max's protection potion before leaving. Hayes was picking them up for the ride to the Warwick Marriott where the meeting was being held. They stood on the graceful porch waiting, remarking about the unseasonably warm weather. Kat nervously fingered the single lion's head button that closed her jacket and worried aloud about still not being able to reach Stuart. She had overcome any reservations about trying to track him down. Roxy wanted more details about what exactly was preventing their connecting but Hayes arrived and Kat sat silent reviewing her copy of the speech.

They were pulling into the drive at the hotel when Hayes handed Kat a copy of that day's *National*. Stuart and several senate candidates were pictured on the political page.

"He said he's tried to call you several times. Not to worry. He's fine. He misses you and will call you from Washington."

The look of horror Kat gave him as she leapt from the car made the hair on Roxy's arms stand up. They scrambled to follow her into the hall.

It was the worst performance Roxy had ever seen her give. Pro-Douglas reporters were scattered around the edges of the huge crowd, many of whom had come to hear Kiley Tomasso speak. They gleefully scratched unflattering descriptions of the candidate that would be entirely justified by the television coverage. The room's lighting accentuated her bleak expression, her voice sounded strained and flat. Occasionally she would raise her head from the pages of the speech and her eyes would be blank. Roxy prayed she would recognize her place when she looked back down.

She thought it could get no worse until she sniffed and smelled.

"Carrie" she hissed, pinching Liz's arm. They spotted her immediately standing near the edge of the front section of chairs. When Liz made a move to go after her, Carrie smiled benignly and vanished behind a pillar and out a side entrance. There was no change in Kat's voice. She must not have seen Carrie staring at her from the audience. Roxy blessed Max for his foresight and hoped his concoction worked. The episode with the gun had shattered her nerves.

★ ★ ★ ★ ★

Kat jumped every time the phone rang. Hayes was in the office handling calls while Liz and Roxy sat around the kitchen table trying to distract her. They were all watching the clock waiting for Max to arrive. Impossible as it later seemed, they had forgotten Max's arrival also meant Celeste's.

Liz whipped up a batch of nachos covered with spicy melted cheese, black olives, hot peppers and sour cream to try and tempt Kat to eat. She added a bowl of fresh guacamole and sat down.

"Can I try out the trivia cards to my Senate Game on you, Kat?"

Roxy could not believe it. Kat had been mute since they returned from the speech and Liz wanted her to answer Rhode Island trivia questions.

After explaining the role of the trivia cards in the game and how sets for each state could be ordered special, Liz began barraging Kat with questions. After a few easy lobs on the early ones, the plan seemed to be working. Kat was interested.

"Now we get to the tough questions." Liz gave Kat a serious look then started humming game show themes.

"I'm ready," Kat responded with more life than they had seen in days.

"How much did Roger Williams pay the Indians for Rhode Island?"

"Nothing. They gave him the land. Williams claimed 'Rhode Island was purchased by love.'"

"Several times in its history, Rhode Island has been considered the national leader in various industries. Name three."

"Candles, textiles, and jewelry."

"Where did the name Rhode Island originate?"

"Giovanni Verrazano was the first recorded European explorer. He spent more than two weeks in Narragansett Bay. The first place he landed was Block Island which he observed was approximately the size of Rhodes."

"Hey, maybe that's why there are so many Italians in the state," Liz observed. "It was discovered by one."

"Christopher Columbus was Italian," Roxy chimed in.

"Yeh, but who could tell from his name? Verrazano is a sure thing. Now here's another question about our favorite ethnic group and political power base. What Rhode Island city boasts—notice that hype, Kat—boasts the highest percentage of Italian population in America?"

"Cranston," Kat whined with the flattened "a" common among natives of the town where she spent her teen-age years and where her brother still lived.

"How many points in Rhode Island are more than one thousand feet in elevation?"

"None," Kat answered quickly.

"That's right! The highest point is only eight hundred twelve feet and that's on the Connecticut boarder. Some slick Yankee probably claimed the spot for Rhode Island illegally so there would be at least one place above sea level in the state."

Liz paused and took a long drink of apple cider.

"This is the big one. This is how they'll choose their senator. What is the mascot of I-95?"

Kat looked blank. Liz started humming time's-almost-up music and smiling devilishly. It was her theory that Rhode Islanders never even noticed the strange apparition that was indelibly printed on the mind of every visitor who saw it.

"I'll give you a hint. There's a statue erected in its honor in….," Liz waved frantically at Roxy who shrugged.

"I don't know if it's Cranston or Providence at that point."

"It doesn't matter," Liz said. "It's right there casting its benevolent glance over the interstate, it's…"

"The roach!" shouted Kat, victoriously. They all laughed about the monster size roach that advertised an extermination firm to the thousands of cars passing up and down the highway, daily.

"You got them all right! It's an omen," Liz said solemnly. "The outcome of your senate race is now assured."

They were still feeling jolly when Max came into the kitchen, three silver dollars spinning across his knuckles.

"Your mother is in the living room," he announced.

★ ★ ★ ★ ★

Kat loosened her grip on the arm of the brocade covered Chippendale easy chair that matched the one in which Celeste sat on the other side of the low cherry table. They had retired to the second floor parlor for privacy. It was one of her favorite rooms in the house, catching the same late afternoon sun as did her library directly above. She used it as a personal office. The inlaid mahogany secretary with lattice glazed bookcase was filled with financial records, stationery, and a selection of books from her collection on myths. Kat allowed the intricate pattern of the peacock blue Persian rug spread on the polished wood floor to calm her mind.

She stared at her mother, searching for the path to connect them. She barely heard Celeste's complaints about Max's urgent summons and completely missed her mother's mention that he finally located her in Key West.

They did not resemble each other. Countless times during her teen-age years, Kat tortured herself into believing she hated her mother because she envied Celeste her looks. She wondered why, as her daughter, she inherited nothing but her flawless complexion. Celeste was the image of the ideal Miss Williams student with her blonde hair, blue eyes and willowy figure. Kat always felt alien: too tall, too dark, too angular and exotic. These exercises in self-flagellation always ended instantly in repentance for her envy and frantic assurances to divine forces that she adored every physical attribute that was a gift from Duke, primarily her hair—and she liked to believe—her heart.

Eventually she concluded she was some form of genetic averaging of her wildly opposing parents, a mutation of sorts, a hybrid. Max theorized her Aquarian energy made her a prototype of the future, confirming the thought that she was a type of mutation. For a while during their period of intimacy he advocated they have a child, claiming both their unique genetic configurations deserved further development and cross-breeding. She decided against the idea; her maternal instincts seemed abstract. She was concerned about children in general, children as the future of the human race, but believed she had no interest in having a child of her own. Now she knew how wrong she was.

Recalling her purpose in summoning her mother, she turned back to Celeste's conversation which was focused on belligerent demands.

"Why am I here?" her mother demanded. "I thought you never wanted to see me again. Is this about money?"

Kat's heart plummeted. Their last encounter flashed in her mind and she quickly repressed it. She did not want to be reminded of her mother's complicity in Duke's death. How could she reach out to this woman? Frantically she searched her memories for a time when her mother was there for her. Race! Celeste shielded her from Race. She willingly kept the information from Duke when he returned, and directed Kat to more suitable companions. Of course, Celeste's direction ultimately led to Jamie and more degradation.

There was no alternative. She had to do this for Beau, for herself, for the child she wanted. She knelt in front of her mother's chair, tears filling her eyes, and plunged into the abyss.

"It's not about money. It's about being a mother."

Celeste was shocked, then her eyes grew cold and spiteful as Kat told her story: about the miscarriage, about her belief that she could not be a mother until she and Celeste were reconciled. Kat refused all questions about the father.

"Well, you've never been very successful with men," was the opening volley in a stream of abuse directed at Kat for her years of neglect, her haughty attitude, her inability to love anyone but her father.

"You're just like him," she screamed. "You treat me as beneath your notice until finally you need me and expect that I'll be there for you. I wasn't there for him, and I won't be there for you either. Neither of you deserve my concern." Celeste pushed Kat aside and stormed from the room.

Kat ran down the main staircase behind her mother reaching the first floor entryway just as Mario came into the house. He nearly collided with Celeste, who was screaming for Max to take her home. When she saw Mario, her mouth twisted. A demented mask of fury settled on her face, blotching her perfect skin.

"You want a mother figure," she screeched venomously, "take his."

She pointed her finger at Mario, looking for all the world like the stepmother in Cinderella.

"Your father did and he was the result. You're just like him, bringing bastard children into the world, except you can't even do that right."

Mario's horrified face acknowledged the truth in Celeste's accusation. Kat collapsed onto the floor, sliding down the carved pillar that marked the end of the staircase. Max hurried Celeste out the front door while Mario knelt beside his sobbing sister.

Roxy and Liz arrived for the concluding scene and watched in disbelief as Kat pushed Mario away.

"How could you know and not tell me? How could you all have known, all those years, all those lies? Get out! Get away from me!"

Her voice was hysterical, her eyes rings of gray and black and white. As Mario backed away, his broken heart visible in his face and soft brown eyes, Liz moved next to Kat and gently helped her up.

"When was the last time you ate?" she said, concerned as she led the staggering woman back into the kitchen.

"Now you know that mother-daughter chats aren't like those in the Tampax commercials," Liz commented as she motioned Kat to the table. Moving towards the refrigerator, she whispered to a stunned Roxy, "You owe me a hundred bucks."

★ ★ ★ ★ ★

While Liz prepared an elaborate omelet, Roxy related Max's tale of breaking the spell Carrie had cast to keep Kat and Stuart out of touch.

"He had this knotted rope, just like the one you saw at the window yesterday. Only it was all muddy. He'd gone to Carrie's house and somehow found it buried. He dug it up and brought it here. While we watched, he pulled out this weird knife and severed the rope between each knot. The knife's handle was a bear jaw bone with the teeth still in it," Roxy hissed. "He said the magic should dissipate in a couple hours and you should be able to call Stuart, or have him get through to you."

Roxy did not like the empty look in Kat's eyes as she sat staring at her clasped hands.

Getting no response, Roxy changed the subject.

"What about tomorrow's schedule? You and Mario are supposed to…." She stopped dead when she saw horror rise in Kat's eyes like muddy flood waters.

"You drive me tomorrow, please Roxy. No Mario."

Kat's voice sounded as if it were coming from a distant cave. Roxy exchanged a panicked glance with Liz. This was not a time for Kat to jettison her most devoted aide, not to mention her… Roxy had difficulty accepting the notion that Liz was again correct, that Mario was Kat's brother.

"I'll be happy to drive. There's a reporter from the Newport paper who wants to travel with you."

Kat shook her head. "No," she croaked. "Not with us. Liz can drive the reporter separately and we'll arrange to rendezvous at specific events or locations."

Liz arranged the heaping platter of food in front of Kat and agreed quickly.

"No problem. I'll take care of everything and indicate on the schedule where you'll be seeing the reporter."

For several moments Kat stared mutely at the plate. Liz attempted another ploy.

"Let's do what my friend Belle and I used to do after school every day."

"What was that?" Roxy bit immediately.

"We'd call up boys! Let's call the vice president. Max said the spell was broken and we could get through. What's his number, Kat?"

"The vice president?" Kat asked vacantly.

"Yeh! Stuart! You remember him don't you?"

"Yes, I remember him." Kat answered as if the question were serious.

The glance Roxy and Liz exchanged was more panicked than before. They were attempting to wordlessly decide what to do next when Kat rose stiffly and moved to the cupboard. She reached in, took out a bottle and walked back to the table. She put it down, saying nothing, her face as vacant as her voice. They watched her go to the refrigerator and take out a bottle of juice.

Standing over them, behind her chair, Kat said, "I think I'm going to get drunk. If I'm very diligent I can deaden some of the pain, at least for a while."

She quickly polished off three glasses of vodka and cranberry juice as the other two women watched dumbfounded. Neither had ever seen her drink more than a glass of wine. The alcohol etched her expressionless face into a carved ivory grief mask. As she moved to pour another, Liz grabbed the bottle and glass and moved over to the sink.

"Don't be ridiculous," she said to Kat. "It doesn't help anything. Trust me, I know."

"And how long did it take you to learn that? How many bottles did you kill before you found truth in one?"

Roxy raised her head from the table as Liz remained silent.

"It took me two years," she finally whispered, pain filling her throat. "I want to save you that."

Kat nodded, tears rolling in a new crevice through her cheek.

"Don't you think I can spare a couple hours to learn it myself?"

Liz walked slowly to the table and put the bottle and glass back down.

"Let's talk about the pain. That will help more than alcohol."

"I feel betrayed—betrayed by everyone." She quickly reached across the table and grabbed both their hands. "Except you. Thank you," she whispered repeatedly. "Without you and Max, I would have lost faith entirely."

Keeping hold on the bottle, Liz asked "Who betrayed you Kat?"

It was a few minutes before she was able to stop crying and answer. There was a weak smile on her face.

"We can skip the obvious villains like Carrie, Race, my mother. I never had hope for any of them. But Jasmine hurt, and now—now…"

Liz poured her a glass of straight cranberry juice as Kat sat, tears still falling, wetting the backs of her hands.

"It was only in my maddest moments that I truly believed my father betrayed me by dying, leaving me alone, not giving me the opportunity to say good-bye. I knew it was the grief that distorted my mind. But he did betray me, and my mother. How could he have a son and not tell me? How could Mario not tell me? Letting me live for years with Mario as part of our family without knowing?"

"He gave you a brother, Kat. Just not by that name. And he protected everyone, even your mother. What was he betraying? Not his heart, not his own purpose. Betrayal is not always what it seems." Liz talked steadily. "What would have happened if Duke told you?"

"I would have hated Mario," Kat finally answered, her voice thick.

"How could you hate Mario? He's your brother. He loves you. That's why he didn't tell you. He would do anything for you. So would Stuart. Do you feel he's betrayed you, too?" There was a long silence.

"Do you feel you've betrayed something or someone by loving him?"

They could scarcely hear Kat's answer.

"No. No. I couldn't stand it if I didn't feel I could trust him completely. But

I'm so afraid for him, for us. All these forces aimed against us, how can we withstand it? I can't even talk to him." Pain and fear abraded her eyes.

"Knotted ropes, black magic, guns, lies. Why? Why is all this happening to me? What can I do? I feel like someone switched the character I was assigned to play. Max says I need to have hope. What can I hope for?"

"A lifetime of being loved by a remarkable man who you love in return. The Senate's not that important. How can you be promoted from goddess?" Liz grinned at Kat who managed to smile in return.

Hayes walked in with the telephone.

"The vice president would like to speak with you," he said. He handed Kat the phone, then turned and walked out of the room. Liz and Roxy followed him as Kat croaked hello almost inaudibly.

"It's bad enough dealing with crowded schedules and busy signals but to have to worry about black magic torturing old Ma Bell—a man has to wade through herds of fire breathing dragons to get to you. But it's worth it, I assure you, Darlin' even if my sword arm is getting a bit tired."

He chuckled and Kat felt security flow back into veins she thought were permanently empty. It would be only a few more days.

"I miss you." She was appalled that the strain sounded so clearly in her voice. She did not want to add to his concern. All lightness was gone as he responded.

"I want to be there cradling you in my arms, telling you it will all be OK, protecting the woman I love. It takes every ounce of will and discipline I can muster to stay away. I feel like I'm under house arrest. Shanley and my boys would chain me to my desk if I tried to escape. When I couldn't call you the ten times every hour I wanted to hear your voice, I reverted back to my old habit of having conversations with you in my head. You're there with me constantly. I can smell you and hear you. It's what got me through all those months when I couldn't see you. Now it's only a few more days."

Kat could barely speak as she choked back her tears.

"I can hang on. I don't want to make anything worse. And, as long as I can talk with you, I'll be fine." She tried to make her voice strong.

"You'll never start another day without hearing my voice. You don't mind if I call you before dawn, do you?"

Kat giggled in relief.

★ ★ ★ ★ ★

All day Thursday, Roxy felt like she was holding her breath, waiting for something more to happen. There was no denying there were weird vibes everywhere. She was exhausted from sitting up late into the night with Mario, offering what comfort she could. She was almost glad it all happened. Hayes went to bed early and she could count another night saved. There were only five more nights to go, then it would be over and she could—what? She fell asleep before she found an answer and now, driving around Aquidneck, felt no closer to a solution.

Although talking with Stuart enlivened Kat somewhat, she still looked like a pale imitation of her former glowing self. The muddy brown coat dress she wore was made from a fabric that absorbed wrinkles from the atmosphere. Her hair was lifeless and she stuffed it under a brown felt hat, disregarding pointed statements about how terrible she looked. She wore the jade Kuan Yin pendant Stuart had given her, rubbing it constantly. By day's end it was the only thing about her that glowed. She moved like a wind-up toy, smile painted on, eyes glassy, arm pumping as they visited shops, stood outside of grocery stores, and spoke to several moderately sized groups organized by her Albright cousin who had the Aquidneck vote well in hand.

Liz spent all morning at the house working the grass roots network in South County. Her methods were simple. She chose the echelon of neighborhood leaders just below their professional field staff and pumped them up. She fed them anecdotes, inspiration, reassured them about the polls, applauded their efforts contacting voters, and reminded them that turning out the vote on election day was the only result that counted. She noted who needed materials or assistance and what sort they needed. By afternoon, she was ready to trick the Newport reporter into believing Kat was as effervescent as usual. She was so successful in charming the woman that the candidate's debilitated state went unmentioned in the next day's feature story.

Kat was thrilled with the result even though Liz received almost twice as many inches of coverage as she, and credit for the best lines.

"You kept her from noticing the empress had no clothes," Kat praised.

They were on their way back to Narragansett at day's end when Kat told Roxy about her encounter with Celeste the previous evening and how disappointed she had been. Roxy began talking about her own mother.

"It doesn't always work that having a perfect mother inspires you to be one. My mother is a perfect … who's the mother goddess?"

"Demeter," Kat answered.

"My mother is a perfect Demeter. She wanted nothing more than to care for my father and me. She was disappointed to have only one child but never let me feel any guilt about it. All through school my friends loved to hang out at our house. My mother never yelled at anyone and always had fresh batches of cookies. She gardened and sewed and did volunteer work with whatever school group needed her. And she never neglected my father.

"She has a collection of Madonna paintings, statues and images that rivals the Vatican. As selfless as her devotion to me and my Dad is, never for a moment do I doubt that she is blissfully happy and totally fulfilled in her life. She never looked at another man, never wondered whether life could be more exciting. They still hold hands when they go for Sunday afternoon walks in the park.

"She was never critical although she could provide insightful and discriminating advice when needed. She seemed to understand perfectly the role of a parent, to guide their child to be the most they can be."

"So what's the downside here, Roxy?"

She looked over at Kat. "How can her daughter, the slut, ever hope to live up to such a model? I don't agree with your assessment that you would be an inadequate mother but at least you'll surpass your own mother in the nurturing department. I've often thought I've avoided motherhood in part because I know I can't be my Mom."

Kat broke their silence. "Did you ever notice how the princesses in the fairy tales fall in love and live happily ever but never talk of pregnancies or babies?"

Roxy wondered why Kat felt being a good mother was somehow inherited, a genetic trait. She looked over at her friend who glanced back, her gray eyes as cloudy as the sky.

"Where do your gray eyes come from?"

Kat looked bemused but answered.

"I often wondered that when I was a little girl. I felt so alien from my mother that for a while I was convinced I was a changeling, a fairy child left in my father's care. That theory immediately crumbled when faced with how obviously I was my father's daughter. My looks encouraged me to explore genetics, evolution, and all that. I eventually stumbled across an anthropological description of North African tribes with gray eyes. Romantically I decided my eyes came from some Berber captive dragged to Italy by a marauding warrior ancestor of mine. My grandmother had these same eyes."

"The grandmother Duke called you Kat after?"

She nodded.

"Maybe you can learn being a mother from her model. You can believe you inherited her Demeter genes. Maybe Celeste did give you the answer you needed when she referred you to someone else's mother."

Kat had tears in her eyes as she beamed appreciation of her friend's wisdom.

★ ★ ★ ★ ★

Carrie watched them in front of the Almart's in Middletown that afternoon, shaking hands, greeting shoppers and asking for their vote. She was pleased to notice how worn and grief stricken Kat looked. There was no trace of life in her and Carrie knew the substance to rid Kat's womb of the fetus had succeeded. She felt emboldened and abandoned her watch to go home and quickly listen to the previous day's phone taps.

She played the segment several times before conceding it was indeed Stuart and Kat. How had they broken the spell? She knew from the conversation that this was the first they had spoken. She could not decide whether Stuart's comment about black magic was serious or not. Running out to the garden area behind her house, she found an empty hole where she buried the knotted rope. Max! He was the only one who could have done this. She would have to neutralize him if her plan was to succeed. Returning to her little fortress she immersed herself in the chapter describing methods for counteracting magical interference. She would save the pleasure of torturing Race with the intimate conversation she recorded until she prepared the spells she would use on Max.

★ ★ ★ ★ ★

Roxy arranged to meet Jake at the Ocean View for dinner. She wanted to be out of the house before Hayes returned from his day of talking to anyone who had an educated opinion to offer. They had not been to the restaurant for weeks and she was pleased to find the "ears," crispy shrimp and tangy chicken were as delectable as ever. She was also unreasonably buoyed by the fact that Kat's autographed photo was still hanging in place of honor on the restaurant's wall. Obviously the dragon lady and her family were not wavering in their support. They sent Roxy off with a care package for Kat.

Once back at Jake's they settled in to watch some television before working on the next four towns: Tiverton, Warren, Warwick and Westerly.

"That leaves us only three more to go and we'll be finished," she said glancing at the list Jake kept by his bed.

"Does that mean no more sex for us?" he asked.

Roxy was shocked to hear the woeful tone in his voice. She was suddenly struck with how great an impact whatever choice she made would have on him. She wondered what Jake wanted from her in the long run. Before she could do more than mutter a few consoling words about how once they were finished with the towns they could make love just for the pleasure of it, the commercial of Kat asking for votes came on. As they watched, the picture on the portable television grew smaller and smaller until it was barely a postage stamp in the center of the screen. Jake snapped it off.

"I didn't want it to fade until she disappeared. What do you think it means?" he asked, disconcerted.

Roxy felt panic rush along her nerves and flip flop in her stomach. She caught herself and said with feigned nonchalance, "probably needs new batteries."

But she could not shake the feeling that all was not well and their work on the vote count definitely suffered. She awakened Jake before dawn and insisted they do the same four towns again hoping quantity might compensate for quality.

"How can I deny anything to a naked goddess in my bed?" Jake asked, his normal optimism restored by a night's sleep.

As she closed the door behind her, she had high hopes for a big vote in Tiverton, Warren, Warwick and Westerly, and thanked the whim of the goddess that brought her to Jake. Without him, she surely would have been over the edge months ago. Or worse, begging for crumbs of attention from Hayes at whatever cost.

★ ★ ★ ★ ★

She had gone up to bed at nine hoping to get enough sleep that she could survive the weekend. At some point she needed to think about what she would say on her statewide telecast Monday night. Roxy had asked about the speech several times. She instructed her to draft the main part of the address that would be a summary of her accomplishments and future vision. When she was still awake at midnight, lying rigidly in bed, shuddering at every banging of tree limbs in the wind, Kat conceded defeat and got up. She slipped on a black silk kimono and went into her library.

Pulling out the clippings file of Stuart that staff assembled for her, Kat spread them out on her walnut table. They covered almost every inch of the dark surface. His face was repeated dozens of times: smiling, looking serious, and her favorite, with a raised eyebrow and gleam in his eye.

She remembered that incident. It was a major televised press conference soon after Stuart was designated vice president. Posturing like a hot shot, a young female reporter asked about opposition to his naming from Swearman and the White House handlers. She seemed to be fishing for personal notice from Stuart. He gave her the look and held it silently long enough that scores of cameras flashed in anticipation.

"I can honestly say that the opportunity to sit across the Cabinet table from Bud Swearman on a day-to-day basis was a prime enticement of the job," was his response. She remembered thinking that day how completely the exchange captured the essence of the man.

Holding the clipping, she stroked the picture and crooned his name as the full moon erased shadows cast by the light over the table.

"If you come over here and do that, I'll give you a prize."

Kat gasped and spun around to face the door. Stuart was standing there grinning. He moved towards her.

Her heart pounded, almost drowning out the roaring in her ears. His lips were burning against hers and she held him tightly. He was solid, everything else whirled and spun at a dizzying rate from the energy they were generating. It was a whirlpool of sensation. She was intoxicated by this closeness, his smell, his body against hers.

When she came to her senses, she was sitting in his arms on the leather couch. She could see his lips moving, talking to her, although nothing made sense except the love in his eyes. She lightly dragged her fingers across his lips and as he kissed them exclaimed, "You're here!"

He laughed and grabbed both her hands. "Welcome back to earth, Darlin'. I'm here."

"But how?"

"I told the president."

She looked at him flabbergasted.

"I figured if I was going to ask for the keys to the car, he deserved to know why."

"What did he say?"

"He said his term of office would be a success if we would consider getting married at the White House."

★ ★ ★ ★ ★

She kept her eyes on him, afraid that if she broke her concentration the magic would end and he would not be there anymore. It would turn out to be a dream, a phantom, demonic torture from Carrie. He talked about the other campaigns he visited, progress on his approval, what he thought about her race from studying the nightly numbers and speaking with her team. He could have been talking ancient Mayan for all she knew. The only thing that registered on her brain was the tone of love in every word. When her silence began to concern him, he prodded her to tell him what had been happening.

Kat looked at him warily. His political world passed for normal. There were polls, press events, issues discussed, voting records compared. Her race never seemed to have functioned like that, contrary to what she planned. She shrugged and proceeded to tell him the saga of her past few days. She felt like a hapless soldier pinned down by enemy artillery fire as she reported the strange happenings: shooting at the apparition of Carrie, Max breaking the spell by severing the knotted rope, her failed attempt at rapprochement with her mother, and the traumatic revelation of her relationship to Mario.

"The direct hits are mild compared to the emotional aftershocks," she concluded.

Pulled back into the emotional chaos that flooded the events, she was so caught up in her story that she missed the growing grin on Stuart's face. When he began laughing, she was shocked.

"The plot thickens. Are all political campaigns in Rhode Island soap operas or was this one specially written for the state's favorite angel?"

Indignant that he would treat the horrors that had been heaped on her so lightly, Kat jumped from the couch and glared at him.

"My life was fine before you appeared in it," she accused.

He leaned back on the couch and laughed again.

"It seems to me that Scarlatti's obsession with you, the bad blood with your mother, and your father's procreative urges long predated my arrival. I'll take some responsibility for your press secretary's subversive actions but since they were directed mostly at having me eradicated, I suppose I've paid that price."

Kat blushed at the mention of Jasmine. Stuart cocked an eyebrow at her obvious discomfort.

"Would you care to enlighten me about why that neurotic bitch hates me so much? I can only assume it's more personal than the misfortune of being born male."

"Fuck you!" Kat muttered and fled out of the room.

He followed her into the bedroom and pulled her into his arms.

"An excellent suggestion," he said, kissing her deeply.

The anger poured fuel back in her veins and his obvious desire ignited it. Kat was thrilled to feel alive again for the first time in days. The force of longing in his eyes as he untied her kimono and slipped it off her shoulders in the bright moonlight that flooded her bedroom almost knocked her over with its intensity.

"What can I do that won't hurt you?" he asked between kisses.

From the sparks that skittered along her nerves, bursting in tiny explosions and setting off even more intense waves of pleasure, she knew it would take little to satisfy her. She led him over to the bed, pulled off his sweater and unzipped his jeans. Gesturing him to lie down on the bed, she smiled serenely.

"Allow me," she said softly, tugging on the cloud of golden hair from which his aroused nakedness stood erect, cocksure and ready for her caresses. As she settled herself comfortably and began pleasuring him, as Roxy would say, she was rewarded with a blissful groan.

"Thank you, God, for making me a man," he muttered stretching himself along the cool sheets, "and giving me a woman like this." He wrapped his fingers in her hair and surrendered to her lips.

As she felt the strange weight and consistency of his balls in her hands, Kat felt anger rise in her again. What was this about balls anyway? The thought pushed her mouth away from him and she sat up still holding the soft sacs in her hand.

There was a brief time lapse, then he groaned, barely lifting his head from the pillow. "What?"

"I have a question."

"Not now, Darlin'. Finish what you started first."

Kat jumped away to stand beside the bed. "No! Now!"

The tone in his voice was not amused as he leaned on one elbow and looked up at her. "What?"

"What makes them so special?"

"What?" His irritation sounded louder.

"Balls! What makes them so special?"

He stared at her for a moment. "This is why you interrupted our pleasure?

"Your pleasure," she said spitefully.

"Pardon me for pointing this out but 'allow me' were your exact words."

Kat snorted then repeated her question. "Well, what makes them so special that you have to have balls to do something?"

"Besides being essential in making that baby you want?"

Cuba and his alleged plans to play hero in a revolution suddenly popped into her mind. Now she knew why she was angry. If he were dead, there could be no child. She recognized the eternal female complaint. Men were always ready to run off and get themselves killed for some dream or another forgetting the women they leave behind, grieving.

"I suppose it was balls that motivated you to sign up for the 1990 invasion of Cuba; the desire to get them shot off. If it weren't for the president demanding you give up the notion, you'd be there on the beaches right now. It means nothing to you that… that… that without you, I would be….." The thought of his body lifeless on some Caribbean beach made it impossible for Kat to continue.

Stuart sat up and folded his arms across his chest as if shielding his heart.

"You prevented me from going to Cuba. The vice presidency offered me an honorable cover. Believe it or not, I feel the same way you do. Once I thought my goal in life was to have a meaningful death, a hero in battle. Not now that I've found you. Except for trying to protect you, which could be a full time job, my warrior days are over. I'd trade away anything for a guarantee that I would have twenty years of loving you, waking up each morning with your hair curled around my fingers."

As Kat stood transfixed by his loving confession, she did not notice his hand snake out until he grabbed her and arced her onto the bed, pinning her against the mattress with his body. He was poised to jam himself into her and she felt a twinge of panic.

"Balls give me the strength and will to do this," he said solemnly, then added, "but love conquers balls." He rolled onto his back and laughed.

Stunned for a moment, Kat too began to giggle and instantly found herself happily re-engaged in what Liz claimed was the best man-bait in the world.

"Are spectacular blow-jobs a prerequisite for being a goddess?" a satisfied Stuart asked later as he wound and unwound her hair around his fingers.

"Liz claims it's the surest way to keep your man."
"Ah, that Liz—what a woman!"

★ ★ ★ ★ ★

There were legions of tiny fairies tickling her skin, making sparks fly from her nerve endings. They careened along her arms, then danced around her feet and along her legs. When the tickling reached the soft skin on the inside of her thigh, Kat moaned and woke up feverish and aroused. The room was darker than it had been when the moon was still up. Dawn was only a hint in the eastern sky.

"What are you doing?" she asked, her voice husky from sleep, and now desire.

His lips were moving slowly along her left leg which he held lightly in his hand, bending it at the knee.

"I'm tasting you and imprinting it. Then I'll always know where I am on your body by the taste. It will also allow me to immediately detect any imposters." He nibbled a spot behind her knee. "Tasty, but not as sweet as this."

He leaned over and ran his tongue across her nipple. Kat gasped for breath and remembered the tantric promise that once attuned, lovers could reach orgasm without any touching. She was not sure she believed that but she now knew how little touching it took. Her body shook and exploded as she pressed herself against him and his tasting concentrated on her lips.

She must have slept briefly. When she opened her eyes again, the room was lighter and Stuart was standing dressed, watching her.

"I'll be back before you miss me," he said bending over to kiss her.

"Not unless you don't leave."

He laughed, then was clambering down the stairs before she could mobilize to get up. Within an instant, she was hugging his still warm pillow and drifting back to dreams of horny fairies threading stars through her pubic hair.

★ ★ ★ ★ ★

There was the barest stripe of magenta on the horizon as Roxy pulled into the circular driveway at Kat's house. She was surprised to see three men walking down from the porch, and more surprised when she realized who they were.

Stuart's Secret Service chief held open the car door and waited as the vice president detoured over to Roxy and gave her a quick peck on the cheek.

"Take care of my lady. I'm counting on you. I'll be back as soon as I can."

Gaping, she watched him climb into the car and jumped when Hayes slid his arm around her waist and stole a kiss.

"Getting him here deserves a reward, don't you think? I'll be around to collect later." He kissed her again and got behind the wheel of his car to drive Stuart and his agent to the airstrip.

Neither Liz nor Kat were anywhere to be seen or heard in the house. Roxy assumed they were still asleep. She hoped Stuart had stayed long enough to do Kat some good. He certainly looked satisfied, she mused, as she set out for a walk on the beach. A happy Kat would certainly make her own day of driving easier.

Roxy was not pleased by the flat gray scene that greeted her. Everything was fuzzy around the edges, as if the ocean oracle was hungover from too much full moon. Thoughts hung suspended in her mind like the mist hovering just above the surf. Only the white lacy foam of the crashing waves broke up the expanse of gray. A small rowboat with two men fishing bounced perilously close to the rocks jutting out from the Coast Guard House.

As fog closed behind her obscuring even the Towers once she passed through, Roxy shivered. Her past vanished, the future was as obscured as the curved line of the beach. She could not quite focus and just drifted onto the beach. It was not raining, but beads of moisture from the laden air collected like seed pearls gleaming on her black sweat suit. She kicked at several of the round, colorless objects that shone in the sand. They looked like the bottoms of soda bottles and she wondered what industrial waste machine dumped them on the beach. Then she realized they were tiny jellyfish, hundreds of them everywhere. She nodded to the old man as he emerged from the grayness. They often met at the same point, he returning from the estuary, she heading towards it.

When she got back, the fog had lifted, and the kitchen was filled with sparkling light. Kat was radiant, happily devouring several waffles heaped with fried apples. Thank heavens they didn't sit around talking about the campaign, thought Roxy as she watched Kat's face alive and mobile again.

"Doesn't the 'just laid look' suit her?" Liz asked as she put a plate of waffles down in front of Roxy. Kat flashed a silly smile and kept on eating. "Sure fire way to put a smile on anyone's face, male or female." Roxy caught Liz's glance and pasted a smile on her own face.

"I'm doing my part," she said, her smile reflecting genuine pleasure as she thought of the two hits Tiverton and alphabetical companions got in the past twelve hours.

They were on the road to their first stop of the morning opening a new community art center in Bristol when Hayes called on the car phone. Believing Stuart's claim that their cellular phone conversations were regularly screened, he insisted they pull off as soon as possible and find a public phone to call him back.

As Kat got out at a Dunkin Donuts to call, Roxy hoped the news, whatever it was, would not drain her restored vigor. She looked graceful and elegant in a gold wool fitted jacket with contrasting facings in a rich brocade. The skirt was long and tapered. Kat was wearing the brooch of Medusa, for strength, Roxy recalled.

"He had good news and bad news," Kat said, her sheen noticeably dulled but not gone. "The good news was that Stuart slipped out before the fog shut down the coast again." She sighed. "There have been so many other dangers, I never thought about worrying whether he was safe flying."

Roxy patted her hand. "What's the bad news?"

Kat sighed more heavily and tossed a copy of the *Ocean State Beacon* on the seat. "Douglas certainly has these boys in his pocket," she said pointing to an article that highlighted medical reports of her emergency room visit.

"How could they have gotten these records?" Roxy asked, horrified.

"I'm sure it wasn't hard. Hospital record clerks don't make millions. Now that they've made a point of this information, questions can be asked. I don't know what to say." Kat's voice was once again raw and strained. "With the numbers from last night showing me at barely fifty-four percent, we have no margin for error."

"Does that mean Douglas is at forty-six percent?" Roxy asked with disbelief.

"It means that every day voters are becoming more undecided and smear tactics like these," she flicked her hand at the paper, "make it more difficult for them to decide in my favor."

★ ★ ★ ★ ★

She almost forgot the problem that started the day. Events presented much worse ones. Mario met up with them outside the Ann & Hope discount store in Cumberland where few people seemed to have read the paper or jumped to any sordid conclusions. The parade of mostly female shoppers who poured in and out of the store greeted her warmly, pledging their support. It felt like old times again, thought Roxy trying to shake off the bad feeling she got when they met with cold faces, avoided eyes.

When she saw Kat flinch and turn her face away as Mario approached, she remembered the old times were gone forever. She promised herself that morning that she would plead Mario's case to Kat, begging her not to blame him. Roxy walked over to join them.

Mario's doe-like eyes were glistening with tears as he handed a sheaf of papers to Kat, who was attempting to ignore him.

"These are letters that were just mailed this morning. They should begin arriving tomorrow. Friends helped us get a sneak preview," he explained with a bleak smile. "They hint pretty directly that a botched abortion landed you in the hospital. We're trying to trace the source, how many have gone out, and to whom. Unfortunately, outright interception is a Federal crime. One they take seriously."

Kat turned to face him, her face ashen. She seemed to crumble and shrink before their eyes and Roxy swore the radiant gold of her suit changed into a putrid brown. He put his arms around her and cried. "I'm sorry Kat, I'm so sorry. About this, about everything. Please let me keep loving you, let me be your brother."

She stiffened and extracted herself from his embrace backing away. Her eyes stared at him, unfocused, then she turned and walked to the car. As if reaching the end of a short leash, she suddenly stopped with a jerk and turned back to Mario. "We're going back to Federal Hill. Let's talk there."

★ ★ ★ ★ ★

Their reconciliation was brief but complete. Roxy saw a few words exchanged, then Kat brushed Mario's beaming face with a soft kiss. There was no time for anything else. The Hose brought more bad news from the streets.

He was out 'round the clock, talking to everyone with the slightest scrap of information or rumor. The Bishop was sending a letter to be read from the pulpit on Sunday condemning Kat for her pro-choice stand. That would allow the Douglas-influenced media to raise the abortion question in every way possible and the accusation in the direct mail piece was bound to come out. When Harry Crast called Mario begging for a meeting that evening to discuss the *Journal*'s expected endorsement of Kat's candidacy, they knew the letter was in the hands of the press.

"Monday night is our window of opportunity," Hayes said. "We need to get it right the first time and that means everyone working on strategy."

Kat surrendered to the insistence of her campaign manager and chief of staff that Gould and Lila needed to know what was going on. He revealed that Liz was already on her way to the airport to pick them up.

"I knew you wouldn't want to waste time," he said in answer to the weak scowl Kat managed.

Initially the only spin their professional spin doctors were able to muster was from their own reeling with shock. Lila recovered sufficiently from her initial amazement to answer questions about the canvassing numbers that reassured them a bit about the solidity of their base support. Her assessment that getting people to the polls was going to be the deciding factor, especially with the Democrats mobilizing behind the straight party ticket, was one they all agreed with. But good ideas aside, Lila was befuddled. Every so often she would look at Kat and mutter Stuart's name as if she were a teenager whose best friend was unexpectedly invited to the prom by the school's football hero.

Gould was relieved the father was not Jake, which caused Kat and Roxy to exchange an amused glance. He advised waiting until the question was asked, answer truthfully that there was no abortion, and announce that she would address all issues relevant to her candidacy on Monday night. By then they would know what the direction of and fallout from Douglas' attacks would be.

"I'm not giving up on the people of Rhode Island," he insisted. "I think they're decent people, they love Kiley, and they'll give her the benefit of the doubt."

Kat frowned. It was not too long ago that he disparaged her for making that same assumption. But it seemed like they had no choice but to watch and wait. The only scheduled event for the weekend was taping a cable show with a friendly host who would not put Kat on the spot. Mario sent out no press advisory on her weekend schedule, waiting for strategy to be decided so there was nothing to cancel.

"She can't look like she's hiding," Gould insisted. They all agreed but had no idea what implementing that meant.

"I have Roxy drafting the body of my statement for Monday night. It's basically a summary of all our pitch lines with a concluding plea to consider their future. I want to show them my strength and give them hope." Kat's voice drifted off as if even she felt her words to be meaningless.

"What do you plan to say about Stuart?" Gould asked the question, but they all were thinking it.

"Nothing." Her face was expressionless. It was obvious they could pull no more information from her.

"Well, if he's exposed, it must be by you, any other way could be fatal," Gould warned. Then he continued wryly. "If I'd known the vice president's mansion was our real goal, we could have approached this campaign differently."

"It's not my goal!" Kat exploded with renewed vigor. "My goal remains what it has been from the beginning. To get elected to the U.S. Senate."

Mario's concerned voice broke the resulting silence. "What do I tell Harry Crast tonight?"

Kat's eyes still smoldered.

"Tell him there was no abortion and I'm prepared to answer that directly to him if need be. Tell him I was assaulted late Saturday night, pushed down an embankment, and suffered internal injuries from my fall. Assure him we know the assailant and will deal with him after the election. That we believe this incident should have no bearing on the support the *Journal* has given me through the years and I hope will continue. Promise him it will not affect my capacity to serve as a member of the U.S. Senate."

"And if that isn't enough?"

"Say nothing about Stuart under any circumstances. If he needs more information, tell him my assailant was Race Scarlatti. That should keep him sufficiently distracted."

SHELLSHOCKED

It was obvious to Roxy from the shocked faces that she and Liz were the only ones besides Kat who knew of Race's involvement in her miscarriage. Bruno snarled savagely and bolted from the room. Liz got up to follow him.

"Tell him not to touch Race until after the election. Then he can check with Stuart," Kat instructed, causing her consultants' jaws to drop even lower.

★ ★ ★ ★ ★

With a prophetic skill that rivaled Max's, Mario had arranged the national press interviews so that the journalists spent most of their time being shepherded around by staff, meeting supporters and voters. Once the campaign began careening down the circles of hell, he managed to stage only a single sitting of Kat for the press. It was scheduled to follow the strategy session.

Singing the opening bars of "Angel in My Heart," Liz announced Kat's reappearance, dressed and made-up for the press. Everyone applauded the transformation. She was dressed in a dramatically draped, lush raspberry silk blouse with raglan sleeves and matching slimly flared suede skirt. Medusa was once again pinned to her breast. Gold chains wrapped her slender waist and gold nuggets studded her ears. For a crowning touch, Liz pulled back her black curls, confining them demurely in a raspberry crocheted net. Kat looked unassailable.

She met the two reporters with their accompanying photographers in the main office of campaign headquarters filled with bustling volunteers making calls and sorting palm cards made from the postcard bearing Kat's picture. Hayes swore poll watchers distributing these cards could influence the vote by as much as ten percent. After a few photographs displaying the activity, obvious enthusiasm of the organization, and walls covered with clippings, photos and memorabilia, they moved into the back office. Hayes, Gould, Mario and Roxy took positions around the walls.

After the opening volley about the impending Republican Senate which Kat returned with her usual statement of independence, the *National* reporter asked about the progress of the panel reviewing Jamie's pornography collection. Kat smiled tightly and nodded to Mario who reported that hundreds of hours of film still had yielded no footage of Kat. He recommended contacting Harry Crast should the *National* require more details.

Kat stiffened when the *National* reporter held up a copy of the *Beacon*'s story on the medical report from Kat's emergency room visit.

"Why do you think the *Beacon* printed these records?"

"You'll have to ask the editor that question. Perhaps they're planning a series on escalating health care costs. I think the real question is the ethical violation of printing confidential records illegally obtained. I am certain South County

Hospital has the matter under investigation since their reputation and business would suffer serious damage should people believe their medical records are readily available to any prying reporter."

The sharp tone in Kat's voice cowed the Boston reporter who sat motionless. Then the *National* reporter mentioned the Bishop's planned letter.

"Do you find the issuance of this letter the final weekend of the campaign a problem?"

"The Bishop is carrying out the precepts of the Church he serves. While I object to his threats against me for exercising my duties as a Member of Congress, I have no quarrel with his rightful duties as shepherd to his flock. It is the position of my opponent who has flip-flopped on this issue which should be questioned, not the Bishop's or mine."

Kat was staring at the reporter and did not blink when he asked the next question although Roxy felt her own stomach plummet.

"Have you ever had an abortion, congresswoman?"

The Boston reporter gaped and quickly turned back to Kat for her reaction.

"It is obvious that even your colleague considers that an unacceptable question. However, knowing well your lack of journalistic ethics, I am certain my refusal to answer would be painted as an affirmative response. I have never had an abortion, nor do I ever contemplate having one. My support of a woman's right to choose what happens to her body has nothing to do with favoring abortion or with personal experience."

"Have you ever been pregnant?"

Kat rose from her chair and stood facing the two men looking like an avenging angel. "Throughout most of this campaign, the press has chosen to turn a blind eye to the many serious policy issues facing our state and our country. Again and again I have tried to seriously discuss a variety of approaches to these problems only to find my ideas ignored in favor of gossip, lies and rumors. I will tolerate it no longer. You have allowed my opponent to rob the people of this state of the opportunity to know what their future holds and to make a well informed choice as to whom they want representing them in this future. If we are not to discuss issues of concern to Rhode Island: the economy, impending banking crises, health care, family leave and a long list of other topics, then this interview is over."

The *National* reporter flashed a cynical smile, nodded and left the room. The man from Boston remained and listened to Kat's plans for economic revitalization of Rhode Island.

★ ★ ★ ★ ★

The taping Saturday morning went well once Kat assured her host that she was prepared to swear she never had an abortion. The segment would be shown repeatedly through election day. By the time they pulled up at Sacred Heart senior housing facility in East Providence and found Kat's young scheduler sobbing hysterically, they knew the letters were on the street.

"They won't let you in," Beth said between gasping sobs. "They said you were a 'brazen hussy'. Why would they believe Douglas' lies?"

Kat left her in Roxy's care and went to confront the lioness in her den, her jeweled cross that she had worn into battle with the Bishop, gleaming on her black sweater.

Sacred Heart became their final public appearance of the day although it was not yet noon. Kat retreated to her room, looking once again haggard and worn. Mario's report that the *Providence Journal* was sticking by its endorsement and also agreed not to bring up the issue of the scurrilous letters until after the election, buoyed everyone's spirits for a while. No one worried that he had been forced to tell Crast about Race.

★ ★ ★ ★ ★

Race was one of the first to see the letter Saturday morning. He was furious and shot the felt slouch hat off the messenger's head.

"Ask your boss why I didn't know before these went out," he hissed as the youth fled. He slowly shifted his unblinking gaze to Carrie who kept her face neutral.

"She is useless to me if the world thinks she is damaged, soiled, profaned." He sat, breathing evenly. "This is Douglas' doing. He's trying to steal my prize by making it worthless." He raised the gun and pointed it over Carrie's head.

"You will do two things," he said, sighting along the barrel. "All the votes we control will today be filled in for Kat. I want these letters stopped. I don't care what the cost."

He lowered the gun without firing. "Don't fail me. I could not forgive that."

Carrie thought that neither of Race's orders fit with her plans. She nodded her agreement and quickly left the house. She would make one call though, to Douglas. She speculated on how much the votes Race controlled would be worth to him. As for the letters, she hoped there was one in her mailbox so she could talk about it on call-in radio. Later, she would return and tell him about Stuart's surprise visit the other night. That would distract him from checking on whether she followed his orders.

21

For I Have Sinned
November 3–5

Rhode Island

The worship of Aphrodite on Saturday night began early for Roxy, sometime in junior high when she and her girlfriends stalked school dances for boys. Being short was definitely an advantage in those days, so were early developing breasts. Later on, Saturday night sin did not mesh with Sunday Mass and Communion so Roxy gave up all but lip service to the church of her childhood. She maintained her devotion to Saturday night through various love affairs and bleak periods. Part of her aversion to married men was their resolute assignment of that night to their wives. Kat's campaign was her first experience with Saturday night interruptus. This one had the earmarks of a sojourn in Hell.

With all crews prepared for an intensive two days of lit drops including copies of the expected *Providence Journal* endorsement, Liz returned to cooking. Her fingers never ceased picking lobster, peeling vegetables or rolling piecrusts as she bitched about the noticeable drop in volunteer enthusiasm.

"Don't they realize this is the home stretch? Everything up to now means nothing if we don't get those people out to the polls."

Roxy smiled. In less than four months Liz had become a campaign expert. Then Hayes weighed in on the side of pessimism.

"It's a known fact that panic travels faster than the speed of light. If people begin to think Kat's going to lose, they'll melt away into the fog and we'll never see them again."

"Kat's not going to lose," Roxy said with a certainty she did not feel. Liz kept slicing apples into her three piecrusts and Hayes shrugged.

"Speaking of knowing outcomes, where's Max been?" Liz asked no one in particular.

Hayes appeared unconcerned and Roxy had no answer. She asked Kat the same question earlier and was surprised to find even she did not know.

"Everything will be ready in half hour," Liz said as she directed Roxy to go up and summon Kat.

"There's no reason for her to pine away in her tower when she could be down here eating and yucking it up with us."

Roxy rose to follow her instructions although she had not noticed much hilarity in the kitchen for the past couple hours. Seeing Mario and the Hose approaching the back door, she hoped the mood might improve.

Kat was leaning on her outstretched arm against the wall of her bedroom, cursing as Roxy walked in.

"I'm so out of balance I can't even stand straight any more."

She knew that meant Kat could not hold her favorite pose for minutes on end, standing on one leg, the sole of her other foot pressed against the inside of her knee like some non-colorized flamingo. She agreed to come down for dinner as soon as she showered.

Roxy bounded down the stairs, startled as Hayes emerged from the empty bedroom on the second floor to block her path.

"I hate these shapeless sweaters," he said, sliding his hand under the wildly printed one she wore over dark wool tights. "Although they may have redeeming value," he amended as his wandering hand reached her bare breasts. Somehow he maneuvered her into the dark room.

Her body was breaking new ground in betrayal of good intentions as he kissed her and rubbed her nipple between his fingers. His free hand inserted itself beneath the elastic of her tights and wiggled down to begin caressing the tight roundness of her cheek. His fingers slipped easily into her moist crotch and Roxy summoned all the will she could in the final moments before her body surrendered.

"No, Hayes, please don't," she moaned. "Not now, not like this."

There were tears on her face and in her voice. She was amazed when he backed away withdrawing his hands. There was just the slightest tinge of disappointment to her gratitude.

"Jake called. He'll be about an hour late."

He smiled archly, blue eyes twinkling as he headed down the front stairs motioning Roxy towards the back ones that led directly into the kitchen.

★ ★ ★ ★ ★

It did not have the jolly atmosphere of some wakes she'd attended but Roxy had to admit the mood was lighter than circumstances would have predicted. Liz deserved full credit for driving depression into some dark corner where Roxy felt certain it would lurk and spring on them unexpectedly during the next couple of days. But for now it was laughing, eating, and no discussion of the campaign.

Mario added a huge platter of homemade raviolis from Yola to the table already covered with several loaves of French bread, trays of sliced raw vegetable and dips and a bowl of lightly dressed lobster chunks for lobster rolls. Creamy quohog chowder steamed in a giant cauldron on the stove and the three pies were cooling on a rack by the window. Two bottle of Rhode Island Red from Sakonnet already lay empty and a third was preparing to join them.

As Kat began to demur about the vast quantities of food, Liz planted her hands on her hips and glared.

"Haven't you learned anything these past few weeks? When your stomach is full you start on a lung. It's easy, watch Bruno. Of course, he is the Hose."

The two grinned lewdly and Roxy was again astonished at how delighted the incongruous pair were in each other. Bruno was slim and graceful, a young dandy whose skewed nose barely prevented him from being pretty. Liz was a fine figure of a mature woman, a true mountain mama.

"It's a known fact, dicks have real bad eyesight," Liz explained one day. At least watching them kept her eyes off the other incongruous pair at the table.

Hayes and Jake sat together across from her, engrossed in discussing the comparative merits of fishing the Atlantic off the Outer Banks and Block Island. It was the first opportunity she had to examine them side by side. No doubt about it, Jake's gleaming smile, dark hair and eyes, perfect features and remarkably expressive eyebrows declared him the more handsome. But it was Hayes' sandy hair, bristly mustache and iridescent blue eyes that were more compelling to her.

Kat and Mario had their dark heads close together reminiscing about historic Tomasso feasts all of which featured Yola's renown raviolis.

They were finishing off one of the apple pies when Kat asked quietly of her newly discovered brother, "How long have you known?" Roxy tuned in to their conversation. She speculated on that point with Liz as they sliced carrots earlier in the day.

"My mother told me the night after Duke died. She felt I should go through the funeral knowing it was a tribute to my father. We wanted to tell you but you were much too fragile for any more shocks. And then after a while it didn't seem to matter to me. The only relationship it would have changed was with Duke and he was gone. I couldn't feel any more like your brother than I already did. And, I knew how you would feel. I didn't want to cause you that pain. I didn't want you to remember Duke as anything but perfect."

"Would you have kept it from me forever?" Kat's slender hand was laced with protruding veins as she gripped the fork tightly.

"Maybe," he answered in a tone full with self-reproach. "I guess the horrible way it happened was my punishment for not telling you sooner. I'm sorry you got caught in the backlash."

Roxy watched tears trickle down Kat's cheek as her own eyes filled.

"You know, we're not the only sordid political gossip in town," Liz announced opening the morning paper. "Here's this state senator, Glen Harri, who was arrested for shoplifting condoms. But the worst part is the bozo was hiding them in his sock."

"Those white bread boys can't do nothin' right," the Hose exclaimed. "He probably thought that's where they went."

Liz allowed Mario and Bruno to indulge in a few minutes of macho boasting about their superior place in Rhode Island's notable ethnic mix before she changed the subject dramatically.

"OK Kat, for months I've been hearing about the goddess and her various characters. I know that as a Catholic this is nothing new for you. You've been worshipping the goddess in the Virgin Mary for years. And I understand the basic plot—the angel, mother, slut series. But, there's something more in the air and I want the short-form explanation in words I've heard at least once before in my life."

Hayes jumped in with his own questions before Kat could compose a response that would meet Liz's stringent requirements.

"Is this goddess stuff another ploy for dominance once 'God is woman' failed?"

"The goddess is definitely not about dominance of any sort. In fact, she offers the opposite—partnership, valuing of both male and female," Kat answered.

"I understand that," Liz chimed in. "Each sex has its own particular equipment and it works best when we put them together." She slapped away the hand Bruno stretched out towards her in agreement.

"We talk about the goddess in ancient vocabulary but actually the need is for a new, mature goddess, a unified image. Aphrodite's sensual nature blended with the wisdom and independence of Athena. She'll cherish the Earth like Artemis and children like Demeter and serve both the inner and outer community as Persephone and Hera."

"She'll need a new name," Roxy said. "Maybe we can call her Star."

Kat nodded and continued.

"There was once a unified Great Goddess who was worshipped as the principle of life. Then nomads swept from the barren corners of the globe with weapons of death and demoted her, sliced her into weakened pieces which are the tradition we inherited. Now is the time when those wounds can be healed and a new goddess Star," she smiled at Roxy, "can usher in the next millennium."

"And she'll rule the world for five thousand years?" Hayes asked.

"No. She'll join with the hero and as partners they'll live in harmony with the world, hopefully forever. Once again humanity will worship life rather than death."

"Oh, I love it when stories end with they lived happily ever after. Roxy's always end that way," Liz chided.

"As a Libran, I love the notion of a balanced world," added Jake, earning a radiant smile from Kat.

"If we could clone a thousand Jakes," she responded, "we'd be well on our way to this splendid new era."

On cue, the phones in the other room began ringing and both Hayes and Mario jumped up to answer them. Seeing her opportunity to leave on a high note, Roxy pulled Jake away. He was a willing captive. They left while Hayes was juggling a phone in each ear.

"All this talk of goddesses makes me want to indulge myself in the perfect emissary she's sent to me," was his farewell comment, inciting applause from both Liz and Kat.

★ ★ ★ ★ ★

"I have a present for you." Jake was grinning broadly as he slipped a video tape into his machine. "It's actually a joint gift from me and Pete."

She sat mystified, waiting to see what would appear on the screen. The opening scene highlighted the title "Check Please," then shifted to Pete and Jake posed in the pagoda shaped entrance of the Ocean View. From there the pace accelerated and Roxy's giggles kept up turning into belly laughs. The two men changed clothes, restaurant locales and postures as they conducted a series of "check please" scenes. They stood up, sat down, and laid on the floor. They waggled fingers, glasses and Pete's pipe. They chanted, they shouted, they yelled in languages that matched the cuisine. They included every restaurant the three of them had visited during the past year and several only she and Jake had sampled.

The finale was filmed at Jack's and included both their favorite waitress Maria, and Max. Once they did the usual "check please" routine, the camera shifted to the magician who deliberately took a five dollar bill and folded it into a heart shape which he puffed out so it made a tiny holder. He palmed the masterpiece, pulled it from behind Maria's ear and handed it to her as a tip.

Roxy was in tears—from hilarity, from sentiment. Kat was right. A thousand Jakes would guarantee a better world.

That night there was an fragrance of roses and a taste of honey she never noticed in their lovemaking previously although they did no ritual preparations, no focusing on vote counts. Realizing she yearned for his hero juices with a passion that rose from her heart rather than elevated kundalini energy, Roxy knew a big step had been taken. She wondered where it would lead besides to the bliss that was her last waking sensation.

SENATE MAGIC

★ ★ ★ ★ ★

Bolting upright in bed, Kat woke from the nightmare, heart pounding, limbs trembling in shock. Election day was over, she missed it, no one told her! She struggled to bring herself fully awake, to escape lingering dream images of sobbing crowds trampling her Kiley for Senate signs littering the ballroom floor. The phone was ringing. She reached to answer it. There was only one person who would call at four a.m.

It was his voice that greeted her from the other end of the line.

"Hi, Darlin'. I was wrong about the diligence of your press secretary. You rate a full page in the *Washington Daily*. Photos, too."

Kat cringed. This was not good news. She pushed a tangled mass of black curls away from her face and moved the phone closer to her ear.

"Do they name you?" she asked, her voice filled with fear-residue from her dream.

"Oh yes, I make the list."

"List?"

"More than a dozen photos of you, each with a different man."

"What? What men?" Kat was stunned.

"It's distinguished company and you look gorgeous in every picture, as usual. You and President Jamison are standing tanned and smiling on the deck of some boat. In the picture with Prince Charles they catch your nose at a bad angle but compared to him you're a sculptor's dream."

Kat groaned as he continued. "And I thought we had something special.

"There's one of you making eyes at Charlie Drummond from ABC. Guess you made it into his little black book after all. Another one has you dueling eyebrows with some Hollywood hunk…"

"I don't want to hear any more," she said attempting to halt his amused recital.

"Wait. The three best are coming up. You and the Dalai Lama, then you and three New Guinea mudmen. I think those three are mudmen, although they could be the Democratic Senate leadership. Finally, there's a picture that must be at least a decade old. Your face is fuller and your hair is long and wild, just the way I like it, and covered with white lace. You're standing with a demure look next to the Pope."

"The Pope! You can't be serious." Kat rubbed her eyes and looked out the window at the dark sky. Was she actually awake?

"It's fortunate I'm a secure man— one with balls, as you well know. I'm not shown until the bottom of the page. We do look good together though, better than you and the Holy Father. I'll admit to a bit of pride that my lady is able to tempt the Supreme Pontiff of the Roman Catholic Church. That should win you a few undecided votes in Rhode Island."

Muttering obscenities under her breath, Kat slid a long leg out from under her crazy quilt and onto the wood floor. She shuddered at the glimpse of her face in the carved walnut dressing mirror that stood near her bed. Patting the hollows beneath her prominent cheekbones, she acknowledged he was right. Her face was more angular, gaunt in fact. The campaign had taken its toll.

Dark eyebrows, high bridged nose, unruly mane of black hair—she resembled a pre-Mosaic Egyptian queen or goddess. Or an albino raccoon, she thought, dismayed as she rubbed the dark smudges beneath her large gray eyes fringed with thick curly black lashes. Her wide mouth, bare of its usual red lipstick cover, added to the impression.

"I'm bringing copies of the paper with me for your memory book. I'll be there in a couple hours. Have someone meet me at the Charlestown airstrip and assemble your team for a meeting probably by 7 a.m." Kat barely heard his words.

There were only two days until the election. What could she do to counter this in such a short time? As if reading her mind, his voice became serious.

"The headline says it all: 'Who's the Lucky Man?' Either their source doesn't know about me or he's waiting to up the suspense—and the price—by exposing us piece meal."

"He? Do you know who…?" Kat's voice was strained.

"Preventive measures have been taken," he said quickly. "I'll tell you when I get there."

An angry flush crawled up her face and emerged in her tone. "What do you mean, 'preventive measures?' What have you done? Why do you refuse to talk with me before going ahead and…."

"There's no other way, Darlin.'" His deep voice was patient but firm as he interrupted. "This is my scandal, too. It's come down to war and I'm committed to getting you out alive. I'm sorry I didn't consult you before drawing my sword. That's the problem with us heroes, we take all this chivalry to heart. I'll be there soon. You can berate me in person."

As he hung up, Kat lowered her head into her hands.

"Men," she muttered, "and their fucking balls!"

★ ★ ★ ★ ★

It was a reflex action. Roxy answered the phone that woke her, realizing too late she was at Jake's. It didn't matter. It was Kat asking her and Jake to be at the house by seven. She wondered what new calamity had developed.

It was dark when they rolled out of bed. Dawn was breaking as they reached the beach. Roxy begged for a quick walk. They had an hour before Kat wanted them. She was enchanted by the galaxies of starfish covering the sand beyond the Dunes Club.

"Can I make a wish?" she asked.

He nodded then took her into his arms and kissed her bow-shaped mouth soundly. Walking over to the nearest starfish he kicked it aside.

"That takes care of my wish on that one. Now it's your turn."

"Do you think there are two hundred and fifty thousand of them here? And will I have enough time to wish for a vote on each one?" she asked plaintively.

Jake laughed and promised that later he would show her a collection of them near Point Judith that would boggle her mind, and provide more than enough wishes for every vote they needed.

★ ★ ★ ★ ★

"Do you know where Max is?"

Roxy was absorbing the scene in the kitchen and ignored Kat's question for which she had no answer anyway. There was a newspaper spread on the table covered with pictures of Kat. Stuart was casually disguised in jeans and a VMI sweatshirt, leaning against the counter, grabbing hot cinnamon rolls from the pan Liz pulled from the oven. He tossed one to Terence Shanley, who settled his giant frame in a chair near the back door. She slipped into the chair next to Kat and picked up the newspaper.

"Who's the Lucky Man?" she read, howling as she saw the pictures. "From the looks on their faces, I'd be inclined to pick Charlie Drummond."

"He looks at all gorgeous brunettes that way," Stuart remarked.

Kat scowled at him. "I'm sure we can make jokes about this all morning but that won't save my race or win you a Republican Senate."

A contrite looked crossed his long face.

"It could be worse," he said, and tossed a manila envelope onto the table.

"A special treat you were saving until later?"

He shrugged.

"I wanted you to see the public version first."

Kat slipped a large glossy photograph from the envelope. She pulled off the note and read it. Roxy snatched the picture, her heart skipping a few beats.

"Wow! This would blow your cover in a second."

"Exactly what the note says." Kat read: "Couldn't stop the story but did manage to switch pictures. This would have made the answer too easy for anyone with eyes. Lucky lady." She lifted her eyes to Stuart. "A fan of yours, I guess. Where did this come from?"

"I found it on my doorstep late yesterday."

Kat waved away the picture and Roxy passed it over to Liz who began humming the opening bars to "The Look of Love." Like the one in the paper, the photo had been taken the day they were at Little Compton. Stuart had the mallet in his hand and he and Kat were gazing at each other with a look that could only be described as rapturous.

Stuart pulled up a chair facing Kat and took both of her hands.

"This is all they have. Whoever is behind this, besides Emmett Douglas, is trying to draw you out, get more concrete proof. The scum that work for this paper can smell a scandal somewhere but don't know quite where. I've tied to plug all the leaks to give you time. Tomorrow night you'll have to tell them something but it will be your show, your agenda."

"What leaks did you plug?"

"The pictures of us came from Carrie. Somehow, she's the link between the various parts. The Hose is convinced she's freelancing on this, that Scarlatti is not behind it. Your friend Race has been assisting you, in fact. Rumor has it that no more letters accusing you of having an abortion will be sent, and many of those already mailed have been—ah, rerouted. Max assures me he has neutralizing Carrie on his list. I gave him a toy that might help."

"My team seems to prefer you as their captain."

"Nobody's forgetting who's the star. I'm getting help from your friends not stealing your team."

It was too much for Kat to absorb. She focused on Max's whereabouts.

"Do you know where he is?" she sounded perplexed.

"He should be here any minute with your mother."

Before Kat could pursue that information, Stuart went on.

"The direct source to the *Daily* was Douglas, courtesy of your ex-husband. I have no idea how he knew but he'll have no more information to trade."

"What have you done with Jamie?" Kat's voice was barely a whisper.

"He's on a fishing trip in the Gulf. He'll be back after the election, unless he pisses off the Cubans who are manning the yacht."

Kat paled.

"That's kidnapping."

"Pardon me, congresswoman, but it's a known fact that the Vice President of the United States does not kidnap people. When Caldwell returns from his cruise, he'll find the U.S. Attorney waiting with a fistful of indictments. I'm sure he'll be grateful for the opportunity to spend a few days at sea before being retired to an empty cell at Raiford."

"But how did he know about anything?"

Before Stuart could answer, Max came in dragging Celeste behind him. Once she caught sight of the vice president a strange smile came over her face.

"Well, I see Jamie was right. How unfortunate he couldn't prove it."

As Kat gasped, Stuart tightened his grip on her hands seeming to will her strength. Her eyes were glassy as she looked back at him.

"My mother?"

Celeste sat, crossing her legs and examining Stuart. She answered her daughter.

"Surely you're not surprised? Your ex-husband has always been far more amiable than you, and much more generous both with his money and himself."

Kat began breathing heavily.

"My nerves are shredded, my mind is mush. I surrender. What do you think I should do?"

"It's not advisable to allow venomous snakes the run of the house, Darlin'. The decision is yours to make but remember we need to buy time."

A light blazed deep in Kat's eyes and she turned resolutely to Max.

"Please escort my mother to the file room on the third floor. It locks from the outside." She shifted her gaze to Celeste who suddenly looked peaked.

"If you touch one thing in that room Mother, I will personally break every bone in both your hands and rearrange your nose. Stop huffing. You'll be released when the polls close Tuesday night. If necessary, you'll be kept—shall we say—sedated. Max has many potions. You may even enjoy it."

By the conclusion of her speech, Kat's voice could have cut diamonds. Celeste's eyes were big as saucers, and she moaned piteously, too terrified to speak as Max led her up the back stairs.

"Who else?"

Stuart shrugged again.

"Jasmine?"

"She's enrolled in a three-week stop smoking program in the mountains of West Virginia. No phones, no contact with the outside world," Liz explained.

"Jasmine doesn't smoke." Roxy immediately regretted her comment as Liz fixed a glance on her.

"Then I guess she'll be the star pupil, won't she," Liz said, disgusted.

"I think we've got our bases covered," Stuart concluded.

Kat stared at him in disbelief.

"How do we keep this from being headline news on television and in tomorrow's papers?"

"This is tabloid trash. You won't confirm anything and no respectable media outlet will proceed with such flimsy evidence. The papers Douglas controls won't be out until Tuesday morning. By then, you'll have told your story. For now, the campaign must go on as usual."

He motioned Mario over.

"What's on her schedule for today?"

Kat stared at them as if they had sprouted an additional pair of heads each. Stuart nodded as Mario explained then addressed Kat very gently.

"You and De Palma should go to Mass and make the usual stops afterwards."

Her head swung back and forth between them.

"You're crazy!" she croaked. "What do I say? I'll be besieged, if not about this then about abortion rumors."

"You smile and announce you'll be making a statement tomorrow night about whatever you don't want to answer and invite them to tune in and watch."

"I don't know that I can control my reactions," Kat said.

"Isn't there something in your little first aid kit for that?"

Discussion seemed to be over as Stuart rose from the chair and began directing the activity, barking orders to everyone. In the same tone, he sent Kat upstairs to calm down and get dressed. Pulling out his phone he began dialing, smiling absently as she stood up.

★ ★ ★ ★ ★

The slate floor felt cold under her thin slippers as she stared at the Jacuzzi, watching it fill with steaming hot water. She must have turned it on. She was the only one in the plant-filled conservatory. As Max touched her arm, she jumped. All her anger and exhaustion poured out.

"He's ignoring me. I'm only the face that accidentally is attached to the senate seat he wants. I feel like I've been plugged into a whole marching band of high tension towers and voltage enough for ten cities is being poured along my nerves. If I put a toe in that water, it'll be ionized in a flash, or turned to steam. What do I do?"

The desperation in her voice was matched by the death lock she put on Max's arm.

"It doesn't take much of a wizard to know the answer to that one, Kat." She looked thoroughly confused.

"You're out of balance and the way back is in the other room. That's why he's here. Use him."

She considered his words then laughed.

"Am I always so blind to the obvious?"

"Sometimes your elevated vision causes you to lose sight of the ground under your feet."

Kat looked like a still-wet pen and ink sketch with her pale face, black silk kimono and wild hair.

"I guess the goddess of chaos needs a lightning bolt to bring her creativity to the surface. If you will excuse me, I'm going to stand under a tree and pray for a thunderstorm." She walked back into the kitchen.

"Hang up," she said to Stuart, no compromise in her voice. He complied immediately and stood waiting.

"If you want a functioning senate candidate to make all this activity worthwhile, you must come with me, now." There was neither question nor surprise in his face as he followed her upstairs.

She stood in her bedroom facing him, clasping and unclasping her hands. "I'm disengaging, flying apart in a million directions. Make love to me, please. I need your strength. I need you inside me. Please, Beau."

"My pleasure, Darlin'." He smiled delightedly. "I'd do anything for you, even play crazy glue."

The humming in her head was rhythmic again, not a dissonant screeching. She ran her fingers across his bare chest, smiling. He rolled on his side to face her, pulling a couple of curls, watching them spring back when he released them.

"Looks like everything is holding together. Was there any pain?"

Kat shook her head.

"No pain, only bliss. But I'm not sure how long it'll last. Maybe we should do it again." She reached over and began fondling him.

"Five minutes. Give me five minutes and I'll be happy to oblige." They both laughed and settled into kissing to pass the time.

"Your ex-husband was wrong again," he observed between kisses. "Human love is evolved from the rutting of animals by the kiss and caress, not by where a man puts his dick."

It took several minutes longer to recover the second time. When Kat slowly opened her eyes, she basked in the satisfied glow radiating from his soft brown eyes. She blessed this man who shone his light and drove the darkness away. He was so generous with his strength, his love, his brilliant mind.

Kat reached out to touch her fingers to his lips. He kissed her fingertips.

"Your eyes are glowing. I'm humbled that I can bring that back to you. Promise you'll always come to me when you feel like this?"

She nodded agreement, knowing she never wanted to be anywhere else but in his arms. However, plans for paradise were still a couple days away and the path clearly led through the lowest circles of Hell.

"What do I say tomorrow night?"

"Check with your old friend Sun Tzu. I believe he says something along the lines of rather than presuming they will not attack, we appear in a place they cannot attack."

"What place is that?"

"The only place that is ever certain, the pinnacle of truth. From there you can demand the best from them in response. Leave them wallowing in the gutter and you've lost. That's Douglas territory."

While Kat was considering what the truth might entail in her televised speech to the state, Stuart got dressed.

"It's time for me to go." He gestured for her to stay in bed.

"Believe it or not, I have other senate races to consider. I'm in Miami tonight, Georgia tomorrow. I'll be at the studio tomorrow night if you need me. Then it's off to spend election day in California."

As Kat began to demur, he waved away her complaint.

"It was the price for my playing hooky this past week. The president refuses to allow me on the same coast as you until the polls are closed. But I haven't forgotten my promise. I'll be there to take you home Tuesday night. I've always wanted to fuck a freshly-elected senator."

He was standing next to the bed when he picked up a small pottery jar and pulled out its cork.

"What's this? It's full of stars," he said, peering in.

"What did you expect?" she laughed, pointing to the word stars written on the jar.

He got that wild look in his eyes and she hoped he would not find it amusing to execute a supernova and scatter the thousands of tiny, multicolor star shapes all over the room. They were impossible to clean up. While she was concerned about the mundane, he had a more sublime prank in mind. He rubbed his fingers along the inside of her thigh then spread the sticky residue of their love around her nipples, showering stars on them as well. They stuck, glittering in the morning light and he smiled down at her surprised face.

"I like my goddess glittery."

★ ★ ★ ★ ★

"How could they leave you out of the line-up? Don't they know she really belongs to you?"

Carrie kept the derision from her voice. Race did not look too stable this morning and she did not want him taking out his frustrations on her. She smiled slightly as he grabbed the paper from her hand, rolled it up and touched a match to it. He held it steady, big chunks of charred paper falling around him, until the heat against his hand forced him to toss the final smoldering strip onto the floor where he stomped it out.

"Douglas again," he said, venom dripping along with a fleck of saliva from the corner of his mouth. His nose started to drip blood and he blotted it automatically. Race was disintegrating nicely, she thought.

"Did you handle the votes?"

She nodded, then jumped to another subject to distract him from further exploration of exactly how she handled the votes. By the time he discovered the thousands of dollars she extorted from Douglas for the five thousand votes he was certain would win him the election, her spells would have worked and Race would be finished. More and more often in these past few days, Carrie saw herself moving into his place, becoming the shadow queen of the underworld. She would keep Race as the front man but merely a shell, a zombie she could direct with the slightest twisting of her thoughts.

"You know she's scheduled to go on television tomorrow night. I think she's going to declare her love for our dashing soon-to-be vice president."

His reaction did not disappoint her.

"No!" He hissed in a burst louder than she had ever heard from him. And his formless white face showed traces of purple beneath the pasty skin. Blood leaked from his nose again. "Stop her."

"What do you have in mind?" Carrie asked, interested in what he saw as the bounds of her skill.

"I don't know. Make her lose her voice, or break a leg, or something."

"It would be safer, and more certain, if you remove her. Just temporarily, of course," she hastened to add.

"Maybe an intimate dinner before the show, in New Hampshire or on Block Island."

His dead eyes got the barest glimmer of hope at this absurd suggestion. Carrie wondered how he could be so dense and still be chief. Then she remembered one of the cardinal rules espoused by Kat's favorite strategist. She purchased a copy of Sun Tzu once she discovered the premier place he held in the campaign hierarchy. The general claimed that once you locate an opponent's deepest desire and threaten it, he must yield. It certainly worked with Kat. The slightest threat to Stuart had her walking into the lion's den. It would work on Race with Kat as bait.

"She'd never agree to go."

"Don't ask."

Carrie was pleased with her resolution. She did not think Race could pull it off and that was fine. She wanted to see Kat expose herself on television. She would enjoy what that would do to Race. Right now, she needed to devote herself to eliminating that fake magician blocking her path.

★ ★ ★ ★ ★

"I feel guilty about having so much fun today. With all that's happening to Kat, it seems only right that I should be suffering, too." Roxy leaned into Jake's arms as they sat against the dunes on a small fringe of sand around the corner from the north end of the beach. It was calm and serene, low tide barely exposing a small sandbar in the middle of the river. There were traces of civilization: fire circles, an abandoned beach chair, burnt out logs. They watched a spectacular sunset over Narrow River as it stretched along the horizon.

"This is a magical spot. One of the few places on the mainland where you can be at the ocean and watch the sun set into the water." Jake rested his face against her soft, golden hair.

FOR I HAVE SINNED

Once Stuart left, they all scattered to various tasks. She and Jake worked the beaches, fishing accesses, and shore towns in South County. They stuck copies of the *Journal* endorsement on car windshields, knocked on doors, accosted people in shops and restaurants. In general the response was positive. Few people in Rhode Island knew about the *Washington Daily* and most seemed content with the familiar image of Kiley Tomasso, protector of their precious ocean. For many along the Atlantic coast, that was all that mattered. There were unpleasant encounters, but they were scattered and weak and most dissipated when they recognized Jake, or at least recognized that he was someone they had seen on television and therefore a celebrity they could use to impress their friends.

They cruised around salt ponds beyond coastal reefs: brackish accumulations of still water transformed by man-made, stone lined channels into flourishing salt ponds that encouraged wildlife and vegetation. The breachways made it possible to flush around these coastal areas, built on a central pillar like an elevator shaft that housed regular bouts of high seas. She was not sure it would work in a serious hurricane, nor was anyone. There had been no major storm in the area since the relatively new burst of development made South County the fastest growing section of the state after decades of seeing its power and population drawn to the cities of the north.

The only sad note that stayed with her throughout the afternoon was their visit to the huge graveyard of starfish just north of the lighthouse at Point Judith. Jake was right. It was mind boggling. Countless starfish corpses filled a huge area of rocks and shallows—mega thousands of dried orange bodies. Jake had no answer as to their origin or the reason for their demise. No matter how reassuring he tried to be, Roxy could not shake the feeling that all those dead starfish were an omen, a signal of lost wishes.

They got up to leave and walk back to the house, Jake lovingly brushing sand from her bottom. She looked longingly across the estuary to the scrub covered hill topped with a weathered shack.

"There're only two days left and I never made it to the other side," she bemoaned.

"For the past year, this typhoon of political activity has rearranged my life, my image, my ideas about what I wanted. In two days that will all disappear but the most important part of it doesn't have to end with the election, Roxy. You don't have to leave. There's lots of Rhode Island left to explore, lots we haven't done yet."

She knew where this conversation was going and panicked. She began to move away but Jake caught her arm.

"I'm prepared to make a commitment but it's hard when you always have your hand on the doorknob, ready to leave."

Roxy said nothing but the refrain in her mind was a familiar one. If she committed herself to Jake did that mean she could never fall in love with anyone else the rest of her life? Would she be capable of doing that? She heard the Dixie-filled music of Hayes' voice in her ears. She could not rely on her will to keep away from him now. What would happen in a year, or five years? She knew from experience that all sensations became dull after a while. There were foods she stopped eating, music she no longer could listen to because their enticement had stopped. But then she considered how different the experience had been with Jake from the beginning. It had not been sensation sweeping her away. It had been something else, something slow and subtle that had grown and developed and surprised her with its strength and tenacity. Maybe it would not go away.

"I want to tell you a story, an Aphrodite lesson." Roxy flinched as Jake broke into her thoughts.

"There are two fountains in Aphrodite's garden. One is sweet, the other bitter. That's the way choices in love can be. The taste may be masked at first, so often it's best to wait."

They walked silently most of the way back to the stairs.

"I don't want to force any decisions on you now, Roxy," he said softly as they leaned against the seawall. "This is hardly the time for rational thought. All I ask is that you don't bolt out of here the day after the election. Give us some time together that's not dominated by vote counts and alphabetical listings of towns.

"And to show how easy I am, I think you should stay at home tonight. Kat needs you more than I do."

★ ★ ★ ★ ★

Liz pounced the instant she walked in the house.

"I hope you're planning to sleep here for a change. I'm leaving for the front lines in a few minutes and don't think Kat should be here without one of us."

She proceeded to bombard Roxy with reports on Kat's day, what she and Bruno had planned for the night, everyone's current location, and what was available to eat. Once she left, Roxy sorted through all the random pieces and assembled a summary of key items.

Two of the aunts, Tillie and Carmella, were camped out in the empty bedroom upstairs, recruited to keep guard on Celeste. Max was off somewhere working on magic and muttering about Carrie. Hayes was dealing with the press, giving them positive poll numbers and predicting the electorate will walk into the voting booth and cut Emmett Douglas' throat.

"The man is perfect for the job," Liz told her, narrowing her blue eyes. "He's just the type of smooth professional liar the press wants."

Hard core volunteers were pouring their hearts into papering the state with the *Journal*'s strong endorsement of Kat's candidacy. Her appearance at Holy

Ghost Church for Mass triggered mixed response, which upset Kat tremendously. Someone alerted the press and she had to flee to avoid the harassing journalists from the *Ocean State Beacon*. She and Mario holed up most of the afternoon at the compound escaping through a back gate at dusk.

"She learned the first rule of survival," claimed Liz. "Have no expectations."

★ ★ ★ ★ ★

"Where have you been?" Kat had been waiting too long for Max to appear.

"We all have our particular roles to play in your mythic drama, and I've been creating props for mine."

As she looked mystified, he pulled a copper wand from a purple velvet bag, unwrapping it from a black silk cloth blazoned with a pattern of stars and crescents. There was a tourmaline obelisk emerging from a dragonfly at one end, a clear quartz crystal in a claw at the other. "Stuart gave me a trinket from his mad scientist friends at DARPA. It's some sort of reflector device for sending sound waves back to their source, amplified. He thinks I can use it to turn back negative energy and wants a full report. I mounted it in the wand so it focuses through the tourmaline.

"I'm considering trying it out on Carrie."

She sat in shocked silence and watched his expressionless square face as he rewrapped the wand, put it in his tunic pocket and pulled out a silver dollar. As it spun across his knuckles he explained.

"I've avoided power magic for years because I was hesitant to take the responsibility. I was afraid I couldn't resist its lure. The time has come."

Forestalling any discussion, Max pulled a deck of tarot cards from the air, and motioned her to sit with him on the rug. They were the goddess cards that Roxy found so revealing.

"Sit in the heart," he directed, "and shuffle the cards. Lay them out the way I tell you. Three across the top, from right to left. These will answer your questions about the telecast tonight. Three more in a second line will tell us about the election. The final line of five will tell us about the long term future."

Kat nodded and spread the cards, her hands shaking slightly. This was the first time she had handled them in months. There was so much at stake. She wondered if she really wanted to know.

Max turned over the first three cards. They were swords. The truth was all that would serve. When she saw the knight racing on horseback, sword upraised, she laughed. Her hero. Who knew all those months ago when this card first appeared it would be so literal.

The second line of three offered no clear resolution. There was the initial card which was filled with vague forms and called Illusion. Kat wondered whose illusion it represented. The second card was the election itself and depicted an unresolved battle with each side standing off surrounded by their swords. The final card, which represented the resulting situation, threw it all to the hand of fate. It was the card called Karma and indicated the cosmic implications of the test she faced.

He stopped her hand as she reached to turn over the third line of cards.

"These must be read against an understanding of the larger times," he began. "This is a remarkable epoch. So much is ending: the Mayan calendar, the Age of Pisces, the most dramatic millennium in the history of mankind. Indicators of our future are everywhere from the pattern of the stars to earthly events that reflect that pattern. The aborigines call it a sacred dreamtime between worlds. Toynbee named it the Time of Troubles: a seed time, the closing of a cycle. It's a time when new heroes appear ready to go adventuring in the dawn of an era, and this time, the goddess has returned at last."

"Is it so important that there be a hero and a goddess?" she asked.

"Their mere existence can give courage and hope." He nodded for her to turn over the final cards.

The message was stunning. The Emperor led off. Roxy was right—the man depicted did look like Stuart, even to the intense concentration on his face as he leaned forward on his throne. The next two cards brought tears of joy to her eyes. They were cards of accomplishment and reward. They featured a blazing couple and another joined by a child. Kat could not believe her eyes as she recognized the familiar death card, called the Close in this deck, and laying reversed. No more deaths, she prayed, not for a long time. When the final card revealed the beautiful World card, the ultimate fulfillment, she relaxed and knew she found the answer to her recurring dream.

She slowly picked up the cards and told Max about the dream.

"It's been happening for weeks. These two blazing stars are speeding through a black sky. They collide in a shattering supernova splashing light everywhere and it results in … I don't know. I can't see. I get stuck in the enormity of the collision. If I could believe this," she picked up the beautiful World card with its star-surrounded lady, "if I knew a universe would result from the joining, no matter how violent it was, I could accept it."

"Trust it, Kat. Have no doubt that your work is with Stuart. You are here each to meet the other and the force you release will change the world."

★ ★ ★ ★ ★

Except for brief encounters when she had a question about some slant or another for the main body of the speech, Roxy did not see Kat until late afternoon when they went for a walk on the beach. Kat was pleased with the eight minutes of facts and vision it had been her assignment to write. "I want to grip each and every heart even if I'm talking about economics."

Roxy was pleased too. The outline was Kat's. She ignored the death topics: no mention of the situation in the Gulf, the war on drugs, or abortion, except later to deny the rumors. The three "E's" were her issues: economics, education and the environment. After building people to a sense of controlling their own destiny, she would point out how tactics during the campaign acted to deprive them of that control. What Kat would say about her hospital stay and "Who's the Lucky Man?" was still undecided.

They turned back from the estuary and Kat asked for her suggestions on what to say in conclusion. Roxy panicked. She could turn Kat's vision into easily accessible prose but revealing the most private emotions to millions was more than she could grasp. She lived on an intimate scale, even her books were read one person at a time. Roxy had no answer.

"What's everyone else advising?" she asked, brushing her hair away from her eyes. She knew Kat spent the day talking with dozens of people.

Kat laughed. "You're turning into a master politician, Roxy. Too much time with Hayes. But a good point. Liz and Bruno want the entire ten minute broadcast to be a three-ring circus. Beau and I would get married center ring while to our right, Race would be ripped to shreds by ravenous rats and Carrie would be burned at the stake on our left. They consider Douglas inconsequential.

"Beau and Max are waving the banner of truth at me; a multilevel answer if I ever heard one. Mario doesn't care what I say as long as I get to live happily ever after. Although he does feel that pointing out Rhode Island would be getting a senator who is in bed with the White House couldn't hurt in the clout department. Gould is concerned about what I'm planning to wear, which I'll show you when we get back, and that I appear graceful and sincere. He referred me to Jake whom he considers the epitome of these two characteristics. And Lila is simply dying to ask about the intimate details of our love life and find out whether our vice president sleeps in the nude."

"Does he?"

"Who knows? I've never spent a normal night with the man.

"The press wants sordid confessions whatever they might be, and the Democrats want a fetus in a bottle. Sun Tzu advises that in a desperate situation one must move fast or die. All my aunts want to know why being Mrs. Vice President isn't more than enough."

Between chuckles, Roxy was keeping track. "What about Hayes?" she asked of the obvious omission.

"He wants to know how much it would cost to buy the race. He quoted Jefferson to me to the affect that you can't lose votes with a speech you don't make."

She looked at Roxy. "What does Jake have to say?"

"I think he's on the side of true love these days."

"Want to talk about it?" Kat asked, hearing the catch in her friend's voice.

"I don't even want to think about it until Wednesday."

Kat stopped, put her arm on Roxy's shoulder, and stood looking down at her. "Professionally, after Tuesday night I don't care what choice you make. Personally, I think Jake is unbeatable."

Before she could reply, Kat's grip tightened.

"Very slowly I want you to switch positions with me and look at the two gorillas in cheap human suits standing at the near end of the parking lot."

She wondered if Kat had lost her mind but followed instructions. As soon as she saw the two men, she understood. They did look like gorillas in cheap human suits.

"They're Race Scarlatti's thugs," Kat said softly.

"They've spotted us and are looking this way, gesturing to each other. What are we going to do?"

Suddenly Kat was leading her back towards the Dunes Club. The men saw them and began scrambling to get around the fence and follow. Kat broke into a run and they trotted up the steps to the Club from the beach and scampered across the beach side lawn. Running around the far side of the complex beyond the swimming pool, they crossed the lower parking area and came up in the scrub by the long hall for staff housing. The deepening dusk made it easy to elude the thugs they could see poking around the building. Hidden by the curves of the long driveway, they ran to Ocean Drive where Kat flagged down the first car she could. They were safely through the Towers before the gorillas emerged.

Between Kat and Liz, they had the house ringed with protectors in minutes.

"I have the feeling that Race doesn't want me to go on television tonight and declare my heart belongs to Stuart," Kat remarked as she took Roxy and Liz upstairs to approve her clothes and start working on her hair. The broadcast was scheduled for the ten minutes preceding the late night news, so they had abundant time to prepare the star.

★ ★ ★ ★ ★

"You'll have to stop making me laugh once we get to the eye make-up or I'll streak."

Liz had been entertaining them with stories of her escapades in what she termed guerilla election fare.

"Bruno collected three of his favorite young protégés. He calls them Harvard boys and lawyers trying to find roots. We set off in a beat-up old station wagon strategically plastered with Democratic bumper stickers. Two of the license plate numbers were obscured. First we went to Douglas headquarters and papered it with Kiley signs. Then we snuck into their parking lot and put Kiley for Senate bumper stickers on all the Douglas staff cars. We were spotted but our look-out and driver were both alert and we lost them in the maze around the underpass to the East Side. We sent other teams out to paper over Douglas signs wherever they found them.

"When we got back to Federal Hill sometime after one a.m., the fax war started. For a while it was low key, mostly want ads and one-liners. Then they sent a copy of the photo of you and Stuart, surrounded by hearts with 'Kiley has a boyfriend' scrawled across it."

Kat stiffened. Liz kept brushing her hair, pulling it back into a loose bun on her neck. Heartbreakingly pure was the look they wanted. Earlier Liz had described her search for the perfect lipstick color.

"I went into the store and asked for 'Pure' but it wasn't quite the right shade. 'Let me try Heartbreakingly' I said and she brought out the perfect color."

"We tricked them though," Liz continued, ignoring Kat's concern. "We sent back the one of you and the Pope. 'Why settle for a mere politician when she can go right to God.'"

Kat groaned.

"Don't worry. That confused them. We got no response for a while so we shut off the fax and went to bed.

"And today, Dolly from Nooseneck reappeared. Mario agreed no one could do anything the last day. I trashed that loser Douglas. I spent all day reciting every dirty trick, every bribe, every criminal associate, every missed vote, every fart. I stopped short of threatening that everyone who voted for Douglas would be turned into a frog. I figured they might connect it with Max."

As Liz pulled a series of tendrils to whorl sweetly along her cheeks and forehead, Kat smiled. The woman was truly a genius with hair.

"Speaking of our favorite magician, I don't suppose you asked about the outcome of this election tomorrow, did you?" Liz stood back to admire her work and to look Kat in the eye.

She smiled sweetly, patted her curls, and said, "I thought it might be fun to be surprised." She returned Liz's steady gaze.

"Thanks. It's exactly the look I wanted."

Kat slipped the dress over her black underwear and turned her back to Liz for zipping. She wore a navy blue velvet long sleeve dress with fitted bodice and waist and a slimly gored skirt. Liz pinned on an intricate lace collar that stretched almost to the tips of her breasts, and attached a delicate onyx cameo at her throat. She wore pearl clusters in her ears and no other jewelry. She slipped her wolf's eye ring into a small crocheted bag along with several other magical charms; she would carry it in her hand.

"Have you decided about your closing yet?" Roxy asked, as the three stood up to leave.

Kat squared her shoulders, smoothed the dark, velvety nap of her dress, and pasted on a courageous smile for which she could produce no collateral.

"No. I have faith as I step off into the abyss I'll think of the right thing to say. It's the kind of faith that springs from total despair."

★ ★ ★ ★ ★

Roxy grabbed the ringing phone as they got to the first floor. It was Pete. He and Jake were out fishing on the wharf about an hour ago. Giant blues started biting just as they arrived. Jake went down on the rocks to get closer and as he did, slid, fell and injured his ankle badly. Before assuring her that Jake was OK, Pete pointed out that through all the pain and shock, Jake picked up his pole, cast, and caught a big bluefish.

The doctor at the emergency room set the ankle and Pete was preparing to take Jake home.

"He's shot up with pain killers and totally spaced out. He said to tell you not to worry. Call him sometime late tomorrow morning. He's not going anywhere. And apologize to Kat. He won't be able to dance at her victory party tomorrow night. He made me promise to tape her speech so he could watch when he rejoined the world of the living."

She worried about Jake all the way to the television studio and what this would mean tomorrow night when only Hayes was around.

★ ★ ★ ★ ★

The director gave Kat a signal indicating three minutes before airtime. The pale blue backdrop provided the perfect contrast to her dark dress. She sat in graceful Miss Williams School for Girls posture on a brocade chair that matched the backdrop curtain, a Victorian cameo come to life. She was a 19th century Madonna, so who would not believe what she said? If Gould's concern had engineered Kat's appearance and setting, he should be applauded for his single-mindedness.

While Kat sat serenely, slender white fingers folded calmly on small pieces of paper invisible in her lap, Roxy shredded pages of script copy with fidgety hands. Liz was sitting beside her grinning like a Cheshire cat, fake eyelashes fluttering. She could sense Hayes standing directly behind her chair. Mario sat on her other side and Kat's cousin John, pastor at Holy Ghost, sat along the back wall flanked by Yola and two of the aunts. The director, cameraman and two station executives made up the remainder of the small audience.

FOR I HAVE SINNED

Outside, the studio entrance was cordoned off by Providence police provided by the outgoing mayor as a favor to the Hose who had threatened to reveal the addresses of the apartments he provided for his three mistresses. It was eerie walking through the crowd of Kat supporters who filled the lawn around the brick building on a dingy side street. They held Kiley for Senate placards and hand-lettered signs pledging their support, but they stood silent even when she stepped from the campaign van and walked up the entranceway. The abyss was yawning at their feet too. Hecklers were nowhere to be seen or heard and Roxy wondered if they had been ousted earlier.

"You never paid me the hundred dollars I won on Mario's parentage."

Roxy looked in horror at Liz. What a time to be discussing that.

"I'll give you a chance to win it back." Liz was leaning on the back of Roxy's chair, whispering loudly in her ear. "A hundred bucks says Stuart will be here for the broadcast."

There were only two minutes left. She would take that bet. Roxy nodded her agreement. Her heart sank as two bulky suits with coiled wires hanging from their ears walked from a dark corridor into the studio. Two more followed close behind. As they spread out along the side wall, Roxy saw a radiant light shine from Kat, transfiguring her face. The tiny lines of fear in the corners of her eyes and lips were erased. She smiled at Stuart. He stood, arms folded across his chest, just outside the perimeter of glaring light flooding the set. His white shirt gleamed.

"One more chance," Liz urged, not bothering to disguise the glee in her voice. "Another hundred says he goes on camera with her."

The director raised his hand, studio lights dimmed, Kat gazed directly at the camera. No way, thought Roxy, as she nodded her acceptance of Liz's bet.

"I am here tonight, talking with you, not as potential voters but as my friends and family—that's how it is in Rhode Island." Kat's voice sounded as clear and perfect as the night she sang at the White House barbecue. There were no audible traces of trauma or fear.

Listening to her opening address, Roxy realized this would be seen by more than the voters of Rhode Island or the people of southern New England. Depending on what happened, scenes from Kat's ten-minute appearance would appear on network newscasts everywhere.

Kat succinctly reviewed her work for the state then launched into an inspired presentation of her vision for the future.

"There is an ideal Rhode Island just beyond the horizon of tomorrow, a state we can create together. It will be a challenge but a new and better life is struggling to be born."

When she heard the slight quiver in Kat's voice, Roxy flinched. In the dozens of times she read and reread that phrase, it never occurred to her what it would mean to Kat personally. The moment passed.

"Our future Rhode Island is one of strong communities and caring families with people doing useful and satisfying work for a just wage. The children of our future state are excited about learning. They play without fear. Their parents and grandparents feel secure about health care and housing.

"Young couples proudly care for their first homes in this state of ours. And there are clean beaches, pure air, clean water and open spaces to be enjoyed freely by everyone. Our Rhode Island-to-be exists in a stable, prosperous and peaceful world. We the people of this state know what's happening in our lives. We take charge, make choices, shape our planet. You can see this vision, I know you can. We can take this leap of imagination together. We can make this future a reality."

There was a brief pause that seemed endless in the tension of the studio. Kat clasped her hands over the pages on her lap, intensified her gaze at the camera, and subtly amplified the power she was sending to her audience.

"Many of you have known me all my life. You know the quality of my ideas, my commitment to public service. I have not lived a flawless life. Who has? I understand that as a public figure—an icon, as some remind me—I have an obligation to rise above my personal feelings, to behave with honor and dignity. You scarcely need to be reminded that I have never betrayed the public trust nor the truth as I know it.

"I will confess to flunking timing in my personal life, but that is a minor infraction, important only to those who measure time by elections and news cycles. The far graver sin has been committed by my opponent and those who applauded and promoted his tactics.

"We could have spent the past seven months discussing the future Rhode Island I sketched earlier, debating the best methods for guaranteeing that vision. Instead we had this right stolen from us by lies, distortions, and rumors spread by my opponent and his cronies. We have been defrauded of our rights as citizens and voters.

"So much depends on your vote tomorrow, on the choice you make. It's a clear choice. Business as usual, meaning corruption, manipulation, lies and fraud or a new way of thinking, a vision that includes you, all of you. Vote for me tomorrow and we will take the path of vision to the future century, the new millennium that is almost upon us.

"You have heard many rumors, many lies about me, about my ideas. I will not give them credibility by repeating them once again, denying them once again. There is only one I must address."

Roxy felt her stomach knot, and saw Kat clasp her hands more tightly. There was a transcendent timbre in her voice and she seemed to be looking through and beyond the camera.

"For several weeks, I was blessed with the greatest of miracles. I carried in my womb a child I desperately wanted. I prayed daily that this life would grow and thrive. For whatever reason, it was not to be. There was no abortion as has been rumored, but a miscarriage, an act of God that I could only accept, not understand. I was devastated. The child I carried meant everything to me. I love the man who fathered this child with all my heart and soul. We plan to marry after the election."

It was worth the money she lost to see the look in Kat's eyes as Stuart stepped into camera range, standing tall and straight at the side of her chair, placing his hand on her shoulder. Tears made the scene waver and blur but Roxy was certain she would see it replayed hundreds of times. She could imagine the collective gasps of disbelief that swept not only Rhode Island, where thousands and thousands of people were glued to their televisions, but all over America and eventually, the world.

Kat's joyous voice brought her back to reality.

"Though I may have flunked timing in my personal life, I promise it will not affect my performance as your senator."

Stuart never took his penetrating gaze off the camera and the millions beyond it. As he began to speak, Roxy wondered whether this was planned or if it sprang from their perfect resonance with each other.

"Rhode Island could have no finer senator than Kiley Tomasso," he said in his rich and stirring voice. Then he reached down and took Kat's hand. Her look clearly said she did not have a clue what he had in mind.

"And a man could have no finer wife." Stuart switched his gaze to her as he slipped a ring on her left hand, positioned perfectly so the camera would not miss the action.

"Now there's a real hero," Liz muttered as the glowing pair stood looking at each other for the few moments left before the director indicated the broadcast was over.

When the red light of the camera switched off, both Mario and Hayes positioned themselves in front of it, backs to the lens, as Stuart raised Kat from the chair and they embraced. Watching the kiss, Roxy felt her heart melt. It was too much love for her to bear.

★ ★ ★ ★ ★

The roller coaster continued as Kat felt the love pulsing through her lips, her body, every inch of nerves and skin. Whatever happened tomorrow would be anticlimactic to this moment. Random thoughts of unusual proposals she had seen or read about splashed through her brain. What could compare to this?

His lips were not on hers and he was saying something. Kat forced her attention back into her head and listened. He took her hand and closed it around a hard object.

"You were wonderful. If they love you only a fraction as much as I do, it'll be a landslide." He smiled adoringly at her. "I'm posting bail," he added. "This will guarantee I'll be back tomorrow night."

He kissed her again.

"And, Darlin' no black underwear. There's nothing more to mourn."

As the suits surrounded him and moved back out through the dark corridor, Kat opened her hand. A magnificent blue sapphire pendant lay there. It was as clear blue as the Paris sky that first morning she knew how much she loved him. She looked at her other hand and saw the ring for the first time. It was a perfect ruby, mounted on a diamond chip encrusted heart. Then there were arms around her leading her out of the dark studio.

★ ★ ★ ★ ★

Why did Max want her at headquarters immediately after the broadcast? Roxy wondered about the note as she scurried to catch up with the entourage. Then the chaotic scene around her demanded all attention.

A squad of beefy men in dark suits materialized under the Hose's direction and formed a square around Kat. Several more held shut the doors into the glassed-in newsroom of the television station where the press had watched the broadcast on monitors. They were banging frantically on the glass as Kat swept by. Mario and Hayes stayed to speak with them as soon as the candidate was safely away. It had been decided earlier that once her speech was made Kat would say nothing more to the press. She would vote as soon as the polls opened in Narragansett the next morning, then spend the day visiting key polling places in the state asking for votes as if this were a routine election.

Her squad opened briefly when she faced the crowd of people who waited outside watching a large monitor through the front window, listening to a simulcast of dozens of radios. She waved automatically and scarcely noticed the varied reactions. There were pockets of stunned silence dotting the crowd where many cheered support and others cried.

As the van and surrounding motorcade sped off to wherever the Hose was taking them for security reasons, Roxy found Mario's car and wound her way across town. She drove under the entry arch that marked the beginning of Federal Hill, glancing to her left at Sister Dominica Manor, a senior high rise across from Garabaldi Park that Mario identified as home of the controlled ballot. In pessimistic moments during the past week, he repeatedly claimed a close election would be decided in places like the Manor all over Providence and a few other cities. She wondered what change in prognostications Kat's appearance tonight would make.

Parking in front of headquarters, she returned to her speculation about why Max summoned her. The few remaining volunteers were leaving as she got out of the car. They looked as cheery as could be expected under the circumstances and assured her Max was inside. Maybe he needed a ride somewhere. She did not care. She would stop and see Jake on the way home then unplug all the phones and hopefully get a little sleep before tomorrow. It was hard to believe there was still the election to get through.

★ ★ ★ ★ ★

She found Max in Mario's darkened office on the first floor pumping air in and out of his chest in some sort of ritual breathing. He looked surprised to see her.

"What message?" he asked perplexed. When a concerned look pulled down the corners of his yellow-white mustache, Roxy felt chills.

"Why are you here?" she asked with trepidation.

Max stood, picked up his bag and hooked a heavy black cape around his neck. "I'm meeting Carrie at midnight."

Roxy gaped. "You've talked to Carrie?"

He shook his head, pulling his white pigtail outside the cape collar. "I just know."

"Where? Here?" Roxy began to get the feeling that somehow she was a planned part of this, planned at least by Carrie.

"I think so. Somewhere around here. I was getting ready to go outside and wait for her to make her move."

She sat heavily into the chair by Mario's desk.

"Why do you think I'm here?"

"Maybe she wanted a witness," Max shrugged.

Roxy pulled her light jacket around her. She was not dressed for the cold night but she was not about to wimp out if she was supposed to be here for Max, for whatever. She was learning about myths all right, and one of the rules seemed to be that all actions had a universal purpose.

★ ★ ★ ★ ★

They walked up and down both sides of the block in front of Kat's Federal Hill headquarters for almost thirty minutes. Roxy was freezing and ready to jump ship and head back to Narragansett when Max slowed and turned to face the opposite sidewalk. Carrie was walking from the shadowy space between the building she had been using to spy on them for months and the one next to it that housed Angostino's Religious Supplies and the widow's apartment upstairs.

Standing in front of the shop window facing them, Carrie looked … Roxy did not know what word to use. Possessed, except she was absolutely calm and focused. Hateful, although again her emotions seemed to be totally controlled and intentional. Triumphant. There was no doubt about that. Whatever Carrie had in mind, Roxy knew she believed she would succeed. She decided to pass on this particular test and remained partially hidden in the headquarters doorway as Max moved into the street to face Carrie.

He flipped back both ends of his heavy cape, spreading out his hands. In his right, he had five coins spinning and whirling across his knuckles. Roxy never saw him do five before, although she knew he could. It was several moments before she could take her eyes off the clanking and sparkling silver blurs. Then she noticed the object in his other hand, the one with the maimed pinky. It was some sort of wand with a spooky light on top. He held it casually as if it were far less important than the spinning coins, but Roxy knew that could not be true. The coins were a decoy. She wondered what the wand did and what Carrie thought of Max's modest defense.

Carrie's face seemed unchanged and then almost imperceptibly she flinched, as if a fly landed on her shoulder. It happened again, and yet again. Her face began to twist and darken and her gaze grew more penetrating. She pointed the index fingers of both hands at Max and began chanting softly. Roxy heard a vague muttering sound but could not make out the words. Against her better judgement, she was drawn out of the doorway. She moved closer to Max. She wanted to hear what Carrie had to say.

Max had not changed position. The coins continued to spin at the same velocity under and over his hand. The wand remained focused on Carrie, although the glow on the top end seemed magnified and a matching glow was coming from the bottom. She could not see his face but the tense stance of his body convinced her that something powerful and dramatic was happening between the two.

She quaked when Carrie uttered the first scream. It took several repetitions for Roxy to realize the now furious woman was shouting particular syllables and words, although not in any language she could understand. Max did not budge but Carrie seemed sporadically rocked, almost as if some sort of wave was hitting against her. As her cries continued to amplify, the rocking became more pronounced.

Roxy looked around the empty street, quickly estimating how long it would be before neighbors and police appeared. She began to hear a low humming that intensified as Carrie continued her curses. A dark cloud gathered around the screaming woman and she rocked almost rhythmically, the humming growing louder and louder. Behind her the window began to radiate a pale light that grew ever more pink. There were ripples of light that flowed up and down the plate glass. The rosy glow extended behind the statues that filled the display area.

Roxy felt the hair on her arms stand up as Carrie's screams changed quality. Yelps of pain punctuated curses and appeared to coincide with the rocking. Something was smashing against Carrie. Her face twisted, her voice grew sharper, the humming increased. Roxy could not imagine what was causing all the activity. Max was rooted to his spot in the center of the street doing nothing more than holding the wand which glowed blindingly. No traffic had passed since the confrontation began.

Suddenly, tiny Mrs. Angostino, wrapped in a black wool coat with a flannel nightgown flapping around her ankles beneath it, came screeching out of the rosy glow through the door of her shop. It all happened so fast Roxy was never quite certain of the sequence of events.

Carrie snapped her head around to face the old lady, breaking her focus on Max. There was a huge explosion, sparks sprayed from the window, and Mrs. Angostino jumped back into the doorway. Shattered glass was everywhere. When Roxy arrived just behind Max, she saw Carrie sprawled on the glass covered sidewalk, lying on her side. A yard long spear of glass protruded from her chest and back.

Blood oozed onto the street. Carrie writhed hysterically and tried to pull at the glass spear, shredding her hands. More blood added to the pool forming beneath her. Max stood watching, holding the wand pointed directly at her round face, now distorted with pain, fear and hate. Roxy looked away from the demented woman dying at her feet and saw an equally hysterical Mrs. Angostino climb through the empty frame on her shop's front window and embrace the feet of a life-size statue of the Virgin Mary that held the place of honor. The rosy glow filled the storefront, gathered itself around the statue, then faded away.

Before the light disappeared completely, a slightly stooped man brushed by Mrs. Angostino and stepped out through the broken window onto the street. The intact streetlight next to the shop revealed his pasty, rounded head with its dull, brown ponytail. As he moved next to Max to face the still twitching body of his minion, Roxy began sobbing. Race Scarlatti! What did he have to do with this? Were they in danger?

Carrie's black eyes froze into a tormented stare, her face a mask of hate and terror. Race kicked at the spear of glass that stuck out from below her heart and laughed as she howled in agony. Then with an incredible effort of will, she spoke, her words garbled by the death rattle in her throat and repeated chokes on blood that poured from her mouth. But they heard the message.

"I sold the votes to Douglas."

Roxy's scream blended with Carrie's as Race stomped on the flat side of the glass spear, leveraging it to rip through her back. She watched the tortured woman's head slump against the bloodstained street, her mouth slack, the curses finally stopped. Carrie was dead.

Roxy was shaking uncontrollably as Max grabbed her and pushed her towards Mario's car parked in front of headquarters. Race's crazed laugh followed them as they sped off. They were taking the Route 4 exit off the interstate by the time Roxy recovered enough from the shock to look over at Max, who was driving intently.

"What happened?" she whispered. "Was Carrie doing magic? Why was Race there?"

He took her hand, and briefly glanced over at her.

"It takes more than knowledge to be a magician. It takes understanding, commitment, practice, and great desire. But to be safe with the power, it takes belief and grace. What happened tonight was justice. Carrie was destroyed by her own negative forces. We were only witnesses."

22

The Judgement
Election Day

Rain was falling in sheets, slashing against the windows, wind whipping the bare branches of the trees. Dawn, less than an hour away, promised little but a change from black to gray in the sky. Roxy felt the weather was an omen all the way to her chilled toes. She did not look forward to shaking hands with Electric Boat workers at 6:15 a.m. She jumped into the shower then dressed in warm leggings, boots and several layers of sweaters. She and Kat converged on the kitchen, drawn by warm smells. Liz had beaten them both out of bed.

By mutual agreement, no one turned on the television. Only CNN would be broadcasting news at this hour and that would tell them nothing about reaction in Rhode Island. The three women were doing Electric Boat alone. By the time they returned to pick up Hayes and take Kat to her polling place to vote, he would know something.

Fortification provided by Liz's hearty breakfast began to fade as Roxy watched the surf from the car window. Kat decided to drive so she gratefully devoted herself to riding shotgun and staring at the churning waves whipped into frenzied peaks by gale winds. The shore was almost obliterated by the sheets of water that hammered the windshield and splashed from the road. Only the sound of the ocean prevailed. It did not take a political genius to guess the effect of weather like this on the number of voters. What was a mystery to Roxy was whether light or heavy turnout favored them more. Another fact she was certain Hayes would know.

It was a grim scene at the factory gates. Rain, wind, guys clutching at their hats, lunch coolers and coffee arguably left no hands to shake Kat's. The placards she and Liz carried were soaked and drooping. It was too windy for an umbrella so Kat stood bareheaded in the rain wordlessly begging men to look her in the eye. She was calm and graceful dancing through the puddles, trying not to miss a hand. That so many shrank away, embarrassed and reluctant, must have broken her heart. Roxy knew every man who came over to Kat or indicated his support was being imprinted on her mind to be thanked later however she could.

They stood drenched and cold until the last few straggled through the gates. Kat walked over to say a final good-bye to the man at the breakfast truck. She returned to the car looking as if she had been slapped.

"What did he say?" Liz asked as Kat directed Roxy to drive back to the house.

"He said he thought I was doing the right thing. That Stuart seemed like a wonderful man and he wished us the best. That I'd be happier married with a family than worrying about the Senate."

"I wonder what planet they beam his television transmissions from," Liz snorted.

Rage quickly replaced hurt. "How did this happen? How could it happen to me? I've spent my whole life studying, working, striving to accomplish as much as I could for the state, and the world. After all these years of watching me, do the people of Rhode Island think I'm incapable of being both a wife and a senator? Is falling in love always such a misfortune?"

"What can you expect of people who voted a giant clam as their state mascot?" Liz quipped. As Kat scowled, Liz continued her analysis. "Rhode Island is like a small town. All those guys feel they know you personally and they're pissed because you're getting laid and it's not by one of them."

★ ★ ★ ★ ★

"The overnight numbers have the race dead even among people planning to vote. The real mind bender is the people who are dropping out, blocking the election from their minds like some terrible nightmare. The weather won't help at all. We'll be lucky if the whole turn-out is the two hundred fifty thousand votes you've been working so diligently to win for Kat."

Hayes was distracted by the bizarre shape the election was taking. Yet he easily shifted into intimate mode and turned their quick conversation in the narrow passage from the kitchen to the front hall into passionate foreplay. At least that was how her tense body interpreted the encounter. Roxy would much rather listen to her body at the moment than consider the news Hayes so considerately shared with her.

"Looks like the first-string is sidelined with injuries and it's time for the bench to have a chance to play," he teased. Backed against the door to the basement, his face only inches from hers, she could not swear to who kissed whom first, but Roxy was certain it was the warmest she had felt in days. Liz's thudding steps down the stairs pushed them apart and towards the front hall.

As they pulled into the school where Kat's polling place was, their stomachs knotted in unison. The rain stopped briefly, though the skies were lead colored and winds whipped signs being held by a platoon of Douglas supporters who ringed the parking lot. It was a press mob scene with reporters and cameras shoving microphones into the faces of the Douglas pickets as well as every voter who ran the gauntlet of flashing bulbs, sound poles, photographers and technicians. There was almost a stampede when they spotted Kat emerging from the van and Roxy hung onto Liz for dear life, knowing she could be trampled if she fell into that melee.

Representatives from CBS were taking exit polls, asking every third person what factors influenced their choice in the U.S. Senate race. Kat was one of those polled. Once she cited the factors of integrity, competence, and vision of the future, she refused any further questions about her relationship with the vice president, whether they had selected a date for their wedding, and what impact she felt her confession would have on his chances to be approved by Congress.

Hayes was busy demanding a van plastered with Douglas posters be removed beyond the designated limit for campaigning near the polling place. He then rescued Kat, hurrying her back to the van, warning of problems ahead.

"Whatever we do today will have to be unscheduled. You're obviously their prime target. They'll be staking you out. We'll have to sneak in and out of headquarters to avoid being the head of a massive media parade."

They cruised past the other polling places in Narragansett. There were no Douglas volunteers or demonstrators at any of them. The show at Kat's polling place was just that, a show of force for the cameras and to harass the candidate. It succeeded. As they scooted around the back streets of Narragansett evading their press tails, Kat grilled Hayes relentlessly about reaction to her speech, the effect of the weather on her vote, and what the overnight polls showed. Previously she claimed she did not want to know.

His report was not an optimistic one although he laced it with disclaimers urging her not to jump to any conclusions until they got to headquarters and were able to check word on the street. Hayes made one prediction with certainty. The massive Democratic effort to turn out voters would guarantee a close race. He predicted it would be decided by less than five thousand votes. That meant Providence was the only place that mattered for them, and turning out their supporters was the only priority. "I think undecideds are all going to stay home," was his final word.

They watched a few minutes of local television reporting but the emphasis on speculative gossip about her relationship with Stuart turned Kat into a crazed Fury. Hayes shut it off and sent her to pack and prepare for the long day and night they had ahead. He hid the *Ocean State Beacon*, knowing the pages of pictures of her and Stuart and their blatantly sensational and distorted headlines and stories would push her to melt-down. Aside from sordid conjecture about secret rendezvous, most of the alleged news items focused on how the relationship with Stuart located Kat solidly in the reactionary Republican camp, raising all the old demons of sex and race discrimination, favoritism for the rich, and neglect of the environment. The bishop's rabid letter condemning Kat for her pro-choice stand was featured prominently.

Plans were for them all to stay at the Marriot where the Republicans would gather for election night returns. Agreeing that she would meet up with them at headquarters later that morning, Roxy went off to see Jake.

★ ★ ★ ★ ★

As she sat on the edge of Jake's bed, his eyes fluttered open and he smiled. Taking her hand, he thanked her for coming over.

"I'm sorry about this," he waved his hand vaguely at the bottom of the bed. "I'll miss not being there with you and Kat tonight, and doing my part to turn out the vote. If you want to leave some phone lists, I think I can do some calling." His face twisted slightly and he squeezed her hand.

"It was my bad ankle," he explained. "The pain is severe but they've given me some serious drugs to deal with it. No more fishing on the rocks for me."

"Will you be able to walk?" Roxy asked, concerned.

"Sure! Eventually. Although I'll probably have a slight limp. Just enough to be sexy. Maybe I'll even get to use a cane. My biggest regret," Jake lifted himself up against the pillows, "is that I can't give a last burst for the vote count. My leg isn't the only thing that's limp, thanks to the pain killers.

"Roxy, will you wait until I'm better?"

She nodded quickly, her eyes filling with tears.

"Will you wait until I'm best?" he said with a shy smile.

"You already are best." As she said it, Roxy knew it was true. The real question was what would she do with the best?

★ ★ ★ ★ ★

A few hardy members of the press braved the torrential rain and clustered outside the front of Kat's headquarters on Federal Hill questioning volunteers who scooted in and out of the building to pick up more palm cards, more lists of calls to make. Inside, the mood was as gray and dreary as the weather.

Radio call-in shows were the worst. Although Kat's team knew the most demeaning and patronizing calls were staged by Douglas supporters, it did little to relieve their depression. Some callers wondered whether the vice president's wife should be allowed to serve in the Senate, others speculated on how improbable it was that Kat would be willing to defend Rhode Island's interest if they came in conflict with her soon-to-be-husband's ambitions. It was on the Carole Ann show that they first heard reference to Kat as a fallen angel.

Liz was the only one who was willing to comment.

"That's not good news," she said bluntly. "There're a lot of sick people out there who are willing to see fallen angels burn at the stake."

The news got worse when Mario arrived.

"No one is voting. Almost literally, no one. All the old timers working the polls claim they've never seen anything like it. They even had poll watchers calling in before dawn begging off their jobs." Mario dropped his head into his hands then raised it to look directly at Kat. "Consensus of streetwise vote watchers is that people are in shock, not just those who were sitting on the fence—they're gone for good—but also lots of your supporters. Liz is right. Being a fallen angel is not a good position. Maybe we shouldn't have waited so long to tell the truth."

Kat dismissed his second guessing.

"It's too late to worry about that now."

As the talk continued, Roxy was stunned. No one seemed to know anything about Carrie. Surely the Hose would have heard. He had been on the streets of Providence since before the telecast the previous night. And where was Max? As if reading her thoughts, Kat turned to her and asked, "Where's Max?"

Roxy shook her head.

Hayes began analyzing the vote patterns, scanning lists of minimum vote goals for each region of the state, working out with Mario what their strategy had to be.

"We mobilize everyone we can to get on the phones. No one but supporters should be called. We have all their names and numbers from our nightly canvassing. They have to go vote. If they're in shock, we have to bust them out of it. Don't you have one of those magic pills that ends shock?"

Roxy giggled at the thought of Hayes and Max conspiring to slip arnica into the water supply and cure mass shock. Hayes meant the question as comic relief. He acknowledged Roxy's appropriate response and continued his commands.

"We need to get watchers out to every key polling place in the state to check off our supporters who come to vote and to call those who have not yet showed. Kat, you have to do Providence. Take Mario and hit every poll in the city."

"Last but not least, it's time to start making deals."

Mario nodded his agreement as Kat stared at her chief of staff blankly.

"Making deals?" she asked.

"Call Race. He has the votes that can win this for you."

Roxy flinched. Carrie's dying words came into her head. She knew that was not true. Before she could marshal her thoughts enough to tell Kat calling Race was a futile effort, Yola burst into the office and snapped on the television.

"Too bad you're not running in California," she said as they all turned to watch.

Stuart was featured at an early morning rally in San Diego with the Republican candidate for governor, the current senator. They were standing on a banner-draped platform, suspended in what appeared to be an endless sea of chanting, screaming people. It was Stuart's name they were chanting.

"Well, I guess those flakes in La La Land know a hero when they see one," Liz said, as she turned up the sound.

A male and female commentator traded breathless analysis that focused on the unprecedented size of the crowd, the tide of hero worship that swept the state when the final two minutes of Kat's appearance the previous night were shown on the late night news, and the impact this would have on the precarious California election. They discussed Stuart's shining future as a presidential contender in '92 and virtually buried their own senator, Matt Steele, as significant competition. Reports from elsewhere in the state showed similar reactions and police were preparing for onslaughts from record crowds at scheduled stops in Los Angeles and San Francisco.

Kat bit her lip and moaned when coverage shifted to taped interviews with Douglas supporters outside her polling place attacking her for abandoning Rhode Island and her virtue. She appeared haggard and besieged as she refused to answer questions about their relationship.

The double standard of behavior was obviously in effect on election day 1990. The female commentator questioned why Stuart was in California campaigning instead of Rhode Island and had the grace to flinch when the male responded off-handedly that perhaps he wanted to avoid a showdown with irate voters who saw him as a despoiler. The commentator then went on to describe Kat's brushes with rumored misconduct after years of being considered above reproach and speculated that her senate race was now a lost cause.

"Late polls show that even without a Kiley Tomasso victory in Rhode Island, the Republicans will have a tied Senate, a tie the new vice president will break in his party's favor," he said, implying it was more important to cast Stuart as a hero than to fight a pointless battle for the Rhode Island seat.

They could almost hear something snap in Kat's head as she jumped up and turned off the television. She began barking orders, agreeing with Hayes' analysis and directing everyone to begin implementing his suggestions for turning out their votes.

"Mario and I will blanket Providence as soon as Liz makes me presentable. Roxy, find Max. I want to know what's ahead."

★ ★ ★ ★ ★

THE JUDGEMENT

Kat looked beautiful and powerful, Roxy thought, as she and Max entered the office where Liz was putting on finishing touches. She could almost see sparks flying from her hair, more curly than ever from the damp weather. Liz had smoothed away or covered all the recently acquired lines in her perfect complexion. The make-up was subtle except for her lips, which blazed red. Kat's eyes looked clear and alert. She was dressed in a crimson wool suit with extended shoulders and a belted waist. The skirt was slightly flared and covered the tops of high heel black boots. Medusa's head was once again pinned to the high neck of a severe white blouse and gold stars gleamed in her ears. As she slipped the wolf's eye ring onto her right hand, they knew she was ready to do battle.

She nodded briefly to Max then quickly dialed a phone number.

"I want the five thousand votes," Kat said peremptorily when Race answered. She flicked the phone to speaker and they all heard his rasping response.

"What do I get?"

"What do you want?" she responded.

"Unconditional surrender."

"Whose?"

"Yours. To me. Now. Before I designate the votes."

Roxy grabbed Max's arm but he gestured for her to relax. He would not let Kat sacrifice herself for nothing.

"What about Stuart?"

"He's a dead man in any case." Race had barely hissed the final syllable when Kat slammed down the phone.

"We'll have to win by at least six thousand votes," she said to the assembled team.

"The votes Race controls have already been signed over to Douglas," Max reported, pulling three coins from his pocket and starting them spinning across his hand.

"Is that a prediction or real-time information?" Mario asked while Kat stared quizzically at the large white-haired man.

"Carrie told us, and Race, last night."

Roxy shrank back against the wall as Max told the story. She had been trying to forget the horrible scene with Carrie's blood spurting on the glass fragments. When no one mentioned anything about her death all day, she hoped it was some magic illusion; that Max had disappeared her until after the election then she would reappear rendered somehow harmless.

Shock and horror dominated the room. Finally Kat put her hand on Max's.

"I'm sorry it came to this."

He shrugged.

"Roxy will have nightmares, not me. I learned a lot."

"That son-of-a-bitch Race tried to hustle me," Kat said, laughing at the absurdity of her position. "Bruno, watch those votes. Get people we trust at the most dicey polls in Providence, Pawtucket and Central Falls. If there's fraud, we'll expose it. "

She faced Max. "I'm planning to go out and win this race. Do you have any advice?"

He plucked a small, white stone from the air and laid it on the desk. It was an arrow, pointed upright.

"The Warrior," he explained. "It's a rune of courage and counsels perseverance. You will ultimately be victorious."

Kat's eyes flashed. "I assume 'ultimately' means tonight." She swept from the room, motioning Mario to follow.

"We're going to conquer Providence," she yelled as they headed for the back door to elude the waiting press.

★ ★ ★ ★ ★

It was depressingly familiar. Runners drove from one poll to another in Jaguars, wrapping their five hundred dollar trench coats around thousand dollar suits. They ran into all three candidates in the Providence mayor's race. As the young man with the mop of unruly hair who had been written off by all observers weeks ago walked into the school to shake hands with voters there, two of his staff sidled over to Kat's car. One asked Mario directly for a job, the other was more subtle in mentioning his skills to Kat. At least there were two men in town who still believed she was going to win, Kat thought. Of course, they probably would have approached Douglas had he driven up while they were around.

Everyone was polite. They encountered none of the random violence at Providence polling places that was reported on the radio. At several Federal Hill locations she and Mario worked the line of "boys" in their dark suits who huddled against the entrance wall accosting voters as they walked by. She was surprised at how easily she could detect the note of insincerity in their protestations that she was a shoo-in. None mentioned her speech of the previous evening or the vice president. She felt like she was in a time warp and it was 1982 during her first election. Except Duke had been with her then.

Duke. She sat in the front seat next to Mario amazed at how much he looked like their father. Except that Mario's hair was soft and straight. What would Duke have done? What advice would he have given her about this race, about her choices? As she started to ask Mario what he thought Duke's reaction would have been, the car phone rang.

"Do you think the political system could withstand the vice president and his senator wife starring in a docudrama of their timeless love affair?"

Kat stared at the phone. He must have lost his mind.

"Too excited to answer, I guess. Think about it. The studio head that made the offer doesn't need an immediate response. He claimed he could get us a million each and a cut of the grosses."

"Does the offer still hold if I lose?" Kat immediately regretted her bitter tone when she heard the corresponding pain in his voice.

"Redcliffe told me the election is being a no-show. I'm sorry. It sounds like you're doing everything that can be done. Darlin', if I could take the lumps for you I would, you know that."

"Easy for you to say when thousands and thousands of screaming women are throwing themselves at your feet like you're Prince Charming come to life. Meanwhile crowds are assembling to stone me at the city gates." Kat broke into tears and handed Mario the phone. When he hung up she waved away his offer to return to headquarters.

"I'm not stopping until the polls close. No one will be able to say I didn't give my all. Unfortunately, I seem to have given too much in the wrong places at least as far as my electorate is concerned. It must be all that Catholic guilt."

Mario nodded agreement. Kat's main chance lay in turning out every vote they could find. Democrats always vote late and if their machine was as geared up as he thought, it was going to be a long night.

They continued their quest for votes up and down the seven hills of Providence. Kat spoke Italian to old ladies on stoops and nodded to Vietnamese and Hmongs in storefronts and back rooms where costume jewelry was assembled. She stood in the cold at Brown University and begged for votes. She called headquarters regularly to get names and numbers of key supporters who needed a special boost from her. And she cursed Carrie for stealing the votes that could have won her the seat.

As that thought scurried across her brain, Kat was horrified. She told Mario. He pulled into the empty parking lot of the Foxy Lady, a strip club near the interstate, and held her in his arms while she cried hysterically.

"What's wrong with me?" she wailed. "Two minutes ago I was actually contemplating how inconsequential sleeping with Race would have been to get those five thousand votes."

The phone rang and Mario answered. Kat choked back her sobs and fought for control.

"It's Stuart," he said, handing her the receiver. She was startled at how hoarse he sounded.

"You sound terrible," she said realizing instantly how she must sound, her throat still tight from crying.

"It's from shouting into microphones while thousands and thousands of screaming women throw themselves at me. What's your excuse?"

"I just came face to face with the demon of ambition and it was ready to drag

me into the mud. I regretted not sleeping with Race Scarlatti to win this election." Her voice broke and she waited for his response. The silence continued for
so long Kat was certain they had been disconnected.

"What time is it there?" His voice sounded distant. She was frightened. She
never should have told him. How stupid! She reported the time.

"I'll be there by midnight." He hung up.

Fifteen minutes later, the phone rang again. It was Hayes.

"Stuart just made a pitch on CNN for Rhode Island not to betray its chance
for a glorious future. He begged them to vote for you."

"Will it help?" she could barely speak.

"Anything can happen in an hour. You should be pleased. It sure beats roses
as a way to say I love you."

★ ★ ★ ★ ★

Roxy leaned her head on the desk. Her fingers ached from dialing, she had
almost no voice left. She must have talked to five hundred people today, cajoling,
threatening, reasoning, ordering them to get out and vote for Kat. No more. She
could not talk to another soul.

"Lying down on the job, you slut? Waiting for your stud to come and juice
you up?" Liz glared at her from the doorway.

Roxy moaned and ignored her. She barely saw Hayes all day and every time
she did, he was juggling at least two phones, fielding the avalanche of press calls
that were coming in from all over the country and the world. A few minutes
ago, he told her that they had Fed Ex-ed nearly fifty video copies of Kat's speech
everywhere. He claimed that, win or lose, Kat would soon be one of the most
famous women in America and their wedding could be the media event of the
year. As long as Stuart's confirmation was not threatened and the Republicans
were going to control the Senate with or without Kat's seat, Hayes was happy.
Secretly he agreed with the segment of Rhode Island voters who wondered why
being married to the vice president would not give Kat access enough to whatever power she felt she needed.

"Do you think Kat should blow off this senate race and be content with Mrs.
Vice President?" Roxy asked.

Liz eyed her suspiciously. "And leave her poor state in the clutches of that
bottom feeder, Douglas?"

"If they elect him, they deserve what they get!"

"What happened to this isn't real life, this is politics? No one deserves the
people they usually elect. Remember Jake's assessment, voting is generally a

choice between two fatal diseases? Speaking of Jake, he just called. He had Pete come and carry him over to the polls so he could vote. Now that's devotion."

She switched on the television and sank into the couch. While clips of world news hotspots flashed by, Liz returned to discussion of Kat.

"I'm not sure she's cut out to be 'wife of the great man.' Frankly, I think she should insist if he runs for president in '92, she's on the ticket as vice president. Think of the money the country could save on housing alone."

Roxy had no time to ponder the suggestion before CNN flashed footage of massive crowds Stuart continued to draw on his tour through California. The coverage shifted to Rhode Island where commentators speculated on why turn-out was the lowest ever recorded since universal suffrage was instituted in the mid-thirties.

"Kiley Tomasso appealed to the alienated from all groups. She was one of the few politicians in what some consider the most corrupt state in the union to possess any integrity. Until her opponent began a series of attacks, her honor was considered above reproach. The shock of her televised confession last night revealing a secret love affair that led to a miscarriage just one week earlier left supporters too shattered to mobilize for her. For many, it was another disappointment, another politician who proved to be less than they claimed, an angel fallen from the heights. And they stayed home in droves."

The commentator's self-righteous tones brought howls of disbelief from both women watching.

"A senate race that less than three weeks ago was considered one of the most certain to fall in the Republican column, lays tonight in shambles."

"They don't even mention Stuart!" Roxy exclaimed. "I can't believe it!"

A news bulletin flashed across the screen and a second, more sonorous voice appeared, attached to a blow-dry guy in an Armani suit.

"We must be in California," commented Liz.

They watched amazed as the vice president appeared on the screen and made an impassioned plea for Rhode Island not to turn their back on Kiley Tomasso. As he finished, with a look that rivaled Jake's for sincere, Liz muttered her appreciation.

"At least he didn't apologize for ruining her."

★ ★ ★ ★ ★

It was 10:15 and the mood among Republicans assembled at the Marriott resembled a testimonial dinner for death row inmates. Democrats swept the state. They knocked off the popular Republican congressman in the first district and won Kat's former seat in the second district. Kat's race remained undecided, the lead switching back and forth moment by moment. It was a tribute to the work they had done and to the depth of love the people of Rhode Island had for her that the race was so close.

Only in the Kiley for Senate suite were people partying. There was still hope for her race. Burhkart men who knew for weeks that the sour attorney general could not hope to beat the young, dynamic mayor of Bristol in the governor's race clustered around the bar in the central living room, trying to pick up devastated young girls from the Magill campaign who were stunned by the upset defeat of their candidate.

Kat's volunteers and supporters surrounded televisions in both bedrooms of the suite, discussing the vote counts which changed by tens and twenties every few minutes.

Roxy came up from the third floor to get some food and drinks for the small group preparing Kat for an appearance before the eleven o'clock news. Hayes emerged from huddling over a telephone in the quietest bedroom where he was checking results from other key races in the country. Pulling her aside, he emptied her hands and directed a rapid fire series of directions at her to take back.

"Burkhart is finally conceding now that eighty percent of the vote is in and he won less than thirty of it. Of course we knew that hours ago but he was posturing his enormous ego. Magill is so staggered by his defeat that he's dysfunctional. His campaign manager is covering up by claiming they plan to wait until the final ballot is cast. They want Kat to go on in fifteen minutes."

"To do what? Surely not to concede." Roxy was horrified at the very thought.

Hayes treated her to a scathing look.

"Kat has a shot at legend-stature. But she has to prove she has what it takes. It doesn't matter what she says, as long as she looks strong and in control. A half-million people, more or less, care what happens in the Rhode Island senate race. Millions and millions all over the world care what happens to Kiley Tomasso and T.J. Stuart. You're a romantic Roxy, you should understand that. Now go up and make sure she's ready. She needs to stop here first and collect everyone to go down to the ballroom with her."

His eyes scanned the room, checking to see who was there, which big contributors, who among Rhode Island's political insiders. Satisfied with the head count, he switched attention back to her and shifted to intimate mode. Pushing her through the crowded open door into the corridor, they moved around the corner where only a few stragglers passed by.

"I have fond memories of the first time I saw you in that dress," he said seductively, reaching around to pull on the tied back tail of blonde hair streaming down her back. "Will you let your hair loose later on? I've been looking forward to running my hands through it for weeks. Eleven weeks to be exact."

Roxy brushed her burning cheeks, checking to see if they were as inflamed as they felt. She was wearing the red dress she had on a year ago when the president came to visit Rhode Island. A year! She could scarcely believe it, or that in a few hours it would all be over.

He rested the back of his hand against her chest as he lifted the antique gold heart locket she wore on a chain. Her heart was beating so hard, she was certain he could feel it. He opened the locket and read the message he placed in it. "November 6, I'll be waiting."

"Can I assume the fact that you're wearing this tonight means the waiting is over?"

Roxy blushed. She had asked herself the same question when she clasped it around her neck. She allowed herself to look into his translucent blue eyes. The desire burning in them demanded she yield.

"I better get word to Kat," she answered evasively as she slipped away, avoiding the press that lurked in the main corridor by the campaign suite.

★ ★ ★ ★ ★

"What's your mother doing here?" Roxy was surprised to see Celeste sitting sullenly in a chair by the window.

"I couldn't ask anyone to miss out on the party tonight to watch her. And Mario insisted I give her another chance." There was no indication in Kat's toneless response what she really felt. Celeste grimaced at the reminder that her husband's bastard son should have anything to say about her activities.

Roxy repeated Hayes message, then settled on the bed to watch Liz put the finishing touches on Kat's hair. Her black curls were intricately braided and wrapped with a silver cord threaded with tiny silver stars that flashed in a shower of sparks as she moved her head one way and another.

"Won't the television cameras hate these little flashes," she said with only the barest trace of malicious glee. Liz's expert fingers pulled loose tendrils to wave softly on her forehead and along her carved cheekbones. Kat's luminous gray eyes had a bluish tone, reflecting the incredible color of the Givenchy dress she wore. She was radiantly beautiful, looking more like a movie star than a senator.

Kat picked up the sapphire pendant Stuart had given her the previous night and clasped it around her neck. It matched perfectly the royal blue velvet dress with a flared satin skirt. An endless row of tiny jeweled buttons closed the tight bodice extending from a plunging sweetheart neckline to a dropped waist.

"I have to do something to compete with all those California blondes who've been flinging themselves at Tommy Jeff." She rolled her eyes dramatically and winked at Liz who was examining her handiwork, looking pleased. Kat stood up and shook out her skirt.

"Do we have any new information about the vote count, Mario?"

He put down the phone.

"We're about a thousand votes ahead." The bemused expression in his eyes reflected their shared thought, how far they had fallen from the days of scoring seventy percent in the polls.

"At least that will keep the kids at the party from jumping out the window in despair," Liz commented.

Kat murmured her agreement then started as a loud knocking came from the door. Liz opened it a crack, jumping out of the way as Bruno barreled through.

"I guess you must have missed me," she said as he ran by with barely a nod and changed the channel on the television, clenching his fists as Douglas' sleek face filled the screen.

"We're delighted the vote count is so close," he squeaked in his high pitch whine, eyes shifting rapidly.

"It shows the people of Rhode Island are not ready to throw over traditional moral values for some fuzzy-headed notion of a brave new world run by conservative Republicans. As I predicted weeks ago," he paused to let his prescience sink in, "this election will be decided by absentee ballots. And we know who's done their homework there."

His repulsive chortle matched the evil glow from his tan-in-a-can face.

The little group exchanged glances. Except for Celeste, they all knew Douglas was counting on Scarlatti's block of votes for his margin of victory.

"Too bad Max didn't get rid of Carrie sooner," Roxy said. She jumped as Liz pinched her hard, nodding towards the window where Celeste sat.

"Sorry," she muttered, chagrined at forgetting there was an enemy present, or at least someone whose loyalty was in question.

"It's OK, Roxy," Kat said soothingly. "Besides, the price on those votes was too high, with or without Carrie."

"I saw him lurking in the parking lot." Everyone's head turned to the Hose.

"Who?" Kat asked.

"Scarlatti. He was sitting in that black Corvette he drives, his goons in the Lincoln behind him." In an instant, Kat's face was a study in black and white.

"Stuart!" she gasped.

"I figured." The Hose beamed proudly. "I sent one of my protégées over with the limo to meet him at the airport. He'll warn the VP. Max went along, too. He said he had a product report to deliver.

"Kat." The Hose's practiced tough guy look softened. "You won't abandon Rhode Island to those scum will you?" He waved vaguely at the television screen which announced the latest numbers showing Kat nearly twelve hundred votes ahead. "Not even for the White House?"

She patted his arm comfortingly as she moved toward the door.

"No, Bruno. I won't abandon you."

THE JUDGEMENT

★ ★ ★ ★ ★

Standing on the sideboard in the campaign suite, the jeweled blue tones of her dress and necklace gleaming, Kat clasped her hands and looked out at dozens of faces, all turned to hear what she had to say. As happened in odd moments during the campaign, she was charged with a feeling she could only call humility. All these people, and thousands more throughout the state, turned to her as their best hope for bringing order and honest dealings to their lives, for making an increasingly hostile government work in their favor. No matter where her path led after tonight, she would honor her pledge to Bruno and all her faithful supporters. She would not abandon them.

Seeing shadows of tension, pain and despair on many faces, she felt the shame and sadness that filled the final days of the campaign. She wondered, standing in the light-filled room, the same thing she wondered in those gray and bleak hours before dawn. What stream of resentment had she touched that so many had been willing to believe the worst lies, the most preposterous charges, and hate her for them? She recalled Stuart's voice on the phone earlier when she asked him why and he repeated the same reason Liz gave.

"You're a fallen angel Darlin' and that's not easy to forgive."

Had someone asked her later what she said, Kat could not have answered. She felt so much emotion that it surged from her like electrical voltage and she could almost smell ozone in the air. She did notice the subtle change in people's faces when she mentioned the attacks, rumors and chaos of recent days. Their eyes no longer shone with adoration for their favorite Madonna. They appeared to doubt that she could do anything to soothe their hurts. The men had sly looks, the women seemed dismayed.

When she began pouring out her gratitude for their love and support, she was pleased to see the light return to most eyes and tears appear in many. She took Mario's hand as he helped her down and reached out to each person as they filed past. She wanted to touch them all, to give them hope, to give them something in return for all they had given her. And she did, silently blessing each as they filed by, murmuring a few words of how she could never have done it without them. Miraculously, every face had a name; many a story, a memory that she could share. She blessed Duke for teaching her the skill she found politically invaluable. Only a few people in the room slipped away to avoid looking her in the eye.

She smiled at Roxy's solemn face as her friend deliberately handed each person a round Kiley for Senate sticker to wear. They took them with a reverence not far from that given the sacrament, wearing them as a badge of honor, the mark of an insider that would allow them up on stage. Businessmen smiled and stuck them on seven hundred dollar suits; women arranged them next to their jewels.

Her inner circle became a packed cube as they squeezed on the elevator, Mario shielding her from being crushed. Kat reached out and pulled Roxy in just as the doors closed, holding her hand as they walked out on the first floor and headed through the lobby to the ballroom.

For moments at a time, she moved blindly through the corridors, lights from dozens of cameras flashing in her face. People were jockeying for position all around her as she clung to Roxy's hand and felt Mario's arm guiding her from the other side. Security men pushed through lines of people bobbing Kiley signs and cheering. At every step, press were crouched in front of the moving group, scurrying backwards like crabs trying to keep her face in focus. She worried that someone would fall and be trampled before they could be pulled back up to their feet. The noise made it impossible to think. All she could hear was her name being screamed over and over.

As they broke through crowds into the ballroom, her theme music began playing "Parade of the Charioteers" from *Ben Hur* summoned her courage with its heroic chords. A path opened and she could pick out an occasional face coming into focus from the fast moving blur of humanity as they bulled their way through.

Once on stage, the lights made it impossible to see, and the heat was stifling. There were nothing but faces bobbing with mouths open in the glaring light. She could hear noise—screaming, deafening sound. How could Beau stand the thousands and thousands who screamed in his face all day? Finally she focused on the signs, weaving and waving on the floor. Her own Kiley for Senate signs with their distinctive blue star and red stripe far outnumbered any others. The few blue Magill signs that remained huddled in a far corner brought tears to her eyes. Ben Magill was a good representative. She was sorry he lost.

She released Roxy's hand and raised her arms to silence the cheering crowd. Lights heated her skin, flashes blinded her eyes, hundreds of upturned faces drifted in front of her. They still loved her, she knew. They believed she could give them hope for the future, courage to face the unknown ahead. They were able to sift through the rhetoric, gossip, rumors, and thirty-second television spots to choose the best leader.

From the corner of her eye she saw tears streaming down Roxy's face and clenched her raised fists. She had to keep the ball in her stomach from rising to her throat or she would be showering the audience with her tears, too. She wanted her vision emblazoned in their minds. She wanted to inspire them to demand that the system work, that the leaders they selected give their best. She did not want to cry in front of the millions she knew were watching. She blessed Liz for insisting she use waterproof mascara. At least she would not streak.

Kat caught a glimpse of her face in the monitors along the edge of the stage and flinched. There were deep creases around her eyes and mouth, creases that were not there three months ago. Badges of honor, Max would say. Mementos of the campaign. She looked away and reached into her heart. She had to give them hope. Whatever happened, that was what they wanted, what they needed the most. They had to believe what she promised Bruno, that she would never abandon them, no matter what.

As the words started, words that were etched in gold and shimmered before her eyes like the words in the ancient sacred books Max described to her, she heard courage in her voice and was grateful. The shouting headlines and slashing attacks faded away and she gave them her magic. They would be winners.

★ ★ ★ ★ ★

There were five agents with drawn guns surrounding the Lincoln with its RACE plates parked around the corner from the Marriott entrance. Three more held guns on Scarlatti who was seated behind the wheel of his Corvette. Stuart casually pushed the barrel of a .38-caliber Smith & Wesson just in front of his ear. The vice president's seal gleamed on gold cufflinks.

"This is the '90s. It's Ladies' Choice, and you lose." Stuart's voice was hoarse. "Disappear, Scarlatti. Consider a long search for your Roman roots. I want you gone. Being vice president means I get my way. It's amazing what can be done with my own SS troops and a bunch of trivial regulations like tax codes."

As Race appeared to relax his death grip on the car wheel, Stuart jammed the barrel tighter against his pasty cheek. His voice became menacing.

"If anything happens to me or Kiley, to any of her family or friends—you're a dead man, no questions asked. I have friends in low places, too."

Seeing Scarlatti flick his eyes to the rear view mirror, Stuart pulled back on the hammer of the small pistol that fit perfectly in his palm.

"You're outnumbered and it's going to stay that way. Any time you want it to be you and me though, call the White House. They'll find me." He slowly tightened his finger on the trigger. The snap of an empty chamber pushed Scarlatti forward to slump against the wheel. Stuart laughed and stepped back.

"I heard this was one of your favorite games."

Guns remained trained on the Corvette as Scarlatti roared off, followed by his thugs. Stuart grinned at Max as they walked into the hotel.

"Don't you love it when the good guys win?"

★ ★ ★ ★ ★

She asked the time every five minutes. It was midnight, then it was later. He still had not arrived. She worried. Then Max was standing in the doorway. They connected and she knew Beau was here, safe. Her passage across the room seemed endless. She wanted to push her way through all the people who reached out to her and run down the stairs. But she murmured thanks for support, accepted expressions of concern, bolstered those in despair, promised no matter what happened she would not abandon Rhode Island. She kept moving. Whenever she looked up, Max was waiting, standing by the door. Finally she was by his side and he whisked her into the hall, shielding her from the press who hung back intimidated by his alien presence.

"He's waiting in your room. There are guards by the door. I'll keep press out of these stairs. If you go up one flight then down by another set of stairs you should be able to slip by."

"What about Scarlatti?"

Max got a peculiar smile on his face and began spinning two coins across his knuckles. Seeing them lounging by the exit door, the press began to relax. Several turned back to interrupted conversations.

"It could be argued that Stuart's seen one too many Clint Eastwood movies. But," Max shrugged, "it's effective."

"What exactly does that mean?"

He laughed, then quickly described the scene in the parking lot. As her eyes widened in horror, he opened the door to the stairwell, pushing her through.

"I don't think he's in the mood to be kept waiting."

★ ★ ★ ★ ★

Kat nodded shyly to Shanley and the other equally large Secret Service agent who stood guard at the door. Her hand shook so badly she could scarcely hold the key in the lock.

Dim light from a small lamp by the bed cast him in shadows as he stood intently watching the returns, shirt sleeves rolled up, collar open. She watched him in silence, desperately searching for what to say. She was so weary, so exhausted from being strong, from holding back the tears. Now it was over. They were together and….what? What did she expect? What could she say? Tears began trickling down her cheeks, then cries she could not hold back. All the emotion from the ballroom, from the people who hoped for so much from her—it poured from her eyes, from her heart.

"Why are you crying?" he said, nodding to the screen. "The votes are almost all in and you're ahead. I'm impressed that fifty percent of the people voted for love."

"Douglas has Race's five thousand votes." She looked at the screen which was flashing the numbers from her race and did some quick calculating. With her twelve hundred vote lead, even if she won every vote left to be counted she would lose if five thousand Douglas ballots suddenly showed up. Despair clutched her throat.

"Maybe not. I saw your boyfriend outside. We had a few words."

"Max told me."

"A fuller version than mine, I'm sure."

She sat on the bed. "The votes were delivered to Douglas by Carrie on her own."

He shrugged and walked over to sit beside her.

"It doesn't matter. Buying votes is the old way. You wouldn't do it that way. That's the point."

Kat could feel the blue sapphire pulsing against the hollow of her throat.

"I called Race this afternoon before I knew he didn't have the votes."

"Did he know?"

"Yes." She quickly sketched events of the previous night.

"Did he tell you?"

She shook her head.

"What did he want from you?"

"Unconditional surrender. Immediately." When Kat realized how hard she was clutching his hand, she willed herself to let go and clasped her hands in her lap.

He took her clenched fists in his hands and leaned over to lightly kiss them. "And?"

"I asked about you."

He looked quizzical.

"He said you were a dead man in any case. I hung up."

He held her in his arms.

"Your pal Athena, goddess of truth, obviously has her ways for keeping you honest."

He sat back and looked at her. He brushed his fingers lightly along her jaw.

"They're glad I'm back," he said as a long curl wound itself around his finger. Eyes shining, he ran his fingers over the jewel at her throat and down the long row of tiny buttons. "You look properly sparkling."

Standing, he pulled her to her feet and spun her partially around and back.

"Unwrapping the package is a favorite part but if those buttons are the only way to get you out of that beautiful wrapping, I'm going to need your help."

Kat laughed and breathed a quick prayer to whomever that her shaking fingers would work. She slipped the satin cuffed long sleeves over her hands and dropped the dress from her shoulders to her waist. The look of pure love he gave her broke into a million tiny star beams that danced across the edge of her skin.

"No black underwear, I see. What color is this? Blushing Venus?" He stroked her bare breast. "Or maybe Porcelain Perfection?" He bent to kiss her. "Whatever, it's my favorite."

The dress fell to the floor and she unclasped the necklace dropping it onto the bed.

His hands moved over her body as if it were his to claim and own. Jasmine was right about how she felt, Kat thought in a random flash. What she could never realize was Kat wanted to be owned by him, wanted him to take every part of her being. Her body, her heart, her mind, her soul—all were her tribute to this hero.

Yet, as he explored her body with his lips and eyes and fingertips, she could feel the adoration pour from him to her. If asked, he would claim to be the possessed not the possessor. When he finally entered her pulsing body, Kat felt a circuit close and the voltage of the connection sent all the millions of tiny stars clustering around them streaming and bursting to fill all the space she could see. In the brilliant sparks she recognized the face of the new goddess. His words brought her back to herself.

"I'm so glad you're a goddess," he whispered against her ear in a teasing tone. "It makes it easy for a mere mortal to retain his dignity while being lost in worship."

He turned her face to look in his eyes.

"You won't devour me and leave my flesh to fertilize the fields like the ancient goddess did, will you?"

★ ★ ★ ★ ★

Every time she got up from the couch, tides of sensation shifted in her body. Hayes had been at her side since Kat left, touching her lightly whenever he could. If desire were indeed fluid, she was ready to burst and drown the room. She wanted to get to it. There was no doubt in her mind that she surrendered hours ago. The liberating troops were taking too long to begin the marching through.

The Hose broke in on her reveries as he reported to Hayes. Absentee ballots were being counted. Kat had loyal people in most key places. They would keep their eyes peeled for fraud and take notes. Results should be complete by dawn. As Liz walked over, throwing a scandalized look at Roxy, Bruno kissed her quickly and said he was needed back on Federal Hill.

"I'll catch up with you after breakfast, that's always my best time," he grinned. She rolled her eyes and fluttered her fake lashes in mock horror.

"Oh, I'm not sure I'm woman enough for your best."

From his pat response as he left the room, Roxy assumed this was a standard routine and she marveled again at the perfect fit of odd pieces. She caught Liz's baleful stare once Bruno was gone and knew she was in for a lecture. She snuggled closer to Hayes who was flipping through the stations looking for returns from the west coast. Shouts came from the other room and several young volunteers scurried in looking horrified. Saved, Roxy thought gratefully as they all ran to see what was happening.

They arrived just in time to witness Kat's mother, obviously drunk and disorderly, pour a pitcher of beer on Mario who was standing with his back to her. As he jumped away, shocked, she picked up an empty wine bottle and began flailing at him. Arms raised to protect himself, he tried to fend her off but she was screaming hysterically, grabbing handfuls of food lying on tables, throwing them at him. Mario bolted through the door to the open bedroom and locked himself in the bathroom. Celeste was beating on the closed door with the bottle by the time Liz threw a death lock on the crazed woman's throat and began dragging her away.

"I'm putting her in your room," Liz muttered to Roxy as she dragged Celeste out towards the hall. "I'm sure you won't be using it."

Having released Mario, and directed several of the partygoers to clean up the damage, Hayes pulled her into a far corner.

"All the barriers are down between you and temptation. May I encourage you to yield?"

Roxy laughed wildly as she pulled his face down to meet her lips. Who needed to be encouraged?

★ ★ ★ ★ ★

"Leave on the locket, please. It's my lucky charm," he said as he unhooked her bra and let her full breasts fall freely into his waiting hands.

She surrendered to the bliss of feeling his mouth everywhere on her skin, demanding response, ignoring the niceties of ritual or sacredness. Her pulses throbbed under his insistent touch so strongly she was afraid they would burst skin. He wanted to fuck her brains out and she wanted him to. In some dark corner of her mind lurked the notion that this would help her choose. Then she thought about her final fortune strip. She opened it while getting dressed earlier. She hated to admit it was the deciding vote in her decision to wear the locket and all that indicated. *Do not feel bound by the old ways* was its advice. Roxy relaxed. No reason why she could not have two boyfriends and love them both enough.

"A standing prick has no conscience as every boy learns in school," Hayes murmured, poised to plunge into her. Nor does a wet pussy, thought Roxy, quivering ecstatically as she felt the soft lips of her sex swallow him up, pulling him deeper and deeper.

SENATE MAGIC

★ ★ ★ ★ ★

His voice startled her. Kat wondered how long he had watched her pace back and forth across the room, his shirt wrapped tightly around her.

"I must be slipping if you're still that tense."

"How could this have happened?" She stood facing him, her hair unbraided and wild, the tiny stars wrapped in it scattered all over the sheets. One of them gleamed on his shoulder. "How could it all come to nothing? The rhetoric, the vision, the ideas that would lead us to a better future—why did no one listen? They voted on the gossip, on whether they believed my feminine virtue was intact or not. They voted on whether love is sufficient excuse or whether it disqualifies me."

"As I mentioned earlier, there's hope for a state where at least half the voting population believes in love."

"Sun Tzu never said anything about love," she quipped.

"Remember Darlin', what works for the wizard can be more ambiguous for us common mortals."

"I can't marry you if I lose. It would feel like a consolation prize."

"Not when you see the perfect house I have for my bride-to-be. Your favorite period. A beautiful Victorian on the best hill in the city. It even has it's own observatory, you should like that. There's a big veranda, large open rooms with sunny windows and it comes with a full staff of Navy stewards who will adore you."

"I'm serious."

"So am I. It does have a few drawbacks, I have to admit. There's video security everywhere but we'll be married so no one'll care what we do. As long as we restrict our passionate sex to the interior there won't be any more skin flicks."

Kat stared at him, propped up against the pillows, smiling benignly. "I won't have a job." It sounded foolish to her but it just came out.

"I'll hire you. Since your net worth is probably more than mine, I hope money doesn't become a stumbling block in these negotiations. You can choose your own title and most of your duties. There's a few I'll require."

She gaped at him and pulled at the shirt she wore. It felt as taut as her nerves.

"You just don't understand," she shouted frustrated. "I'm afraid of becoming an ornament for you, losing myself."

He was out of bed and by her side in an instant.

"I don't want to enslave you. I don't want you to prefer my happiness to yours, to want something because I want it. I don't want you to yield your will to me. I love you because you are willful, strong, independent. I want to share in your spirit, not own it.

"I don't pretend to understand the mystery of marriage but I do know that by yielding we each can be more complete. I know that you possess the essential

600

quality to make me more than I am, and I can only hope that I can do the same for you. Aren't there any married goddesses?"

She knew what he said was true. It vibrated with force and resonance through her whole body. But she could find no words in her chaotic mind to tell him.

"Do you have doubts about us, Kiley?" There was no teasing in his voice, only the slightest tinge of uncertainty.

"Not about you, not about our love. But maybe a little about marriage. We're both strong individuals, used to our own lives. What if we can't become one?"

"We have a lifetime to practice. I'm not worried."

She waved at the stack of newspapers on the dresser featuring their pose at the end of the broadcast Monday night.

"We won't be leading a normal life. We won't have the luxury of time alone to work out our differences. Can we resist all this?"

"We're not exactly Sean and Madonna. I would hope we can behave like adults." He was smiling again. "I think being closed in a small dark space is making us both crazy. Let's go for a walk."

"A walk?"

"Yep." He began pulling off her shirt. "But I'll need my shirt."

She let him unwrap her again and watched satisfied as the look on his face changed to one of rapt pleasure.

"Maybe we're being a little hasty. There are other ways to relieve tension."

Kat danced away. "No. I think your suggestion for a walk was perfect."

She pulled a sweat suit from her bag and escaped laughing into the bathroom.

★ ★ ★ ★ ★

Roxy stood at the window, Hayes' shirt draped from her shoulders. He had been on the phone checking results in the key California race and was calling Kat's room.

"Stuart told me I could call anytime after 5 a.m. but there's no answer."

Roxy smiled. She saw them threading their way through cars in the dark parking lot below, two bulky shadows with coiled wires following discretely.

"I think he's taking his watchdogs for a walk," she said.

There appeared to be a glow around the couple as they scrambled up the gravel embankment and stood at the road deciding which way to turn. Roxy speculated on whether the glow came when you found your perfect mate. A tear trickled down her cheek as she wondered if she would ever know the answer to that from her own experience. Then she giggled. If she found her twin flame, she tried to imagine whose bed he would be in the other half of his time.

SENATE MAGIC

★ ★ ★ ★ ★

"Not that way." Kat grabbed his arm as he started downhill to the left. "Channel 6 is over there, and the morgue. We'll go this way." She moved to the right.

"The morgue, huh? Must be lots of Douglas voters in there."

They crossed the wide overpass and turned into an empty parking lot. Slipping between squat and ugly modern state office buildings they found themselves looking out over the lights of Providence. "The Democrats are celebrating their almost clean sweep of the state," she said pointing to the Biltmore's glowing red rooftop sign. Her heart sank at the thought of the Republican party in shambles, her race a question mark.

Stuart said nothing and guided her across Smith Street to the Capitol, the Independent Man atop the dome standing with his back to them. They skirted the building and reached the manicured Capitol lawn stretching in a gentle slope to the street. The silver dome of the train station gleamed to their left, the Journal building just visible down the avenue. Kat made a mental note to call Harry Crast later that morning to thank him for standing by her. She knew it was only because of him that the *Journal* had not withdrawn their endorsement.

They wandered hand and hand among the trees, sitting finally on a bench staring at the ascending and descending light of the Biltmore's exterior elevator.

"Will you still want to marry me if I lose and you don't have a Republican Senate?"

"Even without your seat the Senate is tied and I get my wish. My vote as vice president will create a Republican Senate." His answer was cheery.

"I have to admit I was looking forward to being married to a senator but I can take the disappointment. At the risk of ruining your drama, may I remind you again that you haven't lost yet?"

Kat ignored him.

"I won't have a job. I won't have a purpose. And if I don't have a purpose everything else will eventually break down. I'll be bored and crazy and you'll hate me."

She blessed him silently when he did not laugh. She knew her position was absurd but it was how she felt. She allowed herself to relax as he put his arm lightly around her shoulder and pulled her towards him.

"The institutions, the old ways are dead for us. You've said that to me dozens of times. Don't you believe it? We're life entrepreneurs, wizards of free enterprise, making our own rules, our own paths, creating our own purpose. From where I sit, your purpose is unchanged: to drag the rest of us kicking and screaming into that glorious future you see so clearly. Frankly it may be easier to do without a job, certainly without a job in an institution that is stuck somewhere in the glory of the 19th century. I know you feel Sun Tzu failed you with his advice but he did say to successfully challenge an opponent you must be emotionally and financially disengaged."

His words brought order to the turmoil in her mind and she submitted to his caressing fingers as he played with her disheveled locks. In his arms it was easy to forget the world. It all came rushing back as they stood to leave.

"I can't leave Rhode Island," she said looking out towards the ocean.

"Darlin', if we can wake up in the same bed at least half the time, I'll be a happy man."

★ ★ ★ ★ ★

"Is it the back door and the press room, or the front door and the lobby?" Stuart asked when they found the door they used to leave the hotel was locked. Deciding on the front entrance, they ran into the Hose as he came charging into the lobby behind them.

"You could see through the ballots where they erased your name to put in Douglas'. They must've used first graders with wet erasers to do it. I couldn't stop the count though. The official announcement will come any minute. You lost by twenty-two hundred votes."

Kat was stunned to see tears in her faithful lieutenant's eyes as he delivered the news. Stuart stood silent, arms folded, waiting for her response.

"Call the Secretary of State. Demand a recount. Tell her we're going to contest every absentee ballot and any cast at the polls that we think are phony. I'm not going to let that son-of-a-bitch steal my senate seat."

Bruno whooped his agreement, kissed her soundly and ran out the front door. Kat turned to find Stuart smiling broadly.

"The body of a pin-up and balls, too. What a woman!"

★ ★ ★ ★ ★

Kat's challenge to the outcome of the election moved slowly through the courts, delayed repeatedly by questionable maneuvers from Douglas who, as the incumbent, retained his seat in the Senate during the process. Finally, she was declared the official winner of the 1990 Rhode Island senate race.

On May 16, 1991 at 3:14 p.m., K.A.T. Stuart was sworn in by the Senate's presiding officer, her husband, Thomas Jefferson Stuart, Vice President of the United States. At a press conference immediately following her swearing-in, Senator Stuart announced the couple was expecting a child in December, making her the first pregnant member of the United States Senate. It was an historic occasion.

Author's Note

Senate Magic was written the year after I completed work on the 1990 U.S. Senate campaign in Rhode Island. It was not published until magic intervened 22 years later. Necessary help appeared. The cosmic pattern of the current time perfectly expressed major themes in the book. Buried in my notebooks of the period was the year 2013 as the fictional (I thought) date of publication—a year determined through an error in addition.

While some of the characters had resonance in real people, the hero and two goddesses are mythic. I breathed life into them by creating specific astrological charts for Stuart, Roxy and Kat. They took control and I marveled at how they lived the campaign year.

There have been no substantial edits in the text of *Senate Magic* as written in 1991 that alter in any way the prescience of the content. That's all magic.

About the Author

Jeanne Mozier is an award-winning writer of both fiction and nonfiction.

She is author of the best-selling *Way Out in West Virginia, a Must-have Guide to the Oddities and Wonders of the Mountain State* (Quarrier Press), now in its 4th edition and available in eBook format. *Way Out in West Virginia* was voted Best Book about West Virginia and Mozier was voted Best West Virginia author by statewide readers.

Mozier co-authored the historical compendium *Images of Berkeley Springs* (Arcadia Publishing) with Betty Lou Harmison.

She wrote the text for two volumes of Steve Shaluta photographs: *West Virginia Beauty: Familiar and Rare* and *Wonders of West Virginia* (Quarrier Press).

She is also author of *Panhandle Paradise*, the sole lifestyle guide to West Virginia's Eastern Panhandle.

Her short stories are included in three volumes of *Tales from the Springs,* and three of her plays have been staged. She was a contributor to the *West Virginia*

Encyclopedia, and is a regular contributor of travel and lifestyle articles to a variety of regional and national publications.

Senate Magic is her first novel.

Mozier's astrological writings have appeared in numerous publications, and her ongoing analysis of current news and daily energy flow posted regularly online.

To order *Senate Magic*, visit www.senatemagic.com. To order Jeanne Mozier's other books and check her astrological writings, go to www.starwv.com.

www.ingramcontent.com/pod-product-compliance
Lightning Source LLC
Chambersburg PA
CBHW020454020726
47493CB00001B/25

* 9 7 8 0 9 8 9 8 0 1 8 0 5 *